QUEEN MARGOT

QUEEN
MARGOT

or

Marguerite de Valois

by Alexandre Dumas

MIRAMAX
B O O K S
HYPERION

NEW YORK

LIBRARY OF CONGRESS CATALOGING-IN-PUBLICATION DATA

Dumas, Alexandre, 1802–1870.
[Reine Margot. English]
Queen Margot, or, Marguerite de Valois / by Alexandre
Dumas.
p. cm.

"A Miramax book from Hyperion"

ISBN 0-7868-8082-1

1. Marguerite, Queen, consort of Henry IV, King of France,
1553–1615—Fiction. 2. Saint Bartholomew's Day, Massacre of,
France, 1572—Fiction. 3. Henry IV, King of France, 1553–1610—
Fiction. 4. France—Kings and rulers—Fiction. 5. Queens—France—
Fiction. I. Title. II. Title: Queen Margot. III. Title:
Marguerite de Valois.
PQ2227.R3E55 1994
843'.7—dc20

94-7600
CIP

DESIGN BY HOLLY McNEELY

FIRST EDITION
10   9   8   7   6   5   4   3   2   1

FICTION
DUMAS
QUE

TABLE OF CONTENTS

v

Contents ~ vii

CHIEF HISTORICAL FIGURES

ALENÇON, FRANÇOIS, DUC D', 1554–84, sixth son of Henri II and Catherine de Médicis, became Duc d'Anjou after his brother acceded to the throne of France as Henri III.

ANJOU, HENRI, DUC D', 1551–89, fifth son of Henri II and Catherine de Médicis; elected king of Poland in 1573, became king of France as Henri III on the death of his brother Charles IX in 1574. Fought against Henri de Navarre and the Protestants, then turned against Guise and had him murdered in Blois in 1588. He then made peace with Henri de Navarre, acknowledging him as his successor. Assassinated by a fanatical monk, Jacques Clément.

BESME, murderer of Coligny; one of Guise's partisans; called a German, but in fact a Czech from Bohemia, hence his name Besme. His real name was Jean Simanowitz.

CATHERINE DE MÉDICIS, 1519–89, daughter of Lorenzo the Magnificent; wife of Henri II, king of France 1547–59. After years without children, she gave birth to ten, three of whom reigned in France.

CHARLES IX, 1550–74, son of Henri II, king of France, and Catherine de Médicis. He succeeded his brother, François II, in 1560, but actually reigned only after 1570, as Catherine was the real ruler until then. He married Elizabeth of Austria and had only one daughter by her. By his mistress, Marie Touchet, he had a son, Charles de Valois, who became the Duc d'Angouléme.

COCONNAS, ANNIBAL DE, Piedmontese nobleman who served the Duc de Guise and murdered a number of Huguenots with ferocious zeal on St. Bartholomew night. Conspired with and for the

Duc d'Alençon and was executed on the scaffold in 1574. He had been the lover of the Duchesse de Nevers.

COLIGNY, GASPARD DE, 1519–72, had the title of Admiral, although he never commanded a fleet, but organized French expeditions in overseas lands. Became a convert to Protestantism while a prisoner of the Spaniards in 1557–59. He was one of the two nephews of Montmorency, the other one being Cardinal Odet de Châtillon.

CONDÉ, HENRI DE, 1552–88, son of Louis de Condé, a close friend of his coreligionist, Henri de Navarre; resisted conversion after St. Bartholomew's Day, but his life was spared. Was perhaps murdered by his own wife later.

CONDÉ, LOUIS DE, 1530–69, became a Protestant and one of the Huguenot leaders; he was captured at the battle of Jarnac and murdered by a captain in the service of the Duc d'Anjou.

DIANE DE POITIERS, 1499–1566, celebrated mistress of King Henri II; a fierce foe of the Protestants, whose ministers had branded her as immoral and sinful; openly flouted the queen, Catherine de Médicis.

ELIZABETH OF AUSTRIA, 1554–92, daughter of Maximilian II, married in 1570 to King Charles IX of France; respected for her dignified and austere manners.

FRANÇOIS, see Alençon.

GUISE, FRANÇOIS, DUC DE, 1519–63, had won fame by recapturing Calais from the English in 1558; a fierce enemy of the Huguenots, whom he helped massacre at Vassy, 1562; assassinated by Poltrot de Méré. The murder was supposed by his family (probably wrongly) to have been instigated by Coligny.

GUISE, HENRI, DUC DE, 1550–88, usually called "le Balafre" or "Scarface" after receiving a deep wound on his face at Dormans in 1575. For a time, lover of Marguerite de Valois; directed the murder of Coligny in 1572; assassinated by order of Henri III in 1588.

GUISE, LOUIS DE, Cardinal of Lorraine, 1555–88, brother of Henri; his assassination followed by one day that of Henri de Guise.

HENRI III, see Anjou.

HENRI DE NAVARRE, 1553–1610, was king of Navarre after 1562 and became King Henri IV of France in 1589. After the battle of Jarnac (1569), he became the chief of the Huguenots. In 1584, on the death of the Duc d'Alençon (the younger brother of Charles IX), he became the pretender to the throne, since King Henri III (formerly the Duc d'Anjou) had no children. Henri III designated Henri de Navarre as his heir in 1589, but he still had to fight against the Catholic leagues before he could conquer his kingdom and enter Paris; he then accepted Catholicism. He was assassinated in 1610.

JEANNE D'ALBRET, 1528–72, wife of Antoine de Bourbon; queen of Navarre and mother of Henri de Navarre. Died, allegedly through poison, a few weeks before her son's marriage to Marguerite de Valois, after having laboriously negotiated the marriage.

LA MOLE, BONIFACE DE, foe, then intimate friend of Coconnas; a convert to Catholicism; conspired with and for the Duc d'Alençon, was betrayed by him and beheaded in 1574. Marguerite de Valois, who loved him, had his head embalmed.

MARGUERITE DE VALOIS (LA REINE MARGOT) was born in 1553 at Saint-Germain-en-Laye, the daughter of Henri II and Catherine de Médicis. She was learned, polished in the arts, and fluent in several languages, and had many notorious love affairs. For political reasons, and in order to pacify the Protestants, she married Henri de Navarre on August 18, 1572, just before the St. Bartholomew Massacre. After Henri III expelled her from the court in 1583, she held a small court of her own at Nérac in southwestern France. She was later imprisoned in central France, and her marriage to Henri de Navarre was annulled. Under his reign as Henri IV she was allowed to return to the court in 1605. She died in 1615, five years after the murder of her former husband.

MONTGOMERY, GABRIEL, COMTE DE, accidentally caused the death of King Henri II in a tournament in 1559; became a Protestant, fought alongside Condé against the Catholics; put to death in 1574.

NEVERS, FRANÇOIS DE CLÈVES, DUC DE, 1516–62, fought against the Huguenots during the reigns of Francis I and Henri II.

NEVERS, MARIE DE, 1553–74, daughter of François de Clèves; renowned for her beauty, loved by the Duc d'Anjou; married her cousin Henri, prince of Condé, and died when giving birth to a child.

PARÉ, AMBROISE, 1517?–90, the greatest surgeon of the time, in whom four kings successively put their trust, although he belonged to the Reformed faith.

RONSARD, PIERRE DE, 1524–85, the greatest French poet of his time, admired by Charles IX, for whom he wrote several long poems advocating tolerance and charity.

TÉLIGNY, CHARLES DE, Coligny's son-in-law, died alongside him in the St. Bartholomew Massacre.

TOUCHET, MARIE, 1549–1638, daughter of a Protestant artisan; her beauty and unreserved devotion profoundly touched Charles IX. She was his mistress for six years, even after his marriage to Elizabeth of Austria.

PART ONE

CHAPTER 1

M. de Guise's Latin

On Monday, the eighteenth of August, 1572, there was a grand fête at the Louvre. The windows of the ancient royal residence, ordinarily so dark, were brilliantly illuminated; and the squares and streets adjacent, usually so solitary after the clock of St. Germain l'Auxerrois had tolled nine, were crowded with people, although it was past midnight.

This great crowd, threatening, pressing, and turbulent, resembled in the gloom a dark and rolling sea, each swell of which increases to a moaning wave; this sea, extending all along the quay, and into the streets Fossés St. Germain and l'Astruce, spent its waves at the base of the walls of the Louvre, on the one hand, and against the Hôtel de Bourbon, which was opposite, on the other. There was, in spite of the royal fête, and perhaps even because of the royal fête, something threatening in the aspect of the multitude; for it was very sure that the festivity which it then witnessed was but the prelude to a festivity of another kind, to occur a week later, to which it would be invited, and in which it would heartily participate.

The court was celebrating the marriage of Madame Marguerite de Valois, daughter of Henri II, and sister of King Charles IX, with Henri de Bourbon, King of Navarre. That same morning the Cardinal de Bourbon had united the young couple with the usual ceremonial observed at the marriages of the royal daughters of France, on a stage erected at the entrance to Notre Dame.

This marriage had astonished everybody, and occasioned much surmise to certain persons who were more discerning than others. They could not comprehend the union of two parties who hated each other so thoroughly as did at this moment the Protestant party and the Catholic party; and they wondered how the young Prince de Condé could forgive the Duc d'Anjou, the king's brother, for the

3

death of his father, assassinated by Montesquiou, at Jarnac. They asked how the young Du de Guise could pardon Admiral de Coligny for the death of his father, assassinated at Orléans by Poltrot de Méré. Moreover, Jeanne de Navarre, the courageous spouse of the weak Antoine de Bourbon, who had conducted his son Henri to the royal espousals which awaited him, had died scarcely two months before, and singular reports had been spread abroad as to this sudden death. It was everywhere whispered, and in some places said aloud, that she had discovered some terrible secret; and that Catherine de Médicis, fearing its disclosure, had poisoned her with perfumed gloves, made by one René, a Florentine very skillful in matters of that kind. This report was the more spread and believed when, after the death of this great queen, at her son's request two physicians, one of whom was the famous Ambroise Paré, were instructed to open and examine the body, but not the skull. As it was by the smell that Jeanne de Navarre had been poisoned, it was the brain alone—the only part of the body excluded from the autopsy—that could present any traces of the crime. We say crime, for no one doubted that a crime had been committed.

This was not all. King Charles, in particular, had pushed on this marriage, which not only would reestablish peace in his king dom, but would draw to Paris the leading Huguenots in France, with a persistence bordering on obstinacy. As the two betrothed belonged, one to the Catholic religion and the other to the Reformed religion, they were obliged to obtain a dispensation from Gregory XIII, who then filled the papal chair. The dispensation was slow in coming, and the delay causing great uneasiness to the late Queen of Navarre, she had one day expressed to Charles IX her fears lest the dispensation should not arrive; to which the king had replied—

"Be under no alarm, my dear aunt. I honor you more than I do the Pope, and I love my sister more than I fear his Holiness. I am not a Huguenot, but neither am I a fool; and if the Pope makes any difficulties, I will myself take Margot by the hand, and unite her to your son in full church."

This speech was soon spread through the Louvre and the city, and while it greatly rejoiced the Huguenots, had given the Catholics wherewithal to reflect upon; and they asked one another in suppressed tones if the king really meant to betray them, or was only playing a part which some fine morning or some fine evening might have an unexpected conclusion.

It was particularly with regard to Admiral de Coligny, who for five or six years had been so bitterly opposed to the king, that the conduct of Charles IX appeared inexplicable. After having put on his head a price of a hundred and fifty thousand golden crowns, the king now swore by him, called him his father, and declared openly that he should in future confide the conduct of the war to him alone. To such a pitch was this carried that Catherine de Médicis herself, who until then had controlled the actions, will, and even desires of the young prince, seemed beginning to be really uneasy, and not without reason; for in a moment of confidence, Charles IX had said to the admiral in reference to the war in Flanders, "My father, there is one other thing in regard to which we must be on our guard; and that is, that the queen, my mother, who likes to poke her nose everywhere, as you well know, shall learn nothing of this undertaking. We must keep it so quiet that she does not hear a word of it, or, meddler as she is, she will spoil all."

Now, wise and experienced as he was, Coligny had not kept this counsel secret; and although he had come to Paris with great suspicions, and although at his departure from Châtillon a peasant had thrown herself at his feet, crying, "Oh, Monsieur, our good master, do not go to Paris, for if you do you will die—you and all who are with you!"—these suspicions were lulled and almost destroyed in his breast and in that of Téligny, his son-in-law, to whom the king was especially kind and attentive, calling him his brother as he called the admiral his father, and behaving to him as he did to his best friends.

The Huguenots, then, excepting some few morose and suspicious spirits, were completely reassured. The death of the Queen of Navarre was understood to have been caused by a pleurisy; and the spacious apartments of the Louvre were filled with those brave Protestants to whom the marriage of their young chief, Henri, promised an unexpected return of good fortune. Admiral de Coligny, La Rochefoucault, the young Prince de Condé, Téligny, in short, all the leaders of the party, were triumphant when they saw so powerful at the Louvre and so welcome in Paris those whom, three months before, King Charles and Queen Catherine would have hanged on gibbets higher than those of assassins.

Marshal de Montmorency alone was looked for in vain among his brethren, for no promise could allure him, no pretense could deceive him; and he remained in retirement in his Château de l'Isle Adam, putting forth in explanation the enduring grief occasioned by the death of his father, Constable Anne de Montmorency, killed by a pistol-shot by Robert Stuart at the battle of St. Denis. But as this had happened more than three years before, and as sensitiveness was a virtue not much in vogue at that time, one could place as much or as little faith as he pleased in that explanation.

Everything seemed to show that the retirement of Marshal de Montmorency was ill-judged; the king, the queen, the Duc d'Anjou, and the Duc d'Alençon did the honors of the royal fête with surprising courtesy and kindness.

The Duc d'Anjou received from the Huguenots themselves well-merited compliments on the two battles of Jarnac and Montcontour, which he had gained before he was eighteen years of age—more precocious in that than either Cæsar or Alexander, to whom they compared him, of course placing the conquerors of Pharsalia and Issus below the living prince. The Duc d'Alençon looked on with his bland, false smile, while Queen Catherine, radiant with joy and diffuse in compliment, congratulated Prince Henri de Condé on his recent marriage with Marie de Clèves; and the M. M. de Guise themselves looked graciously on the formidable enemies of their house, and the Duc de Mayenne discoursed with M. de Tavannes and the admiral on the impending war, which was now more than ever threatened against Philippe II.

In the midst of these groups, his head a little inclined, his ear open to all that was said, moved a young man about nineteen years of age, with a keen eye, black hair cut very close, thick eyebrows, and a nose curved like an eagle's beak, with a sneering smile, and a growing mustache and beard. This young man, who had first distinguished himself at the battle of Arnay le Duc, where he had bravely exposed himself to danger, and who received many compliments, was the dearly beloved pupil of Coligny, and the hero of the day. Three months before, that is to say, when his mother was living, they called him the Prince de Béarn; now he was called the King of Navarre, and in after-time Henri IV.

From time to time a gloomy cloud passed suddenly and rapidly over his brow. Doubtless he recollected that only two months had elapsed since his mother's death; and he less than any one doubted that she had been poisoned. But the cloud was transitory, and disappeared like a fleeting shadow; for they who spoke to him, they who congratulated him, they who elbowed him, were they who had assassinated the brave Jeanne d'Albret.

Some paces distant from the King of Navarre, almost as pensive and gloomy as the king affected to be joyous and frank, was the young Duc de Guise, conversing with Téligny. More fortunate than the Béarnais, at twenty-two years of age he had almost attained the reputation of his father, François, the great Duc de Guise. He was a polished nobleman, very tall, with a high and haughty expression, and gifted with such natural majesty as to occasion the remark that by his side other princes seemed to belong to the people. Young as he was, the Catholics looked up to him as the chief of their party, as the Huguenots considered Henri de Navarre, whose portrait we have just drawn, to be their chief. He had heretofore borne the title of Prince de Joinville, and at the siege of Orléans fought his first fight under his father, who died in his arms, denouncing Admiral de Coligny as his assassin. It was then that the young duke, like Hannibal, took a solemn oath to avenge his father's death on the admiral and his family, and to pursue the foes of his religion without truce or respite, promising God to be His exterminating angel on earth until the very last heretic should be cut off. It was therefore with the deepest astonishment that the people saw this prince, usually so faithful to his word, extend the hand of fellowship to those whom he had sworn to hold as his eternal enemies, and converse familiarly with the son-in-law of the man whose death he had promised to his dying father.

But, as we have said, this was an evening of surprises. Indeed, had an observer been present endowed with that knowledge of the future which, happily, is wanting in man, with that faculty of reading the heart which, unhappily, belongs only to God, he certainly would have enjoyed the most curious spectacle afforded by the annals of the sad comedy of human life.

But that spectator who was not admitted to the galleries of the Louvre; who remained in the street, looking with gleaming eyes and muttering with threatening voice—that spectator was the multitude, which, with its instinct wonderfully sharpened by hatred, observed from a distance the shadows of its implacable enemies, and interpreted their movements as clearly as was possible to a spectator before the windows of a ballroom hermetically closed. Music excites and directs the dancer, while the spectator sees the motion only, and laughs at that pantomime which goes on without reason; for the spectator does not hear the music.

The music which excited the Huguenots was the voice of their pride. The gleams which shot forth from the eyes of the Parisians into the darkness of night were the lightnings of their hatred illumining the future.

Meantime, in the interior all were smiling; and a murmur, more soft and flattering than ever, pervaded the Louvre at the moment when the youthful bride, after having laid aside her toilet of ceremony, her long mantle, and flowing veil, returned to the ballroom, accompanied by the lovely Duchesse de Nevers, her most intimate friend, and led by her brother, Charles IX, who presented her to the principal guests.

The bride was the daughter of Henri II, the pearl of the crown of France, Marguerite de Valois, whom, in his familiar tenderness for her, King Charles IX always called *ma sœur Margot*.

Never was a more flattering reception, never one more merited than that which awaited the new Queen of Navarre. Marguerite at this period was scarcely twenty years old, and already she was the object of all the poets' eulogies, some of whom compared her to Aurora, others to Cytherea; she was, in truth, a beauty without rival in that court in which Catherine de Médicis had assembled the loveliest women of the age and country.

She had black hair, a brilliant complexion, a voluptuous eye veiled by long lids, coral and delicate lips, a graceful neck, a full, enchanting figure, and, concealed in a satin slipper, a tiny foot scarce larger than an infant's. The French, who possessed her, were proud to see so lovely a flower flourishing in their soil, and foreigners who passed through France returned home dazzled with her beauty if they had but seen her, and amazed at her knowledge if they had discoursed with her; for not only was Marguerite the loveliest, she was also the most learned woman of her time. And on all sides was quoted the remark of an Italian savant who had been presented to her, and who after having conversed with her for an hour in Italian,

Spanish, Greek, and Latin, had said on quitting her presence, "To see the court without seeing Marguerite de Valois is to see neither France nor the court."

Thus it may be supposed that addresses to King Charles IX and the Queen of Navarre were not wanting. The Huguenots were much given to speech-making. Many allusions to the past, and many demands as to the future were adroitly slipped into these addresses to the king; but to all such allusions and speeches he replied, with his pale lips and his crafty smile—

"In giving my sister Margot to Henri de Navarre, I give my sister to all the Protestants of the kingdom."

This phrase assured some, and made others smile, for it had really a double sense—the one paternal, which Charles IX could not sincerely intend; the other injurious to the bride, her husband, and even to him who uttered it—for it recalled some scandalous rumors with which the chroniclers of the court had already found means to smirch the nuptial robe of Marguerite de Valois.

Meantime, M. de Guise was conversing, as we have said, with Téligny; he did not, however, pay to the conversation such sustained attention but that he turned away somewhat, from time to time, to cast a glance at the group of ladies in the midst of which shone the Queen of Navarre. When the princess's eye thus met that of the young duke, a cloud seemed to overspread that lovely brow, around which stars of diamonds formed a tremulous circlet, and some agitating thought might be divined in her restless and impatient manner.

The Princess Claude, the elder sister of Marguerite, who had been for some years married to the Duc de Lorraine, had observed this uneasiness, and going up to her, was about to inquire the cause, when all stood aside at the approach of the queen-mother, who came forward, leaning on the arm of the young Prince de Condé; and the princess was thus suddenly shut out from her sister. There was then a general movement, by which the Duc de Guise profited to approach Madame de Nevers, his sister-in-law, and Marguerite.

Madame de Lorraine, who had not lost sight of her sister, then remarked, instead of the cloud which she had before observed on her forehead, a burning blush come into her cheeks. The duke approached still nearer; and when he was within two steps of Marguerite, she appeared rather to feel than see his presence, and turned round, making a violent effort over herself in order to give her features an appearance of calmness and indifference. The duke then, respectfully bowing, murmured in a low tone, *"Ipse attuli"* ("I have brought it").

Marguerite returned the salute of the young duke, and as she bowed, replied in the same tone, *"Noctu pro more"* ("Tonight as usual").

These words, uttered softly, were so lost in the enormous collar which the princess wore as to be heard only by the person to whom they were addressed; but brief as had been the conference, it doubtless comprised all that the young couple had to say—for after this exchange of two words for three, they separated, Marguerite more thoughtful, and the duke with his brow less clouded than when they met. This little scene took place apparently without being noticed by the person most concerned; for on his side, the King of Navarre had eyes but for one individual among those whom Marguerite de Valois had around her, and that was the lovely Madame de Sauve.

Charlotte de Beaune-Semblançay, granddaughter of the unfortunate Semblançay, and wife of Simon de Fizes, Baron de Sauve, was one of the ladies-in-waiting to Catherine de Médicis, and one of the most redoubtable auxiliaries of this queen, who poured forth for her enemies philters of love when she dared not pour out for them Italian poison. Delicately fair, and by turns sparkling with vivacity or languishing in melancholy, always ready for love or intrigue—the two great occupations which for fifty years employed the court of the three succeeding kings—a woman in the full sense of the word, and endowed with all womanly charms, from the blue eye, languishing or beaming fire, to the small and finely formed feet, restless in their slippers of velvet, Madame de Sauve had already for some months captivated the senses of the King of Navarre—then making his début as lover as well as politician—so completely that Marguerite de Valois, a magnificent and royal beauty, had not even excited admiration in the heart of her spouse; and what was more strange, and astonished every one, even in that soul so full of darkness and mystery—Catherine de Médicis, while she prosecuted her project of union between her daughter and the King of Navarre, had not ceased to favor almost openly his amour with Madame de Sauve. But despite this powerful aid, and despite the easy manners of the age, the lovely Charlotte had hitherto resisted; and this resistance, unheard-of, incredible, unprecedented, even more than the beauty and wit of her who resisted, had inspired in the heart of the Béarnais a passion which, ungratified, had recoiled on itself and had destroyed in the young king's heart all timidity, pride, and even that carelessness, half philosophy, half idleness, which formed the basis of his character.

Madame de Sauve had been only a few minutes in the ballroom; from spite or grief, she had at first resolved on not being present at her rival's triumph, and under the pretext of an indisposition, had allowed her husband, who had been for five years secretary of state, to go alone to the Louvre. But when Catherine de Médicis saw the baron without his wife, had learned the cause that kept away her dear Charlotte, and that her indisposition was but slight, she wrote to her a brief summons, which the young woman had instantly obeyed. Henri, sad as he had at first been at her absence, had yet breathed more freely when he saw M. de Sauve enter alone; but at the moment when, not expecting her appearance, he was about to pay some court to the charming creature whom he was condemned, if not to love, at least to treat as his wife, he saw Madame de Sauve arise, as it were, from the farther end of the gallery. He was nailed to the place, his eyes fastened on the Circe who enthralled him as if by magic chains, and instead of continuing his steps toward his wife, by a movement of hesitation which betrayed more astonishment than alarm, he advanced to meet Madame de Sauve.

The courtiers, seeing the King of Navarre, whose inflammable heart they knew, approach the beautiful Charlotte, had not the courage to prevent their meeting, but drew aside complaisantly; so that at the same moment when Marguerite de Valois and M. de Guise exchanged the few words in Latin which we have noted above, Henri, having approached Madame de Sauve, began, in a French very intelligible, although flavored with a Gascon accent, a conversation much less mysterious.

"Ah, my dear!" he said, "you have then come at the very moment when they assured me that you were unwell, and I had lost all hope of seeing you?"

"Your Majesty," replied Madame de Sauve, "would perhaps wish me to believe that it had cost you something to lose this hope?"

"*Sang Diou!* I believe it!" replied the Béarnais; "know you not that you are my sun by day, and my star by night? By my faith! I was in deepest darkness till you appeared and illumined all."

"Then, Monseigneur, I serve you a very ill turn."

"What mean you, my dear?" inquired Henri.

"I mean that he who is master of the handsomest woman in France should only have one desire—that the light should disappear and give way to darkness and to happiness."

"You know, cruel one, that my happiness is in the hands of one woman only, and that she laughs at poor Henri."

"Oh!" replied the baroness, "I believed, on the contrary, that it was this person who was the sport and jest of the King of Navarre."

Henri was alarmed by this unfriendly manner, although he re-flected that it betrayed jealousy, and that jealousy is the mask of love. "By my faith, dear Charlotte, you reproach me very unjustly, and I do not comprehend how so lovely a mouth can be so cruel. Do you suppose, then, that it is I who marry myself? No, *ventre-saint-gris,* it is not I!"

"It is I, perhaps," said the baroness, sharply.

"With your lovely eyes have you not seen farther, Baroness? No, no; it is not Henri de Navarre who weds Marguerite de Valois."

"And who is it, then?"

"Why, *sang Diou!* it is the Reformed religion which marries the Pope; that's all."

"No, no, Monseigneur; I am not to be deceived by your witti-cisms. Your Majesty loves Madame Marguerite. And can I blame you? Heaven forbid! She is beautiful enough to be adored."

Henri reflected for a moment, and as he reflected, a meaning smile curled the corner of his lips.

"Baroness," said he, "you have no right to seek a quarrel with me. What have you done to prevent me from espousing Madame Marguerite? Nothing. On the contrary, you have always driven me to despair."

"And well for me that I have, Monseigneur!" replied Madame de Sauve.

"How is that?"

"Certainly, since today you wed another."

"Ah! I marry her because you do not love me."

"If I loved you, Sire, it would be fatal to me in another hour."

"In another hour! What do you mean? And of what death would you die?"

"Of jealousy! for in an hour from now the Queen of Navarre will send away her women, and your Majesty your gentlemen."

"Is that really the thought that occupies your mind, my dear?"

"I do not say so. I only say that if I loved you it would occupy my mind most tormentingly."

"Well!" cried Henri, full of delight on hearing that avowal, the first that he had received, "if the King of Navarre should not send away his gentlemen this evening?"

"Sire," replied Madame de Sauve, looking at the king with astonishment for once unfeigned, "you say things impossible and incredible."

"What must I do to make you believe them?"

"Give me a proof; and that proof you cannot give me."

"Yes, Baroness, yes! By Saint Henri, I will give it you!" exclaimed the king, gazing amorously on her.

"Oh, your Majesty!" murmured the lovely Charlotte, with downcast eyes, "I do not comprehend. No; it is impossible that you should turn away from the happiness that awaits you."

"There are four Henris in this hall, my adorable!" replied the king—"Henri de France, Henri de Condé, Henri de Guise; but there is only one Henri de Navarre."

"Well?"

"Well; if this Henri de Navarre is with you all night—"

"All night!"

"Yes; then you will be certain that he is not with any other."

"Ah! if you do that, Sire," said Madame de Sauve.

"On the honor of a gentleman, I will do it!"

Madame de Sauve raised her beaming and love-promising eyes and smiled at the king, whose heart was filled with intoxicating delight.

"And then," said Henri, "what will you say?"

"I will say," replied Charlotte, "that your Majesty really loves me."

"*Ventre-saint-gris!* then you shall say it."

"But how can it be managed?" murmured Madame de Sauve.

"Oh, *pardieu!* Baroness, have you not about you some waiting-woman whom you can trust?"

"Yes, Dariole is devoted to me."

"Sang Diou! then say to her that I will make her fortune when I am King of France, as the astrologers prophesy."

Charlotte smiled, for even at this period the Gascon reputation of the Béarnais was already established with respect to his promises.

"Well, then, what do you desire of Dariole?"

"Little for her, a great deal for me. Your apartment is over mine?"

"Yes."

"Let her wait behind the door. I will strike three blows gently; she will open, and you will have the proof I offer you."

Madame de Sauve kept silence for several seconds; and then, as if she had looked around her to observe if she were overheard, she fastened her gaze for a moment on the group which surrounded the queen-mother. Brief as the moment was, it was sufficient for Catherine and her lady-in-waiting to exchange a look.

"Oh, if I were inclined," said Madame de Sauve, in the tone of a siren, which would have melted the wax in Ulysses' ears—"if I were inclined to make your Majesty tell a falsehood—"

"My darling, try!"

"Ah, upon my soul! I confess I am tempted to do so."

"Allow yourself to yield; women are never so strong as after their defeat."

"Sire, I hold you to your promise for Dariole, when you shall be King of France."

Henri uttered an exclamation of joy.

It was at the precise moment when the cry escaped the lips of the Béarnais that the Queen of Navarre replied to the Duc de Guise, *"Noctu pro more."*

Then Henri withdrew from Madame de Sauve as happy as the Duc de Guise when he went from Marguerite de Valois.

An hour after the double scene we have just related, King Charles and the queen-mother also retired to their apartments. Almost immediately the apartments began to empty; in the galleries the bases of the marble columns were exposed to view. The admiral and the Prince de Condé were escorted home by four hundred

Huguenot gentlemen through the middle of the crowd, which groaned as they passed. Then Henri de Guise, with the Lorraine and Catholic gentlemen, left in their turn, greeted by the cries of joy and plaudits of the people.

As to Marguerite de Valois, Henri de Navarre, and Madame de Sauve, they lived in the Louvre.

CHAPTER 2

The Queen of Navarre's Chamber

The Duc de Guise escorted his sister-in-law, the Duchesse de Nevers, to his house in the Rue du Chaume, and then proceeded to his own apartments to change his dress, put on a night cloak, and arm himself with one of those short and sharp poniards which were called *"foi de gentilhomme,"* and were worn without swords; but at the moment when he took it off the table on which it was placed, he perceived a small billet between the blade and the scabbard. He opened it and read as follows:

> I hope that M. de Guise will not return to the Louvre tonight; or if he does, that he will at least take the precaution to provide himself with a good coat-of-mail and a proved sword.

"Ah, ah!" said the duke, turning to his *valet de chambre,* "this is a singular warning, Maître Robin; have the kindness to tell me who have been here in my absence."

"Only one, Monseigneur."

"Who?"

"M. du Gast."

"Ah, ah! In fact, I thought I recognized his writing. You are sure Gast has been here? You have seen him?"

"I have done more, Monseigneur, I have spoken to him."

"Good; then I will follow the advice. My jacket and my sword!"

The *valet de chambre,* accustomed to these changes of costume, brought both. The duke put on his jacket, which was made of rings of steel so fine that it was scarcely thicker than velvet; he then put

16

on a doublet of gray and silver, his favorite colors, drew on long boots reaching to his thighs, put upon his head a black velvet cap, without feather or jewels, enveloped himself in a cloak of dark color, placed a dagger in his belt, and giving his sword to a page, the only attendant he allowed to accompany him, he started for the Louvre. As he stepped upon the threshold of the house, the watchman of St. Germain l'Auxerrois called the hour of one. Late as it was, and unsafe as were the streets at that period, no accident happened to the adventurous prince, and he arrived safely before the colossal pile of the old Louvre, whose lights were all extinguished, and which at that hour arose formidable in its silence and darkness.

In front of the royal château was a deep fosse, looking into which were the chambers of most of the princes who inhabited the palace. Marguerite's apartment was on the first floor, and, easily accessible but for the fosse, was, in consequence of the depth to which that was cut, thirty feet from the bottom of the wall, and consequently out of the reach of robbers or lovers; but nevertheless the Duc de Guise approached it without hesitation.

At the same moment was heard the noise of a window which opened on the ground floor. The window was grated; but a hand appeared, lifted out one of the bars, loosened beforehand, and dropped from it a silken cord.

"Is that you, Gillonne?" said the duke, in a low voice.

"Yes, Monseigneur," replied a female voice, in a still lower tone.

"And Marguerite?"

"Awaits you."

" 'Tis well."

Hereupon the duke made a signal to his page, who, opening his cloak, took out a small rope ladder. The prince attached one end to the silk cord, and Gillonne, drawing it up, made it fast; and the prince, after having buckled his sword to his belt, ascended without accident. When he entered, the bar was replaced and the window closed, while the page, having seen his master quietly enter the Louvre, to the windows of which he had accompanied him twenty times in the same way, laid himself down in his cloak on the grass of the fosse, and beneath the shadow of the wall. The night was dark;

and several large rain-spots fell from the heavy clouds charged with electric fluid.

The Duc de Guise followed his conductress, who was no other than the daughter of Jacques de Matignon, Marshal of France. She was the confidante of Marguerite, who kept no secret from her; and it was said that among the number of mysteries entrusted to her incorruptible fidelity, there were some so terrible as to compel her to keep the rest.

There was no light left either in the lower chamber or in the corridor, only from time to time a livid glare illuminated the dark apartments with a vivid flash, which instantly disappeared. The duke, still guided by his conductress, who held his hand, reached a spiral staircase formed in the thickness of the wall, and which opened by a secret and invisible door into the antechamber of Marguerite's apartment. In this antechamber, which was entirely dark, Gillonne stopped.

"Have you brought what the queen requested?" she inquired in a low voice.

"Yes," replied the Duc de Guise; "but I will only give it to her Majesty in person."

"Come, then, and do not lose an instant!" said a voice from the darkness which made the duke start, for he recognized it as Marguerite's. At the same moment a curtain of violet velvet covered with fleurs-de-lis was raised; and the duke made out the form of the queen, who in her impatience had come to meet him.

"I am here, Madame," he then said; and he passed the curtain, which fell behind him. Gillonne remained in the antechamber.

As if she comprehended the jealousies of the duke, Marguerite led him to the bedchamber, and then paused. "Well," she said, "are you content, Duke?"

"Content, Madame?" was the reply; "and in regard to what?"

"With this proof which I give you," replied Marguerite, with a slight tone of vexation in her voice, "that I belong to a man who, on the very night of his marriage, makes me of such small importance that he does not even come to thank me for the honor I have done him, not in selecting, but in accepting him for my husband."

"Oh, Madame," said the duke, sorrowfully, "be assured he will come—especially if you desire it."

"And is it you who say that, Henri?" cried Marguerite—"you, who better than any know that the truth is contrary to what you say. If I had that desire, should I have asked you to come to the Louvre?"

"You have asked me to come to the Louvre, Marguerite, because you are anxious to destroy every vestige of the past, and because that past lives not only in my memory, but in this silver casket which I bring to you."

"Henri, shall I say one thing to you?" replied Marguerite; "it is that you are more like a schoolboy than a prince. I deny that I have loved you! I desire to quench a flame which will die perhaps, but whose reflection will never die! No, no, Duke; you may keep the letters of your Marguerite, and the casket she has given you. From these letters she asks but one, and that only because it is as dangerous for you as for herself."

"They are all at your disposal," said the duke; "select, then, among them the one you wish to destroy."

Marguerite searched anxiously in the open casket, and with a tremulous hand took, one after the other, a dozen letters, of which she examined the addresses only, as if by the inspection alone of these she could recall to her memory what the letters themselves contained; but after a close scrutiny, she looked at the duke, pale and agitated. "Monsieur," she said, "what I seek is not here. Have you lost it by any accident?"

"What letter do you seek, Madame?"

"That one in which I told you to marry without delay."

"As an excuse for your infidelity?"

Marguerite shrugged her shoulders. "No; but to save your life. That one in which I say to you that the king, seeing our love and my exertions to break off your proposed espousals with the Infanta of Portugal, had sent for his brother, the bastard of Angoulême, and said to him, pointing to two swords, 'With this slay Henri de Guise this night, or with the other I will slay thee in the morning.' Where is that letter?"

"Here," said the duke, drawing it from his breast.

Marguerite snatched it from his hands, opened it anxiously, assured herself that it was really that which she desired, uttered an exclamation of joy, and applied to it the lighted candle. The flames instantly consumed the paper; then, as if Marguerite feared that her imprudent words might be read in the very ashes, she trampled them underfoot.

During all this feverish action, the Duc de Guise had watched his mistress attentively.

"Well, Marguerite," he said, when she had finished, "are you satisfied now?"

"Yes, for now that you have wedded the Princesse de Procian, my brother will forgive me your love; while he never would have pardoned me for revealing a secret such as that which in my weakness for you I had not the strength to conceal from you."

"True," replied Guise; "then you loved me."

"And I love you still, Henri, as much—more than ever!"

"You?"

"Yes, I; for never more than at this moment did I need a sincere and devoted friend. Queen, I have no throne; wife, I have no husband!"

The young prince shook his head sorrowfully.

"I tell you, I repeat to you, Henri, that my husband not only does not love me, but hates—despises me; indeed, it seems to me that your presence in the chamber in which he ought to be is proof of this hatred and of this contempt."

"It is not yet late, Madame, and the King of Navarre requires time to dismiss his gentlemen; if he has not already come, he will come soon."

"And I tell you," cried Marguerite, with increasing vexation— "I tell you that he will not come!"

"Madame!" exclaimed Gillonne, suddenly entering, "the King of Navarre is just leaving his apartments!"

"Oh, I knew he would come!" exclaimed the Duc de Guise.

"Henri," said Marguerite, in a quick tone, and seizing the duke's hand—"Henri, you shall see if I am a woman of my word, and if I may be relied on. Henri, enter that closet."

"Madame, allow me to go while there is yet time, for reflect that the first mark of love you bestow on him, I shall quit the cabinet, and then woe to him!"

"Are you mad? Go in—go in, I say, and I will be responsible for all"; and she pushed the duke into the closet.

It was time. The door was scarcely closed behind the prince when the King of Navarre, escorted by two pages, who carried eight torches of yellow wax in two candelabra, appeared, smiling, on the threshold of the chamber. Marguerite concealed her trouble, and made a low bow.

"You are not yet in bed, Madame," observed the Béarnais, with his frank and joyous look. "Were you by chance waiting for me?"

"No, Monsieur," replied Marguerite; "for yesterday you repeated to me that our marriage was a political alliance, and that you would never thwart my wishes."

"Assuredly; but that is no reason why we should not confer a little together. Gillonne, close the door, and leave us."

Marguerite, who was sitting, then rose and extended her hand, as if to desire the pages to remain.

"Must I call your women?" inquired the king. "I will do so if such be your desire, although I confess that for what I have to say to you I should prefer our being alone"; and the King of Navarre advanced toward the closet.

"No!" exclaimed Marguerite, hastily going before him—"no! There is no occasion for that; I am ready to hear you."

The Béarnais had learned what he desired to know; he threw a rapid and penetrating glance toward the cabinet, as if in spite of the thick curtain which hung before it, he would dive into its obscurity, and then, turning his looks to his lovely wife, pale with terror, he said with the utmost composure, "In that case, Madame, let us confer for a few moments."

"As your Majesty pleases," said the young wife, falling into rather than sitting upon the seat which her husband pointed out to her.

The Béarnais placed himself beside her. "Madame," he continued, "whatever many persons may have said, I think our marriage is a good marriage. I stand well with you; you stand well with me."

"But—" said Marguerite, alarmed.

"Consequently, we ought," observed the King of Navarre, without seeming to notice Marguerite's hesitation, "to act toward each other like good allies, since we have today sworn alliance in the presence of God. Don't you think so?"

"Unquestionably, Monsieur."

"I know, Madame, how great your penetration is; I know how the ground at court is intersected with dangerous abysses. Now, I am young, and although I never injured any one, I have a great many enemies. In which camp, Madame, ought I to range her who bears my name, and who has vowed her affection to me at the foot of the altar?"

"Monsieur, could you think—"

"I think nothing, Madame; I hope, and I am anxious to know that my hope is well founded. It is quite certain that our marriage is merely a pretext or a snare."

Marguerite started, for perhaps the same thought had occurred to her own mind.

"Now, then, which of the two?" continued Henri de Navarre. "The king hates me; the Duc d'Anjou hates me; the Duc d'Alençon hates me; Catherine de Médicis hated my mother too much not to hate me."

"Oh, Monsieur, what are you saying?"

"The truth, Madame," replied the king; "and I wish, in order that it may not be supposed that I am duped concerning the assassination of M. de Mouy and the poisoning of my mother, that some one were here who could hear me."

"Oh, Monsieur," replied Marguerite, with an air as calm and smiling as she could assume, "you know very well that there is no one here but you and myself."

"It is for that very reason that I thus give vent to my thoughts; this it is that emboldens me to declare that I am not duped by the caresses showered on me by the house of France or by those of the house of Lorraine."

"Sire! Sire!" exclaimed Marguerite.

"Well, what is it, my dear?" inquired Henri, smiling.

"Why, Monsieur, such remarks as these are extremely dangerous."

"Not when we are alone," observed the king. "I was saying—"

Marguerite was evidently distressed; she desired to stop every word upon the lips of the king, but he continued with his apparent simplicity, "I was saying that I am menaced on all sides—menaced by the king, menaced by the Duc d'Alençon, menaced by the Duc d'Anjou, menaced by the queen-mother, menaced by the Duc de Guise, by the Duc de Mayenne, by the Cardinal de Lorraine, menaced, in fact, by everybody. One feels that instinctively, as you know, Madame. Well, against all these menaces, which must soon become attacks, I can defend myself by your aid, for you are beloved by all the persons who detest me."

"I?" said Marguerite.

"Yes, you," replied Henri, with easy frankness of manner— "yes, you are beloved by King Charles; you are beloved [he laid strong emphasis on the word] by the Duc d'Alençon; you are beloved by Queen Catherine; and you are beloved by the Duc de Guise."

"Monsieur!" murmured Marguerite.

"Well! what is there astonishing in the fact that all the world loves you? All I have mentioned are your brothers or relatives. To love one's brothers and relatives is to live according to the heart of God."

"But what, then," asked Marguerite, distressed—"what would you have?"

"I would say that if you will—I will not ask you to love me— but if you will be my ally, I can brave everything; while on the other hand, if you become my enemy, I am lost."

"Oh, your enemy! never, Monsieur!" exclaimed Marguerite.

"And my love—never either?"

"Perhaps—"

"And my ally?"

"Certainly." And Marguerite turned round and presented her hand to the king.

Henri took the proffered hand, kissed it gallantly, and retaining it in his own, more from a desire of investigation than from any sentiment of tenderness, said, "Well, Madame, I believe you, and accept the alliance. They married us without our knowing each other, without our loving each other; they married us without consulting us—us whom they united. We therefore owe nothing to each other as man and wife. You see, Madame, that I anticipate your wishes, and that I confirm to you tonight what I told you yesterday. But we ally ourselves freely and without any compulsion. We ally ourselves as two loyal hearts who owe each other mutual protection should ally themselves. Do you so understand the matter?"

"Yes, Monsieur," said Marguerite, endeavoring to withdraw her hand.

"Well, then," continued the Béarnais, with his eyes fixed on the cabinet, "as the first proof of a frank alliance is the most perfect confidence, I will now, Madame, relate to you in all its details the plan I have formed, in order that we may victoriously meet and overcome all these enemies."

"Monsieur!" said Marguerite, turning her eyes toward the closet, while the Béarnais, seeing his trick succeed, laughed in his sleeve.

"This is what I mean to do," he continued, without appearing to remark the uneasiness of his young wife; "I intend—"

"Monsieur," said Marguerite, rising hastily, and seizing the king's arm, "allow me a little air; my emotion—the heat—I am stifling." And, in truth, she was as pale and trembling as if she was about to fall on the carpet.

Henri went straight to a window at some distance and opened it. This window looked on the river. Marguerite followed him. "Silence, Sire! silence, for pity's sake!" she murmured.

"What, Madame!" said the Béarnais, with his peculiar smile, "did you not say we were alone?"

"Yes, Monsieur; but have you not heard me say that by the aid of a tube introduced into the ceiling or the wall everything could be heard?"

"Well, Madame, well," said the Béarnais, earnestly, and in a low voice, "it is true you do not love me; but you are at least an honorable woman."

"What do you mean, Monsieur?"

"I mean that if you were capable of betraying me you would have allowed me to continue, as I might have betrayed myself. You stopped me. I now know that some one is concealed here; that you are an unfaithful wife, but a faithful ally; and at this moment," he added, smiling, "I have more need of fidelity in politics than in love."

"Sire—" murmured Marguerite, confused.

"Good, good; we will talk of this hereafter," said Henri, "when we know each other better." Then, raising his voice, "Well," he continued, "do you breathe more freely now, Madame?"

"Yes, Monsieur! yes!"

"Well, then," said the Béarnais, "I will no longer intrude on you. I owed you my respects, and some advances toward better acquaintance; deign, then, to accept them, as they are offered with all my heart. Good-night, and happy slumbers!"

Marguerite raised to her husband her eyes, brilliant with gratitude, and in her turn extended her hand. "It is agreed," she said.

"Political alliance, frank and loyal?" asked Henri.

"Frank and loyal," was the reply.

The Béarnais went toward the door, drawing Marguerite after him by a look, as if by the power of enchantment. Then, when the curtain had fallen between them and the bedchamber, "Thanks, Marguerite," he said in a quick and low tone, "thanks! You are a true daughter of France. I leave you quite tranquil; though I lack your love, your friendship will not fail me. I rely on you, as you, for your part, may rely on me. Adieu, Madame."

Henri kissed his wife's hand, and pressed it gently. Then with a quick step he returned to his own apartments, saying to himself in a low voice in the corridor, "Who the devil is with her? Is it the king, or the Duc d'Anjou, or the Duc d'Alençon, or the Duc de Guise? Is it a brother or a lover? Is it both? I' faith, I am almost sorry now that I asked the baroness for this rendezvous; but as my word is pledged, and Dariole awaits me, no matter. She will not be so attractive, I fear, since in going to her I have passed through my wife's bedchamber; for *ventre-saint-gris!* this Margot, as my brother-in-law, King Charles, calls her, is an adorable creature." And with a step which betrayed a slight hesitation, Henri de Navarre ascended the staircase which led to Madame de Sauve's apartments.

Marguerite had followed him with her eyes until he disappeared. Then she returned to her chamber, and found the duke at the door of the cabinet. The sight almost touched her with remorse.

The duke was grave; and his knitted brow bespoke bitter reflection. "Marguerite is neutral today," he said; "Marguerite will be hostile in a week."

"Ah! you have been listening?" said Marguerite.

"What else could I do in the cabinet?"

"And did you find that I behaved otherwise than the Queen of Navarre should behave?"

"No; but differently from the way in which the mistress of the Duc de Guise should behave."

"Monsieur," replied the queen, "I may not love my husband;

but no one has the right to require me to betray him. Would you yourself reveal the secrets of the Princesse de Porcian, your wife?"

"Come, come, Madame," answered the duke, shaking his head, "this is very well; I see that you do not love me as in those days when you disclosed to me the plot of the king against me and my party."

"The king was strong and you were weak; Henri is weak and you are strong. You see I play a consistent part!"

"Only you pass from one camp to another."

"That was a right I acquired, Monsieur, in saving your life."

"Good, Madame; and as when lovers separate, they return all the gifts that have passed between them, I will, if the occasion presents itself, save your life in my turn, and we shall be quits." And bowing politely, the duke left the room, nor did Marguerite attempt to retain him. In the antechamber he found Gillonne, who guided him to the window on the groundfloor, and in the fosse he found his page, with whom he returned to the Hôtel de Guise.

Marguerite went to the opened window. "What a marriage-night!" she murmured to herself; "the husband flies, the lover forsakes me!" She shut the window, and called Gillonne to help her to undress and retire to bed.

CHAPTER 3

The Poet-King

The morrow and the following days were passed in a succession of balls, tournaments, and banquets. The same union continued to be exhibited between the two parties. Attentions and caresses were lavishly bestowed on the leading Huguenots. The king seemed to have laid aside his usual melancholy, and the queen-mother was so occupied with embroidery, ornaments, and plumes that she could not sleep.

The Huguenots, in some measure appeased by that new Capua, began to assume silken doublets, wear devices, and parade before certain balconies, as if they were Catholics. On every side the reaction in favor of the Protestants was so great that it seemed as if the court were about to become Protestant itself. Even the admiral, in spite of his discernment, was deceived, and was so carried away that one evening he forgot for two whole hours to chew his toothpick—an occupation to which he usually abandoned himself from two o'clock, when he finished his dinner, until eight o'clock at night, when he sat down to supper.

The evening on which the admiral thus deviated from his usual habit, King Charles IX had invited Henri de Navarre and the Duc de Guise to sup with him. After the repast he went into his chamber, and was busily explaining to them the mechanism of a wolftrap he had invented, when, interrupting himself, "The admiral does not come tonight," said he; "who has seen him today, and can tell me anything about him?"

"I have," said the King of Navarre; "and should your Majesty be anxious about his health, I can reassure you, for I saw him this morning at six, and this evening at seven o'clock."

"Ah, ah!" replied the king, whose eyes were instantly fixed

with a searching expression on his brother-in-law; "for a newly married man, Henriot, you are very early."

"Yes, Sire," answered the King of Navarre; "I wished to inquire of the admiral, who knows everything, whether some gentlemen I expect are on their way hither."

"More gentlemen! why, you had eight hundred on the day of your wedding, and new ones join you every day. You are surely not going to invade us?" said Charles IX, smiling.

The Duc de Guise frowned.

"Sire," returned the Béarnais, "a war with Flanders is spoken of; and I am collecting round me all those gentlemen of my country who I think can be useful to your Majesty."

The duke, calling to mind the project of which Henri had spoken to Marguerite the day of their marriage, listened more attentively.

"Well, well," replied the king, with his sinister smile, "the more the better; let them all come. But who are these gentlemen? Brave ones, I trust?"

"I know not, Sire, if my gentlemen will ever equal those of your Majesty, of the Duc d'Anjou, or of the Duc de Guise; but I know that they will do their best."

"Do you expect many?"

"Ten or twelve, perhaps."

"What are their names?"

"Sire, I cannot at this moment call any of them to mind, with the exception of one whom Téligny recommends to me as a most accomplished gentleman, and whose name is La Mole."

"La Mole!" said the king, who was well acquainted with the genealogy of all the noble families of France; "is he not a Lerac de la Mole, a Provençal?"

"Exactly so, Sire; you see, I recruit even in Provence."

"And I," added the Duc de Guise, with a sarcastic smile, "go still farther than the King of Navarre, for I seek even in Piedmont all the brave Catholics I can find."

"Catholic or Huguenot," interrupted the king, "it little matters to me, so they are brave."

The expression of the king's face, while he uttered these words, which thus united Catholics and Huguenots in his thoughts, was so full of indifference that the duke himself was surprised.

"Your Majesty is talking of the Flemings?" said the admiral, to whom Charles had some days previously accorded the privilege of entering without being announced, and who had overheard the king's last words.

"Ah! here is my father, the admiral!" cried Charles, opening his arms. "We were speaking of battles, of gentlemen, of brave men—and *he* comes. It is like the lodestone that attracts the iron. My brother-in-law of Navarre and my cousin of Guise expect reinforcements for your army. That was the subject of our conversation."

"And these reinforcements are approaching," said the admiral.

"Have you any intelligence of them, Monsieur?" asked the Béarnais.

"Yes, my son, and particularly of M. de la Mole; he was at Orléans yesterday, and will be in Paris tomorrow or the day after."

"The devil! You must be a sorcerer, Monsieur the Admiral," said the Duc de Guise, "to know what is passing at thirty or forty leagues' distance. For my part, I should like to know with as much certainty what will happen, or what has happened at Orléans."

Coligny remained unmoved by this speech, which evidently alluded to the death of François de Guise, the duke's father, killed before Orléans by Poltrot de Méré, and not without a suspicion of the admiral's having been concerned in the murder.

"Monsieur," replied he, coldly, and with dignity, "I am a sorcerer whenever I wish to know anything that concerns my own affairs or those of the king. My courier arrived an hour ago from Orléans, having traveled, thanks to the post, thirty-two leagues in a day. As M. de la Mole has only his own horse, he rides but ten leagues a day, and cannot arrive in Paris until the twenty-fourth. Here is all my magic."

"Bravo, my father! well answered!" cried Charles IX. "Teach these young men that it is wisdom as well as age that has whitened your hair and beard; so now we will send them to talk of love and tournaments, and we will ourselves discourse of our wars. Good advisers make good kings. Leave us, gentlemen; I wish to talk with the admiral."

The two young men left the apartment—the King of Navarre first, then the Duc de Guise; but outside the door they separated, after a formal salute. Coligny followed them with his eyes, not without disquietude; for he never saw these two men meet, who cherished so deadly a hate against each other, without a dread that some spark would kindle a conflagration. Charles saw what was passing in his mind, and said, laying his hand on his arm—

"Fear nothing, my father; I am here to preserve peace and obedience. I am really a king, now that my mother is no longer queen; and she is no longer queen since Coligny became my father."

"Oh, Sire!" responded the admiral, "the Queen Catherine—"

"Is a mischief-maker. Peace is impossible with her. These Italian Catholics are furious, and will hear of nothing but extermination; now, for my part, I not only wish to pacify, but I wish to give power to those who profess the Reformed religion. The others are too dissolute, and scandalize me with their amours and their revels. Shall I speak frankly to you?" continued Charles, with increasing effusiveness. "I mistrust every one about me, except my new friends. I suspect the ambition of Tavannes; Vieilleville cares only for good wine, and would betray his king for a cask of Malvoisie; Montmorency thinks only of the chase, and lives among his dogs and falcons; the Comte de Retz is a Spaniard; the Guises are Lorraines. I think there are no true Frenchmen in France except myself, my brother-in-law of Navarre, and yourself; but I am chained to the throne, and cannot command the army. It is as much as I can do to hunt at St. Germain or Rambouillet. My brother-in-law of Navarre is too young and too inexperienced; besides, he seems to me exactly like his father Antoine, who was always abandoned to women. There is but you, my father, who can be called at the same time brave as Cæsar and wise as Plato; so that I scarcely know what to do—keep you near me as my adviser, or send you to the army as its general. If you counsel me, who will command? If you command, who will counsel me?"

"Sire," said Coligny, "we must conquer first, and take counsel after the victory."

"That is your advice; so be it. Monday you shall leave for Flanders, and I for Amboise."

"Your Majesty leaves Paris, then?"

"Yes; I am weary of this confusion, and of these fêtes. I am not a man of action; I am a dreamer. I was not born to be a king; I was born to be a poet. You shall form a sort of council, which will govern while you are away fighting; and if my mother has no part in it, all will go well. I have already sent word to Ronsard to meet me;

and there, we two—far from noise, far from the world, far from the wicked, under the great forest-trees, on riverbanks, by murmuring streams—will talk together of the things of God, the only compensation which this world affords for the deeds of men. At this moment I must go and reply to a sonnet my dear and illustrious poet has sent me. I cannot, therefore, now give you the documents necessary to make you acquainted with the question at issue between Philippe II and myself. There is, besides, a plan of the campaign drawn up by my ministers. I will find it all for you and give it to you tomorrow."

"At what o'clock, Sire?"

"At ten o'clock; and if by chance I am busy making verses, or in my cabinet writing, well, you will find all the papers in this red portfolio. The color is remarkable, and you cannot mistake it. I am now going to write to Ronsard."

"Adieu, Sire!"

"Adieu, my father!"

"Your hand?"

"What! my hand? In my arms, in my heart, there is your place! Come, my old soldier, come!" And Charles, drawing Coligny toward him as he inclined himself before him, pressed his lips to his forehead.

The admiral wiped away a tear as he left the room. Charles followed him with his eyes as long as he could see him, and listened as long as he could catch a sound; and when he could no longer see or hear him, he turned and entered his armory. This armory was the favorite apartment of the king. It was there he took his fencing lessons with Pompée, and his lessons in poetry with Ronsard. He had gathered there all the most costly arms he had been able to collect. The walls were hung with axes, shields, spears, halberds, pistols, and muskets, and that day a famous armorer had brought him a magnificent arquebus, on the barrel of which were encrusted in silver these four lines, composed by the royal poet himself:

> POUR MAINTENIR LA FOY,
> JE SUIS BELLE ET FIDÈLE:
> AUX ENNEMIS DU ROY,
> JE SUIS BELLE ET CRUELLE.

Charles entered this room, as we have said; and after having shut the door by which he had entered, he raised the tapestry that masked a passage leading into a little chamber, where a woman, kneeling, was saying her prayers. As this movement was quietly made, and the footsteps of the king were deadened by the thick carpet, the woman heard no sound, and continued to pray. Charles stood for a moment pensively looking at her.

She was a woman of thirty-four or thirty-five years of age, whose masculine beauty was set off by the costume of the peasants in the neighborhood of Caux. She wore the high cap so much the fashion at the court of France during the time of Isabel of Bavaria, and her bodice was red and embroidered with gold, like those of the *contadines* of Nettuno and Sora. The apartment which she had occupied for nearly twenty years was close to the bedchamber of the king, and presented a singular mixture of elegance and rusticity. The palace had encroached upon the cottage, and the cottage upon the palace; so that the chamber presented an appearance combining the simplicity of the peasant and the luxury of a woman of rank. The prie-dieu on which she knelt was of oak, beautifully carved, covered with velvet, and embroidered with gold; while the Bible (for she was of the Reformed religion) from which she was reading was very old and torn, like those found in the poorest cottages. Everything was in keeping with that prie-dieu and that Bible.

"Eh, Madelon!" said the king.

The kneeling woman lifted her head with a smile on hearing that well-known voice; and rising from her knees, "Ah! it is you, my son," said she.

"Yes, Nurse; come here."

Charles IX let fall the curtain and sat down on the arm of a large chair. The nurse appeared. "What do you want with me, Charles?" she said.

"Come near, and answer in a low tone."

The nurse approached him with a familiarity which might spring from that maternal tenderness which a woman conceives for the child she has nursed, but to which the pamphlets of the period assign an origin far less pure.

"Here I am," said she; "speak!"

"Is the man here for whom I sent?"

"He has been here half an hour."

Charles rose from his seat, approached the window, looked to assure himself there were no eavesdroppers, went toward the door, and looked out there also, shook the dust from his trophies of arms, patted a large greyhound which followed him wherever he went, stopping when he stopped, and moving when he moved, then returning to his nurse, "Let him come in, Nurse," said he.

The nurse disappeared by the same passage by which she had entered, while the king went and leaned against a table on which were scattered arms of every kind. Scarcely had he done so, when the tapestry was again lifted, and the person whom he expected entered. He was a man about forty years old, his large gray eyes full of treachery and falsehood, his nose curved like the beak of a screech-owl, his cheekbones prominent. His face sought to assume an expression of respect; but only a hypocritical smile appeared on his lips blanched by fear.

Charles gently put his hand behind him, and grasped the butt of a pistol of a new construction, that was discharged, not by a match, as formerly, but by a flint brought in contact with a wheel of steel. He fixed his dull eyes steadily on the newcomer, while he whistled, with striking correctness and even melody, one of his favorite hunting airs.

After a pause of some minutes, during which the expression of the stranger's face grew more and more discomposed, "You are the person," said the king, "called François de Louviers-Maurevel?"

"Yes, Sire."

"Commander of petardeers?"

"Yes, Sire."

"I wished to see you."

Maurevel bowed.

"You know," continued Charles, laying a stress on each word, "that I love all my subjects equally?"

"I know," stammered Maurevel, "that your Majesty is the father of your people."

"And that the Huguenots and Catholics are equally my children."

Maurevel remained silent; but his agitation was manifest to the piercing eyes of the king, although he was almost concealed in the obscurity.

"This displeases you," said the king, "who are so great an enemy to the Huguenots."

Maurevel fell on his knees. "Sire," he stammered, "believe that—"

"I believe," continued Charles, fixing on Maurevel a look which, glassy at first, now seemed almost flaming—"I believe that you had a great desire at Moncontour to kill the admiral who has just left me; I believe you missed your aim, and that then you entered the army of my brother, the Duc d'Anjou; I believe that you enlisted into the company of M. de Mouy de St. Phale."

"Oh, Sire!"

"A brave gentleman from Picardy."

"Sire, Sire!" cried Maurevel, "do not overwhelm me!"

"He was a brave soldier," continued Charles, whose features assumed an aspect of almost ferocious cruelty, "who received you as if you had been his son—fed you, lodged you, and clothed you."

Maurevel uttered a despairing sigh.

"You called him your father, and a tender friendship existed between you and the young Mouy."

Maurevel, still on his knees, bent himself more and more; the king stood immovable, like a statue whose lips only are endowed with vitality.

"By the way," continued the king, "M. de Guise was to give you ten thousand crowns if you killed the admiral, was he not?"

The assassin struck his forehead against the floor.

"One day when your father, the Sieur de Mouy, reconnoitered near Chevreux, he let his whip fall, and dismounted to pick it up. You were then alone with him; you took a pistol from your holster and shot him in the back; then, seeing he was dead—for you killed him on the spot—you escaped on the horse he had given you. This is your history, I believe?"

And as Maurevel remained mute under this accusation, every detail of which was true, the king began to whistle again, with the same correctness and melody, the same hunting air.

"Now, then, Master Assassin," said he, "do you know I have a great mind to hang you?"

"Oh, Sire!" cried Maurevel.

"Young Mouy entreated me to do so only yesterday; and I scarcely knew what answer to make him, for his demand was but just."

Maurevel clasped his hands.

"All the more just, since I am, as you have said, the father of my people; and since, as I answered you, now that I am reconciled to the Huguenots, they are as much my children as the Catholics."

"Sire," said Maurevel, in despair, "my life is in your hands; do with it what you will."

"You are quite right; and I would not give a farthing for it."

"But, Sire," asked the assassin, "is there no way of redeeming my crime?"

"I know of none; only if I were in your place—but thank God I am not—"

"Well, Sire, were you in my place?" murmured Maurevel.

"I think I could extricate myself," said the king.

Maurevel raised himself on one knee and one hand, fixing his eyes upon Charles.

"I am very fond of young Mouy," said the king; "but I am equally fond of my cousin of Guise. And if my cousin asked me to spare a man whom the other wanted me to hang, I confess I should be embarrassed; but for the sake of policy as well as of religion I should comply with Guise's request—for Mouy, although a brave captain, is but a petty personage compared with a prince of Lorraine."

During these words Maurevel slowly rose, like a man who comes to life.

"Now, the important thing for you, in your present desperate situation, is to secure the favor of my cousin of Guise; and speaking of him, I am reminded of something he told me last night." Maurevel drew nearer. " 'Imagine, Sire,' said he to me, 'that every morning at ten o'clock my deadliest enemy passes down the Rue St. Germain l'Auxerrois, on his return from the Louvre. I see him from a barred window in the room of my old preceptor, the Canon Pierre Piles; and I pray the Devil to open the earth and swallow him in its abysses.' Now, then, Maître Maurevel, if you were the Devil, or if for a moment you could take his place, that would perhaps be agreeable to my cousin of Guise."

Maurevel recovered his infernal smile, and from his lips, still pale with fright, dropped the words, "But, Sire, I cannot make the earth open."

"You opened it, however, if I remember correctly, to the brave Mouy. After that, you will tell me that it was done with a pistol. Have you that pistol no longer?"

"I am a better marksman, Sire, with an arquebus than a pistol," replied Maurevel, now quite reassured.

"Never mind," said the king; "I am sure M. de Guise will not care how it is done, so it be done."

"But," said Maurevel, "I must have a weapon I can rely on, as perhaps I shall have to fire from a long distance."

"I have ten arquebuse in this chamber," replied Charles IX, "with which I hit a crown-piece at a hundred and fifty paces; will you try one?"

"Most willingly, Sire!" cried Maurevel, advancing toward the one placed in a corner, and which that very day had been brought to the king.

"No, not that one," said the king; "I reserve that for myself. Someday I will have a grand hunt, and then I hope to use it. Take any other you like."

Maurevel took one from a rack. "And who is this enemy, Sire?"

"How should I know?" replied Charles, with a contemptuous look.

"I must ask M. de Guise, then," faltered Maurevel.

The king shrugged his shoulders. "Do not ask," said he; "for M. de Guise will not answer. Does any one answer such questions as that? It is for those who do not wish to be hanged to guess."

"But how shall I know him?"

"I tell you he passes the canon's window every morning at ten o'clock."

"But many pass that window; would your Majesty deign to give me a sign of some kind?"

"Oh, that is very easy. Tomorrow, for example, he will carry a red morocco portfolio under his arm."

"That is sufficient, Sire."

"You have still the horse M. de Mouy gave you, have you not?"

"Sire, I have a horse that is fleeter than any other in France."

"Oh, I am not anxious about you; only it is as well to let you know there is a back door."

"Thanks, Sire; pray Heaven for me!"

"Eh! thousand demons! pray to the Devil rather; for by his aid only can you escape a halter."

"Adieu, Sire."

"Adieu! By the way, M. Maurevel, remember that if I hear of you before ten tomorrow, or do not hear of you afterward, there is an oubliette at the Louvre."

And Charles began to whistle tranquilly, and more correctly than ever, his favorite air.

CHAPTER 4

The Evening of August 24, 1572

Our readers have not forgotten that in the previous chapter Henri was anxiously expecting the arrival of a gentleman named La Mole.

This young gentleman, as the admiral had anticipated, entered Paris by the gate of St. Marcel, the evening of Aug. 24, 1572; and bestowing a contemptuous glance on the numerous hostelries that displayed their picturesque signs on either side of him, he rode on into the heart of the city, and after having passed through the Place Maubert, the Petit Pont, the Pont Notre Dame, and along the quays, he stopped at the end of the Rue de l'Arbre Sec.

The name pleased him, no doubt, for he entered the street; and finding on his left a large plate of iron swinging, creaking on its hinges, he stopped and read these words, "La Belle Etoile," written on a scroll beneath the sign, which was a most attractive one for a hungry traveler; it represented a fowl roasting in the midst of a black sky, while a man in a red cloak reached toward that novel kind of star with his arms, his purse, and his longings.

"Here," said the gentleman to himself, "is an inn that promises well, and the landlord must be a most ingenious fellow. I have always heard that the Rue de l'Arbre Sec was near the Louvre; and provided that the interior agrees with the exterior, I shall be admirably lodged."

While this monologue was going on, another person entered the other end of the street, and stopped also to admire the sign of the Belle Etoile.

The gentleman, whom we already know, at least by name, rode a white horse, and wore a black doublet ornamented with jet; his cloak was of violet velvet, his boots were of black leather, and the hilts of his sword and dagger were of steel, beautifully worked.

He was a man from twenty-four to twenty-five years old, of dark complexion, with blue eyes, a delicate mustache, and shining teeth that seemed to light up his face when his finely formed lips were parted in a smile of melancholy sweetness.

Nothing could form a greater contrast with him than the second traveler. Beneath his slouched hat appeared a profusion of hair of a brown-red color, and large gray eyes that on the slightest occasion sparkled so fiercely that they seemed to be black. He had a fair complexion, a light mustache, and splendid teeth; with his white skin and tall form and broad shoulders, he was what is generally termed a handsome cavalier, and during the last hour which he had employed in staring up at all the windows on the pretext of looking for signs, the women had honored him with considerable attention. As to the men, although they were inclined to laugh on seeing his short coat, his tight breeches, and his boots of an antique fashion, they changed their rising laughter to a "God preserve you!" courteously spoken, on a nearer view of that countenance, which took on in one minute ten different expressions, but not, however, the expression of goodwill commonly worn by the embarrassed provincial. He it was who first addressed the other gentleman, who was, as we have said, looking at the sign of the Belle Etoile.

"Mordi, Monsieur!" said he, with the accent that characterizes the natives of Piedmont, "we are close to the Louvre, are we not? At all events, I think your choice is the same as mine, and I am highly flattered by it."

"Monsieur," replied the other, with a provincial accent that rivaled that of his companion, "I believe this inn is near the Louvre; but I have not yet made up my mind to enter it."

"You are undecided, Monsieur? The house is tempting, nevertheless. You must allow the sign is very inviting."

"Very! and it is for that very reason I mistrust it, for I am told that Paris is full of sharpers, and they may cheat you by a sign as well as by anything else."

"Mordi!" replied the Piedmontese, "I don't care a fig for their tricks; and if the host does not serve me a chicken as well roasted as the one on his sign, I will put him on the spit and roast him instead. Come, let us go in."

"You have decided me," said the Provençal, laughing; "precede me, I beg."

"Impossible, Monsieur; I could not think of it, for I am only your most obedient servant, the Comte Annibal de Coconnas."

"And I, Monsieur, but the Comte Joseph-Hyacinthe Boniface de Lerac de la Mole, entirely at your service."

"And so, Monsieur, let us take each other's arm, and enter together."

The result of this proposition was that the two young men got off their horses, threw the bridles to the hostler, linked arms, adjusted their swords, and advanced toward the door of the inn, on the threshold of which stood the innkeeper. But contrary to usage in such cases, the worthy proprietor did not seem to notice them, so busy was he talking with a tall man, wrapped in a large drab cloak, like an owl buried in her feathers. The two gentlemen were so near the host and his friend in the dun-colored cloak that Coconnas, impatient at the small degree of importance accorded to him and his companion, touched the landlord's sleeve, who seemed then to arouse himself with a start, and dismissed his friend with an "Au revoir! come soon, and at any rate, let me know the hour appointed."

"Well, Monsieur Jackanapes," said Coconnas, "do not you see that we have business with you?"

"I beg pardon, gentlemen," said the host; "I did not see you."

"Eh, *mordi!* then you ought to have seen us; and now that you do see us, say, if you please, 'Monsieur the Count,' and not 'Monsieur.' "

La Mole stood in the background, leaving Coconnas, who seemed to have taken charge of the affair, to speak; but it was plain from the expression of his face that he was fully prepared to act upon occasion.

"Well, what is your pleasure, Monsieur the Count?" asked the landlord, in a quiet tone.

"Ah, that's better; is it not?" said Coconnas, turning to La Mole, who inclined his head affirmatively. "Monsieur the Count and myself wish to sup and sleep here tonight."

"Gentlemen," said the host, "I am very sorry, but I have only one chamber; and I am afraid that would not suit you."

"So much the better," said La Mole; "we will go and lodge somewhere else."

"No, no; I shall stay here," said Coconnas. "My horse is tired. I will have the room, since you will not."

"Ah! that is quite different," replied the host, with the same impertinent coolness. "If there is to be only one of you, I cannot lodge you at all."

"Mordi!" cried Coconnas, "here's a pretty fellow! Just now you could not lodge us because we were two, and now you have not room for one. You will not lodge us at all then?"

"Since you take this high tone, gentlemen, I will answer you frankly."

"Answer, then; but answer quickly."

"Well, then, I would rather not have the honor of lodging you at all."

"For what reason?" asked Coconnas, growing white with rage.

"Because you have no servants, and for one master's room full, I should have two servants' rooms empty; so that if I let you have the master's room, I run the risk of not letting the others."

"M. de la Mole," said Coconnas, "do you not think we ought to thrash this fellow?"

"Decidedly," said La Mole, preparing himself, as did Coconnas, to lay his whip over the host's back.

But the landlord, despite this demonstration, contented himself with retreating a step or two. "It is easy to see," said he, in a tone of raillery, "that these gentlemen are from the provinces. At Paris it is no longer the fashion to kill innkeepers; only great men are killed nowadays. And if you make any disturbance, I will call my neighbors; and instead of your beating me, you will be beaten yourselves—which will be rather humiliating to two gentlemen."

"Mordi!" cried Coconnas, in a rage; "he is laughing at us."

"Grégoire, my arquebus," said the host to his servant, in the same voice in which he would have said, "Give these gentlemen a chair."

"Trippe del papa!" roared Coconnas, drawing his sword; "warm up, then, M. de la Mole!"

"No, no; for while we warm up, our supper will grow cold."

"What! you think—" cried Coconnas.

"I think that M. de la Belle Etoile is right. Only he does not know how to treat his guests, especially when they are gentlemen; for instead of saying coarsely, 'Gentlemen, I do not want you,' he should have said politely, 'Enter, gentlemen'—at the same time reserving to himself the right to charge in his bill—'Master's room, so much; servant's room, so much.' " With these words La Mole gently pushed aside the host, who was looking for his arquebus, and entered with Coconnas.

"Well," said Coconnas, "I am sorry to sheathe my sword before I have ascertained that it is as sharp as that rascal's larding-needle."

"Patience, my dear friend," said La Mole. "All the inns in Paris are full of gentlemen come to attend the King of Navarre's marriage, or for the threatened war in Flanders; and we should have great difficulty in finding another apartment. Besides, perhaps it is the custom to receive strangers at Paris in this manner."

"*Mordi!* how quiet you are, M. de la Mole!" muttered Coconnas, curling his red mustache with rage. "But let the scoundrel take care; for if his meat be not excellent, if his bed be hard, his wine less than three years in bottle, and his waiter be not as pliant as a reed—"

"There, there, my gentleman," said the landlord, whetting his knife on a strap, "you may make yourself easy; you are in a land of plenty." Then in a low tone he added, shaking his head, "It is some Huguenot; they have grown so insolent since the marriage of their Béarnais with Mademoiselle Margot!" Then, with a smile that would have made his guests shudder had they seen it, "How strange it would be if I were to have two Huguenots come to my house, just when—"

"Now, then," interrupted Coconnas, "are we going to have any supper?"

"Yes, as soon as you please, Monsieur," returned the host, softened, no doubt, by the last reflection that had occurred to him.

"Well, then, the sooner the better," said Coconnas. Then, turning to La Mole, "Pray, Monsieur the Count," said he, "while our room is being prepared, tell me, do you think Paris seems a gay city?"

"Faith! no," said La Mole. "Thus far I seem to have seen only scared and sullen faces. Perhaps they are afraid of the storm. You see the sky is dark and the air is heavy."

"Tell me Count, you are looking for the Louvre, are you not?"

"Yes; and you also, I think, M. de Coconnas."

"Well, let us look for it together."

"It is rather late to go out, is it not?" said La Mole.

"Early or late, I must go out; my orders are peremptory—to come instantly to Paris, and on arriving, to communicate with the Duc de Guise."

At the name of the Duc de Guise, the landlord drew nearer.

"I think the rascal is listening to us," said Coconnas, who could not forgive the host his rude reception of them.

"I am listening, gentlemen," replied he, taking off his cap; "but it is to serve you. I heard the great duke's name mentioned, and I came immediately. What can I do for you?"

"Ah! that name is magical, it seems, since it changes your insolence to politeness. *Mordi!* Maître—Maître—what is your name?"

"La Hurière," replied the host, bowing.

"Well, Maître la Hurière, do you think my arm is lighter than that of the Duc de Guise, who makes you so civil?"

"No, Monsieur the Count; but it is not so long. Besides, I must tell you that the great Henri is the idol of the Parisians."

"What Henri?" asked La Mole.

"It seems to me that there is only one," said the innkeeper.

"Pardon, my friend, there is another, of whom I beg you not to speak disrespectfully; it is Henri de Navarre. And there is also Henri de Condé, who has his share of merit."

"I do not know them," said the landlord.

"But I do; and as I am directed to the King of Navarre, I desire you not to speak slightingly of him before me."

The host, without replying to M. de la Mole, carelessly touched his cap and continued his attentions to Coconnas. "Monsieur," he said, "is going to see the great Duc de Guise? Monsieur is very fortunate; he has come, no doubt, for—"

"For what?" asked Coconnas.

"For the fête," replied the host, with a singular smile.

"For the fêtes, you ought to say," replied Coconnas; "for according to what I hear, Paris is gorged with fêtes. At least, no one talks of anything but balls, festivities, and carousals. People enjoy themselves in Paris, hey?"

"Only moderately—up to the present time, at least; but they are going to enjoy themselves, I hope."

"The marriage of the King of Navarre has brought a great many people to Paris, however, has it not?" said La Mole.

"A great many Huguenots, yes," replied La Hurière, roughly; but suddenly changing his tone, "Pardon me, gentlemen," said he; "perhaps you are of that religion?"

"I of that religion!" cried Coconnas; "come, now, I am as good a Catholic as our holy Father the Pope."

La Hurière turned toward La Mole, as if to question him; but either La Mole did not understand the movement or he judged it inexpedient to reply except by another question. "If you do not know his Majesty the King of Navarre, Maître la Hurière," said he, "perhaps you know the admiral. I have heard he has some influence at court; and as I have letters for him, perhaps you will so far sully your mouth as to tell me where he lives."

"He lived in the Rue de Béthisy," replied the host, with a satisfaction he could not conceal.

"He lived?" said La Mole. "What do you mean? Has he moved, then?"

"Yes; out of this world perhaps."

"What!" cried both the gentlemen together, "the admiral dead?"

"What! M. de Coconnas," continued the host, with a wicked smile, "are you a friend of the Duc de Guise, and do you not know that about the admiral?"

"Know what?"

"That day before yesterday, as the admiral was passing before the house of the Canon Pierre Piles, he was fired at—"

"And killed?" said La Mole.

"No, he had his arm broken and two fingers taken off; but it is hoped the balls were poisoned."

"How, wretch!" cried La Mole; "hoped?"

"Believed, I mean," said the host. "We won't quarrel about a word; my tongue tripped." And Maître la Hurière, turning his back to La Mole, put out his tongue at Coconnas in a jeering way, accompanying that action with a glance full of meaning.

"Really!" said Coconnas, joyfully.

"Really!" said La Mole, sorrowfully.

"It is just as I tell you, gentlemen," said the host.

"In that case," said La Mole, "I must go instantly to the Louvre. Shall I find the King of Navarre there?"

"Most likely, since he lives there."

"And I," said Coconnas, "must also go to the Louvre. Shall I find the Duc de Guise there?"

"Most likely; for he has this instant passed with two hundred gentlemen."

"Come, then, M. de Coconnas," said La Mole.

"I am ready," returned he.

"But your supper, gentlemen?" cried La Hurière.

"Ah," said La Mole, "I shall perhaps sup with the King of Navarre."

"And I," said Coconnas, "with the Duc de Guise."

"And I," said the host, after having seen the two gentlemen take the road to the Louvre—"I will go and burnish my steel cap, put a match to my arquebus, and sharpen my partisan; for no one knows what may happen."

CHAPTER 5

Of the Louvre in Particular, and of Virtue in General

The two young men, directed by the first person they met, went by way of the Rue d'Averon and the Rue St. Germain l'Auxerrois, and soon found themselves before the Louvre, whose towers were beginning to be lost in the darkness of the night.

"What is the matter with you?" asked Coconnas of La Mole, who stopped before the old château, and gazed with a sacred respect on the drawbridges, the narrow windows, and the pointed belfries suddenly presented to his view.

"I scarcely know," said La Mole; "my heart beats strangely. I am not timid; but—I know not why—this palace seems to me gloomy and—yes, terrible!"

"For my part," replied Coconnas, "I feel in excellent spirits. My dress is perhaps somewhat disordered," continued he, glancing at his traveling costume, "but, bah! it is the distinguished manner that tells. Besides, my orders commanded prompt action; I shall therefore have my welcome, since I shall have promptly obeyed."

The two young men continued their way, each influenced by the feelings he had expressed.

The Louvre was guarded with more than usual care, and the number of the sentinels was doubled. Our cavaliers were therefore at first somewhat embarrassed; but Coconnas, who had remarked that the Duc de Guise's name acted like a talisman on the Parisians, approached the sentinel, and making use of the duke's name, demanded permission to enter. The name seemed to produce its ordinary effect upon the soldier, who, however, asked Coconnas if he had the countersign. Coconnas was forced to confess that he had not.

"Stand back, then," said the soldier.

At this moment a person who was talking with the officer of

the guard when Coconnas demanded leave to enter, advanced to him. "What do you want with M. de Guise?" asked he, with a strong German accent.

"I wish to see him," said Coconnas.

"Impossible; the duke is with the king."

"But I have a letter for him."

"Ah, that is different. What is your name?"

"The Comte Annibal de Coconnas."

"Will M. Annibal give me the letter?"

"On my word," said La Mole to himself, "I hope I may find another gentleman, equally polite, to conduct me to the King of Navarre."

"Give me the letter," said the German gentleman, holding out his hand toward Coconnas.

"Mordi!" replied the Piedmontese, "I scarcely know whether I ought, as I have not the honor of knowing you."

"It is M. de Besme," said the sentinel; "you may safely give him your letter. I'll answer for it."

"M. de Besme!" cried Coconnas; "with the greatest pleasure. Here is the letter. Pardon my hesitation; but when one is entrusted with an important commission, one ought to be careful."

"There is no need of any excuse," said Besme.

"Monsieur," said La Mole, advancing in his turn, "since you are so obliging, will you take charge of my letter, as you have taken that of my companion?"

"Who are you, Monsieur?"

"The Comte Lerac de la Mole."

"I don't know you."

"It is very natural that I should not have the honor of being known to you, Monsieur; I am a stranger, and like the Comte de Coconnas, I have arrived this evening from a far distance."

"Where do you come from?"

"From Provence."

"With a letter?"

"Yes."

"For the Duc de Guise?"

"No; for his Majesty the King of Navarre."

"I am not in the service of the King of Navarre," said Besme, with a sudden coldness; "and therefore I cannot take your letter."

And turning on his heel, he entered the Louvre, bidding Coconnas follow him.

La Mole was left alone. At this moment a troop of cavaliers, about a hundred in number, came out from the Louvre.

"Ah, ah!" said the sentinel to his comrade, "here comes Mouy and his Huguenots! See how joyous they all are. The king has promised them, no doubt, to put to death the assassin of the admiral; and as it was he who murdered Mouy's father, the son will kill two birds with one stone."

"Pardon," said La Mole, addressing the soldier, "but did you not say, my good fellow, that this officer is M. de Mouy?"

"Yes, indeed, my gentleman."

"And that those with him—"

"—Are heretics, yes."

"Thank you," said La Mole, without seeming to notice the term of contempt employed by the sentinel; "that is all I wished to know." Immediately approaching the leader of the party, "Monsieur," he said, "I am informed that you are M. de Mouy."

"Yes, Monsieur," returned the officer, courteously; "may I inquire whom I have the honor of addressing?"

"The Comte Lerac de la Mole."

The young men bowed to each other.

"What can I do for you, Monsieur?" asked Mouy.

"Monsieur, I have just arrived from Aix, bearing a letter from M. d'Auriac, Governor of Provence, for the King of Navarre. How can I give it to him? How can I enter the Louvre?"

"Nothing is easier than to enter the Louvre," replied Mouy; "but I fear the King of Navarre will be unable to see you at this hour. I will, however, if you please, conduct you to his apartments, and then you must manage for yourself."

"A thousand thanks!"

"Come, then, Monsieur," said Mouy.

Mouy dismounted, advanced toward the wicket, passed the sentinel, conducted La Mole into the château, and opening the door leading to the king's apartments, "Enter, and inquire for yourself, Monsieur," said he. And saluting La Mole, he retired.

La Mole, left alone, looked around. The anteroom was vacant; one of the doors on the inner side was open. He advanced a few paces and found himself in a passageway. He knocked and called;

but no one answered. The profoundest silence reigned in that part of the Louvre. "Who, then, told me," he thought, "of that formalism so rigorously exclusive? Any one may go and come in this palace as in a public place." He called again, without any better result than before. "I will walk straight on," thought he; "I must meet some one at last." And he went into the corridor, which became darker as he proceeded.

Suddenly the door opposite that by which he had entered opened, and two pages appeared, lighting a lady of noble bearing and exquisite beauty. The glare of the torches fell full on La Mole, who stood motionless. The lady stopped also. "What do you want, Monsieur?" said she, in a voice which sounded in his ears like delicious music.

"Oh, Madame," said La Mole, lowering his eyes, "pardon me! I have just left M. de Mouy, who was so good as to conduct me hither, and I wish to see the King of Navarre."

"His Majesty is not here, Monsieur; he is, I think, with his brother-in-law. But in his absence, could you not say to the queen—"

"Oh, yes, Madame," returned La Mole, "if I could obtain audience of her."

"You have it already, Monsieur."

"How is that?" cried La Mole.

"I am the Queen of Navarre."

La Mole made so abrupt a movement of surprise and alarm that the queen smiled.

"Speak, Monsieur," said Marguerite; "but speak quickly, for the queen-mother is waiting for me."

"Oh, Madame! if you are expected so immediately, permit me to withdraw, for it is impossible for me to speak to you at this moment. I am incapable of bringing together two ideas; the sight of you has dazzled me. I no longer think; I admire."

Marguerite, full of grace and beauty, advanced toward the handsome young man, who, without knowing it, had acquitted himself like a finished courtier.

"Recover yourself, Monsieur," said she; "I will wait, and let them wait for me."

"Oh, pardon me, Madame," said La Mole, "that I did not at once salute your Majesty with all the respect which your Majesty has the right to expect from one of her most humble servants; but—"

"But," interrupted Marguerite, "you took me for one of my ladies?"

"No, Madame; but for the shade of the beautiful Diana of Poitiers, who is said to haunt the Louvre."

"Come, Monsieur," said Marguerite, "I see that you will make your fortune at court. You have a letter for the king, you say? It was very useless. But no matter; where is it? I will give it to him. Only hasten, I beg of you."

In an instant La Mole threw open his doublet and drew from his breast a letter enveloped in silk. Marguerite took the letter and glanced at the writing. "Are you not M. de la Mole?"

"Yes, Madame. Oh! is it possible? Is it my happiness that my name is known to your Majesty?"

"I have heard my husband and the Duc d'Alençon, my brother, speak of you. I know they expect you."

And she placed in her corsage, glittering with gold and diamonds, that letter which left the young man's doublet, and which was still warm with the warmth of his breast. La Mole followed eagerly with his eyes every movement of Marguerite.

"Now, Monsieur," said she, "descend to the gallery below, and wait until some one comes to you from the King of Navarre. One of my pages will show you the way." With these words Marguerite continued on her way. La Mole placed himself against the wall; but the corridor was so narrow, and the skirts of the Queen of Navarre were so ample that her silk dress brushed against the young man, while a penetrating perfume diffused itself where she had passed. La Mole shuddered through all his frame, and perceiving that he was about to fall, leaned against the wall for support. Marguerite disappeared like a vision.

"Are you coming, Monsieur?" cried the page who was to conduct La Mole to the lower gallery.

"Oh, yes, yes!" cried La Mole, intoxicated; for as the page led him the same way that Marguerite had gone, he hoped that by hastening he should see her again.

And in fact, as he reached the top of the staircase, he perceived her below; and either by chance, or because she heard his step. she looked around, and La Mole saw her features a second time. "Oh!"

said he, as he followed the page, "she is not a mortal; she is a goddess. As Virgilius Maro says, *'Et vera incessit patuit dea.'* "

"Well?" asked the young page.

"I am coming," said La Mole; "pardon, I am coming."

The page preceding La Mole descended a story lower, opened one door, then another, and stopping, "Here you are to wait," said he.

La Mole entered the gallery, the door of which closed after him. The gallery was unoccupied, except for the presence of a gentleman who was sauntering up and down, and seemed also waiting for some one.

It was so dark that though not twenty paces apart it was impossible for either to recognize the other's face. La Mole drew nearer. "By Heaven!" muttered he, "here is M. de Coconnas again!"

At the sound of footsteps, Coconnas had already turned, and was looking at him with the same astonishment.

"Mordi!" he cried. "The devil take me, but here is M. de la Mole! Ah! what am I doing?—swearing in the king's palace! But, bah! it seems that the king swears even worse than I do, and even in the church. Eh, here we are at last, then, in the Louvre?"

"As you see. M. de Besme introduced you?"

"Yes. A charming German is that M. de Besme. And you, who introduced you?"

"M. de Mouy. I told you the Huguenots were no longer without favor at court. And have you seen M. de Guise?"

"No, not yet. Have you obtained an audience of the King of Navarre?"

"No; but I soon shall. I was conducted here and told to wait."

"Ah, you will see we shall be invited to some grand supper, and placed side by side. What a strange chance! Two hours ago we were married by fate—but what is the matter? You seem preoccupied."

"I!" said La Mole, quickly, with a start—for he still continued as if dazed by the vision which had appeared to him; "no, but the place in which we now are awakens in my mind a crowd of reflections."

"Philosophical, are they not? That is like me. When you came in just now I was calling to mind the recommendations of my tutor. Monsieur the Count, are you acquainted with Plutarch?"

"Of course," said La Mole, smiling; "he is one of my favorite authors."

"Very well," continued Coconnas, gravely, "that great man seems to me not mistaken when he compares the gifts of nature with brilliant but ephemeral flowers, while he regards virtue as a balsamic plant, of an imperishable perfume, and of a sovereign efficacy for the cure of wounds."

"Do you know Greek, M. de Coconnas?" said La Mole, looking steadily at his interlocutor.

"No; but my tutor knew it, and he strongly advised me, when I should be at court, to discourse upon virtue. That, he said, gives one a good appearance. So I am fortified on that subject, I forewarn you. By the way, are you hungry?"

"No."

"And yet you seemed anxious to taste the good cheer of the Belle Etoile. As for me, I am dying of starvation."

"Well, M. de Coconnas, here is a good opportunity to utilize your arguments upon virtue and to prove your admiration for Plutarch; for that great writer says somewhere, 'It is good to exercise the soul with grief, and the stomach with hunger' ('Prepon esti tên men psychen odune, ton de gastera semo askeïn')."

"Ah, there! you know Greek, then?" cried Coconnas, stupefied.

"Of course," replied La Mole; "my tutor taught it to me."

"Mordi! Count, your fortune is in that case assured. You can make verses with King Charles IX, and can talk Greek with Queen Marguerite."

"Without reckoning," added La Mole, smiling, "that I can also talk Gascon with the King of Navarre."

At this moment the door communicating with the king's apartments opened, and M. de Besme entered. He scrutinized both young men, in order to recognize his own, and then motioned to Coconnas to follow him. Coconnas waved his hand to La Mole. Besme traversed a gallery, opened a door, and stood at the head of a staircase.

He looked cautiously around, and said, "M. de Coconnas, where are you staying?"

"At the Belle Etoile, Rue de l'Arbre Sec."

"Ah, that is close by. Return to your hotel, and tonight—" He again looked around.

"Well, tonight?"

"Come here with a white cross in your hat. The password is 'Guise.' Hush! not a word."

"What time am I to come?"

"When you hear the tocsin."

"Good; I shall be here," said Coconnas. And saluting Besme, he withdrew, asking himself in a low tone, "What in the devil does he mean? and for what is the tocsin to sound? No matter; I hold to my opinion—a charming Tédesco is M. de Besme. Shall I wait for the Comte de la Mole? Ah! of course not; he will probably sup with the King of Navarre." And Coconnas directed his steps toward the Rue de l'Arbre Sec, whither the sign of the Belle Etoile drew him like a lodestone.

In the meantime the door of the King of Navarre's apartment opened, and a page appeared. "You are the Comte de la Mole?" said he.

"That is my name."

"Where do you lodge?"

"At the Belle Etoile."

"Good! that is close to the Louvre. Listen; his Majesty the King of Navarre has desired me to inform you that he cannot at present receive you. Perhaps he will send for you tonight; but at all events, if tomorrow morning you have not heard from him, come to the Louvre."

"But the sentinel will refuse me admission."

"True. The countersign is 'Navarre'; utter that word and all the doors will open before you."

"Thanks."

"Wait, my gentleman. I am ordered to conduct you to the gate, that you may not lose yourself in the Louvre."

"By the way, where's Coconnas?" said La Mole to himself when outside the palace. "Oh! he has stayed to take supper with the Duc de Guise." But the first person La Mole saw on entering the inn was Coconnas seated before a large omelet.

"Oh, oh!" cried Coconnas, with a loud burst of laughter, "I see you have not dined with the King of Navarre any more than I have supped with the Duc de Guise."

"Well, no."

"Are you hungry now?"

"I believe I am."

"In spite of Plutarch?"

"Monsieur the Count," said La Mole, smiling, "Plutarch says in another place, 'Let him who has share with him who has not.' Will you, for love of Plutarch, share your omelet with me? While eating, we will talk of virtue."

"Oh! by my soul, no. That will do at the Louvre, when one is afraid he may be overheard, and when his stomach is empty. Sit down and let us have supper."

"I see that fate makes us inseparable. Do you sleep here?"

"I know nothing about it."

"Nor do I."

"I know, at any rate, where I shall pass the night."

"Where?"

"Wherever you do; that is inevitable."

They both laughed and fell to work on the omelet of Maître la Hurière.

CHAPTER 6

The Debt Paid

Now, if the reader is curious to know why M. de la Mole had not been received by the King of Navarre, why M. de Coconnas had not seen M. de Guise, and why both, instead of supping at the Louvre on pheasants, partridges, and kid, supped at the Belle Etoile on an omelet, he must kindly accompany us to the old palace of kings, and follow Queen Marguerite of Navarre, of whom La Mole had lost sight at the entrance of the grand gallery.

While Marguerite was descending that staircase, Duc Henri de Guise, whom she had not seen since the night of her marriage, was in the king's cabinet. To that staircase which Marguerite was descending there was an outlet; to the cabinet in which M. de Guise was, there was a door; and this door and this outlet gave entrance to a corridor which led to the apartments of the queen-mother, Catherine de Médicis.

Catherine de Médicis was alone, seated near a table, with her elbow leaning on a prayerbook half-open, and her head leaning on a hand still remarkably beautiful—thanks to the cosmetics with which she was supplied by the Florentine, René, who united the double duty of perfumer and poisoner to the queen-mother.

The widow of Henri II was clothed in mourning, which she had not thrown off since her husband's death. At this period she was about fifty-two or fifty-three years of age, and preserved a figure full of freshness and still of considerable beauty. Her apartment, like her costume, was that of a widow; everything was of a sombre color. By her side was a small Italian greyhound, called Phébé, a present from her son-in-law, Henri de Navarre.

Suddenly, and at a moment when the queen-mother appeared plunged in some thought that brought a smile to her lips, colored with carmine, a man opened the door, raised the tapestry, and showing a pale face, said, "All goes badly."

Catherine raised her head, and recognized the Duc de Guise. "How 'all goes badly'?" she replied. "What mean you, Henri?"

"I mean that the king is more than ever taken with the accursed Huguenots; and if we await his leave to execute the great enterprise, we shall wait a very long time, and perhaps forever."

"What, then, has happened?" inquired Catherine, still preserving the tranquillity of countenance that was habitual to her, and yet to which, when occasion served, she could give so different an expression.

"Why, just now, for the twentieth time, I opened the conversation with his Majesty as to whether he would still permit all those bravados which the gentlemen of the Reformed religion indulge in since the wounding of their admiral."

"And what did my son reply?" asked Catherine.

"He replied, 'Monsieur the Duke, you must necessarily be suspected by the people as the author of the attempted assassination of my second father, the admiral; defend yourself from the imputation as best you may. As to me, I will defend myself properly, if I am insulted'; and then he turned away to feed his dogs."

"And you made no attempt to detain him?"

"Yes; but he replied to me in that tone which you so well know, and looking at me with the gaze peculiar to him, 'Monsieur the Duke, my dogs are hungry; and they are not men, whom I can keep waiting.' Whereupon I came straight to you."

"And you have done right," said the queen-mother.

"But what is now to be done?"

"Try a last effort."

"And who will try it?"

"I! Is the king alone?"

"No; M. de Tavannes is with him."

"Await me here; or rather, follow me at a distance."

Catherine rose and went to the chamber, where, on Turkey carpets and velvet cushions, were the favorite greyhounds of the king. On perches ranged along the wall were two or three select falcons and a small pied hawk, with which Charles IX amused himself in bringing down the small birds in the garden of the old Louvre and that of the Tuileries—this last palace being in the process of construction.

On her way the queen-mother had brought a distressed expression to her face, down which rolled a last, or rather a first, tear. She approached Charles IX noiselessly, as he was giving his dogs fragments of cakes cut into equal portions. "My son," she said with a trembling of the voice so skillfully affected that the king started.

"What would you, Madame?" said Charles, turning round suddenly.

"I would, my son," replied Catherine, "request your leave to retire to one of your châteaux—no matter which, so that it be far from Paris."

"And wherefore, Madame?" inquired Charles IX, fixing on his mother that glassy eye which on certain occasions became so penetrating.

"Because every day I receive new insults from persons of the new faith; because today I hear that you have been menaced by the Protestants, even in your own Louvre, and I do not desire to be present at such scenes."

"But then, Madame," said Charles IX, with an expression full of conviction, an attempt has been made to kill their admiral. An infamous murderer has already assassinated the brave M. de Mouy. *Mort de ma vie,* Mother, there must be justice in a kingdom!"

"Oh, be easy on that head, my son," said Catherine; "justice will not be wanting to them, for if you should refuse it, they will still have it in their own way—on M. de Guise today, on me tomorrow, and yourself hereafter."

"Oh, Madame!" said Charles, allowing a first accent of doubt to break through, "do you think so?"

"Eh, my son," replied Catherine, giving way entirely to the violence of her thoughts, "do you not see that it is no longer a question of the death of François de Guise or the admiral, of Protestant religion or Catholic, but simply of the substitution of the son of Antoine de Bourbon for the son of Henri the Second?"

"Come, come, Mother, you are falling again into your usual exaggeration," said the king.

"What, then, is your intention, my son?"

"To wait, Mother—to wait. All human wisdom is in that sin-

gle word. The greatest, the strongest, the most skillful is he who
knows how to wait."

"Do you wait, then; but for my part, I will not wait."

And on this Catherine bowed, and advancing toward the door,
was about to return to her apartments. Charles IX stopped her.
"Well, then, really, what is best to be done, Mother?" he asked; "for
I am just, before everything, and I would have every one satisfied
with me."

Catherine turned toward him. "Come, Count," she said to
Tavannes, who was caressing the pied hawk, "and tell the king your
opinion as to what should be done."

"Will your Majesty permit me?" inquired the count.

"Speak, Tavannes! speak!"

"What does your Majesty do when in the chase the wounded
boar turns on you?"

"*Mordieu,* Monsieur! I await him, with firm foot and hand,"
replied Charles, "and stab him in the throat with my sword."

"Simply that he may not hurt you," remarked Catherine.

"And to amuse myself," said the king, with a smile which indicated courage pushed even to ferocity—"but I will not amuse myself with killing my subjects; for after all, the Huguenots are my
subjects as well as the Catholics."

"Then, Sire," said Catherine, "your subjects, the Huguenots,
will do like the wild boar who escapes the sword thrust at his throat;
they will bring down the throne."

"Bah! Do you really think so, Madame?" said Charles IX, with
an air which denoted that he did not place great faith in his mother's
predictions.

"But have you not seen M. de Mouy and his party today?"

"Yes; I have seen them, and indeed just left them. But what
does he ask for that is not just? He has requested the death of his father's murderer and the admiral's assassin. Did we not punish M. de
Montgomery for the death of my father and your husband, although
that death was a simple accident?"

" 'Tis well, Sire," said Catherine, piqued; "let us say no more.
Your Majesty is under the protection of that God who gives
strength, wisdom, and confidence. But I, a poor woman, whom
God abandons, no doubt on account of my sins—I fear, and give
way." And Catherine bowed again and left the room, making a sign

to the Duc de Guise, who had at that moment entered, to remain in her place, and try a last effort.

Charles IX followed his mother with his eye, but this time did not recall her. He then began to caress his dogs, whistling a hunting air. He suddenly paused. "My mother," said he, "is a right royal spirit, and hesitates at nothing. Really now, it is a cool proposal, to kill off some dozens of Huguenots because they come to demand justice! Is it not their right, after all?"

"Some dozens!" murmured the Duc de Guise.

"Ah! you are there, Monsieur?" said the king, appearing to see him for the first time. "Yes, some dozens. A tolerable waste of life! Ah! if any one came to me and said, 'Sire, you shall be rid of all your enemies at once, and tomorrow there shall not remain one to reproach you with the death of the others,' why, then, I do not say—"

"Well, Sire!"

"Tavannes," said the king, "you will tire Margot; put her back on her perch. There is no reason, because she bears the name of my sister, the Queen of Navarre, that all the world should caress her."

Tavannes put the hawk on her perch, and amused himself by playing with a greyhound's ears.

"But, Sire," said the Duc de Guise, "if any one should say to your Majesty, 'Sire, your Majesty shall be delivered from all your enemies tomorrow'?"

"And by the intercession of what saint would this miracle be effected?"

"Sire, we are today at the twenty-fourth of August, and it will therefore be by the intercession of Saint Bartholomew."

"A worthy saint," replied the king, "who allowed himself to be skinned alive."

"So much the better; the more he suffered, the more he will have cherished a desire for vengeance on his executioners."

"And is it you, my cousin," said the king—"is it you, with your pretty little gold-hilted sword, who will tomorrow slay ten thousand Huguenots? Ah, ah! *mort de ma vie!* you are very amusing, M. de Guise!" And the king burst into loud laughter, but a laughter so forced that the room echoed with its sinister sound.

"Sire, one word, one only," continued the duke, shuddering in spite of himself at the sound of this laugh, which had nothing human in it—"one sign, and all is ready. I have the Swiss and eleven hundred gentlemen; I have the light-horse and the citizens. Your Majesty has your guards; your friends, the Catholic nobility. We are twenty to one."

"Well, then, cousin of mine, since you are so strong, why the devil do you come to batter my ears with all this? Act without me—act!" And the king turned again to his dogs.

Then the tapestry suddenly moved aside, and Catherine reappeared. "All goes well," she said to the duke; "insist, and he will yield." And the tapestry fell on Catherine, without the king seeing, or at least appearing to see her.

"But yet," continued Guise, "it is necessary that I should know whether in acting as I desire, I shall act agreeably to your Majesty's views."

"Really, Cousin Henri, you put your knife to my throat! But I shall resist. *Mordieu!* am I not the king?"

"No, not yet, Sire; but if you will, you shall be so tomorrow."

"Ah, what!" continued Charles, "you would kill the King of Navarre, the Prince de Condé, in my Louvre—ah!" Then he added in a voice scarcely audible, "Without the walls, I do not say—"

"Sire," cried the duke, "they are going out this evening to join in a revel with your brother, the Duc d'Alençon."

"Tavannes," said the king, with well-affected impatience, "do not you see that you annoy Actæon? Here, boy! here!"

And Charles IX left the apartment, without waiting to hear more, leaving Tavannes and the Duc de Guise almost as uncertain as before.

Another scene was taking place in Catherine's apartments, who, after she had given the Duc de Guise her counsel to remain firm, had returned to her rooms, where she found assembled the persons who usually assisted at her going to bed.

Her face was now as full of joy as it had been downcast when she went out. One by one she dismissed her women; and there remained only Madame Marguerite, who, seated on a chest near the open window, was looking at the sky, absorbed in thought. On finding herself alone with her daughter, the queen-mother two or three times opened her mouth to speak, but each time a gloomy thought suppressed the words ready to escape her lips. Suddenly the tapestry moved, and Henri de Navarre appeared. The little greyhound, which was asleep on a sofa, leaped toward him at a bound.

"You here, my son?" said Catherine, starting. "Do you sup in the Louvre tonight?"

"No, Madame," replied Henri; "we are going into the city tonight, with M. M. d'Alençon and de Condé. I almost expected to find them here."

Catherine smiled. "Ah! you men are so happy to have such liberty! Are they not, dear daughter?"

"Yes," replied Marguerite; "liberty is so glorious, so sweet a thing."

"Would you imply that I restrict yours, Madame?" inquired Henri, bowing to his wife.

"No, Monsieur; it is not for myself that I complain, but for women in general."

"Perhaps you intend calling on the admiral, my son?" said Catherine.

"Yes, perhaps."

"Do so; it will be a good example, and tomorrow you can give me news of him."

"I will go then, Madame, since you approve."

"I!" said Catherine, "I approve nothing. But who is there? Send them away."

Henri started toward the door to execute the order, but at the same moment the tapestry was raised, and Madame de Sauve showed her lovely head.

"Madame," she said, "it is René, the perfumer, whom your Majesty sent for."

Catherine cast a glance as quick as lightning at Henri de Navarre. The young prince turned slightly red and then fearfully pale. The name of his mother's assassin had been mentioned in his presence; he felt that his face betrayed his emotion, and he leaned against the bar of the window. The little greyhound growled. At the same moment two persons entered—the one announced, and the other having no need to be.

The first was René, the perfumer, who approached Catherine with all the servile obsequiousness of Florentine servants. He held in his hand a box, which he opened, and all the compartments were seen filled with powders and flasks.

The second was Madame de Lorraine, the eldest sister of Marguerite. She entered by a small private door which led from the king's cabinet, and all pale and trembling, and hoping not to be observed by Catherine, who was examining, with Madame de Sauve, the contents of the box brought by René, seated herself beside Marguerite, near whom the King of Navarre was standing, with his hand on his brow, like one who tries to rouse himself from some sudden shock.

At this instant Catherine turned round. "Daughter," she said to Marguerite, "you may retire to your chamber. My son, you may go and enjoy yourself in the city."

Marguerite rose, and Henri turned half round. Madame de Lorraine seized Marguerite's hand. "Sister," she whispered hastily, "in the name of the Duc de Guise, who now saves you, as you saved him, do not go hence; do not go to your apartments."

"Eh! what say you, Claude?" inquired Catherine, turning round.

"Nothing, Mother."

"What did you whisper to Marguerite?"

"Only to bid her goodnight, and to give her a message from the Duchesse de Nevers."

"And where is the lovely duchess?"

"With her brother-in-law, M. de Guise."

Catherine looked suspiciously at her two daughters, and frowned. "Come here, Claude," she said.

Claude obeyed, and the queen seized her hand. "What have you said to her, indiscreet girl that you are?" she murmured, squeezing her daughter's wrist until she almost made her shriek.

"Madame," said Henri to his wife, having lost nothing of the movements of the queen, Claude, and Marguerite. "Madame, will you allow me the honor of kissing your hand?"

Marguerite extended her trembling hand.

"What did she say to you?" murmured Henri, as he stooped to imprint a kiss on her hand.

"Not to go out. In the name of Heaven therefore, do not you go out either!"

It was only a flash; but by its light, brief as it was, Henri at once saw through the whole plot.

"This is not all," added Marguerite; "here is a letter, which a country gentleman brought."

"M. de la Mole?"

"Yes."

"Thanks," he said, taking the letter, and putting it under his doublet; and passing in front of his bewildered wife, he placed his hand on the shoulder of the Florentine.

"Well, Maître René!" he said, "and how is business?"

"Pretty good, Monseigneur—pretty good," replied the poisoner, with his perfidious smile.

"I should think so," said Henri—"with men who, like you, supply all the crowned heads at home and abroad."

"Except that of the King of Navarre," replied the Florentine, impudently.

"*Ventre-saint-gris,* Maître René," replied the king, "you are right; and yet my poor mother, who also bought of you, recommended you to me with her dying breath. Come to me tomorrow, or the day after tomorrow, and bring your best perfumes."

At this moment, the Duchesse de Lorraine, who could no longer contain herself, burst into loud sobs. Henri appeared not to hear her.

"Sister dear, what is the matter?" cried Marguerite, going to her.

"Nothing," said Catherine, passing between the two young women—"nothing; she has those nervous attacks, for which Mazille prescribed aromatic preparations"; and again, and with more force than before, she pressed her eldest daughter's arm. Then, turning toward the youngest, "Why, Margot," she said, "did you not hear me request you to retire to your room? If that is not sufficient, I command you."

"Pardon me, Madame," replied Marguerite, trembling and pale; "I wish your Majesty goodnight."

"I hope your wishes may be heard. Goodnight; goodnight!"

Marguerite withdrew, staggering with terror, and in vain seeking a glance from her husband, who did not even turn toward her.

There was a moment's silence, during which Catherine remained with her eyes fixed on the Duchesse de Lorraine, who, without speaking, looked at her mother with clasped hands.

Henri's back was still turned, but he was watching the scene in a glass, while seeming to curl his mustache with a pomade which René had given to him.

"And you, Henri, do you mean to go?" asked Catherine.

"Ah, yes! that's true," exclaimed the King of Navarre. "Upon my soul! I forgot that the Duc d'Alençon and the Prince de Condé are waiting for me. These are admirable perfumes. They quite overpower one, and destroy one's memory. Au revoir, Madame."

"Au revoir! Tomorrow you will bring me tidings of the admiral, will you not?"

"Without fail. Well, Phébé, what is it?"

"Phébé!" said the queen-mother, impatiently.

"Call her, Madame," said the Béarnais, "for she will not allow me to go out."

The queen-mother rose, took the little greyhound by the collar, and held her while Henri left the apartment, with his features as calm and smiling as if he did not feel in his heart that his life was in imminent peril. Behind him the little dog, set free by Catherine de Médicis, leaped to overtake him; but the door was closed, and Phébé could only put her long nose under the tapestry, and give a long and mournful howl.

"Now, Charlotte," said Catherine to Madame de Sauve, "go and find M. de Guise and Tavannes, who are in my oratory, and bring them here to be company for the Duchesse de Lorraine, who has the vapors."

CHAPTER 7

The Night of August 24, 1572

When La Mole and Coconnas had finished their meager supper, Coconnas stretched his legs, leaned one elbow on the table, and drinking a last glass of wine, said, "Do you mean to go to bed at once, M. de la Mole?"

"Upon my word, I am very much inclined to do so, for it is possible that I may be called up in the night."

"And I, too," said Coconnas; "but it appears to me that under the circumstances, instead of going to bed and making those wait who are to come to us, we should do better to call for cards and play a game. They will then find us quite ready."

"I would willingly accept your proposal, Monsieur, but I have very little money for play. I have scarce a hundred gold crowns in my valise for my whole treasure."

"A hundred gold crowns!" cried Coconnas, "and you complain? *Mordi!* I have but six!"

"Why," replied La Mole, "I saw you draw from your pocket a purse which appeared not only full, but I should say brim-full."

"Ah," said Coconnas, "that is to defray a debt which I am compelled to pay to an old friend of my father, whom I suspect to be like yourself somewhat of a Huguenot. Yes, there are here a hundred rose nobles," he added, slapping his pocket; "but these hundred rose nobles belong to Maître Mercandon. As to my personal patrimony, that, as I tell you, is limited to six crowns."

"How, then, can you play?"

"Why, it is for that very reason that I wish to play. Besides, an idea occurs to me."

"What is it?"

"We both came to Paris on the same errand."

"Yes."

"We have each a powerful protector."

"Yes."

"You rely on yours as I rely on mine."

"Yes."

"Well, then, it has occurred to me that we should play at first for our money, and afterward for the first favor which may come to us, either from the court or from our mistress."

"Really, a very ingenious idea," said La Mole, with a smile; "but I confess I am not such a gamester as to risk my whole life on a card or a turn of the dice; for the first favor which may come either to you or to me will in all probability involve our whole life."

"Well, then, let us set aside the first favor of the court, and play for the first favor of our mistress."

"I see but one inconvenience in that," said La Mole.

"What is it?"

"That I have no mistress."

"Nor I; but I shall not be slow in getting one. Thank God I am not formed in a way to be long in want in that direction!"

"As you say, you will succeed, M. de Coconnas; but as I have not the same confidence in my star of love, it would be sheer robbery to stake my fortune against yours. Let us play, then, until your six crowns be lost or doubled; and if lost, and you desire to continue the game, you are a gentleman, and your word is as good as gold."

"Done," replied Coconnas; "you are right, Monsieur; a gentleman's word is gold, especially when he has credit at court. Thus, believe me, I did not risk too much when I proposed to play for the first favor we might receive at court."

"Doubtless, and you might lose it, but I could not gain it; for being with the King of Navarre, I could not receive anything from the Duc de Guise."

"Ah, the heretic!" murmured the host, while rubbing up his old helmet, "what! I smelt you out, did I?" and he interrupted himself to make the sign of the cross.

"Well, then," continued Coconnas, shuffling the cards which the waiter brought him, "you are of the—"

"What?"

"New religion."

"I?"

"Yes, you."

"Well, say that I am," said La Mole, with a smile; "have you anything against us?"

"No, thank God! I hate Huguenotry with all my heart; but I do not hate the Huguenots, for they are in fashion."

"Yes," replied La Mole, smiling, "as witness the shooting at the admiral; but let us play."

"Yes, let us play, and do not fear; for should I lose a hundred crowns of gold against yours, I shall have wherewithal to pay you tomorrow morning."

"Then your fortune will come while you sleep."

"No; I shall go and find it."

"Where? I'll go with you."

"To the Louvre."

"Are you going back there tonight?"

"Yes; I have tonight a private audience with the great Duc de Guise."

Since Coconnas had mentioned the Louvre, La Hurière had left off cleaning his headpiece, and placed himself behind La Mole's chair, so that Coconnas alone could see him, and made signs to him which the Piedmontese, absorbed in his game and the conversation, did not remark.

"Well, it is very strange," remarked La Mole; "and you were right to say that we were born under the same star. I also have an appointment at the Louvre tonight, but not with the Duc de Guise; mine is with the King of Navarre."

"Have you a countersign?"

"Yes."

"A rallying sign?"

"No."

"Well, I have one, and my countersign is—"

At these words of the Piedmontese, La Hurière made so significant a gesture that Coconnas, who had just raised his head, was greatly astonished, even more than by the game, at which he had lost three crowns. On seeing the astonishment depicted on the face of his partner, La Mole turned round; but he saw nothing behind him but his host, with his arms crossed, and on his head the helmet which he had been furbishing.

"What then is the matter?" said La Mole to Coconnas.

Coconnas looked at the host and at his companion without replying; he did not at all comprehend the redoubled gesticulation of Maître la Hurière. La Hurière saw that he must come to his assistance, and hastily said, "I also am fond of play, and as I drew near to see the play on which you had just won, Monsieur noticed my warlike helmet, and that on the head of a poor bourgeois astonished him."

"You make a fine appearance, in fact!" cried La Mole, bursting into laughter.

"Eh, Monsieur!" replied La Hurière, with a simplicity admirably put on, and a movement of his shoulders expressing a sense of his inferiority, "we citizens are not brave, and we have not the distinguished appearance. It is proper enough for brave gentlemen like you to brighten up your gilded helmets and delicate rapiers; and provided we mount guard punctually—"

"Ah, ah!" said La Mole, shuffling the cards; "you mount guard?"

"Eh! to be sure, Monsieur the Count; I am sergeant in a company of citizen militia." And having thus spoken, while La Mole was occupied in dealing the cards, La Hurière withdrew, putting his finger to his lips to recommend prudence to Coconnas, more bewildered than ever. Doubtless that caution was the cause of his losing the second game almost as quickly as he had the first.

"Well," observed La Mole, "this makes exactly your six crowns. Will you play for revenge on the strength of your future fortune?"

"Willingly," replied Coconnas, "willingly."

"But before you begin—did you not say you had an appointment with the Duc de Guise?"

Coconnas turned his looks toward the kitchen, and saw the great eyes of La Hurière repeating the same warning. "Yes," he replied; "but it is not yet the hour. But now let us talk a little about yourself, M. de la Mole."

"We shall do better, I think, by talking of the game, my dear M. de Coconnas; for unless I am very much mistaken, you are in a fair way of losing six more crowns."

"*Mordi!* that is true! I always heard that the Huguenots had good luck at cards. Devil take me, if I haven't a good mind to turn Huguenot!"

The eyes of La Hurière sparkled like two coals; but Coconnas, absorbed in his play, did not notice him.

"Do, Count, do," said La Mole; "and you shall be well received among us."

Coconnas scratched his ear. "If I was sure that your good luck came from that," he said, "I would, for I really do not hold so entirely with Mass; and as the king does not think so much of it either—"

"Then it is such a beautiful religion," said La Mole; "so simple, so pure—"

"And moreover it is in fashion," said Coconnas, "and it brings good luck at cards; for, devil take me, if you do not hold all the aces, and yet I have watched you closely, and you play very fairly. It must be the religion—"

"You owe me six crowns more," said La Mole, quietly.

"Ah, how you tempt me!" said Coconnas; "and this very night, if I am not satisfied with M. de Guise—"

"Well?"

"Well! tomorrow I will ask you to present me to the King of Navarre; and be assured, if once I turn Huguenot I shall be more Huguenot than Luther, than Calvin, than Melancthon, than all the reformers on earth."

"Hush!" said La Mole, "you will get into a quarrel with our host."

"Ah, that is true," said Coconnas, turning his eyes toward the kitchen; "but, no, he is not listening. He is too much occupied at this moment."

"What is he doing?" inquired La Mole, who could see nothing from his place.

"He is talking with—devil take me! it is he!"

"Who?"

"Why, that night bird with whom he was talking when we arrived—the man in the yellow doublet and drab cloak. *Mordi!* how earnestly he talks! Eh! say there, Maître la Hurière, are you talking politics, perchance?"

But this time the reply of Maître la Hurière was a gesture so forcible and imperative that in spite of his love for cards, Coconnas rose and went to him.

"What is the matter?" asked La Mole.

"You want wine, my gentleman?" said La Hurière, seizing eagerly the hand of Coconnas; "they will get it for you. Grégoire! wine for the gentlemen!" Then, whispering in his ear, "Silence, for your life! and get rid of your companion."

La Hurière was so pale, the sallow man was so sinister, that Coconnas shuddered, and turning toward La Mole, "My dear M. de la Mole," said he, "I must beg you to excuse me. I have lost fifty crowns in no time. I am in bad luck tonight."

"Well, Monsieur, as you please," replied La Mole; "besides, I shall not be sorry to lie down for a time. Maître la Hurière!"

"Monsieur the Count!"

"If any one comes for me from the King of Navarre, wake me immediately; I shall be dressed, and consequently ready."

"So shall I," said Coconnas; "and that I may not keep his Highness waiting, I will prepare the sign. Maître la Hurière, some white paper and scissors!"

"Grégoire!" cried La Hurière, "some white paper to write a letter, and scissors to cut out an envelope."

"Ah, decidedly," said the Piedmontese to himself, "something mysterious is going on."

"Goodnight, M. de Coconnas," said La Mole; "and you, landlord, be so good as to light me to my room. Good luck, my friend!" and La Mole disappeared up the staircase, followed by La Hurière.

Then the mysterious personage, taking Coconnas by the arm, said to him hastily, "Monsieur, you have very nearly betrayed a secret on which depends the fate of a kingdom. One word more, and I should have brought you down with my arquebus. Now that we are alone, listen."

"But who are you who speak to me in that tone of command?" said Coconnas.

"Did you ever hear any one speak of Maurevel?"

"The assassin of the admiral?"

"And of Captain de Mouy."

"Yes, certainly."

"Well, I am Maurevel."

"Ah, ah!" said Coconnas.

"Listen to me, then."

"*Mordi!* of course I listen."

"Hush!" said Maurevel, putting his finger on his mouth.

Coconnas remained quiet, with open ears. At this moment he heard the landlord close the door of a chamber, then the door of a corridor, and bolt it, and then return precipitately to the two interlocutors. He offered a seat to Coconnas and a seat to Maurevel, taking a third for himself. "All is close now," he said; "and you may speak out, M. Maurevel."

Eleven o'clock struck by St. Germain l'Auxerrois; Maurevel counted each stroke of the clock, which sounded full and dull in the night, and when the last sound had died away, "Monsieur," he said, turning to Coconnas, who was amazed at all the precautions taken, "are you a good Catholic?"

"I believe so," replied Coconnas.

"Monsieur, are you devoted to the king?"

"Body and soul! You offend me, Monsieur, by asking such a question."

"We will not quarrel about that; only, will you follow us?"

"Whither?"

"That is of no consequence—let me guide you; your fortune, and perhaps your life, are concerned in the result."

"I tell you, Monsieur, that at midnight I have an appointment at the Louvre."

"That is just where we are going."

"M. de Guise awaits me there."

"And us also!"

"But I have a special password," continued Coconnas, feeling a little ashamed to share the honor of his audience with Maurevel and La Hurière.

"And so have we!"

"But I have a sign of recognition."

Maurevel smiled and drew from beneath his doublet a handful of crosses in white stuff, of which he gave one to La Hurière, one to Coconnas, and took another for himself. La Hurière fastened his to his helmet. Maurevel attached his to the side of his hat.

"Ah, then," said Coconnas, amazed, "the appointment, the countersign, and the rallying mark were for everybody?"

"Yes, Monsieur—that is to say, for all good Catholics."

"Then there is a fête at the Louvre—some royal banquet, is there not?" said Coconnas; "and they wish to exclude those hounds

of Huguenots. Good! Capital! Excellent! They have had the best of
it too long."

"Yes, there is a fête at the Louvre," said Maurevel, "a royal
banquet; and the Huguenots are invited, and more, they will be the
heroes of the fête, and will pay for the festival, and if you will be one
of us, we will begin by going to invite their principal champion—
their Gideon, as they call him."

"The admiral!" cried Coconnas.

"Yes, old Gaspard, whom I missed like a fool, although I aimed
at him with the king's arquebus."

"And this, my gentleman, is why I was furbishing my helmet,
sharpening my sword, and putting an edge on my knives," said La
Hurière, with a strident voice, affecting warlike tones.

At these words, Coconnas shuddered and turned very pale, for
he began to comprehend. "Then really," he exclaimed, "this fête—
this banquet is a—"

"You are a long time guessing, Monsieur," said Maurevel,
"and it is easy to see that you are not so weary of these insolent
heretics as we are."

"And you take on yourself," he said, "to go to the admiral and
to—"

Maurevel smiled, and drawing Coconnas to the window, he
said, "Look there! do you see, in the small square at the end of the
street, behind the church, a troop drawn up quietly in the shadow?"

"Yes."

"The men who form that troop have, like Maître la Hurière,
you, and me, a cross in their hats."

"Well!"

"Well, these men are a company of Swiss, from the smaller
cantons, commanded by Toquenot; you know they are friends of
the king."

"Ah, ah!" said Coconnas.

"Now look at that troop of horse passing along the quay; do
you recognize their leader?"

"How can I recognize him," asked Coconnas, with a shudder,
"when it was only this evening that I arrived in Paris?"

"Well, then, it is he with whom you have a rendezvous at the
Louvre at midnight. See, he is going to wait for you!"

"The Duc de Guise?"

"Himself! His escorts are Marcel, the ex-provost of the trades-men, and Jean Choron, the present provost. These two are going to summon their companies; and see, here is the captain of the quarter entering the street. See what he will do!"

"He knocks at each door; but what is there on the doors at which he knocks?"

"A white cross, young man, such as that which we have in our hats."

"But at each house at which he knocks they open, and from each house there come out armed citizens."

"He will knock here in turn, and we shall in turn go out."

"But," said Coconnas, "all the world on foot to go and kill one old Huguenot! *Mordi!* it is shameful! It is an affair of cutthroats, and not of soldiers."

"Young man," replied Maurevel, "if the old are objectionable to you, you may choose young ones—you will find plenty for all tastes. If you despise daggers, use your sword, for the Huguenots are not the men to allow their throats to be cut without defending themselves; and you know that Huguenots, young or old, are hard-lived."

"But are they going to kill them all, then?" cried Coconnas.

"All!"

"By order of the king?"

"By order of the king and M. de Guise."

"And when?"

"When you hear the clock of St. Germain l'Auxerrois strike."

"Oh, it was for that, then, that the amiable German who is with M. de Guise told me to hasten at the first sound of the tocsin."

"You have then seen M. de Besme?"

"I have seen and spoken to him."

"Where?"

"At the Louvre."

"Look there!"

"Mordi! 'tis he himself."

"Would you speak with him?"

"Why, really, I should like to do so."

Maurevel opened the window instantly; Besme was passing at the moment with twenty soldiers.

"Guise and Lorraine!" said Maurevel.

Besme turned round; and perceiving that it was himself who was accosted, he came under the window. "Oh, is it you, M. Maurevel?"

"Yes, 'tis I; what seek you?"

"I am seeking the hostelry of the Belle Etoile, to find a certain M. de Coconnas."

"I am here, M. de Besme," said the young man.

"Good, good! are you ready?"

"Yes; to do what?"

"Whatever M. Maurevel may tell you, for he is a good Catholic."

"Do you hear?" inquired Maurevel.

"Yes," replied Coconnas, "but, M. de Besme, where are you going?"

"I am going to say a word to the admiral."

"Say two, if necessary," said Maurevel; "and this time, if he gets up again at the first, do not let him rise at the second."

"Make yourself easy, M. Maurevel, and put the young gentleman in the right path."

"Ah, have no fear for me; the Coconnas have keen scent, and good dogs follow their race."

"Adieu! begin the chase! We shall be in at the death."

Besme went on, and Maurevel closed the window.

"You hear, young man," said Maurevel; "if you have any private enemy, although he is not altogether a Huguenot, you can put him on your list, and he will pass with the others."

Coconnas, more bewildered than ever with what he saw and heard, looked by turns at the host, who posed in formidable attitudes, and at Maurevel, who quietly drew a paper from his pocket. "Here's my list," said he—"three hundred. Let each good Catholic do this night one-tenth part of the business I shall do, and tomorrow there will not remain one heretic in the kingdom."

"Hush!" said La Hurière.

"What is it?" inquired Coconnas and Maurevel together.

They heard the first stroke of the bell of St. Germain l'Auxerrois vibrate.

"The signal!" exclaimed Maurevel. "The hour is anticipated, then; it was appointed for midnight. So much the better. When the interest of God and the king is at stake, clocks that are fast are better than those that are slow."

In fact the sinister sound of the church bell was distinctly heard. Then a shot was fired, and in an instant the light of several torches blazed up like flashes of lightning in the Rue de l'Arbre Sec. Coconnas passed his hand over a brow damp with perspiration.

"It has begun!" cried Maurevel. "Now to work! away!"

"One moment, one moment!" said the host. "Before we begin, let us protect the camp, as they say in war. I do not wish to have my wife and children killed in my absence. There is a Huguenot here."

"M. de la Mole!" said Coconnas, starting.

"Yes, the heretic has thrown himself into the wolf's throat."

"What!" said Coconnas; "would you attack your guest?"

"It was for him I gave an extra edge to my rapier."

"Oh, oh!" said the Piedmontese, frowning.

"I never yet killed anything but rabbits, ducks, and chickens," replied the worthy host; "and I do not know very well how to kill a man. Well, I will go and practice on him, and if I am clumsy, no one will be there to laugh at me."

"Mordi! it is hard," said Coconnas. "M. de la Mole is my companion; M. de la Mole has supped with me; M. de la Mole has played with me."

"Yes; but M. de la Mole is a heretic," said Maurevel. "M. de la Mole is doomed; and if we do not kill him, others will."

"Not to say," added the host, "that he has gained fifty crowns from you."

"True," said Coconnas; "but fairly, I am sure."

"Fairly or not, you must pay them, while if I kill him, you are quits."

"Come, come!" cried Maurevel; "make haste, or we shall not be in time with the aid we have promised M. de Guise at the admiral's."

Coconnas sighed.

"I'll make haste!" cried La Hurière; "wait for me!"

"Mordi!" cried Coconnas, "he will make the poor fellow suffer, and perhaps rob him. I must be present to finish him, if necessary, and to keep any one from touching his money."

And impelled by this happy thought, Coconnas followed La Hurière upstairs, and soon overtook him; for the latter, doubtless as a result of reflection, slackened his pace as he approached the intended victim. As he reached the door, Coconnas still following, several discharges of musketry in the street were heard. Then they heard La Mole leap from his bed, and the floor creak under his feet.

"The devil!" muttered La Hurière, somewhat disconcerted; "that has awakened him, I think."

"I should say so," said Coconnas.

"And he will defend himself?"

"He is capable of it. Suppose, now, Maître la Hurière, he were to kill you—that would be droll, eh?"

"Hum, hum!" responded the host, but knowing himself to be armed with a good arquebus, he plucked up courage and dashed the door in with a kick of his foot.

La Mole, without his hat, but dressed, was entrenched behind his bed, his sword between his teeth, and his pistols in his hands.

"Ah, ah!" said Coconnas, his nostrils expanding like those of a wild beast who smells blood; "this grows interesting, Maître la Hurière. Forward!"

"Ah, you would assassinate me, it seems!" cried La Mole, with flashing eyes; "and it is you, wretch!"

Maître la Hurière replied to this apostrophe only by taking aim at the young man with his arquebus; but La Mole was on his guard, and as he fired, went on his knees, and the ball passed over his head.

"Help!" cried La Mole; "help, M. de Coconnas!"

"Help, M. Maurevel, help!" cried La Hurière.

"Faith! M. de la Mole," replied Coconnas, "all I can do in this affair is not to join the attack against you. It seems all the Huguenots are to be put to death tonight in the king's name. Get out of it as well as you can."

"Ah, traitors! assassins! is it so? Well, then, take this!" And La Mole, aiming in his turn, fired one of his pistols. La Hurière, who had kept his eye on him, moved suddenly on one side; but Coconnas, not anticipating such a reply, had not stirred, and the ball grazed his shoulder.

"Mordi!" he exclaimed, grinding his teeth, "I have it. Well,

then, let it be between us two since you will have it so!" and drawing his rapier, he rushed on La Mole.

Had he been alone, La Mole would doubtless have awaited his
attack; but Coconnas had La Hurière to aid him, who was reloading
his gun, and Maurevel, who in response to the innkeeper's call was
coming rapidly up the stairs. La Mole therefore dashed into a cabinet, which he bolted inside.

"Ah, coward!" cried Coconnas, furious, and striking at the
door with the pommel of his sword. "Wait, wait! and I will make as
many holes in your body as you have gained crowns of me tonight.
Ah, I came to prevent your suffering! Oh, I came so that no one
should rob you! And you reward me by sending a bullet into my
shoulder! Wait for me, poltroon! wait for me!"

La Hurière approached, and striking with the butt of his gun,
made the door fly open. Coconnas rushed into the cabinet, but it
was empty, and the window was open.

"He has thrown himself out," said the host, "and as we are on
the fourth story, he must be killed."

"Or he has escaped by the roof of the next house," said
Coconnas, putting his leg over the bar of the window, and preparing to follow him over this narrow and slippery route; but Maurevel
and La Hurière drew him back into the chamber.

"Are you mad?" they both exclaimed at once; "you will kill
yourself!"

"Bah!" said Coconnas, "I am a mountaineer, and used to tra-
verse the glaciers; besides, when a man has once offended me, I will
go up to heaven or descend to hell with him, by whatever route he
pleases. Let me do as I wish."

"Well," said Maurevel, "he is either dead or a long way off by
this time. Come with us, and if he escape you, there will be a thousand others in his place."

"You are right," cried Coconnas. "Death to the Huguenots! I
want revenge, and the sooner the better"; and the three descended
the staircase like an avalanche.

"To the admiral's!" cried Maurevel.

"To the admiral's!" shouted La Hurière.

"To the admiral's, then, if it must be so!" shouted Coconnas.
And all three, leaving the Belle Etoile in charge of Grégoire and the

other waiters, hastened toward the Rue de Béthisy, a bright light, and the report of firearms guiding them in that direction.

"Who comes here?" cried Coconnas. "A man without his doublet or scarf!"

"It is someone escaping," said Maurevel.

"Fire! fire!" exclaimed Coconnas; "you who have arquebuses."

"Faith! not I," replied Maurevel. "I keep my powder for better game."

"You, then, La Hurière!"

"Wait, wait!" said the innkeeper, taking aim.

"Oh, yes, wait, and he will escape!" replied Coconnas. And he rushed after the unhappy wretch, whom he soon overtook, as he was wounded; but at the moment when in order that he might not strike him behind, he exclaimed, "Turn, turn!" the report of an arquebus was heard, a ball whistled by Coconnas's ears, and the fugitive rolled over like a hare struck by the bullet of a sportsman.

A cry of triumph was heard behind Coconnas. The Piedmontese turned round, and saw La Hurière brandishing his weapon.

"Ah, now," he exclaimed, "I have made my maiden shot!"

"And only just missed making a hole in me from one side to the other."

"Take care! take care!" cried La Hurière.

Coconnas sprang back. The wounded man had risen on his knee, and, bent on revenge, was about to stab Coconnas with his poniard when the host's warning put the Piedmontese on his guard.

"Ah, viper!" shouted Coconnas; and rushing at the wounded man, he thrust his sword through him three times up to the hilt.

"And now," cried he, leaving the Huguenot in the agonies of death, "to the admiral's! to the admiral's!"

"Ah, ah! my gentleman," said Maurevel, "it seems to work."

"Faith, yes!" replied Coconnas. "I do not know if it is the smell of gunpowder that makes me drunk or the sight of blood which excites me, but, *mordi!* I am eager for slaughter. It is like a *battue* of men. I have as yet had only *battues* of bears and wolves, and on my honor a *battue* of men seems more amusing." And the three went on their way.

CHAPTER 8

The Victims

The hotel of the admiral was, as we have said, situated in the Rue de Béthisy. It was a large house, opening on a court in front, flanked by two wings. One principal and two small gates afforded entrance into this courtyard.

When our three cutthroats entered the Rue de Béthisy, which forms part of the Rue des Fossés St. Germain l'Auxerrois, they saw the hotel surrounded with Swiss soldiers and citizens, armed to the teeth, all holding in their right hands swords, pikes, or arquebuses, and some, in their left hands, torches that threw a fitful and lurid glare on this sea of human heads and naked weapons. The work of destruction was proceeding all around the hotel and in the Rues Tirechappe, Etienne, and Bertin Poirée. Long cries were heard; there was the rattling sound of musketry; and from time to time some unfortunate fugitive, half-naked, pale, and bloody, came bounding like a hunted deer into the circle of funereal light, where a multitude of demons seemed to be at work.

In an instant Coconnas, Maurevel, and La Hurière, accredited by their white crosses, and received with cries of welcome, were in the midst of the tumult, though they could not have entered the throng had not Maurevel been recognized. Coconnas and La Hurière followed him, and all three contrived to enter the court. In the center of this court, the three doors of which were burst open, a man around whom a body of Catholics formed a respectful circle stood leaning on his drawn rapier, and eagerly looking up at a balcony about fifteen feet above him, which extended in front of the principal window of the hotel. This man stamped impatiently on the ground, and from time to time questioned those around him.

"Nothing yet!" murmured he. "No one. He has been warned, and has escaped. What do you think, Gast?"

"Impossible, Monseigneur."

"Why? Did you not tell me that just before we arrived a man, bare-headed, with a drawn sword in his hand, came running, as if pursued, knocked at the door, and was admitted?"

"Yes, Monseigneur, but M. de Besme came up immediately, broke open the doors, and surrounded the hotel. The man went in, sure enough; but he has not gone out."

"Why," said Coconnas to La Hurière, "if my eyes do not deceive me, it is M. de Guise I see!"

"Himself, Monsieur. Yes; the great Henri de Guise has come in person to watch for the admiral and serve him as he served the duke's father. Everyone has his day, and it is our turn now."

"Holloa, Besme!" cried the duke, with his powerful voice, "have you not finished yet?" And he struck his sword so forcibly against the stones that sparks flew out. At this instant cries were heard in the hotel, then several shots, then a clashing of swords; and then all was again silent. The duke was about to rush into the house.

"Monseigneur, Monseigneur!" said Gast, detaining him, "your dignity commands you to wait here."

"You are right, Gast. I must stay here; but I am dying with anxiety. If he were to escape!"

Suddenly the windows of the first floor were lighted up with what seemed the reflection of torches. The window on which the duke's eyes were fixed opened, or rather was shattered to pieces, and a man, his face and collar stained with blood, appeared on the balcony. "Ah! at last, Besme!" cried the duke; "what news?"

"Here, here!" replied the German, with the greatest *sangfroid*, lifting, as he spoke, a heavy body.

"But where are the others?" demanded the duke.

"The others are finishing the rest."

"And what have you done?"

"You shall see. Stand back a little!"

The duke retreated a few paces. The object that Besme was trying to lift was now visible; it was the body of an old man. He raised it above the balcony, and threw it by a powerful effort at his master's feet. The heavy fall, and the blood that gushed forth, startled even the duke himself; but curiosity soon overpowered fear, and the light of the torches was speedily thrown on the body. A white beard, a venerable countenance, and limbs contracted by death were then visible.

"The admiral!" cried twenty voices, as instantaneously hushed.

"Yes, the admiral!" said the duke, approaching the corpse, and contemplating it with silent satisfaction.

"The admiral! the admiral!" repeated in hushed tones the witnesses of this terrible scene, timidly approaching the grand old man, majestic even in death.

"Ah, here you are at last, Gaspard!" said the Duc de Guise, triumphantly. "You murdered my father; I avenge him." And he dared place his foot on the breast of the Protestant hero.

But immediately the dying warrior opened his eyes, his bleeding and mutilated hand was clenched for the last time, and the admiral, with a sepulchral voice, said to the duke—

"Henri de Guise, one day the foot of the assassin shall be planted on thy breast! I did not kill thy father, and I curse thee!"

The duke, pale, and trembling in spite of himself, felt a cold shudder come over him. He passed his hand across his brow, as if to dispel the fearful vision; and when he dared again to glance at the admiral, his eyes were closed, his hand unclenched, and a stream of black blood poured over his silvery beard from that mouth which had so lately uttered the terrible denunciation against his murderer. The duke lifted his sword with a gesture of desperate resolution.

"Are you satisfied, Monseigneur?" asked Besme.

"Yes," returned Henri; "for thou hast avenged—"

"The Duc François!" said Besme.

"The Catholic religion," continued Henri, in a gloomy tone. Then, turning to the soldiers and citizens who filled the court and street, "To work, my friends, to work!"

"Good evening, M. de Besme," said Coconnas, approaching the German, who stood on the balcony, wiping his sword.

"It was you, then, who settled him!" cried La Hurière; "how did you manage it?"

"Oh, very easily; he heard a noise, opened his door, and I ran him through the body. But I think they are killing Téligny now, for I hear him cry out."

At this moment, indeed, several cries of distress were heard, and the windows of the long gallery that formed a wing of the hotel were lighted up with a red glare; two men were seen flying before a body of assassins. An arquebus shot killed one; the other sprang boldly, and without stopping to look at the distance from the ground, through an open window into the court below, heeding not the enemies who awaited him there.

"Kill! kill!" cried the assassins, seeing their prey about to escape them.

The fugitive picked up his sword, which in his leap had fallen from his hand, dashed through the soldiers, upset three or four, ran one through the body, and amid the pistol shots and imprecations of the furious Catholics, darted like lightning by Coconnas, who stood ready for him at the door.

"Touché!" cried the Piedmontese, piercing his arm with his sharp blade.

"Coward!" replied the fugitive, striking him on the face with the flat of his weapon, for want of room to thrust at him with its point.

"A thousand devils!" cried Coconnas; "it's M. de la Mole!"

"M. de la Mole!" reechoed La Hurière and Maurevel.

"It is he who warned the admiral!" cried several soldiers.

"Kill him; kill him!" was shouted on all sides.

Coconnas, La Hurière, and half a score of soldiers rushed in pursuit of La Mole, who, covered with blood, and having attained that state of desperation which is the last resource of human strength, dashed wildly through the streets with no other guide than instinct. The sound of footsteps behind him and the shouts of his pursuers gave him wings. Occasionally a ball whistled by his ear, and made him dart forward with redoubled speed. He no longer seemed to breathe; it was a hoarse rattle which came from his chest. Soon his doublet seemed too close for the pulsations of his heart, and he tore it off; then his sword became too heavy for his hand, and he threw it away. The blood and perspiration matted his hair, and trickled in heavy drops down his face. Sometimes it seemed to him that he was gaining on his pursuers, and that their steps sounded farther away; but at their cries, other assassins started up at every turn and contin- ued the chase. Suddenly he perceived on his left the river, rolling silently on. He felt, like the stag at bay, a strong desire to plunge into it; the supreme power of reason alone restrained him. On his right was the Louvre, dark and frowning, but full of strange and ominous sounds; soldiers on the drawbridge came and went, and helmets and cuirasses glittered in the moonlight. La Mole thought of the King of Navarre as he had before thought of Coligny; they were his only protectors. He collected all his strength, looked toward the heavens, and inwardly vowing to abjure his faith should he escape massacre, he rushed by the soldiers onto the drawbridge, received another poniard-stab in the side, and despite the cries of "Kill! kill!" that resounded on all sides, and the opposing weapons of the sentinels, darted like an arrow through the court into the vestibule, mounted the staircase, then up two stories higher, recognized a door, and leaned against it, striking it violently with his hands and feet.

"Who is there?" asked a woman's voice.

"Oh, my God!" murmured La Mole; "they are coming—I hear them! they are here—I see them! 'Tis I! 'tis I!"

"Who are you?" said the voice.

La Mole recollected the password. "Navarre! Navarre!" cried he.

The door instantly opened. La Mole, without thanking, or even seeing Gillonne, dashed into the vestibule, then along a corridor, through two or three chambers, until at last he entered a room lighted by a lamp suspended from the ceiling. Beneath curtains of velvet with gold fleurs-de-lis, in a bed of carved oak, a woman, half-naked, raised herself on her arm, and opened her eyes, staring with fright. La Mole precipitated himself toward her. "Madame," he cried, "they are killing, they are butchering my brothers! they seek to kill me also! You are queen; save me!" And he threw himself at her feet, leaving on the carpet a large track of blood.

At the sight of a man, pale, exhausted, and bleeding at her feet, the Queen of Navarre rose in great fear, clasped her hands over her eyes, and shrieked for help.

"Madame," cried La Mole, making an effort to rise, "for the love of Heaven, do not call! If you do, I am lost, for my murderers are at hand; they are on the stairs! Hark! I hear them now!"

"Help!" cried the queen, beside herself—"Help!"

"Ah!" said La Mole, despairingly, "it is you who have killed me. I did not think it possible to die by so sweet a voice, so fair a hand!"

At the same time the door flew open, and a troop of men, panting, furious, their faces covered with blood and blackened with powder, their swords drawn, and their pikes and arquebuses leveled, rushed into the chamber. Coconnas was at their head—his red hair bristling, his eye flashing fire, and his cheek cut open by La Mole's sword. The Piedmontese was terrible to behold. *"Mordi!"* cried he, "we have him at last!"

La Mole looked round him for a weapon, but in vain; he glanced at the queen, and saw profound commiseration depicted in her face. He at once felt that she alone could save him; he threw his arms around her.

Coconnas advanced, and with the point of his long rapier again wounded his enemy's shoulder; and the crimson drops of warm blood stained the white and perfumed sheets of Marguerite's couch.

Marguerite saw the blood flow and felt the shudder that ran through La Mole's frame; she threw herself with him into the recess between the bed and the wall. It was time, for La Mole was incapable of flight or resistance; his head leaned on Marguerite's shoulder, and his hand convulsively seized and tore its thin cambric covering.

"Oh, Madame," murmured he, "save me!"

He could say no more. A mist came over his eyes, his head sank back, his arms fell at his side, and he sank on the floor, bathed in his blood, and dragging the queen with him.

At this moment Coconnas, excited by the sight of blood and exasperated by the long pursuit, advanced toward the recess; in another instant his sword would have pierced La Mole's heart, and perhaps that of Marguerite also.

At the sight of the bare steel, and even more moved by that brutal insolence, the daughter of kings drew herself up to her full height, and sent forth such a cry of fear, indignation, and rage that Coconnas stood petrified.

Suddenly a door in the wall opened, and a young man of sixteen or seventeen, dressed in black, and his hair in disorder, rushed in. "Hold! hold!" cried he; "I am here, my sister! I am here!"

"François! François!" cried Marguerite; "help! help!"

"The Duc d'Alençon!" murmured La Hurière, grounding his arquebus.

"Mordi! a son of France!" growled Coconnas, drawing back.

The duke glanced round him. He saw Marguerite disheveled,

more lovely than ever, leaning against the wall surrounded by men, fury in her eyes, large drops of perspiration on her forehead, and foam on her lips.

"Wretches!" he cried.

"Save me, my brother!" said Marguerite, exhausted. "They are going to kill me!"

The duke's pallid face became crimson. He was unarmed; but sustained, no doubt, by the consciousness of his rank, he advanced with clenched teeth and hands toward Coconnas and his companions, who retreated, terrified at the lightning darting from his eyes. "Ha! and will you murder a son of France, too?" cried the duke. Then as they recoiled, "Without there! captain of the guard! Hang me everyone of these ruffians!"

More alarmed at the sight of this weaponless young man than he would have been at the aspect of a company of *reitres* or of *lansquenets,* Coconnas had already reached the door. La Hurière sprang after him like a deer, and the soldiers jostled and pushed one another in the vestibule, in their endeavors to escape, finding the door far too small for their great desire to be outside it. Meantime Marguerite had instinctively thrown the damask coverlid of her bed over La Mole, and withdrawn from him. No sooner had the last murderer departed than the duke turned to his sister. "Are you hurt?" cried he, seeing Marguerite covered with blood. And he darted toward his sister with an anxiety that would have done credit to his fraternal tenderness had not that tenderness been charged with being more than brotherly.

"No," said she; "I think not; or if I am, it is but slightly."

"But this blood," said the duke, passing his trembling hands over the body of Marguerite; "whence comes it?"

"I know not," replied she; "one of those wretches put his hand upon me. Perhaps he had been wounded."

"What!" cried the duke, "dare to touch my sister! Oh, had you but shown him to me! did I but know where to find him—"

"Hush!" said Marguerite.

"And why?" said François.

"Because if anyone should know that you were in my chamber at this hour—"

"Cannot a brother visit his sister, Marguerite?"

The queen bestowed on the Duc d'Alençon a look so fixed and threatening that the young man recoiled. "Yes, yes, Marguerite," he said, "you are right; yes, I will go; but you cannot remain alone this dreadful night. Shall I call Gillonne?"

"No, no! leave me, François; leave me!"

The prince obeyed; and hardly had he disappeared when Marguerite, hearing a groan from the recess, quickly bolted the door of the secret passage, and then hastening to the other entrance, closed it just as a troop of archers dashed by in hot chase of some other Huguenot residents in the Louvre. After glancing round to assure herself she was really alone, she lifted the covering that had concealed La Mole from the Duc d'Alençon, and tremblingly drawing the apparently lifeless body, by great exertion, into the middle of the room, and finding that the victim still breathed, sat down, placed his head on her knees, and sprinkled his face with water.

Then it was that the mask of blood, dust, and gunpowder which had covered his face being removed, Marguerite recognized the handsome cavalier who, full of life and hope, had but three or four hours before solicited her protection and that of the King of Navarre, and while dazzled by her own beauty, had attracted her attention by his own.

Marguerite uttered a cry of terror, for now it was more than mere pity that she felt for the wounded man; it was interest. He was no longer a stranger; he was almost an acquaintance. By her care, La Mole's fine features soon reappeared, free from stain, but pale and distorted by pain. A shudder ran through her whole frame, as she tremblingly placed her hand on his heart. It still beat. She then took a smelling-bottle from the table, and applied it to his nostrils.

La Mole opened his eyes. "Oh, *mon Dieu!*" murmured he, "where am I?"

"Saved!" said Marguerite. "Reassure yourself; you are saved."

La Mole turned his eyes on the queen, gazed earnestly for a moment, and murmuring, "Oh, loveliest of the lovely!" closed his lids, as if overpowered, and sent forth a long deep sigh.

Marguerite started. He had become still paler than before, if that were possible, and she feared that sigh was his last.

"Oh, Heaven!" she cried, "have pity on him!"

At this moment a violent knocking was heard at the door.

Marguerite half raised herself, still supporting La Mole. "Who is there?" she cried.

"Madame, it is I; it is I," replied a female voice—"the Duchesse de Nevers."

"Henriette!" cried Marguerite. "Oh! there is no danger; it is my friend. Do you hear me, Monsieur?"

La Mole contrived to raise himself on one knee.

"Endeavor to support yourself while I open the door," said the queen.

La Mole, resting his hand on the ground, managed to keep his equilibrium. Marguerite advanced toward the door, but stopped suddenly.

"Ah, you are not alone?" she said, hearing the noise of arms outside.

"No, I have twelve guards that my brother-in-law, M. de Guise, assigned me."

"M. de Guise!" murmured La Mole. "The assassin! the assassin!"

"Silence!" said Marguerite. "Not a word!" And she looked round to see where she could conceal the wounded man.

"A sword! a dagger!" muttered La Mole.

"To defend yourself? Useless! Did you not hear? They are twelve, and you alone."

"Not to defend myself, but that I may not fall alive into their hands."

"No, no!" said Marguerite. "I will save you. Ah! this cabinet! Come! come!"

La Mole made an effort, and supported by Marguerite, dragged himself to the cabinet. Marguerite locked the door upon him, and hid the key in her alms-purse. "Not a sound, not a movement," whispered she, through the latticework, "and you are saved!" Then hastily throwing a mantle round her, she opened the door for her friend, who tenderly embraced her.

"Ah!" cried Madame de Nevers, "nothing has happened to you, then?"

"Nothing," replied Marguerite, wrapping the mantle still more closely round her, to conceal the blood on her dress.

"So much the better. However, since M. de Guise has given

me twelve of his guards to escort me to his hotel, and since I do not need so many, I will leave six with your Majesty. Six of the duke's guards are worth a regiment of the king's tonight."

Marguerite dared not refuse; she placed the soldiers in the corridor, and embraced the duchess, who then returned to the Hôtel de Guise, where she resided in her husband's absence.

CHAPTER 9

The Murderers

Coconnas had not fled, he had retreated; La Hurière had not fled, he had flown. The one had disappeared like a tiger, the other like a wolf.

The consequence was that La Hurière had already reached the Place St. Germain l'Auxerrois when Coconnas had only just left the Louvre.

La Hurière, finding himself alone with his arquebus in the midst of passersby who were running, bullets that whistled, and bodies falling from windows—some of them in one mass, and others in pieces—began to be afraid and to entertain prudent thoughts of regaining his hostelry; but as he turned the corner, in the Rue de l'Arbre Sec, he fell in with a troop of Swiss and light-horse, led by Maurevel.

"Well!" exclaimed the latter, who had christened himself the King's Killer, "have you finished already? What the devil have you done with our Piedmontese gentleman? Has any mischance happened to him? It would be a pity, for he went to work like a hero."

"I think not," replied La Hurière; "and probably he will rejoin us."

"Whence do you come?"

"From the Louvre; and I must say that we were rather rudely tumbled out."

"By whom?"

"M. le Duc d'Alençon. Is he, then, not in this affair?"

"Monseigneur le Duc d'Alençon is in nothing that does not touch him personally. Propose to him to treat his two elder brothers as Huguenots, and he will favor it—provided that the work may be done without compromising him. But do you not accompany these brave fellows, Maître la Hurière?"

"And where are they going?"

"Oh! to Rue Montorgueil. There is a Huguenot minister of my acquaintance there; he has a wife and six children. These heretics breed enormously; it is a curious thing."

"And you, where do you go?"

"Oh, I have a small private affair."

"Then let me go with you," said a voice which made Maurevel start; "for you know all the good places."

"Ah! it is our Piedmontese," said Maurevel.

"It is M. de Coconnas," said La Hurière. "I thought you were following me."

"*Peste!* you scampered off too fast for that; and besides, I turned a little from the direct course to throw into the river a frightful child who cried 'Down with the Papists! Long live the admiral!' Unfortunately, I believe the rascal knew how to swim. If one wishes to drown these pestilent heretics, he must throw them into the water like kittens, before they can see clearly."

"Ah! you have come from the Louvre. Did your Huguenot, then, take refuge there?" asked Maurevel.

"*Mon Dieu!* yes."

"I gave him a pistol-shot at the moment when he was picking up his sword in the admiral's courtyard, but I somehow or other missed him."

"I," added Coconnas, "did not miss him; I gave him such a thrust in the back that my sword was wet five inches up the blade. Besides, I saw him fall into the arms of Madame Marguerite—a fine woman, *mordi!* Yet I confess I should not be sorry to hear he was really dead; the vagabond is infernally spiteful, and capable of bearing me a grudge all his life. But did you not say you were going somewhere?"

"Do you mean to go with me?"

"Why, I do not like standing still. *Mordi!* I have only killed three or four as yet, and when I get cold my shoulder pains me. Forward! forward!"

"Captain," said Maurevel to the commander of the troop, "give me three men, and go on your own way with the rest."

Three Swiss were detached and joined Maurevel, who, followed by Coconnas and La Hurière and his three men, went toward the Rue St. Avoye.

"Where the devil are you leading us?" asked Coconnas.

"I am leading you to an enterprise brilliant and useful at the same time. After the admiral, after Téligny, after the Huguenot princes, I can offer you nothing better. Our affair is in the Rue du Chaume, and we shall be there in a moment."

"Tell me," said Coconnas, "is not the Rue du Chaume near the Temple?"

"Yes, why?"

"Because an old creditor of our family lives there, one Lambert Mercandon, to whom my father has desired me to hand over a hundred rose nobles I have in my pocket for that purpose."

"Well," replied Maurevel, "this is a good opportunity for squaring matters with him."

"How so?"

"This is the day for settling old accounts. Is your Mercandon a Huguenot?"

"Oh, I understand!" said Coconnas; "he probably is."

"Hush! here we are."

"What is that large hotel, with its entrance in the street?"

"The Hôtel de Guise."

"Truly," returned Coconnas, "I ought not to have failed of coming here, as I am under the patronage of the great Henri. But *mordi!* all is so very quiet in this quarter, we might fancy ourselves in the country. Devil take me, everybody is asleep!"

And indeed the Hôtel de Guise seemed as quiet as in ordinary times. All the windows were closed; and a solitary light burned behind the blind of the principal window, over the entrance. At the corner of the Rue des Quatre Fils, Maurevel stopped.

"This is the house of him we seek," he said. "Do you, La Hurière, with your sleek look, knock at the door; hand your arquebus to M. de Coconnas, who has been ogling it this last half-hour. If you are introduced, you must ask to speak to M. de Mouy."

"Oh!" said Coconnas, "now I understand; you have a creditor in the Quartier du Temple, it would seem."

"Exactly so," responded Maurevel. "You will go up to him in the character of a Huguenot, and inform M. de Mouy of all that has passed; he is brave, and will come down."

"And once down?" asked La Hurière.

"Once down, I will beg of him to cross swords with me."

La Hurière, without making any reply, knocked at the door, and the sounds echoing in the silence of the night caused the doors of the Hôtel de Guise to open, and several heads to appear at the windows; it was then evident that the hotel was quiet after the fashion of citadels—that is to say, because it was filled with soldiers. The heads were instantly withdrawn, their owners doubtless divining correctly the occasion of the noise.

"Does your M. de Mouy live here?" inquired Coconnas, pointing to the house at which La Hurière continued to knock.

"No; but his mistress does."

"*Mordi!* how gallant you are, to give him an occasion to draw sword in the presence of his lady-love! We shall be the judges of the field. I should like very well to fight myself; my shoulder burns."

"And your face?" asked Maurevel; "it is considerably damaged, is it not?"

Coconnas uttered a kind of growl. "*Mordi!*" he said, "I hope he is dead; if I thought he was not, I would return to the Louvre and finish him."

La Hurière continued knocking. Soon the window on the first floor opened, and a man appeared in the balcony in a nightcap and drawers, and unarmed. "Who's there?" cried he.

Maurevel made a sign to the Swiss, who retreated into a corner, while Coconnas stood close against the wall.

"Ah, M. de Mouy!" said the innkeeper, in his blandest tones, "is that you?"

"Yes; what then?"

"It is he!" said Maurevel, joyfully.

"Well, then, Monsieur," continued La Hurière, "do you not know what is going on? They are murdering the admiral, and all of our religion. Hasten to their assistance!"

"Ah!" exclaimed Mouy, "I feared something was plotted for this night. I ought not to have left my brave comrades. I will come, my friend; wait for me."

And without closing the window, through which issued the voice of a frightened woman uttering tender supplications, M. de Mouy put on his doublet, cloak, and weapons.

"He is coming down! he is coming down!" murmured Maurevel, pale with joy. "Attention, you fellows!" he whispered to the Swiss. Then, taking the arquebus from Coconnas, and blowing on the match to assure himself that it was lighted, "Here, La Hurière," he said to the innkeeper, who had fallen back on the group, "take your arquebus."

"Mordi!" cried Coconnas, "there is the moon coming out of a cloud to see this beautiful fight. I would give a great deal if Lambert Mercandon were here to serve as M. de Mouy's second."

"Wait, wait!" said Maurevel; "M. de Mouy is equal to ten men by himself, and it is likely that we six shall have enough to do to despatch him. Forward, my men!" continued Maurevel, making a sign to the Swiss to stand by the door in order to strike Mouy as he came forth.

"Ah, ah!" said Coconnas, as he watched these arrangements, "it appears that this will not come off quite as I expected."

Already was heard the sound of the bar, which Mouy moved aside. The Swiss were at the door; Maurevel and La Hurière came forward on tiptoe, while, from a feeling of honor, Coconnas remained where he was, when the young woman, whom they had neglected to keep in mind, appeared in her turn in the balcony, and gave a terrible shriek when she saw the Swiss, Maurevel, and La Hurière. Mouy, who had already half opened the door, paused.

"Return, return!" cried the damsel. "I see swords glitter, and the match of an arquebus; there is treachery!"

"Ah, ah!" said the young man, "let us see, then, what all this means." And he closed the door, replaced the bar, and went upstairs again.

Maurevel's order of battle was changed as soon as he saw that Mouy did not come out. The Swiss went and posted themselves on the other side of the street, and La Hurière, with his arquebus in his hand, awaited the reappearance of the enemy at the window. He did not wait long. Mouy came forward, holding before him two pistols of such respectable length that La Hurière, who was already taking aim, suddenly reflected that the Huguenot's balls had no farther to go in reaching him than had his to reach the balcony. "It is true," said he, "I may kill the gentleman; but it is equally true that the gentleman may kill me!" and this reflection determined him to retreat into an angle of the Rue de Braque so far off as to make any aim of his at Mouy somewhat uncertain. Mouy cast a glance around him, and advanced like a man preparing to fight a duel; but seeing nothing, he exclaimed—

"Why, it appears, my friend, that you have forgotten your arquebus at my door! I am here. What do you want with me?"

"Ah, ah!" said Coconnas to himself; "this is a brave fellow!"

"Well," continued Mouy, "friends or enemies, whichever you are, do you not see I am waiting?"

La Hurière kept silence, Maurevel made no reply, and the three Swiss remained in covert. Coconnas waited a moment; then, seeing that no one continued the conversation begun by La Hurière and followed by Mouy, he left his station, and advancing into the middle of the street, took off his hat and said—

"Monsieur, we are not here for an assassination, as you seem to suppose, but for a duel. I accompany hither one of your enemies, who wishes to have a little encounter with you to end honorably an ancient dispute. Eh, *mordi!* come forward, M. Maurevel, instead of turning your back. The gentleman accepts."

"Maurevel!" cried Mouy—"Maurevel, the assassin of my father! Maurevel, the King's Killer! Ah, *pardieu!* yes, I accept." And taking aim at Maurevel, who was about to knock at the Hôtel de Guise to request a reinforcement, he sent a ball through his hat.

At the noise of the report and Maurevel's cries, the guard which had escorted Madame de Nevers came out, accompanied by three or four gentlemen, followed by their pages, and approached the house of young Mouy's mistress. A second pistol-shot, fired into the midst of the troop, killed the soldier next to Maurevel; after which Mouy, having no longer any loaded arms, sheltered himself within the gallery of the balcony. Meantime, windows began to be opened in every direction, and according to the respective dispositions of their pacific or bellicose inhabitants, were closed again, or bristled with muskets and arquebuse.

"Help! my worthy Mercandon," shouted Mouy, making a sign to an old man who, from a window which opened opposite to the Hôtel de Guise, was trying to make out the cause of the confusion.

"Is it you who call, M. de Mouy?" cried the old man; "is it you they are attacking?"

"They attack me—you—all the Protestants; and there is the proof!"

Indeed, at that moment Mouy had seen La Hurière aiming his arquebus at him. It was fired; but the young man stooped, and the ball broke a pane of glass over his head.

"Mercandon!" exclaimed Coconnas, who, in his delight at sight of the tumult, had forgotten his creditor, but was reminded of him by this apostrophe of Mouy—"Mercandon, Rue du Chaume; that is it! Ah, he lives there! Good! We shall have an affair each with our man!"

And while the people from the Hôtel de Guise broke in the doors of Mouy's house, and Maurevel, torch in hand, tried to set it on fire; while, the doors once broken, there was a fearful struggle with an antagonist who at each rapier-thrust brought down his foe—Coconnas tried, by the help of a paving stone, to break in the door of Mercandon, who, unmoved by this solitary effort, was doing his best with his arquebus at his window.

And now all this deserted and obscure quarter was lighted up, as if by open day—peopled like the interior of an ant-hive; for from the Hôtel de Montmorency six or eight Huguenot gentlemen, with their servants and friends, issuing forth, made a furious charge, and began, supported by the firing from the windows, to repulse Maurevel's and the Guise's force, whom at length they drove back to the place whence they had come.

Coconnas, who had not yet managed to drive in Mercandon's door, though he tried to do so with all his might, was surprised in this sudden retreat. Placing his back to the wall, and grasping his sword firmly, he began not only to defend himself, but to attack his assailants, with cries so terrible that they were heard above all the uproar. He struck right and left, hitting friends and enemies, until a wide space was cleared around him. In proportion as his rapier made a hole in some breast, and the warm blood spurted over on his hands and face, he, with dilated eye, expanded nostrils, and clenched teeth, regained the ground he had lost, and approached the beleaguered house.

Mouy, after a terrible combat in the staircase and hall, had at length, in the manner of a true hero, come forth from the burning house. In the midst of all the struggle he had not ceased to cry, "Here, Maurevel! Maurevel, where are you?" insulting him by the most opprobrious epithets. He finally appeared in the street, supporting on one arm his mistress, half-naked and nearly fainting, and holding a poniard between his teeth. His sword, flaming by the sweeping action he gave it, traced circles of white or red, according as the moon glittered on the blade, or its bloody stains were reflected in the torchlight. Maurevel had fled. La Hurière, driven back by Mouy as far as Coconnas, who did not recognize him, and received him at sword's point, entreated mercy on both sides. At this moment Mercandon perceived him, and knew him by his white scarf to be one of those engaged in the massacre. He fired. La Hurière shrieked, threw up his arms, dropped his arquebus, and after having vainly attempted to reach the wall in order to support himself, fell, face downward, to the ground. Mouy, profiting by this circumstance, turned down the Rue de Paradis, and disappeared.

Such had been the resistance of the Huguenots that the Guise party, defeated, had retired into their hotel, fearing to be besieged and taken in their own habitation.

Coconnas, who, drunk with blood and riot, had reached that degree of excitement when, with the men of the South more especially, courage changes into madness, had not seen or heard anything, and was going toward a man lying with his face in a pool of blood, and whom he recognized as La Hurière, when the door of the house he had in vain tried to burst in opened, and old Mercandon, followed by his son and two nephews, rushed upon him.

"Here he is! here he is!" cried they all, with one voice.

Coconnas was in the middle of the street, and fearing to be surrounded by these four men who assailed him at once, gave one of those chamois-bounds which he had so often practiced in his native mountains, and in an instant found himself with his back against the wall of the Hôtel de Guise. Once at ease as to not being surprised from behind, he put himself in a posture of defense, and said jestingly, "Ah, ah! Daddy Mercandon, don't you know me?"

"Wretch!" cried the old Huguenot, "I know you well; you against me—me, the friend and companion of your father!"

"And his creditor, are you not?"

"Yes; his creditor, as you say."

"Well, then," said Coconnas, "I have come to settle the account."

"Seize him, bind him!" said Mercandon to the young men who accompanied him, and who at his bidding rushed toward the Piedmontese.

"One moment! one moment!" said Coconnas, laughing; "to

seize a man you must have a writ, and you have forgotten that."
And with these words, he crossed his sword with that of the young
man nearest to him, and at the first blow cut off his hand. The
wounded man retreated with a cry of pain.

"That will do for one!" said Coconnas.

At the same moment the window under which Coconnas had
sought shelter opened. He sprang on one side, fearing an attack from
behind; but instead of an enemy, it was a woman he beheld; instead
of the enemy's weapon he was prepared to encounter, it was a
nosegay that fell at his feet.

"Ah!" he said, "a woman!" He saluted the lady with his sword,
and stooped to pick up the bouquet.

"Be on your guard, brave Catholic! be on your guard!" cried
the lady.

Coconnas rose, but not before the dagger of the second
nephew had pierced his cloak, and wounded his other shoulder.
The lady uttered a piercing shriek. Coconnas thanked her, assured
her by a gesture, and then made a pass at the nephew, which he par-
ried; but at the second thrust, his foot slipped in the blood, and
Coconnas, springing at him like a tiger-cat, drove his sword through
his breast.

"Good! good! brave cavalier!" exclaimed the lady of the Hôtel
de Guise; "good! I will send you succor."

"Do not give yourself any trouble about that, Madame," was
Coconnas's reply; "rather look on to the end, if it interests you, and
see how the Comte Annibal de Coconnas pacifies the Huguenots."

At this moment the son of old Mercandon placed a pistol almost close to Coconnas, and fired. The count fell on his knee. The
lady at the window uttered a cry; but Coconnas rose instantly. He
had only knelt to avoid the ball, which struck the wall about two
feet beneath where the lady was standing.

Almost at the same moment there issued a cry of rage from the
window of Mercandon's house, and an old woman who recognized
Coconnas as a Catholic, by his white scarf and cross, threw a flower-
pot at him, which struck him above the knee.

"Bravo!" said Coconnas; "one throws me flowers, and the
other flowerpots. Thanks, Mother; thanks!"

"Go on, Wife, go on," said old Mercandon; "but take care of
yourself."

"Wait, M. de Coconnas, wait," said the young lady in the Hôtel de Guise; "I will have them fire at the windows."

"Ah!" said Coconnas, "the women are in arms, then, some for me, and others against me! *Mordi!* let us end this!"

The scene, in fact, was much changed, and evidently drew near its close. Opposed to Coconnas, wounded, it is true, but in all the vigor of four-and-twenty, used to arms, and irritated rather than weakened by the three or four scratches he had received, there remained only Mercandon and his son, an old man of sixty or seventy years, and a stripling of sixteen or eighteen. The latter, pale, fair, and weak, having discharged his pistol, which was consequently useless, was brandishing a sword half the length of that of the Piedmontese; the father, armed only with a dagger and a discharged arquebus, was calling for help. An old woman, the young man's mother, looking out of the window, held a piece of marble in her hand, which she was preparing to hurl down. Coconnas, excited on the one hand by menaces, and on the other by encouragements, proud of his twofold victory, drunk with powder and blood, lighted by the reflection of a house in flames, warmed by the idea that he was fighting under the eyes of a woman whose beauty seemed to him as superior as her rank appeared unquestionable—Coconnas, like the last of the Horatii, felt his strength redouble, and seeing the young man falter, rushed on him and crossed his small weapon with his terrible and bloody rapier. Two blows sufficed to drive it out of his hands. Then Mercandon tried to drive Coconnas back, so that the projectiles thrown from the window might be sure to strike him; but Coconnas, to defeat the double attack of the old man, who tried to stab him with his dagger, and the mother of the young man, who was endeavoring to break his skull with the stone she was ready to throw, seized his adversary by the body, presenting him against all the blows as a buckler, and well-nigh strangling him in his herculean grasp.

"Help! help!" cried the young man, "he is crushing my chest! help! help!" and his voice grew faint in a low and choking groan.

Then Mercandon ceased to attack, and began to entreat. "Mercy, mercy! M. de Coconnas, mercy! he is my only child!"

"He is my son, my son!" cried the mother—"the hope of our old age! Do not kill him, Monsieur! do not kill him!"

"Really," cried Coconnas, bursting into laughter, "not kill

him! What did he mean then to do with me, with his sword and pistol?"

"Monsieur," said Mercandon, clasping his hands, "I have at home your father's undertaking; I will return it to you. I have ten thousand crowns of gold; I will give them to you. I have the family jewels; they shall be yours. But do not kill him! do not kill him!"

"And I have my love," said the lady in the Hôtel de Guise, in a low tone; "and I promise it you."

Coconnas reflected a moment, and said suddenly, "Are you a Huguenot?"

"Yes," murmured the youth.

"Then you must die!" replied Coconnas, frowning, and putting to his adversary's breast his keen and glittering dagger.

"Die!" cried the old man; "my poor child, die!" And the shriek of the mother resounded so piercingly and loud that for a moment it shook the savage resolution of the Piedmontese.

"Oh, Madame the Duchess!" cried the father, turning toward the lady at the Hôtel de Guise, "intercede for us, and every morning and evening you shall be remembered in our prayers."

"Then let him be a convert," said the lady.

"I am a Protestant," said the boy.

"Then die!" exclaimed Coconnas, lifting his dagger; "die! since you will not accept the life which that lovely mouth offers to you."

Mercandon and his wife saw the blade of that deadly weapon gleam like lightning above the head of their son.

"My son! my Olivier!" cried his mother, "abjure, abjure!"

"Abjure, my dear boy!" cried Mercandon, going on his knees to Coconnas; "do not leave us alone on the earth!"

"Abjure all together," said Coconnas; "for one *Credo,* three souls and one life."

"I will!" said the youth.

"We will!" cried Mercandon and his wife.

"On your knees then," said Coconnas, "and let your son repeat after me, word for word, the prayer I shall say."

The father obeyed first. "I am ready," said the son, also kneeling.

Coconnas then began to repeat in Latin the words of the *Credo.* But whether from chance or calculation, young Olivier knelt close to where his sword had fallen. Scarcely did he see this weapon within his reach, when, not ceasing to repeat the words which Coconnas dictated, he stretched out his hand to take it up. Coconnas watched the movement, although he pretended not to see it; but at the moment when the young man touched the handle of the sword with his fingers, he rushed on him, knocked him over, and plunged his dagger in his throat, exclaiming, "Traitor!"

The youth uttered one cry, raised himself convulsively on his knee, and fell dead.

"Ah, ruffian!" shrieked Mercandon, "you slay us to rob us of the hundred rose nobles you owe us."

"Faith! no," said Coconnas; "and here's the proof"; and so saying, he threw at the old man's feet the purse which his father had given him before his departure to pay his creditor.

"And here's your death!" cried the old woman from the window.

"Take care, M. de Coconnas; take care!" called out the lady at the Hôtel de Guise.

But before Coconnas could turn his head to comply with this advice, or get out of the way of the threat, a heavy mass came hissing through the air, falling on the hat of the Piedmontese, breaking his sword, and prostrating him on the pavement. He was overcome, crushed, so that he did not hear the double cry of joy and distress which came from the right and left.

Mercandon instantly rushed, dagger in hand, on Coconnas, bereft of sense; but at this moment the door of the Hôtel de Guise opened, and the old man, seeing swords and partisans gleaming, fled, while the lady he had called the duchess, whose beauty seemed terrible by the light of the flames, all dazzling as she was with gems and diamonds, leaned half out of the window in order to direct the newcomers, her arm extended toward Coconnas.

"There! there! in front of me—a gentleman in a red doublet. There! that is he—yes, that is he."

Death, Mass, or the Bastille

Marguerite, as we have said, had shut the door and returned to her chamber. But as she entered, all breathless, she saw Gillonne, who, terror-struck, was leaning against the door of the cabinet, gazing on the traces of blood on the bed, the furniture, and the carpet.

"Oh, Madame," she exclaimed, "is he then dead?"

"Silence, Gillonne!" and Gillonne was silent.

Marguerite then took from her purse a small gold key, opened the door of the cabinet, and pointed to the young man. La Mole had succeeded in raising himself and going toward the window; on hearing the door open, he had seized a small poniard, such as women of the period carried.

"Fear nothing, Monsieur," said Marguerite; "for on my soul, you are safe!"

La Mole sank on his knees. "Oh, Madame," he cried, "you are more than a queen, you are a goddess!"

"Do not agitate yourself, Monsieur," said Marguerite; "your blood is still flowing. Oh, look, Gillonne, how pale he is! Let us see where you are wounded."

"Madame," said La Mole, trying to fix on certain parts of his body the pain which pervaded his whole frame, "I think I have a dagger-thrust in my shoulder, another in my chest; the other wounds are mere trifles."

"We will see," said Marguerite. "Gillonne, bring me my casket with the balms in it."

Gillonne obeyed, and returned, holding in one hand a casket, and in the other a silver basin and some fine Holland linen.

"Help me to raise him, Gillonne," said Queen Marguerite; "for in attempting to raise himself, the poor gentleman has lost all his strength."

"But, Madame," said La Mole, "I am overwhelmed. Indeed, I cannot allow—"

"But, Monsieur, I think you will allow things to take their course," said Marguerite. "When we can save you, it would be a crime to let you die."

"Oh!" cried La Mole, "I would rather die than see you, the queen, stain your hands with blood as unworthy as mine. Oh, never, never!" And he shrank back respectfully.

"Your blood, Monsieur," replied Gillonne, with a smile, "has already stained the bed and apartments of her Majesty."

Marguerite folded her mantle over her cambric dressing gown, all bespattered with small red spots. That movement, full of feminine modesty, recalled to La Mole the fact that he had held that beautiful queen in his arms and pressed her against his heart, and at the remembrance a fugitive blush passed over his pale cheeks. "Madame," he stammered, "can you not leave me to the care of the surgeon?"

"Of a Catholic surgeon?" said the queen, with an expression which La Mole comprehended, and which made him shudder. "Do you not know, then," continued the queen, with a voice and smile of ineffable sweetness, "that we, the daughters of France, are taught to know the use of herbs, and to compound healing balms? For our duty, as women and as queens, is to mitigate sufferings; and so we are equal to the best physicians in the world—according to our flatterers, at least. Come, Gillonne, let us to work!"

La Mole again endeavored to resist, and repeated that he would rather die than allow the queen to perform a task which, though begun in pity, must end in disgust; but this exertion completely exhausted his strength, and falling back, he fainted a second time.

Marguerite, then seizing the poniard which he had dropped, quickly cut the lacing which fastened his doublet; while Gillonne, with another blade, ripped open the sleeves. Then Gillonne, with a cloth dipped in fresh water, stanched the blood which escaped from his shoulder and breast, and Marguerite, with a silver needle with a round point, probed the wounds with all the delicacy and skill that Ambroise Paré could have displayed.

"A dangerous, but not mortal wound—*acerrimum humeri vulnus, non autem lethale,*" murmured the lovely and learned lady surgeon; "hand me the salve, Gillonne, and get the lint ready."

Gillonne had already dried and perfumed the young man's chest and arms, shaped like the classic models, his shoulders, which fell gracefully back, and his neck shaded by thick hair, which seemed rather to belong to a statue of Parian marble than the mangled frame of a dying man.

"Poor young man!" murmured Gillonne.

"Is he not handsome?" said Marguerite, with royal frankness.

"Yes, Madame; but I think we should lift him on the bed."

"Yes," said Marguerite, "you are right"; and the two women, uniting their strength, raised La Mole, and deposited him on a kind of large sofa in front of the window, which they partly opened. This movement aroused La Mole, who heaved a sigh, and opening his eyes, began to experience that indescribable feeling of comfort which attends the sensations of a wounded man, when on his return to consciousness, he finds freshness instead of burning heat, and the perfume of healing salves instead of the noisome odor of blood. He muttered some unconnected words, to which Marguerite replied by a smile, placing her finger on her mouth. At this moment several blows were struck at the door.

"Some one knocks at the secret passage," said Marguerite; "I will go and see who it is. Do you remain here, and do not leave him for a single moment."

Marguerite went into the chamber, and closing the door of the cabinet, opened that of the passage which led to the king's and queen-mother's apartments.

"Madame de Sauve!" she exclaimed, retreating suddenly, and with an expression which resembled hatred, if not terror; so true it is that a woman never forgives another for carrying off from her even a man whom she does not love—"Madame de Sauve!"

"Yes, your Majesty!" she replied, clasping her hands.

"You here, Madame?" exclaimed Marguerite, more and more surprised, and at the same time more and more imperious.

Charlotte fell on her knees. "Madame," she said, "pardon me! I know how guilty I am toward you; but if you knew—the fault is not wholly mine. An express command of the queen-mother—"

"Rise!" said Marguerite; "and as I do not suppose you have come with the hope of justifying yourself to me, tell me why you have come at all?"

"I have come, Madame," said Charlotte, still on her knees,

and with a look of wild alarm, "I came to ask you if he were not here?"

"Here! who? Of whom are you speaking, Madame? for I really do not understand."

"Of the king!"

"Of the king? What, do you follow him to my apartments? You know very well, however, that he never comes hither."

"Ah, Madame!" continued the Baronne de Sauve, without replying to these attacks, or even seeming to comprehend them; "ah, would to Heaven he were here!"

"And wherefore?"

"Eh, *mon Dieu!* Madame, because they are murdering the Huguenots, and the King of Navarre is the chief of the Huguenots."

"Oh!" cried Marguerite, seizing Madame de Sauve by the hand, and compelling her to rise—"oh! I had forgotten! Besides, I did not think a king could be exposed to the same dangers as other men."

"More, Madame; a thousand times more!" cried Charlotte.

"In fact, Madame de Lorraine had warned me; I had begged him not to leave the Louvre. Has he done so?"

"No, Madame, he is in the Louvre; but if he is not here—"

"He is not here!"

"Oh!" cried Madame de Sauve, with a burst of agony, "then he is a dead man, for the queen-mother has sworn his destruction!"

"His destruction! ah," said Marguerite, "you terrify me! impossible!"

"Madame," replied Madame de Sauve, with that energy which passion alone can give, "I tell you that no one knows where the King of Navarre is."

"And where is the queen-mother?"

"The queen-mother sent me to seek M. de Guise and M. de Tavannes, who were in her oratory, and then dismissed me. Then, forgive me, Madame, I went up to my room, and according to custom, I waited—"

"For my husband?" said Marguerite.

"He did not come, Madame. Then I sought him everywhere, and asked everybody for him. One soldier told me he thought he had seen him in the midst of the guards who accompanied him, with his drawn sword in his hand, some time before the massacre began; and the massacre began an hour ago."

"Thanks, Madame," said Marguerite; "and although perhaps the sentiment which impels you is an additional offense toward me—yet again, thanks!"

"Oh, forgive me, Madame," she said; "and I shall return to my apartments fortified by your pardon, for I dare not follow you, even at a distance."

Marguerite extended her hand to her. "I will seek Queen Catherine," she said; "return to your apartments. The King of Navarre is under my safeguard; I have promised him my alliance, and I will be faithful to my promise."

"But suppose you cannot obtain access to the queen-mother, Madame?"

"Then I will go to my brother Charles, and I will speak to him."

"Go, Madame, go," said Charlotte; "and may God guide your Majesty!"

Marguerite passed quickly along the passage; but on reaching the end, she turned to assure herself that Madame de Sauve did not remain behind. Madame de Sauve followed her. The Queen of Navarre saw her turn to her own apartments, and then went herself toward the queen's chamber. Here all was changed. Instead of the crowd of eager courtiers who usually opened their ranks before the queen and respectfully saluted her, Marguerite met only guards with red partisans and garments stained with blood, or gentlemen in torn mantles, their faces blackened with powder, bearing orders and despatches—some going in, others going out; all these entrances and exits made a great and frightful confusion in the galleries. Marguerite, however, went boldly on until she reached the ante-chamber of the queen-mother, which was guarded by a double file of soldiers, who allowed only those to enter who had the proper countersign. Marguerite in vain tried to pass this living barrier. Several times she saw the door open and shut; and through the opening she could see Catherine moving and excited, as if she were only twenty years of age, writing, receiving letters, opening them, addressing a word to one, a smile to another; and those on whom she smiled most graciously were those who were the most covered with dust and blood. Without the walls was heard from time to time the report of firearms.

"I shall never reach him!" said Marguerite, after having made several vain attempts to pass the soldiers. "Rather than lose my time here, I will go and find my brother."

At this moment M. de Guise passed; he had come to inform the queen of the murder of the admiral, and was returning to the butchery.

"Oh, Henri!" cried Marguerite, "where is the King of Navarre?"

The duke looked at her with a smile of astonishment, bowed, and without any reply, passed on.

"Ah, my dear René," said the queen, recognizing Catherine's perfumer, "is that you? You have just left my mother; do you know what has become of my husband?"

"His Majesty the King of Navarre is no friend of mine, Madame—that you know very well. It is even said," he added with a smile that resembled a grimace, "that he ventures to accuse me of having been the accomplice of Queen Catherine in poisoning his mother."

"No, no!" cried Marguerite; "my good René, do not believe that!"

"Oh, it is of little consequence, Madame!" said the perfumer; "neither the King of Navarre nor his party are any longer to be feared!" And he turned his back on Marguerite.

"Ah, M. de Tavannes!" cried Marguerite, "one word, I beseech you!"

Tavannes stopped.

"Where is Henri de Navarre?"

"Faith," he replied in a loud voice, "I believe he is somewhere in the city with the M. M. d'Alençon and de Condé." And then he added in a tone so low that the queen alone could hear, "Your Majesty, if you would see him—to be in whose place I would give my life—go and knock at the king's armory."

"Thanks, Tavannes, thanks!" said Marguerite; "I will go there." And she went on her way thither, murmuring, "Oh, after all I promised him, after the way in which he behaved to me when that ingrate, Henri de Guise, was concealed in the closet, I cannot let him perish!" And she knocked at the door of the king's apartments, but they were begirt within by two companies of guards.

"No one is admitted to the king," said the officer, coming forward.

"But I—" said Marguerite.

"The order is general."

"I, the Queen of Navarre! I, his sister!"

"I dare make no exception, Madame." And the officer closed the door.

"Oh, he is lost!" exclaimed Marguerite, alarmed at the sight of all the sinister countenances she had seen. "Yes, yes! I comprehend all. I have been used as a bait. I am the snare which has entrapped the Huguenots! Oh! I will enter, or they shall kill me!" And she ran like a mad creature through the corridors and galleries, when suddenly while passing by a small door, she heard a low chanting, almost as melancholy as it was monotonous. It was a Calvinistic psalm, sung by a trembling voice in an adjacent chamber.

"The nurse of my brother the king—the good Madelon; it is she!" exclaimed Marguerite. "God of the Christians, aid me now!" And full of hope, Marguerite knocked at the little door.

Soon after the counsel which Marguerite had conveyed to him, after his conversation with René, after leaving the queen-mother's chamber—poor Phébé, like a good genius, opposing—Henri de Navarre had met some worthy Catholic gentlemen, who, under a pretext of doing him honor, had escorted him to his apartments, where a score of Huguenots awaited him, who had rallied round the young prince, and having once rallied, would not leave him—so strongly for some hours had the presentiment of that night weighed on the Louvre. They had remained there, without any one attempting to disturb them. At last, at the first stroke of the bell of St. Germain l'Auxerrois, which resounded through all hearts like a funeral knell, Tavannes entered, and in the midst of a deathlike silence, announced that King Charles IX desired to speak to Henri.

It was useless to attempt resistance, and no one thought of it. They had heard the ceilings, galleries, and corridors creak beneath the feet of the assembled soldiers, who were in the courtyards as well as in the apartments to the number of two thousand. Henri, after having taken leave of his friends, whom he might never again see, followed Tavannes, who led him to a small gallery near the king's apartments, where he left him alone, unarmed, and a prey to mistrust.

The King of Navarre counted here alone, minute by minute, two mortal hours—listening, with increasing alarm, to the sound of the tocsin and the discharge of firearms; seeing through a small window, by the light of the flames and torches, the victims and their assassins pass; understanding nothing of these shrieks of murder, these cries of distress; not even suspecting, in spite of his knowledge of Charles IX, the queen-mother, and the Duc de Guise, the horrible tragedy at this moment performed.

Henri had not physical courage; but he had better than that—he had moral force. Fearing danger, he yet smiled at and faced it; but it was danger in the field of battle, danger in the open air, danger in the eyes of all, and attended by the noisy harmony of trumpets and the loud and vibrating beat of drums. But now he was without arms, shut up, immured in a half-light which was scarcely sufficient to enable him to see the enemy who might glide toward him, and the weapon that might be raised to strike him. These two hours were perhaps the most painful of his life.

In the hottest of the tumult, and as Henri was beginning to comprehend that in all probability this was some organized massacre, a captain came to seek the prince, and conducted him to the king. As they approached, the door opened, and behind them it closed, as if by enchantment. The captain then led Henri to the king, who was in his armory. When they entered, the king was seated in an armchair, his two hands placed on the two arms of the seat, and his head inclined forward. As they entered, Charles looked up, and on his brow Henri observed the perspiration in large beads.

"Good evening, Henriot," said the king, roughly. "La Chastre, leave us."

The captain retired, and a profound silence ensued. Henri looked around him with uneasiness, and saw that he was alone with the king. Charles suddenly arose. *"Mordieu!"* said he, passing his hands through his light-brown hair, and wiping his brow at the same time, "you are glad to be with me, are not you, Henriot?"

"Certainly, Sire," replied the King of Navarre, "I am always happy to be with your Majesty."

"Happier than if you were down there, eh?" continued

Charles, following his own thoughts, rather than replying to Henri's compliment.

"I do not understand, Sire," replied Henri.

"Look out, then, and you will soon understand."

And with a quick gesture, Charles moved, or rather sprang toward the window, and drawing his brother-in-law toward him, who became more and more alarmed, he pointed out to him the horrible outlines of the assassins, who, on the deck of a boat, were cutting the throats or drowning the victims brought them at every moment.

"In the name of Heaven!" cried Henri, "what is going on tonight?"

"On this night, Monsieur," replied Charles IX, "they are ridding me of all the Huguenots. Look down there, over the Hôtel de Bourbon, at the smoke and flames; they are the smoke and flames of the admiral's house, which has been fired. Do you see that body, which these good Catholics are drawing on a torn mattress. It is the corpse of the admiral's son-in-law—the carcass of your friend, Téligny."

"Oh, what is the meaning of it?" cried the King of Navarre, seeking vainly by his side for the hilt of his dagger, and trembling equally with shame and anger; for he felt that he was at the same time laughed at and menaced.

"It means," cried Charles IX, suddenly furious, and turning white in a frightful manner, "that I will no longer have any Huguenots about me. Do you hear me, Henri? Am I king? Am I master?"

"But, your Majesty—"

"My Majesty kills and massacres at this moment all that is not Catholic; it is my pleasure. Are you Catholic?" exclaimed Charles, whose anger rose like an excited sea.

"Sire," replied Henri, "remember your own words, 'What matters the religion of those who serve me well!' "

"Ah, ah, ah!" cried Charles, bursting into a ferocious laugh; "you tell me to remember my words, Henri! *'Verba volant,'* as my sister Margot says. And had not all those"—and he pointed to the city with his finger—"served me well also? Were they not brave in battle, wise in council, deeply devoted? They were all useful subjects; but they were Huguenots, and I want none but Catholics."

Henri remained silent.

"Well! do you understand me now, Henriot?" asked Charles.

"I understand, Sire."

"Well?"

"Well, Sire! I do not see why the King of Navarre should not do what so many gentlemen and poor folk have done. For if they all die, poor unfortunates, it is because the same terms have been proposed to them which your Majesty proposes to me; and they have refused, as I refuse."

Charles seized the arm of the young prince, and fixed on him a look whose vacancy suddenly changed into a fierce and savage scowl. "What!" he said, "do you believe that I have taken the trouble to offer the alternative of the Mass to those whose throats are cut down there?"

"Sire," said Henri, disengaging his arm, "will you not die in the religion of your fathers?"

"Yes, *mordieu!* and you?"

"Well, Sire, I will do the same!" replied Henri.

Charles uttered a cry of fierce rage, and seized with trembling hand his arquebus lying on the table. Henri, who, leaning against the tapestry with the perspiration streaming from his brow, was yet, owing to his self-control, apparently calm, followed with the stupefied gaze of a bird fascinated by a serpent every movement of the terrible king. Charles cocked his arquebus, and stamping his foot with blind rage, cried, as he dazzled Henri's eyes with the polished barrel of the brandished weapon, "Will you accept the Mass?" Henri remained silent. Charles IX shook the vaults of the Louvre with the most terrible oath that ever issued from the lips of man, and grew more livid than before. "Death, Mass, or the Bastille!" he cried, taking aim at the King of Navarre.

"Oh, Sire!" exclaimed Henri, "will you kill me—me, your brother?"

Henri thus eluded by his incomparable tact, which was one of his most conspicuous gifts, the answer which the king demanded; for doubtless had this reply been in the negative, Henri had been a dead man.

As immediately after the last paroxysms of rage there is always the beginning of reaction, Charles IX did not repeat the question he had addressed to the Prince de Navarre; and after a moment's hesitation, during which he uttered a hoarse growl, he turned toward the open window, and aimed at a man who was running along the quay in front. "I must kill someone!" he cried, ghastly as a corpse, his eyes injected with blood; and firing as he spoke, he prostrated the man who was running. Henri uttered a groan. Then, animated by a frightful ardor, Charles loaded and fired his arquebus without cessation, uttering cries of joy every time he hit his man.

"It is all over with me!" said the King of Navarre to himself; "when he sees no one else to kill, he will kill me!"

"Well!" said a voice behind the princes, suddenly, "is it done?"

It was Catherine de Médicis, who had entered as the king fired his last shot.

"No, thousand thunders of hell!" said the king, throwing his arquebus on the floor—"no, the obstinate blockhead will not consent!"

Catherine made no reply. She turned slowly toward the part of the chamber in which Henri was, as motionless as one of the figures of the tapestry against which he was leaning. She then gave a glance to the king, which seemed to say, "Then why is he alive?"

"He lives, he lives," murmured Charles IX, who well understood the glance, and replied to it without hesitation—"he lives because he—is my relative."

Catherine smiled. Henri saw the smile, and felt then assured that it was with Catherine he must struggle. "Madame," he said to her, "all comes from you, I see very well, and nothing from my brother-in-law Charles. It is you who have laid the plan for drawing me into a snare. It is you who made your daughter the bait which was to destroy us all. It is you who have separated me from my wife, that she might not see me killed before her eyes."

"Yes, but that shall not be!" cried another voice, breathless and impassioned, which Henri recognized in an instant, and which made Charles start with surprise, and Catherine with rage.

"Marguerite!" exclaimed Henri.

"Margot!" said Charles IX.

"My daughter!" muttered Catherine.

"Monsieur," said Marguerite to Henri, "your last words were an accusation against me, and you were both right and wrong— right, for I am the means by which they attempted to destroy you; wrong, for I did not know that you were going toward destruction.

I myself, Monsieur, owe my life to chance—to my mother's not thinking of me perhaps; but as soon as I learned your danger, I remembered my duty, and a wife's duty is to share the fortunes of her husband. If you are exiled, Monsieur, I will be exiled, too; if they imprison you, I will be your fellow captive; if they kill you, I will also die." And she extended her hand to her husband, which he eagerly seized, if not with love, at least with gratitude.

"Oh, my poor Margot!" said Charles, "you had much better desire him to become a Catholic!"

"Sire," replied Marguerite, with that lofty dignity which was so natural to her, "for your own sake do not ask any prince of your house to commit a base action."

Catherine darted a significant glance at Charles.

"Brother," cried Marguerite, who, as well as Charles IX, understood the terrible dumb-show of Catherine, "remember, you made him my husband!"

Charles was for a time stupefied between the imperative look of Catherine and the supplicating regard of Marguerite; but after a pause he said in a whisper to Catherine, "Faith, Madame, Margot is right; and Henriot is my brother-in-law."

"Yes," was Catherine's reply, in a similar whisper to her son— "yes, but if he were not—"

The Hawthorn of the Cemetery of the Innocents

When she had reached her own apartments, Marguerite vainly endeavored to divine the words which Catherine de Médicis had whispered to Charles IX, and which had cut short the terrible interview on which hung life and death. A part of the morning was employed by her in attending to La Mole, and the other in searching that problem which her mind could not solve.

The King of Navarre remained a prisoner in the Louvre. The pursuit of the Huguenots was hotter than ever. To the terrible night had succeeded a day of massacre still more horrible. It was no longer the tocsin and bells that sounded, but the "Te Deum"; and the echoes of this joyous anthem, resounding in the midst of fire and slaughter, were perhaps more sad by the light of the sun than had been the knell of the previous night sounding in darkness. This was not all. Strange to say, a hawthorn tree, which had blossomed in the spring, and which, according to custom, had lost its odorous flowers in the month of June, had reblossomed during the night; and the Catholics, who saw in this even a miracle, and who by spreading abroad the report of this miracle would make God their accomplice, went in procession, cross and banner at their head, to the Cemetery of the Innocents, where this hawthorn was blooming. This approval, as it were, sent from heaven, had increased the zeal of the assassins; and while the city continued to present in each street and thoroughfare a scene of desolation, the Louvre had become the common tomb for all Protestants who had been shut up there when the signal was given. The King of Navarre, the Prince de Condé, and La Mole were the only survivors.

Assured as to La Mole, whose wounds, though severe, were not mortal, Marguerite was occupied now with the one idea of saving her husband's life, which was still threatened. No doubt the first sentiment which actuated the wife was one of generous pity for a man to whom, as to the Béarnais, she had sworn, if not love, at least alliance; but there was besides another less pure sentiment which had penetrated the queen's heart. Marguerite was ambitious, and had foreseen almost a certainty of royalty in her marriage with Henri de Bourbon. Navarre, harassed on one side by the kings of France, and on the other by the kings of Spain, who had finally seized half its territory, might, if Henri de Bourbon should fulfill the hopes awakened by the courage he had displayed on the rare occasions when he had drawn the sword, become a veritable kingdom, with the Huguenots of France for subjects. Should she lose Henri, she would lose not only a husband but a throne.

While wrapped in her reflections, she heard a knock at the secret door. She started, for three persons only came by that door—the king, the queen-mother, and the Duc d'Alençon. She half-opened the door of the cabinet, made a gesture of silence to Gillonne and La Mole, and then went and opened the door to her visitor. It was the Duc d'Alençon. The young prince had disappeared during the evening. For a moment Marguerite had had the idea of claiming his intercession for the King of Navarre; but a terrible idea restrained her. The marriage had taken place contrary to his wishes. François detested Henri, and had maintained neutrality toward the Béarnais only because he was convinced that Henri and his wife had remained strangers to each other. Any sign of interest in her husband shown by Marguerite would therefore bring nearer to his breast one of the three daggers which threatened him. She therefore shuddered on perceiving the young prince more than she had on seeing the king or even the queen-mother. D'Alençon was attired with his usual elegance. His clothes and linen gave forth those perfumes which Charles IX despised, but of which the Ducs d'Anjou and d'Alençon made continual use. He entered in his accustomed manner, and approached his sister to embrace her. But instead of offering to him her cheeks as she would have done to King Charles or the Duc d'Anjou, she inclined her head and offered him her brow. The Duc d'Alençon sighed and pressed his pale lips on Marguerite's forehead. Then, sitting down, he began to relate to his sister the bloody particulars of the night—the lingering and terrible death of the admiral, the instantaneous death of Téligny, pierced by a ball. He paused and emphasized all the terrible details of this night with that love of blood peculiar to himself and his two brothers; Marguerite allowed him to run on. At last, having told everything, he paused.

"It was not to tell me this only that you came hither, Brother?" said Marguerite.

The Duc d'Alençon smiled.

"You have something else to say to me?"

"No," replied the duke; "I am waiting."

"Waiting! for what?"

"Did you not tell me, dearest Marguerite," said the duke, drawing his chair close up to that of his sister, "that this marriage with the King of Navarre was contracted against your will?"

"Yes, no doubt. I did not know the Prince de Béarn when he was proposed to me as a husband."

"And after you knew him did you not say that you felt no love for him?"

"I said so, and it is true."

"Was it not your opinion that this marriage would make you miserable?"

"My dear François," said Marguerite, "when a marriage is not extremely happy, it is almost always extremely miserable."

"Well, then, my dear Marguerite, as I said to you, I am waiting."

"But for what are you waiting?"

"Until you display your joy."

"What have I to be joyful for?"

"The unexpected occasion which offers itself for you to resume your liberty."

"My liberty?" replied Marguerite, who was resolved on allowing the prince to disclose all his thoughts.

"Yes; your liberty! You will now be separated from the King of Navarre."

"Separated!" said Marguerite, fastening her eyes on the young prince.

The Duc d'Alençon tried to sustain his sister's look; but his eyes soon sank in embarrassment.

"Separated!" repeated Marguerite; "and how, Brother, for I should like to comprehend all you mean, and by what method it is proposed to separate us?"

"Why," murmured the duke, "Henri is a Huguenot."

"No doubt; but he made no mystery of his religion, and they knew that when we were married."

"Yes; but since your marriage, Sister," asked the duke, allowing, in spite of himself, a ray of joy to illumine his countenance; "what has been Henri's behavior?"

"Why, you know better than anyone, François; for he has passed his days almost perpetually in your society—sometimes at the chase, sometimes at mall, sometimes at tennis."

"Yes, his days, no doubt," replied the duke; "his days—but his nights?"

Marguerite was silent; it was now her turn to cast down her eyes.

"His nights," repeated the Duc d'Alençon—"his nights?"

"Well?" inquired Marguerite, feeling that it was requisite that she should say something in reply.

"Well, he has passed them with Madame de Sauve!"

"How do you know that?" exclaimed Marguerite.

"I know it, because I had an interest in knowing it," replied the young prince, turning pale and picking the embroidery of his sleeves.

Marguerite began to understand what Catherine had whispered to Charles, but affected to remain in ignorance. "Why do you tell me this, Brother?" she replied with a well-affected air of melancholy. "Was it for the sake of recalling to me that no one here loves me and is loyal to me—neither those whom nature has given to me as protectors, nor he whom the Church has given me as my spouse?"

"You are unjust," said the Duc d'Alençon, drawing his chair still nearer to his sister; "I love you and protect you!"

"Brother," said Marguerite, looking steadfastly at him, "you have something to say to me on the part of the queen-mother?"

"I? You mistake, Sister, I swear to you; what can make you think that?"

"What can make me think that? Why, because you break the intimacy that binds you to my husband; you abandon the cause of the King of Navarre."

"The cause of the King of Navarre!" replied the Duc d'Alençon, surprised.

"Yes, certainly. Come, François, let us speak freely. You have admitted twenty times that you cannot raise yourself, or even sustain yourself without his aid. That alliance—"

"Has now become impossible, Sister," interrupted the Duc d'Alençon.

"And why?"

"Because the king has designs on your husband. Pardon me; in saying 'your husband' I am in error—on Henri de Navarre, I should say. Our mother has divined everything. I allied myself to the Huguenots, because I believed the Huguenots were in favor; but now they kill the Huguenots, and in another week there will not remain fifty in the whole kingdom. I held out my hand to the King of Navarre because he was—your husband; but now it appears that he is not your husband. What can you say to that—you who are not only the loveliest woman in France, but have the clearest head in the kingdom?"

"Why, I have to say," replied Marguerite, "that I know our brother Charles. I saw him yesterday in one of those fits of frenzy, every one of which shortens his life ten years. I have to say that these attacks are unfortunately very frequent, and that thus in all probability our brother Charles has not very long to live. I have to say, finally, that the King of Poland is just dead, and the question of electing a prince of the house of France in his stead is much discussed. When circumstances are thus shaped, it is not the moment to abandon allies who in the moment of struggle might support us with the strength of a nation and the power of a kingdom."

"And you!" exclaimed the duke, "do you not act much more treasonably to me in preferring a stranger to your own house?"

"Explain yourself, François! in what and how have I acted treasonably to you?"

"You yesterday begged the life of the King of Navarre from King Charles."

"Well?" said Marguerite, with affected simplicity.

The duke rose hastily, paced round the chamber twice or thrice with a bewildered air, then came and took Marguerite's hand. "Adieu, Sister!" he said. "You would not understand me; do not therefore complain of whatever may happen to you."

Marguerite turned pale, but remained fixed in her place. She saw the Duc d'Alençon go away, without making any attempt to detain him; but scarcely had she lost sight of him in the corridor, when he returned.

"Listen, Marguerite," he said; "I had forgotten one thing—it is that tomorrow, at a certain hour, the King of Navarre will be dead."

Marguerite uttered a cry, for the idea that she was the instrument of assassination caused in her a fear she could not subdue.

"And you will not prevent this death?" she said; "you will not save your best and most faithful ally?"

"Since yesterday, the King of Navarre is no longer my ally."

"Then who is?"

"M. de Guise. By destroying the Huguenots, M. de Guise has become the king of the Catholics."

"And is it a son of Henri II who recognizes as his king a duke of Lorraine?"

"You are in a bad mood, Marguerite, and will not understand anything."

"I confess that I seek in vain to read your thoughts."

"Sister, you are of as good a house as the Princesse de Porcian; Guise is no more immortal than the King of Navarre. Well, Marguerite, now suppose three things, all possible: first, that Monsieur is elected King of Poland; second, that you should love me as I love you—well! I am King of France, and you—and you—Queen of the Catholics."

Marguerite was overwhelmed at the depth of the views of this youth, whom no one at court thought possessed of even common understanding. "Then," she said after a moment of silence, "you are not jealous of the Duc de Guise, as you are of the King of Navarre?"

"What is done is done," said the Duc d'Alençon, in a gloomy tone; "and if I had reason to be jealous of the Duc de Guise—well, I have been so."

"There is only one thing which can prevent this capital plan from succeeding."

"And what is that?"

"That I no longer love the Duc de Guise."

"And whom, then, do you love?" asked the duke.

"No one."

D'Alençon looked at Marguerite with the astonishment of a man who in his turn does not comprehend, and left the apartment, pressing his cold hand on his forehead, which ached to bursting.

Marguerite was alone and thoughtful. The situation began, in her view, to assume clear and definite outlines. The king had permitted the massacre; Queen Catherine and the Duc de Guise had instigated it. The death of the King of Navarre would be a natural consequence of the great catastrophe. The Duc de Guise and the Duc d'Alençon were about to join forces in order to secure to themselves the greatest possible advantage. The King of Navarre dead, they would take possession of his kingdom. Marguerite then would be a widow, without a throne, without power, with nothing before her but a cloister, where she would not have even the melancholy satisfaction of weeping for a spouse who had never been her husband.

Marguerite was at this point in her meditations when Queen Catherine sent to know if she would accompany her in a pilgrimage to the hawthorn of the Cemetery of the Innocents. Her first impulse was to refuse to join that cavalcade; but reflecting that the excursion might afford opportunity to learn something about the fate of the King of Navarre, she sent word that if they would prepare a horse, she would most readily accompany their Majesties.

A few minutes after, the page came to tell her that all was ready; and after a sign to Gillonne to take care of La Mole, she went forth.

The king, the queen-mother, Tavannes, and the principal Catholics, were already mounted. Marguerite cast a rapid glance over the group, which was composed of about twenty persons, but the King of Navarre was not of the party.

Madame de Sauve was there, and she exchanged a glance with her which convinced the Queen of Navarre that her husband's mistress had something to tell her.

On seeing the king, Queen Catherine, and the more prominent Catholics, the people gathered, and followed the cortège like an increasing wave, crying, "Vive la roi! Vive la messe! Mort aux Huguenots!" These cries were accompanied by the brandishing of reddened swords and still smoking arquebuses—which showed the part which each had taken in the sinister event that had taken place.

When they reached the top of the Rue des Prouvelles, they met some men who were dragging a corpse without a head. It was that of the admiral. The men were going to hang it by the feet at Montfaucon.

They entered the Cemetery of Saints Innocents, and the clergy, forewarned of the visit of the king and the queen-mother, awaited their Majesties, to deliver addresses to them.

Madame de Sauve profited by a moment when Catherine was listening to a discourse to approach the Queen of Navarre, and beg leave to kiss her hand. Marguerite extended her arm toward her, and Madame de Sauve, as she kissed the queen's hand, secretly put a small piece of paper up her sleeve. Quick and well managed as was Madame de Sauve's proceeding, yet Catherine perceived it, and turned round at the moment when the maid of honor was kissing Marguerite's hand. The two women saw that look, which struck them like lightning, but both remained unmoved; only Madame de Sauve left Marguerite, and resumed her place near Catherine. When the address was finished, Catherine made a gesture smilingly to the Queen of Navarre, who went toward her.

"Eh, my daughter," said the queen-mother in her Italian patois, "are you, then, on such intimate terms with Madame de Sauve?"

Marguerite smiled in turn, and gave to her lovely countenance the bitterest expression she could, as she said, "Yes, Mother; the serpent came to bite my hand!"

"Ah, ah!" replied Catherine, with a smile, "you are jealous, I think!"

"You mistake, Madame," replied Marguerite; "I am no more jealous of the King of Navarre than the King of Navarre is jealous of me, only I know how to distinguish my friends from my enemies. I like those who like me, and detest those who hate me. If not, Madame, should I be your daughter?"

Catherine smiled in a manner which satisfied Marguerite that if she had had any suspicion it had vanished.

At this moment arrived other pilgrims. The Duc de Guise came with a troop of gentlemen all warm still with recent carnage. They escorted a litter covered with rich tapestry, which stopped in front of the king.

"The Duchesse de Nevers!" cried Charles IX, "let that lovely and vigorous Catholic come and receive our compliments. Why, they tell me, Cousin, that from your window you made war on the Huguenots, and killed one with a stone."

The Duchesse de Nevers blushed. "Sire," she said, in a low

tone, and kneeling before the king, "it was, on the contrary, a wounded Catholic, whom I had the good fortune to rescue."

"Good; good, my cousin! there are two ways of serving me—one by exterminating my enemies, the other by aiding my friends. One does what one can; and I am sure that if you had had opportunity to do more you would have done it."

During this time the people, seeing the signs of harmony between the house of Lorraine and Charles IX shouted, "Vive le roi! Vive le Duc de Guise! Vive la messe!"

"Do you return to the Louvre with us, Henriette?" said the queen-mother to the lovely duchess.

Marguerite touched her friend on the elbow, who, understanding the sign, replied, "No, Madame, unless your Majesty desire it; for I have business in the city with her Majesty the Queen of Navarre."

"And what are you going to do together?" inquired Catherine.

"To see some very rare and curious Greek books found at an old Protestant pastor's, and which have been taken to the Tower of St. Jacques la Boucherie," replied Marguerite.

"You would do much better to see the last Huguenot flung from the top of Pont aux Meuniers into the Seine," said Charles IX; "that is the place for all good Frenchmen."

"We will go if it be your Majesty's desire," replied the Duchesse de Nevers.

Catherine cast a look of distrust on the two young women. Marguerite, on the watch, remarked it, and turning herself round uneasily, looked about her. This assumed or real disquietude did not escape Catherine.

"What are you looking for?"

"I am seeking—I do not see—" she replied.

"Whom are you seeking?"

"Madame de Sauve," said Marguerite; "she must have returned to the Louvre."

"Did I not say you were jealous!" said Catherine, in her daughter's ear. "Oh, *bestia!* Come, come, Henriette," she added; "begone, and take the Queen of Navarre with you."

Marguerite still pretended to look about her; then, turning toward her friend, she said in a whisper, "Take me away quickly; I have matters of great importance to say to you."

The duchess saluted the king and queen-mother respectfully, and then, inclining before the Queen of Navarre, "Will your Majesty condescend to come into my litter?" said she.

"Willingly, only you will have to take me back to the Louvre."

"My litter, like my servants and myself, are at your Majesty's orders."

Queen Marguerite entered the litter; and upon a sign from her, the Duchesse de Nevers entered and placed herself respectfully by her side. Catherine and her gentlemen returned to the Louvre, and during the route, she spoke incessantly to the king, pointing several times to Madame de Sauve; and every time she did so the king laughed, as Charles IX could laugh—that is, with a laugh more sinister than a threat.

As to Marguerite, as soon as she felt the litter in motion, and had no longer to fear the searching gaze of Catherine, she quickly drew from her sleeve the note of Madame de Sauve, and read as follows:

I have received orders to send tonight to the King of Navarre two keys—one is that of the chamber in which he is shut up; and the other is the key of my chamber. When once in my apartment, I am enjoined to keep him there until six o'clock in the morning.

Let your Majesty reflect; let your Majesty decide; let your Majesty esteem my life as nothing.

"There is now no doubt," murmured Marguerite; "and the poor woman is the tool of which they wish to make use to destroy us all. But we will see if the Queen Margot, as my brother Charles calls me, is so easily to be made a nun."

"And what is that letter about?" inquired the Duchesse de Nevers.

"Ah, Duchess, I have so many things to say to you!" replied Marguerite, tearing the note into a thousand bits, and scattering them to the winds.

CHAPTER 12

Confidences

"And first, where are we going?" asked Marguerite; "not to the Pont des Meuniers, I suppose—I have seen enough slaughter since yesterday."

"I have taken the liberty to conduct your Majesty—"

"First and foremost, my Majesty requests you to forget my Majesty; you are taking me—"

"To the Hôtel de Guise, unless you decide otherwise."

"No, no, let us go there, Henriette; the duke and your husband are not there?"

"Oh, no," cried the duchess, her bright eyes sparkling with joy—"no; neither my husband, my brother-in-law, nor anyone else. I am free—free as air, free as a bird; free, my queen! Do you understand the happiness there is in that word 'free'? I come, I go, I command. Ah, poor queen, you are not free; you sigh."

"You come, you go, you command; is that all, then? Is that all the use of liberty? Come, you are very happy over being only free."

"Your Majesty promised me that you would begin our confidences."

"Again 'your Majesty'! I shall be angry soon, Henriette. Have you forgotten our agreement?"

"No; your respectful servant in public, in private your madcap confidante. Is it not so, Marguerite?"

"Yes, yes," said the queen, smiling.

"No family rivalry, no perfidies of love, all fair and open. An offensive and defensive alliance for the sole purpose of seeking, and if we can, seizing that ephemeral thing called happiness."

"Precisely, my duchess; and to renew the compact, kiss me."

And the two beautiful women, the one so roseate, so fair, so animated, the other so pale, so full of melancholy, united their lips as they had united their thoughts.

"What is there new?" asked the duchess, fixing her eyes upon Marguerite.

"Everything is new since two days ago, is it not?"

"Oh, I am speaking of love, not of politics. When we are as old as your mother Catherine, we will think of politics; but at twenty, my beautiful queen, let us think of something else. Tell me, are you altogether married?"

"To whom?" said Marguerite, smiling.

"Ah, you reassure me."

"Well, Henriette, that which reassures you alarms me. Duchess, I must be married."

"When?"

"Tomorrow."

"Oh, poor Marguerite! and is it necessary?"

"Absolutely."

"*Mordi!* as an acquaintance of mine says, this is very sad."

"You know someone who says *mordi?*" asked Marguerite, smiling.

"Yes."

"And who is this someone?"

"You ask questions instead of answering them. Finish your story, and then I will begin."

"In two words, it is this: The King of Navarre is in love, and not with me; I am not in love, and certainly not with him; yet we must both of us change, or seem to change, before tomorrow."

"Well, do you change, and he will soon do the same."

"That is quite impossible, for I am less than ever inclined to change."

"Only with respect to your husband, I hope."

"Henriette, I have a scruple."

"A scruple! about what?"

"About religion. Do you make any difference between Huguenots and Catholics?"

"In politics?"

"Yes."

"Of course."

"And in love?"

"Ma chère, we women are such heathens that we admit every kind of sect, and recognize many gods."

"In one, eh?"

"Yes," replied the duchess, her eyes sparkling; "him who is called Eros, Cupido, Amor; who has a quiver on his back, wings on his shoulders, and a bandage over his eyes. *Mordi, vive la devotion!"*

"Nevertheless, you have a way of worshipping peculiarly your own, you throw stones on the heads of the Huguenots."

"Let them talk. Ah, Marguerite! how the finest ideas, the no blest actions, are spoiled in passing through the mouths of the vulgar!"

"The vulgar! why, it was my brother Charles who congratulated you on your exploits."

"Your brother Charles is a mighty hunter, who blows the horn all day, which makes him very thin. I reject his compliments; besides, I gave him his answer. Did you not hear what I said?"

"No; you spoke so low."

"So much the better. I shall have more news to tell you. Now then, finish your story, Marguerite."

"Why—why—"

"Well?"

"Why, in truth," said the queen, laughing, "if the stone my brother spoke of be a fact, I should not care to tell you my story at all."

"Ah!" cried Henriette, "you have chosen a Huguenot. Well, to reassure your conscience, I promise you to choose one myself on the first opportunity."

"Ah, you have chosen a Catholic, then?"

"Mordi!" replied the duchess.

"I see, I see."

"And what is this Huguenot of yours?"

"I have not adopted him. He is nothing, and probably never will be anything to me."

"But of what sort is he? You can tell me that; you know how curious I am about these matters."

"A poor young fellow, beautiful as Benvenuto Cellini's Nisus, and who took refuge in my apartments."

"Oh, oh! of course without any suggestion on your part?"

"Do not laugh, Henriette; at this very moment he is between life and death."

"He is ill, then?"

"He is severely wounded."

"A wounded Huguenot is very disagreeable, especially in these times; and what have you done with this wounded Huguenot, who is not, and never will be anything to you?"

"He is hid in my cabinet; I would save him."

"He is young, handsome, and wounded; you hide him and wish to save him. He will be very senseless if he does not prove to be grateful."

"He is already, I fear, more grateful than I could wish."

"And this poor young man interests you?"

"Only for humanity's sake."

"Ah! humanity's precisely the virtue that undoes all us women."

"Yes; and you see the king, the Duc d'Alençon, my mother, or even my husband may at any moment enter the apartment—"

"Ay, you want me to hide your Huguenot so long as he is ill, upon condition I send him back to you when he is cured."

"No," said Marguerite, "I do not look forward so far; but if you could conceal the poor fellow, if you could preserve the life I have saved, I should be most grateful. You are free at the Hôtel de Guise; you have no one to watch you. Besides, behind your chamber there is a cabinet like mine, into which no one is entitled to enter; lend me this cabinet for my Huguenot, and when he is cured, open the cage, and let the bird fly away."

"There is only one difficulty, my dear; the cage is already occupied."

"What, have you also saved somebody?"

"That is exactly what I answered to your brother."

"Ah, ah! that's why you spoke so low that I could not hear you."

"Listen, Marguerite; the story is no less poetical and romantic than yours. After I had left to you six of my guards, I returned with the rest to the Hôtel de Guise. I was looking at a house that was burning opposite, when I heard the voices of men swearing, and of women crying. I went out on the balcony and saw first a sword whose flashes seemed to light all the scene. I admired that furious blade—for I have a passion for brave deeds; then of course I searched for the arm that gave it motion and for the body to which the arm belonged. In the midst of the blows and cries I at length distinguished the man, and I saw—a hero, an Ajax Telamon. I became excited, palpitating, starting at every stroke which threatened him, at every blow he dealt. I had a quarter of an hour of an emotion, you see, my queen, such as I had never experienced or thought possible. So there I was, panting, exalted, dumb, when suddenly my hero disappeared."

"How?"

"Struck down by a stone an old woman threw at him. Then, like Cyrus, I found my voice, and screamed, 'Help! help!' My guards went out, lifted him up, and bore him to my chamber, which you now ask of me for your protégé."

"Alas! I can the better understand this history because it is so nearly my own."

"With this difference, my queen, that as I have served the king and the Catholic religion in succoring him, I have no reason to send M. Annibal de Coconnas away."

"His name is Annibal de Coconnas!" said Marguerite, laughing.

"A terrible name, is it not? Well, he who bears it is worthy of it. Put on your mask, for we are now at the hotel."

"Why put on my mask?"

"Because I wish to show you my hero."

"Is he handsome?"

"He seemed to me magnificent during the conflict. In the morning, I must confess, he did not look quite so well as at night by the light of the flames. But I do not think you will find great fault with him."

"Then my protégé is rejected at the Hôtel de Guise; I am sorry for it, for that is the last place where they would look for a Huguenot."

"Oh, no, your Huguenot shall come; he shall have one corner of the cabinet, and Annibal the other."

"But when they recognize each other, the one for a Protestant, the other for a Catholic, they will fight."

"Oh, there is no danger. M. de Coconnas has had a cut down

the face that prevents him from seeing very well; your Huguenot is wounded in the chest, which will perhaps repress his activity; and besides, you have only to tell him to be silent on the subject of religion, and all will go well."

"So be it."

"It's a bargain; and now let us go in."

"Thanks," said Marguerite, pressing her friend's hand.

"Here, Madame," said the duchess, "you are again 'your Majesty'; suffer me, then, to do the honors of the Hôtel de Guise fittingly for the Queen of Navarre."

And the duchess, descending from the litter, almost bent her knee as she aided Marguerite to alight; then, pointing to the gate guarded by two soldiers, arquebus in hand, she followed the queen respectfully into the hotel. Arrived at her chamber, the duchess closed the door, and calling to her waiting-woman, a thorough Sicilian, said to her in Italian, "How is Monsieur the Count?"

"Better and better," replied she.

"What is he doing?"

"At this moment he is taking some refreshment, Madame."

"It is always a good sign," said Marguerite, "when the appetite returns."

"Ah, I forgot you were a pupil of Ambroise Paré. Leave us, Mica."

"Why do you send her away?"

"That she may be on the watch."

Mica went out.

"Now," said the duchess, "will you go in to see him, or shall I have him come here?"

"Neither the one nor the other. I wish to see him without his seeing me."

"What matters it? You have your mask."

"He may recognize me by my hands, my hair, my ring."

"Oh! how cautious we are, since we've been married!"

Marguerite smiled.

"Well," said the duchess, "I see only one way."

"What is that?"

"To look through the keyhole."

"Take me to the door, then."

The duchess led Marguerite to a door covered with tapestry; raising this, she knelt down and applied her eye to the keyhole.

" 'Tis as you could wish; he is sitting at table, with his face turned toward us."

The queen took her friend's place; Coconnas was, as the duchess had said, sitting at a table well provided, and despite his wounds, was doing ample justice to the good things before him.

"Ah, *mon Dieu!*" cried Marguerite, drawing back.

"What is the matter?" asked the duchess.

"Impossible! no! yes! 'tis he himself!"

"Who?"

"Hush," said Marguerite; " 'tis he who pursued my Huguenot into my apartment, and would have killed him in my arms! Oh, Henriette, how fortunate he did not see me."

"Well, then, you have seen him in battle; is he not handsome?"

"I do not know," said Marguerite, "for I was looking at him he pursued."

"What is his name?"

"You will not mention it before the count?"

"No."

"Lerac de la Mole."

"And now what do you think of him?"

"Of La Mole?"

"No, of M. de Coconnas."

"Upon my word!" said Marguerite, "I confess I think—" She stopped.

"Come, come," said the duchess, "I see you cannot forgive his wounding your Huguenot."

"Why, so far," said Marguerite, smiling, "my Huguenot owes him nothing; the cut he gave him on his face—"

"They are quits, then; and we can reconcile them. Send me your wounded man."

"Not now; by and by."

"When?"

"When you have found yours a fresh chamber."

"Which?"

Marguerite looked meaningly at her friend, who after a moment's silence laughed.

"So be it," said the duchess; "alliance firmer than ever."

"Friendship ever sincere!"

"And the word, in case we need each other?"

"The triple name of your triple god—Eros-Cupido-Amor."

And the two women separated after one more embrace, and pressing each other's hand for the twentieth time.

How There Are Keys That Open Doors They Are Not Meant For

The Queen of Navarre, on her return to the Louvre, found Gillonne in great excitement. Madame de Sauve had come in her absence. She had brought a key sent her by the queen-mother. It was the key of the chamber in which Henri was confined. It was evident that the queen-mother wished the Béarnais to pass the night in Madame de Sauve's apartment. Marguerite took the key, and turned it and turned it; she made Gillonne repeat Madame de Sauve's every word, weighed them, letter by letter, and at length thought she detected Catherine's plan. She took pen and ink and wrote—

> Instead of going to Madame de Sauve tonight, come to the Queen of Navarre.
>
> Marguerite

She rolled up the paper, put it in the pipe of the key, and ordered Gillonne, as soon as it was dark, to slip the key under the king's door. This done, she thought of the wounded man, closed all the doors, entered the cabinet, and to her great surprise found La Mole dressed in all his clothes, torn and bloodstained as they were. On seeing her he strove to rise, but could not stand, and fell back upon the sofa which had served for his bed.

"What is the matter, Monsieur?" asked Marguerite; "and why do you thus disobey the orders of your physician? I recommended you repose, and instead of following my advice, you do just the contrary."

"Oh, Madame," said Gillonne, "it is not my fault; I have entreated Monsieur the Count not to commit this folly, but he declares that nothing shall keep him any longer at the Louvre."

"Leave the Louvre!" said Marguerite, astonished. "Why, it is impossible! you can scarcely stand; you are pale and weak; your knees tremble. Only a few hours ago the wound in your shoulder still bled."

"Madame," said the young man, "as earnestly as I thanked your Majesty for having saved my life, as earnestly do I pray you to suffer me to depart."

"I scarcely know what to call such a resolution," said Marguerite, in astonishment; "it is worse than ingratitude."

"Oh," cried La Mole, clasping his hands, "think me not ungrateful; my gratitude will cease only with my life."

"It will not last long, then," said Marguerite, moved at these words, the sincerity of which it was impossible to doubt; "for your wounds will open, and you will die from loss of blood, or you will be recognized for a Huguenot, and killed ere you advance fifty yards in the street."

"I must nevertheless quit the Louvre," murmured La Mole.

"Must!" returned Marguerite, fixing her full, speaking gaze upon him, then turning slightly pale; "ah, yes! forgive me, I understand. Doubtless, there is one who anxiously awaits you. That is natural, M. de la Mole, and I understand it. Why did you not speak of it at once, or rather, why have I not myself thought of it? It is a duty of hospitality to protect the affections as well as to cure wounds, and to take care of the soul at the same time with the body."

"Alas, Madame!" said La Mole, "you are strangely mistaken; I am well-nigh alone in the world, and altogether so in Paris, where no one knows me. My pursuer is the first man I have spoken to in this city; your Majesty the first woman who has addressed me."

"Then why would you go?"

"Because," replied La Mole, "last night you had no rest, and tonight—"

Marguerite blushed. "Gillonne," said she, "it is time to take that key to the King of Navarre."

Gillonne smiled and left the room.

"But," continued Marguerite, "if you are alone, without friends, what will you do?"

"Madame, I soon shall have friends, for while I was pursued I thought of my mother, who was a Catholic. I thought I saw her form glide before me, a cross in her hand, on the way to the Louvre;

and I made a vow that if God would spare my life I would embrace my mother's religion. God has done more than save my life; he has sent me one of his angels to make life dear to me."

"But you cannot walk; you will faint before you have gone a hundred steps."

"Madame, I have tried to walk in the cabinet; I walk slowly and with pain, it is true, but let me go only to the Place du Louvre. Once outside, let come what will."

Marguerite leaned her head on her hand, and reflected for an instant. "And the King of Navarre," said she, with significance, "you do not speak of him. In changing your religion, have you also changed your desire to enter his service?"

"Madame," returned La Mole, turning pale, "you approach the true cause of my wish to depart. I know that the King of Navarre is in great danger, and that all the influence of your Majesty as daughter of France will hardly suffice to save his head."

"What!" said Marguerite, "how know you that?"

"Madame," returned La Mole, after some hesitation, "one can hear everything in this cabinet."

" 'Tis true," said Marguerite to herself; "M. de Guise told me so before.

"Well," added she aloud, "what have you heard?"

"In the first place, the conversation between your Majesty and your brother."

"With François?" said Marguerite.

"With the Duc d'Alençon, yes, Madame; and after your departure that of Gillonne and Madame de Sauve."

"And it is these two conversations?"

"Yes, Madame; married scarcely a week, you love your husband. Tonight he will come in his turn in the same way that the Duc d'Alençon and Madame de Sauve have come; he will discourse with you of his affairs. I do not wish to hear; I might be indiscreet, and I cannot—I ought not—especially, I will not be so."

By the tone in which La Mole uttered these last words, by the hesitation in his voice and the embarrassment of his manner, Marguerite was suddenly enlightened, as by a revelation.

"Ah!" said she, "you have heard everything that has been said in this chamber?"

"Yes, Madame." These words were uttered in a sigh.

"And you wish to depart tonight to avoid hearing any more?"

"This moment, if it please your Majesty."

"Poor fellow!" said Marguerite, with an accent of tender pity.

Astonished at so gentle an apostrophe, when he expected an abrupt reply, La Mole lifted his head timidly; his eyes encountered those of the queen, and remained fixed as by a magnetic power under the clear and searching look of the queen.

"You are, then, incapable of keeping a secret, M. de la Mole?" said the queen, who, seated in a large chair, could watch La Mole's face while her own remained in the shadow.

"Madame," said La Mole, "I am of an envious disposition. I distrust myself; the happiness of another gives me pain."

"The happiness of whom? Ah, yes! of the King of Navarre! Poor Henri!"

"You see," cried La Mole, passionately, "he is happy."

"Happy?"

"Yes, for your Majesty pities him."

Marguerite played with the golden tassels of her alms-purse.

"You will not, then, see the King of Navarre; you are quite resolved?"

"I fear I should be troublesome to his Majesty at present."

"But," said Marguerite, "the Duc d'Alençon, my brother?"

"Oh, no!" cried La Mole, "the Duc d'Alençon even less than the King of Navarre."

"Why so?" asked Marguerite.

"Because, although I am already too bad a Huguenot to be a faithful servant of the King of Navarre, I am not a sufficiently good Catholic to be friendly with the Duc d'Alençon and M. de Guise."

Marguerite cast down her eyes; what La Mole had said struck to her very heart.

At this instant Gillonne returned; Marguerite, with a look, interrogated her, and Gillonne, in the same manner, answered in the affirmative; the King of Navarre had received the key. Marguerite turned her eyes toward La Mole, who stood, his head drooping on his breast, sad, pale, grief-laden, as one suffering alike in mind and in body. "M. de la Mole is so proud," said she, "that I hesitate to make him an offer I fear he will repel."

La Mole rose and advanced a step toward Marguerite; but a

feeling of faintness came over him, and he caught at a table to save himself from falling.

"You see, Monsieur," cried Marguerite, hastening to him and supporting him in her arms, "that I am still necessary to you."

"Oh, yes!" murmured La Mole, "as the air I breathe, as the light of heaven."

At this moment three knocks were heard at the outer door.

"Do you hear, Madame?" cried Gillonne, alarmed.

"Already!" murmured Marguerite.

"Shall I open?"

"Wait! it is the King of Navarre perhaps."

"Oh, Madame!" cried La Mole, recalled to himself by these words, which the queen hoped had been heard by Gillonne alone, "I implore, I entreat you, let me depart—yes, dead or alive, Madame! Oh, you do not answer me! Well, I will tell you all, and then you will drive me away, I hope."

"Be silent," said Marguerite, who found an indescribable charm in the reproaches of the young man—"be silent!"

"Madame," replied La Mole, who did not find that anger he expected in the voice of the queen—"Madame, I tell you again, one can hear everything from this cabinet. Oh, do not make me perish by tortures more cruel than the executioner could inflict—"

"Silence! silence!" said Marguerite.

"Oh, you are merciless! you will not understand me. Know, then, that I love you—"

"Silence, I tell you!" said Marguerite, placing on his mouth her white and perfumed hand, which he seized, and pressed eagerly to his lips.

"But—" murmured he.

"Be silent, child! Who is this rebel that refuses to obey his queen?"

Then, hastily leaving the cabinet, she leaned against the wall, seeking to repress with trembling hand the beatings of her heart. "Open, Gillonne," said she.

Gillonne left the apartment, and an instant after the fine, intellectual, and somewhat anxious countenance of the King of Navarre appeared.

"You have sent for me, Madame?"

"Yes, Monsieur. Your Majesty received my letter?"

"And not without some surprise, I confess," said Henri, look-ing around with distrust, which, however, almost instantly vanished from his mind.

"And not without some uneasiness?" added Marguerite.

"I confess it! But still, surrounded as I am by deadly enemies, by friends still more dangerous perhaps than my open foes, I recol-lected that one evening I had seen a noble generosity radiant in your eyes—'twas the night of our marriage; that one other evening I had seen the star of courage shining there,—'twas yesterday, the day fixed for my death."

"Well, Monsieur?" said Marguerite, smiling, while Henri seemed striving to read her heart.

"Well, Madame," returned the king, "thinking of these things, I said to myself when I read your letter, 'Without friends, for he is a disarmed prisoner, the King of Navarre has but one means of dying nobly, of dying a death that will be recorded in history—it is to die betrayed by his wife'; and I have come."

"Sire," replied Marguerite, "you will change your tone when you learn that all this is the work of a woman who loves you, and whom you love."

Henri started back at these words, and his piercing gray eyes were fixed on the queen with earnest curiosity.

"Oh, reassure yourself, Sire," said the queen, smiling; "I have not the presumption to say that I am that person."

"But, Madame," said Henri, "it is you who sent me this key, and this is your writing."

"It is my writing, I confess; but the key is a different matter. Let it suffice you to know that it has passed through the hands of four women before it reached you."

"Of four women?"

"Yes," said Marguerite; "those of Queen Catherine, Madame de Sauve, Gillonne, and myself."

Henri pondered over this enigma.

"Let us speak plainly," said Marguerite. "Report says that your Majesty has consented to abjure. Is that true?"

"Report is somewhat premature; I have not yet consented."

"But your mind is made up?"

"That is to say, I am deliberating. At twenty, and almost a king, *ventre-saint-gris!* there are many things that are well worth a Mass."

"Life, for instance?"

Henri smiled.

"You do not tell me all your thought, Sire," said Marguerite.

"I have reservations for my allies, Madame; and you know we are but allies as yet. If, indeed, you were both my ally and—"

"And your wife, Monsieur?"

"Faith, yes! and my wife—"

"What then?"

"Why, then it might be different, and I perhaps might resolve to remain King of the Huguenots, as they call me. But, as it is, I must be content to live."

Marguerite looked at Henri in so peculiar a manner that it would have awakened suspicion in a less acute mind than his. "And are you quite sure of retaining even that?" she asked.

"Why, almost; but you know in this world nothing is certain."

"Truly, your Majesty shows such moderation, such disinterestedness, that after having renounced your crown, your religion, you may be expected to satisfy the hopes of some people, and renounce your alliance with a daughter of France!"

These words carried so deep a significance that Henri shuddered in spite of himself. But quickly subduing that emotion, he said, "Recollect, Madame, that at this moment I am not my own master; I shall therefore do what the King of France orders me. As to myself, were I consulted the least in the world on this question, affecting as it does my throne, my honor, and my life, rather than build my future hopes on this forced marriage of ours, I would enter a cloister or turn gamekeeper."

This calm resignation, this renunciation of the world alarmed Marguerite. She thought perhaps this rupture of the marriage had been arranged between Charles IX, Catherine, and the King of Navarre. Why should they not treat her as a dupe, or as a victim? Because she was sister to the one, and daughter to the other? Experience showed her that there was nothing in that on which to establish her safety. Ambition, then, gnawed at the heart of the young woman, or rather, of the young queen—too far above vulgar weaknesses to be led by a petty vanity. When a woman loves, her love exempts her from those small miseries; for true love is itself an ambition.

"Your Majesty," said Marguerite, with a sort of disdainful

raillery, "has no confidence, it appears, in the star that shines over every king's head!"

"Ah," said Henri, "I cannot see mine; it is hidden by the storm that now threatens me!"

"And suppose the breath of a woman were to dispel this threatened tempest, and make the star reappear, brilliant as ever?"

" 'Twere difficult."

"Do you deny the existence of this woman, Monsieur?"

"No, I deny only her power."

"You mean her will."

"I said her power, and I repeat the word. A woman is only powerful when love and interest are combined within her in equal degrees; if either sentiment predominates, she is, like Achilles, vulnerable. Now, in regard to the woman in question, if I mistake not, I cannot rely on her love."

Marguerite made no reply.

"Listen," said Henri. "At the last stroke of the bell of St. Germain l'Auxerrois, you most likely thought of regaining your liberty sacrificed to the interests of your party. For myself, I thought of saving my life; that was the essential point. We lose Navarre, indeed; but what is that compared with your being enabled to speak aloud in your chamber, which you dared not do when you had someone listening to you in yonder cabinet?"

Marguerite could not refrain from smiling. The king rose and prepared to seek his own apartments; for it was eleven, and everybody at the Louvre was, or seemed to be, asleep.

Henri advanced toward the door, then, as if suddenly recollecting the motive of his visit, "By the way, Madame," said he, "had you not something to communicate to me, or did you desire to give me an opportunity of thanking you for the respite which your courageous presence in the king's armory yesterday secured to me? In truth, Madame, it was time, I cannot deny it; and you came upon the scene like a goddess of antiquity, just in time to save my life."

"What!" exclaimed Marguerite, seizing her husband's arm; "do you not see that nothing is saved, neither your liberty, your crown, nor your life? Blind fool! poor fool! Did you, then, see nothing in my letter but an amorous rendezvous?"

"I confess, Madame," said Henri, astonished—"I confess—"

Marguerite shrugged her shoulders with an expression impossible to describe. At this instant a strange sound was heard, like a sharp scratching, at the secret door. Marguerite led the king thither. "Listen," said she.

"The queen-mother is leaving her apartments," said a trembling voice outside, which Henri instantly recognized as that of Madame de Sauve.

"Where is she going?" asked Marguerite.

"She is coming to your Majesty."

And then the rustling of silk showed that Madame de Sauve was hastening rapidly away.

"Oh, oh!" said Henri.

"I was sure of this," said Marguerite.

"And I," replied Henri, "feared it, as this will prove." And half opening his doublet of black velvet, he showed the queen that he had beneath it a shirt of mail and a long Milan poniard, which instantly glittered in his hand.

"As if there could be any occasion here for steel and cuirass!" cried Marguerite. "Come, Monsieur, come, hide that dagger. It is the queen-mother, indeed, but the queen-mother only."

"Yet—"

"Silence! I hear her."

And she whispered in Henri's ear a few words which the young king heard with attention and surprise. Then he concealed himself behind the curtains of the bed.

Marguerite sprang into the cabinet, where La Mole awaited her, and pressing his hand in the darkness, "Silence," said she, approaching her lips so near that he felt her breath; "silence!"

Then, returning to her chamber, she tore off her headdress, cut the lacing of her dress with her poniard, and sprang into bed. It was time; the key turned in the lock. Catherine had a key for every door in the Louvre.

"Who is there?" cried Marguerite, as Catherine placed on guard at the door the four gentlemen by whom she was attended.

And as if frightened by this intrusion into her chamber, Marguerite sprang out of bed in a white dressing gown, and then, seeming to recognize Catherine, came to kiss her hand with so well-feigned a surprise that the wily Florentine herself was deceived.

CHAPTER 14

Catherine and Marguerite

The queen-mother surveyed the chamber with eager and curious eyes; but the sight of Marguerite's velvet slippers at the foot of the bed, her vestments thrown negligently upon the chairs, and her well-feigned drowsiness, convinced Catherine that she had really roused her daughter from her slumbers. Smiling, therefore, the self-complacent smile of one whose plan of attack has been successful, she drew a chair toward her, saying, "Let us sit down, my child, and have a little talk together."

"I am all attention, Madame."

"It is time," said Catherine, shutting her eyes and speaking with that slowness peculiar to persons of great reflection or great dissimulation—"it is time, my daughter, that you should know how ardently your brother and myself desire to see you happy."

This was a somewhat alarming preface for one who was acquainted with Catherine's real disposition.

"What can she be about to say?" thought Marguerite.

"Certainly," continued the Florentine, "in marrying you, we fulfilled one of those acts of policy frequently peremptorily demanded for the interest of the kingdom and those who govern it; but I must honestly confess to you, my poor child, that we had no expectation that the repugnance manifested by the King of Navarre for one so young, so lovely, and so fascinating as yourself would have been so persistent."

Marguerite arose, and folding her *robe de chambre* around her, made a ceremonious bow to her mother.

"I have heard tonight only (otherwise I should have paid you an earlier visit) that your husband is far from showing you those attentions you have a right to claim, not merely as a beautiful woman, but as a daughter of France."

Marguerite gently sighed, and Catherine, encouraged by this mute approval, proceeded:

"I am even assured that the King of Navarre has a liaison with one of my maids of honor, and that he openly avows his disgraceful passion for her. Now, that he should despise the affection of the superior being we have bestowed upon him is unfortunately one of those evils which, powerful as we are, we have no means of remedying, although the meanest gentleman of our kingdom would quickly demand satisfaction for so great an insult."

Marguerite lowered her head. Her mother continued. "For some time past, my daughter, I have been well assured by your red and swollen eyes, as well as the bitterness of your sallies against Madame de Sauve, that, try as you may, your poor wounded heart is not content to bleed and break in silent sorrow."

Marguerite started; a slight movement had agitated the curtains of the bed, but fortunately it passed unperceived by Catherine.

"That wound," she said with increasing affection and tenderness, "it belongs to a mother to heal. Those who, expecting to secure your happiness, appointed your marriage, and who in their solicitude for you have noticed that every night Henri de Navarre goes to the wrong apartment; those who cannot permit that a knight like him should insult every moment a woman of your beauty, of your rank, and of your merit, by contempt of your person and disregard for posterity; those who, in short, see that at the first wind which he thinks favorable that foolish and insolent fellow will turn against our family and drive you from his house—have not those persons the right, by separating your interests from his, to assure your future in a manner more worthy of you and of your rank?"

"Nevertheless, Madame," replied Marguerite, "notwithstanding those observations, all impressed with maternal love, and which lift me to summits of delight and honor, I must have the boldness to remind your Majesty that the King of Navarre is my husband."

Catherine started with rage; then, drawing closer to Marguerite, she said, "He your husband? Do the few words pronounced over you by a priest warrant your styling him your husband? Were you Madame de Sauve, indeed, you might make that assertion. But, wholly contrary to our expectations, since you permitted to Henri de Navarre the honor of calling you his wife, it is to another that he has given himself; and at this very moment," said

Catherine, raising her voice, "come, come with me. This key opens the door of Madame de Sauve's apartments; accompany me thither, and you will see."

"Oh, not so loud, Madame! not so loud, I beseech you!" said Marguerite; "for not only are you mistaken, but—"

"But what?"

"I fear you will awaken my husband!"

As she said these words, Marguerite gracefully arose, her white dress fluttering loosely around her, while the large open sleeves displayed her matchless hand and arm; carrying one of the rose-colored tapers toward the bed, she gently drew back the curtain, and smiling at her mother, pointed to the King of Navarre, who, stretched in easy negligence upon the couch, seemed buried in profound repose.

Pale and wonder-stricken, her body thrown back as though to avoid some abyss that had opened at her feet, Catherine uttered not a cry, but a half-suppressed groan.

"You perceive, Madame," said Marguerite, "you were misinformed."

Catherine alternately gazed from her daughter to the sleeping king, and again scrutinized the features of Marguerite; but the countenance of the latter bore unshrinkingly the searching glances of the queen-mother, who bit her thin lips in silent rage.

Marguerite allowed her mother to contemplate for a moment that scene which had on her the effect of Medusa's head. Then she let fall the curtain, and walking on tiptoe back to her chair, resumed her place beside Catherine, saying, "You would advise, then, Madame?"

The Florentine again fixed her piercing looks on Marguerite, as though she would read her very thoughts; but baffled and disconcerted by the calm placidity of her daughter's face, "Nothing," she said, and hastened precipitately from the chamber.

No sooner had the sound of her departing footsteps died away in the vast corridor than the bed-curtains opened a second time, and Henri, with sparkling eye, trembling hand, and panting breath, went and kneeled at Marguerite's feet. He was dressed in only his nether garments and his coat of mail; so that on seeing him in that garb, Marguerite, pressing his hand heartily, could not suppress a burst of laughter.

"Ah, Madame! ah, Marguerite!" exclaimed the king, "how

shall I ever repay your goodness?" And he covered her hand with kisses, which gradually ascended from her hand to her arm.

"Sire," replied Marguerite, gently drawing back, "do you forget that a poor woman to whom you owe your life is at this moment in dire uneasiness on your account? Madame de Sauve," added she, in a lower tone, "has forgotten her jealousy in sending you to me; and to that sacrifice she may probably have to add her life, for no one knows better than yourself how terrible is the anger of my mother."

Henri shuddered, and rising, was about to leave the room.

"Upon second thoughts," said Marguerite, "I see no cause for alarm. The key was given to you without any directions, and you will be considered as having given me the preference tonight."

"And so I do, Marguerite! Consent but to forget—"

"Not so loud! not so loud, Sire!" replied the queen, employing the same words she had a few minutes before used to her mother; "anyone in the adjoining cabinet can hear you. I must beg of you to use a lower tone."

"Oh!" said Henri, half-smiling, half-gloomy, "that's true! I forgot that I am probably not the person with whom the interesting events of today are to close! This cabinet—"

"Let me beg of your Majesty to enter there," said Marguerite; "for I wish to have the honor of presenting to you a brave gentleman, wounded during the massacre, while endeavoring to make his way to the Louvre, for the purpose of apprising your Majesty of the danger that threatened you."

The queen advanced toward the door, followed by Henri. She opened it, and the king was thunderstruck at beholding a man in this cabinet predestined to surprises. But La Mole was even more surprised on thus unexpectedly finding himself in the presence of Henri de Navarre. The king cast an ironical glance on Marguerite, who bore it without flinching.

"Sire," said she, "I am in dread that this gentleman may be murdered even here, in the sanctuary of my apartments; he is devoted to the service of your Majesty, and I commend him to your royal protection."

"Sire," continued the young man, "I am the Comte Lerac de la Mole; the same your Majesty expected, recommended to you by M. de Téligny, who was killed by my side."

"Ah, ah!" said Henri, "I remember; the queen gave me his letter. But have you not also a letter from the Governor of Languedoc?"

"Yes, Sire, with orders to give it to your Majesty immediately on my arrival."

"And wherefore did you delay?"

"Sire, I was at the Louvre yesterday evening for that purpose; but your Majesty was too much occupied to give me audience."

"True!" answered the king; "but in that case why not send the letter to me?"

"Because M. d'Auriac had strictly charged me to give it into no other hands than those of your Majesty, since it contained, he said, information so important that he feared to entrust it to any ordinary messenger."

"The contents are indeed of a serious nature," said the king, when he had received and perused the letter, "advising my instant withdrawal from the court of France, and retirement to Béarn. M. d'Auriac, although a Catholic, was always a staunch friend of mine; and it is possible that, acting as governor of a province, he got scent of what was in the wind here. *Ventre-saint-gris,* Monsieur! why was not this letter given to me three days ago, instead of now?"

"Because, as I before assured your Majesty, using all the speed and diligence in my power, it was wholly impossible to arrive before yesterday."

"That is very unfortunate," murmured the king; "for had you done so, we should at this time have been in security, either at Rochelle, or in some broad plain surrounded by two or three thousand trusty horsemen."

"Sire," said Marguerite, in an undertone, "what is done is done, and instead of losing your time in useless recrimination, it is expedient for you to make the best arrangements you can for the future."

"Then," replied Henri, with his glance of interrogation, "I am to suppose that in my place you would not despair?"

"Certainly not; I should consider myself as playing a game of three points, of which I had lost only the first."

"Ah, Madame," whispered Henri, "if I could hope that you would go halves with me in the game."

"Had I intended to side with your adversaries," replied Marguerite, "I should scarcely have delayed till now."

"True!" replied Henri, "I am ungrateful; and, as you say, the past may still be repaired. But, Madame," continued he, attentively observing La Mole, "this gentleman cannot remain here without causing you considerable inconvenience, and being himself subject to very unpleasant surprises. What will you do with him?"

"But, Sire, could we not get him out of the Louvre? for I am precisely of your opinion."

"It is difficult."

"Then, could not your Majesty find accommodation for M. de la Mole in your own apartments?"

"Alas, Madame! you speak as though I were still king of the Huguenots, and had subjects to command. You are aware that I am half converted and have no subjects at all."

Anyone but Marguerite would have promptly answered, "And he also is a Catholic." But the queen wished Henri himself to ask her to do the very thing she was desirous of effecting; while La Mole, perceiving the reserve of his protectress, and not yet knowing where to place his foot on the slippery ground of a court so dangerous as was that of France, remained silent.

"But what is this the governor says in his letter?" said Henri, again casting his eyes over the missive he held in his hand. "He states that your mother was a Catholic, and from that circumstance originates the interest he has in you."

"And what were you telling me, Monsieur the Count," said Marguerite, "respecting a vow you had formed to change your religion? I confess my recollection on the subject is somewhat confused. Have the goodness to assist me, M. de la Mole. Did not your conversation refer to something of the nature his Majesty appears to desire?"

"Alas, yes! but what I said about that was so coldly received by your Majesty, that I have not dared—"

"Simply because it in no way concerned me," answered Marguerite. "But explain yourself to the king."

"What is the vow you refer to?" asked the king. "Let me hear."

"Sire," said La Mole, "when pursued by assassins, myself unarmed, and almost expiring with pain and agony from my wounds, I fancied I beheld the spirit of my mother, holding a cross in her hands, and guiding me toward the Louvre. Then I vowed that if my life were preserved I would adopt the religion of my mother, who had been permitted to leave her grave to serve me as a guide in that horrible night. God has conducted me hither, Sire. I find myself here under the double protection of a daughter of France and the King of Navarre. My life has been saved by a miracle; I have, then, only to fulfill my vow, Sire. I am ready to become a Catholic."

Henri frowned. Skeptic as he was, he could well understand a change of religion from motives of interest, but as a matter of faith and conscience, it was wholly beyond his comprehension.

"It is all over!" thought Marguerite; "the king evidently will have nothing to do with my protégé."

La Mole continued timid and embarrassed between the two opposing wills. He perceived, too, the ridiculous aspect of his position. Marguerite's tact and woman's wit came again happily to his relief. "Sire," said she, "we both forget that the poor wounded gentleman has need of repose. For myself, I am half-asleep. See! he is growing pale, as though he would faint."

La Mole did indeed turn pale; but it was at Marguerite's last words, which he had interpreted according to his own ideas.

"Well, Madame," answered Henri, "nothing can be easier than for you and me to retire, and leave M. de la Mole to take the repose he so much needs."

The young man fixed a supplicating look on Marguerite, and, spite of the august presence in which he stood, sank upon a chair, overcome with fatigue and pain. Marguerite fully comprehended all the love in that look and all the despair in that weakness.

"Sire," said she, "your Majesty is bound to confer on this young man, who periled his life for his king—since it was while coming hither to acquaint you with the death of the admiral and Téligny that he received his wounds—is bound, I repeat, to confer on him an honor, for which he will be ever grateful."

"What is it, Madame?" asked Henri. "Command me; I am ready."

" 'Tis to permit M. de la Mole to repose tonight at the feet of your Majesty, who will sleep on this couch. With the permission of my august spouse," added Marguerite, smiling, "I will summon

Gillonne, and return to bed; for I can assure you I am not the least wearied of us three."

Henri had shrewd sense and a quick perception; friends and enemies subsequently found fault with him for possessing too much of both. He fully admitted that she who thus banished him from the nuptial bed was well justified in so doing by the indifference he had himself manifested toward her; and then, too, she had just repaid this indifference by saving his life. He therefore did not allow his wounded self-love to dictate his answer, but replied, "If, Madame, M. de la Mole were capable of coming to my apartments, I would give him up my own bed."

"Yes," said Marguerite, "but your apartments would be safe for neither of you at this hour, and prudence directs that your Majesty should remain here until the morning."

Then, without awaiting any further reply from the king, she summoned Gillonne, and bade her prepare the necessary cushions for the king, and to arrange a bed at the king's feet for M. de la Mole, who appeared so happy and contented with the honor done him as almost to forget his wounds.

Then Marguerite, with a ceremonious bow to the king, passed into the adjoining chamber, the doors of which were well furnished with bolts, and threw herself on the bed.

"One thing is certain," said Marguerite, mentally, "that tomorrow M. de la Mole must have a protector at the Louvre; and he who tonight will see and hear nothing may change his mind tomorrow."

Then, calling Gillonne, she said in a whisper, "Gillonne, you must contrive to bring my brother D'Alençon here tomorrow morning before eight o'clock."

The loud peal of the Louvre clock chimed the second hour after midnight. La Mole, after a short parley with the king on political subjects, was left to his own reflections; for Henri fell asleep in the midst of one of his own speeches, and snored as lustily as though he had been reposing on his own leathern couch in Béarn. La Mole would perhaps have slept like the king, but Marguerite did not sleep; she turned and turned again upon her bed, and that sound disturbed the ideas and the sleep of the young man.

"He is very young and timid," murmured the wakeful queen; "but his eyes are rich with manly expression, and his form is one of nobleness and beauty. But if he should not prove to be brave! He fled; he abjures. It is a pity; the dream began well—But come, let us stop thinking and commend ourselves to the triple god of that mad Henriette." And toward morning Marguerite fell asleep, murmuring, "Eros-Cupido-Amor."

CHAPTER 15

What Woman Wills, God Wills

Marguerite was right. The rage accumulated in Catherine's heart by that comedy whose plot she could perceive, without being able to change its conclusion, must be discharged upon someone. Instead, therefore, of retiring to her own apartments, the queen-mother proceeded to those of her lady-in-waiting.

Madame de Sauve was expecting two visits—she hoped for one from Henri; she dreaded one from the queen-mother. Reclining on her bed only partially undressed, while Dariole kept watch in the antechamber, she heard a key turn in the lock. Then slow steps approached, which would have been loud had not their sound been deadened by the thick carpet. They were not the light and eager steps of Henri. She surmised that Dariole had been prevented from coming to warn her; leaning on her hand, her eyes open, and ears alert, she waited.

The curtain which covered the doorway was raised, and Catherine de Médicis appeared. She seemed calm; but Madame de Sauve, accustomed for two years to the study of her crafty and deceitful nature, well knew what sinister thoughts and vengeful purposes might be concealed beneath that apparent tranquillity.

At sight of Catherine, Madame de Sauve was about to spring from her bed, but Catherine signed to her to remain where she was; and poor Charlotte remained fixed in her place, mustering all her resources to face the silently gathering storm.

"Did you convey the key to the King of Navarre?" inquired Catherine, in her usual tone of voice; but the lips with which these words were uttered became whiter every moment.

"I did, Madame," answered Charlotte, in a voice that vainly sought to imitate the firm, assured manner of Catherine.

"And have you seen him?"

"Whom?" asked Madame de Sauve.

"The King of Navarre."

"No, Madame; but I expect him. And when I heard the sound of a key in the lock, I thought he was coming."

This reply, which indicated either a blind confidence or profound dissimulation on the part of Madame de Sauve, enraged Catherine beyond all power of concealment; she literally shook with passion, and clenching her small plump hand, she said with her malignant smile, "And yet you knew well, Carlotta, that the King of Navarre would not come tonight."

"I, Madame, I knew that?" cried Charlotte, with a well-assumed accent of surprise.

"Yes, you knew it."

"If he does not come he must be dead!" replied the young woman, shuddering at the idea. What gave her courage for such dissimulation was her fear of some terrible vengeance in case her treason should be discovered.

"But did you not write to the king, my Carlotta?" inquired Catherine, with the same cruel and unnatural smile.

"No, Madame," answered Charlotte, with admirable naïveté, "I cannot recollect receiving your Majesty's commands to do so."

A short silence followed, during which Catherine continued to gaze on Madame de Sauve as the serpent gazes on the bird it wishes to fascinate.

"You think yourself a beauty and a skillful maneuverer, do you not?" asked Catherine.

"No, indeed, Madame," answered Charlotte; "I only remember that there have been times when your Majesty has been graciously pleased to commend both my personal attractions and my address."

"Well, then," said Catherine, growing eager and animated, "you deceived yourself if you believed that, and I lied if I said it; you are but a hideous dolt when compared to my daughter Margot."

"Oh, Madame," replied Charlotte, "that is a fact I seek not to deny—least of all in your presence."

"It follows, then, that the King of Navarre prefers my daughter to you—a circumstance, I presume, not to your wishes, and certainly not what we agreed upon."

"Alas, Madame!" cried Charlotte, bursting into a torrent of tears, which now flowed from no feigned source, "if it be so, I can but say I am very unfortunate!"

"It is the fact," said Catherine, stabbing the heart of Madame de Sauve with the rays from her eyes, as with a double-bladed dagger.

"But what reason has your Majesty for coming to this conclusion?"

"Proceed to the apartments of the Queen of Navarre, you incredulous simpleton! and you will find your lover there."

"Oh!" said Madame de Sauve.

Catherine shrugged her shoulders. "Are you jealous, then?" she said.

"I jealous?" said Madame de Sauve, recalling her fast-failing strength and courage.

"Yes, you! I have a curiosity to see how a Frenchwoman demonstrates that passion."

"Nay," said Madame de Sauve, "why should your Majesty suppose I am wounded in any other feeling than my vanity, since all the interest I feel in the King of Navarre arises from my wish to be of service to your Majesty."

Catherine looked at her a moment with thoughtful eyes. "You may be speaking the truth," said she. "Am I, then, to consider you as wholly devoted to my service?"

"Command me, Madame, and you will see."

"Well, then, Carlotta, since you devote yourself to my service, you must (in my service, understand) affect the utmost affection for the King of Navarre, and, above all, a violent jealousy—an Italian jealousy."

"And in what manner, Madame, do the Italian women evince their jealousy?"

"I will instruct you," replied Catherine, who, after remaining some moments with bowed head, left the apartment slowly and noiselessly as she had entered it.

Thankful to be freed from the oppressive gaze of eyes that seemed to expand and dilate like those of the cat or panther, Charlotte permitted her to depart without attempting to utter a word; nor did she breathe freely till Dariole came to tell her that the terrible visitant had finally departed. She then bade the waiting-maid to bring an armchair beside her bed and to remain with her through the night, fearing, as she said, to be left alone. Dariole obeyed; but despite the company of her faithful attendant, despite the bright light from a lamp illumined by her orders, Madame de Sauve still heard the metallic tones of Catherine's voice, and did not close her eyes in sleep till the dawn of day.

Notwithstanding the late hour at which Marguerite's slumbers had begun, she awoke at the first sound of the hunting horns and dogs, and instantly rising, dressed herself in a costume so *négligé* as to indicate design. She then summoned her maids, and caused the ordinary attendants of the King of Navarre to be shown into an antechamber adjoining that in which he had passed the night. Then, opening the door of the chamber which contained both Henri and La Mole, she cast an affectionate glance on the latter, and said to her husband—

"It is not sufficient, Sire, to have persuaded my mother that matters are different from what they seem; you must also impress upon your whole court a belief in the good understanding existing between us. But make yourself quite easy," added she, laughing, "and remember my words, rendered the more impressive by the circumstances under which I utter them—today is the very last time your Majesty will be subjected to so severe a trial."

Henri smiled, and desired that the officers of his suite should be admitted; but at the very moment of returning their salutation, he feigned suddenly to recollect having left his mantle on the queen's bed, and begged their excuse for receiving them ere fully dressed. Then, taking his mantle from the hands of Marguerite, who stood blushing by his side, he clasped it on his shoulder. Next, turning to his gentlemen, he carelessly inquired what was stirring abroad.

Marguerite's quick eye readily caught the expression of astonishment impressed on every countenance on discovering the intimacy between herself and the King of Navarre; and ere they had recovered from it, an attendant entering announced the arrival of the Duc d'Alençon, with three or four officers of his suite. To induce him to come, Gillonne had needed only to inform him that the king had passed the night in the queen's apartments; and so hurried was the manner of François in entering that he narrowly escaped knocking against every person he met in his way. His first glance was directed to Henri; his next to Marguerite. The former replied to him by a courteous salutation, while the calm, composed features of Marguerite exhibited the utmost serenity and happiness. Again the sharp scrutiny of the duke traveled round the chamber, and he quickly observed the two pillows placed at the head of the bed, the derangement of its tapestried coverings, and the king's plumed hat carelessly thrown on a chair beside it. At this sight the color forsook his cheeks; but quickly recovering himself, he said, "Does my brother Henri join this morning with the king in his game of tennis?"

"Does his Majesty do me the honor to select me as his partner," inquired Henri, "or is it only a little attention on your own part, my brother-in-law?"

"His Majesty has not so said, certainly," replied the duke, somewhat embarrassed; "but as you play with him so habitually, I considered—"

Henri smiled, for so many and so serious events had occurred since he last played with the king that he would not have been astonished to learn that the king had changed his habitual companions at the game.

"I shall certainly join the king in his sport," said Henri, with a smile.

"Then come," cried the duke.

"Are you going away?" inquired Marguerite.

"Yes, my sister."

"Are you in great haste to be gone?"

"In very great haste!"

"Might I venture to ask you to grant me a few minutes ere you depart?"

Such a request from Marguerite was so rare that her brother looked at her, turning red and pale alternately.

"What can she intend saying to him?" thought Henri, taken as much by surprise as the duke himself.

Marguerite, as if she had divined her husband's thought, turned toward him. "Monsieur," she said with a charming smile, "you can, if you please, rejoin his Majesty; for the secret I am about to reveal to my brother is already known to you, since I preferred to you yesterday a request relating to that secret which was almost refused by

your Majesty. I would not therefore annoy your Majesty by expressing in your presence a wish that seems inconvenient to you."

"What is it all about?" asked François, looking at them with astonishment.

"Ah, ah!" said Henri, blushing with spite, "I know what you
wish to say, Madame. Indeed, I regret that I am not more at liberty.
But if I cannot offer to M. de la Mole a hospitality which would assure his safety, I can at least recommend, with you, to my brother
D'Alençon the person in whom you are interested. Perhaps even,"
he added, to give more force to his words, "my brother will devise
some plan which will enable you to keep M. de la Mole here—near
to you; which would be best of all, would it not, Madame?"

"Come, come," said Marguerite to herself, "between them
they will do what neither of them would do alone." And she
opened the door of the cabinet, and beckoned forth the wounded
man, saying to Henri, "It is for your Majesty to explain to my
brother the reason for our taking an interest in M. de la Mole."

Henri, caught in the snare, briefly related to M. d'Alençon—
half Protestant for the sake of opposition, as he himself was half
Catholic from prudence—the arrival of M. de la Mole at Paris, and
how the young man had been severely wounded while bringing to
him a letter from M. d'Auriac. As the duke turned round after listening to this recital, he perceived the hero of the tale standing before him. At the sight of his pale, handsome countenance, rendered
still more captivating by the marks of recent weakness and suffering,
a new feeling of anger and distrust shot through his heart.
Marguerite held him by his jealousy and by his vanity at once.

"Brother," said Marguerite, "I will engage for this young gentleman that he will render himself serviceable to whosoever may
employ him. Should you accept his services, he will obtain a powerful protector, and you a faithful, zealous servitor. In such times as the
present, Brother," continued she, "we cannot be too well surrounded by devoted friends; more especially," added she, lowering
her voice so as to be heard only by the duke, "when one is ambitious, and has the misfortune to be only third in the succession to
the throne." Then, placing her finger significantly on her lip, she in-
timated to D'Alençon that she had not revealed the whole of her
views and ideas on the subject, but had the most important part still

buried within her own breast. "Perhaps," she added, "you may differ from Henri in considering it not decorous or befitting that this young gentleman should remain so immediately in the vicinity of my apartments."

"Sister," replied François, eagerly, "M. de la Mole, if it be agreeable to him, shall in half an hour be installed in my apartments, where, I think, he can have no cause to fear. Let him love me, and I will love him."

François lied, for already he detested La Mole from the bottom of his heart.

"Excellent," murmured Marguerite to herself, as she saw the frown that hung over the brow of the King of Navarre. "Ah, I see plainly enough that to lead you both as I would have you go, it is necessary to make one lead the other." Then, completing her thought, " 'Good, Marguerite,' Henriette would say."

And in half an hour after this, La Mole, having been gravely lectured by Marguerite, kissed the hem of her robe, and ascended to D'Alençon's apartments with a step wondrously light and agile for one who had been so recently wounded.

Two or three days passed away, in which the harmony apparently existing between Henri and his wife appeared to become still further established. Henri had obtained permission not to make a public renunciation of his religion; but he had formally recanted in the presence of the king's confessor, and every day went openly to Mass. At night he took ostensibly the way to his wife's apartments, entered by the principal door, and after remaining some time in conversation with her, left by the secret door, and ascended to the chamber of Madame de Sauve, who had duly informed him of the visit of the queen-mother, as well as of the imminent danger which threatened him. Thus warned and protected on both sides, Henri redoubled his mistrust and his caution against Catherine, and with greater vigilance for the reason that Catherine had begun to smile upon him. One morning Henri saw on her pale lips an expression of goodwill, and all that day he could hardly persuade himself to eat anything but eggs of his own cooking, or to drink anything but water which he had himself seen drawn from the river.

Though the massacres still continued, their extent and violence were naturally lessened, and bade fair soon to end; for so great had been the butchery of the Huguenots that the supply began to fail, and additional victims were not easily found. The greater part of those unfortunate people were already sacrificed. Many had found safety in flight, and others were in concealment. Occasionally a great outcry would arise in some neighborhood, when one of them was discovered; and the execution was either public or private, according as the unhappy victim was penned up in a place without issue, or in a place admitting a possibility of flight. In the latter case there was great joy in the quarter where the incident took place; for instead of being quieted by the extinction of their enemies, the Catholics became more and more ferocious—the smaller the remnant the more savagely they pursued that remnant.

Charles IX had taken great pleasure in hunting down the Huguenots, and when he could no longer continue the chase himself, he took delight in the noise of others hunting. One day, returning from playing at mall, which with tennis and hunting were his favorite amusements, he went to his mother's apartments in high spirits, followed by his usual train of courtiers.

"Mother," he said, embracing the Florentine, who, observing his joy, endeavored to detect its cause—"Mother, good news! Death of all the devils! Do you know that the illustrious carcass of the admiral, which it was said was lost, has been found."

"Ah, ah!" said Catherine.

"Oh, *mon Dieu!* yes. You thought as I did, Mother—did you not?—that the dogs had eaten a wedding dinner off him; but it was not so. My people, my dear people, my good people, had a clever idea, and have hung the admiral up at the gibbet of Montfaucon.

"FROM HIGH TO LOW GASPARD
WAS THROWN,
AND NOW FROM LOW TO HIGH
HAS FLOWN."

"Well?" said Catherine.

"Well, my good mother," replied Charles IX, "I have a strong desire to see him again, dear old man, now that I know he is really dead! It is very fine weather, and the flowers seem to smell very sweet today. The air is full of life and perfume, and I feel better than

I ever did. If you like, Mother, we will get on horseback, and go to Montfaucon."

"Willingly, my son," said Catherine, "if I had not an appointment that I cannot defer; and besides, to pay a visit to a man of such importance as the admiral, we should assemble the whole court. It will be an occasion for observers to make very curious remarks. We shall see who comes and who stays away."

"Faith! you are right, Mother, and it will be better tomorrow; so send out your invitations, and I will send mine, or rather, do not let us invite anyone. We will only say that we are going, and then all will be free to do as they please. Adieu, Mother! I am going to play on the horn."

"You will exhaust yourself, Charles, as Ambroise Paré is always telling you; and he is right. It is too trying an exercise for you."

"Bah! bah! bah!" said Charles; "I wish I was sure nothing else would kill me; I would then bury everybody here, including Henriot, who will one day succeed us all, as Nostradamus prophesies."

Catherine frowned. "My son," she said, "mistrust more especially all things that appear impossible; and in the meanwhile take care of yourself."

"Only two or three blasts to rejoice my dogs, who are wearied to death with doing nothing, poor things! I ought to have let them loose on the Huguenots; that would have done them good!" And Charles IX left his mother's apartments, went into his armory, took down a horn, and sounded it with a vigor that would have done honor to Roland himself. It was difficult to understand how so weak a frame and such pale lips could blow a blast so powerful.

Catherine, in truth, was awaiting someone, as she had told her son. A minute after he had left her, one of her women came and spoke to her in a low voice. The queen smiled, rose, and saluting the persons who formed her court, followed the messenger.

René the Florentine, he whom on the eve of Saint Bartholomew the King of Navarre had accosted so diplomatically, entered the oratory.

"Ah! is it you, René?" said Catherine. "I have impatiently awaited you."

René bowed.

"Did you receive yesterday the little note I wrote to you?"

"I had that honor."

"Have you renewed, as I desired, the trial of the horoscope drawn by Ruggieri, and which agrees so well with the prophecy of Nostradamus, which says that all my three sons shall reign? Within the last few days affairs are so changed that I have thought it possible that destiny had become less threatening."

"Madame," replied René, bowing, "your Majesty is well aware that affairs can never change destiny; on the contrary, destiny governs affairs."

"You have at any rate repeated the sacrifice, have you not?"

"Yes, Madame," replied René; "for it is my duty to obey you in all things."

"Well; and the result?"

"Still the same, Madame."

"What, the black lamb has again uttered three cries?"

"Again, Madame."

"The sign of three cruel deaths in my family," murmured Catherine.

"Alas!" said René.

"What then?"

"Then, Madame, there was in its entrails that strange displacing of the liver, which we had already observed in the first two."

"A change of dynasty still—still—still!" muttered Catherine; "yet this must be resisted, René," she added.

René shook his head. "I have told your Majesty," he said, "that destiny rules all."

"Is that your opinion?" asked Catherine.

"Yes, Madame."

"Do you remember Jeanne d'Albret's horoscope?"

"Yes, Madame."

"Repeat it, I have quite forgotten it."

"*Vives honorata,*" said René; "*morieris reformidata; regina amplificabere.*"

"Which means, I believe," said Catherine, "*Thou shalt live honored*—and she lacked common necessaries; *Thou shalt die feared*—and we laughed at her; *Thou shalt be greater than thou hast been as a queen*—and she is dead, and sleeps in a tomb on which we have not even engraved her name."

"Madame, your Majesty does not translate the *vives honorata* rightly. The Queen of Navarre lived honored; for all her life she enjoyed the love of her children and the respect of her partisans—respect and love all the more sincere in that she was poor."

"Yes," said Catherine, "I pass over the *vives honorata:* but *morieris reformidata*—how will you explain that?"

"Nothing more easy: *Thou shalt die feared.*"

"Well, did she die feared?"

"So much so that she would not have died had not your Majesty feared her. Then, *As a queen thou shalt be greater;* or, *Thou shalt be greater than thou hast been as a queen.* This is equally true, Madame, for in exchange for a terrestrial crown, she has doubtless as a queen and martyr a celestial crown; and, besides, who knows what the future may reserve for her posterity?"

Catherine was superstitious to excess; she was more alarmed at René's cool pertinacity than at the persistence of the auguries and she said suddenly to him without any other transition than the working of her own thoughts, "Have any Italian perfumes arrived?"

"Yes, Madame."

"Send me a box full."

"Of which?"

"Of the last of those—" Catherine stopped.

"Of those the Queen of Navarre was so fond of?" asked René.

"Exactly."

"I need not prepare them, for your Majesty is now as skillful in that as I am."

"You think so?" said Catherine. "The point is that they succeed."

"Your Majesty has nothing more to say to me?" asked the perfumer.

"Nothing," said Catherine to him, thoughtfully; "only if there is any change in the sacrifices, let me know it. Let us leave the lambs, and try the hens."

"Alas, Madame! I fear that in changing the victim we shall not change the presages."

"Do as I tell you."

The perfumer bowed and left the apartment. Catherine mused for a short time, then rose, and returning to her bedchamber, where her women awaited her, announced the pilgrimage to Montfaucon for the morrow.

The news of this party of pleasure threw the palace and city into no small bustle. The ladies prepared their most elegant toilets, the gentlemen their finest arms and steeds; the tradesmen closed their shops, and the populace killed a few straggling Huguenots, in order to furnish company to the dead admiral. There was a great stir during all the evening and a good part of the night.

La Mole had passed a miserable day, and this miserable day had followed three or four others equally miserable. M. d'Alençon, to please his sister, had installed him in his apartments, but had not since seen him; he felt himself like a poor deserted child, deprived of the tender cares, the soothing attentions of two women, the recollections of one of whom occupied him perpetually. He had news of her through Ambroise Paré, whom she had sent to him; but that news, brought by a man fifty years old, who was ignorant—or feigned to be ignorant—of the interest taken by La Mole in the smallest details concerning Marguerite, was very incomplete and unsatisfying. Gillonne, indeed, had come once, as if of her own accord, to ask after him, and the visit was to him like a sunbeam darting into a dungeon; but although two days had elapsed, Gillonne had not repeated it.

As soon, then, as he heard of this splendid assemblage of the court on the morrow, La Mole requested of M. d'Alençon the favor of being allowed to accompany it. The duke did not even trouble himself to inquire whether La Mole was sufficiently recovered to bear the fatigue, but merely answered, "Very well, let him have one of my horses."

This was all La Mole wanted. Maître Ambroise Paré came to dress his wounds; and La Mole explained to him the necessity he was under of mounting on horseback, and prayed him to dress his wounds with more than usual care. The two wounds were closed, both that on the breast and that on the shoulder, and the latter alone pained him. They were both in a fair way of healing; Maître Ambroise Paré covered them with gummed taffetas—a remedy greatly in vogue then—and promised La Mole that if he did not exert himself too much, everything would go well.

La Mole was in an ecstasy of delight. Aside from a certain feebleness caused by loss of blood, and a slight giddiness owing to the same cause, he found himself in as good condition as he could expect to be. Besides, Marguerite would be in the cavalcade; he would see her. And when he thought of the good done him by a sight of Gillonne, he did not doubt that the sight of her mistress would prove far more efficacious. He employed a part of the money he had received when he left his family in purchasing a very handsome white satin doublet, and one of the richest embroidered cloaks he could procure. He also bought a pair of boots of perfumed leather, worn at that period. He dressed himself quickly, looked in his glass, and found that he was suitably attired, arranged, and perfumed.

While he was thus engaged in the Louvre, another scene, of a similar kind, was going on at the Hôtel de Guise. A tall gentleman, with red hair, was examining before a glass a red mark which went across his face very disagreeably. He colored and perfumed his mustache, and as he did so, in vain tried to conceal this scar; in spite of all the cosmetics applied, it would still appear. The gentleman put on a magnificent dress which a tailor had brought to his apartment without any commands from him. Thus attired, scented, and armed from head to foot, he descended the staircase, and began to pat a large black horse, whose beauty would have been matchless but for a small scar in the flank, caused by a sword wound.

Yet, enchanted with his horse as he was with himself, the gentleman, whom, no doubt, our readers have recognized, was in the saddle a quarter of an hour before the rest of the company, and made the courtyard of the Hôtel de Guise resound with the neighings of his horse, to which responded, in proportion as he obtained the mastery, *Mordis* in all tones. After a short time the horse, completely subdued, recognized by his obedience and subjection the control of the cavalier; but the victory had not been obtained without noise, and this noise (perhaps our gentleman had counted on it) had drawn to the windows a lady whom the cavalier saluted respectfully, and who smiled at him in the most agreeable manner.

Five minutes later Madame de Nevers asked her steward whether Coconnas had breakfasted comfortably, and was told that he had indeed. "Good!" said the duchess. Turning then toward her first gentleman, "M. d'Arguzon," she said, "let us set out for the Louvre; and keep an eye, I beg, on the Comte Annibal de

Coconnas, for he is wounded, and consequently still weak. I would not for all the world any accident should happen to him. That would make the Huguenots laugh, for they owe him a spite since the blessed night of Saint Bartholomew." And Madame de Nevers, mounting her horse, went joyfully toward the Louvre, which was the general rendezvous.

CHAPTER 16

The Body of a Dead Enemy Always Smells Sweet

It was two o'clock in the afternoon when a file of cavaliers, glittering with gold, jewels, and shining garments, appeared in the Rue St. Denis.

Nothing can be imagined more splendid than this spectacle. The rich and elegant silk dresses, bequeathed as a splendid fashion by François I to his successors, had not yet been changed into those formal and somber vestments which came into fashion under Henri III; so that the costume of Charles IX, less rich, but perhaps more elegant than those of preceding reigns, was brilliant in its perfect harmony. In our days an approach to the splendors of such a cortège is no longer possible; for we are reduced to depend, for magnificence in parade, on symmetry and uniformity. Pages, esquires, gentlemen of low degree, dogs, and horses, on the flanks and in the rear, transformed the royal cortège into an army. Behind this army came the people, or rather, the people were everywhere.

That morning, in presence of Catherine and the Duc de Guise, Charles had, as a perfectly natural thing, spoken before Henri de Navarre of going to visit the gibbet of Montfaucon, or rather, the mutilated corpse of the admiral, which had been suspended to it. Henri's first impulse had been to decline to accompany them; this Catherine had expected. At the first words he said, expressing his repugnance, she exchanged a glance and smile with the Duc de Guise. Henri surprised both, and understood them; then suddenly changing his mind, he said, "But why should I not go? I am a Catholic, and am bound to my new religion." Then, addressing the king, "Your Majesty may reckon on me," he said; "and I shall be always happy to accompany you wheresoever you may go"; and he threw a sweeping glance around, to see whose brows might be frowning.

Perhaps of all this cortège, the person who was looked at with

the greatest curiosity was this son without a mother, this king without a kingdom, this Huguenot turned Catholic. His long and
marked countenance, his somewhat vulgar figure, his familiarity
with his inferiors, which he carried to a degree almost derogatory to
a king—a familiarity acquired by the mountaineer habits of his
youth, and which he preserved till his death—marked him out to
the spectators, some of whom cried, "To Mass, Henriot! To Mass!"

To which Henri replied, "I attended it yesterday, today, and I
shall attend it again tomorrow. *Ventre-saint-gris!* surely that is sufficient."

Marguerite was on horseback—so lovely, so fresh, so elegant,
that around her there was a concert of admiring exclamations, some
of which, it must be admitted, were addressed to her companion,
the Duchesse de Nevers, whose white horse, as if proud of the
weight he carried, shook his head furiously.

"Well, Duchess!" said the Queen of Navarre, "what news?"

"Why, Madame," replied the duchess, aloud, "I know of
none." Then in a lower tone, "And what has become of the
Huguenot?"

"I have found him a retreat almost safe," replied Marguerite.
"And the wholesale murderer, what have you done with him?"

"He wished to be present, and so we mounted him on M. de
Nevers's warhorse, a creature as big as an elephant. He is a terrible
cavalier. I allowed him to be present today, as I reflected that your
Huguenot would be prudent enough to keep his chamber, and that
there was no fear of their meeting."

"Oh, upon my word!" replied Marguerite, smiling, "if he were
here, and he is not, I do not think a rencontre would ensue. My
Huguenot is remarkably handsome, but nothing more—a dove, and
not a hawk; he coos, but does not bite. After all," she added, with a
gesture impossible to describe, and shrugging her shoulders
slightly—"after all, perhaps we have thought him a Huguenot,
while he is only a Brahmin, and his religion forbids him to shed
blood."

"But where, then, is the Duc d'Alençon?" inquired Henriette;
"I do not see him."

"He will come. He had trouble with his eyes this morning and
was unwilling to come; but as it is well known that for the sake of
not being of the same opinion with his brother Charles and his

brother Henri, he leans toward the Huguenots, he was made to understand that his absence might be construed by the king to his disadvantage, and that decided him. But see, they are looking; they shout down there. It is he, doubtless, passing the Porte Montmartre."

"Yes; it is he, and he seems in good spirits today," said Henriette; "he is in love, perchance. And see how nice it is to be a prince of the blood; he gallops over everybody, and everybody draws on one side."

"Yes," said Marguerite, laughing, "he will ride over us. But draw your attendants on one side, Duchess, for here comes one who will be killed if he does not give way."

"It is my hero!" cried the duchess; "look, only look!"

Coconnas had quitted his rank to approach the Duchesse de Nevers; but at the moment when his horse was crossing the exterior boulevard which separates the street from the Faubourg St. Denis, a cavalier of the suite of the Duc d'Alençon, trying in vain to rein in his excited horse, dashed full against Coconnas, who, shaken by the collision, well-nigh lost his seat; his hat nearly fell off, and as he put it on firmer, he turned round furiously.

"Dieu!" said Marguerite, in a low tone to her friend, "M. de la Mole!"

"That handsome, pale young man?" exclaimed the duchess, unable to repress her first impression.

"Yes, yes; he who nearly upset your Piedmontese."

"Oh," said the duchess, "something terrible will happen! they look at each other, recollect each other!"

Coconnas had indeed recognized La Mole, and in his surprise dropped his bridle; for he believed he had killed his old companion, or at least put him *hors de combat* for some time. La Mole had also recognized Coconnas, and all his blood rushed up into his face. For some seconds, which sufficed for the expression of all the sentiments which these two men felt toward each other, they gazed on each other in a way that frightened the two women. After which, La Mole having looked about him, and seeing that the place was ill chosen for any explanation, spurred his horse and rejoined the Duc d'Alençon. Coconnas remained stationary for a moment, twisting his mustache until the point almost entered his eye; then, seeing La Mole dash off without a word, he did the same.

"Ah, ah!" said Marguerite, with painful contempt, "I was not deceived, then! it is really too much"; and she bit her lips till the blood came.

"He is very handsome," added the Duchesse de Nevers, with commiseration.

Just at this moment, the Duc d'Alençon reached his place behind the king and the queen-mother, so that his suite, in following him, were obliged to pass before Marguerite and the Duchesse de Nevers. La Mole, as he passed, raised his hat, saluted the queen, and, bowing to his horse's neck, remained uncovered until her Majesty should honor him with a look. But Marguerite turned her head aside disdainfully. La Mole no doubt comprehended the contemptuous expression of the queen's features; already pale, he became livid, and that he might not fall from his horse, was compelled to hold on by the mane.

"Ah, ah!" said Henriette to the queen; "look, cruel that you are! He is going to faint."

"Good," said the queen, with a smile of disdain; "it only needs that. Where are your salts?"

Madame de Nevers was mistaken. La Mole, with an effort, recovered himself, and sitting erect on his horse, took his place in the Duc d'Alençon's suite.

As they went forward they at length saw the fearful outline of the gibbet, erected and first used by Enguerrand de Marigny. Never had it been so conspicuously adorned as at that time. The guards advanced and formed a large ring around the spot; at their approach the crows perched on the gibbet flew away, croaking and angry.

The crowd advanced; the king and Catherine arrived first, then the Duc d'Anjou, the Duc d'Alençon, the King of Navarre, M. de Guise, and their followers; then Madame Marguerite, the Duchesse de Nevers, and all the women who composed what was called the queen's flying squadron; then the pages, esquires, attendants, and people—in all, ten thousand persons.

To the principal gibbet was suspended a misshapen mass, stained with coagulated blood and with mud whitened by layers of dust. The corpse was headless, and they had hung it up by the legs. The people, ingenious as they always are, had replaced the head with a bunch of straw, on which they had put a mask; and in the mouth of this mask some wag, knowing the admiral's habit, had introduced a toothpick.

It was a sight at once strange and appalling, as all these elegant lords and handsome ladies defiled in the midst of those blackened carcasses and those gibbets with their long fleshless arms. Many could scarcely support this horrible spectacle; and by his paleness might be distinguished, in the center of rallied Huguenots, Henri, who, however great his control over himself, and his power of dissimulation, could not bear it any longer. He made as his excuse the strong smell which emanated from those human remains, and going toward Charles, who, with Catherine, had stopped in front of the admiral's dead body, he said, "Sire, does not your Majesty find this poor carcass smelling so strongly that it is impossible to remain near it any longer?"

"Do you find it so, Henriot?" inquired the king, his eyes sparkling with ferocious joy.

"Yes, Sire."

"Well, then, I am not of your opinion; the body of a dead enemy always smells sweet."

"Faith, Sire," said Tavannes, "since your Majesty knew that we were to make a little visit to Monsieur the Admiral, you should have invited Pierre Ronsard, your master of poetry; he would have composed offhand an epitaph for old Gaspard."

"There is no need of him for that," said Charles IX, "and we will even do it ourselves. For example, listen, gentlemen," said he, after reflecting a moment:

> "HERE LIES—BUT THAT IS NOT
>   QUITE TRUE;
> OF HIM THAT WORD IS NOT
>   WELL SAID—
> HERE IS THE ADMIRAL IN VIEW,
>   HUNG BY THE FEET FOR WANT
>   OF HEAD."

"Bravo! bravo!" cried the Catholic gentlemen, with one voice, while the Huguenots bent their brows in silence. As to Henri, he was talking with Marguerite, and pretended not to have heard.

"Come, come, Sire!" said Catherine, who, in spite of the perfume with which she was covered, began to be incommoded with the putrid odor. "Come, however agreeable company may be, it must be left at last; let us therefore bid adieu to the admiral and return to Paris."

She made with her head an ironical gesture, in imitation of a leave-taking from a friend, and going to the front of the columns, regained the road, while the cortège defiled before the corpse of Coligny. The sun was fast sinking in the horizon. The crowd followed so rapidly that in ten minutes after the departure of the king there was no one near the mutilated corpse of the admiral, which was now blown upon by the first breezes of the evening.

When we say no one, we mistake. A gentleman mounted on a black horse, and who, doubtless, could not contemplate at his ease the misshapen and mutilated trunk when it was honored by the presence of princes, had remained behind, and was examining in all their details the bolts, stone pillars, and chains of the gibbet, which no doubt appeared to him (but lately arrived in Paris, and ignorant of the perfection to which things could be brought in the capital) the paragon of all that man could invent in the way of horrible ugliness.

We need hardly inform our readers that this man was our friend Coconnas.

The eye of a woman had in vain sought him in the ranks—and not hers alone. A gentleman noticeable for his white satin doublet and flowing plume, after having looked around him on all sides, thought of looking behind, and at length caught sight of the tall figure of Coconnas and the vast outline of his horse, in strong profile against the sky reddened by the last rays of the setting sun. Then the gentleman in the white satin doublet left the course which the main body was taking, and turning to the right and describing a semicircle, returned toward the gibbet. Almost at the same moment the woman whom we have recognized as the Duchesse de Nevers, approached Marguerite and said to her, "We were both deceived, Marguerite, for the Piedmontese has remained behind, and M. de la Mole has gone to him."

"Mordi!" replied Marguerite, laughing, "then something is going to happen. Faith! I confess I shall not be sorry to have occasion to change my opinion of him."

Marguerite then turned round, and saw La Mole execute the maneuver we have described. The two princesses left the main body at the first favorable occasion, and turned down a path, bordered on both sides by hedges, which led back to within thirty paces of the gibbet. Madame de Nevers said a word in her captain's ear, Marguerite made a sign to Gillonne; and the four persons went by the crossroad to ensconce themselves behind the bushes nearest to the spot in which the event was to occur which they desired to witness. Marguerite alighted, as did Madame de Nevers and Gillonne; the captain in his turn dismounted and took charge of the four horses. A space in the hedge allowed the three women to see all that occurred.

La Mole had reached Coconnas, and stretching out his hand, tapped him on the shoulder. The Piedmontese turned round.

"Oh!" said he, "then it was not a dream! You are still alive!"

"Yes, Monsieur," replied La Mole; "yes, I am still alive. It is no fault of yours, but I am still alive."

"Mordi! I know you again well enough," replied Coconnas, "in spite of your pale face. You were redder than that the last time we met!"

"And I," said La Mole, "I also recognize you, in spite of that yellow line across your face. You were paler than that when I made that mark for you!"

Coconnas bit his lips; but resolved on continuing the conversation in a tone of irony, he said, "It is curious, is it not, M. de la Mole, particularly for a Huguenot, to be able to look at the admiral suspended from an iron hook? And yet they say that we are guilty of killing even the small Huguenots who were sucking at the breast."

"Count," said La Mole, bowing, "I am no longer a Huguenot; I have the happiness to be a Catholic!"

"Bah!" exclaimed Coconnas, bursting into loud laughter; "you are a convert, eh, Monsieur? Well, that's well managed!"

"Monsieur," replied La Mole, with the same seriousness and the same politeness, "I made a vow to become a convert if I escaped the massacre."

"Count," said the Piedmontese, "that was a very prudent vow, and I beg to congratulate you. Made you no others?"

"Yes," answered La Mole, "I made a second." And as he said so he quietly patted his horse.

"And what might that be?" inquired Coconnas.

"To hang you up there by that small nail which seems to await you beneath M. de Coligny."

"What! as I am now," asked Coconnas—"alive and merry?"

"No, Monsieur, but after having passed my sword through your body!"

Coconnas became purple, and his eyes darted flames. "Do you mean it?" he asked jeeringly—"to that nail?"

"Yes," replied La Mole, "to that nail."

"You are not tall enough to do it, my little man!"

"Then I'll get on your horse, my great manslayer," replied La Mole. "Ah, you believe, my dear M. Annibal de Coconnas, that one may with impunity assassinate people under the loyal and honorable cover of a hundred to one, forsooth! But the day comes when a man finds his man, and I believe that day has come now. I should very well like to send a bullet through your ugly head; but, bah! I might miss you, for my hand is still trembling from the traitorous wounds you inflicted upon me."

"My ugly head!" shouted Coconnas, dismounting hastily. "Down—down from your horse, Monsieur the Count, and draw!" And he drew his sword.

"I believe that your Huguenot said 'ugly head,'" the Duchesse de Nevers whispered to Marguerite. "Do you think him ugly?"

"He is charming!" said Marguerite; "and I am obliged to say that anger makes M. de la Mole unjust. But hush! look!"

La Mole alighted as calmly as Coconnas had precipitately; he took off his cherry-colored cloak, laid it leisurely on the ground, drew his sword, and put himself on guard.

"Ah!" he said, as he stretched out his arm.

"Oh!" muttered Coconnas, as he did the same; for both, as it will be remembered, had been wounded in the shoulder.

A burst of laughter, ill-repressed, came from the clump of bushes. The two princesses had suddenly found it impossible to refrain from breaking out when they saw the two champions rubbing their shoulders and making grimaces. That burst of laughter reached the ears of the two gentlemen, who were ignorant that they had witnesses, and who, on turning round, beheld their ladies. La Mole resumed his guard as firm as an automaton, and Coconnas crossed his blade with an emphatic *Mordi!*

"Ah, then! now they will murder each other in real earnest, if we do not interfere. There has been enough of this. Holloa, gentlemen!—holloa!" cried Marguerite.

"Let them be; let them be!" said Henriette, who, having seen Coconnas fight, hoped in her heart that he would make as short work with La Mole as he had done with the two nephews and the son of Mercandon.

"Oh, they are really beautiful so!" exclaimed Marguerite. "Look! they seem to breathe fire!"

The combat, begun with railleries and mutual provocations, became silent as soon as the champions had crossed their swords. Both distrusted their strength, and each, at every quick pass, was compelled to restrain an expression of pain occasioned by his old wounds. With his eyes fixed and burning, his mouth half open, and his teeth set, La Mole advanced with short and firm steps toward his adversary, who, seeing in him a most skillful swordsman, retreated step by step. They both thus reached the edge of the ditch, on the other side of which were the spectators; then, as f his retreat had been only a simple stratagem to draw nearer to his lady, Coconnas took his stand, and on a motion of his blade a little too wide by his adversary, with the quickness of lightning made a direct thrust, and in a moment the white satin doublet of La Mole was stained with a spot of blood which kept growing larger.

"Courage!" cried the Duchess.

"Ah, poor La Mole!" exclaimed Marguerite, with a cry of distress.

La Mole heard this cry, darted at the queen one of those looks which penetrate the heart even deeper than the sword's point, and taking advantage of a false parade, thrust vigorously at his adversary. This time the two women uttered two cries which seemed like one. The point of La Mole's rapier had appeared, all covered with blood, behind Coconnas's back.

Yet neither fell. Both remained erect, looking at each other with open mouth, and feeling that on the slightest movement they must lose their balance. At last the Piedmontese, more dangerously wounded than his adversary, and feeling his senses forsaking him with his blood, fell on La Mole, grasping him with one hand, while with the other he endeavored to unsheathe his poniard. La Mole, on his part, roused all his strength, raised his hand, and let fall the pommel of his sword on Coconnas's forehead, who, stupefied by the blow, fell, but in his fall drew down his adversary with him, and both rolled into the ditch.

Then Marguerite and the Duchesse de Nevers, seeing that, dying as they were, they were still struggling to destroy each other, hastened toward them, followed by the captain of the guards; but before they could reach them, their hands unloosened their mutual clutch, their eyes closed, and the combatants, letting go their grasp of their weapons, stiffened as in their final agony. A large stream of blood flowed from each.

"Oh, brave, brave La Mole!" cried Marguerite, unable any longer to repress her admiration. "Ah! pardon me a thousand times for having a moment doubted your courage!" And her eyes filled with tears.

"Alas! alas!" murmured the duchess, "gallant Annibal! Did you ever see two more intrepid heroes, Madame?" And she sobbed aloud.

"Indeed, they were ugly thrusts," said the captain, endeavoring to stanch the streams of blood. "Holloa, you, there! come here as quickly as you can! here, I say—" He addressed a man who, seated on a kind of tumbril, or cart, painted red, was singing a snatch of an old song. "Holloa!" repeated the captain. "Come, then, when you are called! Do you not see that these gentlemen need help?"

The carter, whose repulsive exterior formed a singular contrast with the sweet and sylvan song he was singing, stopped his horse, came toward the two bodies, and looking at them, said, "These be terrible wounds, sure enough, but I have made worse."

"Who, then, are you?" inquired Marguerite, feeling in spite of herself a certain vague terror which she could not overcome.

"Madame," replied the man, bowing down to the ground, "I am Maître Caboche, headsman to the provostry of Paris, and I have come to hang up at the gibbet some companions for Monsieur the Admiral."

"Well! and I am the Queen of Navarre," replied Marguerite; "cast your corpses down there, spread in your cart the housings of our horses, and bring these two gentlemen softly behind us to the Louvre."

The Rival of
Maître Ambroise Paré

The tumbril in which were La Mole and Coconnas took the road to the Louvre, following at a distance the group that served as a guide. It stopped at the Louvre, and the driver was amply rewarded. The wounded men were carried to the Duc d'Alençon's lodgings, and Maître Ambroise Paré sent for. When he arrived, they were both insensible. La Mole was the least hurt of the two. The sword had pierced him below the right armpit, but without touching any vital part. As for Coconnas, he was run through the lungs, and the air that escaped from his wound made the flame of a candle waver. Ambroise Paré would not answer for his recovery.

Madame de Nevers was in despair. She it was who, relying on Coconnas's courage and skill, had prevented Marguerite from interposing. She would have been glad to have Coconnas carried to the Hôtel de Guise, so that she might on this second occasion repeat the care she had bestowed on him before; but her husband might at any moment arrive from Rome, and would not understand, perhaps, the installation of an intruder in the conjugal abode.

In order to conceal the cause of their wounds, Marguerite, in having the young men transported to her brother's apartments, where one of them was already installed, said they were two gentlemen who had been thrown from their horses; but the real story became known, in consequence of the admiration of the captain who had witnessed the duel, and who related all the particulars; and our two heroes had soon a brilliant reputation at court.

Attended by the same surgeon, they both passed through the different stages of convalescence arising from the nature of their wounds. La Mole was the first who came to himself. As for Coconnas, he was in a high fever, and his return to life was marked by all the signs of delirium.

Although in the same room as Coconnas, La Mole had not perceived his companion, or at least had given no indication of having done so. Coconnas, on the contrary, when he opened his eyes, fixed them on La Mole with an expression that proved that the blood he had lost had not modified the passions of his fiery temperament.

Coconnas thought he was dreaming, and that in his dream he saw again the enemy he imagined he had twice slain; only this dream was prolonged beyond measure. After having observed La Mole laid, like himself, on a couch, and his wounds dressed by the surgeon, he saw him rise up in bed, while he himself was still too weak to move, then get out of bed, then walk, first leaning on the surgeon's arm, and then on a cane, and in the end, without assistance. Coconnas, still delirious, viewed these different stages of his companion's recovery with eyes sometimes fixed, at others wandering, but always threatening.

All this offered to the fevered mind of the Piedmontese a frightful mixture of fancy and reality. To him La Mole was dead— dead indeed; dead twice rather than once. And yet he found the shade of that La Mole lying on a bed like his own; then, as we have said, he saw that shade rise, then walk, and—fearful sight—walk toward his bed! That shade, from which Coconnas would have been glad to flee, even to the depths of hell, came straight to him, and paused by his bed, looking down at him; there was on his face an expression of gentleness and compassion which Coconnas took for an expression of infernal derision. Then arose in his mind, more wounded than his body, a blind passion for vengeance. He was wholly occupied with one idea—that of procuring some weapon, and piercing this vision that so cruelly persecuted him. His clothes, stained with blood, had been placed on a chair by his bed, but were afterward removed, it being thought imprudent to leave them in his sight; but his poniard still remained on the chair, for it was imagined it would be some time before he would want to use it.

Coconnas saw the poniard. Three nights, profiting by La Mole's slumbers, he strove to reach it; three nights his strength failed him, and he fainted. At length, on the fourth night, he clutched it convulsively, and groaning with the pain of the effort, concealed the weapon beneath his pillow.

The next day he saw something unheard of until then. The shade of La Mole, that every day seemed to gain strength, while he, occupied with his design, seemed to lose his—the shade of La Mole, becoming more and more active, walked thoughtfully up and down the room three or four times, then, after having adjusted his mantle, buckled on his rapier, put on a large hat, opened the door and went out. Coconnas breathed again. He thought that he had got rid of his ghost. For two hours his blood circulated more freely in his veins than it had since the duel. One day's absence of La Mole would have recalled Coconnas's senses; a week's absence would have cured him perhaps. Unfortunately, La Mole returned at the end of two hours.

This reappearance of La Mole was a poniard stab for Coconnas; and although La Mole did not return alone, Coconnas did not give a single look at his companion. That companion was nevertheless worth looking at. He was a man forty years old, short, thickset, and vigorous, with black hair cut short, and a black beard, which, contrary to the fashion of the period, thickly covered the chin; but he seemed one who cared little for the fashion. He wore a leather jerkin, stained and spotted with blood, red hose and leggings, thick shoes coming above the ankle, a cap of the same color as his stockings, and a girdle, from which hung a large knife in a leather sheath.

This singular personage, whose presence in the Louvre seemed so unaccountable, threw his brown mantle on a chair, and unceremoniously approached Coconnas, whose eyes, as if fascinated, remained fixed upon La Mole, who remained at the other end of the room. He looked at the sick man, and shaking his head, said to La Mole, "You haven't hurried yourself."

"I could not get out sooner."

"Why did you not send for me?"

"Whom had I to send?"

"True, I forgot where we are. Ah, if my prescriptions had been followed instead of those of that ass, Ambroise Paré, you would have been by this time in a condition to go in pursuit of adventures together, or exchange another sword thrust if you liked; but we shall see. Does your friend hear reason?"

"Scarcely."

"Hold out your tongue, Monsieur."

Coconnas put out his tongue at La Mole with so frightful a grimace that the examiner again shook his head.

"Oh, oh!" he murmured; "contraction of the muscles; there is no time to lose. This evening I will send you a potion; you must make him take it in three doses an hour apart—at midnight, at one o'clock, and at two."

"Very well."

"But who will administer it?"

"I will."

"You yourself?"

"Yes."

"You promise me?"

"On my honor."

"And if the doctor seeks to obtain any of it to analyze it?"

"I will throw it away to the last drop."

"On your honor?"

"I swear it!"

"But how will my messenger reach you?"

"That is provided for; he will say that he comes on the part of M. René the perfumer."

"That Florentine who lives on the Pont St. Michel?"

"Precisely. He has the privilege of entering the Louvre at all hours of day or night."

The man smiled. "In fact," said he, "that is the least the queen-mother can do for him. Well, it is understood; someone will come as from Maître René the perfumer. I may surely take his name for once; he has often, without a license, practiced my profession."

"Then," said La Mole, "I rely on you."

"You may."

"And as for the payment?"

"Oh, we will arrange about that when the gentleman is well again."

"You may be quite easy on that score, for I am sure he will pay you nobly."

"No doubt. But," he added with a strange smile, "as it is not customary for those who have business with me to be grateful, I shall not be at all surprised if when he is once on his feet he should forget, or rather should not trouble himself to think of me."

"In that case," said La Mole, smiling in his turn, "I shall be at hand to refresh his memory."

"Good! In two hours you will have the potion."

"Au revoir!"

"You say?"

"Au revoir!"

The man smiled. "I," he said, "have the habit of saying 'Adieu.' Adieu, then, M. de la Mole. In two hours you will have the potion. You understand, it must be given at midnight—in three doses, from hour to hour." So saying, he left the room, and La Mole was alone with Coconnas.

Coconnas had heard the whole conversation, but remembered nothing except the word "midnight." He continued to watch La Mole, who remained in the room, pacing thoughtfully up and down.

The unknown doctor kept his word, and at the appointed time sent the potion, which La Mole placed on a small heater, and then lay down.

The clock struck twelve. Coconnas opened his eyes; his breath seemed to scorch his lips, and his throat was parched with fever; the night-lamp shed a faint light, and made thousands of phantoms dance before his eyes. He saw La Mole rise from his couch, walk about a few moments, and then advance toward him, threatening him, as he thought, with his clenched hand. Coconnas seized his poniard, and prepared to plunge it into his enemy.

La Mole approached.

Coconnas murmured, "Ah! 'tis you! 'tis you, then! Ah, you menace me! you show your fist! you smile! Come, come, come, that I may kill you!"

And suiting the action to the word, as La Mole leaned toward him, Coconnas drew the poniard from under the clothes; but the effort exhausted him, and he fell back upon his pillow.

"Come, come," said La Mole, supporting him, "drink this, my poor fellow, for you are burning."

It was in fact a cup that La Mole presented to Coconnas, and which he had mistaken for his fist. But at the nectarous sensation of this blessed draught, soothing his lips and cooling his throat, Coconnas resumed his reason, or rather, his instinct; a feeling of comfort pervaded his frame. He fixed his eyes on La Mole, who was supporting him in his arms, and smiled gratefully on him; and from those eyes so lately glowing with fury, a tear rolled down his burning cheek.

"Mordi!" murmured Coconnas. "If I get over this, M. de la Mole, you shall be my friend."

"And you will get over it, my comrade," said La Mole, "if you will drink the other two cups, and have no more ugly dreams."

An hour afterward La Mole, obedient to his instructions, rose again, poured a second dose into the cup, and carried it to Coconnas, who, instead of receiving him with his poniard, opened his arms, eagerly swallowed the potion, and then fell asleep tranquilly for the first time.

The third cup had a no less marvelous effect. The sick man's breathing became more regular, his limbs supple, a gentle perspiration diffused itself over his skin; and when Ambroise Paré visited him the next morning, he smiled complacently, saying, "I answer for M. de Coconnas now; and this will not be one of the least difficult cures I have effected."

The result of this scene was that the friendship of the two gentlemen, begun at the Belle Etoile, and violently interrupted by the events of the night of Saint Bartholomew, now surpassed that of Orestes and Pylades.

Old and new wounds, slight or serious, were at last in a fair way of cure. La Mole, though quite well, would not abandon his post of nurse until Coconnas was also recovered. He raised him in bed, and helped him when he began to walk, until by the aid of Comte Annibal's naturally vigorous constitution, he was restored to perfect convalescence.

However, one and the same thought occupied both the young men. Each had in his delirium seen the woman he loved approach his couch, and yet, since they had recovered their senses, neither Marguerite nor Madame de Nevers had appeared. That, however, was easily understood. Could they—the one, wife of the King of Navarre, the other, sister-in-law of the Duc de Guise—give so public an indication of interest in two simple gentlemen? No. And so reasoned La Mole and Coconnas. But that absence, which might indicate total forgetfulness, was none the less grievous. It is true that the gentleman who had witnessed the combat had come several times, as if of his own accord, to inquire after them; it is also true that Gillonne had done the same. But La Mole had not ventured to speak to the one concerning the queen; Coconnas had not ventured to speak to the other of Madame de Nevers.

CHAPTER 18

The Visit

During some time the two young men kept their secret confined each to his own breast. At last, on a day of warm and mutual feeling, the thought which had so long occupied them escaped their lips; and both cemented their friendship by that final proof, without which there is no friendship—namely, perfect confidence.

They were both madly in love—one with a princess, and the other with a queen. There was something appalling to those two lovers in the almost insuperable distance which separated them from the objects of their desires. And yet hope is a sentiment so deeply rooted in the heart of man that though their hope seemed foolish, still they hoped.

They both, as they recovered from their illness, took great pains with their personal appearance. Every man, even the most indifferent to physical appearance, has at certain times mute interviews with his looking glass, interchanging with it signs of intelligence, after which he withdraws from his confidant quite satisfied with the conversation. Now our two young friends were not men whose mirrors gave them no encouragement. La Mole, thin, pale, and elegant, had the beauty of distinction; Coconnas, powerful, large-framed, and fresh-colored, had the beauty of strength. He had more, for his recent illness had been of advantage to him. He had become thinner, grown paler, and the famous scar, which had annoyed him so much by its prismatic resemblance to a rainbow, had disappeared, announcing probably a long succession of calm days and quiet nights.

The most delicate attentions continued to be lavished on the two wounded men, and on the day when each was well enough to rise, he found a *robe de chambre* on the easy chair nearest his bed, and on the day when he was able to dress himself, a complete suit of clothes; moreover, in the pocket of each doublet was a well-filled purse, which they each kept, intending, of course, to return it, when occasion should permit, to the unknown protector who watched over them.

This unknown protector could not be the prince with whom the two young men resided, for not only had the prince never once paid them a visit, but he had not even sent to make any inquiry after them. A vague hope whispered to each heart that this unknown protector was the woman he loved. The two wounded men therefore awaited with intense impatience the moment when they could go out. La Mole, stronger and sooner cured than Coconnas, could have done so long before, but a kind of tacit convention bound him to his friend. It was understood between them that their first outing should be devoted to making three visits—the first, to the unknown doctor whose medicine had operated so beneficially on the inflamed lungs of Coconnas; the second, to the hotel of the late Maître la Hurière, where they each had left a valise and a horse; the third, to Florentine René, who united to his title of perfumer that of magician, and not only sold cosmetics and poisons, but even concocted philters and delivered oracles.

At length, after two months passed in convalescence and confinement, the long-looked-for day arrived, and about two o'clock in the afternoon, on a fine day in autumn, such as Paris sometimes offers to her astonished population, who have already made up their minds to the winter, the two friends, leaning on each other's arms, left the Louvre.

La Mole undertook to be the guide of Coconnas; and Coconnas allowed himself to be guided without resistance or reflection. He knew that his friend meant to conduct him to the unknown doctor's, whose potion, not patented, had cured him in a single night when all the drugs of Maître Ambroise Paré were killing him slowly. He had divided the money in his purse into two parts, and intended a hundred rose nobles for the unknown Æsculapius to whom his recovery was due. Coconnas was not afraid of death; but he was not the less satisfied to be alive and well, and was prepared to recompense generously his preserver.

La Mole directed his steps toward the Place des Halles. Near the ancient fountain was an octagon stone building, surmounted by a vast lantern of wood, which was again surmounted by a pointed roof, on the top of which was a weathercock. This wooden lantern had eight openings, traversed, as that heraldic piece which they call the *fascis* traverses the field of blazonry, by a kind of wheel of wood, which was divided in the middle, in order to admit in the holes cut in it for that purpose the head and hands of the sentenced person or persons who were exposed at one or other of these eight openings.

This singular construction, in no way resembling the surrounding buildings, was called the pillory. An ill-constructed, irregular, crooked, one-eyed, limping house, the roof covered with moss like the skin of a leper, had, like a toadstool, sprung up at the foot of this species of tower. This house was the executioner's.

A man was exposed in the pillory, and was thrusting out his tongue at the passersby; he was one of the robbers who had been following his profession beneath the gibbet of Montfaucon, and had by ill luck been arrested in the exercise of his functions. Coconnas believed that his friend had brought him to see this singular spectacle, and mingled in the crowd of spectators who replied to the grimaces of the patient by vociferations and taunts. Coconnas was naturally cruel, and the sight very much amused him; only he would have preferred that instead of taunts and vociferations, stones had been cast at a culprit so insolent as to thrust out his tongue at noblemen who did him the honor to visit him. So when the moving lantern was turning on its base, in order to show the exhibited to another portion of the multitude, and the crowd were following, Coconnas would have accompanied them had not La Mole checked him, saying in a low tone, "It was not for this that we came here." And he led Coconnas to a small window in the house which abutted on the tower, and at which a man was leaning.

"Ah, ah! is it you, Messeigneurs?" said the man, raising his blood-red cap, and showing his black and thick hair, which descended to his eyebrows. "You are welcome."

"Who is this man?" inquired Coconnas, endeavoring to recollect, for he believed he had seen his face during one of the crises of his fever.

"Your preserver, my dear friend," replied La Mole; "he who brought to you at the Louvre that refreshing drink which did you so much good."

"Oh, oh!" said Marguerite; "in that case, my friend—" And he held out his hand to him.

But the man, instead of returning the gesture, stood up and re-treated a pace from the two friends. "Monsieur," he said to Coconnas, "thanks for the honor you offer me, but it is most prob-able that if you knew me you would not vouchsafe it."

"Faith!" said Coconnas, "I declare that even if you were the Devil himself, I am very greatly obliged to you, for I owe you my life."

"I am not exactly the Devil," replied the man in the red cap; "but yet there are frequently persons who would rather see the Devil than me."

"Then who are you?"

"Monsieur," replied the man, "I am Maître Caboche, the exe-cutioner of the provostry of Paris—"

"Ah!" said Coconnas, withdrawing his hand.

"You see!" said Maître Caboche.

"No, no; I will touch your hand, or may the devil take me! Hold it out!"

"Really?"

"Wide open."

"Here it is!"

"Open it—wider—there!" And Coconnas took from his pocket the handful of gold he had prepared for his anonymous physician, and placed it in the executioner's hand.

"I would rather have had your hand entirely and solely," said Maître Caboche, shaking his head; "for I am not in want of money, but of hands to touch mine. Never mind! God bless you, my gentle-man!"

"So, then, my friend," said Coconnas, looking at the execu-tioner with curiosity, "it is you who give men pain, who put them on the wheel, rack them, cut off heads, and break bones. Ah, ah! I am very glad to have formed your acquaintance."

"Monsieur," said Maître Caboche, "I do not do all myself. Just as you have lackeys, you noble gentlemen, to do what you do not choose to do yourself, so have I my assistants, who do the coarser work and make preparations. Only when by chance I have to do with folks of quality, like you and that other gentleman, for instance, ah! it is then a very different thing, and I take a pride in doing every-thing myself, from first to last—that is to say, from the first putting of the question to the beheading!"

In spite of himself Coconnas felt a shudder pervade his veins, as if the actual wedge pressed his legs, as if the edge of the axe was against his neck. La Mole, without being able to account for it, felt the same sensation. But Coconnas overcame the emotion, of which he was ashamed, and wishing to take leave of Maître Caboche with a jest on his lips, said to him—

"Well, Master, I hold you to your word, and when it is my turn to mount the gallows of Enguerrand de Marigny, or the scaffold of M. de Nemours, you alone shall lay hands on me."

"I promise you."

"Then, this time here is my hand, as a pledge that I accept your promise," said Coconnas. And he extended to the headsman his hand, which the headsman touched timidly with his own, although it was evident that he had a great desire to grasp it warmly. At this light touch Coconnas turned rather pale, but the same smile still remained on his lips; while La Mole, ill at ease, and seeing the crowd turn with the lantern and come toward them, pulled him by his cloak. Coconnas, who really had as great desire as La Mole to put an end to this scene, in which, by the natural tendency of his character, he had got himself engaged more deeply than he wished, nodded to the executioner, and turned away.

"Faith!" said La Mole, when he and his companion had reached the Cross du Trahoir, "we breathe more freely here than in the Place des Halles!"

"Decidedly," replied Coconnas; "but I am not the less glad at having made Maître Caboche's acquaintance. It is well to have friends everywhere."

"Even at the sign of the Belle Etoile," said La Mole, smiling.

"Oh! as to poor Maître la Hurière," said Coconnas, "he is certainly dead. I saw the flame from the arquebus; I heard the stroke of the bullet, which sounded as if it had hit the bell of Notre Dame; and I left him lying in a stream of blood which flowed from his nose and mouth. If we are to speak of him as a friend, it must be as a friend in the other world."

Conversing in this manner, the two young men entered the Rue de l'Arbre Sec and drew near to the sign of the Belle Etoile, which still creaked in its old place, and still offered to the traveler its appetizing allurements.

Coconnas and La Mole were expecting to find the house in despair, the widow in mourning, and the servants with crepe on their arms; but to their great astonishment they found the house in full tide of business, Madame la Hurière magnificent, and the servants more jolly than ever.

"Oh, the unfaithful woman!" said La Mole; "she has married again!" Then, addressing himself to the new Artemisia, "Madame," he said, "we are two acquaintances of poor M. la Hurière. We left here two horses and two valises, which we have come to recover."

"Gentlemen," replied the mistress of the house, after an effort to recall some remembrance of them, "since I have not the honor to recognize you, I will, if you please, send for my husband. Grégoire, go and call your master."

Grégoire passed through the first kitchen, which was the general pandemonium, into the second, which was the laboratory in which were concocted the dishes which Maître la Hurière, while living, judged worthy to be prepared by his own skillful hands.

"The devil take me!" murmured Coconnas, "it goes to my heart to see this house so lively when it ought to be so sad. Poor La Hurière!"

"He tried to kill me," said La Mole; "but I forgive him with all my heart."

La Mole had hardly uttered these words when a man appeared, holding in his hand a stewpan in which he was cooking some onions, which he turned with a wooden spoon. La Mole and Coconnas uttered a cry of surprise. At that cry the man raised his head, and answering with a similar exclamation, let fall his stewpan, keeping in his hand only his wooden spoon.

"*In nomine Patris*," said the man, waving his wooden spoon as if it were a holy-water sprinkler, "*et Filii, et Spiritus Sancti*—"

"Maître la Hurière!" cried the two young men.

"M. M. de Coconnas and de la Mole!" exclaimed La Hurière.

"You are not dead, then?" said Coconnas.

"You are, then, still living?" said the host.

"I saw you fall, nevertheless," said Coconnas; "I heard the noise of the bullet which hit something about you, I know not what. I left you lying in the gutter losing blood from the nose, the mouth, and even from the eyes."

"All that is true as the Gospel, M. de Coconnas. But the noise which you heard was that of the bullet striking my helmet, on which, fortunately, it was flattened; but the shock was none the less violent, for, as you see," added La Hurière, raising his cap and showing his head bald as a knee, "I haven't a hair left."

The two young men burst into laughter on seeing his grotesque appearance.

"Ah, ah! you laugh!" said La Hurière, a little reassured. "You have not come, then, with hostile intentions?"

"And you, Maître la Hurière, are you cured of your warlike tastes?"

"Yes, by my soul, yes, gentlemen; and now—"

"Well? now—"

"Now I have made a vow never to see any other fire but that of my kitchen."

"Bravo!" said Coconnas; "in that you are wise. Now, then," added the Piedmontese, "we have left in your stables two horses, and in your chambers two valises."

"Ah, the devil!" said the host, scratching his ear.

"Well?"

"Two horses, do you say?"

"Yes, in the stable."

"And two valises?"

"Yes, in the chamber."

"The trouble is, you see—You thought I was dead, did you not?"

"Certainly."

"You will admit that since you have been mistaken, I, too, might be."

"In believing us also dead? You were entirely free to do so."

"Ah, there it is! Since you died intestate—"

"Well?"

"I thought—I was wrong, I see now that I was—"

"What did you think? let us have it."

"I thought that I might inherit from you."

"Ah, ah!" exclaimed the young men.

"I am not the less pleased that you are living, gentlemen."

"And so you have sold our horses?" said Coconnas.

"Alas!" replied La Hurière.

"And our valises?" continued La Mole.

"Oh! the valises? no," cried La Hurière, "but only what was in them."

"Say then, La Mole," said Coconnas, "this fellow seems to me an impudent rascal; shall we disembowel him?"

This threat seemed to have a great effect on Maître la Hurière, who ventured to say, "But, gentlemen, it can be arranged, I think."

"Listen," said La Mole; "it is I who have the most to complain of against you."

"Certainly, Monsieur the Count, for I remember that in a moment of folly I had the audacity to threaten you."

"Yes, with a bullet that passed within two inches of my head."

"You think so?"

"I am sure of it."

"If you are sure of it, M. de la Mole," said La Hurière, picking up his stewpan with an innocent air, "I am too much your servant to contradict you."

"Well," said La Mole, "for my part I claim nothing from you."

"How so, my gentleman?"

"Except—"

"Oh, oh!" said La Hurière.

"Except a dinner for myself and my friends whenever I am in this neighborhood."

"Only that?" cried La Hurière, delighted. "At your orders, my gentleman, at your orders!"

"So, then, it is agreed?"

"With all my heart. And you, M. de Coconnas," continued the host, "do you agree to the bargain?"

"Yes; but like my friend, I must add a slight condition."

"What is it?"

"That you restore to M. de la Mole the fifty crowns I owe him, which I confided to your keeping."

"To me, Monsieur? When was that?"

"Quarter of an hour before you sold my horse and my valise."

La Hurière made a sign of intelligence. "Oh! I understand," he said, and going to a closet he took out, one after another, fifty crowns, which he handed to La Mole.

"Very good, Monsieur," said that gentleman; "serve us an omelet. The fifty crowns will go to Grégoire."

"Oh!" cried La Hurière, "indeed, my gentlemen, you have princely souls, and I am yours for life or for death."

"In that case," said Coconnas, "make us the omelet called for, and spare neither butter nor lard." Then, looking at the clock, "Faith, you are right, La Mole. We have still three hours to wait, and may as well spend them here as elsewhere—especially since at this point we are nearly halfway to Pont St. Michel."

The two young men sat down at the table in the little end-room, in the same places they had occupied on that famous evening of Aug. 24, 1572, during which Coconnas had proposed to La Mole that they should play for their respective mistresses. It must be stated to their credit that on this evening neither of them thought of making such a proposition.

CHAPTER 19

The Abode of Maître René, Perfumer to the Queen-Mother

At the period of this history there existed in Paris, for passing from one part of the city to another, but five bridges, some of stone and the others of wood, and they all led to the Cité; among these five bridges, each of which has its history, we shall now speak more particularly of the Pont St. Michel.

In the midst of the houses which bordered the line of the bridge, facing a small islet, was a house remarkable for its panels of wood, over which a large roof impended, like the lid of an immense eye. At the only window which opened on the first story, over the window and door of the ground floor, closely shut, was observable a reddish light, which attracted the attention of the passersby to the low façade, large, and painted blue, with rich gold moldings. A kind of frieze, which separated the ground floor from the first floor, represented groups of devils in the most grotesque postures imaginable; and a large plain strip, painted blue like the façade, ran between the frieze and the window, with this inscription:

RENÉ, FLORENTINE,
PERFUMER TO HER MAJESTY
THE QUEEN-MOTHER

The door of this shop was, as we have said, closely bolted; but it was defended from nocturnal attacks better than by bolts by the reputation of its occupant, so redoubtable that the passengers over the bridge usually kept away from contact with the building, as if they feared that the smell of the perfumes might reach them through the wall.

From similar motives, the neighbors on the right and left of René, fearing, doubtless, to be compromised by that proximity, had, since the installation of Maître René on the Pont St. Michel, abandoned their houses, which were thus entirely deserted. Yet, in spite of this solitude, belated passersby had frequently seen, glittering through the crevices of the shutters of these empty habitations, certain rays of light, and had heard certain noises like groans, which proved that some beings frequented these abodes, although they did not know whether they belonged to this world or the other.

It was doubtless owing to the privilege which the dread of him, widely circulated, had procured for him, that Maître René had dared to keep up a light after the prescribed hour. No roundsman or guard, however, would have dared to molest him—a man doubly dear to her Majesty as her fellow countryman and her perfumer.

The shop on the ground floor had been dark and deserted since eight o'clock in the evening—the hour at which it closed, not again to open until next morning. That was the place of the daily sale of perfumery, unguents, cosmetics, and all the wares of a skillful chemist. Two apprentices aided him in the retail business, but did not sleep in the house. In the evening they went out an instant before the shop was closed, and in the morning waited at the door until it was opened.

In the shop, which was large and deep, there were two doors, each leading to a staircase. One of these staircases was in the wall itself, and the other was exterior and visible from the Quai des Augustins and from what is now called the Quai des Orfévres. Both led to a room on the first floor, of the same size as the ground floor, except that it was divided into two compartments by tapestry suspended in the center. At the end of the first compartment opened the door which led to the exterior staircase. On the side face of the second opened the door of the secret staircase. This door was invisible, being concealed by a large carved cupboard fastened to it by iron cramps, and moving with it when pushed open. Catherine alone, besides René, knew the secret of this door, and by it she came and departed; and with eye or ear placed against the cupboard, in which were several small holes, she saw and heard all that took place in the chamber.

Two other doors, visible to all eyes, presented themselves at the sides of the second compartment. One opened to a small chamber lighted from the roof, and having nothing in it but a large stove, alembics, retorts, and crucibles—it was an alchemist's laboratory; the other opened into a cell of stranger appearance than the other rooms, for it was not lighted at all, and had neither carpet nor furniture, but only a kind of stone altar. The floor sloped from the center to the ends, and from the ends to the base of the wall was a kind of gutter ending in a funnel, through whose orifice might be seen the somber waters of the Seine. On nails driven into the walls were suspended instruments of singular shape, all keen and trenchant, with points as fine as a needle and edges as sharp as a razor. Some shone like mirrors; others, on the contrary, were of a dull gray or murky blue. In a corner were two black fowls, struggling with each other, tied together by the claws. This was the Sanctuary of Augury.

Let us return to the middle chamber, that with two compartments. It was here that the vulgar clients were introduced; here Ibises of Egypt, mummies, with gilded bands, the crocodile, yawning from the ceiling, death's heads with eyeless sockets and gumless teeth, old musty volumes, torn and rat-eaten, presented to the eye of the visitor a scene of confusion whence resulted varying emotions which prevented thought from following a direct course. Behind the curtain were phials, singularly shaped boxes, and vases of sinister appearance—all lighted up by two small silver lamps which, supplied with perfumed oil, cast their yellow flame up to the somber vault, to which each was suspended by three blackened chains.

René alone, his arms crossed, was pacing up and down the second compartment with long strides, and shaking his head. After a lengthened and painful musing he paused before an hourglass.

"Ah, ah!" he said, "I forgot to turn it; and perhaps the sand has all passed a long time since." Then looking at the moon, as it struggled through a heavy black cloud which seemed to hang over Notre Dame, he said, "It is nine o'clock. If she comes, she will come, as usual, in an hour or an hour and a half; then there will be time for all."

At this moment a noise was heard on the bridge. René applied his ear to the long tube, the extremity of which reached unto the street. "No," he said, "it is neither she nor they. It is men's footsteps, and they stop at my door; they are coming hither."

Immediately three knocks were heard at the door. René rapidly descended and placed his ear against the door, without opening it. The blows were repeated. "Who's there?" asked René.

"Is it necessary that we should mention our names?" inquired a voice.

"Absolutely indispensable," replied René.

"Then I am the Comte Annibal de Coconnas," said the same voice.

"And I am the Comte Lerac de la Mole," said another voice.

"Wait; wait a second, gentlemen, and I am at your service"; and at the same moment, René, drawing the bolts and lifting the bars, opened the door to the two young men, locking it after them. Then, conducting them by the exterior staircase, he introduced them into the second compartment.

La Mole, as he entered, made the sign of the cross under his cloak. He was pale, and his hand trembled; he was able to repress this symptom of weakness. Coconnas looked at everything, one after the other; and seeing the door of the cell, tried to open it. "Allow me to observe, Monsieur," said René, in a serious tone, and placing his hand on that of Coconnas, "that those who do me the honor of a visit have access to this apartment only."

"Oh, very well," replied Coconnas; "besides, I want to sit down"; and he placed himself on a chair.

There was profound silence for the next minute, Maître René expecting that one of the young men would open the conversation. During this silence one could hear the whistling respiration of Coconnas, whose wounds were not fully healed.

"Maître René," at length said Coconnas, "you are a very skillful man, and I pray you tell me if I shall always remain a sufferer from my wound—that is, always experience this shortness of breath, which prevents me from riding on horseback, practicing feats of arms, and eating rich omelets?"

René put his ear to Coconnas's chest, and listened attentively to the play of the lungs. "No, Count," he replied, "you will be cured."

"Really?"

"Yes, I assure you."

"Well, I am happy to hear it."

Again all was silent.

"Is there nothing else you would desire to know, Monsieur the Count?"

"I wish to know," said Coconnas, "if I am really in love?"

"You are," replied René.

"How do you know?"

"Because you ask the question."

"Mordi! you are right. But with whom?"

"With her who now, on every occasion, uses the oath you have just uttered."

"Ah!" said Coconnas, amazed; "Maître René, you are a wonderful man! Now, La Mole, it is your turn."

La Mole blushed, and seemed embarrassed. "I, M. René," he stammered, and speaking more firmly as he proceeded, "do not desire to ask you if I am in love, for I know that I am, and do not seek to conceal it from myself; but tell me, shall I be beloved in return? for in truth, all that at first seemed propitious now turns against me."

"Perchance you have not done all you should do."

"What is there to do, Monsieur, but to testify by our respect and devotion to the lady of our thoughts that she is really and profoundly beloved?"

"You know," replied René, "that these demonstrations are frequently very insignificant."

"Then must I despair?"

"By no means; we must have recourse to science. There are in human nature antipathies to be overcome, sympathies which may be forced. Iron is not the lodestone; but by magnetizing it, we make it in its turn attract iron."

"Yes, yes," muttered La Mole; "but I have an objection to all these sorceries."

"Ah, then, if you have any such objections, you should not come here," answered René.

"Come, come, this is child's play!" interposed Coconnas. "Maître René, can you show me the Devil?"

"No, Monsieur the Count."

"I'm sorry for that; for I had a few words to say to him, and it might have encouraged La Mole."

"Well, then, let it be so," said La Mole; "let us go to the point at once. They have spoken to me of figures modeled in wax after the resemblance of the beloved object. Is this a method?"

"An infallible one."

"And in the experiment there is nothing which can in any way affect the life or health of the person beloved?"

"Nothing."

"Let us try, then."

"Shall I make first trial?" said Coconnas.

"No," said La Mole, "since I have begun, I will go through to the end."

At this moment, some one rapped lightly at the door, so lightly that Maître René alone heard the noise—doubtless because he had been expecting it. Without affecting any concealment, he put his ear to the tube, meantime idly questioning La Mole. He heard sounds of voices which seemed to fix his attention.

"Think intently of your wish," he said, "and call the person whom you love."

La Mole knelt, as if about to name a divinity; and René, going into the other compartment, went out noiselessly by the exterior staircase, and an instant afterward light steps trod the flooring of his shop.

La Mole rose, and beheld before him Maître René. The Florentine held in his hand a small figure in wax, very indifferently modeled, and wearing a crown and mantle.

"Do you desire to be always beloved by your royal mistress?" demanded the perfumer.

"Yes, if my life, my soul, should be the sacrifice!" replied La Mole.

"Well," said the Florentine, taking with the ends of his fingers some drops of water from a pitcher, sprinkling them over the figure, and muttering a few Latin words. La Mole shuddered, believing that some sacrilege was committed.

"What are you doing?" he inquired.

"I am christening this figure with the name of Marguerite."

"For what purpose?"

"To establish a sympathy."

La Mole opened his lips to prevent his going any further, but a bantering look from Coconnas stopped him. René, who had seen the movement, waited. "It must be with your full and free consent," he said.

"Go on," replied La Mole.

René then traced on a small strip of red paper certain cabalistic characters, put it into the eye of a steel needle, and with the needle pierced the small wax model in the heart. Strange to say, at the orifice of the wound appeared a small drop of blood. He then lighted the paper. The warmth of the needle melted the wax around it and dried up the spot of blood.

"Thus," said René, "by the force of sympathy, your love shall pierce and burn the heart of the woman whom you love."

Coconnas, as the bolder of the two, laughed, and in a low tone jested at the whole affair; but La Mole, amorous and superstitious, felt a cold dew start from the roots of his hair.

"And now," continued René, "press your lips to the lips of the figure, and say, 'Marguerite, I love thee! Come, Marguerite, come!'"

La Mole obeyed. At this moment they heard the door of the second chamber open, and light steps approach. Coconnas, curious and incredulous, drew his poniard, and fearing a rebuke from René if he raised the tapestry, cut it with his dagger, and applying his eyes to the opening, uttered a cry of astonishment, to which two female voices responded.

"What is it?" exclaimed La Mole, nearly dropping the waxen figure, which René caught from his hands.

"Why," replied Coconnas, "the Duchesse de Nevers and Madame Marguerite are there!"

"Well, then, incredulous!" replied René, with an austere smile, "do you still doubt the force of sympathy?"

La Mole was petrified on seeing the queen; Coconnas was amazed at beholding Madame de Nevers. One believed that the sorceries of René had evoked the spectre of Marguerite; the other, seeing the door half-open by which the lovely phantoms had entered, had found at once a worldly and substantial explanation of the mystery.

While La Mole was crossing himself and sighing, Coconnas, who by the aid of his strong powers of incredulity had driven away all ideas of the interference of the foul fiend, having observed, through the chink in the curtain, the astonishment of Madame de Nevers and the somewhat caustic smile of Marguerite, judged it to be a decisive moment, and understanding that a man may say in behalf of a friend what he cannot say for himself, instead of going to Madame de Nevers, went straight to Marguerite; and bending his knee, after the fashion of the great Artaxerxes as represented in the show, he cried with a voice to which the whistling of his wound gave a certain accent not without effect, "Madame, this very moment, at the demand of my friend the Comte de la Mole, Maître René evoked your spirit; and to my utter astonishment, your spirit has appeared, accompanied by an attractive body which I recommend to my friend. Shade of her Majesty the Queen of Navarre, will you desire the body of your companion to go to the other side of the curtain?"

Marguerite laughed heartily, and made a sign to Henriette, who passed to the other side.

"La Mole, my friend," said Coconnas, "be as eloquent as Demosthenes, as Cicero, as the Chancellor de l'Hôpital! and be assured that my life will be periled if you do not persuade the body of Madame de Nevers that I am her most devoted, most obedient, and most faithful servant."

"But—" stammered La Mole.

"Do as I say! And you, Maître René, watch, that we may not be interrupted."

René did as Coconnas desired him.

"*Mordi!* Monsieur," said Marguerite, "you are a man of sense. I listen to you. What have you to say?"

"I have to say to you, Madame, that the shadow of my friend (for he is a shadow, and he proves it by not uttering a single syllable), I say, then, that this shadow has supplicated me to use the faculty of speaking intelligibly which material bodies possess, and to say to you: Lovely Shadow, the gentleman who has thus lost his corporeality has lost it by the rigor of your eyes. If you were yourself, I would ask Maître René to plunge me in some sulphurous hole rather than hold such language to the daughter of Henri II, the sister of King Charles IX, and the wife of the King of Navarre; but shades are freed from all terrestrial pride, and are not annoyed by being loved. Therefore, pray of your body, Madame, to bestow a little love on poor La Mole—a soul in trouble, if ever there was one; a soul first persecuted by friendship, which three times thrust into him several inches of cold steel; a soul burned by the fire of your eyes— fire a thousand times more consuming than all the flames of Tartarus! Have pity, then, on this poor soul! Love a little what was the handsome La Mole; and if you no longer possess speech, ah! bestow a gesture, a smile upon him. The soul of my friend is a very intelligent soul, and will easily comprehend. Be kind to him, then; or, *mordi!* I will pass my sword through the body of René, in order that by virtue of the power which he possesses over spirits, he may force yours, which he has already so opportunely evoked, to do things scarcely becoming to an honest shade, such as you appear to be."

At that peroration, delivered in the character of Æneas in the realm of shades, Marguerite could not repress a great burst of laughter; but preserving the silence proper for a royal shade, she presented her hand to Coconnas, who took it tenderly in his own, and calling to La Mole, said, "Shade of my friend, come hither instantly!"

La Mole, amazed, overcome, silently obeyed.

" 'Tis well," said Coconnas, taking him by the back of the head; "and now bring the shadow of your handsome brown countenance into contact with the white and vaporous hand before you."

And Coconnas, suiting the action to the word, placed this most delicate hand to La Mole's lips, and kept them for a moment respectfully united; nor did the hand seek to withdraw itself from the sweet constraint.

Marguerite had not ceased to smile. But Madame de Nevers, still excited by the unexpected appearance of the two gentlemen, did not smile. Her uneasiness was increased by all the fire of a nascent jealousy; for to her it seemed that Coconnas should not thus neglect his own affairs for those of others. La Mole saw the contraction of her brow, caught the menacing flash of her eyes, and, intoxicated as he was by the pleasure which was overpowering his senses, he understood the danger incurred by his friend, and that it devolved upon him to attempt a rescue. Rising, therefore, and leaving the hand of Marguerite in that of Coconnas, he took himself that of the Duchesse de Nevers, and bending his knee, said—

"Loveliest, most adorable of women!—I speak of living women, and not of shades!" and he turned a look and a smile to Marguerite—"allow a soul released from its mortal trappings to repair the absence of a body fully absorbed by material friendship. M. de Coconnas, whom you see, is but a man—a man of bold and hardy frame, of flesh handsome to gaze upon perchance, but perishable, like all flesh. Yet although a stalwart and right knightly gentleman, who, as you have seen, distributes as heavy blows as were ever seen in wide France, this champion, so full of eloquence in presence of a shade, dares not speak to a woman. 'Tis therefore he has addressed the shade of the queen, charging me to speak to your lovely body, and to tell you that he lays at your feet his soul and heart; that he entreats from your divine eyes a look of pity, from your rosy fingers to beckon him with a sign, and from your musical and heavenly voice to say those words which one never forgets. He has also begged another thing, and that is that in case he should not soften you, you will pass for the second time my sword—which is a real blade, for swords have no shades but in the sunshine—pass my sword through his body; for he can live no longer if you do not authorize him to live exclusively for you."

Henriette's eyes turned from La Mole, to whom she had listened, toward Coconnas, to see if the expression of that gentleman's countenance harmonized with the amorous address of his friend. It seemed that she was satisfied, for blushing, breathless, conquered, she said to Coconnas, with a smile which disclosed a double row of pearls enclosed in coral, "Is this true?"

"Mordi!" exclaimed Coconnas, fascinated by her look, "it is true indeed. Oh, yes, Madame, it is true—true on my life; true on my death!"

"There, then," said Henriette, extending to him her hand, while her eyes proclaimed the feelings of her heart.

Coconnas and La Mole each approached his ladylove, when suddenly the door at the bottom opened, and René appeared.

"Silence!" he exclaimed, in a voice which at once damped all the ardor of the lovers; "silence!"

And they heard in the solid wall the sound of a key in a lock, and of a door grating on its hinges.

"But," said Marguerite, haughtily, "it seems to me that no one has the right to enter while we are here!"

"Not even the queen-mother?" murmured René in her ear.

Marguerite instantly rushed out by the exterior staircase, leading La Mole after her; Henriette and Coconnas, half-embracing, followed them. They all four fled, as fly at the first noise the birds we have seen engaged in loving parley on the boughs of a flowering shrub.

The Black Hens

It was time for the two couples to disappear. Catherine turned the key in the lock just as Coconnas and Madame de Nevers closed the end door, and she could hear their steps on the stairs. She cast a suspicious glance around, and then fixing her eyes on René, who stood motionless before her, said, "Who was that?"

"Only some lovers, who are quite content with the assurance I gave them, that they are really in love."

"Never mind them," said Catherine, shrugging her shoulders; "is there no one here?"

"No one but your Majesty and myself."

"Have you done what I ordered you?"

"About the two black hens?"

"Yes."

"They are ready, Madame."

"Ah," muttered Catherine, "if you were a Jew!"

"Why a Jew, Madame?"

"Because you could then read the Hebrew treatises concerning sacrifices. I have had one of them translated, and I found that it was not in the heart or liver, as among the Romans, that the Hebrews sought for omens, but in the brain, and the letters traced there by the all-powerful hand of destiny."

"Yes, Madame; so I have heard from an old rabbi."

"There are," said Catherine, "characters thus marked that reveal all the future. Only the Chaldæan seers recommend—"

"What?" asked René, seeing the queen hesitate.

"That the experiment shall be tried on the human brain, as more developed and more nearly sympathizing with the wishes of the consulter."

"Alas!" said René, "your Majesty knows it is impossible."

"Difficult, at least," said Catherine; "if we had known this at the Saint Bartholomew what a rich harvest we might have had. But I will think of it the first time anybody is to be hanged. Meantime, let us do what we can. Is the chamber of sacrifice prepared?"

"Yes, Madame."

"Let us go there."

René lighted a taper made of strange substances and emitting strong odors, and preceded Catherine into the cell. Catherine selected from among the sacrificial instruments a knife of blue steel, while René took up one of the fowls that were crouched in the corner.

"How shall we proceed?"

"We will examine the liver of the one and the brain of the other. If these two experiments lead to the same result with the former, we must needs be convinced."

"With which shall we commence?"

"With the liver."

"Very well," said René, and he fastened the bird down to two rings attached to the little altar, so that the creature, turned on its back, could only struggle, without stirring from the spot. Catherine opened its breast with a single stroke of her knife; the fowl uttered three cries, and after some convulsions, expired.

"Always three cries!" said Catherine—"three signs of death." She then opened the body. "And the liver inclining to the left, always to the left—a triple death, followed by a downfall. 'Tis terrible, René."

"We must see, Madame, whether the presages from the second correspond with those of the first."

René threw the dead fowl into a corner, and went toward the other, which, endeavoring to escape, and seeing itself pent up in a corner, flew suddenly over René's head, and in its flight extinguished the magic taper Catherine held.

"You see, René," said the queen; "so shall our race be extinguished. Death shall breathe upon it and destroy it from the face of the earth! Yet three sons! three sons!" she murmured sorrowfully.

René took from her the extinguished taper, and went to relight it. On his return, he found the hen hiding its head in a funnel.

"This time," said Catherine, "I will prevent the cries, for I will cut off the head at once."

Accordingly, as soon as the hen was bound, Catherine severed the head at a single blow; but in the last agony the beak opened three times, and then closed forever.

"See!" said Catherine, terrified, "instead of three cries, three sighs! Three, always three! All three will die. Let us now inspect the brain."

She severed the comb from the head, and carefully opening the skull, endeavored to trace a letter formed in the bloody cavities that divide the brain.

"Always so!" she cried, clasping her hands; "and this time clearer than ever. See here!" René approached.

"What is this letter?" asked Catherine.

"An H," replied René.

"How many times repeated?"

René counted. "Four," said he.

"Ay, ay! I see it! that is to say, Henri IV. Oh," cried she, casting the knife from her, "I am accursed in my posterity!"

She was terrible, that woman, pale as a corpse, lighted by the dismal taper, and clasping her bloody hands.

"He will reign!" she exclaimed with a sigh of despair; "he will reign!"

"He will reign!" repeated René, buried in meditation.

The gloomy expression of Catherine's face soon disappeared in the light of a thought which seemed to spring up in the depths of her mind.

"René," said she, without lifting her head from her breast— "René, do you recollect the terrible history of a doctor at Perugia, who killed at once, by the aid of a pomade, his daughter and his daughter's lover?"

"Yes, Madame."

"And this lover was—" continued Catherine, still meditating.

"Was King Ladislas, Madame."

"Ah, yes!" murmured she; "have you any account of this history?"

"I have an old book that mentions it," replied René.

"Well, let us go into the other chamber, and then you can show it to me."

They left the cell, the door of which René closed after him.

"Has your Majesty any other orders to give me concerning the sacrifices?"

"No, René, none; I am satisfied for the present. We will wait till we can procure the head of someone condemned; and on the day of the next execution you must arrange for it with the executioner."

René bowed and approached the shelves where the books stood; he mounted a chair and took down one of them, and handed it to the queen-mother.

Catherine sat down at a table, René placed the magic taper close to her, and by its dim and lurid glare she read a few lines.

"Good!" said she; "this is all I wanted to know."

She rose from her seat, leaving the book on the table, but bearing away the idea that had germinated in her mind, and which would ripen there. René waited respectfully, taper in hand, until the queen, who seemed about to retire, should give him additional orders or ask other questions. Catherine walked up and down several times without speaking. Then, suddenly stopping before René, and fixing on him her eyes, round and piercing as those of a bird of prey, "Confess you have given her some love-draught," said she.

"Whom?" asked René, starting.

"La Sauve."

"I, Madame?" said René; "never!"

"Never?"

"I swear it."

"There must be some magic in it, however, for he is desperately in love with her, though he is not famous for his constancy."

"Who, Madame?"

"He, Henri the accursed; he who is to succeed my three sons; he who shall one day sit upon the throne of France and be called Henry IV, and is yet the son of Jeanne d'Albret." And Catherine accompanied these last words with a sigh that made René shudder, for he thought of the famous gloves he had prepared by Catherine's order for the Queen of Navarre.

"He runs after her still, then?" said René.

"Still," replied the queen.

"I thought that the King of Navarre was quite in love with his wife now."

"All a farce, René. I know not why, but everybody is seeking to deceive me. My daughter Marguerite is leagued against me; perhaps she, too, is looking forward to her brothers' death; perhaps she hopes to be Queen of France."

"Yes, perhaps," said René, falling back into his reverie, and echoing Catherine's terrible doubt.

"Ha! we shall see," said Catherine, advancing toward the great door, for she doubtless judged it useless to descend the secret stair, after René's assurance that they were alone. René preceded her, and in a few minutes they stood in the laboratory of the perfumer.

"You promised me some fresh cosmetics for my hands and lips, René; the winter is approaching, and you know how tender my skin is."

"I have already thought of that, Madame; and I intended to bring you some tomorrow."

"I shall not be visible before nine o'clock tomorrow evening; I shall be occupied with my devotions during the day."

"I will be at the Louvre at nine o'clock, then, Madame."

"Madame de Sauve has beautiful hands and lips," said Catherine, in a careless tone. "What pomade does she use?"

"Heliotrope."

"For her hands?"

"Yes."

"What for her lips?"

"She is going to try a new composition of my invention, and of which I intended to bring your Majesty a box at the same time."

Catherine mused an instant. "She is certainly very beautiful," said she, pursuing her secret thoughts; "and this passion of the Béarnais for her is not at all surprising."

"And so devoted to your Majesty."

Catherine shrugged her shoulders. "When a woman loves," she said, "is she faithful to anyone but her lover? You must have given her some love-spell, René."

"I swear I have not, Madame."

"Well, well; we'll say no more about it. Show me this opiate you spoke of, that is to make her lips still more rosy."

René approached a shelf, and showed Catherine six small silver boxes of a round shape, ranged side by side.

"This is the only spell she ever asked me for," observed René; "it is true, as your Majesty says, I have composed it expressly for her, for her lips are so tender that the sun and wind affect them equally."

Catherine opened one of the boxes; it contained a beautiful carmine paste.

"Give me some paste for my hands, René," said she; "I will take it with me."

René took the taper, and went to seek in a private drawer what the queen asked for. As he turned, he fancied that he saw the queen conceal a box under her mantle. He was, however, too familiar with the queen's pilferings to fall into the imprudence of seeming to perceive the movement; so, wrapping the cosmetic she demanded in a paper bag ornamented with fleur-de-lis, "Here it is, Madame," he said.

"Thank you, René," returned the queen; then, after a moment's silence, "Do not give Madame de Sauve that paste for a few days; I wish to make the first trial of it myself." And she approached the door.

"Shall I have the honor of escorting your Majesty?" asked René.

"Only to the end of the bridge," replied Catherine; "my gentlemen and my litter wait for me there."

They left the house, and at the end of the Rue Barillerie four gentlemen on horseback and a plain litter were in attendance.

On his return, René's first care was to count his boxes of opiates; one was wanting.

Madame de Sauve's Chamber

Catherine had calculated rightly in supposing that Henri would speedily resume his habit of passing his evenings with Madame de Sauve. 'Tis true that the utmost caution was at first observed in making these visits, but by degrees all precaution was laid aside; and so openly did the King of Navarre avow his preference for the society of Madame de Sauve that Catherine found no difficulty in ascertaining that the Queen of Navarre continued to be nominally Marguerite, in fact, Madame de Sauve.

We have already made a slight mention of Madame de Sauve's apartments, but for the reader's better information, we will state that they were situated on the second floor of the palace, almost immediately above those occupied by Henri himself, and in common with the suites of rooms occupied by such as were officially employed by the royal family, were small, dark, and inconvenient; the door opened upon a corridor, feebly lighted by an arched window, which even in the brightest days of summer admitted only a dim light. In winter it was necessary to light a lamp there at three o'clock in the afternoon; and as the lamp contained only a given quantity of oil, it was burned out by ten o'clock in the evening, affording thus an especial security to the two lovers.

A small antechamber, hung with yellow damask; a receiving room, with hangings of blue velvet; a sleeping room, with its bed of curiously carved wood, and heavy curtains of rose-colored satin, enclosing a recess ornamented by a mirror set in silver, and by paintings representing the loves of Venus and Adonis—these were the rooms, as we should say today, the nest, of the lovely Charlotte de la Sauve, lady-in-waiting to her Majesty Queen Catherine.

A more careful examination of the apartments we have just been describing discovered a toilet provided with all the accessories of female beauty, nearly opposite to which was a small door opening into a kind of oratory, where, at an elevation of two steps from the ground, stood a carved prie-dieu. Against the walls were suspended, as if to offset the two mythological pictures we have mentioned, three or four paintings of a most elevated spiritual tone. Among these paintings, on gilded nails were hung weapons adapted to woman's use; for in these times of mysterious intrigue, women carried arms as well as men, and very frequently employed them as skillfully.

The evening on which we have introduced the reader to Madame de Sauve's apartments was the one following the scenes in which Maître René had played so conspicuous a part; and the fair Charlotte, seated beside Henri in her sleeping chamber, was eloquently discoursing of her fears and affection, and touched on the devotion she had exhibited the night succeeding the massacre of Saint Bartholomew—the night which Henri had spent in Marguerite's apartments. Henri expressed to her his gratitude. Madame de Sauve was charming that evening in her simple white dressing gown, and Henri was very grateful. In the midst of it all, Henri, though loving, was dreamy; and Madame de Sauve, who had come to cherish with all her heart that love enjoined by Catherine, watched Henri to see if his eyes were in harmony with his words.

"Come, Henri," said Madame de Sauve, "be frank. During that night spent in the cabinet of her Majesty the Queen of Navarre, with M. de la Mole at your feet, had you no regret that that worthy gentleman was between you and the chamber in which lay the queen?"

"Yes, indeed, my darling," said Henri, "for it was absolutely necessary to pass through that chamber to come to this, where I like to be, and where I am so happy at this moment."

Madame de Sauve smiled. "And you have not been there since?"

"How many times I have told you!"

"You will never return there without telling me?"

"Never."

"Would you swear it?"

"Yes, certainly, if I were still a Huguenot, but—"

"But what?"

"But the Catholic religion, whose doctrines I am now learning, teaches me that one ought never to swear."

"Gascon!" said Madame de Sauve, shaking her head.

"But in your turn, Charlotte," said Henri, "if I question you, will you answer my questions?"

"Certainly," replied the young woman. "I have nothing to hide."

"Well, Charlotte," said the king, "explain to me in good faith how it happens that after that desperate resistance before my marriage you have become less cruel to me, who am an awkward Béarnais, an absurd provincial, a prince too poor, in short, to keep in order the jewels of his crown?"

"Henri," said Charlotte, "you ask me the secret which philosophers of all lands have sought for three thousand years. Henri, never ask a woman why she loves you; be content to ask her, 'Do you love me?' "

"Do you love me, Charlotte?" asked Henri.

"I love you," replied Madame de Sauve, with a charming smile, and placing her beautiful hand in that of her lover.

Henri held her hand in his. "But," replied he, pursuing his thought, "suppose I had divined that secret which philosophers have sought in vain three thousand years—at least, as regards you, Charlotte."

Madame de Sauve blushed.

"You love me," continued Henri; "consequently I have nothing else to ask of you, and I consider myself the happiest man in the world. But, you know, to happiness there is always something lacking. Adam, in the midst of Paradise, did not find himself entirely happy, and he ate of that wretched apple which has entailed upon us the curiosity which leads every one to spend his life seeking something unknown. Tell me, sweetheart, to aid me in my own quest, did not Queen Catherine tell you, in the first place, to love me?"

"Henri," said Madame de Sauve, "speak low when you speak of the queen-mother."

"Oh!" said Henri, with a careless confidence which deceived even Madame de Sauve, "it was wise formerly to distrust her—that good mother—when we were not agreed; but now that I am the husband of her daughter—"

"The husband of Madame Marguerite!" said Madame de Sauve, blushing with jealousy.

"Speak low in your turn," said Henri. "Now that I am the husband of her daughter, we are the best friends in the world. What did they want? Apparently, that I should turn Catholic. Very well, grace has touched me, and by the favor of Saint Bartholomew I have become a Catholic. We live now harmoniously, as good Christians."

"And Queen Marguerite?"

"Queen Marguerite?" said Henri; "she is the tie that binds us."

"But you told me, Henri, that the Queen of Navarre, in gratitude for my devotion to her, had been generous to me. If you told me what was true, if that generosity for which I have felt so much gratitude is real, she is only a conventional bond of union, easy to break. You cannot, therefore, rest on that support, for you deceive no one with that pretended intimacy."

"I rest on it, nevertheless; and for three months it is the pillow on which I have slept."

"Then, Henri," cried Madame de Sauve, "you have deceived me; and Madame Marguerite is in all things your wife."

Henri smiled.

"There, Henri!" said Madame de Sauve, "there is one of those smiles which exasperate me, which inspire me sometimes with a savage impulse to tear your eyes out, king though you are."

"Then," said Henri, "I have succeeded in deceiving someone with that pretended intimacy, since you sometimes wish to tear out my eyes, king though I am, because you believe that it exists!"

"Henri! Henri!" said Madame de Sauve, "I believe that God himself does not know what you really think."

"I think, my dear," said Henri, "that in the first place Catherine told you to love me, and that then your heart told you to; and that when those two voices speak, you hear only the voice of your heart. Now, for my part, I love you, and with all my soul. And it is for that very reason that I keep from you secrets, the knowledge of which might compromise you—for the friendship of the queen is changeable; it is that of a mother-in-law."

This was not what Charlotte had counted on; it seemed to her that the veil which thickened between her and her lover whenever she attempted to sound the fathomless depths of his heart, had assumed the solidity of a wall, and separated them from each other. On receiving that answer she felt the tears coming into her eyes; and as at that moment the clock struck ten, "Sire," she said, "it is my hour for retiring, and I must be with the queen-mother very early tomorrow morning."

"You drive me away then tonight, my dear?" said Henri.

"Henri, I am sad; and you would think me cross, and would love me no longer. You see yourself that it is much better that you should withdraw."

"So be it," said Henri. "I will go if you insist on it; but, *ventre-saint-gris!* you will give me the privilege of assisting at your toilet?"

"Does not your Majesty fear the displeasure of Queen Marguerite, should you protract your departure?"

"Charlotte," answered Henri, with a serious air, "we agreed never to allude to or mention the name of the Queen of Navarre, and it seems to me as though tonight we had talked of nothing else."

Madame de Sauve arose with a sigh, and seated herself before her toilet table, while Henri, drawing a chair beside her, placed one knee on the seat, and leaning on the back, exclaimed—

"*Mon Dieu!* how many things you have here, my pretty Charlotte!—scent bottles, powders, pots of perfume, odoriferous pastilles, phials, washes!"

"It seems a great deal," said Charlotte, with a sigh; "and yet it is not enough, since with all that, I have not yet found the way to reign alone in your Majesty's heart."

"Come, come, sweetheart," interrupted Henri, "do not let us fall back on politics. What is the use of this delicately small pencil? Is it to paint the brows of my Olympian Jupiter?"

"Yes, Sire," replied Madame de Sauve, smiling; "you have hit it the first time."

"And that pretty little ivory rake?"

"It is for tracing the line of the hair."

"And this charming little silver box, with the lid so elegantly wrought and embossed?"

"That, Sire, was sent to me by René; it contains the lip salve so long promised by him, to sweeten still further the lips which your Majesty has the goodness to think sometimes are sweet enough."

Henri, as if to attest the words of the charming woman, whose face brightened in proportion as she took again the ground of co-quetry, applied his lips to those which the baroness was attentively considering in the mirror.

Charlotte put her hand on the box of which they had been speaking, doubtless to show Henri how the paste was used, when a sudden knocking at the door made the lovers start.

"Madame," said Dariole, introducing her head through the curtains that hung before the entrance to the chamber, "someone knocks."

"Go see who it is, and return quickly," said her mistress.

During the absence of the confidante, Henri and Charlotte exchanged looks of considerable alarm, the former contemplating a hasty retreat to the oratory, which had before now afforded him a safe hiding place when similarly surprised.

"Madame!" cried Dariole, "it is Maître René the perfumer."

At this name a frown darkened the brow of Henri, and his lips were involuntarily compressed.

"Shall I send him away?" asked Charlotte.

"By no means," answered Henri; "Maître René is one of those persons who do nothing without a motive; if he comes to see you he has some reason for it."

"Do you wish to conceal yourself?"

"On no account," replied Henri; "for Maître René, who knows everything, knows that I am here."

"But are there not reasons why his presence should be unpleasant to your Majesty?"

"No!" answered Henri, vainly striving to conceal his emotion, "none whatever. 'Tis true there was a coolness between us; but since the night of Saint Bartholomew, we have made up all our differences."

"Show Maître René in," said Madame de Sauve to Dariole. A moment later René entered the chamber, casting around him a quick, searching glance that took in all the chamber. He found Madame de Sauve sitting before her toilet, and Henri reclining on the sofa at the opposite end of the room, so that while the full light fell upon Charlotte, Henri remained in shadow.

"Madame," said René, with a sort of respectful freedom, "I come to offer my apologies to you."

"And wherefore, my good René?" asked Madame de Sauve, with that air of condescension which pretty women exhibit to the world of attendants who surround them and contribute to their beauty.

"Because I promised so long ago to invent a new beautifier for those lovely lips, and—"

"And have delayed fulfilling that promise until this very day—

that is what you mean, is it not, my worthy Maître René?" inquired Charlotte.

"Until today?" repeated René.

"Yes, indeed, 'twas but this evening, not long since, that I received this box from you."

"Ah, truly; I had indeed forgotten it," said René, gazing with a singular expression on the small ointment box lying on Madame de Sauve's toilet table, and which exactly resembled those in his shop. "I was sure of it!" he murmured; "and may I inquire whether you have yet made trial of it?"

"Not yet; I was just about to do so when you entered."

The countenance of René became thoughtful, a change which did not escape the observation of Henri, whom, indeed, few things escaped.

"Well, René, what are you thinking of?" inquired the king.

"Nothing, Sire," answered René. "I was but waiting till your Majesty should condescend to address me ere I took my leave of Madame."

"Come," answered Henri, smiling, "do you need words of mine to assure you that I am always happy to see you?"

René glanced around him, and seemed as though searchingly examining each nook and corner of the apartment; then, suddenly ceasing his survey, he so placed himself that he could see at the same time both Madame de Sauve and Henri. "I do not know," he said.

Warned by that admirable instinct which like a sixth sense guided him in all the earlier part of his life through the dangers which surrounded him that some strange and conflicting struggle was going on in the mind of the perfumer, Henri turned toward him; and still remaining in the shade, while the face of the Florentine was fully revealed, he said, "By the way, what brings you here so late tonight, Maître René?"

"Have I been so unfortunate as to disturb your Majesty by my visit?" replied the perfumer, taking a step backwards.

"Not in the least, but I should like to know one thing."

"What is that, Sire?"

"Did you expect to find me here?"

"I was quite sure of it."

"You were seeking me, then?"

"I am at least very happy to have met your Majesty."

"You have something to say to me?" persisted Henri.

"Perhaps, Sire," said René.

Charlotte blushed, for she feared that the revelation the perfumer seemed tempted to make to Henri might relate to her previous conduct toward the king; feigning therefore so entire an absorption in the duties of her toilet as not to have heard a word that had passed, she interrupted the conversation by exclaiming, as she opened the box of lip salve:

"René, you are a charming man; the color of this ointment is wonderful. Since you are here, I will, in your honor, make a trial of your new production in your presence."

So saying, she dipped the tip of her finger in the vermilion paste, and was just about to raise it to her lips. René shuddered. The hand of the baroness had almost touched her lips. René turned pale. Henri, concealed in deep shadow, watching with fixed and glowing eyes, lost not a movement of the one nor a shudder of the other. René became ghastly pale as the distance between the finger of Charlotte and her lips was diminished to the smallest possible space; then suddenly springing forward, he arrested her arm at the very instant that Henri arose with the same intention. The king instantly fell back on the sofa without the slightest noise.

"One moment, Madame!" cried René, with a forced smile, "but this ointment must not be used without very particular directions."

"And who will supply me with these directions?"

"I will."

"And when?"

"As soon as I have finished saying what I have to say to his Majesty the King of Navarre."

Charlotte opened her eyes, understanding nothing of the mysterious words uttered in her presence, and remained holding the pot of salve in one hand, and looking at the end of her finger tinged by the roseate ointment.

Henri arose, and moved by an idea which, like all the thoughts of the young king, had two sides—the one apparently superficial, and the other profound—went straight to Charlotte, and taking her hand, reddened as it was with the ointment, feigned to be about to carry it to his lips.

"Wait one minute!" exclaimed René, eagerly; "but an instant!

Be kind enough, Madame, to wash your beautiful hands with this Naples soap, which I quite forgot to send when I sent the ointment, and which I have had the honor of bringing to you myself." And drawing from its silver envelope a cake of greenish soap, he put it into a gilt basin, poured water upon it, and bending one knee to the ground, he presented the whole to Madame de Sauve.

"Why, really, Maître René," cried Henri, "your gallantry quite astonishes me; you put our court beaux quite out of the field!"

"Oh, what a delicious odor!" exclaimed Charlotte, rubbing her fair hands with the pearly froth that arose from the balmy soap.

René, unmoved by Henri's raillery, continued to fulfill his self-imposed duties with the most rigorous exactitude. Putting aside the basin he had held, he presented Charlotte with a towel of the most delicate texture, and when she had thoroughly dried her hands, said, "And now, Monseigneur, act according to your pleasure."

Charlotte held out her hand to Henri, who kissed it and returned to his seat, more convinced than ever that something most extraordinary was going on in the mind of the Florentine.

"Well?" said Charlotte.

The Florentine appeared as though trying to collect all his resolution, and after a short hesitation, turned toward Henri.

CHAPTER 22

"Sire, You Will Be King!"

"Sire," said René to Henri, "I wish to speak to you on a matter which has for a long time occupied my attention."

"Of perfumes?" asked Henri, with a smile.

"Well, yes, Sire; of perfumes," replied René, with a singular sign of acquiescence.

"Well, then, speak on; for it is a subject which has much interested me."

René looked at the king, endeavoring to read his impenetrable thoughts; but seeing that his scrutiny was unavailing, he continued, "One of my friends, Sire, has just arrived from Florence; this friend has devoted much of his time to astrology."

"Yes," said Henri, "I know it is a Florentine pursuit."

"And he has, in association with the leading wise men of the world, drawn the horoscopes of the principal personages in Europe."

"Indeed!" said Henri.

"And as the house of Bourbon is among the leading houses, descending, as it does, from the Comte du Clermont, fifth son of Saint Louis, your Majesty may well suppose that yours has not been forgotten."

Henri listened still more attentively. "And do you recollect this horoscope?" he said with a smile as indifferent as he could make it.

"Oh!" answered René, shaking his head; "your horoscope is one not easily forgotten."

"Really!" said Henri, with an ironical look.

"Yes, Sire; your Majesty, according to the indications of this horoscope, is called to the most brilliant destiny."

The eyes of the young prince emitted an involuntary flash, extinguished immediately in a cloud of indifference. "All these Italian oracles are flatterers," he said, "and he who flatters, lies. Are there not some who say I shall command armies?" And he burst into loud laughter. But an observer less occupied than René would have marked and comprehended the effort this laugh had cost.

"Sire," said René, coolly, "the horoscope announces better than that."

"Does it announce that at the head of one of these armies I shall gain battles?"

"Better than that, Sire."

"Well, then," said Henri, "at all events I shall be a conqueror."

"Sire, you will be king!"

"Eh, *ventre-saint-gris!*" said Henri, repressing a violent palpitation of the heart; "am I not so already?"

"Sire, my friend knows what he promises; not only will you be king, but you will reign."

"And then," said Henri, in the same strain of raillery, "your friend wants ten golden crowns, does he not, René? For such a prophecy in such times is indeed an ambitious one. Well, well, René, I am not rich; so I will give your friend five at once, and the other five when the prophecy shall be realized."

"Sire," said Madame de Sauve, "do not forget what you have already promised to Dariole, and do not overload yourself with promises."

"Madame," said Henri, "when the time comes I hope I may be treated as a king, and that everyone will be well satisfied if I keep half of my promises."

"Sire," said René, "allow me to proceed."

"What, is not that all?" said Henri. "Well, if I am an emperor, I will give double."

"Sire, my friend came from Florence with his horoscope, which he has renewed in Paris, and which gives again the same result; and he has confided to me a secret."

"A secret that concerns his Majesty?" inquired Charlotte, eagerly.

"I believe so," replied the Florentine.

"He hesitates," Henri said to himself, without offering René any help. "It appears that the affair is difficult to disclose."

"Then say it," answered the Baronne de Sauve. "What is it?"

"It is," said the Florentine, weighing each of his words well—

"it is in reference to the reports of poisoning which have been circulated for some time."

A slight expansion of the nostrils was the only indication which the King of Navarre exhibited of his increased attention upon this sudden change in the conversation.

"And does your friend, the Florentine," inquired the king, "know anything of these poisonings?"

"Yes, Sire."

"How can you confide to me a secret which is not your own, René—and particularly when it is so important?" inquired Henri, in the most natural tone he could assume.

"My friend has some advice to ask of your Majesty."

"Of me?"

"What is there astonishing in this, Sire? When my friend confided his secret to me, your Majesty was the first chief of the Calvinistic party, and M. de Condé the second."

"Well?" observed Henri.

"This friend hoped you would use your all-powerful influence with the Prince de Condé to persuade him not to be hostile toward him."

"Explain yourself, René, if you would have me comprehend you," replied Henri, without manifesting the least alteration in his features or voice.

"Sire, your Majesty will comprehend at the first word; this friend knows all the particulars of the attempt to poison Monseigneur le Prince de Condé."

"What! did they attempt to poison the Prince de Condé?" exclaimed Henri, with well-acted surprise. "Indeed! and when was that?"

René looked steadfastly at the king, and replied in these words only, "A week since, your Majesty."

"Some enemy?" inquired the king.

"Yes," replied René; "an enemy whom your Majesty knows, and who knows your Majesty."

"Yes, now I remember," said Henri; "I must have heard this spoken of, but I am ignorant of the details—which your friend would disclose to me, you say."

"Well, a scented apple was offered to the Prince de Condé, but fortunately his physician was there when it was brought to him; he took it from the messenger, and smelt it. Two days afterwards a gangrenous humor formed in his face; then an extravasation of blood, and then a cancerous sore which ate into his cheeks, were the price of his devotion, or the result of his imprudence."

"Unfortunately, being already half a Catholic," answered Henri, "I have lost all my influence over M. de Condé, and therefore your friend would gain nothing by addressing me."

"It was not only with M. de Condé that your Majesty might by your influence be useful to my friend, but with the Prince de Porcian, brother of him who was poisoned."

Henri understood that René was anxious to make some point that he could not yet see clearly.

"What!" observed the king, "do you also know the details of the poisoning of the Prince de Porcian?"

"Yes," was the reply. "They knew that he burned every night a lamp near his bed; they poisoned the oil, and he was stifled by the odor."

Henri clasped his hands moist with perspiration. "Thus, then," he replied, "he whom you term your friend knows not only the details of this poisoning, but the author of it also?"

"Yes; and that is why he wished to ascertain from you if you had sufficient influence with the present Prince de Porcian to induce him to pardon the murderer of his brother?"

"Unfortunately," replied Henri, "being still half Huguenot, I have no influence over the Prince de Porcian; your friend was wrong therefore to address me."

"But what do you think of the inclinations of M. le Prince de Condé and M. de Porcian?"

"How should I know their inclinations, René? God has not, to my knowledge, given me the privilege of reading hearts."

"Your Majesty may ask yourself the question," said the Florentine, calmly—"has there not been in your Majesty's life some event so gloomy that it may serve as a test of clemency; so painful that it may be a touchstone for generosity?"

These words were pronounced in a tone that made Charlotte shudder. The allusion was so direct, so manifest, that the young lady turned aside to hide her flushed face and avoid Henri's look.

Henri made a powerful effort over himself, smoothed his brow, which during the Florentine's address had been heavy with menace, and throwing off the noble filial sorrow which oppressed him, he said with an air of vague meditation, "In my life, a gloomy event! no, René, no; I only recollect the folly and recklessness of my youth mixed with the necessities, more or less cruel, imposed by the demands of nature and the discipline of life."

René mastered himself in his turn and directed his glance from Henri to Charlotte, as if to excite the one and restrain the other—for Charlotte, going toward her toilet to conceal her weariness of this conversation, again extended her hand toward the box of ointment.

"But if, Sire, you were the brother of the Prince de Porcian, or the son of the Prince de Condé, and your brother had been poisoned, or your father assassinated?"

Charlotte uttered a cry, and again was about to apply the ointment to her lips. René saw the movement, but this time sought neither by word nor by gesture to arrest it; but he cried out, "In Heaven's name, answer, Sire! If you were in their place, what would you do?"

Henri collected himself, wiped with tremulous hand his forehead bedewed with drops of cold perspiration, and raising his figure to its full height, replied in the midst of the breathless silence of René and Charlotte, "If I were in their place, and were sure of being king—that is to say, of representing God on earth—I would do like God: I would forgive!"

"Madame," exclaimed René, snatching the opiate from Madame de Sauve's hands—"Madame, give me that box! I see that my assistant made a mistake in bringing it to you; tomorrow I will send you another."

CHAPTER 23

A New Convert

On the following day there was to be a hunt in the forest of St. Germain. Henri had desired that there should be ready, at eight o'-clock in the morning, saddled and bridled, a small horse of the Béarn breed, which he intended as a present for Madame de Sauve, but which he first wished to try. The horse was duly brought; and as the clock struck eight, Henri descended.

The horse, full of life and fire, in spite of its small size, was plunging about in the courtyard. It was cold, and a slight hoarfrost covered the ground. Henri was about to cross the courtyard in order to reach the stables, where the horse and his groom were waiting, when, as he passed before a Swiss soldier who was on guard at the door, the sentinel presented arms to him, saying, "God preserve his Majesty the King of Navarre!"

At this wish, and particularly the accent and emphasis of the voice that uttered it, the Béarnais started and took a step backward. "Mouy!" he murmured.

"Yes, Sire, Mouy."

"And what are you doing here?"

"Seeking you."

"What would you?"

"I must speak to your Majesty!"

"Rash man!" said the king, going close to him, "do you know that you risk your head?"

"I know it."

"Well?"

"Well, I am here."

Henri turned slightly pale, for he knew that he shared the danger incurred by the zealous young man. He therefore looked anxiously around, and recoiled a second time, no less quickly than before. He saw the Duc d'Alençon at a window. Then, changing his manner, Henri took the musket from Mouy, and appeared to be examining it.

"Mouy," he said, "it is some very powerful motive that makes you come thus to throw yourself into the wolf's throat."

"It is, Sire, and for eight days I have been on the watch. It was only yesterday I learned that your Majesty meant to try this horse this morning, and I took my post accordingly at this door of the Louvre."

"Why under this costume?"

"The captain of the company is a Protestant, and one of my friends."

"Take your musket, and continue your guard. We are watched. As I return, I will endeavor to say a word to you; but if I do not speak to you, do not stop me. Adieu!"

Mouy resumed his measured tread, and Henri advanced toward the horse.

"What is that pretty creature?" inquired the Duc d'Alençon from his window.

"A horse I plan to try this morning."

"But it is not a man's horse."

"It is intended for a pretty woman."

"Be careful, Henri—you are about to commit an imprudence; for we shall see this pretty woman at the chase, and if I do not know whose chevalier you are, I shall at least learn whose esquire you may be."

"Eh, *mon Dieu!* you will not know," said Henri, with his pretended simplicity; "for this pretty woman being very unwell this morning, she cannot ride today." And he sprang into the saddle.

"Ah, bah!" said D'Alençon, laughing; "poor Madame de Sauve!"

"François! François! it is you who are indiscreet."

"And what ails the lovely Charlotte?" inquired the duke.

"Why," answered Henri, "I hardly know. A kind of heaviness in the head, as Dariole informed me; a weakness in all her limbs—a general feebleness, in short."

"And will that prevent you from accompanying us?" inquired D'Alençon.

"Why should it?" was Henri's reply. "You know how madly I love a hunt, and that nothing would make me miss one."

"You will miss this, however, Henri," replied the duke, after turning round and speaking to someone whom Henri could not see, "for I learn from his Majesty that the chase cannot take place."

"Bah!" said Henri, with the most disappointed air in the world; "why not?"

"Very important letters have arrived from M. de Nevers; and the king, the queen-mother, and my brother the Duc d'Anjou are in council."

"Ah, ah!" said Henri to himself, "is there any news from Poland?" Then he added aloud, "In that case it is useless for me to run any more risk on this slippery ground. Au revoir, Brother." Then pulling his horse up short near Mouy, "My friend," he said, "call one of your comrades to finish your guard. Help the groom to take the saddle off my horse, put it on your head, and carry it to the goldsmith of the royal stable; there is some embroidery to do to it, which he had not time to finish. You can bring me back his answer."

Mouy hastily obeyed, for the Duc d'Alençon had disappeared from his window, and it was evident that he had conceived some suspicion. Scarcely, indeed, had the Huguenot chief left the wicket when the duke appeared. A real Swiss had taken Mouy's place.

D'Alençon looked attentively at the new sentinel, then turning to Henri, he said, "This is not the man with whom you were conversing just now, is it, Brother?"

"The other was a young fellow of my house, for whom I obtained a post among the Swiss. I gave him a commission which he has gone to execute."

"Ah!" said the duke, as if satisfied with the answer; "and how is Marguerite?"

"I am just going to inquire, Brother."

"Haven't you seen her since yesterday?"

"No. I went last night at eleven o'clock; but Gillonne told me she was much fatigued and asleep."

"You will not find her in her apartments; she has gone out."

"Yes," replied Henri, "most likely. She was going to the Convent of the Annonciade."

There was no way of pushing the conversation further, as Henri appeared determined only to reply. The two brothers-in-law then separated—the Duc d'Alençon to go and hear the news, as he said, and the King of Navarre to return to his apartments. He had been there hardly five minutes when he heard someone knocking.

"Who is there?" he asked.

"Sire," replied a voice which Henri recognized as that of Mouy, "it is the answer from the goldsmith."

Henri, visibly agitated, admitted the young man, and closed the door behind him. "It is you, Mouy!" said he. "I hoped that you would reflect."

"Sire," replied Mouy, "I have been reflecting for three months—that is enough; now it is time to act."

Henri made a movement of uneasiness.

"Fear nothing, Sire—we are alone; and I will be quick, for time is very precious. Your Majesty may now by a single word restore to us all that we have lost for our holy religion during this disastrous year. Let us be explicit; let us be brief; let us be frank."

"I listen, my gallant Mouy," replied the king, seeing that it was impossible any longer to avoid an explanation.

"Is it true that your Majesty has abjured the Protestant religion?"

"It is true," said Henri.

"Yes; but is it an abjuration of the lips or of the heart?"

"We are always grateful to God when he has saved our life," replied Henri, evading the question, as he was accustomed to do in such cases; "and God has visibly spared me in that cruel danger."

"But, Sire," continued Mouy, "confess that your abjuration is not a matter of conviction, but of calculation. You have abjured that the king may let you live, and not because God has spared your life."

"Whatever may be the cause of my conversion, Mouy," answered Henri, "I am not the less a Catholic."

"Yes; but shall you always continue to be one? On the first opportunity of resuming freedom of life and of conscience, will you not resume it? Well, this occasion presents itself at this moment. Rochelle is insurgent; Roussillon and Béarn only await the signal to act; and in Guienne all is ripe for revolt. Only avow that you were a Catholic on compulsion, and I will answer for all the rest."

"My dear Mouy, a gentleman of my birth is never forced; what I have done, I have done freely."

"But, Sire," continued the young man, his heart oppressed at this unexpected resistance; "you do not reflect that in acting thus you abandon us—you betray us!"

Henri remained unmoved.

"Yes," Mouy continued, "you betray us, Sire; for very many of us have come at the peril of our lives to save your honor and liberty. We have prepared everything to give you a throne, Sire—not only liberty, but power, a throne of your choice; for in two months you may choose between France and Navarre."

"Mouy," replied Henri, looking downwards for an instant to conceal the joy that sparkled in his eyes—"Mouy, I am safe. I am a Catholic; I am the husband of Marguerite; I am the brother of King Charles; I am son-in-law of my good mother Catherine; and when, Mouy, I took all these relations upon me, I not only calculated the chances, but also the obligations."

"But, Sire," replied Mouy, "what am I to believe? They say that your marriage is incomplete; they say that you are free in your own heart; they say that Catherine's hatred—"

"Lies, lies, lies all!" interrupted the Béarnais, hastily; "you have been impudently deceived, my friend. My dearest Marguerite is indeed my wife; Catherine is truly my mother; King Charles IX is really the lord and master of my life and of my heart."

Mouy started, and a smile almost contemptuous passed over his lips. "Then, Sire," said he, dropping his arms with an air of discouragement, and endeavoring to fathom with his eyes that soul full of mystery, "this is the answer I shall bear to my brothers in arms. I shall say that the King of Navarre extends his hand and gives his heart to those who cut our throats; I shall say that he has become the flatterer of the queen-mother, and the friend of Maurevel."

"My dear Mouy," said Henri, "the king is just breaking up the council; and I must go and learn what are the important reasons which have postponed the hunt. Adieu! imitate me, my friend; renounce politics, swear allegiance to the king, and take the Mass." And Henri led, or rather pushed the young man to the door of his antechamber, while Mouy's amazement was fast giving way to rage.

Scarcely was the door closed, when, unable to resist his desire of visiting his vengeance on something for want of somebody,

Mouy squeezed his hat between his hands, threw it on the ground, and trampled it under foot, as a bull does the cloak of a matador, " 'Sdeath!" he cried, "he is a cowardly prince, and I have a great mind to kill myself on this very spot, that my blood may forever stain him and his name."

"Hush, M. de Mouy!" said a voice which came from behind a half-opened door; "hush! or someone else will hear you besides myself."

Mouy turned round suddenly, and perceived the Duc d'Alençon, enveloped in his mantle, and thrusting his pale face into the corridor to ascertain if he and Mouy were really alone.

"The Duc d'Alençon!" cried Mouy; "then I am lost!"

"On the contrary," said the prince, in a subdued tone, "you have perchance found that which you have been seeking; and in proof of this, I would not have you kill yourself here, as you propose. Believe me, your blood may be better employed than in reddening the threshold of the King of Navarre." And the duke opened wide the door which had been hitherto ajar.

"This chamber belongs to two of my gentlemen," said the duke; "and no one will come to seek you here, so we may converse at our ease. Come, Monsieur."

"I am here, Monseigneur," said the conspirator, stupefied; and he entered the chamber, the duke closing the door after him quickly and securely.

Mouy entered, furious, enraged, and desperate; but gradually the cold and steady gaze of the young Duc François had the effect on the young Huguenot captain that ice has upon intoxication.

"M. de Mouy," said François, "I thought I recognized you in spite of your disguise, as you presented arms to my brother Henri. Well, Mouy, you are not satisfied, then, with the King of Navarre?"

"Monseigneur!"

"Come, come! speak frankly to me, and you may find I am your friend."

"You, Monseigneur!"

"Yes, I; but speak."

"I know not what to say to your Highness. What I had to tell the King of Navarre touched on interests impossible to be understood by you; besides," added Mouy, with a manner which he strove to render indifferent, "it was about trifles."

"Trifles!" exclaimed the duke.

"Yes, Monseigneur."

"Trifles! when for this you have exposed your life by returning to the Louvre, when you well know your head is worth its weight in gold! For it is well known that you, like the King of Navarre and the Prince de Condé, are one of the principal leaders of the Huguenots."

"If you think so, Monsigneur, act toward me as the brother of King Charles and the son of Queen Catherine."

"Why would you have me act so, when I tell you I am your friend? Tell me but the truth, and—"

"Monseigneur, I swear to you—"

"Do not swear, Monsieur; the Reformed religion forbids oaths, and especially false ones."

Mouy frowned.

"I tell you I know all," continued the duke.

Mouy was still silent.

"Do you doubt it?" proceeded the prince, with earnestness. "Well, then, my dear Mouy, I must convince you, and you will see if I am mistaken. Have you, or not, proposed to my brother-in-law Henri, there, just now"—and the duke extended his hand toward Henri's apartments—"your aid, and that of your allies, to reestablish him in his kingdom of Navarre?"

Mouy looked at the duke in amazement.

"Propositions which he refused in alarm?"

Mouy remained stupefied.

"Did you not then invoke your ancient friendship, the remembrance of your common religion? Did you not then seek to lure on the King of Navarre by a very brilliant hope and prospect, so brilliant that he was dazzled at it—the hope of obtaining the crown of France? Eh! am I well informed? Was it not this that you came to propose to the Béarnais?"

"Monseigneur," exclaimed Mouy, "it is so precisely all that occurred that I ask myself at this moment whether I ought not to say to your Highness that you lie, provoke you in this very chamber to a combat without mercy, and so by the death of both, assure the extinction of this terrible secret."

"Gently, my brave Mouy, gently," replied D'Alençon, without changing countenance, or making the slightest motion at this menace; "this secret will be better kept between us two if we both live than if one of us were to die. Listen to me, and do not thus grip the handle of your sword; for the third time I tell you, you are with a friend. Reply, then, as to a friend. Tell me, did not the King of Navarre refuse your offers?"

"He did, Monseigneur; and I confess it, because the avowal can compromise no one but myself."

"And are you still of the same opinion you were when you quitted my brother Henri's chamber, and said he was a cowardly prince, and unworthy any longer to remain your leader?"

"I am, Monseigneur, and more so than ever."

"Well, then, M. de Mouy, am I, the third son of Henri II—I, a son of France—am I good enough to command your soldiers? Let us see. Do you think me so loyal that you can rely on my word?"

"You, Monseigneur! you the chief of the Huguenots!"

"Why not? This is the epoch of conversions, as you know; and if Henri has become a Catholic, why may not I turn Protestant?"

"Unquestionably, Monseigneur; but perhaps you will explain to me—"

"Nothing more simple; I will unfold to you in two words everybody's politics. My brother Charles kills the Huguenots that he may reign more absolutely. My brother D'Anjou lets him kill them, because he is to succeed my brother Charles, and, as you know, my brother Charles is often ill. But I, it is very different with me, who will never reign over France—at least, I have two elder brothers before me—with me, whom the hatred of my mother and brothers, more even than the law of nature, alienates from the throne; with me, who see before me no family affection, no glory, no kingdom; with me, who yet have a heart as noble as my brothers. And therefore I, Mouy, would fain cut myself out a throne with my sword in this France which they are staining with gore. And this is what I would do, Mouy, listen: I would be King of Navarre, not by right of birth, but by election! And observe well, you can have no objection to make me so, for I am no usurper; my brother refuses your offers, and, buried in torpor, declares openly that this kingdom of Navarre is but a fiction. With Henri de Béarn, you have nothing now in common; with me you may have a sword and a name. François d'Alençon, son of France, can protect all his companions or all his accomplices, as you may please to call them. Well, then! what say you to this offer, M. de Mouy?"

"I say that it bewilders me, Monseigneur."

"Mouy, Mouy, we shall have many obstacles to overcome; do not, then, show yourself at the start so scrupulous and difficult with the son of a king and the brother of a king, who comes to you."

"Monseigneur, the thing should be done at once if I were the only person to decide. But we have a council; and how brilliant soever may be the offer, perhaps the leaders will not accede to it without condition."

"That is another matter; and the reply is that of an honest heart and a prudent mind. By the way in which I have acted, Mouy, you must see that I am frank and honorable; treat me, then, on your part, like a man you esteem, and not a prince whom you would flatter. Mouy, have I any chance?"

"On my word, Monseigneur, and since your Highness desires to have my opinion, you have every chance, since the King of Navarre refuses the offer I have just made him. But I repeat to you, Monseigneur, it is indispensable that I should have a consultation with our leaders.

"Of course, Monsieur," was D'Alençon's reply; "but when shall I have the answer?"

Mouy considered the prince with silent attention, and then coming to a resolution, said, "Monseigneur, give me your hand; it is necessary that the hand of a son of France should touch mine, to be sure I shall not be betrayed."

The duke not only extended his hand to Mouy, but seized his and clasped it in his own.

"Now, Monseigneur, I am assured," said the young Huguenot; "if we should be betrayed I should acquit you of all participation. Otherwise, Monseigneur, however little you were concerned in such treachery, you would be dishonored."

"Why do you say that, Mouy, before telling me when you will bring me the reply of your chiefs?"

"Because, Monseigneur, in asking when the answer shall be given, you ask me in that question where our leaders are; and if I replied, 'This evening,' you would know that the chiefs were concealed in Paris." And as he said these words, with a gesture of distrust, Mouy fixed his piercing eye on the face of the false and vacillating young prince.

"What! you have still your doubts, Mouy? but yet what right have I to your confidence at a first interview! You will know me better by and by. You say this evening, then, M. de Mouy?"

"Yes, Monseigneur, for time presses. This evening. But where?"

"Here, in the Louvre. In this chamber, if that suits you."

"This chamber is occupied?" said Mouy, looking at the two beds placed opposite to each other.

"By two of my gentlemen, yes."

"Monseigneur, it seems to me imprudent for me to return to the Louvre."

"Why so?"

"Because others may recognize me as well as your Highness. Yet if you will accord me a safe-conduct I will return to the Louvre."

"Mouy," replied the duke, "my safe-conduct seized on your person would destroy me, and would not save you; I cannot. The least evidence of concert between us, before my mother or brothers, would cost me my life. Make, therefore, another trial of your own courage. I will guarantee your safety; try on my word what you tried without my brother's word. Come to the Louvre this evening."

"But how?"

"I think I see the means before me; here!"

And the duke saw on the bed La Mole's outer garment spread out—a magnificent cherry-colored cloak, embroidered with gold, also a hat with a white plume, surrounded by a string of pearls, with gold and silver between them, and a gray satin doublet worked with gold.

"Do you see this cloak, feather, and doublet?" said the duke. "They belong to M. de la Mole, one of my gentlemen, and a fop of the first water. This dress creates quite a sensation at court, and M. de la Mole is recognized a hundred yards off when he wears it. I will give you his tailor's address, and if you pay him twice what it is worth he will bring you a similar suit this evening. Remember the name—M. de la Mole."

The duke had scarcely done speaking when a step was heard of someone approaching, and a key was turned in the lock of the door.

"Who's there?" inquired the duke, hastening toward the door, which he secured with the bolt.

"Pardieu!" replied a voice from without, "that is a very odd question; who are you? It is rather pleasant, i' faith, to come to one's own room and be asked, 'Who's there?'"

"Oh! it is you, M. de la Mole?"

"Of course it is. But who are you?"

D'Alençon turned round suddenly, and said to Mouy, "Do you know M. de la Mole?"

"No, Monseigneur."

"Does he know you?"

"I should say no."

"Then all will go well. Just appear to be looking out of the window."

Mouy obeyed, and the duke opening the door, La Mole entered hastily, but when he saw the duke he retreated, surprised, and saying, "Monseigneur the Duke! Your pardon; your pardon, Monseigneur!"

"It needs not, Monsieur; I wished to see a person, and made use of your chamber."

"Pray do, Monseigneur. But allow me to take my cloak and hat, for I lost both last night on the Quai de la Grève where I was attacked by thieves."

"Really! You must have had an encounter with determined robbers."

The duke handed the young gentleman the desired articles, and La Mole retired to dress himself in the antechamber. On his return in a few moments, "Has your Highness heard or seen anything of the Comte de Coconnas?" he asked.

"No, Monsieur the Count; and yet he should have been on duty this morning."

"Then they have murdered him!" said La Mole to himself, as he made his obeisance and rushed out again.

The duke listened to his retreating footsteps, and then opening the door, said to Mouy, "Look at him, and try to imitate his easy and peculiar gesture."

"I will do my best," replied Mouy; "unfortunately I am not a fine gentleman, but only a soldier."

"I shall expect you before midnight in this corridor. If the chamber of my gentlemen is free, I will receive you here; if not, we will find another."

"Tonight, before midnight!"

"Ah! by the way, Mouy, swing your right arm as you walk; it is a peculiarity of M. de la Mole."

CHAPTER 24

The Rue Tizon and the Rue Cloche Percée

La Mole ran out of the Louvre, and went in search of poor Coconnas. First he went to the Rue de l'Arbre Sec, to the house of Maître la Hurière, for he remembered that he had often quoted to the Piedmontese a certain Latin saying which went to show that Love, Bacchus, and Ceres are divinities of the first importance; and he hoped that Coconnas, to follow out the Roman aphorism, would have resorted to the Belle Etoile, after a night probably as fully occupied by him as it had been by La Mole. But La Mole found nothing there but a breakfast offered with tolerably good grace, in recognition of an assumed obligation, and to which, despite his inquietude, he did ample justice.

His appetite appeased, La Mole went along the Seine. Arrived at the Quai de la Grève, he recognized the spot where he had been stopped three or four hours before, and found on the field of battle a fragment of his hat-plume. La Mole had ten feathers, each handsomer than the other; he stopped, nevertheless, to pick up this, or rather the only fragment that remained of it, and was looking at it with a piteous air when an authoritative voice bade him stand aside. La Mole looked up and perceived a litter, preceded by two pages, and followed by an esquire. La Mole thought he recognized the litter, and stood on one side. He was not mistaken.

"M. de la Mole?" said a sweet voice from the litter, while a hand, white and soft as satin, put aside the curtains.

"Yes, it is I, Madame," replied La Mole, bowing.

"M. de la Mole with a plume in his hand," said the lady. "Are you in love, then, and do you seek here lost traces of your mistress?"

"Yes, Madame," returned La Mole; "I am in love, and to desperation. As for these relics, they are my own, though not those I seek. But permit me to inquire after your Majesty's health."

"Excellent—never better; which is probably owing to the fact that I passed the night in a convent."

"Ah, in a convent!" said La Mole, looking at Marguerite with a singular expression.

"Yes; what is there so astonishing in that?"

"May I venture to inquire in what convent?"

"Certainly; I make no mystery of it—at the Convent of the Annonciade. But what are you doing here, with so wild an air?"

"Madame, I also spent the night in and near the same convent. This morning I am searching for my friend, and in looking for him I find this plume."

"Which belongs to him? You really alarm me for him; the place has a bad reputation."

"Your Majesty may be reassured; the plume is mine. I lost it here this morning, at about half-past five, in escaping from four bandits who tried, I think, to assassinate me."

Marguerite suppressed an exclamation of terror. "Oh, tell me all about it!" she said.

"A simple matter, Madame. It was as I said, about half-past five—"

"And at half-past five you were already out?"

"Nay, Madame, I had not yet gone home."

"Ah!" said Marguerite, with a smile that to everyone else would have seemed malicious, but which La Mole thought adorable, "returning home so late! You are rightly served."

"I do not complain, your Majesty," said La Mole; "and had I been killed, I should still have enjoyed more happiness than I deserve. But, in short, I was returning late—or early, if your Majesty will have it so—from that blessed convent where I had spent the night, when four scoundrels rushed on me, armed with long knives. Grotesque, is it not, Madame? I was obliged to run, for I had forgotten my sword."

"Oh, I understand," said Marguerite, with an exquisite air of simplicity; "you are going to fetch your sword."

La Mole looked at Marguerite doubtingly. "Madame," said he, "I should be glad to return thither, for my sword is an excellent blade; but I do not know where the house is."

"What, Monsieur!" said Marguerite, "you do not know where the house is where you spent the night?"

"No, Madame; Satan exterminate me if I have the least idea!"

"Oh! that is very strange. Your story, then, is quite a romance?"

"A veritable romance, Madame."

"Relate it to me."

"It is somewhat long."

"No matter, I have plenty of time."

"And very incredible."

"Go on, I am very credulous."

"Your Majesty commands me?"

"Yes, if necessary."

"I obey; last night, after leaving two adorable women with whom we had spent the evening, on Pont St. Michel, we supped at Maître la Hurière's."

"In the first place," asked Marguerite, with a beautiful simplicity, "who is Maître la Hurière?"

"Maître la Hurière, Madame," answered La Mole, with another look of doubt at the queen, "is the landlord of the Belle Etoile, Rue de l'Arbre Sec."

"Ah, I understand; well, you were supping at La Hurière's—with your friend Coconnas, no doubt?"

"Yes, Madame, with my friend Coconnas, when a man entered, and gave each of us a letter."

"Alike?"

"Exactly."

"And which contained—"

"But one line: 'You are waited for in the Rue St. Antoine, opposite the Rue de Jouy.' "

"And no signature?"

"None, but three words—three delicious words that promised a triple happiness."

"And what were these three words?"

"Eros—Cupido—Amor."

"Three soft, pretty names, by my faith; and did they fulfill what they promised?"

"Oh, more, Madame!" cried La Mole, animatedly, "a hundredfold more!"

"Continue. I am anxious to know what awaited you at the Rue St. Antoine."

"Two duennas, who stipulated that our eyes should be bandaged. Your Majesty may imagine we made no great difficulty. My guide led me to the right, my friend's led him to the left."

"And then?" asked Marguerite.

"I do not know where they took my friend, perhaps to the infernal regions," said La Mole; "but I was taken to Paradise."

"And whence your too great inquisitiveness no doubt got you expelled."

"Exactly so; your Majesty has the gift of divination. I waited until day should come to show me where I was, when the duenna entered, blindfolded me again, and led me away out of the house, and some hundred paces on, and then made me promise not to take off the bandage till I had counted fifty. I counted fifty, and then, on taking off the handkerchief, found myself in the Rue St. Antoine, opposite the Rue de Jouy."

"And then—"

"Then, Madame, I started on my return so joyous that I was taken off my guard by the four scoundrels from whom I escaped with so much difficulty. Now, Madame, on finding here a fragment of my plume, my heart bounded, and I picked up the fragment, intending to cherish it as a souvenir of that happy night. But one thing disquiets me—what can have become of my friend?"

"He is not at the Louvre, then?"

"Alas, no; and I have sought him at the Belle Etoile, at the tennis court, and everywhere, but there is no Annibal to be found."

As he said this, and accompanied his lamentation by throwing up his arms, La Mole disclosed his doublet, which was torn and cut in several places.

"Why, you have been completely riddled!" said Marguerite.

"Riddled—that is the exact word," said La Mole, not sorry to make the most of the danger he had incurred. "See, Madame, see!"

"Why did you not change your doublet at the Louvre when you got back?"

"Why," said La Mole, "because there was someone in my chamber."

"How, someone in your chamber?" said Marguerite, whose eyes expressed the greatest astonishment. "Who?"

"His Highness—"

"Hush!" said Marguerite.

The young man obeyed.

"Qui ad lecticam meam stant?" ("Who are with my litter?")

"Duo pueri et unus eques." ("Two pages and a groom.")

"Optime, barbari," said she. *"Dic, Moles, quem inveneris in cubiculo tuo?"* ("Good, they won't understand us. Tell me, La Mole, whom did you find in your chamber?")

"Franciscum ducem." ("Duc François.")

"Agentem?" ("What was he doing?")

"Nescio quid." ("I don't know.")

"Quocum?" ("Who was with him?")

"Cum ignoto." ("A man I don't know.")

"Singular," said Marguerite. "So you have not found Coconnas?" she continued, evidently with her mind elsewhere.

"No, Madame, and I am dying with anxiety."

"Well," said Marguerite, "I will not further delay your search; but I have an idea he will be found before long. But, nevertheless, go and look for him."

And the queen placed her finger on her lip. Now, as Marguerite had not communicated any secret to La Mole, he comprehended that this charming sign must have another meaning.

The cortège pursued its way; and La Mole proceeded along the quay, till he came to the Rue du Long Pont, which took him into the Rue St. Antoine.

He stopped opposite the Rue de Jouy.

It was there, the previous evening, that the duennas had blindfolded Coconnas and himself. He well remembered that he had turned to the right and counted twenty paces; he did so again, and found himself opposite a house, or rather a wall, with a house behind it. In the middle of the wall was a door studded with large nails and provided with loopholes.

The house was in the Rue Cloche Percée—a little narrow street that starts from the Rue St. Antoine, and ends in the Rue du Roi de Sicile.

"Sangbleu!" said La Mole. "This is it; I could swear to it. In reaching out my hand as I left the house, I touched the nails; then I went down two steps. That man who ran by crying 'Help!' and who was killed in the Rue du Roi de Sicile, passed at the moment that I put my foot on the first step. Let us see."

La Mole knocked at the door. A porter with a large mustache opened it.

"*Was ist das?*" said he. ("What's that?")

"Ah," said La Mole to himself, "we are German, it seems. My friend," continued he, "I want my sword, which I left here last night."

"*Ich verstehe nicht,*" said the porter. ("I don't understand you.")

"My sword—"

"*Ich verstehe nicht.*"

"—That I left—"

"*Ich verstehe nicht.*"

—"In this house, where I passed the night."

"*Gehe zum Teufel.*" ("Go to the devil!") And he shut the door in his face.

"*Mordieu!*" said La Mole, "had I my sword, I would pass it cheerfully through that fellow's body. But I haven't it, and the matter must lie over to some other day."

La Mole then struck into the Rue du Roi de Sicile, turned to the right, counted fifty paces, turned to the right again, and found himself in the Rue Tizon, a little street parallel with the Rue Cloche Percée, and exactly like it. The resemblance went farther. Scarcely had he taken thirty steps when he found the little door studded with nails, the narrow loopholes, the two steps, and the wall.

La Mole then reflected that he might have mistaken his right for his left, and he knocked at this door. But this time he knocked in vain; no one opened the door. He walked round the same way several times, and then arrived at the natural conclusion that the house had two entrances—one in the Rue Tizon, the other in the Rue Cloche Percée. But this reasoning, though logical, did not restore to him his sword or his friend.

He had for an instant an idea of purchasing another rapier, and pinking the rascally porter who persisted in speaking only German; but he was checked by the reflection that if he belonged to Marguerite she doubtless had her reasons for selecting him, and would be vexed were she deprived of him. Now La Mole would not for the world have done anything to vex Marguerite. To avoid the temptation he returned to the Louvre.

This time his apartment was empty; and being in no small haste to change his doublet, which was somewhat dilapidated, he hastened to the bed to take down his fine gray satin one, when to his intense amazement he saw lying near it the identical sword he had left in the Rue Cloche Percée. He took it and examined it; it was indeed the same.

"Ah, ah!" said he, "there is some magic in this." Then, with a sigh, "Ah, if Coconnas would come back like this sword!"

Two or three hours afterwards the door in the Rue Tizon opened. It was five o'clock, and consequently dark. A woman enveloped in a long furred mantle, accompanied by a servant, came out, glided rapidly into the Rue du Roi de Sicile, knocked at a little door of the Hôtel d'Argenson, entered the hotel, left it again by the great gate that opens into the Vieille Rue du Temple, reached a private door of the Hôtel de Guise, opened it with a passkey, and disappeared.

Half an hour afterwards a young man, his eyes bandaged, came out of the same door of the same house, led by a woman, who took him to the corner of the Rue Geoffroy Lasnier and de la Mortellerie. There she bade him count fifty paces, and then take off the handkerchief. The young man complied scrupulously with these directions, and at the prescribed number took off the bandage.

"Mordi!" cried he, "I'll be hanged if I know where I am! Six o'clock! Why, where can La Mole be? I'll run to the Louvre; I shall perhaps hear of him there."

So saying, Coconnas started off, running, and arrived at the Louvre in less time than an ordinary horse would have needed to cover that distance. He questioned the Swiss and the sentinel. The Swiss thought he had seen M. de la Mole enter in the morning; but he had not seen him go out. The sentinel had been on guard only an hour and a half and had seen nothing.

Coconnas ran upstairs, entered La Mole's room, and found nothing but his torn doublet, which redoubled his anxiety. He then betook himself to La Hurière's. La Hurière had seen M. de la Mole; M. de la Mole had breakfasted there. Reassured by these tidings, Coconnas ordered supper, which occupied him until eight o'clock, when, recruited by a good meal and two bottles of wine, he again started in search of his friend.

For an hour Coconnas traversed the streets near the Quai de la Grève, the Rue St. Antoine, and the Rues Tizon and Cloche Percée. At last he returned to the Louvre, determined to watch under the gate there until La Mole's return.

He was not a hundred paces from the Louvre, and was assisting a woman to rise whose husband he had upset just before, when by the light of a large lamp he perceived the cherry-velvet mantle and white plume of his friend, who, like a ghost, disappeared beneath the portal of the Louvre. The cherry-colored mantle was too well known to be for an instant mistaken.

"*Mordi!*" cried Coconnas; "it is he at last! Eh, La Mole! Why does he not answer? Fortunately my legs are as good as my voice."

He dashed after Cherry Mantle, but only in time to see him, as he entered the court, disappear in the vestibule.

"La Mole!" cried Coconnas; "stop! stop! it is I, Coconnas! Why in the devil are you in such haste? Are you running away from me, perchance?"

Cherry Mantle mounted the second story as if he had wings.

"Ah! you do not wish to hear!" cried Coconnas. "Ah, you are angry with me! Well, go to the devil, *mordi!* as for me I can go no farther."

Coconnas ceased the pursuit, but followed with his eyes the fugitive, who now arrived at the apartments of the Queen of Navarre; suddenly a woman appeared and took Cherry Mantle by the hand.

"Oh," said Coconnas, "that's Queen Marguerite; now I know why he would not wait."

After a few whispered words, Cherry Mantle followed the queen into her apartments.

"Good!" said Coconnas, "I was not mistaken. There are times when your best friend is in the way; this is one, and I'll not interrupt the old fellow." He ascended the stairs quietly, and sat down on a bench covered with velvet, saying, "I'll stop here for him; or stay, he's with the queen, and I may stop long enough. It is cold here, *mordi!* and I may just as well wait for him in his room; he must come there at last."

At this moment he heard a quick step on the stairs above, and a voice singing a little air so much like his friend that Coconnas looked up. It was La Mole himself, who, perceiving the Piedmontese, ran down the stairs four steps at a time, and threw himself into his arms.

"*Mordi!* it is you!" said Coconnas. "How in the devil did you come out?"

"Why, by the Rue Cloche Percée."

"No. I don't mean there."

"Whence, then?"

"From the queen."

"From the queen?"

"Ay, from the queen."

"I have not been with her."

"Come, come!"

"My dear Annibal," said La Mole, "you are crazy! I have this instant left my room, where I have been waiting for you these two hours."

"You have just left your room?"

"Yes."

"It was not you I ran after from the Place du Louvre?"

"When?"

"Just now."

"No."

"It was not you who disappeared under the gateway ten minutes ago?"

"No."

"It was not you who dashed up the stairs as if the Devil was after you?"

"No."

"Mordi!" replied Coconnas. "The wine of the Belle Etoile has not turned my head to that extent. I tell you that I saw your cherry mantle and white plume enter the Louvre; that I followed the one and the other to the bottom of this staircase; and that your mantle, your plume, apparently yourself, even to your swinging arm, were awaited here by a lady who I strongly suspect was the Queen of Navarre, who led the apparition to yonder door, which, if I am not mistaken, is that of the beautiful Marguerite."

"Mordieu!" exclaimed La Mole, turning very pale. "Can there be treachery already?"

"Ah, swear as much as you like," returned Coconnas, "but don't tell me I was mistaken."

La Mole hesitated an instant, and then, carried away by his jealousy, rushed to the queen's door and knocked furiously.

"You'll get us both arrested," said Coconnas. "I say—do you think there are ghosts at the Louvre, La Mole?"

"I do not know," said the young man; "but I've always wanted to see one, and would like to find myself face-to-face with this ghost, if ghost it really be."

"Very good," said Coconnas; "but don't knock so loud, or you'll alarm him."

Enraged as La Mole was, he yet saw the justice of this observation, and though he continued to knock, knocked less violently.

CHAPTER 25

The Cherry Mantle

Coconnas was not deceived. The lady who had stopped the cavalier in the cherry mantle was indeed the Queen of Navarre; the cavalier in the cherry mantle was, as our readers have doubtless guessed, no other than Mouy.

On recognizing the Queen of Navarre, the young man saw there was some mistake, but he feared to say anything, lest a cry from the queen should betray him. He therefore suffered himself to be led into the apartment, resolved, once there, to say to his fair guide, "Silence for silence, Madame."

Marguerite had gently pressed the arm of him whom in the darkness she mistook for La Mole, and whispered in his ear in Latin, *"Sola sum; introito, carissime."* ("I am alone; come in, dearest.")

Mouy entered in silence; but scarcely was he in the antechamber, and the door closed, than Marguerite perceived that it was not La Mole, and she then uttered that very cry which the prudent Huguenot had dreaded. Happily, it was no longer to be feared.

"M. de Mouy!" she cried, starting back.

"Myself, Madame," returned the young man; "and I entreat your Majesty to suffer me to proceed, without informing anyone of my presence at the Louvre."

"Oh, M. de Mouy," said the queen, "I was mistaken, then."

"Yes, so I comprehend," returned Mouy; "your Majesty mistook me for the King of Navarre. My dress is the same as his, and my height and figure, I have been told by those who would flatter me, are not unlike his."

Marguerite looked fixedly at him. "Do you know Latin?" she asked.

"I did once, but I have forgotten it," replied the young man.

Marguerite smiled. "You may rely upon my discretion, M. de

Mouy; and as I think I know the person you seek, I will, if you wish, conduct you to him."

"Madame," replied Mouy, "I see that you are mistaken, and that you are completely ignorant who the person is that I wish to see."

"What!" cried Marguerite, "is it not the King of Navarre you seek?"

"Alas, Madame, it is with regret I have to beseech you especially to conceal my presence in the Louvre from the king your husband."

"M. de Mouy," said Marguerite, "I have always considered you one of the steadiest partisans of my husband, and one of the most zealous Huguenot leaders. Am I, then, mistaken?"

"No, Madame, for I was, up to this morning, all that you say."

"And why have you changed?"

"Madame," returned Mouy, "I entreat you to excuse my replying, and to receive my adieu." And Mouy firmly but respectfully proceeded toward the door.

Marguerite stopped him. "Yet, Monsieur," said she, "if I should venture to ask a word of explanation, my promise is good, is it not?"

"Madame," returned Mouy, "my duty bids me be silent; I need hardly say that it is an imperious duty which prevents my obeying your Majesty."

"Yet, Monsieur—"

"Your Majesty can ruin me, but you cannot require me to betray my new friends."

"Have your old friends no claims on you?"

"Those who have remained faithful, yes; those who not only have abandoned us, but have abandoned themselves, no."

Marguerite, thoughtful and uneasy, was about to pursue her interrogatories, when Gillonne rushed in.

"The King of Navarre, Madame!"

"Which way is he coming?"

"By the secret passage."

"Then let this gentleman out by the other door."

"Impossible, Madame; someone is knocking there."

"Who is it?"

"I do not know."

"Go and see."

"Madame," said Mouy, "permit me to observe that I am lost if the King of Navarre sees me in the Louvre at this hour and in this costume."

Marguerite seized his hand, and leading him to the famous cabinet, "Enter there," said she; "you are as safe as in your own house, for you are under the guarantee of my word."

Mouy sprang in, and hardly had he done so when Henri appeared. He entered with that cautious observation that made him, even when in the least danger, remark the most trifling circumstances. He instantly perceived the cloud on Marguerite's brow. "You were occupied, Madame?" said he.

"Yes, Sire, I was thinking."

"And with good reason, Madame; thoughtfulness becomes you. I too have been thinking, and came to communicate my thoughts to you."

Marguerite inclined her head in token of welcome, and pointing to a seat, placed herself in an ebony chair beautifully carved. There was a moment's pause; Henri first broke the silence. "I remembered, Madame," said he, "that my dreams as to the future had this in common with yours, that though separated as husband and wife, we yet wished to unite our fortunes."

"It is true, Sire."

"I also understood that in all my plans for our common elevation, I should find in you not only a faithful but an active ally."

"Yes, Sire; and I only ask to have an early opportunity of proving it to you."

"I am delighted to find you so well disposed; and I believe that you have not for an instant mistrusted that I have lost sight of those plans I resolved upon the day when, thanks to your courage, my life was saved."

"Monsieur, I believe that your indifference is merely a mask; and I have confidence not only in the predictions of astrologers, but also in your genius."

"What should you say, then, were someone to come in and thwart our plans, and threaten to destroy our hopes?"

"I would reply that I am ready to strive with you, openly or in secret, against him, be he who he may."

"Madame," returned Henri, "you have the right of entering

the Duc d'Alençon's apartments at all times, have you not? You have his confidence, and he has a warm liking for you. Might I request of you to go and see if he be not in secret conference with someone?"

Marguerite was startled. "With whom?" she said.

"With Mouy."

"Why?" replied Marguerite, suppressing her emotion.

"Because if it be so, adieu to all our plans—all mine, at least."

"Speak lower, Sire," said Marguerite, pointing to the cabinet.

"Oh, oh! someone there again?" said Henri. "By my faith, that cabinet is so often inhabited that it renders your chamber uninhabitable."

Marguerite smiled.

"Is it M. de la Mole, still?" said Henri.

"No, Sire; it is M. de Mouy."

"Mouy!" cried Henri, joyfully. "He is not, then, with the Duc d'Alençon. Oh, let me speak to him!"

Marguerite ran to the cabinet, and without further ceremony presented Mouy to the king.

"Ah, Madame," said the young Huguenot, reproachfully, "you have not kept your promise. Suppose I were to revenge myself by saying—"

"You will not avenge yourself, Mouy," said Henri, pressing his hand; "at least, not before you have heard me. Madame, have the kindness to see that no one overhears us."

Scarcely were these words uttered, when Gillonne entered all aghast, and said something to Marguerite that made her bound from her seat. While she hastened to the antechamber with Gillonne, Henri, not troubling himself as to the cause of her abrupt departure, lifted the tapestry, sounded the walls, and looked into every recess. As for Mouy, somewhat alarmed by these precautions, he loosened his sword in the scabbard.

Marguerite, on leaving her bedchamber, had darted into the antechamber, and found herself in the presence of La Mole, who, in spite of Gillonne, was forcing his way in. Behind him stood Coconnas, ready to advance or retreat with him, as the case might be.

"Ah, is it you, M. de la Mole?" said the queen. "What is the matter with you? and why so pale and trembling?"

"Madame," said Gillonne, "M. de la Mole knocked so loud that in spite of your Majesty's orders, I was forced to admit him."

"Ha!" said the queen, angrily. "Is this true, M. de la Mole?"

"Madame, I wished to inform your Majesty that a stranger, a robber perhaps, had entered your apartments, wearing my mantle and hat."

"You are mad, Monsieur," returned Marguerite; "for I see your mantle on your shoulders; and moreover, by my faith, I see your hat on your head, though you are speaking to a queen."

"Forgive me, Madame!" cried La Mole, hastily uncovering. "God knows it is not want of respect—"

"No; but want of faith," said the queen.

"Oh, Madame," said La Mole, "when a man enters your apartments in my dress, perchance under my name—"

"A man!" said Marguerite, pressing her lover's hand. "Very fine, M. de la Mole; look through that opening, and you will see two men."

And she gently raised the velvet curtains, and showed to La Mole and Coconnas, who, moved with curiosity, came forward, Henri speaking to the cavalier in the cherry-colored mantle, whom Coconnas at once recognized as Mouy.

"Now that you are satisfied," said Marguerite, "place yourself at that door, and let no one enter; if anyone even approaches, let me know."

La Mole, docile as an infant, obeyed, and both he and Coconnas found themselves outside the door before they had well recovered from their amazement.

"Mouy!" cried Coconnas.

"Henri!" muttered La Mole.

"Mouy, with your scarlet cloak and your white plume!"

"Zounds!" said La Mole, "this is some plot."

"Ah, here we are in politics again!" grumbled Coconnas. "Fortunately, I do not see Madame de Nevers mixed up in the matter."

Marguerite returned to her bedroom; she had been absent scarcely a minute, but she had made good use of her time. Gillonne guarding the secret passage, and the two gentlemen outside the principal entrance, afforded full security.

"Madame," said Henri, "do you think it possible anyone can overhear us?"

"Sire," returned Marguerite, "the walls are all double-paneled, and lined between with mattresses."

"Ay, ay, that will do," said Henri, smiling. Then, turning to Mouy, "Now, then," said he, in a low tone, as notwithstanding Marguerite's assurances, his fears were not dissipated, "what are you come here for?"

"Here!" repeated Mouy.

"Yes, here—to this chamber?"

"He did not come for anything," said Marguerite; "it was I who brought him here."

"You knew then—"

"I guessed."

"You see, Mouy, people can guess."

"M. de Mouy," continued Marguerite, "was with Duc François this morning in the chamber of two of his gentlemen."

"You see, Mouy," repeated Henri, "we know all."

"It is true," said Mouy.

"I was sure," replied the king, "that D'Alençon had got hold of you."

"It is your fault, Sire. Why did you refuse so obstinately what I offered."

"Ah, you refused!" said Marguerite. "My presentiments, then, were true?"

"Madame," said Henri, "and you, my brave Mouy, you make me smile with your exclamations. What! a man comes to me, and talks to me of thrones and revolutions, and overthrowing States—to me, Henri, a prince tolerated only because I humble myself; a Huguenot, spared only because I pretend to be a Catholic—and thinks I am going to accept his propositions made in a chamber without double panels, and not lined with mattresses. *Ventre-saint-gris!* you are children, or you are mad!"

"But, Sire, your Majesty might have given me some hope—if not in words, by a gesture, a sign."

"What did my brother-in-law say to you, Mouy?" asked Henri.

"Oh, Sire, that is not my secret."

"Oh, *mon Dieu!*" said Henri, impatient at having to deal with a man who did not understand him. "I do not ask you what proposals he made you. I only asked you if he had listened, and if he had overheard?"

"He had listened, Sire, and he had overheard."

"He listened and overheard!—you admit that yourself. Poor conspirator that you are! Had I spoken a word, you had been undone—for if I did not absolutely know he was there, I suspected as much; and if not he, someone else—D'Anjou, the king, or the queen-mother. The walls of the Louvre have good ears; and knowing that, do you think I should speak? I wonder you offer a crown to the King of Navarre, when you give him credit for so little good sense."

"But, Sire," said Mouy, "had you made me a sign, I should not have lost all hope."

"Eh, *ventre-saint-gris!*" cried Henri. "If he listened, could he not see also? At this very instant I dread lest we may be overheard when I say to you, Mouy, repeat to me your proposals."

"Sire," said Mouy, mournfully, "I am now engaged with M. d'Alençon."

Marguerite beat her fair hands together violently. "It is, then, too late?" said she.

"On the contrary," said Henri, "the hand of Providence is visible in this, for the duke will save us all. He will be a buckler protecting us; whereas the name of the King of Navarre would involve you all, by degrees, in destruction. Get fast hold of him; secure proofs; but, silly politician that you are, you have doubtless engaged yourself already without using any precautions."

"Sire," cried Mouy, "despair made me join his party, and fear also, for he held our secret."

"Then hold his in your turn. What does he want—the kingdom of Navarre? Promise it him. To quit the court? Supply him with the means. When the time comes for us to fly, he and I will fly together; when it is time to reign, I will reign alone."

"Distrust the duke," said Marguerite; "he is alike incapable of hatred and friendship—ever ready to treat his enemies as friends, and his friends as enemies."

"He awaits you?" said Henri, without heeding his wife's remark.

"Yes, Sire."

"At what hour?"

"Until midnight."

"It is not yet eleven," said Henri; "you are not too late, Mouy."

"We have your word, Monsieur," said Marguerite.

"Come, come," said Henri, with that air of confidence he so well knew how to show to certain persons and on certain occasions; "with M. de Mouy this is needless."

"You do me justice, Sire," returned the young man. "But I must have your word that I may tell our leaders that I have received it. You are not, then, a Catholic?"

Henri shrugged his shoulders.

"You do not renounce the kingdom of Navarre?"

"I do not renounce any kingdom, only I would select that which suits you and me the best."

"And in the meantime, were your Majesty to be arrested, and they should dare so to violate the regal dignity as to torture you, will you swear to reveal nothing?"

"Mouy, I swear it."

"One word, Sire. How shall I see you?"

"From tomorrow you will have a key of my chamber, and you can come in when you will. The duke must explain your presence at the Louvre. Meanwhile, go up by the little staircase; I shall serve as your guide. While we are so engaged, the queen will bring in here the other Cherry Mantle, who was just now in the antechamber. No difference must be discernible between you; it must not be supposed you are double; eh, Mouy? eh, Madame?"

Henri laughed as he said this, and looked at Marguerite.

"Yes," replied she, without any emotion; "for you know this M. de la Mole is one of the gentlemen of the Duc d'Alençon."

"Try and get him to our side, then," said Henri, with entire gravity; "spare neither gold nor promises. I place all my treasures at his disposal."

"Well, then," said Marguerite, with one of those smiles that belong only to Boccaccio's heroines, "since such is your desire, I will do my best to promote it."

"Very good, Madame; and now to the duke, Mouy, and hook him."

CHAPTER 26

Margarita

During this conversation La Mole and Coconnas remained on guard—the former somewhat vexed, and Coconnas somewhat uneasy. La Mole had had time for reflection, and Coconnas had most liberally assisted him.

"What do you think of all this?" asked La Mole.

"I think," replied the Piedmontese, "that it is some intrigue of the court."

"And are you disposed to play a part in it?"

"My dear fellow!" returned Coconnas, "listen to what I shall say, and take advantage from it. In all these royal maneuverings we are, and should be, but shadows; where the King of Navarre would lose only the end of his feather, or the Duc d'Alençon the skirt of his cloak, you and I would lose our lives. The queen has a fancy for you, and you have a fancy for her—nothing could be better; lose your head in love, my dear fellow, but don't lose it in politics."

That was wise advice; but it was received by La Mole with the sadness of a man who knows that, placed between reason and folly, he will pursue folly.

"I have not a fancy for the queen, Annibal; I love her, and, happily or unhappily, I love her with all my soul. It is folly, I admit; but you, Coconnas, who are prudent, must not suffer by my folly. Seek our master, and do not compromise yourself."

Coconnas reflected an instant; then, shaking his head, "My dear fellow!" said he, "what you say is very just; you are in love, and you act like a lover. I am ambitious, and think life worth more than the smile of a woman. When I risk my life I will make my own terms, and do you, on your part, do the same." So saying, Coconnas pressed La Mole's hand, and left him.

About ten minutes later, the door opened cautiously and

Marguerite appeared. Without speaking a word she led La Mole into her apartments, closing the doors with a care that showed the importance of the conversation she was about to open. Arrived in her chamber, she sat down in her ebony chair, and taking La Mole's hand in hers, "Now that we are alone, my friend," said she, "we will talk seriously."

"Seriously, Madame?" said La Mole.

"Or lovingly, if you like the word better. There may be serious things in love, especially in the love of a queen."

"Let us speak seriously, then; but on condition that your Majesty be not offended with what I shall say."

"I shall be offended at only one thing, La Mole, and that is, if you call me 'Madame' or 'your Majesty'; for you I am only Marguerite."

"Yes, Marguerite! yes, Margarita! yes, my pearl!" cried the young man, gazing passionately at the queen.

"That is well," said Marguerite; "and so you are jealous, my fine gentleman?"

"Oh, madly!"

"Ah! and of whom?"

"Of everyone."

"But of whom in particular?"

"First, of the king."

"I thought, after what you had seen and heard, you were easy on that score."

"Of this M. de Mouy, whom I saw this morning for the first time, and whom I find this evening on such intimate terms with you."

"And what makes you jealous of Mouy?"

"Listen; I have recognized him by his hair, his figure, by a natural feeling of hate. It is he who was with M. d'Alençon this morning."

"Well, what has that to do with me?"

"That I know not. But in any case, Madame, be frank with me; a love like mine is entitled to frankness on your part. See, Madame, at your feet I implore you! If what you have felt for me is but a temporary inclination, I give you back your faith and your promises; I will resign my post to M. d'Alençon, and go and seek death at the siege of Rochelle, if love does not kill me before I arrive there!"

Marguerite listened with a smile to these tender reproaches;

then, leaning her head on her burning hand, "You love me?" she said.

"Oh, yes, Madame, more than life, more than safety, more than all things! But you—you do not love me."

"Silly fellow!" she murmured; "and so the sole interest of life with you is your love, dear La Mole?"

"It is indeed, Madame."

"You love me, then, and would remain with me?"

"My only prayer is that I may never part from you."

"Were I to tell you I love you, would you be wholly devoted to me?"

"Am I not so already?"

"Yes; but you still doubt."

"Oh, I am an ingrate, or rather, I am mad; but tell me, why was M. de Mouy this morning with the Duc d'Alençon; why here tonight? What meant the white plume, the cherry-colored mantle, the imitating my walk and manner? Ah, Madame! it is not you whom I suspect, but your brother."

"Can you not guess? The Duc d'Alençon would kill you with his own hand, did he know you were here at my feet, and that, instead of ordering you to quit my presence, I said to you as I now say, stay where you are, for I love you. Yes, I repeat, he would kill you."

"Great God!" cried La Mole, starting back, and looking at Marguerite with terror, "is it possible?"

"All is possible, my friend, in our time and in our court. Now, a single word. It was not for me that M. de Mouy came here in your hat and cloak—it was for M. d'Alençon; but I mistook him for you. I spoke to him, thinking it was you; I led him hither, thinking it was you. He possesses our secret, La Mole, and must be managed cautiously."

"I would rather kill him," said La Mole; " 'tis the shortest and safest way."

"And I," said the queen, "would rather he should live and that you should know all; for his life is not only useful to us, but necessary. Listen, and weigh well your words before answering; do you love me enough to rejoice if I were to become really a queen—that is, mistress of a veritable kingdom?"

"Alas, Madame," said La Mole, "I love you enough to desire whatever you desire, though it involved myself in utter misery!"

"Will you, then, aid me to realize this object?"

"Oh, I shall lose you!" cried La Mole, burying his face in his hands.

"No; only, instead of being the first of my servants, you will become the first of my subjects."

"Oh, speak not of interest, of ambition! Do not dishonor the sentiment I have for you!—of devotion, ardent, unmixed devotion!"

"Noble nature!" said the queen; "I will accept your devotion, and, be assured, will repay it." And she held out her hands, which La Mole covered with kisses. "Well!" said she.

"Well, yes," replied La Mole; "I now begin to understand the project spoken of by the Huguenots before the Saint Bartholomew—the project, to aid in which I, with so many others, came to Paris. You desire a real kingdom of Navarre instead of a fictitious kingdom. King Henri urges you; Mouy conspires with you; but what has the Duc d'Alençon to do with all this? Where is there a throne for him in this affair? I see none. Now is the Duc d'Alençon sufficiently your friend to aid you without demanding anything in return?"

"The duke conspires for himself. Let him go on his own way; his life answers for ours."

"But how can I, who am in his service, betray him?"

"Betray him! how so? What has he entrusted to you? Has he not betrayed you, by giving Mouy your mantle and hat to enable him to come here? Were you not in my service before you were in his? Has he given you a greater proof of love than you have received from me?"

La Mole rose, pale and agitated. "Coconnas was right," murmured he; "I am becoming entangled in the net of intrigue, and it will destroy me."

"Well?" said Marguerite.

"This is my answer," returned La Mole. "Even at the extremity of France, where the reputation of your beauty reached me, and gave me my first desire to visit Paris that I might see you, I have heard it said that you have loved more than once and that your love has always been fatal to its objects; death, doubtless jealous of their happiness, removed them from you."

"La Mole!"

"Do not interrupt me, Marguerite. It is added that you have

ever with you the embalmed hearts of these departed ones, and that at times you bestow on these sad remains a piteous sigh, perchance a tear. You sigh, my queen, your eyes are lowered to the ground; it is true, then? Well, make me the most loved and the most happy of your favorites. In the case of others you pierced the heart, and that heart you have preserved; with me, you do more—you expose my head. Marguerite, swear to me before the image of that God who even in this place saved my life, swear to me that if—as a sombre presentiment assures me I shall—I perish beneath the executioner's stroke in your service, you will preserve that head which I shall forfeit, and will sometimes look upon it. Swear this, and the prospect of such a reward, made by my queen, will make me silent, traitor and coward when necessary—that is to say, entirely devoted as one should be who is your lover and associate."

"Oh, gloomy foreboding, my dear soul!" said Marguerite; "oh, fatal thought, my sweet love!"

"Swear—on this cross-surmounted coffer."

"I swear," said Marguerite, "that if—may God forbid!—your sombre presentiment be realized, you shall be near me, living or dead, so long as I myself shall live; if I cannot save you in the peril you incur for me, you shall have the poor consolation you ask, and which you will have so well merited."

"One word more, Marguerite. I can now die happily, but I may live; we may triumph, and not fall. The King of Navarre may become king; you will then be queen. He will take you hence; the vow of separation between you may one day be broken, and lead to my separation from you. Oh, dearest Marguerite, reassure me also on this point."

"Fear not, I am yours, body and soul," cried Marguerite, placing her hand on the cross. "If I go, you shall accompany me; if the king refuses to take you, I myself will not depart."

"But you will not dare resist him."

"Dear Hyacinthe," said Marguerite, "you do not know the king. Henri thinks but of one thing—that is, of becoming a king—and to that desire he would at this moment sacrifice all that he possesses, and with the more reason, what he does not possess; farewell!"

"But where am I to go?"

"True! Besides, I must talk to you about this conspiracy."

From this evening La Mole was no longer a common favorite, and he could proudly hold up that head, for which, living or dead, so high a destiny was reserved. Yet sometimes his eyes were fixed on the ground, his cheek grew pale, and deep meditation drew furrows on the brow of the young man, once so gay, now so happy.

CHAPTER 27

The Hand of Providence

As Henri left Madame de Sauve, he said to her, "Charlotte, confine yourself to your bed; pretend to be exceedingly ill, and do not receive any person during the day under any pretext at all!"

Charlotte, knowing that Henri had secrets which he revealed to no one, complied with all his directions, certain that his conduct, however strange, had a purpose. In the evening, she complained to her attendant Dariole of a heaviness in the head, accompanied with faintness, these being the symptoms Henri had requested her to feign. The next morning she seemed desirous of rising, but scarcely had she placed her foot on the floor, when she complained of general weakness, and returned to her bed.

This indisposition, which Henri had already adverted to when speaking to the Duc d'Alençon, was the first information that Catherine received, when she inquired with a calm air why La Sauve did not attend her, as usual, when she arose.

"She is ill," said Madame de Lorraine, who was present.

"Ill?" repeated Catherine, while not a muscle of her face announced the interest she took in the reply; "a little indolent, perhaps?"

"No, Madame," replied the princess; "she complains of a violent pain in the head and a weakness that prevents her from moving."

Catherine made no reply, but to conceal her joy, no doubt, turned toward the window; and seeing Henri crossing the courtyard after his conversation with Mouy, she said, as she looked at him, to her captain of the guards, "Do you not think that my son Henri looks paler than usual this morning?"

It is true that Henri was considerably disturbed in mind, but he was physically in good condition.

Catherine's suite left her, and the instant she was alone she closed the door securely, and going to a secret cupboard she drew from a concealed corner a book, whose crumpled leaves proved how frequently it was made use of. She placed the volume on a table, opened it, and after consulting its pages for a minute, exclaimed, "Yes, it is so—headache, general weakness, pains in the eyes, swelling of the palate. As yet they only mention headache and weakness; but the other symptoms will appear. Then follow inflammation of the throat, which extends over the stomach, surrounds the heart with a circle of fire, and makes the brain burst like a stroke of lightning."

She read on in a low tone, and then said, "The fever lasts six hours, the general inflammation twelve hours, the gangrene twelve hours, the final agony six hours—in all, thirty-six hours. Well, then, let us suppose that absorption is a slower process than swallowing; instead of thirty-six hours we shall have forty, or perhaps forty-eight—yes, forty-eight must be sufficient. But he—he—Henri—how is it that he is able to keep up? Why, because he is a man with a robust habit, and perhaps drank something after he had kissed her, and wiped his lips after drinking."

Catherine impatiently awaited the dinner-hour—Henri dined daily at the king's table. When he came he complained of giddiness in the head, and did not eat, but withdrew immediately after dinner, saying that as he had been up nearly all the night before, he felt a great desire to sleep.

Catherine listened to Henri's retreating and staggering step, and desired someone to follow him, which was done; and the queen-mother was informed that the King of Navarre had gone toward Madame de Sauve's apartments.

"Henri," she said to herself, "will there complete the work of death which unlucky accident may hitherto have rendered incomplete."

The King of Navarre had gone to Madame de Sauve's apartments to request her to continue to play her part.

Next day Henri did not leave his chamber during the morning, nor did he dine at the royal table. Madame de Sauve, it was reported, was worse and worse; and the rumors of Henri's illness, prompted by Catherine herself, spread like one of those presentiments which no one can explain, but which travel in the air.

Catherine awaited, then, with a composed countenance the moment when some attendant, pale and aghast, should enter her apartments, and cry, "Your Majesty, the King of Navarre is dying, and Madame de Sauve is dead."

The clock struck four, and Catherine was feeding with crumbs of bread some rare birds which she herself attended to. Although her features were calm and even melancholy, her heart beat violently at the least sound. Suddenly the door opened.

"Madame," said the captain of the guards, "the King of Navarre is—"

"Ill?" inquired Catherine, suddenly.

"No, Madame, thank God! his Majesty seems excellently well."

"What, then, have you to say?"

"That the King of Navarre is here."

"What would he with me?"

"He brings your Majesty a small monkey of a very rare sort."

And at this moment Henri entered, holding in his hand a basket, and caressing a marmoset that was in it. Henri smiled as he entered, and appeared quite occupied with the small animal he had brought; but yet, preoccupied as he appeared to be, he gave a glance which was sufficient under his peculiar circumstances. As to Catherine, she was very pale—deadly pale, indeed—as she saw the cheeks of the young man who approached her glowing with color and health.

The queen-mother was stupefied by that blow. She accepted mechanically the present he made her, and complimenting him in a troubled voice on his healthy appearance, added, "I am the more pleased to see you in such health, my son, for having heard that you were ill; and I remember you complained of indisposition in my presence. But I see now," she continued, trying to force a smile, "it was only an excuse that you might have your time more freely to yourself."

"Why, I really was very unwell, Madame," replied Henri; "but a specific used in our mountains, and which my mother gave me, cured my illness."

"Ah! you will give me the prescription, won't you, Henri?" said Catherine, really smiling this time, but with irony half concealed.

"Some counterpoison," she muttered; "or he was on his guard. Seeing Madame de Sauve ill, he had some distrust. Really, it would seem that the hand of Providence is extended over this man."

Catherine waited for night most impatiently. Madame de Sauve did not appear; and it was stated that she was still worse. All the evening the queen-mother was uneasy; and every one asked what could be the thoughts that thus disturbed a countenance usually so little agitated.

Everyone retired. Catherine was undressed by her women, and went to bed; but when all was hushed in the Louvre, she rose, put on a long black dressing gown, and with a lamp in her hand, having selected the key that opened Madame de Sauve's door, went to the apartments of her maid of honor.

Had Henri anticipated this visit? Was he in his own apartments? Was he hidden somewhere? At any rate, the young woman was alone.

Catherine opened the door with precaution, passed through the antechamber, entered the salon, placed the lamp on a table, for there was a night-light burning near the invalid, : .d like a shadow she glided into the sleeping apartment. Dariole, extended in a large armchair, was sleeping near her mistress's bed, which was closed in by curtains.

The breathing of the young woman was so light that for an instant Catherine thought she did not breathe at all. At length she heard a light respiration, and with malignant joy she raised the curtain that she might herself witness the effect of the terrible poison, shuddering at the anticipated aspect of the livid paleness or the devouring purple of the mortal fever she hoped to see; but instead of that—calm, her eyes gently covered by their ivory lids, her mouth rosy and half-opened, her soft cheek reposing on one of her arms, gracefully rounded, while the other, fresh and beautiful, was extended on the crimson damask counterpane—the young lady was sleeping with a smile on her lovely features.

Catherine could not repress a cry, which aroused Dariole for an instant. The queen-mother threw herself behind the bed-curtains. Dariole opened her eyes, but being drowsy, she did not even try to account to herself for the cause of her awaking, and her heavy eyelids dropping, she slept again.

Catherine then coming from behind the curtain, looking all

around, saw on a small table a flask of Spanish wine, some sweet-meats, and two glasses. Henri had supped with the baroness, who, apparently, was as well as himself.

Catherine, then going to the toilet-table, took up the small box, which was one-third empty. It was the same which she had sent, or was very similar to it. She took from it a morsel the size of a pearl, at the end of a gold pin, returned to her own apartments, and offered it to the small monkey which Henri had presented to her the same evening. The animal, tempted by the aromatic odor, seized and swallowed it greedily, and curling himself up in his basket, went to sleep. Catherine waited a quarter of an hour. "With half such a piece," she said, "my dog Brunot died in a minute. I have been tri-fled with. Can it be René? René! that is impossible. Then, it is Henri! Oh, fatality! It is clear; as he must reign, he cannot die. But perhaps it is only poison against which he is proof; let us, then, try cold steel."

Catherine went to her couch, turning over in her mind this new idea, which she resolved on putting into execution the next day; and in the morning, summoning the captain of her guards, she gave him a letter to convey to its address, and to be handed only to the person whose name it bore.

It was addressed to "Sire de Louviers de Maurevel, Captain of the King's Petardeers, Rue de la Cerisaie, near the Arsenal."

CHAPTER 28

The Letter from Rome

Some days had elapsed since the events we have related, when one morning a litter, escorted by several gentlemen wearing the colors of M. de Guise, entered the Louvre; and it was announced to the Queen of Navarre that the Duchesse de Nevers desired to pay her respects to her.

Marguerite was receiving a visit from Madame de Sauve. It was the first time the lovely baroness had gone out since her pretended illness. Marguerite congratulated her on her convalescence, and said, "You will come, I hope, to the great hunt, which will certainly take place tomorrow."

"Why, Madame," replied the baroness, "I do not know that I shall be well enough."

"Bah!" replied Marguerite, "you must make an effort; and as I myself am a regular warrior, I have authorized the king to place at your disposal a small Béarn horse, which I was to have ridden, and which will carry you famously. Have you not heard of it?"

"Yes, Madame, but I was ignorant that the little horse had been destined to the honor of being offered to your Majesty; had I known that I would not have accepted him."

"Through pride, Baroness?"

"No, Madame; on the contrary, through humility."

"Then you will come?"

"Your Majesty overwhelms me; and I will be present, as you desire it."

At this moment the Duchesse de Nevers was announced.

"Tomorrow, then," said Marguerite to Madame de Sauve. "Apropos, you know, Baroness," continued Marguerite, "that in public I detest you, seeing that I am horribly jealous of you."

"But in private?" asked Madame de Sauve,

"Oh! in private I not only forgive you, but even thank you."

"Then your Majesty will allow me—"

Marguerite extended her hand, which the baroness kissed respectfully, made a profound reverence, and went out.

The Duchesse de Nevers entered. Gillonne, at the desire of her mistress, fastened the door, and the duchess having taken a seat without ceremony, Marguerite said to her with a smile, "Well! and our famous swordsman, what do we make out of him?"

"My dear queen," replied the duchess, "he is really a mythological being; he is incomparable in his mind, and inexhaustible in his humor. I am really fond of him. And what are you doing with your Apollo?"

"Alas!" said Marguerite, with a sigh.

"Ah, ah! that 'alas' frightens me, dear queen."

"This 'alas' refers only to myself," replied Marguerite.

"And what does it mean?"

"It means, dear duchess, that I have an awful fear that I love him in real earnest."

"Really?"

"On my faith!"

"Ah, so much the better!" cried Henriette. "The joyous life that we shall lead! To love a little was my dream; to love much was yours. It is so pleasant, dear and learned queen, to rest the mind through the heart, and after the delirium to have the smile. Ah, Marguerite! I have a presentiment that we shall pass an agreeable year."

"Do you think so?" said the queen. "I, on the contrary, do not know how it is, but I seem to see everything as it were through a crepe. All these political turmoils torment me terribly. By the way, learn if your Annibal is as much devoted to my brother as he appears to be. It is important to know this."

"He devoted to anyone or to anything! Ah! I see you do not know him as I do. If he is ever devoted, it will be to ambition, and nothing else. Is your brother a man to make him great promises? then he will be devoted to your brother. But let your brother, son of France though he be, take care to fulfill his promises to him; otherwise, my faith! let your brother beware!"

"Really!"

"It is as I say. In fact, Marguerite, there are moments when this tiger whom I have trained makes me afraid for myself. The other day I said to him, 'Annibal, mind and do not be false to me, for if you are false to me—' "

"Well?"

"Well, what do you suppose was his reply? Why, he said, 'And if you are false to me, do you take care; for although you are a princess—' and as he said this he threatened me not only with his eyes but with his finger—his finger, straight and pointed, armed with a nail cut like a spear-point, which he put quite close under my nose. Really, my dear queen, I confess his countenance was so threatening that I trembled; and you know that ordinarily I am no trembler."

"Did he really dare to threaten you, Henriette?"

"Yes, *mordi!* but I had threatened him, you see."

"Have you any news for me?"

"Yes, indeed; I have received news from Rome."

"Well! and matters in Poland?"

"Progress most favorably; and in all probability you will in a few days be freed from your brother D'Anjou."

"The pope, then, has ratified the election?"

"Yes, my dear."

"Why did you not tell me sooner? Come, quick, quick!—all the details."

"Oh, really! I have none but what I have told you. But here is Nevers's letter. No, that is not it; that is a letter from me which I will beg of you to ask La Mole to give to Annibal. This is the duke's letter."

Marguerite opened and read it eagerly, but it told no more than she knew before from the lips of her friend.

"And how did you receive this letter?" continued the queen.

"By one of my husband's couriers, who had his orders to stop at the Hôtel de Guise on his way to the Louvre, and hand me this letter before the king had his. I knew the importance which my queen attached to this news, and wrote to M. de Nevers to act thus. And now in all Paris none but the king, you, and I know this news, unless the man who followed our courier—"

"What man?"

"Oh, what a horrible business! Only imagine this poor messenger, arriving tired, dusty, and jaded, after traveling for a whole week, day and night incessantly, constantly followed by a man of fierce visage, who had relays like his own, and traveled as fast as he for these four hundred leagues, our courier expecting every moment to have a ball in his back. They both arrived at the Barrière St. Marcel at the same time; both descended the Rue Mouffetard at a gallop; both crossed the Cité; but at the end of the bridge Notre Dame, our courier turned to the right, while the other turned to the left by the Place du Châtelet, and passed along the Quais toward the Louvre, like a bolt from a bow."

"Thanks! thanks! dearest Henriette," cried Marguerite; "you are right, and your information is indeed interesting. To whom this other courier went I will find out. Leave me now; we meet tonight in the Rue Tizon, do we not, and tomorrow at the hunt? I will tell you tonight what I wish you to learn from your Coconnas."

"Do not forget my letter."

"No, no; be easy, he shall have it in time."

Madame de Nevers went away, and Marguerite instantly sent for Henri, who hastened to her; and she gave him the letter and told him of the two couriers.

"Yes," said Henri; "I saw one enter the Louvre."

"Perhaps for the queen-mother."

"No, for I went into the corridor, and no one passed."

"Then," said Marguerite, looking at her husband, "it must be for—"

"Your brother D'Alençon, eh?" said Henri.

"Yes; but how to ascertain?"

"Can we not," asked Henri, negligently, "send for one of the two gentlemen, and learn from him—"

"You are right, Sire," replied Marguerite, set at ease by her husband's proposition. "I will send for M. de la Mole"; and calling Gillonne, she desired her to seek that gentleman, and bring him thither.

Henri seated himself at a table, on which was a German book with Albrecht Dürer's engravings, which he looked at with so much attention that when La Mole appeared he did not seem to hear him, not even raising his head.

Marguerite went to La Mole, and said, "M. de la Mole, can you tell me who is on guard today at M. d'Alençon's?"

"Coconnas, Madame," was the reply.

"Endeavor to learn if he has introduced to his master a man covered with mud, who seemed to have ridden a long and rapid journey."

"Madame, I am afraid he will not tell me, for he has been uncommonly taciturn during the last few days."

"Really? Well, but if you give him this letter I should think he would owe you something in exchange."

"From the duchess? Oh! with that letter I will make the attempt."

"Add," said Marguerite, lowering her voice, "that the letter will serve him as safe-conduct for entering this evening the house which you know."

"And I, Madame," said La Mole, in a low voice, "what is to be mine?"

"Give your name; it will be sufficient."

"Give me the letter, Madame," said La Mole, trembling with love; "I will answer for all."

"We shall know tomorrow if the Duc d'Alençon is informed of the affair of Poland," said Marguerite, turning toward her husband.

"This M. de la Mole is really a very capital servant," said the Béarnais, with his own peculiar smile, "and, by the Mass! I will make his fortune."

CHAPTER 29

The Departure

When the red rayless sun rose next morning over Paris, the court had already been in motion for two hours.

A splendid barb, agile as a deer, the swelling veins of whose neck indicated his high breeding, pawed impatiently in the court, awaiting the king; but his impatience was less than his master's, detained by his mother, who had stopped him in the passageway, to speak to him, she said, on a matter of importance.

They were both in the great gallery—Catherine pale and cold as ever; Charles IX biting his nails, and chastising the two favorite dogs which stood by him, clothed in the coat of mail which protected them from the boar's tusks. A shield emblazoned with the arms of France was attached to their chests, like that on the breasts of the royal pages who more than once had envied the privileges of those happy favorites.

"Listen, Charles," said Catherine. "None but you and I are aware of the approaching arrival of the Polish ambassadors; and yet the King of Navarre acts as if he knew of it. In spite of his pretended abjuration, he keeps up a correspondence with the Huguenots. Have you remarked how frequently he has gone out within the last few days? He has money—he who never before had any; he purchases horses and weapons, and when it rains, he practices fencing."

"Bah, Mother!" cried Charles, impatiently; "do you think he is going to kill D'Anjou or myself? He must take a few more lessons first—for yesterday I touched with my foil the buttons on his doublet eleven times, though there are but six of them; and D'Anjou is even more skillful than I, or at least he says so."

"Attend, Charles," said Catherine; "and do not treat your mother's warnings with such levity. These ambassadors will soon arrive; once here, you will see Henri doing his best to gain their attention. He is very insinuating and cunning; and his wife, who now abets him, I don't understand why, will chatter Latin and Greek, Hungarian, and I know not what else, with them. I tell you, Charles, and I am never mistaken, there is something in hand."

At this moment the clock struck. Charles listened. *"Mort de ma vie!* seven o'clock!" he said. "An hour to get there, an hour more at cover; zounds! it will be nine before we are at it! Indeed, Mother, you are causing me to lose time. Down, Risquetout! down, you rascal!" And as he spoke, a vigorous lash drew from the poor hound, astonished at receiving chastisement instead of a caress, a yell of agony.

"Charles," resumed Catherine, "attend to me, in God's name, and do not put to hazard your own fortune and that of France. The chase! the chase! you will have time enough for the chase, when you have performed your duty as king."

"Come, come, Mother," said Charles, pale with impatience; "explain yourself quickly, for you make me boil. Indeed, there are times when I cannot understand you." He paused, striking his boot with the handle of his whip.

Catherine saw the favorable moment had arrived, and determined not to let it slip. "My son," said she, "we know that M. de Mouy is again in Paris; M. Maurevel has seen him. He can be here only for the King of Navarre's purposes. Here is good ground for increased suspicion."

"Ah, here you are again at poor Henriot! I suppose you want me to kill him?"

"Oh, no!"

"To banish him? But don't you perceive that he would be more formidable at a distance than here in the Louvre, where we know everything he does?"

"No, I don't want to banish him."

"What then? Come, quick!"

"I would have him confined while the Poles are here—in the Bastille, for instance."

"Oh, faith! no," cried Charles IX. "We are going to hunt the boar this morning; Henri is one of my best assistants. The chase would be nothing without him. *Mordieu!* you do nothing but annoy me."

"My son, I do not say this morning. The embassy will not arrive until tomorrow or the day after. Arrest him when the chase is over—this evening, tonight."

"Ah, that is different; we will speak again of this, after the hunt, say. Adieu! Come, Risquetout, don't be sulky!"

"Charles," said Catherine, taking hold of his arm, spite of the explosion she knew might follow, "I think it would be best to sign the warrant at once, although we do not execute it until tonight."

"Sign! write an order! go and look for seal and parchment, when I am going to hunt! Devil take me if I do!"

"Nay, I love you too much to delay you; I have everything prepared." And Catherine, agile as a girl, opened the door of her private cabinet, and showed the king an inkstand, a pen, a parchment, and a lighted taper.

The king rapidly ran his eye over the parchment: "Order, etc., to arrest and conduct to the Bastille our brother Henri of Navarre." "There!" said he, hastily affixing his name to it. "Adieu, Mother." And he sprang out of the cabinet, glad to escape so easily.

Charles was waited for impatiently; and as his punctuality in hunting arrangements was well known, his nonappearance occasioned no small surprise. The instant he appeared the hunters saluted him with cheers, the whippers-in with their horns, the horses with neighings, and the hounds with their cries. Charles for a moment was young and happy amid all this noise, and the color mounted up into his pallid cheeks.

He scarcely gave himself time to return the salutations of the brilliant assembly. He nodded to D'Alençon, waved his hand to Marguerite, passed Henri without seeming to observe him, and sprang upon the horse that awaited him. The noble animal bounded impatiently, but soon comprehending with what sort of an equestrian it had to deal, became quiet. The horns once more sounded; and the king left the Louvre, followed by the Duc d'Alençon, the King of Navarre, Marguerite, Madame de Nevers, Madame de Sauve, Tavannes, and the chief nobles of the court. It need not be said that La Mole and Coconnas were of the party. As for the Duc d'Anjou, he had been at the siege of Rochelle for the last three months.

While waiting for the king, Henri had approached his wife,

who whispered, "The courier from Rome was conducted by M. de Coconnas to the Duc d'Alençon a quarter of an hour before the Duc de Nevers's messenger saw the king."

"Then he knows all."

"He must know all. Look at him; despite his accomplished dissimulation, he cannot conceal his joy."

"Ventre-saint-gris!" said the Béarnais, "he is hunting three thrones today—France, Poland, and Navarre, without reckoning the boar."

Then, saluting his wife, Henri returned to his place, and called one of his servants—a Béarnais whom he was used to employing in his love-affairs.

"Orthon," said he, "take this key and carry it to that cousin of Madame de Sauve whom you know, who is at the house of his mistress on the corner of the Rue des Quatre Fils. Tell him his cousin wishes to see him this evening; that he is to go to my chamber. If I am not there, he is to wait for me; and if I am late, he can lie down in my bed."

"There is no answer, Sire?"

"None, except to tell me if you have seen him. The key is for him only, you understand?"

"Yes, Sire."

"Stop, blockhead, you must not go off now; it would create observation. Before we leave Paris, I will call you, as if my girth was slackened; then you can wait behind, discharge your commission, and join us at Bondy."

Orthon bowed and drew back.

The cavalcade passed down the Rue St. Honoré, the Rue St. Denis, then the Faubourg. At the Rue St. Laurent, Henri's saddle became ungirthed; Orthon galloped up, and everything passed as the king had arranged. The royal cortège passed down the Rue des Récollets, and the faithful valet dashed into the Rue du Temple.

When Henri rejoined the king, he was busy talking to D'Alençon about the expected boar, and either did not perceive or affected not to perceive that Henri had stayed behind. Madame Marguerite remarked that her brother seemed embarrassed whenever he glanced at Henri. Madame de Nevers was in high glee, for Coconnas was in capital vein with his jests.

At a quarter past eight the cortège arrived at Bondy. Charles's first care was to inquire whether the boar had broken cover. The boar, however, the huntsman assured him, was still in his lair.

A collation was prepared. The king drank a glass of Hungarian wine; then, inviting the ladies to seat themselves, he went to inspect the kennels and the mews, having first given strict orders that his horse should not be unsaddled meanwhile. During his absence, the Duc de Guise arrived; he was armed as if for war, rather than for the chase, and was attended by twenty or thirty gentlemen in similar array. He went to seek the king, and returned conversing with him.

At nine o'clock, the king himself sounded the signal for departure, and every one mounting, hastened to the place of meeting.

During the journey, Henri again approached his wife. "Well," said he, "anything new?"

"Nothing, except that my brother looks very strangely at you."

"I have remarked it myself."

"Have you taken your precautions?"

"I have my shirt of mail on, and an excellent Spanish hunting knife, sharp as a razor, pointed as a needle, with which I can pierce a crown-piece."

"Well," said Marguerite, "may God guard us!"

The huntsman gave a signal; they were at the boar's lair.

CHAPTER 30

Maurevel

While the glittering cortège proceeded toward Bondy, the queen-mother, rolling up the parchment the king had signed, gave orders to have introduced to her presence the man to whom the captain of her guards had remitted a letter some days previously, to "Rue de la Cerisaie, Quartier de l'Arsenal."

A large band of sarcenet covered one of his eyes, and only just left the other visible. His cheekbones were high, and his nose curved like the beak of a vulture; a grizzled beard covered his chin; he wore a large thick cloak, beneath which were evident the hilts of a whole arsenal of weapons. He had at his side a heavy broadsword, with a basket hilt, and one of his hands grasped underneath his cloak a long poniard.

"Ah, you are here, Monsieur!" said the queen, seating herself. "I promised to reward you for the services you rendered us the night of the Saint Bartholomew, and I have found an opportunity of so doing."

"I humbly thank your Majesty," replied the man.

"An opportunity, such as may never again present itself, of distinguishing yourself."

"I am ready, Madame; but I fear from the preamble that—"

"That the commission is a rough one. It is indeed; it is one which might be coveted by a Guise or a Tavannes."

"Madame, whatever it be, I am at your orders."

"Read that," said Catherine; and she gave him the parchment.

He read it and turned pale. "What!" he cried; "an order to arrest the King of Navarre?"

"Well, what is there so very astonishing in that?"

"But a king, Madame! I doubt if I am gentleman enough to arrest a king."

"The confidence I repose in you makes you the first gentleman in my court."

"I thank your Majesty," returned the assassin, with some hesitation, however.

"You will obey me, then?"

"If your Majesty commands me, it is my duty to obey."

"I do command you."

"Then I obey."

"How will you proceed?"

"I scarcely know; I would be guided by your royal Majesty."

"You dread a commotion."

"I confess it."

"Take twelve men, or even more, if necessary."

"I understand; your Majesty permits me to make use of every advantage. But where shall I seize the King of Navarre?"

"Where would you prefer?"

"I should prefer some place where my responsibility—"

"Ah, I understand; a royal palace—the Louvre, for instance."

"Oh, if your Majesty would permit this it would be a great favor."

"Arrest him in the Louvre, then."

"In what part?"

"In his own apartments."

Maurevel bowed. "And when, Madame?"

"Tonight."

"It shall be done, Madame. But deign to tell me what regard I am to have for his rank."

"Regard! rank!" said Catherine. "You seem not to know that the king of France owes no regard to anyone in his kingdom, since there is no one of a rank equal to his own."

"Yet one other question, Madame. Should the king contest the authenticity of this order—it is not likely—but—"

"On the contrary, it is certain—"

"That he will contest it?"

"Without doubt."

"And that consequently he will refuse to obey it?"

"I fear so."

"And will resist it?"

"Most likely."

"Oh, the devil!" said Maurevel; "in that case—"

"In what case?" asked Catherine.

"In case he resists; what shall I do?"

"What do you do when you have the king's warrant—that is, when you represent the king—and some one resists you?"

"Why, Madame," said the bravo, "when I am honored with such an order, and that order concerns a simple gentleman, I kill him."

"I told you just now that everyone in France is in the king's eyes but a simple gentleman."

Maurevel turned pale, for he began to understand.

"Oh, oh!" said he, "kill the King of Navarre!"

"Who spoke of killing him? This order is only to conduct him to the Bastille. If he suffers himself to be arrested quietly, well and good; but if he resists, and seeks to kill you—"

Maurevel grew still paler.

"You will of course defend yourself. A brave soldier like you cannot be expected to suffer himself to be killed; and then, in your own defense, happen what will—you understand?"

"Yes, Madame; but yet—"

"Come, you want me to write on the order the words, 'Dead or alive'?"

"I confess that would remove my scruples."

"Well, I must do it, I suppose."

And unrolling the warrant with one hand, with the other she wrote, "Dead or alive."

"Is the order sufficiently formal now?" she asked.

"Yes, Madame; but I pray you, let me have the execution of it entirely to myself."

"Will anything I have said interfere?"

"Your Majesty bade me take twelve men."

"Well?"

"I request your permission to take only six."

"Why?"

"Because, Madame, if any misfortune should happen to the king, as is probable, six men would be excused for fearing that their prisoner might escape; but no one would excuse twelve guards for not suffering half their number to be killed before laying violent hands on a king."

"Fine king, my faith! without a kingdom!"

"Madame," said Maurevel, "it is not the kingdom which makes the king; it is birth."

"Do as you will," said Catherine. "Meantime, you must not leave the Louvre."

"But how shall I collect my men?"

"Have you no person you can employ in this?"

"There is my servant, a trusty fellow, who sometimes aids me in such things."

"Send for him and arrange your plans. You will breakfast in the king's armory. When he returns from hunting, you can go to my oratory, and wait there till the hour comes."

"How shall we get into the chamber? The King of Navarre doubtless has his suspicions, and fastens the door within."

"I have keys that open all the doors in the Louvre; and the bolts have been removed from his door. Adieu, M. Maurevel. Remember that any failure would compromise the king's honor."

And Catherine, without leaving Maurevel time to reply, called M. de Nancey, the captain of her guards, and bade him conduct Maurevel into the king's armory.

"Mordieu!" said Maurevel. "I am rising in my profession. First I killed a simple gentleman, then I shot at an admiral, now 'tis a king without a crown; who knows but someday I may have to settle a king with a crown."

CHAPTER 31

The Boar Hunt

The huntsman was not deceived when he affirmed that the game had not broken covert. Scarcely had the hounds entered, when the boar, which was, as the huntsman had said, one of the largest size, appeared.

The animal passed within fifty paces of the king, followed only by the hound which had roused him; but twenty dogs were speedily uncoupled and laid on his track.

The chase was Charles's passion; and scarcely had the animal appeared than he dashed after him, followed by the Duc d'Alençon and Henri, who had received a sign from Marguerite warning him not to lose sight of the king. The other huntsmen followed.

In a quarter of an hour some impassable thickets presented themselves, and Charles returned to the glade, cursing and swearing as was his wont—

"Well, D'Alençon, well, Henriot, here you are, calm and tranquil as nuns following the abbess in procession. Do you call that hunting? You, D'Alençon, look as if you had just come out of a box; you are so perfumed that if you get between the boar and the dogs, you will spoil the scent. And you, Henriot, where is your boar-spear? Where is your arquebus?"

"Sire," said Henri, "what is the use of an arquebus? I know your Majesty likes to shoot the boar at bay. As for the boar-spear, it is never used in my country, where we hunt the bear with the simple poniard."

"*Mordieu!*" replied Charles, "you must send me a cartload of bears when you go back to the Pyrenees. It must be glorious sport to contend foot to foot with an animal that may strangle one in a minute. Hark! I think I hear them. No!"

The king blew a blast on his horn that was answered by several others. At this moment a huntsman appeared, and sounded another note.

"Seen! seen!" cried the king; and he set spurs to his horse, followed by all around him.

The huntsman was right; as the king advanced, the pack, now composed of more than sixty dogs, was heard distinctly. The king no sooner saw the boar pass a second time than he pursued him at full speed, blowing his horn with all his might.

The princes followed him some time; but the king's horse was so strong, and bore him over such difficult ways, through such thick coverts, that first the ladies, then the Duc de Guise and the gentlemen, and then the two princes, were obliged to draw rein. Tavannes followed him a while longer, but he, in his turn, was compelled to give it up.

All then, except the king and a few huntsmen, incited by the hope of reward, found themselves near the glade they had started from. The two princes were side by side in a long, broad forest path, the Duc de Guise and his attendants at some little distance beyond.

"Does it not seem," said the Duc d'Alençon to Henri, "that this man, with his armed retinue, is the real king? He does not deign to glance at us poor princes."

"Why should he treat us better than we are treated by our own relatives? You and I are but the hostages of our party at the court."

The duke started and looked at Henri, as if calling for further explanation, but the latter had been more frank than was customary with him, and remained silent.

"What mean you?" asked François, evidently chagrined at his brother-in-law's compelling him to pursue the subject.

"I mean," returned Henri, "that all these armed men who appear to have been instructed not to lose sight of us, seem like guards stationed to prevent two persons from escaping."

"From escaping! Why? how?" asked the duke, with admirably affected surprise.

"You have a magnificent genet there, D'Alençon," said Henri, affecting to change the conversation, and yet adroitly pursuing the subject; "I am sure he would do fourteen miles in an hour, and forty between this and midday. See what a beautiful crossroad there is that way; does it not invite you to loosen rein? As for me, I should like a gallop vastly."

François made no reply, but turned red and pale alternately, and affected to listen for the hunters.

"The news from Poland has taken effect," thought Henri. "My dear brother-in-law has a plan of his own. He is willing enough I should be off; but I don't fly alone, he may rely upon it." At this moment, several converts from Protestantism, who had been but a short time at the court, came up and saluted the princes with a meaning smile. The Duc d'Alençon needed but to say one word, to make but one sign; for it was evident that the thirty or forty cavaliers collected as if by chance round him, were ready to oppose M. de Guise's troop, and favor his flight. The duke, however, turned his head, and placing his horn to his lips, blew a recall.

Still, the newcomers, as if they believed that the duke's hesitation arose from the presence of the Guisards, gradually placed themselves between that party and the princes, in a manner that showed they were well accustomed to military maneuvers. In order to reach the Duc d'Alençon and the King of Navarre, it would be necessary for the Guise party to pass through them; while as far as the eye could reach, the crossroad was free.

Suddenly, between the trees, at ten paces from the King of Navarre, appeared a gentleman whom the two princes had not yet seen. While Henri was conjecturing who he could be, he raised his hat, and displayed the features of the Vicomte de Turenne, one of the Protestant leaders, who was believed to be in Poitou. The viscount made a sign that asked, "Will you come?"

But Henri, after consulting the immovable visage of the Duc d'Alençon, turned his head two or three times, as if something in his collar hurt him. The viscount understood him, and instantly disappeared.

Suddenly the hounds were again heard; and at the extremity of the alley in which the princes were the boar passed, and then the dogs, and then, looking like the Wild Huntsman, Charles, bareheaded, and blowing his horn furiously. Three or four huntsmen rode after him; Tavannes was not there.

"The king!" cried D'Alençon, and he instantly galloped after him.

Reassured by the presence of his friends, and making a sign to them not to withdraw, Henri advanced to the ladies.

"Well?" said Marguerite, taking some steps toward him.

"Well, Madame," said Henri, "we are hunting the boar."

"Is that all?"

"The wind has changed since the morning, as I predicted to you it would."

"These changes of the wind are very bad for hunting, are they not, Sire?" said Marguerite.

"Yes; sometimes they disturb all our arrangements, and we have to form a new plan altogether."

The pack was now heard rapidly approaching, and a sort of tumultuous vapor warned the hunters to be on their guard. Every one raised his head and stood on the alert. Suddenly the boar broke out of the wood, and dashed by the ladies and their gallants. Behind him, close on his haunches, came forty or fifty hounds, and then the king, bareheaded, without hat or mantle, his dress torn by the thorns, his hands and face all bloody; only one or two huntsmen kept up with him. "*Hallali! hallali!*" cried he, as he passed, placing his horn to his bleeding lips; and boar, dogs, and king disappeared like a vision. Immediately after them came D'Alençon and two or three *piqueurs*. Everyone followed, for it was plain the boar would soon be brought to bay.

And so it happened. In less than ten minutes the boar, coming to an open spot, placed his back against a rock, and prepared himself for a desperate struggle. On hearing the cries of Charles, who had followed him, all the party ran in. The most interesting moment of the chase had arrived; the dogs, though well-nigh breathless with a chase of more than three hours, rushed upon the boar with a fury that redoubled the cries and curses of the king.

All the hunters ranged themselves in a circle—the king a little in advance, the Duc d'Alençon behind him with his arquebus, and Henri, who had only his hunting knife. The Duc d'Alençon lighted the match of his arquebus; Henri loosened his knife in its sheath. The Duc de Guise, who despised all such sports, remained in the background with his party. At some distance was a *piqueur,* who with difficulty held back the king's two huge boar-hounds, which, struggling and baying, awaited anxiously the moment when they should be let loose upon their prey.

The animal fought most gallantly; attacked at once by forty

dogs, surrounding him like a raging sea, he at every stroke of his tusk hurled into the air one of the gallant creatures, torn and dying. In ten minutes twenty dogs were killed or disabled.

"Let loose the hounds!" cried the king.

The *piqueur* opened the swivel of the leashes, and the two huge animals, protected by their coats of mail, dashed through the thickest of the fray, and seized the boar each by an ear.

"Bravo, Risquetout! bravo, Duredent!" cried Charles. "A boar-spear! a boar-spear!"

"Will you have my arquebus?" said D'Alençon.

"No, no!" cried the king, "there is no pleasure in shooting him; but it is delicious to feel the spear going in. A spear! a spear!"

One was presented to him.

"Take care, Charles!" said Marguerite.

"To him! to him! Do not miss him, Sire. Pierce the heretic through and through!" cried the Duchesse de Nevers.

"Never fear!" replied the king; and leveling his spear, he rushed at the boar. But at the sight of the glittering steel, the animal made so sudden a movement that the spear glanced off his shoulder and broke against the rock. *"Milles noms d'un diable!* I have missed!" cried Charles, impatiently. "Another spear!" And backing his steed, like a knight of old in a tournament, he cast away the broken weapon. A *piqueur* advanced to offer him another.

But at that moment, as if he foresaw his fate and sought to avoid it, the boar, by a violent effort, burst from the dogs; and his hair bristling, his mouth foaming with rage, and clashing his tusks together, he rushed with lowered head at the king's horse. The king was too good a sportsman not to have foreseen this attack. Pulling hard on the rein, he made his horse rear; but either from the curb being too tightly pressed, or from fear, the animal fell back upon his rider. A cry burst from every one; the king's thigh was caught between the saddle and the ground.

"Let the bridle go, Sire!" cried Henri.

The king abandoned his hold of the rein, seized the saddle with his left hand, and with his right strove to draw his hunting knife, but in vain—the sheath was so tightly pressed by his body as to render that impossible.

"The boar! the boar!" cried Charles. "Help, help, D'Alençon!"

The horse, as if he comprehended the danger of his master, strained his muscles and had already succeeded in raising himself on three feet, when Henri saw D'Alençon, on his brother's appeal, turn ghastly pale as he placed his arquebus to his shoulder and fired. The ball, instead of hitting the boar, struck the foreleg of the king's horse, which instantly fell again.

"Oh!" murmured D'Alençon, his lips blanched with fear, "I think that D'Anjou is King of France and I King of Poland!"

And, in fact, the boar's tusk already grazed Charles's thigh, when the king felt his arm raised and saw a bright blade flash before his eyes, and bury itself up to the hilt behind the boar's shoulder, while a hand, gloved in iron, was dashed against the mouth of the monster.

Charles had by this time freed himself from his struggling horse, and rose with difficulty; when he saw his dress streaming with blood, he grew still paler than before.

"Sire," said Henri, who, still on one knee, kept his knife in the boar's breast, "you are not hurt; I turned the tusk aside in time." He then rose, leaving the knife in the boar, which turned over dead, bleeding still more profusely from the mouth even than from the wound.

Charles, surrounded by a crowd of courtiers, all sending forth cries of terror, which would have disturbed the calmest courage, seemed for a moment about to fall by the dead boar; but recovering himself, he turned to the King of Navarre, and seized his hand, his eyes beaming with the first ray of sensibility that had touched his heart for full four-and-twenty years.

"Thanks, Henriot!" said he.

"My poor brother!" said D'Alençon coming up to him.

"Ah, is that you, D'Alençon!" cried the king. "Well, famous marksman that you are, where is your ball?"

"It must have flattened upon the boar, no doubt."

"Eh, *mon Dieu,*" said Henri, with an air of surprise admirably feigned, "your ball has broken the leg of the king's horse; it is wonderful!"

"Ah! is that so?" said the king.

"Perhaps," replied the duke, all consternation; "my hand trembled so."

"Humph! for a first-rate marksman you made a most curious shot, D'Alençon," said Charles frowning: "once more, Henriot, thanks!"

Marguerite advanced to congratulate Henri.

"Oh, by my faith, Margot, you may well thank him heartily," said Charles; "but for him the King of France would be Henri III."

"Alas, Madame," returned Henri, "M. d'Anjou, who is already my enemy, will be more than ever so now; but everyone does what he can. Ask M. d'Alençon else—"

And, stooping down, he withdrew his knife from the body of the boar, and plunged it several times into the earth to cleanse it from the blood.

"And now, ladies and gentlemen," said the king, "homeward! I have had enough for one day."

PART TWO

CHAPTER 1

Fraternity

In saving the life of Charles, Henri had done more than save the life of a man; he had prevented three kingdoms from changing sovereigns. Had Charles IX been killed, the Duc d'Anjou would have been King of France, and the Duc d'Alençon most probably King of Poland. As to Navarre, as the Duc d'Anjou was enamored of Madame de Condé, that crown would in all probability have paid the husband for the complaisance of his wife.

In all this change nothing beneficial would have arisen for Henri. He would have changed his master, that was all; and instead of Charles IX, who tolerated him, he would have seen the Duc d'Anjou on the throne, who, having but one head and one heart with his mother Catherine, had sworn his death and would have kept his oath. These were the ideas that floated through his brain when the wild boar had rushed on King Charles, and we have seen the result of this reflection, rapid as lightning, that the life of Charles IX was bound up with his own existence.

Charles IX, then, was saved by a devotion whose spring and action he could not comprehend. Marguerite, however, had comprehended it fully, and had admired the strange courage of Henri, which, like lightning, shone only in the storm.

Henri, as he returned from Bondy, reflected deeply on his situation, and when he reached the Louvre he had resolved on his plan of action. Without taking off his boots, but all dusty and covered with blood as he was, he went to the Duc d'Alençon, whom he found greatly agitated, and pacing hastily up and down his chamber. The prince started when he saw him.

"Yes," said Henri to him, taking both his hands, "I understand, my good brother; you are angry with me because I was the first to call the king's attention to the fact that your ball struck his horse's leg instead of hitting the boar, as you intended. But what could you expect? It was impossible to repress a word of surprise. Besides, the king himself must have perceived it, must he not?"

"Doubtless, doubtless!" muttered D'Alençon; "yet I cannot but attribute to a bad intention your pointing out this fact, which you must have seen has made my brother Charles suspicious of my purpose, and thrown a cloud between us."

"We will talk of this anon; and as to my good or bad intention, I have come now expressly to enable you to judge of it."

"Well," said D'Alençon, with his customary reserve, "speak, Henri; I will hear you."

"When I shall have spoken, François, you will see clearly of what sort are my intentions; for the confidence which I am about to repose in you excludes all reserve and caution, and when I shall have finished you can destroy me with a word."

"What is it, then?" said François, who began to be troubled.

"My brother, your interests are too dear to me to allow me to keep from you that the Huguenots have made me certain proposals."

"Proposals? what sort of proposals?"

"One of the leaders, M. de Mouy de Saint-Phale, son of the brave Mouy assassinated by Maurevel, has been with me at the risk of his life, to prove to me that I am in captivity."

"Ah, indeed! and what reply did you make?"

"My brother, you know how tenderly I love Charles, who saved my life; and that the queen-mother has been like my own mother to me. I have therefore refused all the offers he made me."

"And what were these offers?"

"The Huguenots wish to rehabilitate the throne of Navarre; and as in reality this throne belonged to me by inheritance, they offered it to me."

"Yes, and M. de Mouy, instead of the adhesion he had entreated, received your refusal?"

"Most decidedly; but since then—"

"You have repented, my brother?" interrupted D'Alençon.

"No; but I have found that M. de Mouy, enraged at my refusal, has cast his eyes in another direction."

"Whither?" asked François, quickly.

"I do not know; on the Prince de Condé, perchance."

"Very probably," was the reply.

"I have, however, a certain means of ascertaining the chief he has selected."

François became very pale.

"But," continued Henri, "the Huguenots are divided among themselves; and Mouy, brave and loyal as he is, represents but one half the party. Now, the other half, which is not to be despised, has not lost all hope of seeing on the throne that Henri de Navarre who, having hesitated in the first instance, may have reflected since."

"Do you think so?"

"I have daily proofs of this. The troop that joined us at the hunt—did you notice the men who composed it?"

"Yes; they were converted gentlemen."

"The chief of this troop who made me a sign—did you recognize him?"

"Yes; it was the Vicomte de Turenne."

"Did you understand what they wished?"

"Yes; they proposed to you to fly."

"Then," said Henri, "it is evident that there is a second party with different views from M. de Mouy, and that a very powerful one; so that in order to succeed it is requisite to unite the two parties, Turenne and Mouy. The conspiracy strengthens; troops are ready; they await only the signal from me. Now, in that critical situation, which requires on my part prompt action, I am debating in my mind two purposes, between which I hesitate. I have come to submit these plans to you as to a friend."

"Say rather, as a brother!"

"First let me expose the state of my mind, my dear François. I have no desire, no ambition, no capacity. I am a commonplace country gentleman—poor, indolent, and timid. The role of conspirator presents to me a chance of disgrace, badly compensated by even the assurance of attaining to a crown."

"Ah, my brother!" said François, "you do yourself injustice; nothing can be more pitiable than the position of a prince whose fortune is limited by a landmark, or by some individual in the career of honor. I cannot therefore credit what you say."

"Yet I speak only the truth, my brother," was Henri's reply.

"And if I could believe that I had a real friend, I would resign in his favor all the power which the party attached to me would confer; but," he added with a sigh, "I have not such a friend."

"Perhaps you are mistaken."

"No, *ventre-saint-gris!*" cried Henri. "Except yourself, Brother, I see no one who is attached to me; and then, rather than see a movement miscarry amid frightful commotions, because in the interest of someone who is unworthy, I prefer to inform my brother the king of all that is going on. I will name no person, I will not mention country or date; but I will prevent the catastrophe."

"Great God!" exclaimed D'Alençon, who could not repress his alarm; "what are you saying? What! you, the sole hope of the party since the admiral's death; you, a converted Huguenot—scarce converted, it would seem—would you raise the knife against your brothers? Henri, Henri, in doing that you will hand over to a second Saint Bartholomew all the Calvinists of the kingdom! Do you know that Catherine only awaits such an opportunity to exterminate all the survivors?" And the trembling duke, his face marked with red and livid spots, pressed Henri's hand, in his eagerness to make him promise to renounce a resolution which must destroy him.

"What!" said Henri, with an air of much surprise, "do you think, François, that so many misfortunes must then occur? Yet it seems to me that with the king's guarantee I could save the imprudent partisans."

"The guarantee of King Charles IX, Henri? Did not the admiral have it—Téligny, yourself? Ah, Henri! I tell you, if you do this, you destroy them all—not only them, but also all directly or indirectly connected with them."

Henri appeared to reflect for a moment. "If," he said, "I were an important prince at court, I should act otherwise; in your place, for instance, François, a son of France, and probable heir to the throne—"

François shook his head ironically and said, "What would you do in my place?"

"In your place, my brother," replied Henri, "I should put myself at the head of this movement. My name and credit would answer to my conscience for the life of the seditious; and I would derive from it something useful for myself in the first instance, and then for the king; and this from an enterprise which otherwise may terminate in great mischief for France."

D'Alençon listened to these words with a joy which expanded all the muscles of his face, and replied, "Do you think this practicable, and that it will avoid all those evils which you foresee?"

"I do," said Henri. "The Huguenots like you; your modest exterior, your situation, elevated and interesting at the same time, and the kindness you have always evinced to those of the Reformed faith, induce them to serve you."

"But," said D'Alençon, "there is a schism in the party; will those who are for you be for me?"

"I will undertake to conciliate them on two grounds."

"What are they?"

"In the first place, through the confidence which the chiefs have in me; then, through their fear that your Highness, knowing their names—"

"But those names, who will give them to me?"

"I will, *ventre-saint-gris!*"

"You will do that?"

"Listen, François; I have told you that in this court I love only you. That comes, doubtless, from the fact that you are persecuted like myself. And then my wife also loves you with an affection that has no parallel."

François blushed with pleasure.

"Believe me, my brother," continued Henri; "take up this matter. Reign in Navarre; and if you keep for me a place at your table and a good forest for hunting, I shall be perfectly happy."

"Reign in Navarre!" said the duke; "but if—"

"If the Duc d'Anjou is named King of Poland, you would say?"

François looked at Henri with some alarm.

"Well, listen," said Henri—"since nothing escapes your observation; it is precisely on that supposition that I have reasoned. If the Duc d'Anjou is nominated King of Poland, and our brother Charles (whom God preserve!) should die, it is but two hundred leagues from Pau to Paris, while it is four hundred from Paris to Cracow; and you would be here to claim the inheritance at the moment when the King of Poland would only have learned of its being vacated. Then, if you are satisfied with me, François, you may give me this kingdom of Navarre, which will then be only one of the off-shoots of your crown. Under these circumstances I would accept it. The worst that could happen to you would be to remain king down there starting a royal branch, and living *en famille* with me and my wife; while here, what are you? A poor, persecuted prince, a poor third son of the king, a slave of two elder brothers, whom a caprice may send to the Bastille."

"Yes, yes," said François. "I feel all this so deeply that I cannot understand how you renounce all the hopes that you propose for me. Nothing beats there, then?" and the Duc d'Alençon placed his hand on his brother's heart.

"There are," said Henri, with a smile, "burdens too heavy for certain hands. I shall not try to lift this one. Fear of the fatigue annuls the desire of possession."

"Then, Henri, you really renounce?"

"I said so to Mouy, and I repeat it to you."

"But in such cases, Brother," said D'Alençon, "men do not say, they prove."

Henri drew a long breath, like a wrestler who perceives the strength of his adversary giving way. "I will give you proof," he said, "this evening. At nine o'clock the list of the chiefs and the plan of the enterprise shall be in your hands. I have already sent to Mouy a formal renunciation."

François took Henri's hand, and pressed it with fervor. At the same moment Catherine entered the apartment, and, as usual, without being announced. "Together!" she said with a smile, "like two loving brothers!"

"I hope so, Madame," replied Henri, with the utmost composure, while the Duc d'Alençon turned pale with agony. Henri then withdrew a few steps, leaving Catherine free to talk with her son.

The queen-mother then took from her purse a magnificent jewel, and said to François, "This clasp comes from Florence, and I give it you to put on your sword-belt." Then she added in a low voice, "If you should hear any noise this evening in the apartments of your good brother Henri, do not heed it."

François grasped his mother's hand and said, "Will you allow me to show him the handsome present you have just made me?"

"Do still better; give it to him in your own and my name, for I had ordered a second for that purpose."

"Do you hear, Henri?" said François; "my good mother brings me this jewel, and redoubles its value by allowing me to offer it to you."

Henri went into raptures at the beauty of the jewel, and was profuse in his thanks.

"My son," said Catherine, "I do not feel well, and am going to bed. Your brother Charles is much shaken by his fall, and wishes to do the same thing. We shall not, therefore, all sup together. Ah, Henri! I forgot to compliment you on your courage and skill; you have saved your king and brother, and you must be recompensed for such high service."

"I am recompensed already," replied Henri, with a bow.

"By the feeling that you have done your duty?" was Catherine's reply; "but that is not enough for Charles and myself, and we must devise some means of requiting our obligations toward you."

"All that may come from you and my good brother must be welcome, Madame," was Henri's reply; and bowing, he left the apartment.

"Ah, my worthy brother François!" thought Henri, as he went out; "now I am sure not to go away alone; and the conspiracy, which had a heart, has now found a head, and what is still better, this head is responsible to me for my own. Only let us be on our guard. Catherine has made me a present; Catherine promises me a recompense. There is some deviltry brewing; I will have a conversation this evening with Marguerite."

The Gratitude of King Charles IX

Maurevel had remained for a portion of the day in the king's armory; and when Catherine saw the moment approach of the return from the chase, she had desired him and his satellites to pass into her oratory. Charles IX, informed by his nurse on his arrival who the man was, and remembering the order his mother had extracted from him in the morning, understood everything.

"Ah, ah!" he murmured, "the time is ill-chosen—on the very day on which he has saved my life." And he was about to go to his mother, but suddenly changed his intention.

"*Mordieu!*" he exclaimed, "if I speak to her of it, what a discussion will ensue! We had better act each independently. Nurse," he continued, "shut all the doors, and inform the Queen Elizabeth [Charles IX was married to Elizabeth of Austria, daughter of Maximilian] that being rather unwell from my fall, I shall sleep alone tonight."

The nurse obeyed; and as the hour for his plan had not arrived, Charles began to write verses. It was the occupation in which his time passed most rapidly; and thus nine o'clock struck when Charles thought it was only seven. He counted the strokes one after the other, and at the last he rose. "Devil's name!" he exclaimed, "it is precisely the time."

Taking his cloak and hat, he went out by a secret door which he had made in the paneling, and of the existence of which Catherine herself was ignorant.

He went straight to Henri's apartments. Henri had gone thither only to change his dress when he left the Duc d'Alençon, and had then left it immediately.

"He must have gone to sup with Marguerite," said the king to himself; "he seemed to be on the best possible terms with her today"; and he went toward Marguerite's apartments.

Marguerite had invited to her rooms the Duchesse de Nevers, Coconnas, and La Mole, and they were enjoying a repast of pastry and confectionery.

Charles knocked at the door. Gillonne went to open it, and was so frightened at the sight of the king that she could scarcely make her obeisance to him; and instead of running to inform her mistress of the august visit which was paid her, she allowed Charles to pass her without any other signal than the cry she had uttered. The king crossed the antechamber, and guided by the shouts of laughter, advanced toward the dining room.

"Poor Henriot!" he ejaculated, "he is making merry, quite unconscious of his danger."

" 'Tis I!" he said, raising the tapestry, and presenting a smiling face.

Marguerite uttered a terrible cry. All joyous as was the king's face, it produced on her the effect of a Medusa's head. Sitting facing the curtain, she had recognized Charles. The two men had their backs turned to the king.

"His Majesty!" she exclaimed in a tone of affright; and she rose from her seat.

Coconnas, while the three others felt quite bewildered, was the only one who preserved his presence of mind. He also rose, but with well-contrived awkwardness upset the table, with its glass, plate, and wax lights; instantly there was complete darkness and the silence of death.

"Steal off!" said Coconnas to La Mole; "quick, quick, and cleverly!"

La Mole did not wait for a second hint, but feeling along the wall with his hands, groped his way into the bedchamber, that he might hide in the cabinet which he knew so well. But as he entered the sleeping room he came in contact with a man who entered by the secret passage.

"What can all this mean?" said Charles, in the dark, with a voice that was beginning to sound very impatient. "Am I an intruder, that on my appearance such a scene of confusion takes place? Henriot! Henriot! where are you? Answer me!"

"We are saved!" whispered Marguerite, taking a hand which she supposed to be that of Coconnas; "the king thinks that my husband is one of the guests."

"And he shall think so still, Madame, be assured," said Henri to the queen in the same tone.

"Great God!" exclaimed Marguerite, suddenly dropping the hand she held, which was that of the King of Navarre.

"Hush!" said Henri.

"Thousand names of the devil! what are you all whispering for?" cried Charles. "Henri, answer; where are you?"

"I am here, Sire," said the voice of the King of Navarre.

"The devil!" said Coconnas, who was with the Duchesse de Nevers in a corner; "the plot thickens."

"And we are doubly lost," added the Duchesse de Nevers.

Coconnas, brave even to rashness, had reflected that at last the candles must be lighted, and thinking the sooner the better, abandoned the hand of the Duchesse de Nevers, which he had hitherto held in his own, picked up a taper, and going to the stove, lighted it. The room was thus again illuminated, and Charles cast an inquiring glance around.

Henri was close to his wife; the Duchesse de Nevers was alone in a corner; and Coconnas, standing in the middle of the chamber with his candle in his hand, lighted up the whole scene.

"Excuse us, Brother," said Marguerite; "we did not expect you."

"And so your Majesty, as you may see, has frightened us not a little," said Henriette.

"For my part," added Henri, who at once comprehended the whole, "I was so startled that in rising I upset the table."

Coconnas gave the King of Navarre a look which implied, "I like that! here's a husband who understands at half a word."

"What a terrible confusion!" said Charles. "Henriot, your supper is upset; so come with me, and you shall finish it elsewhere. I mean to carry you off this evening."

"What, Sire!" said Henri; "your Majesty will do me that honor?"

"Yes, my Majesty will do you the honor to take you from the Louvre. Lend him to me, Marguerite, and I will bring him back again tomorrow morning."

"Ah, Brother," replied Marguerite, "you have no need of my permission for that; you are master here, as everywhere else."

"Sire," said Henri, "I will just go for another cloak, and return immediately."

"There's no occasion; the one you have on is quite good enough."

"But, Sire—" said the Béarnais.

"I tell you not to return to your apartments; thousand names of a devil! don't you hear what I say? Come along!"

"Yes, yes, go!" said Marguerite, pressing her husband's arm, for a singular look of Charles's had convinced her that something remarkable was going on.

"I am ready, Sire," said Henri.

But Charles was looking very steadfastly at Coconnas, who continued his office of torch-bearer by lighting the other candles.

"Who is this gentleman?" he inquired of Henri, still looking at the Piedmontese. "It would not, by any chance, be M. de la Mole?"

"Who has mentioned M. de la Mole to him?" thought Marguerite.

"No, Sire," replied Henri; "M. de la Mole is not here, and I regret it the more, as I cannot have the honor of presenting him to your Majesty as well as his friend, M. de Coconnas. They are inseparable, and are both in the suite of M. d'Alençon."

"Ah, ah! of our famous marksman?" said Charles. Then frowning, he added, "Is not M. de la Mole a Huguenot?"

"Converted, Sire," said Henri; "and I answer for him as for myself."

"When you answer for anyone, Henriot, after what you have done today, I have no right to doubt you. But no matter. I should have liked to see M. de la Mole, but some other time will do"; and then, looking again around the chamber, Charles kissed Marguerite, and took away the King of Navarre, holding him by the arm. At the gate of the Louvre, Henri stopped to speak to someone.

"Come, come along quickly, Henriot," said Charles. "When I tell you the air of the Louvre is not good for you this evening, why the devil don't you believe me?"

"*Ventre-saint-gris!*" murmured Henri, "and Mouy will be all alone in my room; if the air is not good for me, it must be worse for him."

"Well," said the king, when he and Henri had crossed the drawbridge, "it is all arranged, then, Henriot, that the gentlemen of M. le Duc d'Alençon shall pay court to your wife?"

"How is that, Sire?"

"Yes, is not that M. de Coconnas paying attentions to Margot?"

"Who has told you that?"

"No matter," replied the king; "someone has told me."

"A hoax, pure and simple, Sire. M. de Coconnas, it is true, has a tenderness for someone, but it is for Madame de Nevers."

"Ah, bah!"

"I can assure your Majesty that it is as I say."

Charles broke out into loud laughter. "Very well," said he; "if the Due de Guise gives me an opportunity I will relate to him the exploits of his sister-in-law. After all," he continued, meditating, "I don't know whether it was M. de Coconnas or M. de la Mole who was mentioned to me."

"Neither the one nor the other, Sire," said Henri. "I can answer to you for the sentiments of my wife."

"Good, Henriot, good!" said the king. "I would rather find you in this mood than in any other. Upon my honor, you are a brave lad, and I think that presently I shall be unable to get along without you."

On saying these words the king gave a peculiar whistle, and four gentlemen who were waiting in the Rue de Beauvais joined them, and they all advanced into the city as the clock struck ten.

"Well!" said Marguerite, when the king and Henri had gone, "let us sit down again to table."

"No, faith!" said the duchess; "I am too much frightened. The little house in the Rue Cloche Percée forever! No one can enter there without laying a regular siege; and our brave friends could use their swords. But what are you looking for, M. de Coconnas, under the tables and in the closets?"

"I am looking for my friend La Mole," said the Piedmontese.

"Search in the direction of my chamber, Monsieur," said Marguerite. "There is a certain cabinet there—"

"Good!" said Coconnas, "I will go there"; and he went into the chamber.

"Well!" said a voice in the darkness, "where are we?"

"Eh, *mordi!* we are now at the dessert."

"And the King of Navarre?"

"Has seen nothing. As a husband he is perfect; I wish my wife might have one like him. But I fear it would have to be by a second marriage."

"And King Charles?"

"Ah, the king has taken off the husband."

"No, really?"

"Yes, and the ladies have a pilgrimage to make toward the Rue du Roi de Sicile, and we must guard the pilgrims."

"Impossible! you know that—"

"Why impossible?"

"Why, then, are we not in the service of his royal Highness?"

The two friends represented their position to their fair companions, and Madame de Nevers said, "Well, then, we will go without you."

"And may we know where you are going?" asked Coconnas.

"Oh, you are too inquisitive," said the duchess. *"Quælre, et invenies."* ("Seek, and you will find.")

The two young men made their bows, and proceeded to the Duc d'Alençon, who seemed to be awaiting them.

"You are rather late, gentlemen," was his remark.

"Scarcely ten o'clock, Monseigneur," replied Coconnas.

The duke looked at his watch. "True," he said, "but yet everybody in the Louvre is in bed."

"Monseigneur," said Coconnas, "your Highness no doubt will go to bed, or write—"

"No, gentlemen, I can dispense with your services until tomorrow morning."

"Come, come," whispered Coconnas to La Mole; "the court sleeps out of bed this evening, it seems. The night will be devilishly fine. Let us take our share of it."

The two young men ran upstairs as speedily as possible, took their cloaks and night-swords, and hastening out of the Louvre, overtook the two ladies at the corner of the Rue du Coq St. Honoré.

Meantime the Duc d'Alençon, shut up in his chamber, waited, with eyes open and ears on the alert, the events which his mother had promised.

CHAPTER 3

Man Proposes, but God Disposes

As the duke had said to the young men, the most profound silence reigned throughout the Louvre. Marguerite and Madame de Nevers had gone to the Rue Tizon; Coconnas and La Mole had followed them; the king and Henri were roving about in the city; the Duc d'Alençon was anxiously awaiting the occurrence of the events his mother had alluded to; and Catherine was in bed, listening to Madame de Sauve, who read to her certain Italian tales, at which the worthy queen laughed heartily.

Catherine had not been in so good spirits for a long time. After partaking with good appetite of a collation with her attendants, she had held a conference with her physician, had gone over the daily household accounts, and then had ordered a service of prayer for the success of a certain enterprise which she said was important to the happiness of her children. It was a habit of Catherine—a habit quite Florentine—to have prayers and masses said, of which none but God and herself knew the purpose. Then she had revisited René, and had selected several novelties from his rich assortment.

"Let someone ascertain," said Catherine, "if my daughter, the Queen of Navarre, is in her apartments, and if she is, beg her to come and keep me company."

The page to whom this order was addressed left the room, and soon returned, accompanied by Gillonne.

"I sent for the queen," said Catherine, "not for her attendant."

"Madame," replied Gillone, "I thought it my duty to come myself to inform your Majesty that the Queen of Navarre is gone out with the Duchesse de Nevers."

"Out at this hour!" said Catherine, frowning; "where is she gone?"

"To a meeting of alchemists, at the Hôtel de Guise, in the apartments of Madame de Nevers."

"And when will she return?"

"The meeting will not break up until very late," replied Gillonne, "so that it is probable her Majesty will sleep at the Hôtel de Guise."

"She is very happy," murmured Catherine. "She has friends, and is a queen; she wears a crown and is called your Majesty, and she has no subjects; she is very fortunate."

After that sally, which made her hearers smile inwardly, "Besides," she murmured, "since she has gone out—for she has gone out, you say?"

"Half an hour ago, Madame."

"So much the better; go."

Gillonne saluted, and left the room.

"Go on, Charlotte," said the queen.

Madame de Sauve obeyed. In ten minutes Catherine stopped her. "Oh, by the way," said she, "dismiss the guards in the gallery."

This was the signal agreed upon with Maurevel. The order was executed, and Madame de Sauve continued. She had read for a quarter of an hour, when a long and piercing cry was heard, that made the hair of all in the chamber stand on end. A pistol shot followed.

"Well," said Catherine, "why do you not go on reading?"

"Madame," replied Charlotte, turning pale, "did not your Majesty hear?"

"What?" asked Catherine.

"That cry!"

"And that pistol shot?" added the captain of the guards.

"A cry and a pistol shot!" said Catherine. "I heard nothing; besides, a cry and a pistol shot are not so very extraordinary at the Louvre. Read on, Carlotta."

"But listen, Madame," said Madame de Sauve, while M. de Nancey stood grasping his sword-hilt, not daring to leave the apartment without the queen's permission; "I hear struggling, imprecations—"

"Shall I go and see, Madame?" asked Nancey.

"No, Monsieur," returned Catherine. "Who will be here to protect me in case of danger? It is only some drunken Swiss quarreling."

The tranquillity of the queen contrasted so strangely with the alarm of everyone else that Madame de Sauve, timid as she was, fixed her eyes inquiringly on her. "But, Madame," said she, "it is as if they were killing someone."

"Whom do you think they are killing?"

"The King of Navarre, Madame; for the noise comes from the direction of his apartments."

"The fool!" murmured the queen, whose lips, spite of the control she had over herself, were strangely agitated, for she was muttering a prayer—"the fool! she sees her King of Navarre everywhere."

"Mon Dieu! mon Dieu!" said Madame de Sauve, sinking into her chair.

"It is over," said Catherine. "Captain," continued she, addressing M. de Nancey, "I hope that tomorrow you will inquire into this, and punish the culprits severely. Continue, Carlotta." And Catherine sank back on her pillow in a state that seemed near akin to fainting, for her attendants remarked large drops of perspiration on her face.

Madame de Sauve obeyed; but her eyes and her voice alone were engaged. She fancied she saw him most dear to her surrounded by deadly perils; and after a mental struggle of some minutes, her voice failed her, the book fell from her hands, and she fainted.

Suddenly a still more violent noise than before was heard, a hasty step shook the corridor, two more pistol-shots made the windowpanes shake. Catherine, astonished at this renewal of the strife, rose; she was deadly pale, her eyes were dilated, and at the moment Nancey was about to rush from the apartment she seized his arm, saying, "Let everyone stay here; I will go myself and see what is the matter."

Thus it was: Mouy had received that morning from the hands of Orthon the key of Henri's chamber; in the key he remarked a small roll of paper, which he took out and found it to contain the password at the Louvre for the night. Orthon had moreover given him the king's directions to be at the Louvre at ten o'clock. At half-past nine Mouy had put on his armor, buttoned a silken doublet on it, buckled on his sword, placed his pistols in his belt, and covered all with the famous cherry mantle.

We have seen how Henri thought fit to pay Marguerite a visit before entering his own apartments, and how he arrived by the secret passage just in time to run against La Mole in Marguerite's chamber and to take his place in the supper room. Precisely at this moment Mouy passed the wicket of the Louvre, and thanks to the password and the cherry mantle, entered the palace without obstacle. He went straight to the King of Navarre's apartments, imitating, as well as he could, La Mole's walk and manner. He found Orthon waiting for him in the antechamber.

"M. de Mouy," said the mountaineer, "the king has gone out, but he has ordered me to conduct you to his chamber, where you are to wait; should he not come until late, he desires you will lie down on his bed."

Mouy entered, without asking further explanation. In order to fill up the time he took pen and paper, and approaching an excellent map of France that hung on the wall, set himself to count the stages from Paris to Pau. This did not occupy him long, and when he had finished he was at a loss what to do. He walked up and down the room a few times, yawned, and then, profiting by Henri's invitation, and justified too by the familiarity that then existed between princes and their gentlemen, he placed his pistols and the lamp on the table, laid his drawn sword by his side, and secure against surprise, for an attendant was watching in the outer chamber, soon slept soundly. Mouy snored like a trooper, and in that respect could rival the King of Navarre himself.

It was then that six men, sword and dagger in hand, glided noiselessly along the corridor that communicated with Henri's apartments. One of these men walked in front; besides his sword and dagger, he had pistols attached to his belt by silver hooks. This man was Maurevel. Arrived at Henri's door, he stopped.

"Are you quite sure all the sentinels of the corridor have gone?" he asked.

"There is not one at his post," replied his lieutenant.

"Good," said Maurevel; "now let us see whether he whom we come for is here."

"But," said the lieutenant, arresting the hand which Maurevel was placing on the doorknob, "Captain, these are the King of Navarre's apartments."

"Who said anything to the contrary?" replied Maurevel.

The men looked at one another with an air of surprise, and the lieutenant recoiled a step. "What!" said he, "are we to make an arrest at this hour in the Louvre, and in the apartments of the King of Navarre?"

"What would you say," replied Maurevel, "if I should tell you that he whom you are about to arrest is the King of Navarre himself?"

"I should say, Captain, that it is a serious matter, and that without an order signed by the king—"

"Read," said Maurevel; and taking from his doublet the order given him by Queen Catherine, he handed it to the lieutenant.

"All right," said the latter, after reading it. "I have nothing more to say."

"And are you ready?"

"I am."

"And you?" continued Maurevel, turning to the five others.

They saluted respectfully.

"Listen to me, then, gentlemen," said Maurevel; "this is the plan: two of you will remain at this door, two at the door of the bedchamber, and two will go in with me."

"And then?" said the lieutenant.

"Listen well to this: we are commanded to prevent the prisoner from calling, crying out, or resisting; any breach of that order is to be punished with death."

"Come, come, he has *carte blanche,*" said the lieutenant to the man appointed with him to go in with Maurevel to the king.

"Complete," said Maurevel.

"Poor devil of a king!" said one of the men; "it is written on high that he should not escape."

"And here also," said Maurevel, taking from the lieutenant Catherine's order, which he returned to his doublet.

Maurevel placed the key Catherine had given him in the lock, and leaving two men at the outer door, passed with the four others into the antechamber.

"Ah," said he, hearing even from that distance the loud breathing of the sleeper; "it appears that we shall find here the man we are looking for."

Orthon, thinking it was his master returning, advanced, and found himself in the presence of five armed men. At the sight of their sinister faces, and more particularly at that of Maurevel, who was called "the King's Killer," he recoiled, and planted himself before the second door.

"Who are you?" said Orthon; "and what do you want?"

"In the king's name," said Maurevel, "where is your master?"

"The King of Navarre is not here."

"A pretext, a lie!" replied Maurevel. "Stand back."

Orthon seized the handle of the door.

"You shall not enter!" cried he.

At a sign from Maurevel the four men grasped the faithful page, tore him from his hold, and as he was about to cry out, Maurevel placed his hand on his mouth. Orthon bit the assassin furiously, who uttered a suppressed cry and struck him on the head with the pommel of his sword. Orthon fell, crying, "Treason! treason!" His voice failed him and he fainted. The assassins passed over his body; two stationed themselves at the second door, and the two others, led by Maurevel, entered the bedchamber. By the light of the lamp they saw the bed; the curtains were closed.

"Oh," said the lieutenant, "he snores no longer!"

"Now, then, upon him!" cried Maurevel.

At this voice a hoarse cry more like the roar of a lion than the voice of a human being was heard; the curtains were violently drawn back; and a man in a cuirass and steel cap appeared, sitting on the bed, a pistol in each hand, and his drawn sword on his knees. When Maurevel saw that face and recognized Mouy, his hair stood on end; he turned deadly pale, and recoiled as if he had seen a spectre.

Suddenly the armed figure rose and advanced toward Maurevel as he started back, so that the threatener seemed to retreat, and the threatened to pursue.

"Ah, scoundrel!" said Mouy; "you have come to murder me, as you murdered my father!"

The two guards who were with Maurevel alone heard these terrible words; but as they were uttered one of Mouy's pistols was leveled at Maurevel's head. The ruffian sank on his knees at the instant Mouy pulled the trigger, and one of the guards, whom he uncovered by this movement, fell with a bullet in his heart; Maurevel instantly fired in return, but the ball glanced off Mouy's cuirass.

Then, measuring the distance and calculating his spring, Mouy, with a back stroke of his large sword, cleft the skull of the second guard, and turning to Maurevel, crossed weapons with him. The combat was terrible, but brief. At the fourth pass Maurevel felt Mouy's sword in his throat; he uttered a low groan and fell, upsetting the lamp, which was extinguished in the fall.

Agile and powerful as one of Homer's heroes, Mouy sprang

boldly forward, favored by the obscurity, into the antechamber, felled one of the guards, sent the other staggering from him, passed like lightning between the two at the outer door, escaped two pistol-shots fired at him, the balls of which grazed the wall of the corridor, and was then safe, for besides the sword with which he had dealt such fearful blows, he had one pistol still loaded. He hesitated an instant whether he should enter D'Alençon's apartments, the door of which seemed ajar, or escape from the Louvre. Resolving upon the latter course, he sprang down the stairs, arrived at the wicket, pronounced the password, and darted out, crying, "Go upstairs! they are killing on the king's account." Availing himself of the stupefaction produced by the report of the pistols and by his own words, he disappeared in the Rue du Coq, without having received a scratch.

It was at this moment that Catherine stopped M. de Nancey, saying, "Let everyone stay here; I will go myself and see what is the matter."

"But, Madame," said the captain, "the danger to which your Majesty is exposed compels me to follow."

"Stay, Monsieur!" said Catherine, in a tone more imperious than before; "stay! Around the paths of kings there is a protection more powerful than the sword of man."

The captain remained. Then, taking a lamp, and pushing her naked feet into slippers, Catherine advanced, impassive and cold as a spectre, along the corridor, still full of smoke, toward Henri's apartments. She arrived at the first door, entered, and found Orthon senseless on the threshold.

"Oh," said she, "here is the servant; we shall soon find the master"; and she approached the second door. There her foot struck against a corpse; she turned the light upon it. It was the guard whose skull had been cleft; he was quite dead. A little beyond lay the lieutenant, with the death-rattle in his throat. Beside the bed was a man, who, pale as death, was bleeding fast from a double wound in his throat, and who, clenching his hands convulsively, strove to raise himself. It was Maurevel.

Catherine shuddered; she saw the bed deserted. She looked round the room, and in vain sought among the three men lying there in their blood for the corpse which she hoped to see.

Maurevel recognized Catherine; his eyes dilated horribly, and he stretched out his hand toward her with a gesture of despair.

"Well," said she, in suppressed tones; "where is he? What has become of him? Wretch, have you allowed him to escape?"

Maurevel strove to speak, but an unintelligible whistling sound came from his wound, a bloody foam covered his lips, and he shook his head to indicate his inability and his suffering.

"Speak!" cried the queen; "speak, if it be but one word!"

Maurevel pointed to his wound, and after a desperate effort to utter something, fainted.

Catherine looked around her; there were none but the dead and the dying there; blood flowed in every direction, and silence reigned in the chamber. She spoke again to Maurevel, but in vain; a paper had dropped from his doublet—it was the order for Henri's arrest. Catherine seized it, and concealed it beneath her robe. At this moment she heard a slight noise behind her, and turning round, she perceived D'Alençon, who had been drawn thither by the noise.

"You here, François?" said she.

"Yes, Madame. For God's sake, what does this mean?"

"Retire to your apartments; you will know soon enough."

D'Alençon, however, was not so ignorant of what had occurred as Catherine imagined. On hearing steps in the corridor he had listened. Seeing men enter the King of Navarre's apartments, he had recalled the words of Catherine, had understood what was to happen, and was secretly rejoiced at having so dangerous a friend disposed of by a hand more powerful than his own.

Soon the noise of firearms and the steps of a fugitive attracted his attention, and he had seen, as it was disappearing, a red mantle, too familiar to him not to be recognized.

"Mouy!" cried he; "Mouy with my brother-in-law! But no, it is impossible! Can it be La Mole?"

He began to feel alarmed. He remembered that the young man had been recommended to him by Marguerite herself. Wishing to assure himself, he ascended to the chamber of the two young men; no one was there, but the cherry-colored mantle was hanging against the wall. It was, then, Mouy. Pale as death, and trembling lest Mouy had been taken prisoner and would betray the secrets of the conspiracy, he rushed to the wicket, where he was informed that the man in the red mantle had escaped safe and sound, saying that someone was being killed on the king's account.

"He was mistaken," muttered D'Alençon; "it is on the queen-mother's account." And returning to the scene of combat, he found Catherine prowling like a hyena among the dead. On the command given him by his mother he returned to his rooms, affecting a quiet obedience notwithstanding the tumultuous ideas agitating his mind.

Catherine, in despair at the failure of this new attempt, called Nancey, had the bodies removed and Maurevel conveyed to his own house, and forbade them to wake the king.

"Oh," she murmured, as she entered her apartments, her head sinking on her bosom, "he has again escaped; the hand of God protects him. He will reign; he will reign!"

Then, as she opened her door, she assumed a smile.

"Oh, Madame, what was the matter?" exclaimed all but Madame de Sauve, who was too frightened to ask any questions.

"Oh, nothing," replied the queen; "only a noise—nothing more."

"Oh!" cried Madame de Sauve, suddenly, pointing with her finger. "Your Majesty says it is nothing, and at every step leaves a track on the carpet!"

CHAPTER 4

The Two Kings

Charles IX walked arm in arm with Henri, followed by his four gentlemen, and preceded by two torch-bearers.

"When I go out from the Louvre," said the poor king, "I experience a pleasure like that I feel when I enter a fine forest—I breathe, I live, I am free!"

Henri smiled. "Your Majesty would be happy in my mountains in Béarn, then?" was his reply.

"Yes, and I can understand how desirous you are to return there; but if the desire comes very strong upon you, Henriot," added Charles, laughing, "be careful, for my mother Catherine is so very fond of you that she really cannot do without you."

"What does your Majesty propose to do this evening?" said Henri, giving a turn to that dangerous conversation.

"I wish to introduce you to someone, Henriot; you will give me your opinion."

"I am at your Majesty's orders."

"To the right! to the right! we will go to the Rue des Barres."

The two kings, followed by their escort, had reached the Hôtel de Condé, when they observed two men, wrapped in long cloaks, come forth from a private door, which one of them closed carefully.

"Oh, oh!" said the king to Henri, who, according to his custom, looked also, but without speaking, "this deserves our attention."

"Why do you say that, Sire?" asked the King of Navarre.

"It is not on your account, Henriot. You are sure of your wife," he added with a smile, "but your cousin Condé is not so sure of his; or if he is sure, devil take me! he is wrong."

"But how do you know, Sire, that it is Madame de Condé these gentlemen have come to visit?"

"A presentiment. They have seen us and try to avoid notice, and then the peculiar cut of one of their mantles. *Pardieu!* it would be strange!"

"What?"

"Nothing—only an idea that occurred to me; but let us advance toward them." And he went toward the two men, who, thus seeing that they must be accosted, made several steps in a contrary direction.

"Holloa, Messieurs!" said the king; "stop!"

"Do you address us?" said a voice which made Charles and his companion start.

"Ah, Henriot!" said Charles, "do you recognize that voice now?"

"Sire," replied Henri, "if your brother, the Duc d'Anjou, were not at Rochelle, I would swear it was he who just spoke."

"Well, then," said Charles, "he is not at Rochelle, that is all."

"But who is with him?"

"You do not recognize his companion?"

"No, Sire."

"He is, nevertheless, a man whose figure can hardly be mistaken. Holloa! I say," continued the king, "did you not hear me?"

"Are you the watch, to apprehend us?" asked the taller of the two men, freeing his arm from the folds of his mantle.

"Assume that we are the watch," said the king, "and stand when you are desired." Then, whispering to Henri, he added, "Now you will see the volcano spit forth flames."

"There are eight of you," replied the taller of the two men, showing not only his arm but his face; "but were you a hundred, I bid you keep your distance."

"Ah, ah! the Duc de Guise!" said Henri.

"Ah! our cousin of Lorraine!" said the king; "it is you, is it? How fortunate!"

"The king!" exclaimed the duke.

As to the other personage, he wrapped himself up still closer in his mantle, and remained motionless, after having first uncovered his head respectfully.

"Sire," said the Duc de Guise, "I have just been paying a visit to my sister-in-law, Madame de Condé."

"Yes, and have brought one of your gentlemen with you. Who is he?"

"Sire," replied the duke, "your Majesty does not know him."

"Then we will make his acquaintance now," said the king; and going toward him, he desired the two men to approach with their torches.

"Pardon, my brother!" said the Duc d'Anjou, opening his mantle, and bowing with ill-concealed vexation.

"Ah, ah, Henri! What, is it you? But no, it cannot be possible; I am mistaken. My brother of Anjou would never have gone to see anyone before coming to see me. He is not ignorant that for princes of the blood there is only one entrance in Paris, and that is by the gate of the Louvre."

"Pardon me, Sire," said the Duc d'Anjou. "I entreat your Majesty to forgive this breach of etiquette."

"Of course," replied the king, in a jeering tone; "and what were you doing, Brother, at the Hôtel de Condé?"

"Why," said the King of Navarre, with his peculiar air, "what your Majesty alluded to but just now"; and inclining to the ear of the king, he finished with a burst of laughter. He laughed loudly.

"What is it, then?" asked the Duc de Guise, with hauteur, for like the rest of the world, he behaved very rudely to the poor King of Navarre. "Why should I not visit my sister-in-law; does not the Duc d'Alençon visit his?"

Henri colored slightly.

"Eh? What sister-in-law?" remarked Charles; "I do not know of any he has but the Queen Elizabeth."

"Your pardon, Sire; it was his sister, I should have said—Madame Marguerite, whom we saw as we came hither half an hour since, in her litter, accompanied by two gallants, one on each side."

"Really?" said Charles; "what do you say to that, Henri?"

"That the Queen of Navarre is free to go where she pleases; but I doubt her having left the Louvre."

"And I am sure of it," said the Duc de Guise.

"And I also," said the Duc d'Anjou; "and the litter stopped in the Rue Cloche Percée."

"Your sister-in-law, then—not this one," said Henri, pointing to the Hôtel de Condé, "but the other," and he turned his finger in the direction of the Hôtel de Guise—"must also be of the party, for we left them together, and they are, as you know, inseparable."

"I do not understand what your Majesty implies," replied the Duc de Guise.

"Now to me," observed the king, "nothing can be more clear; and that is why there was a gallant on each side of the litter."

"Well," said the duke, "if there be any scandal on the part of the queen and of my sister-in-law, we call on the justice of the king to put an end to it."

"Eh, *pardieu!*" said Henri, "let us have done with Mesdames de Condé and de Nevers. The king has no uneasiness about his sister; I have none for my wife."

"No, no," interposed Charles. "I will have the affair cleared up; but let us manage it ourselves. The litter, you say, Cousin, stopped in the Rue Cloche Percée?"

"Yes, Sire."

"You know the spot?"

"Yes, Sire."

"Well, then, let us go thither; and if it be necessary to burn down the house to know who is in it, why, we will do so."

It was with these inclinations, very discouraging for those concerned, that the four principal princes of the Christian world proceeded toward the Rue St. Antoine. When they reached the Rue Cloche Percée, Charles, who wished to confine the thing to his family, dismissed his attendants, desiring them to be near the Bastille at six o'clock in the morning with two horses.

There were only three houses in the Rue Cloche Percée; and therefore the search was less difficult, inasmuch as at two of these there was no refusal to open. At the third it was another matter; it was the house guarded by the German porter, and the German porter was not very tractable. Paris seemed destined to offer that night most memorable examples of fidelity on the part of servants. M. de Guise in vain threatened him in the purest Saxon; Henri d'Anjou in vain offered him a purse of gold; Charles in vain went so far as to tell him that he was lieutenant of the watch—the brave German gave no heed either to promises or threats. Seeing that they insisted in a manner that was becoming importunate, he thrust between the bars of iron the end of a certain arquebus—a demonstration which was only amusing to three of the four visitors (for Henri de Navarre stood apart as if he had no concern in the affair), since the weapon, confined by the bars to a single direction, could be dangerous only to one who should be blind enough to place himself directly in line with it.

When he found that they could neither intimidate nor corrupt the porter, the Duc de Guise, pretending to go away, went to the corner of the Rue St. Antoine, and there picked up one of those stones such as Ajax Telamon and Diomede lifted three thousand years before, and dashed it with violence against the door, which flew open with the concussion, knocking down the German, who fell heavily and with a loud cry that aroused the garrison, which else ran a great risk of being surprised.

Just at that moment La Mole was translating with Marguerite an idyl of Theocritus, and Coconnas was drinking, under pretext that he also was Greek, Syracusan wine with Henriette. Both conversations were violently interrupted. La Mole and Coconnas blew out all the lights instantly, and opening the windows, went out into the balcony, when seeing four men in the darkness they began to shower down upon them all the projectiles within reach, and make a noise by striking the stone walls with the flat of their swords. Charles, the most eager of the assailants, received a silver ewer on his shoulder, the Duc d'Anjou a basin containing a jelly of oranges and cinnamon, and the Duc de Guise a haunch of venison.

Henri received nothing; he was quietly questioning the porter whom M. de Guise had tied to the door, and who replied by his eternal *"Ich verstehe nicht."*

The women ably backed the besieged army and handed projectiles to them, which fell like hail.

"By the devil's death!" cried Charles, as he received on his head a stool which knocked his hat over his eyes and upon his nose, "if they do not open this moment I'll hang them all."

"My brother!" said Marguerite to La Mole, in a low voice.

"The king!" said he to Henriette.

"The king! the king!" said she to Coconnas, who was drawing a large chest to the window, intending it especially for the Duc de Guise, whom, without knowing him, he had picked out as his peculiar antagonist—"the king, I tell you!"

Coconnas let go the chest with an air of amazement. "The king?" said he.

"Yes, the king!"

"Then sound a retreat."

"Well, be it so. Marguerite and La Mole are off already."

"Which way?"

"Come this way, I tell you!" and taking him by the hand, Henriette led Coconnas by the secret door which led to the adjoining house, and having closed it after them they all four fled by the way that gave access to the Rue Tizon.

"Ah, ah!" said Charles, "I think the garrison surrenders."

They waited several minutes; but no sound reached them.

"They are preparing some trick," said the Duc de Guise.

"More probably they have recognized my brother's voice and decamped," said the Duc d'Anjou.

"At any rate they will have to come this way," said Charles.

"Yes," replied the Duc d'Anjou, "unless the house has two exits."

"Cousin," said the king, "take up the stone again, and serve the inner door as you have the outer."

The duke burst the other door in with his foot.

"The torches! the torches!" said the king; and the lackeys having relighted them, came forward, and the king, taking one, handed the other to the Duc d'Anjou. The Duc de Guise went first, sword in hand; Henri brought up the rear.

They reached the first story, and in the dining room found the relics of supper, with candelabra upset, furniture thrown over, and all the dishes except those of silver broken in pieces. They went into the salon, but there found no better clue to the identity of the persons than in the other room.

"There must be another way of egress," observed the king.

"Most probably," replied D'Anjou.

They searched on all sides, but found no door.

"Where is the porter?" inquired the king.

"I fastened him to the door," replied the Duc de Guise.

"Question him, Cousin."

"He will not answer."

"Bah! Have a little fire of dry wood kindled about his legs," said the king, smiling, "and he will certainly answer."

Henri looked out of the window, and observed, "He is there no longer."

"Who has set him free?" asked the Duc de Guise, quickly.

"Devil's death!" said the king, "we shall learn nothing now."

"In fact," said Henri, "you see plainly, Sire, that nothing proves that my wife and the Duc de Guise's sister-in-law have been in this house."

"That is true," said Charles. "Scripture teaches us that there are three things that leave no tracks: the bird in the air, the fish in the sea, and the woman—no, I am wrong—the man with—"

"So," interrupted Henri, "the best thing we can do—"

"—Is," said Charles, "for me to foment my bruise, D'Anjou to wipe away the marks of the orange-jam, and Guise to rub the grease from off his ruff."

They all went away without so much as closing the door after them. When they reached the Rue St. Antoine the king said to M. d'Anjou and the Duc de Guise, "Which way are you going, gentlemen?"

"Sire, we are going to Nantouillet's, who expects my cousin of Lorraine and myself to supper. Will your Majesty deign to accompany us?"

"No, I thank you; our way lies in an opposite direction. Will you have one of my torch-bearers?"

"No, I thank you, Sire," was D'Anjou's reply.

"Good! He is afraid I should watch him," whispered Charles in Henri's ear. Then, taking him by the arm, he said, "Come, Henriot, I will find you a supper tonight."

"Then we are not going back to the Louvre?" Henri asked.

"No, I tell you, you threefold thickhead! Come with me when I tell you; come, come!" And he conducted Henri by the Rue Geoffroy Lasnier.

CHAPTER 5

Marie Touchet

By way of the Rue Geoffroy Lasnier and the Rue Garnier sur l'Eau the two kings came to the Rue des Barres. There, after taking a few steps toward the Rue de la Mortellerie, they stopped before a small lone house in the middle of a garden, enclosed by high walls. Charles took a key from his pocket and opened the door; and then desiring Henri and the torch-bearer to enter, he closed the door after him. One small window only was lighted, to which Charles with a smile called Henri's attention.

"Sire, I do not understand," said the latter.

"You will soon understand, Henriot."

The King of Navarre looked at Charles with astonishment. His voice, his features, had an expression of gentleness so inconsistent with his character that Henri could hardly recognize him.

"Henriot," said the king to him, "I told you that when I go out from the Louvre I go out from hell. When I enter here I enter Paradise."

"Sire," said Henri, "I am glad that your Majesty deems me worthy to make the voyage to heaven in your company."

"The way is narrow," said the king, ascending a small stairway; "but it is so that nothing may be wanting to the comparison."

"And who is the angel that guards the entrance to your Eden, Sire?"

"You will see," replied Charles IX; and making a sign to Henri to follow him without noise, he pushed open a first door, then a second, and paused on the threshold.

"Look!" he said.

Henri did so, and remained with his eyes fixed on as charming a picture as he had ever seen. It was a woman of eighteen or nineteen years of age, reposing at the foot of a bed, on which was a sleeping infant, whose two feet she held in her hands near her lips, while her long chestnut hair fell down like waves of gold. It was like a picture by Albani, representing the Virgin and the infant Jesus.

"Oh, Sire," said the King of Navarre, "who is this charming creature?"

"The angel of my Paradise, Henriot—the only being who loves me for myself."

Henri smiled.

"Yes," said Charles, "for myself; for she loved me before she knew I was the king."

"Well, and since—"

"Well, and since," said Charles, with a sigh, which proved that this glittering royalty was sometimes a burden to him—"since she has known it, she still loves me. Watch!"

The king approached her gently, and on the lovely cheek of the young woman impressed a kiss as light as that of the bee on a lily, yet it awoke her.

"Charles!" she murmured, opening her eyes.

"You see," said the king, "she calls me Charles; the queen says Sire."

"Oh," exclaimed the young girl, "you are not alone, my king!"

"No, my good Marie, I have brought you another king, happier than myself, for he has no crown; more unhappy than I, for he has no Marie Touchet. God provides compensation for everything."

"Sire, it is, then, the King of Navarre?"

"Himself, my child. Come here, Henriot."

Henri went toward her, and Charles took his right hand. "Look at this hand, Marie," said he; "it is the hand of a good brother and a loyal friend. And but for this hand—"

"Well, Sire!"

"But for this hand, this day, Marie, our boy had been fatherless."

Marie uttered a cry, fell on her knees, seized Henri's hand, and kissed it.

"Well done, Marie! well done!" said Charles.

"And what have you done to thank him, Sire?"

"I have done the same by him."

Henri looked at Charles with astonishment.

"You will know someday what I mean, Henriot; meantime, come and look."

The king went to the bed where the child was still asleep. "Eh!" said he, "if this stout boy slept in the Louvre instead of sleeping in this small house, he would change the aspect of things at present, and perhaps for the future."*

"Sire," said Marie, "without offense to your Majesty, I prefer his sleeping here—he sleeps better."

"Then we will not disturb his sleep," said the king. "It is so good to sleep without dreaming."

"Well, Sire?" said Marie, pointing toward one of the doors.

"Yes, you are right, Marie; let us have supper."

"My dear Charles," said Marie, "you will beg the king your brother to excuse me, will you not?"

"And for what?"

"Because I have sent away our servants. Sire," she continued, addressing the King of Navarre, "you must know that Charles will be waited upon only by me."

"*Ventre-saint-gris!*" said Henri, "I can easily believe it."

The two men went into the dining room, while the mother, anxious and careful, covered with a warm wrapper the little Charles, who, thanks to his sound sleep of infancy which his father had envied, did not awake. Then she too went into the dining room.

"Here are only two covers!" said the king.

"Allow me," said Marie, "to wait upon your Majesties."

"Come," said Charles, "see how you bring misfortune to me, Henriot."

"How, Sire?"

"Don't you see?"

"Pardon, Charles, pardon!" said Marie.

"I forgive you; but place yourself there, next to me, between us two."

*This natural child was afterwards the famous Duc d'Angoulême, who died in 1650, and had he been legitimate, would have supplanted Henri III, Henri IV, Louis XIII, Louis XIV. What would he have given us instead? The mind is confounded and overwhelmed in the obscurities of the question.

Marie brought a plate and sat between the two kings, serving both.

"Is it not well, Henriot," asked Charles, "to have a place in the world in which one can venture to eat and drink without the necessity of anyone tasting your viands before you eat them yourself?"

"I believe, Sire," was Henri's rejoinder, "that I can appreciate that better than anyone."

"Assure her, Henriot, that in order to continue thus happy it is better for her to keep free of politics, and especially to avoid making acquaintance with my mother."

"Queen Catherine does indeed love your Majesty so much that she might easily be jealous of any other love," replied Henri, finding in that subterfuge a way of escape from the dangerous confidence of the king.

"Marie," said the king, "I present to you one of the most shrewd and intelligent men I know. At the court—and that is saying a great deal—he has deceived everyone; I alone, perhaps, have seen clearly into his mind, if not into his heart."

"Sire," said Henri, "I hope that in exaggerating the one you have no doubt of the other."

"I do not exaggerate anything, Henriot," replied the king; "and someday you will be known." Then, turning toward the young woman, "He is, for one thing, a capital master of anagrams. Bid him make one on your name, and I will answer for it he will."

"Oh, what can you find in the name of a poor girl like me? What pleasing idea could such a name as Marie Touchet suggest?"

"Sire," said Henri, "the anagram of that name is too easy; there is no merit in finding it."

"What! done already?" said Charles. "You see, Marie."

Henri took his tablets from the pocket of his doublet, tore out a page of the paper, and beneath the name "Marie Touchet," he wrote, *"Je charme tout"* ("I charm all"), and then handed the leaf to the young girl.

"Really," she exclaimed, "it is impossible!"

"What has he found?" inquired Charles.

"Sire, I dare not repeat it."

"Sire," said Henri, "in the name of Marie Touchet there is letter for letter, only changing the I into J, which is customary, the words, *'je charme tout.'* "

"So it does," cried Charles, "letter for letter! This shall be your device, Marie, and never was device better merited. Thanks, Henriot! Marie, I will give it to you written in diamonds."

The supper was finished as it struck two o'clock by Notre Dame. "Now, Marie," said Charles, "in recompense for the compliment, give him an armchair in which he may sleep till daybreak—a long way off from us, though, for he snores fearfully. If, Henriot, you wake before me, rouse me, for we must be at the Bastille by six o'clock. Goodnight; make yourself as comfortable as you can. But," added the king, placing his hand on Henri's shoulder, "on your life, Henriot, on your life, understand, do not leave this house without me, especially to return to the Louvre!"

Henri had suspected too much to disregard this caution.

Charles IX went to his chamber, and Henri, the hardy mountaineer, settled down in his armchair, and speedily justified the precaution his brother-in-law had taken in keeping him at a distance. In the morning Charles aroused Henri, and as he was dressed, his toilet did not occupy him very long. The king was happy and smiling as he was never seen to be at the Louvre. The hours spent by him in that little house in the Rue des Barres were his hours of happiness.

They passed through the bedchamber, where the young woman was sleeping in her bed, and the baby in its cradle. They both were smiling as they slept. Charles looked at them very tenderly, and turning to the King of Navarre, said to him, "Henriot, if you should ever learn what service I have this night rendered you, and any misfortune should happen to me, remember this child which rests here in its cradle." Then kissing them both, he said, "Adieu, my angels!" and left the apartment. Henri followed, buried in thought.

Two horses, held by gentlemen of the king, awaited them at the Bastille; Charles made a sign to Henri to mount, and placed himself in the saddle. Going by the garden of the Arbalète, they went toward the exterior boulevards.

"Where are we going?" asked Henri.

"We are going," Charles replied, "to see if the Duc d'Anjou has returned only on account of Madame de Condé, or if—as I gravely suspect—there is in his heart as much ambition as love."

Henri did not understand the explanation; he followed Charles without speaking.

When they reached the Marais, where they were sheltered by the palisades, Charles directed Henri's attention through the thick haze of the morning to some men wrapped in long mantles and wearing fur caps, who were on horseback beside a wagon heavily laden. As they advanced, these men formed in lines, and among them, on horseback like the rest, and talking with them, appeared another man, wearing a long brown mantle and, shading his forehead, a French hat.

"Ah, ah!" said Charles, smiling, "I thought so."

"Eh, Sire," observed Henri, "I cannot be mistaken; that horseman in the brown mantle is the Duc d'Anjou."

"Himself," said Charles. "Keep back, Henriot! don't let them see us."

"And who are the other men, and what is in the wagon?"

"The men are the Polish ambassadors, and in the wagon is a crown; and now," he added, putting his horse to a gallop, "come, Henriot, for I have seen all I wished to see."

CHAPTER 6

The Return to the Louvre

When Catherine believed that all was arranged in the King of Navarre's chamber—that the dead soldiers were removed, Maurevel conveyed away, and the carpets washed—she dismissed her maids, for it was nearly midnight. She tried to sleep; but the shock had been too severe, the deception too great. The detested Henri continually escaped her plots, well laid and deadly as they were; he seemed protected by some invincible power, which Catherine persisted in calling Chance, although in the depths of her heart a voice told her that the real name of this power was Destiny. That idea, that the rumor of this new attempt, spreading through the Louvre and beyond the Louvre, would give to Henri and the Huguenots a greater confidence in the future than ever, exasperated her; and at that moment, if the chance against which she so unhappily contended had delivered to her her enemy, with the little Florentine dagger which she wore at her side she would no doubt have baffled that fatality so favorable to the King of Navarre.

The hours of the night—those hours so slow to him who wakes and watches—sounded one after another, and still Catherine could not close her eyes. A world of new projects were unfolded during those hours of the night in her mind filled with visions. At last, at the break of day she rose, dressed herself without assistance, and took her way toward the apartments of Charles IX. The guards, who were accustomed to her visiting the king at all hours of day or night, allowed her to pass. She crossed the antechamber and entered the armory. There she found Charles's nurse.

"My son?" said the queen.

"Madame, he has forbidden that anyone should enter his chamber before eight o'clock."

"That order, Nurse, is not for me."

"It is for everyone, Madame."

Catherine smiled.

"Yes, I know well," continued the nurse, "that no one here has any right to obstruct your Majesty; I beseech you, then, to hear the prayer of a poor woman, and go no farther."

"Nurse, it is necessary that I should speak to my son."

"Madame, I will not open the door except on the formal order of your Majesty."

"Open, Nurse, I command you."

The nurse, at this voice, more respected and more dreaded than that of Charles himself, presented the key to Catherine; but Catherine had no need of it. She took from her pocket a key of her own, which opened her son's door in an instant.

The chamber was unoccupied; Charles's bed was undisturbed; and his greyhound, Actæon, stretched on a bearskin at the foot of the bed, rose and licked Catherine's ivory hands.

"Ah!" said the queen, frowning, "he has gone out; I will await him."

And she seated herself gloomily in the recess of a window which looked into the principal court of the Louvre. For two hours she remained there, pale and immovable as a marble statue, when at length she saw a troop of cavaliers enter the gate, at the head of whom she beheld Charles and Henri de Navarre. Then she comprehended all.

Charles, instead of debating with her as to the arrest of his brother-in-law, had carried him off, and thus saved him.

"Blind, blind, blind!" she murmured; and she waited where she was.

A moment later steps resounded in the adjoining room, which was the armory.

"Now, Sire," said Henri, "now that we have returned to the Louvre, tell me why you made me go away, and what is the service you have rendered me?"

"No, no, Henriot," replied Charles, laughing. "You will know someday perhaps; meantime it is a secret. But you may know that in all probability you will have cost me a rough quarrel with my mother."

In saying these words Charles lifted the tapestry and found himself in the presence of his mother. Behind him, and looking over his shoulder, was the pale and uneasy countenance of the Béarnais.

"Ah! you here, Madame?" said Charles IX, frowning.

"Yes, my son; I wish to speak with you."

"To me?"

"You, and alone."

"Well, well," said Charles, turning toward his brother-in-law, "since it cannot be avoided, the sooner the better."

"I leave you, Sire," said Henri.

"Yes, yes, do," replied Charles; "and since you are a Catholic, Henriot, go and hear Mass on my behalf; as for me, I shall stay and hear the sermon."

Henri bowed and went out. Charles IX, anticipating the questions which his mother would address to him, said, trying to turn the affair into a jest, "Well, Madame, *pardieu!* you are going to scold me, are you not? I made your little plot fail most signally. Eh! death of a devil! I really could not allow to be arrested and conveyed to the Bastille the man who had just saved my life; nor could I allow myself to quarrel with you—I am a good son. And then," he added in a lower tone, "the good God punishes those who quarrel with their mother. Forgive me, then, frankly, and admit that it was a good joke."

"Sire," replied Catherine, "your Majesty is mistaken; it was not a joke."

"Yes, yes, and so you will say, or the devil take me!"

"Sire, you have by your own fault caused the failure of a plan which would have led to a great discovery."

"Bah! a plan? Is it possible that you are annoyed by the failure of a plan—you, Mother? You will make twenty others, and among them—well, I promise you my help."

"It is too late; for he is warned and will be on his guard."

"Come," said the king, "come, let us know all about it. What have you to complain of against Henriot?"

"Why, that he is in a conspiracy."

"Yes, of course, that is your everlasting accusation; but doesn't everyone conspire more or less in this charming royal residence called the Louvre?"

"But he conspires more than anyone else; he is more dangerous than anyone suspects."

"You see," said Charles, "the Lorenzino!"

"Listen," said Catherine, her face darkening at the mention of that name, which recalled one of the most bloody catastrophes in Florentine history—"listen: there is a way to prove to me that I am wrong."

"Well, how, Mother?"

"Ask Henri who was in his chamber last night; and if he tells you, I am ready to confess that I was wrong."

"But if it were a woman, we cannot require—"

"A woman?"

"Yes, a woman."

"A woman who killed two of your guards and has wounded, perhaps mortally, M. Maurevel!"

"Ah, ah!" said the king, "this grows serious. There has been blood spilled, then?"

"Three men were left lying upon the floor."

"And he who left them in this condition—"

"Escaped safe and sound."

"By Gog and Magog!" cried Charles, "he was a gallant fellow, and you are right, Mother; I should like to know him."

"Well, I tell you beforehand you will not learn who it is, at least from Henri."

"But from you, Mother. This man did not escape without leaving some traces—without some portion of his dress being re-marked?"

"Nothing was observed but the elegant cherry-colored mantle which he wore."

"Ah, ah! a cherry-colored mantle!" said Charles; "I know but one at court so remarkable as to arrest attention."

"Precisely," said Catherine.

"Well?" replied Charles.

"Well," answered Catherine, "await me here, my son, while I go to see if my orders have been executed."

Catherine went out, leaving Charles alone, who paced up and down thoughtfully, whistling a hunting air, with one hand in his doublet, and letting the other hang down for his dog to lick every time he paused.

As to Henri, he had left his brother-in-law's apartments very uneasy, and instead of going along the usual corridor, he had ascended the small private staircase we have before referred to, and which led to the second story; but scarcely had he gone up four steps when he saw a shadow. He stopped, and put his hand to his dagger, but immediately recognized a woman, who seized his hand, while a charming voice familiar to his ear said, "Heaven be praised, Sire! you are safe and sound. I was in great alarm about you, but Heaven has heard my prayer."

"What, then, has happened?" inquired Henri.

"You will know when you reach your apartments. Do not be uneasy about Orthon; I have taken care of him"; and the young woman descended the stairs rapidly, passing Henri as if she had met him accidentally.

"This is very strange," said Henri to himself; "what can have happened? What has befallen Orthon?"

The question, unfortunately, could not reach Madame de Sauve, for Madame de Sauve was already out of hearing. At the top of the staircase Henri saw another shadow; it was that of a man.

"Hush!" said this man.

"Ah, ah! is that you, François?"

"Do not mention my name."

"What has happened?"

"Go into your rooms, and you will see; then go quietly into the corridor, look carefully about and be sure that no one sees you, and come to me. My door will be ajar." And he disappeared, in his turn, down the staircase, like the ghosts which at the theater sink right through the floor.

"*Ventre-saint-gris!*" muttered the Béarnais, "the mystery grows thicker; but as the solution is to be found in my apartments, let us go thither."

He reached the door, and listened; there was not a sound. Charlotte had told him to go there, and it was thus evident there was nothing to fear. He entered, and cast a glance around the antechamber; it was unoccupied, and nothing indicated that anything had taken place.

"It is true, Orthon is not here," he remarked, and went to the inner chamber. Here all was explained. In spite of the water which had been copiously used, large red spots stained the floor; a piece of furniture was broken; the hangings of the bed were hacked with sword-cuts; a Venetian mirror was broken by the blow of a bullet; and a bloodstained hand had leaned against the wall and left against it a terrible imprint, announcing that this chamber had been the mute witness of a mortal struggle. Henri gazed with haggard eye at all these different details, and passing his hand over his brow, moist with perspiration, he murmured, "Ah! now I understand the service which the king has done me; they came to assassinate me, and— ah!—Mouy! what have they done with Mouy? Wretches! they have murdered him!"

Eager to receive the information which the Duc d'Alençon was to give him, Henri, after giving once more a sorrowful glance to the objects around him, hastened out of the chamber, gained the corridor, and after assuring himself that he was unobserved, went quickly to the duke's apartments. The duke awaited him in the first room. He eagerly took Henri's hand, and placing his finger on his lips, led him to a small room in the tower, completely isolated, where, therefore, they would be safe against discovery.

"Oh, my brother," he said, "what a horrible night!"

"What has happened?" asked Henri.

"They sought to arrest you."

"Me?"

"Yes, you."

"And why?"

"I know not; where were you?"

"The king took me last night away with him into the city."

"Then he was aware of it," said D'Alençon. "But since you were not here, who was in your rooms?"

"Was anyone there?" inquired Henri, as if ignorant of the fact.

"Yes, a man. When I heard the noise I ran to bring you succor, but it was too late."

"Was the man arrested?" inquired Henri, anxiously.

"No; he escaped, after having dangerously wounded Maurevel and killed two guards."

"Ah, brave Mouy!" cried Henri.

"Was it, then, Mouy?" said D'Alençon, quickly.

Henri saw that he had made a blunder. "At least, I presume so," he replied, "for I had given him an appointment to arrange with him as to your flight, and to tell him that I had ceded to you all my rights to the throne of Navarre."

"Then if the affair is known," said D'Alençon, turning pale, "we are lost."

"Yes; for Maurevel will tell."

"Maurevel has been wounded in the throat, and I have learned from the surgeon that he will not speak a word for eight days."

"Eight days! that is a longer time than Mouy requires to reach a place of safety."

"But it may be some other, and not M. de Mouy."

"Do you think so?" asked Henri.

"Yes; this person disappeared very swiftly, and nothing was seen but a cherry-colored cloak."

"Why, really," remarked Henri, "a cherry-colored cloak is a thing for a fop, not a soldier; no one would suspect Mouy of appearing in a cherry-colored cloak."

"No; and if anyone were suspected," said D'Alençon, "it would rather be——" He paused.

"M. de la Mole," said Henri.

"Certainly; since I, who saw him myself, doubted for a moment!"

"You doubted? Well, then, it might be M. de la Mole."

"Does he know nothing?" inquired D'Alençon.

"Nothing important."

"Brother," said the duke, "now I really believe it was he."

"The devil!" observed Henri, "if it be he, it will greatly annoy the queen, who takes an interest in him."

"An interest, say you?" said D'Alençon, amazed.

"Unquestionably. Do you not remember, François, that it was your sister who recommended him to you?"

"It was, indeed," said the duke, gloomily; "and so, being inclined to do him a service, and fearing that his red mantle might compromise him, I went up to his room and brought it away."

"Oh, oh!" said Henri; "that was doubly wise. And now I would not wager, I would swear that it was he."

"Do you mean that seriously?"

"Faith, yes; he came to bring me some message from Marguerite."

"If I were sure that you would support me, I myself would almost accuse him."

"If you accuse him," replied Henri, "understand, Brother, I shall not contradict you."

"But the queen?" said D'Alençon.

"Ah, yes! the queen."

"We must know what she will do."

"I will undertake that commission."

"Plague take it, Brother! she will be wrong to give us the lie, for here is a brilliant reputation for valor readymade for that young man; and it will not have cost him much, for he will have bought it on credit. It is true, indeed, that he may be called on to pay capital and interest at once."

"Devil take it! what would you have?" inquired Henri. "In this world we have nothing for nothing"; and saluting D'Alençon, he cautiously looked out into the corridor, and being certain that no one listened he glided along and disappeared on the secret stairway that led to Marguerite's apartments.

The Queen of Navarre was hardly more at ease than her husband. The expedition of the night, directed against herself and Madame de Nevers by the king, the Duc d'Anjou, the Duc de Guise, and Henri, whom she had recognized, had greatly disturbed her. Doubtless there was no evidence that could compromise her; the porter declared that he had betrayed nothing. But four noblemen like those had not gone out of their way by chance, or without having a reason for so doing. Marguerite, then, had returned home at break of day, after spending the remainder of the night with the Duchesse de Nevers. She had gone to bed, but she could not sleep, and trembled at every sound. In the midst of these anxieties she heard someone knocking at the secret door, and ordered Gillonne to admit the visitor.

Henri paused at the door. Nothing in him announced the injured husband; his habitual smile was on his well-defined lips, and not a muscle of his countenance betrayed the severe emotions he had undergone. He looked at Marguerite to ascertain if she would allow him to remain alone with her, and Marguerite motioned Gillonne to retire.

"Madame," said Henri, "I know how deeply you are attached to your friends, and I fear I bring you unwelcome tidings."

"What are they, Sire?" asked Marguerite.

"One of our best-loved servitors is greatly compromised at this moment."

"Who?"

"Our dear Comte de la Mole."

"And how?"

"In consequence of the adventure of last night."

Marguerite, in spite of her self-command, could not refrain from blushing. "What adventure?" she said.

"What!" said Henri; "did you not hear all the noise that was made at the Louvre last night?"

"No, Monsieur."

"Then I congratulate you, Madame," said Henri, with charming simplicity; "that shows how well you sleep."

"Well, what happened, then?"

"Why, our good mother had ordered M. Maurevel and six of her guards to arrest me."

"You, Monsieur; you?"

"Yes, me."

"And for what reason?"

"Ah! who can tell the reasons of such a mind as your mother's? I suspect them, but do not know them."

"And you were not in your chamber?"

"No, by accident you have guessed rightly, Madame. Last evening the king invited me to accompany him. But if I was not in my chamber, some other person was."

"And who was that other person?"

"It appears that it was the Comte de la Mole."

"The Comte de la Mole!" said Marguerite, amazed.

"*Tudieu!* only imagine what a stout fellow the Provençal was," continued Henri. "Why, he wounded Maurevel and killed two of the guards."

"Wounded M. Maurevel and killed two of the guards! Impossible!"

"What, do you doubt his courage, Madame?"

"No; but I say that M. de la Mole could not be in your apartments."

"Why not?"

"Because—because," answered Marguerite, greatly embarrassed—"because he was elsewhere."

"Ah, if he can prove an alibi," observed Henri, "that is another thing. He will say where he was, and there's an end."

"Where he was?" said Marguerite, quickly.

"Assuredly. Before the day is over he will be arrested and questioned. But unfortunately, as they have proofs—"

"Proofs! What?"

"Why, the man who made this desperate defense wore a red cloak."

"But is M. de la Mole the only man who wears a red cloak? I know another person also."

"So do I; but then see what will happen. If it was not M. de la Mole, it was some other man in a red cloak like him, and you know who that man is."

"Heavens!"

"This is the breaker ahead of us. You have seen it as I have, Madame; and your emotion proves it. Let us, then, talk this matter over like two persons who speak of a thing the most coveted in the world—a throne; of a thing more precious—life. Mouy arrested, we are lost!"

"Yes; I understand that."

"While M. de la Mole can compromise nobody—unless you think him capable of inventing some tale, as, for example, that he was with a party of ladies—"

"Monsieur," said Marguerite, "if you fear only that, be assured; he will not say it."

"What!" said Henri, "will he be silent, even if silence cost him his life?"

"He will, Monsieur."

"You are sure?"

"I will answer for him."

"Then all is for the best," said Henri, rising.

"You are leaving?" cried Marguerite.

"Ah, *mon Dieu!* yes. That is all I had to say to you."

"Then you go, Monsieur—"

"To endeavor to get us out of the danger into which this devil of a man in the red cloak has plunged us."

"Ah, *mon Dieu! mon Dieu!* poor young man!" exclaimed Marguerite, in a paroxysm of grief, and wringing her hands.

"Really," said Henri, as he retired, "this dear M. de la Mole is a very faithful and gentlemanly servitor!

CHAPTER 7

Interrogatories

Charles had entered smiling and jesting into his apartments, but after ten minutes' conversation with his mother, it was she who had recovered her good humor, and he who was serious and thoughtful.

"M. de la Mole!" said Charles, "M. de la Mole! we must summon Henri and D'Alençon—Henri, because this young man is a Huguenot; D'Alençon, because he is in his service."

"Summon them if you will, my son; you will learn nothing. I fear there exists a better understanding between Henri and François than you imagine. If you question them you arouse their suspicions. If you wait a few days; if you give the culprits time to recover breath; if you allow them to believe that they have escaped your vigilance—then, bold, triumphant, they will furnish you an occasion for severity; then we shall know all."

Charles walked up and down rapidly, biting his lips and pressing his hand to his heart, as if to restrain his wrath.

"No, no," said he, "I will not wait! You don't know what it is to wait, attended as I am by phantoms. Besides, these fops are becoming more insolent every day. Even last night did not two of them dare to oppose our will? If M. de la Mole is innocent—good; but I shall not be sorry to know where M. de la Mole was last night when my guards were assailed in the Louvre, and I was attacked in the Rue Cloche Percée. Let someone, then, go for the Duc d'Alençon, then for Henri. I will interrogate them separately. As for you, you can stay if you please."

The Duc d'Alençon entered. His conversation with Henri had prepared him for this interview; he was therefore quite self-possessed. His answers were precise. Warned by his mother not to leave his apartments, he was ignorant of the events of the night. Only, as those apartments were in the same corridor as the King of Navarre's he had heard footsteps, then the sound of a door opening, and the report of firearms; he had ventured to open his door slightly, and had seen a man in a red mantle escape. Charles and the queen looked at each other.

"In a red mantle?" said the king.

"In a red mantle," replied D'Alençon.

"And did not this mantle suggest to you any suspicions as to who the person was?"

D'Alençon collected all his presence of mind in order to lie more naturally. "I confess," said he, "I thought I recognized the mantle of one of my gentlemen."

"Which of them?"

"M. de la Mole."

"Why was he not in attendance on you as his duty required?"

"I had given him leave of absence."

"That will do; go."

The duke advanced toward the door.

"No; this way," said Charles, pointing to the door which led to his nurse's apartments. He did not wish François and Henri to meet. He was ignorant that they had already met for a few moments, and that those few moments had sufficed to arrange their plans.

As D'Alençon went out, Henri entered, on a signal given by Charles. He did not wait for Charles to question him. "Sire," said he, "you have done well to send for me, for I was coming to seek you, to demand justice."

Charles frowned.

"Yes, justice!" said Henri. "I begin by thanking your Majesty for having taken me with you last night, for I now know that by so doing you saved my life; but what have I done to deserve being assassinated?"

"It was not an assassination," said Catherine; "it was an arrest."

"Well!" returned Henri, "what crime have I committed that I should be arrested? I am as guilty today as yesterday. What is my crime, Sire?"

Charles looked at his mother, somewhat embarrassed for an answer.

"My son," said Catherine, "you hold communication with suspected persons."

"Well," said Henri, "and these suspected persons compromise me, is it not so, Madame?"

"Yes, Henri."

"Name them, then; name them to me! Confront me with them!"

"Indeed," said Charles, "Henriot has the right to ask an explanation."

"And I demand one," said Henri, who saw his advantage, and resolved to use it—"I demand one from my good brother Charles, from my good mother Catherine. Since my marriage, have I not been a good husband? Ask Marguerite. A good Catholic? Ask my confessor. A good brother? Ask all those who were at the hunt yesterday."

"It is true, Henriot," replied the king; "but they say you conspire."

"Against whom?"

"Against me."

"Sire, were that true, I needed only to have let events take their course when the boar was on you."

"Eh, *mort diable!* he is right, Mother."

"But who was last night in your apartments?"

"Madame," returned Henri, "in a time when so few can answer for themselves, I will not undertake to answer for others. I left my apartments at seven o'clock in the evening, and the king took me away with him at ten. I was with him all night. I could not be with him and at the same time know what was taking place in my apartments."

"But," said Catherine, "it is not the less true that someone of your followers killed two of the king's guards, and wounded M. Maurevel."

"One of my followers!" cried Henri. "Name him, then, Madame; name him!"

"Every one accuses M. de la Mole."

"M. de la Mole is not in my service, but in that of the Duc d'Alençon, to whom Marguerite recommended him."

"But," said Charles, "was it M. de la Mole who was there, Henriot?"

"How should I know, Sire? I do not say yes or no. M. de la

Mole is a very gallant gentleman, devoted to the Queen of Navarre; and he often brings me messages from Marguerite, to whom he is very grateful for having recommended him to the Duc d'Alençon, or from the duke himself. I cannot say that it was not M. de la Mole."

"It was he," said Catherine; "he was recognized by his red mantle."

"Ah, he has a red mantle?" asked Henri.

"Yes."

"And the man who so maltreated my two guards and M. Maurevel—"

"Had a red mantle?" asked Henri.

"Precisely," said Charles.

"I have nothing to say to that," answered the Béarnais. "But it seems to me that instead of sending for me, it was M. de la Mole who should have been sent for; but there is one thing I would remark."

"What is that?"

"If it had been myself who, seeing an order signed by my king, had refused to obey that order, I should have been culpable and deserving of punishment; but it was not I—it was a person unknown, whom that order did not concern. They tried to arrest him without authority, and he defended himself; he had a right to do so."

"Yet—" murmured Catherine.

"Madame," demanded Henri, "was the order to arrest me?"

"Yes; and the king himself had signed it."

"But was it in the order to arrest anyone found in my place?"

"No," said Catherine.

"Well, then," continued Henri, "unless it can be proved that I am plotting against the king, and that the man in my chamber is plotting with me, he is innocent. Sire," continued he, turning to Charles IX, "I do not leave the Louvre. I am ready at your Majesty's orders to retire to any state-prison you may think fit to indicate; but in the meantime, and until proof to the contrary, I have a right to declare myself the loyal subject and brother of your Majesty." And saluting them with an air of dignity Charles had never before seen in him, Henri withdrew.

"Bravo, Henriot!" cried Charles.

"Bravo! because he has beaten us?"

"And why not? When he hits me in fencing, don't I cry bravo? Mother, you are wrong to despise this young man."

"My son," said Catherine, seizing the king's hand, "I do not despise, I fear him."

"Well, you're wrong. Henriot is my friend; and as he said, if he were really plotting against me, he need only have let the boar alone yesterday."

"Yes," said Catherine, "and so have made D'Anjou, his personal enemy, King of France."

"Never mind what motive made him save my life; suffice it, he did save it, and, death of all the devils! I will not have him meddled with. As for M. de la Mole, I will speak to D'Alençon about him."

Catherine withdrew, trying to fix definitely her wandering suspicions. M. de la Mole was of too little consequence to satisfy the requirements of her plans. On reentering her chamber, she found Marguerite waiting for her. "Ah, ah!" said she, "it is you, my daughter; I sent for you last night."

"I know, Madame. I had gone out."

"And this morning?"

"This morning, Madame, I come to tell your Majesty that you are about to commit a great injustice."

"What is it?"

"You are going to arrest M. de la Mole."

"You are mistaken, my daughter; I arrest no one. It is the king who arrests, not I."

"Let us not play with words, Madame, when the circumstances are so grave. M. de la Mole is to be arrested, is he not?"

"It is probable."

"Accused of having killed two of the king's guards, and wounded M. Maurevel last night, in the King of Navarre's chamber?"

"That is indeed the crime of which he is accused."

"He is wrongfully accused; M. de la Mole is not guilty."

"Not guilty!" cried Catherine, joyfully; for she hoped to learn something from what Marguerite was about to tell her.

"No," returned Marguerite; "he cannot be guilty, for he was not there."

"Where was he, then?"

"With me, Madame."

"With you?"

"Yes, with me."

Catherine, instead of exhibiting consternation and anger at such a confession by a daughter of France, quietly folded her hands in her lap.

"And," she said after a moment of silence, "if they arrest M. de la Mole and question him—"

"He will say where and with whom he was, Mother," said Marguerite, although certain that he would not.

"Since that is so, you are right, my child; it is best that M. de la Mole should not be arrested."

Marguerite shuddered, for there seemed to be in her mother's manner as she said these words a mysterious and ominous significance; but Marguerite had nothing to say, for what she had come to demand had been granted.

"But, then," said Catherine, "if it was not M. de la Mole, it was someone else."

Marguerite was silent.

"Do you know who it was?"

"I do not," returned Marguerite, hesitatingly.

"Come, do not tell me the truth by halves."

"I tell you, Madame, I do not know," said Marguerite, turning pale in spite of herself.

"Well, well," said the queen-mother, with an air of indifference, "we shall find out. Go, my child; your mother watches over your honor."

Marguerite retired.

"Ah!" murmured Catherine, "Henri and Marguerite have an understanding together—provided she is silent, he is blind. Ah, my children, you think yourselves strong in your union, but I will crush you. Besides, all must be known the day when Maurevel can write or pronounce six letters." And hereupon Catherine returned to the royal apartments, where she found Charles in conference with D'Alençon.

"You here, Mother?" said Charles.

"Why not say again, for that was in your thoughts?"

"I keep my thoughts to myself," returned the king, with that harsh tone he sometimes adopted, even to Catherine. "What have you to say?"

"That you were right, Charles; and you, D'Alençon, wrong."

"How?" cried both together.

"It was not La Mole who was in the King of Navarre's apartments."

"Ah, ah!" said François, turning pale.

"And who was it, then?" asked Charles.

"We shall know when Maurevel is recovered; but let us speak of La Mole."

"What do you want with him, since he was not with the King of Navarre?"

"No," said Catherine, "he was not with the king, but he was with—the queen."

"With the queen!" cried Charles, bursting into a troubled laugh.

"With the queen!" murmured D'Alençon, becoming as pale as a corpse.

"Why, no, no!" said Charles, "Guise told us he met her litter."

"Just so," said Catherine; "she has a house in the city."

"Rue Cloche Percée?" cried the king.

"Oh, oh! that is too much!" said D'Alençon, digging his nails into his flesh. "And she recommended him to me!"

"Ah! now I think of it," said the king, suddenly, "it is he who defended himself against us last night, and who threw a dish on my head—the scoundrel!"

"Oh, yes!" repeated François, "the scoundrel!"

"You are right, my children," said Catherine; "for the least indiscretion of this gentleman might occasion a horrible scandal, involving a daughter of France! It needs but a moment of intoxication—"

"Or of vanity," said François.

"Doubtless," returned Charles; "but we cannot carry the cause before the judges until Henri consents."

"My son," said Catherine, significantly, "a crime has been committed, and there may be scandal. But it is not by judges and executioners that crimes of this sort against the royal majesty are punished. Were you simple gentlemen, I should need say nothing to you, for you are both brave; but you are princes, and cannot cross swords with an inferior in rank. Think, then, how to avenge yourselves as princes."

"Death of all the devils! you are right, Mother; I will think of it."

"And I will help you, Brother," cried François.

"I leave you," said Catherine; "but I leave you this to represent me." As she spoke, she untied the silken cord that passed thrice round her waist, and of which the two tassels fell to her knees, and cast it at the feet of the two princes.

"Ah," said Charles, "I understand."

"This cord—" said D'Alençon.

"Is punishment and silence," replied Catherine, victorious; "but, first, it will be as well to mention the thing to Henri." And she retired.

"Pardieu!" replied D'Alençon, "a good suggestion; and when Henri learns that his wife betrays him—So," he added, turning to the king, "you have adopted the advice of our mother?"

"In all respects," said Charles, not suspecting that he plunged a thousand daggers in D'Alençon's heart. "That will annoy Marguerite, but it will please Henriot."

Then calling an officer of the guards he ordered that Henri should be summoned; but changing his mind, "No," said he, "I will see him myself; do you inform D'Anjou and Guise."

And leaving the room, he ascended the private staircase which led to Henri's chamber.

CHAPTER 8

Projects of Vengeance

Henri had profited by the moment's respite from the examination he had undergone so successfully to fly to Madame de Sauve's. There he found Orthon quite recovered; but Orthon could tell him nothing, except that some armed men had entered the apartments, and that one of them had struck him with the hilt of his sword.

As for Orthon, no one had taken any heed to him; Catherine had seen him senseless, and believed he was dead. On coming to himself, in the interval between her departure and the arrival of the captain of the guard, he had taken refuge with Madame de Sauve.

Henri besought Charlotte to let the young man remain with her until he heard from Mouy, who would certainly write to him. He would then despatch Orthon to him, and instead of one, have two men on whom to rely in any emergency. This plan formed, he had returned to his apartments, and was walking up and down in meditation when the door opened, and Charles entered.

"Your Majesty!" cried Henri, hastening to meet the king.

"I myself. Henriot, you are an excellent fellow, and I find that I love you more and more."

"Sire," said Henri, "you overwhelm me."

"You have but one fault."

"If your Majesty will explain yourself, I will seek to correct it," said Henri, who saw by the king's face that he was in an excellent humor.

"It is that having good eyes you do not use them."

"Bah!" said Henri; "am I, then, nearsighted without knowing it?"

"Worse than that, Henriot, worse than that—you are blind."

"Ah! that may be," said the Béarnais; "but perhaps that misfortune comes to me only when I close my eyes."

"Yes, very likely," said Charles; "you are indeed capable of it. But now I am going to open your eyes."

"God said, 'Let there be light!' and there was light. Your Majesty is the representative of God in this world; you can do therefore on earth what God does in the heavens. I listen."

"When Guise told you last night that he saw your wife pass with a gallant, you would not believe it."

"Sire, how could I believe your Majesty's sister would commit such an indiscretion?"

"When he told you your wife had gone to the Rue Cloche Percée, you would not believe that."

"How could I believe, Sire, that a daughter of France would thus publicly risk her reputation?"

"When we besieged the house, and I received a silver dish on my shoulder, D'Anjou a plate of orange-jam on his head, and Guise a haunch of venison in his face, did you not see two men and two women?"

"I saw nothing, Sire; your Majesty may remember that I was questioning the porter."

"Eh, *corbœluf!* I did, then."

"Ah, if your Majesty saw anything, that makes it another matter."

"That is, I saw two men and two women. Well, I now know beyond a doubt that one of the women was Margot, and one of the men La Mole."

"But," said Henri, "if M. de la Mole was in the Rue Cloche Percée, he could not be here."

"No, no, he was not here; but never mind that, we shall know who was here when that blockhead Maurevel can write or speak. The question is whether Margot is deceiving you."

"Bah!" said Henri, "don't trust to lying rumors."

"I said well that you are more than nearsighted, that you are blind! Devil's death! won't you believe me once, you stubborn fellow? I tell you that Margot deceives you, and that this evening we are going to strangle the object of her affections."

Henri started, and looked with an air of bewilderment at the king.

"You won't be sorry for that, I know, Henriot. Margot will cry like a thousand Niobes; but I won't have you made a fool of. Let D'Anjou deceive Condé, I do not care—Condé is my enemy; but you are my brother, my friend."

"But, Sire—"

"I will not have you molested. You are deceived, as may happen to anyone; but you shall have such a reparation that tomorrow everyone shall say, 'Thousand names of a devil! The king loves his brother Henriot, for he twisted M. de la Mole's neck finely for his sake last night.'"

"Are you quite resolved, Sire?" asked Henri.

"Resolved, decided, determined. The fop will have nothing to complain of; we make an expedition—myself, D'Anjou, D'Alençon, and Guise—a king, two sons of France, and a sovereign prince, without counting you."

"How, without counting me?"

"Of course you will be with us."

"I?"

"Yes, you? Stab the fellow for me in royal fashion while we strangle him."

"Sire," said Henri, "your goodness overwhelms me; but are you sure?"

"Eh! horn of the devil! it appears that the fellow boasts of it. He goes sometimes to see her at the Louvre, sometimes at the Rue Cloche Percée. They make verses together—I should like to see that fop's verses—pastorals; they talk of Bion and Moschus, of Daphnis and Corydon. Ah, bah! take a dagger with you at least."

"Sire," said Henri, "upon reflection, your Majesty will comprehend that I cannot take part in this expedition. I am too much interested in it not to have my presence ascribed to a desire of vengeance. Your Majesty punishes a man who calumniates your sister; and Marguerite, whom I maintain innocent, is not dishonored. But if I am associated with it, my cooperation converts an act of justice into an act of vengeance. It is no longer an execution, it is an assassination; and my wife is no longer calumniated, she is guilty."

"*Mordieu*, Henriot! you speak words of gold; I told my mother

just now that you have the intelligence of a demon." And Charles
regarded his brother-in-law complacently. Henri bowed in acknowledgment of the compliment.

"Nevertheless," added Charles, "you will be pleased to get rid
of that fop?"

"Whatever your Majesty may do will be well done," replied
the King of Navarre.

"Well, well, leave all to me. It shall not be the worse executed."

"I leave it all in your hands, Sire," said Henri.

"At what time does he usually go to your wife's apartments?"

"About nine o'clock."

"And at what hour does he leave?"

"Before I come, for I never see him."

"What time is that?"

"About eleven."

"Good! come down this evening at midnight; all will be over."
And Charles, after shaking Henri's hand, and renewing his protestations of friendship, left the apartment, whistling a favorite hunting
air.

"*Ventre-saint-gris!*" said the Béarnais, following Charles with his
eyes, "I will wager anything that the queen-mother is at the bottom
of all this deviltry. She knows no better than to try to get up a quarrel between my wife and myself—and such a pretty scheme!" And
Henri laughed as he could laugh when no one was near to hear him.

At seven o'clock the same evening, a young man who had just
left the bath, perfumed and attired himself, humming a gay air the
while. Beside him slept, or rather reclined on the bed, another
young man.

The one was our friend La Mole, who had been so much an
object of interest through the day, and still drew to himself more attention than he dreamed of; and the other was his companion
Coconnas.

In fact, all that storm had been going on around him without
his hearing the growling of the thunder, or seeing the lightning
flashes. Returning home at three o'clock in the morning, he had
stayed in bed till three o'clock in the afternoon, half sleeping, half
dreaming, building castles on that moving sand we call the future;
then he had risen, spent an hour at some fashionable baths, had

dined at Maître la Hurière's, and on returning to the Louvre, had completed his preparations for his customary visit to the queen.

"And you say you have dined?" said Coconnas, yawning.

"Faith, yes; and with a good appetite."

"Why didn't you take me with you, egotist?"

"Faith, you were so sound asleep that I was unwilling to wake you. But we will have supper instead of dinner. Don't forget to ask Maître la Hurière for that Anjou wine which he has lately received."

"Is it good?"

"Try it; I will say no more."

"And you, where are you going?"

"Where am I going?" said La Mole, surprised that his friend should ask the question. "I am going to the queen."

"Ah, true! I forgot. Here is your mantle."

"No, that is the black; I want the cherry one; the queen prefers me in that."

"Ah, upon my word!" said Coconnas; "look for yourself. I do not see it."

"Not see it!" replied La Mole; "where can it be, then?"

At this moment, when after having turned everything upside down La Mole was beginning to abuse the thieves who dared even rob in the Louvre, the door opened, and a page of the Duc d'Alençon appeared with the mantle in question.

"Ah!" said La Mole, "here it is."

"Yes, Monsieur, Monseigneur sent for it to decide a wager about its color."

"Oh!" said La Mole. "I wanted it only because I was going out; but if his Highness wishes to keep it—"

"No, Monsieur the Count, it is all over."

The page retired, and La Mole clasped on his cloak.

"Well," said he to Coconnas, "what are you going to do?"

"I do not know."

"Shall I find you here this evening?"

"How can I tell you that?"

"You don't know what you will be doing in two hours?"

"I know what I shall do, but don't know what will be done to me."

"The Duchesse de Nevers?"

"No, the Duc d'Alençon."

"In fact," said La Mole, "I notice that for some time past he seems particularly friendly to you."

"Well, yes," said Coconnas.

"Then your future is made," said La Mole, smiling.

"Bah!" said Coconnas, "a cadet!"

"Oh!" said La Mole, "he has such a desire to become the heir that perhaps Heaven will work a miracle in his favor. So you don't know where you will be this evening?"

"No."

"To the devil, then—or rather, adieu."

"That La Mole is a terrible fellow," thought Coconnas, "he's always wanting to know where one is going, as if one knew"; and he composed himself to sleep.

As for La Mole, he betook himself to the Queen of Navarre's apartments. In the corridor he met the Duc d'Alençon.

"Ah, it is you, La Mole?" said he.

"Yes, Monseigneur."

"Are you going out of the Louvre?"

"No, your Highness, I am going to pay my respects to the Queen of Navarre."

"At what time shall you leave her?"

"Has Monseigneur any orders for me?"

"No, but I shall have this evening."

"At what hour?"

"From nine to ten."

"I will not fail to wait on your Highness."

"Well, I rely upon you."

La Mole bowed, and went on.

"It is very strange," thought he; "the duke is pale sometimes as a corpse."

And he knocked at the door. Gillonne, who seemed to be watching for his arrival, opened it, and conducted him to the queen. Marguerite was occupied with something that seemed to fatigue her greatly; a paper covered with erasures, and a volume of Isocrates lay before her. She signed to La Mole to let her finish the sentence, and then casting aside her pen, invited him to sit by her.

La Mole had never seemed so handsome and so gay. "Greek!" cried he, glancing at the volume; "Isocrates! what are you doing?

Ah, and on this paper Latin—'*Ad Sarmatiæ legatos reginæ Margaritæ concio*'—you are going to harangue these barbarians in Latin, then?"

"I must, since they do not understand French."

"But how can you compose the answer without having the address?"

"A person more cunning than I might make you believe in an improvisation; but for you, my Hyacinthe, I have no such trickery; they have given me the address in advance, and I respond to it."

"Are these ambassadors, then, about to arrive?"

"Better still, they arrived this morning."

"But no one knows it?"

"They have come incognito. Their formal entrance is appointed for day after tomorrow, I believe. As for the rest, you will see," said Marguerite, with a slight air of pedantry, "that what I have written is Ciceronian enough; but let us drop these vanities. Let us talk of what has happened to you."

"To me?"

"Yes."

"What has happened to me?"

"Ay, what has happened to you? you look pale."

"I confess it, but it is from too much sleep."

"Come, do not boast, I know all."

"Tell me what you mean, my pearl, for I know nothing."

"Come, answer me frankly. What has the queen-mother asked of you?"

"The queen-mother, of me? Had she, then, something to say to me?"

"What! have you not seen her?"

"No."

"And King Charles?"

"No."

"And the King of Navarre?"

"No."

"But the Duc d'Alençon, you have seen him?"

"Yes, just now. I met him in the corridor."

"What did he say to you?"

"That he had some orders to give me, between nine and ten o'clock this evening."

"Nothing else?"

"Nothing."

"It is strange!"

"But tell me, what is strange?"

"That you have heard nothing."

"What, then, has happened?"

"It has happened, unhappy man, that all this day you have been suspended over an abyss."

"I?"

"Yes, you."

"How so?"

"Listen; Mouy, surprised last night in the apartments of the King of Navarre, whom they wished to arrest, killed three men, and escaped without being recognized, except by the red mantle he wore."

"Well?"

"This red mantle, which once deceived me, has deceived others also. You are suspected of this triple murder. This morning you would have been arrested, tried—who knows?—condemned perhaps; for to save yourself you would not have told where you were, would you?"

"Told where I was?" cried La Mole; "compromise you—you, my beautiful queen? Oh, never, never! I would have died joyfully to spare your glorious eyes but one tear."

"Alas, my poor friend!" replied the queen, "my glorious eyes would have wept many, many tears!"

"But how was this storm appeased?"

"Guess."

"I cannot."

"There was but one way of proving that you were not in the king's chamber."

"And that was—"

"To say where you were."

"Well!"

"And I said it."

"To whom?"

"To my mother."

"And Queen Catherine—"

"Knows that you are my lover."

"Oh, Madame, after having done so much for me, my life belongs to you!"

"I hope so, for I have snatched it from those who wished to take it; but now you are saved."

"Saved by you!" cried the young man; "by you whom I adore—"

At this moment a sharp noise made them both start. La Mole recoiled in undefined terror, and Marguerite, uttering a cry, fixed her eyes on a broken pane in the window. By this pane a stone of the size of an egg had entered, and lay on the floor.

La Mole saw the broken window, and comprehending the cause of the noise, "Who has dared to do this?" he cried, and darted toward the window.

"Stay," said Marguerite; "it seems to me something is fastened to the stone."

"It looks like a letter," replied La Mole.

Marguerite eagerly caught up the stone, round which was wound a slip of paper. The paper was fastened to a thread which passed out of the window. Marguerite opened and read it.

"Oh, Heaven!" cried she, holding out the paper, "La Mole!"

He looked and read:

M. de la Mole is waited for by long swords in the corridor
leading to M. d'Alençon's apartments; perhaps he would
prefer leaving the Louvre by this window, and joining M.
de Mouy at Mantes.

"But," said La Mole, "are these swords longer than mine?"

"No, but there are perhaps ten against one."

"And who is the friend who sends us this letter?" asked La Mole.

Marguerite looked at it attentively.

"The writing of the King of Navarre," said she. "If he warns us, the danger is real; fly, then, fly!"

"How?"

"Does it not mention the window?"

"Command, and I will leap from the window, were it twenty times as high!"

"Stay," said Marguerite, "it seems to me that this string sup-
ports a weight."

"Let us see."

And both, drawing toward them the string, saw with unspeak-
able joy the end of a ladder of silk.

"Ah, you are saved!" said Marguerite.

"It is a miracle of Heaven!"

"No, it is a gift of the King of Navarre."

"What if it were a snare laid for me," said La Mole; "what if
this ladder were to break beneath me! Have you not today avowed
your love for me, Marguerite?"

Marguerite, to whose cheeks joy had restored the color, became deadly pale. "You are right," said she; "it is possible." And she
darted toward the door.

"Where are you going?" cried La Mole.

"To assure myself that you are really waited for in the corridor."

"Never, lest their vengeance fall on you!"

"What can they do to me? A queen and a woman, I am doubly
inviolable."

The queen said this with so much dignity that La Mole felt that
she ran no risk, and that it was best to let her do as she wished.
Marguerite entrusted La Mole to Gillonne, leaving it to her sagacity
to decide according to circumstances whether he should fly or await
her return. She advanced into the corridor that led to the library
and a suite of reception rooms, which opened into the king's and
queen-mother's apartments and to the private staircase leading to
D'Alençon's apartments. Although it was hardly nine o'clock, all the
lights were extinguished, and except for a slight glimmer at the end,
the corridor was quite dark. The queen advanced with a firm step;
but arrived halfway, she heard a sound of voices whispering, to
which the effort of suppression gave a mysterious and hollow sound.
But all noise soon ceased, as if at the command of a superior, and the
light, feeble as it was, seemed to diminish. Marguerite advanced,
going straight to the danger which, if it existed, awaited her; she
seemed calm, but in reality the clenching of her hands showed violent nervous agitation. As she approached the lights, the silence
seemed to grow more intense, and a shadow like a hand obscured

the flickering ray. Suddenly a man sprang forward, uncovered a taper, and exclaimed, "Here he is!"

Marguerite found herself face-to-face with her brother Charles. Behind him stood D'Alençon, a cord of silk in his hand. At the back two shadows were visible, with swords in their hands. Marguerite saw all this at a glance, and replied, smilingly, "You mean, here *she* is."

Charles recoiled; the rest stood motionless. "You here, Margot? Where are you going at this hour?" said he.

"At this hour?" said Marguerite, "is it, then, so late?"

"I ask you where are you going?"

"To get one of the volumes of Cicero, which I think I left in our mother's apartments."

"Without a light?"

"I thought the corridor was lighted."

"And you come from your own apartments?"

"Yes."

"What are you doing, then, this evening?"

"Preparing my speech for the Polish ambassadors. Is there not to be a council tomorrow; and is it not understood that everyone will submit his address to your Majesty?"

"Is anyone helping you?"

Marguerite made a violent effort. "M. de la Mole," replied she. "He is very learned."

"So much so," said D'Alençon, "that I requested him when he should have finished with you to come and help me, who am not so clever as you are."

"You are waiting for him?"

"Yes," returned D'Alençon, impatiently.

"Then," said Marguerite, "I will send him to you, Brother— for we have finished."

"And your book?" said Charles.

"Gillonne can fetch it."

The two brothers interchanged a sign.

"Go, then," said Charles. "We will continue our round."

"Your round?" asked Marguerite. "Whom are you looking for, then?"

"The little red man," returned Charles; "do you not know he

is said to haunt the Louvre? D'Alençon says he has seen him; and we are in search of him."

"Success to your chase!" said Marguerite; and she withdrew, casting a look behind. She saw upon the wall of the corridor the four shadows reunited as if for conference. In a second she was at her door. "Open, Gillonne!" cried she.

Gillonne obeyed. Marguerite sprang into the apartment, and found La Mole resolute and calm, his sword drawn.

"Fly!" said the queen; "fly instantly! There is no time to be lost! They await you in the corridor to murder you."

"You command it?" said La Mole.

"I wish it. We must separate now, that we may meet again."

During her absence La Mole had attached the ladder, and he now stepped on it, after having tenderly embraced the queen. "Should I perish, remember your promise!" said he.

"It is not a promise, but an oath. Adieu!"

Encouraged by these words, La Mole glided down the ladder. At this moment someone knocked at the door. Marguerite did not leave the window until she had seen La Mole reach the ground in safety.

"Madame!" said Gillonne; "Madame!"

"Well."

"The king is knocking at the door."

"Open it."

Gillonne did so.

The four princes, doubtless impatient with waiting, stood at the threshold; Charles entered. Marguerite advanced to meet him with a smile on her lips.

The king cast a quick glance around.

"Whom are you seeking, Brother?" asked the queen.

"Whom am I seeking?" said Charles. *"Corbœuf!* I am seeking M. de la Mole."

"M. de la Mole?"

"Yes; where is he?"

Marguerite took her brother's hand, and led him to the window. At this moment two men from beneath the window started off on horseback at full speed; one of them detached his white satin scarf, and waved it in the air. They were La Mole and Orthon. Marguerite pointed them out with her finger to Charles.

"What does this mean?" asked he.

"It means," returned Marguerite, "that M. d'Alençon may put his cord in his pocket, and M. M. d'Anjou and de Guise may sheathe their swords, for M. de la Mole will not pass through the corridor tonight."

CHAPTER 9

The Atrides

Since his return to Paris, Henri d'Anjou had not had a confidential interview with his mother Catherine, of whom, as everybody knows, he was the favorite son. That interview would not be to him an empty subservience to etiquette, nor a ceremonial disagreeable to perform, but the fulfillment of a duty very pleasant to that son, who, if he did not love his mother, was sure, at least, of being tenderly loved by her.

In fact Catherine really preferred this son, either for his courage or for his beauty—for there was in Catherine something of the woman as well as mother—or in short, because, according to certain chronicles of scandal, Henri d'Anjou recalled to the Florentine a happy period of secret amours.

She alone knew of his return to Paris, of which Charles IX would have remained ignorant if chance had not conducted him to the Hôtel de Condé at the moment when his brother was leaving it. Charles had not expected him until the next day, and Henri d'Anjou had hoped to conceal from him the two motives which had hastened his arrival by a day; namely, his visit to the lovely Marie de Clèves, Princesse de Condé, and his conference with the Polish ambassadors.

When the Duc d'Anjou, so long expected, entered his mother's apartments, Catherine, usually so cold and unmoved, and who, since the departure of her son, had embraced no one with warmth except Coligny, who was to be murdered next day, opened her arms to the child of her love, and pressed him to her breast with an effusion of maternal affection astonishing to find in that withered heart.

"Ah, Madame," said he, "since Heaven gives me the satisfaction of embracing my mother without witness, pray console the most wretched man in the world."

"Eh, *mon Dieu!* my dear child," cried Catherine, "what has happened to you?"

"Nothing that you do not know, Mother. I am in love, I am beloved; but this very love, which would form the bliss of any other, causes my misery."

"Explain yourself, my son," said Catherine.

"Ah, Mother, these ambassadors, this departure."

"Yes," said Catherine, "the ambassadors have arrived; the departure is nigh at hand."

"It needs not be nigh at hand, but my brother urges it; he hates me. I am in his way, and he wishes to be rid of me."

Catherine smiled. "By giving you a throne? Unhappy crowned head!"

"Oh, I do not want it, Mother!" replied Henri, in agony; "I do not wish to go. I, a son of France, brought up in the refinement of polished manners, beside a tender mother, beloved by one of the most charming women on earth—must I go, then, to those snows at the farthest extremity of the earth, to die by inches among coarse, rough people, who are intoxicated from morning till night, and gauge the capacities of their king as they do those of a cask, by the quantity he can hold? No, no, my mother, I will not go; I will die first!"

"Courage, Henri," said Catherine, pressing his hands between her own, "let us inquire into the real reason."

Henri lowered his eyes, as if he dared not let his mother read what was in his heart.

"Is there no other reason," she asked, "less romantic, more reasonable, more public?"

"Mother, it is not my fault if this idea dwells in my mind, and perchance retains a place it should not hold; but have you not said yourself that the horoscope of my brother Charles prophesies that he will die young?"

"Yes," replied Catherine; "but a horoscope may lie, my son. I myself at this moment hope that all horoscopes are not true."

"But did not his horoscope declare this?"

"His horoscope spoke of a quarter of a century, but did not say if it were for his life or for his reign."

"Well, then, dear mother, contrive that I remain; my brother is nearly four-and-twenty, and another year must decide."

Catherine pondered deeply. "Yes, assuredly," she said, "it would be better if it could be so arranged."

"Oh, judge then, my mother," cried Henri, "what despair for me, if I were to exchange the crown of France for the crown of Poland!—to be tormented there with the idea that I might reign at the Louvre in the midst of this lettered and elegant court, near the best mother in the world, whose counsels would save me one half of my fatigue and labors, who, accustomed to bear with my father a portion of the burden of the State, would kindly bear it also with me. Ah, my mother, I should have been a great king!"

"Come, come, my dearest child," said Catherine, to whom this prospect had always been a very sweet hope, "come, do not despair. Have you thought of any way this could be arranged?"

"Yes, assuredly; and that is the principal reason why I returned two or three days before I was expected, making my brother Charles believe that it was for Madame de Condé; then I have formed an acquaintance with Lasco, the principal envoy, doing all that I could to make myself unpopular and disliked, and I hope I have succeeded."

"Ah, my dear son," said Catherine, "that is bad; we must always put the interest of France before your petty dislikes."

"Mother, does the interest of France require, in case of any misfortune happening to my brother Charles, that D'Alençon or the King of Navarre should ascend the throne?"

"Oh, the King of Navarre! Never! never!" murmured Catherine.

"Upon my word!" continued Henri, "my brother D'Alençon is no better, and does not love you more."

"Well," asked Catherine, "and what said Lasco?"

"Lasco hesitated when I pressed him to seek an audience. Oh, if he would write to Poland, and annual the election!"

"Folly, my son; very madness! What a Diet has consecrated is sacred."

"But then, Mother, could not these Poles be induced to accept my brother in my stead?"

"This is difficult, if not impossible."

"Never mind; try. Speak to the king, Mother; ascribe all to my love for Madame de Condé; say I am mad, crazy about her. He saw me, besides, leave the hotel of the prince with Guise, who does me every service in that quarter."

"Yes, in order to make his league; you do not perceive this, but I do."

"Yes, Mother, yes; but in the meantime I make use of him. Should we not be glad when a man serves us while serving himself?"

"And what said the king when he met you?"

"He seemed to believe what I told him, which was that love only had brought me back to Paris."

"But has he not asked you for any account of the rest of the night?"

"Yes, Mother; but I went to sup at Nantouillet's, where I made a great riot, so that the king might hear of it, and have no suspicion as to where I was."

"Then he knows nothing of your visit to Lasco?"

"Nothing."

"So much the better. I will try, then, to speak for you, my poor boy; but you know the intractable disposition of him with whom I have to deal."

"Charles will not allow me to remain. He detests me."

"He is jealous of you, my beautiful hero! Why are you so brave and fortunate? Why, at scarcely twenty years of age, have you gained battles like Alexander and Cæsar? But do not open your heart to everyone. Pretend to be resigned, and pay your court to the king. Today, even, there is to be a private council for reading and discussing the addresses to be delivered at the ceremony. Act the King of Poland and leave all the rest to me. By the way, how succeeded your expedition of last night?"

"It failed, Mother. The gay gallant was warned, and escaped by the window."

"Someday," said Catherine, "I shall learn who is the bad genius who thus counteracts all my projects. In the meanwhile, I have my suspicion. Malediction be on him!"

"Then, Mother—" said the Duc d'Anjou.

"Leave me to manage all"; and she kissed Henri tenderly on the eyes and pushed him out of her cabinet.

The princes of the house then arrived. Charles was in a capital humor; for the audacity of his sister Marguerite had rather pleased than vexed him. He felt no resentment against La Mole, and had awaited him with some ardor in the corridor simply because it was a kind of chase. D'Alençon, on the other hand, was much preoccupied. The repulsion he had always felt for La Mole had changed into hate from the moment he knew that he was beloved by his sister. Marguerite was at the same time meditative and alert. She had to remember and to watch. The Polish deputies had sent a copy of the harangues to be pronounced.

Marguerite, to whom no more mention had been made of the occurrences of the previous evening than if they had never taken place, read the discourses; and except Charles, everyone discussed what the replies should be. Charles allowed Marguerite to reply as she pleased. He was somewhat difficult in his choice of words for D'Alençon; but as to the discourse of Henri d'Anjou, he attacked it bitterly, and made endless corrections and additions.

This meeting, without having any decisive issue, tended to envenom the feelings of all. Henri d'Anjou, who had to rewrite nearly all his discourse, went out to perform his task. Marguerite, who had not heard of the King of Navarre since he had broken her windowpane, returned to her apartments, in the hope of finding him there. D'Alençon, who had read the hesitation in his brother D'Anjou's eyes, and surprised a meaning look between him and his mother, withdrew to ponder over what might be the fresh plot. Charles was going to his forge to finish a boar-spear he was making for himself, when Catherine stopped him. Expecting some opposition to his will from his mother, he paused, and gazed sternly on her. "Well," said he, "and what now?"

"One other word, Sire; we had forgotten it, and yet it is of much importance. What day do you fix for the public reception?"

"True!" said the king, seating himself; "let us talk it over, Mother. Well, what day shall it be?"

"I thought," replied Catherine, "that in your Majesty's silence, your apparent forgetfulness, there was something of deep calculation."

"Why so, Mother?"

"Because," added the queen-mother, very quietly, "there is no need, my son, as it appears to me, that the Poles should see us crave their crown with such avidity."

"On the contrary, Mother," said Charles, "they have hastened by forced marches from Warsaw hither. Honor for honor, politeness for politeness!"

"Your Majesty may be right in one sense, as in another I am not wrong. Your opinion, then, is, that the public reception should be hastened?"

"Certainly; and is it not yours also?"

"You know that I have no opinions but such as are connected with your glory; I tell you, then, that thus hastening the affair, I should fear that you might be accused of profiting very quickly by this occasion which presents itself for relieving the house of France of the charges which your brother imposes on it, but which assuredly he repays to it in glory and devotion."

"Mother," said Charles, "when my brother leaves France, I will so richly endow him that no one will even dare to think what you fear they may say."

"Well," said Catherine, "I give up, since you have such good answers to all my objections; but to receive this warlike people, who judge of the power of States from exterior signs, you must have a considerable display of troops; and I do not think that there are yet enough assembled in the Ile de France."

"Excuse me, Mother, but I had foreseen this event, and was prepared for it. I have recalled two battalions from Normandy, one from Guienne; my company of archers arrived yesterday from Brittany; the light-horse spread over Lorraine will be in Paris in the course of the day; and while it is supposed that I can scarcely command four regiments, I have twenty thousand men ready to appear."

"Ah, ah!" said Catherine, surprised, "then there is only one thing wanting; but that you will procure."

"What is that?"

"Money; I imagine that you have not a superabundance."

"On the contrary, Madame, on the contrary," said Charles IX, "I have fourteen hundred thousand crowns in the Bastille; my private estates have this week brought me in eight hundred thousand crowns, which I have buried in my cellars in the Louvre; and in case of need, Nantouillet has three hundred thousand crowns, besides, at my disposal."

Catherine trembled, for she had before seen Charles violent and passionate, but never provident.

"Well, then," she added, "your Majesty thinks of everything—admirable! and if the tailors, embroiderers, and jewelers use despatch, your Majesty will be ready to give this audience in less than six weeks."

"Six weeks!" exclaimed Charles, "why, Mother, the tailors, embroiderers, and jewelers have been hard at work since the day when my brother's nomination was announced. On a pinch everything might have been ready for today; certainly everything will be ready in three or four days."

"Ah!" murmured Catherine; "you are in greater haste than I thought, my son."

"Honor for honor, as I have already said."

"Good; then it is this honor done to the house of France that flatters you, is it not?"

"Assuredly."

"And to see a son of France on the throne of Poland is your chief desire?"

"Precisely so."

"Then it is the fact and not the man that interests you; and whoever may reign there—"

"No, no, Mother; *corbœuf!* no. Let us be as we are! The Poles have made a good choice; they are skillful, clever fellows! A military nation, a people of soldiers, they take a captain for their ruler. *Peste!* D'Anjou is their man. The hero of Jarnac and Moncontour fits them like a glove. Whom would you have me send them—D'Alençon? A coward! he would give them a fine idea of the house of Valois! D'Alençon! he would flee at the noise of the first ball that whistled by his ears; while Henri d'Anjou is a warrior bold and tried, always sword in hand, always on the march, on his warhorse or on foot. Forward! cut down, thrust, crush, slay! Ah, he is a man, my brother D'Anjou; a gallant soldier, who'll give them fighting from morning till night—from the first of January to the thirty-first of December! He is not a hard drinker, it is true; but he will do his work in cold blood, you see. He will be in his element, the dear Henri! On, on, to the field of battle! bravo, trumpets and drums! Long live the king! Long live the conqueror! Long live the general! They will proclaim him emperor three times a year! This will be admirable for the house of France and the honor of the Valois! he may be killed perchance, but *ventre-mahon!* it will be a glorious death."

Catherine shuddered, and her eyes flashed fire. "Say," she cried, "that you wish to send your brother, Henri d'Anjou, away. Say you do not love your brother."

"Ah, ah, ah!" exclaimed Charles, laughing nervously; "what! have you divined that I wished to send him away? Have you divined that I do not love him? And suppose it were so? Love my brother! why should I love my brother? Ah, ah, ah! do you speak jestingly?" and as he spoke, his pale cheeks were animated with feverish red. "Does he love me? Do you love me? Is there, except my dogs, Marie Touchet, and my nurse—is there anyone who has ever loved me? No, no, I do not love my brother. I love only myself; do you understand? And I do not prevent my brother from doing as I do."

"Sire," said Catherine, becoming animated in her turn, "since you unfold your heart to me, I must open mine to you. You act like a weak king, like an ill-advised king; you send away your brother, the natural support of your throne, who is in all respects fit to succeed you if any misfortune happened to you, leaving, in that event, your crown in jeopardy; for, as you said, D'Alençon is young, incapable, weak—more than weak, cowardly!—and the Béarnais is waiting in the background!"

"Well, death of all the devils!" cried Charles, "how does it concern me what will happen when I am dead? The Béarnais is waiting in the background, say you? *Corbœuf!* so much the better! I said I loved no one—I was wrong; I love Henriot—yes, I love the good Henriot, with his free air and his warm hand, while I see around me none but false eyes, and touch none but ice-cold hands. He is incapable of treason toward me, I will swear! Besides, I owe a recompense; they poisoned his mother, poor fellow—some persons of my family too, it is said. Besides, I am in good health; but if I fell sick, I would send for him, and he should not leave my side. I would take nothing but from his hand; and should I die, I would make him King of France and of Navarre, and, *ventre du pape!* instead of laughing at my death, as my brother would do, he would weep, or at least appear to do so."

Had a thunderbolt fallen at Catherine's feet, she would have been less alarmed than at these words. She remained aghast, looking at Charles with a haggard eye; and then, at the end of a few seconds, she cried, "Henri de Navarre! Henri de Navarre King of France, to the prejudice of my children! Ah, *sainte Madone!* we will see! It is for this you would send away my son?"

"Your son! and what then am I—a son of the wolf, like Romulus?" cried Charles, trembling with rage, and his eye sparkling as if it were on fire. "Your son! You are right; and the King of France, then, is not your son. The King of France has no brothers; the King of France has no mother; the King of France has only subjects! The King of France has no need of sentiment; he has will. He can do without being loved; but he will be obeyed!"

"Sire, you have mistaken my words. I called him my son who is about to leave me. I love him better at this moment because it is he whom at this moment I fear to lose. Is it a crime for a mother to desire that her son should not leave her?"

"And I—I tell you he shall leave you. I tell you he shall leave France and go to Poland, and that in two days; and if you add one word, in one day—tomorrow. And if you do not bow your head, if you do not change that threatening expression of your eyes, I will strangle him tonight, as you would have strangled your daughter's lover yesternight; only I will not miss him as we did La Mole."

At this threat Catherine bent down her head, and then again instantly raised it. "Ah, poor child!" she said, "your brother would kill you; but be tranquil, your mother will defend you."

"Ah! I am defied!" cried Charles. "Well, then, by the blood of Christ! he shall die—not this evening, but this very moment. Ah! a weapon! a dagger! a knife!—ah!"

Charles, after having vainly sought all round for what he demanded, saw the small stiletto which his mother wore at her girdle, seized it, drew it from its shagreen and silver case, and rushed out of the chamber, with the determination of striking Henri d'Anjou wherever he found him; but on reaching the vestibule his overexcited strength gave way suddenly, and extending his arm, he let fall the keen weapon, which stuck in the floor, and uttering a lamentable cry, he swooned and fell on the floor, while the blood spurted copiously from his nose and his mouth.

"Jesus!" he said, "they are killing me! help! help!"

Catherine, who had followed, saw him fall, looked at him for a moment without moving or calling, and then recalled to herself, not by maternal instinct, but by the difficulty of her situation, she opened a door, and cried, "The king is taken ill. Help! help!"

At this cry, a crowd of servants, officers, and courtiers hastened to the young king; but foremost of all a woman rushed on, pushing aside the crowd, and raised Charles, who was as pale as a corpse.

"They are killing me, Nurse! they are killing me!" murmured the king, bathed in perspiration and blood.

"They are killing you, my Charles?" cried the good creature, looking everyone in the face in a way that made even Catherine retreat; "and who is killing you?"

Charles uttered a sigh and fainted.

"Ah!" said the doctor, Ambroise Paré, whom they had sent for; "ah! the king is very ill."

"Now, by choice or by compulsion," said the implacable Catherine to herself, "he must accede to a delay"; and she left the king to go to her second son, who was awaiting in the oratory the result of that interview so important to himself.

CHAPTER 10

The Horoscope

On leaving the oratory, where she had informed Henri d'Anjou of what had taken place, Catherine found René in her chamber. She had written to him the evening before, and he had come in response to her letter.

"Well," asked the queen, "have you seen him?"

"Yes."

"How is he?"

"Rather better."

"Can he speak?"

"No, the sword pierced the larynx."

"I told you to make him write."

"I tried, but his hand had formed only two letters, almost illegible, when he fainted; the jugular vein has been cut into, and the loss of blood has greatly weakened him."

"Have you seen these letters?"

"Here they are."

René took a paper from his pocket, and presented it to the queen, who hastily opened it.

"An *m* and an *o,*" said she. "Can it be, after all, M. de la Mole, and that the confession of Marguerite was only to avert suspicion?"

"Madame," returned René, "if I may venture an opinion, I should say that M. de la Mole is too much in love to trouble his head about politics, and, above all, too much in love with Madame Marguerite to serve her husband very devotedly—for there is no deep love without jealousy."

"You think him in love, then?"

"Desperately."

"Has he had recourse to you?"

"Yes; I made him a waxen image."

"Pierced to the heart?"

"To the heart."

"Have you it still?"

"At my house."

"I wonder," said Catherine, "if these cabalistic preparations have really the power attributed to them?"

"Your Majesty knows even more than I what their influence is."

"Does Marguerite love La Mole?"

"Sufficiently to ruin herself for him. Yesterday she saved him at the risk of her honor and her life; you see all this, and yet you doubt."

"Doubt what?"

"Science."

"I doubt because science has deceived me," looking fixedly at René.

"On what occasion?"

"Oh! you know what I mean—unless, perchance, it is the scholar and not the science."

"I don't know what you mean, Madame," replied the Florentine.

"René, have your perfumes lost their odor?"

"No, Madame—not when they are employed by me; but it is possible that in passing through the hands of others—"

Catherine smiled and shook her head. "Your opiate has done wonders, René," she said; "Madame de Sauve's lips are fresher and redder than ever."

"That must not be attributed to my opiate, Madame, for the Baronne de Sauve, availing herself of a pretty woman's right to be capricious, did not speak to me again about that opiate; and after the suggestion your Majesty made to me, I concluded not to send it to her. The boxes, therefore, are all in my house, just as you left them—except one which has disappeared without my knowing what person took it, or what that person intended to do with it."

"Well, well," said Catherine, "we will speak of that some other time. Tell me what is necessary to arrive at an idea of the probable length of a person's life?"

"To know first the day of his birth, his age, and what constellation he was born under."

"Next?"

"To have some of his blood and hair."

"If I bring you some of his blood and tell you his age, can you tell me the probable time of his death?"

"Yes, within a few days."

"I have his hair, and I will procure some of his blood."

"Was he born in the day, or during the night?"

"At twenty-three minutes past five in the evening."

"Be with me tomorrow at five o'clock; the experiment must be made at the precise hour of the birth."

"Good!" said Catherine. "We will be there."

René saluted, and retired without appearing to notice the "we," which indicated that contrary to her custom the queen would not come alone.

The next morning, at daybreak, Catherine entered her son Charles's apartments; she had inquired after him at midnight, and was informed that Maître Ambroise Paré was with him, and intended bleeding him if the same nervous agitation continued. Shuddering even in his slumbers, pale from loss of blood, Charles slept, his head resting on his faithful nurse's shoulder, who, leaning against the bed, had not changed her position for three hours, fearing to disturb him. Catherine asked if her son had not been bled. The nurse replied that he had, and so abundantly that he had twice fainted.

The blood was in a basin in the adjoining room. Catherine entered under pretense of examining it, and while so doing she filled with it a phial she had brought with her for the purpose; then she returned, hiding her red fingers, that would otherwise have betrayed her, in her pockets. As she reappeared, Charles opened his eyes and perceived his mother; then, recollecting the events of the previous evening, "Ah! it is you, Madame," said he; "well, you may tell your dear son, your Henri d'Anjou, that it will be tomorrow."

"It shall be when you please, my dear Charles; compose yourself, and go to sleep."

Charles closed his eyes, and Catherine left the room; but no sooner had she gone out than Charles, raising himself, cried, "Send for the chancellor, the court! I want them all!"

The nurse replaced his head upon her shoulder, and sought to lull him to sleep.

"No, no, Nurse!" said he, "I shall not sleep anymore. Summon my people; I wish to work today."

When Charles spoke thus no one dared to disobey, and even the nurse, spite of the privileges she enjoyed, did not venture to dispute his orders. The chancellor was summoned and the audience was appointed, not for the morrow, which was impossible, but for the fifth day from that time.

At five o'clock the queen and the Duc d'Anjou proceeded to René's, who, in expectation of their visit, had prepared everything for the experiment. In the chamber on the right—that is, in the chamber of sacrifice—a blade of steel, covered with singular arabesques, was heating in a brazier of charcoal. On the altar lay the book of fate; and as the previous night had been very clear, René had been enabled to consult the stars.

Henri d'Anjou entered first. He had false hair, and his face and figure were concealed beneath a mask and large cloak. His mother followed him, and had she not known in advance that it was her son who awaited her there, she would not have recognized him. The queen took off her mask; D'Anjou, however, did not follow her example.

"Have you consulted the stars?" asked Catherine.

"I have, Madame, and they have already informed me of the past. The person whose fate you desire to know has, like all persons born under Cancer, a fiery and ardent disposition. He is powerful; he has lived nearly a quarter of a century; Heaven has granted him wealth and power. Is it not so, Madame?"

"Perhaps."

"Have you his hair and blood?"

"Here they are."

And Catherine gave the magician a lock of fair hair and a small phial of blood.

René took the phial, shook it, and let fall on the glowing steel blade a large drop of blood that boiled for a second, and then spread itself into a thousand fantastic shapes.

"Oh!" cried René, "I see him convulsed with agony! Hark! how he groans, how he calls for help! See how all around him turns to blood! See how, around his deathbed, combats and wars arise! And see, here are the lances and swords!"

"Will this be long delayed?" asked Catherine, seizing the hand of her son, who, in his anxiety to see, had leaned over the brazier.

René approached the altar, and repeated a cabalistic prayer; then he rose, and announcing that all was ready, took in one hand the phial and in the other the lock of hair, and bidding Catherine open at hazard the book of fate, he poured on the steel blade all the blood, and cast the hair in the fire, pronouncing a mystic formula as he did so.

Instantly the Due d'Anjou and Catherine saw on the blade a figure resembling a corpse wrapped in a winding-sheet. Another figure, that of a woman, leaned over it. At the same time the hair burned, casting out one jet of flame like a fiery tongue.

"A year," cried René, "scarce a year, and this man shall die! One woman alone shall lament over him; and yet, no—at the end of the blade is another woman, with an infant in her arms."

Catherine looked at her son, as if though herself the mother of the man whose death was announced, she would ask him who these two women could be. But scarcely had René finished when the forms disappeared. Then Catherine opened the book at hazard, and read with a voice that trembled in spite of herself the following distich:

> Ains a peri cil que l'on redoutoit,
> Plus tôt, trop tôt, si prudence n'étoit.

"And for him that you know of," said Catherine, "what say the signs for this month?"

"Favorable as ever; unless Providence interposes to thwart his destiny, he is sure to be fortunate, but—"

"But what?"

"One of the stars composing his pleiad was covered by a black cloud during my observations."

"Ah, a black cloud! there is then some hope?"

"Of whom speak you, Madame?" asked D'Anjou.

Catherine drew her son away from the light of the brazier, and spoke to him in a low voice. During this interval, René, kneeling by the brazier, poured into the hollow of his hand one last drop of blood remaining at the bottom of the phial.

"Strange contradiction!" murmured he, "which proves how

little can human knowledge compete with ours. To everyone but me, even to Ambroise Paré, this blood, so pure, so full of health, promises years of life; and yet all that vigor will soon depart, all that life will be extinguished within a year."

Catherine and Henri turned and listened. The eyes of the prince shone through his mask.

"Ah!" continued René, "to the uninitiated the present is manifest, but to us the future is also manifest."

"He will die, then, before the year be over?" said the queen-mother.

"As surely as there are three persons present who must one day repose in the grave."

"Yet you say the blood indicates a long life?"

"Yes, if things were to follow the natural course; but an accident—"

"Ah, yes, you hear," whispered Catherine to Henri; "an accident."

"Alas!" said he, "the greater reason for staying."

"Oh! as to that, think of it no longer, it is impossible."

"Thanks," said the young man, turning to René, and disguising the tone of his voice; "take this purse."

"Come, Count," said Catherine, purposely using this title, to divert René's suspicions. And they left the chamber.

"Mother," cried Henri, "you hear?—an accident. Should it happen, I shall be four hundred leagues away."

"Four hundred leagues may be accomplished in eight days."

"Yes; but who knows if they will suffer me to return?"

"Perhaps," replied the queen, "this illness of the king's is the accident of which René spoke. Go, Henri, go, and beware of irritating your brother, should you see him."

CHAPTER 11

Mutual Confidences

The first thing the Duc d'Anjou learned on reaching the Louvre was that the solemn entry of the ambassadors was fixed for the fifth day. The tailors and jewelers waited on the prince with magnificent dresses and superb ornaments which the king had ordered for him.

While he fitted them on with an anger that brought tears to his eyes, Henri de Navarre was adorning himself with a splendid collar of emeralds, a gold-hilted sword, and a very valuable ring, which Charles had sent him that morning. D'Alençon had just received a letter, and had retired to his chamber in order to read it at his leisure.

As to Coconnas, he was asking for his friend from every echo in the Louvre. Although not much surprised at La Mole's absence through the night, he had begun in the morning to feel somewhat uneasy about him; and he had started out to search for him, beginning at the Belle Etoile, going thence to the Rue Cloche Percée, to the Rue Tizon, to the Pont St. Michel, and so back to the Louvre. That search had been conducted in a manner sometimes so original, sometimes so imperative—as may easily be conceived, when one considers the eccentric character of Coconnas—that it had occasioned between him and three noblemen of the court explanations, which were ended, after the fashion of the period, on the dueling-ground.

Coconnas had entered upon these encounters with as much zeal as he usually gave to affairs of that sort. He had killed the first adversary and wounded the two others, saying, "That poor La Mole! he knew Latin so well!" so that the last man of the three, Baron de Boissey, had said as he fell, "Ah, for the love of Heaven, Coconnas, vary a little; say at least that he knew Greek."

At length a rumor of the affair in the corridor began to be

bruited about. Coconnas was in the utmost grief; for a moment he believed that all these kings and princes had killed his friend and thrown his body into some dungeon. He learned that D'Alençon had been of the party, and overlooking the dignity that encompassed a prince of the blood, he went to him to demand an explanation, with as little ceremony as if he had been a private gentleman.

D'Alençon, at first, was inclined to show to the door an impertinent who came to ask an account of his actions; but Coconnas spoke so sternly, his eyes were so flaming with rage, and the adventure of three duels in less than twenty-four hours had placed the Piedmontese so high that the duke paused, and instead of giving way to his first impulse, replied with a charming smile, "My dear Coconnas, it is true that the king, furious at having received on his shoulder a silver ewer, the Duc d'Anjou, angry at having orange-jam poured on his head, and the Duc de Guise, humiliated by having been assailed with a haunch of venison, combined to kill M. de la Mole; but a friend of your friend's averted the blow, and I assure you the enterprise failed."

"Ah," said Coconnas, breathing as loudly at this information as a smith's bellows; "ah, *mordi!* Monseigneur, that is well; and I should like to know this friend, to prove my gratitude."

D'Alençon made no reply, but smiled more agreeably still, which made Coconnas believe that this friend was none other than the prince himself.

"Well, Monseigneur," he continued, "since you have done so much as to tell me the beginning of this story, will you complete the obligation by relating to me the conclusion? They wished to kill him, but did not kill him, you say; very well, what did they do with him? I am brave; come, tell me. I know how to support bad news. They have thrown him into some dungeon, have they not? So much the better; it will teach him prudence. He is never willing to take my advice. And besides, we will get him out, *mordi!* stones are not hard to everyone."

D'Alençon shook his head. "The worst of all," he said, "my brave Coconnas, is that since that adventure your friend has not been seen, and no one knows where he went."

"*Mordi!*" cried the Piedmontese, again turning pale, "but I will know where he is, even if he has gone to hell!"

"Go to the Queen Marguerite," said D'Alençon, who was as

anxious as Coconnas to learn where La Mole was; "she will know what has become of the friend you lament."

"I had already thought of doing so," replied Coconnas, "but did not dare; for besides the fact that Madame Marguerite impresses me more than I can tell, I was afraid of finding her in tears. But since your Highness assures me that La Mole is not dead, and that her Majesty will know where he is, I will muster up courage and go to her."

"Go, my friend, go," said Duc François; "and when you have gained information pass it over to me; for I am really as anxious as you are. Only bear in mind one thing, Coconnas."

"What is it?"

"Do not say it was by my advice; for if you are so imprudent, you may not obtain any information."

"Monseigneur," said Coconnas, "as your royal Highness recommends me to secrecy on this point, I will be as mute as a fish, or the queen-mother. Good prince! excellent prince! magnanimous prince!" he murmured, as he went to the Queen of Navarre.

Marguerite was awaiting Coconnas; for the noise of his despair had reached her, and on learning by what exploits his despair had been manifested, she almost forgave him his somewhat coarse behavior to Madame de Nevers, whom the Piedmontese had not visited, in consequence of a dispute between them two or three days previously. He was therefore introduced to the queen as soon as announced.

Coconnas entered, not altogether able to surmount the embarrassment which he had told D'Alençon he always felt in the presence of the queen, and which was occasioned more by the superiority of her intelligence than by that of her rank; but Marguerite greeted him with a smile which instantly reassured him.

"Ah, Madame!" he exclaimed, "restore my friend to me, I entreat you; or at least tell me what has become of him, for without him I cannot live. Suppose Euryalus without Nisus, Damon without Pythias, or Orestes without Pylades, and have pity on my misfortune at the loss of my dear friend."

Marguerite smiled, and after having bound Coconnas to secrecy, told him all about the escape by the window. As to the place of his concealment, although Coconnas urged her to reveal it with all earnestness, she decidedly refused. That only half satisfied

Coconnas; he therefore had recourse to the diplomatic tentatives practiced in a higher sphere. The result was that Marguerite clearly perceived that the Duc d'Alençon shared in the desire of his gentleman to know what had become of La Mole.

"Well," said the queen, "if you wish to learn something positive as to your friend, ask the King of Navarre, who is the only person who has a right to speak. As for me, all I can tell you is that he you are seeking lives; have faith in my word!"

"I have faith in something still more sure, Madame; those lovely eyes have not been weeping."

Then, thinking he could not add anything to a saying that had the double advantage of conveying his thought and of expressing his high opinion of La Mole's merit, he retired, meditating a reconciliation with Madame de Nevers, not on her account, but simply to learn from her what he had been unable to learn from Marguerite.

Great griefs are abnormal experiences, the burden of which the mind shakes off as soon as possible. The idea of leaving Marguerite had almost broken La Mole's heart; and it was rather to save the reputation of the queen than to preserve his own life that he had consented to fly. And therefore the next day he had returned to Paris, to see Marguerite at her balcony. Marguerite, on her side, as if a secret voice had informed her that he would be there, had passed the evening at her window; and thus they had seen each other with that indescribable happiness which accompanies forbidden pleasures. There was even more; the melancholy and romantic disposition of La Mole found a certain charm in his misfortune. Nevertheless, as a lover truly devoted is happy only when he sees or possesses, and suffers through all the time of absence, La Mole, eager to revisit Marguerite, occupied himself in organizing with all possible despatch the event which would restore her to him; namely, the flight of the King of Navarre.

Marguerite, having thus seen La Mole, and being aware of his safety, was at ease with respect to him, but fearing that he might be watched and followed, she pertinaciously refused to give him any other meeting than these *à l'Espagnole,* which took place every evening until the night before the reception of the ambassadors. On this evening, about nine o'clock, when all the persons in the Louvre were preoccupied with the preparations for next day, Marguerite opened her window and went into the balcony; but scarcely was she there when the note she expected, according to La Mole's usual custom, was thrown with his usual skill, and fell at the feet of his royal mistress. As he had generally awaited her missive, Marguerite understood by his anticipating her that he had some important intelligence to communicate; and she read the note with all haste. On the first page it contained these words:

MADAME—I must speak to the King of Navarre; it is on a most urgent matter. I am waiting.

And on the second page, which could be detached from the other, was written:

MY LADY AND QUEEN—Manage that I may give you one of those kisses that I send you. I am waiting.

Marguerite had scarcely finished the second side of this letter when she heard the voice of Henri de Navarre, who, with his usual reserve, tapped at the door and asked Gillonne if he might be allowed to enter. The queen instantly divided the sheet of paper, put one of the pages in her bosom and the other in her pocket, ran to the window, which she shut, and going quickly to the door, said, "Come in, Sire."

Gently, quickly, and cleverly as Marguerite had closed the window, the sound had reached the ears of Henri, whose senses were always on the alert, and who had in the society he so much mistrusted acquired that exquisite delicacy of hearing and sight possessed by men living in a savage state. But the King of Navarre was not one of those tyrants who wish to prevent their wives from taking the air and gazing at the stars. He was smiling and urbane as usual.

"Madame," he said, "while our people of the court are trying on their fine apparel, I have come to have a few words with you as to my affairs, which you still regard as your own, do you not?"

"Most assuredly, Monsieur," replied Marguerite; "are not our interests always identical?"

"Yes, Madame; and therefore I wished to ask your opinion as to the effort which D'Alençon had made for several days to avoid me, and which he has carried so far that since the day before yesterday he has betaken himself to St. Germain. Do you not think from this that it is his intention either to go away alone, or not to go at all? Let me, if you please, have your ideas on this point; for it would have great weight with me if your opinion should coincide with mine."

"Your Majesty is quite right to feel uneasy as to my brother's silence. I have thought of it all day; and it is my opinion that, circumstances having changed, he has changed with them."

"That is to say, that seeing King Charles ill, and the Duc d'Anjou King of Poland, he would not be sorry to remain in Paris to watch for the crown of France."

"Precisely so."

"I agree with you. This is all as I wish it," continued Henri. "Let him remain; but that entirely changes our plan—for I require, to go alone, thrice the guarantees I should have asked had your brother accompanied me, whose name and presence in the enterprise would have been my safeguards. The only thing that astonishes me is not having any tidings of Mouy. It is not like him to remain so long without stirring. Have you any intelligence of him, Madame?"

"I, Sire!" said Marguerite, astonished. "How could I possibly—"

"Eh, *pardieu,* my dear, nothing can be more natural. You were so kind as to oblige me by saving young La Mole's life. He was sure to go to Mantes; and if one can go thither he certainly can return."

"Ah! that gives me the solution to a riddle the meaning of which I have sought for in vain," replied Marguerite. "I had left my window open, and found on my return a kind of note on the carpet."

"There, now!" said Henri.

"A note which at first I could not comprehend, and to which I attached no importance," continued Marguerite. "Perhaps I was wrong, and it comes from that quarter."

"Very possible," said Henri; "I would even venture to say that it is probable. Might I see this note?"

"Certainly, Sire," replied Marguerite, handing to the king the half-sheet of paper which she had put in her pocket.

The king looked at it. "Is not this," he asked, "the writing of M. de la Mole?"

"I do not know," was Marguerite's reply; "the writing appears to me disguised."

"Never mind; let us read." And he read:

MADAME—I must speak to the King of Navarre; it is on a most urgent matter. I am waiting.

"Ah, do you see?" said Henri; "he says he is waiting!"

"Yes, I see he says so; but what then?"

"Why, *ventre-saint-gris!* I wish him to come here."

"Come here!" exclaimed Marguerite, fixing on her husband her beautiful eyes, full of amazement; "how can you say such a thing, Sire? A man whom the king has sought to kill, who is marked down, menaced! Let him come, do you say! Is that possible? Were doors made for those who have been—"

"Obliged to escape by the window, you would say."

"Precisely so; you complete my thought."

"Well, but if they know the way by the window, they may take that road again, since it is impossible for them to enter by the door. That is simple enough, surely."

"Do you think so?" said Marguerite, blushing with pleasure at the thought of again having La Mole near her.

"I am sure of it."

"But how can he ascend?" inquired the queen.

"Did you not preserve the rope-ladder I sent you?"

"Yes, Sire," said Marguerite.

"Then the whole thing will be capitally managed. Fasten it to your balcony, and let it hang. If it be Mouy who awaits—and I am inclined to think it is—he will mount the ladder." And without losing his gravity, Henri took the taper to light Marguerite in her search for the ladder. The search was not of long duration; the ladder was discovered in a cupboard in the famous cabinet.

"Here it is," said Henri. "And now, Madame, if it is not too much to ask of your complaisance, tie it, I beg, to the balcony."

"Why I and not you, Sire?" asked Marguerite.

"Because the best conspirators are the most prudent; the sight of a man might alarm your correspondent, you see."

Marguerite smiled, and fastened the ladder.

"There," said Henri, ensconcing himself in a corner of the

apartment; "show yourself plainly; now let the ladder be dropped. Capital! I am sure Mouy will come up."

In fact, ten minutes later, a man intoxicated with joy placed his leg over the balcony; but seeing that the queen did not approach him, he remained for some moments in hesitation, and then Henri advanced.

"Ah!" said he, urbanely, "it is not Mouy; it is M. de la Mole. Good-evening, M. de la Mole. Enter, I entreat you."

La Mole was for a moment stupefied. Perchance, had he still been on the ladder, instead of having his feet firmly on the balcony, he would have fallen backwards.

"You desired to speak to the King of Navarre on an urgent affair," said Marguerite; "I have informed him, and here he is."

Henri went to the window and closed it.

"I love thee!" whispered Marguerite, pressing the young man's hand ardently.

"Well, Monsieur," said Henri, handing a chair to La Mole, "what have we to say?"

"I have to say, Sire," he replied, "that I have left M. de Mouy at the barrier. He desires to know if Maurevel has spoken, and if his presence in your Majesty's chamber is known."

"Not yet; but it must be before long. We must therefore make haste."

"His opinion coincides with your Majesty's, Sire; and if tomorrow, during the evening, M. d'Alençon is ready to depart, Mouy will be at the Porte St. Marcel with a hundred and fifty men; five hundred will await you at Fontainebleau, and then you will gain Blois, Angoulême, and Bordeaux."

"Madame," said Henri, turning to his wife, "tomorrow I shall be ready; shall you?"

La Mole's eyes were fixed on Marguerite's with intense anxiety.

"You have my word," replied the queen. "Whithersoever you go, I follow you; but you know M. d'Alençon must go at the same time. There is no middle path for him: he is with us, or he betrays us; if he hesitates, we will not stir."

"Does he know anything of this proposed plan, M. de la Mole?" inquired Henri.

"He had a letter from Mouy several days since."

"Ah, ah!" said Henri, "and never mentioned it to me!"

"Be on your guard, Monsieur; be on your guard!" said Marguerite.

"Be easy; I am on my guard. But how to return an answer to Mouy?"

"Do not be under any anxiety. Tomorrow, on the right hand or left hand of your Majesty, visible or invisible, during the reception of the ambassadors, he will be there; one word in the queen's address will make him understand whether you consent or not— whether he should flee, or await you. If the Duc d'Alençon refuses, he requires a delay of only a fortnight to reorganize everything in your name."

"Really," replied Henri, "Mouy is an invaluable man. Can you introduce the expected phrase in your discourse, Madame?"

"Nothing easier," replied Marguerite.

"Well, then," said Henri, "I shall see M. d'Alençon tomorrow; let Mouy be at his post, and understand from half a word."

"He will be there, Sire."

"Well, then, M. de la Mole, go and bear him my reply. You have, doubtless, a horse and servant somewhere near at hand."

"Orthon awaits me on the quay."

"Go to him, Count. Oh, not by the window! that is very well on extreme occasions; but you might be seen, and as it would not be known that it was for me that you exposed yourself, it would compromise the queen."

"But how then, Sire?"

"If you could not enter the Louvre alone, you can at least go out of it with me, who have the password. You have your cloak, I have mine; we will wrap ourselves up well, and shall pass the wicket without difficulty. Besides, I shall be glad to give Orthon certain instructions. Wait here while I see if the corridors are free."

Henri, with the most natural air in the world, went out to examine if the way was clear. La Mole remained alone with the queen. "Oh, when shall we meet again?" said he.

"Tomorrow evening, if we flee; an evening soon in the Rue Cloche Percée, if we do not flee."

"M. de la Mole," said Henri, returning, "you may come; there is no one there."

La Mole bowed respectfully before the queen.

"Give him your hand to kiss, Madame," said Henri; "M. de la Mole is no common servitor."

Marguerite obeyed.

"By the way," added Henri, "put away the rope-ladder carefully; it is a very precious instrument for conspirators, and at the moment we least think of it may be useful. Come, M. de la Mole, come!"

CHAPTER 12

The Ambassadors

Next morning the whole population of Paris poured toward the Faubourg St. Antoine, by which it was decided that the Polish ambassadors should enter; a line of soldiers restrained the crowd, and a regiment of horse escorted the nobles and ladies of the court.

Soon appeared, close by the Abbey St. Antoine, a troop of cavaliers dressed in red and yellow, with furred mantles and caps, and bearing large sabers curved like Turkish scimitars. Behind this troop came a second, clothed with Oriental magnificence. They preceded the ambassadors, who, four in number, gorgeously sustained the reputation of their chivalrous country.

One of the ambassadors was the Bishop of Cracow; his costume was half-ecclesiastical, half-military, resplendent with gold and jewels. Next the bishop rode the Palatine Lasco, a powerful noble, nearly related to the royal family, rich as a king, and as proud. Behind these two principal ambassadors, who were accompanied by two other palatines of high rank, came a number of gentlemen, whose steeds, all glittering with gold and precious stones, excited the clamorous admiration of the populace. In fact, the French horsemen, notwithstanding the richness of their appointments, were completely eclipsed by these visitors whom they disdainfully regarded as barbarians.

Up to the last moment Catherine had hoped that the reception would be deferred and that the decision of the king would yield to his weakness, which still continued. But when the day arrived, when she saw Charles, pale as a spectre, assume the royal robes, she saw that she must in appearance at least yield to his iron will, and began to believe that the safest plan for Henri d'Anjou was to depart into the splendid exile to which he was condemned.

Charles, except for the few words he had spoken when on

opening his eyes he had seen his mother coming from the cabinet, had not spoken to Catherine since the scene which had led up to the crisis which had broken him down. Everyone in the Louvre knew that there had been a terrible quarrel, without knowing the occasion of it; and the boldest among them trembled before that coldness and that silence as birds tremble in the threatening calm which precedes the storm.

The large reception chamber had been prepared; and as such ceremonies were usually public, the guards and sentinels had received orders to admit as many persons into the apartments as they could possibly contain.

As for Paris, it presented the same aspect that every great city presents on similar occasions—that is, confusion and curiosity; only, had anyone attentively examined the population, he would have remarked a considerable number of men in cloaks, who exchanged glances and signs when at a distance and, when they met, a few rapid words in a low tone. They seemed much occupied with the procession, following it closely, in advance of the rest; and they apparently received their orders from an old man whose keen black eyes, spite of his long white beard and grizzly eyebrows, bespoke a vigorous activity. This old man, either by his own efforts or by his followers' assistance, gained an entrance to the Louvre; and thanks to the commander of the Swiss guard—a worthy Huguenot, hardly turned Catholic in spite of his conversion—obtained a place behind the ambassadors, and opposite Henri and Marguerite.

Henri, informed by La Mole that Mouy in some disguise would be present, looked round on every side. At last his eyes encountered those of the old man, and remained fixed on him. A sign from Mouy put an end to Henri's uncertainties, for Mouy was so well disguised that the King of Navarre himself could hardly believe that this old man with a white beard was the intrepid Huguenot chief who a few days before had made so desperate a defense.

A word from Henri fixed Marguerite's attention on Mouy. Then her beautiful eyes wandered round the chamber in search of La Mole. La Mole was not there.

The delivery of the addresses was begun. The first was to the king; Lasco, in the name of the Diet of Poland, demanded his consent that the crown of Poland should be offered to a prince of the house of France.

The king responded with an acquiescence short and to the point—presenting to them the Duc d'Anjou, of whose courage he made a high eulogium. He spoke in French, and an interpreter translated what he said at the end of each sentence. While the interpreter took his turn, the king might have been seen touching his lips with a handkerchief, which thus became tinged with blood.

When Charles had finished, Lasco turned to D'Anjou, and offered him the throne in the name of the Polish nation. Lasco's address was in Latin.

The duke replied in the same language, and in a voice he in vain strove to render firm, that he gratefully accepted the honor offered to him. During all this time Charles, who remained standing, with lips compressed, fixed his eyes on him, motionless and threatening, like the eyes of an eagle.

When the duke had finished, Lasco took the crown of the Jagellos from the velvet cushion on which it rested, and while two Polish nobles invested the duke with the royal robe, he placed the crown in Charles's hands. Charles signed to his brother. D'Anjou knelt before him, and with his own hands Charles placed the crown on his head; and the two brothers interchanged a kiss full of bitter hate.

A herald then cried, "Alexandre Edouard Henri de France, Duc d'Anjou, is crowned King of Poland. God save the King of Poland!" All the assembly repeated, "God save the King of Poland!"

Then Lasco turned to Marguerite. The address of the beautiful queen had been reserved for the last. Now, as this was a courtesy accorded to her to bring out more brilliantly her fine genius, as it was called, everyone was prepared to give special attention to that response, which was to be in Latin. We have seen that Marguerite had prepared it herself.

Lasco's address was rather a eulogy than an oration. He had yielded, Sarmatian as he was, to the admiration with which the beautiful Queen of Navarre inspired all hearts; and borrowing the language of Ovid and the style of Ronsard, he said that, starting from Warsaw in the middle of a dark night, he and his companions could not have found their way if there had not been two stars which guided them, as the Magian kings were guided—stars which appeared more and more brilliant as they came nearer to France, and which they now discovered to be the two beautiful eyes of the

Queen of Navarre. Finally, passing from the Gospel to the Koran, from Syria to Arabia Petræa, from Nazareth to Mecca, he closed by saying that he was quite ready to do as the ardent disciples of the prophet had done, who, having once had the happiness of looking upon his tomb, destroyed their eyes—thinking that after enjoying so fair a sight they would find nothing else in the world worthy of admiration. His discourse was applauded by all—by those who understood Latin, because they shared the opinion of the orator; by those who did not understand it, because they wished it to appear as if they did.

Marguerite, having made a gracious inclination to the ambassador, fixed her eyes on Mouy, and began thus: *"Quod nunc hâc in aulâ insperati adestis exsultaremus ego et conjux, nisi ideo immineret calamitas, scilicet non solum fratris, sed etiam amici orbitas."* ("Your unlooked-for presence in this court would overwhelm my husband and myself with joy, did it not threaten us with a great misfortune; that is, not only the loss of a brother, but also that of a friend.")

These words had a double meaning, and while intended for Mouy, were supposed to refer to the Duc d'Anjou. The latter, accordingly, bowed in token of acknowledgment. Charles did not recollect having read this sentence in Marguerite's speech when submitted to him some days before, but he attached no great importance to the words of Marguerite in a speech of simple courtesy; and, besides, he understood Latin very imperfectly.

Marguerite continued: *"Adeo dolemur a te dividi ut tecum proficisci maluissemus; sed idem fatum quo nunc sine ullâ morâ Lutetiâ cedere juberis, hâc in urbe detinet. Proficiscere ergo, frater; proficiscere, amice; proficiscere sine nobis; proficiscentem, sequuntur spes et desideria nostra."* (We are grieved to be separated from you, for we should have preferred going with you; but the same fate that compels you to quit Paris without delay, retains us in that city. Go, dear brother; go, then, dear friend—go without us. Our hopes and our wishes follow you.")

It is easy to understand how attentively Mouy had listened to these words, which though addressed to the Duc d'Anjou were meant for him alone. Henri had indeed already turned his head negatively two or three times as a sign to the young Huguenot that D'Alençon had refused; but that movement, which might be the effect of chance, would have seemed to Mouy an insufficient indication had it not been confirmed by Marguerite's words. Now, while he looked at Marguerite and listened to her with all his soul, his black eyes shone so brightly under their gray brows as to arrest Catherine's attention, who started as if struck by an electric shock, and continued looking in that direction.

"That is a strange face," she murmured, as she continued to retain the ceremonial expression on her face. "Who can this man be who watches Marguerite so attentively, and whom Henri and Marguerite, on their part, look at with such earnestness?"

The Queen of Navarre continued her discourse, which from that point was a response to the courteous expressions of the Polish envoy. While Catherine strove in vain to divine the name of this strange old man, the master of the ceremonies came behind her, and presented to her a little satin bag; she opened it, and found a paper containing these words:

"Maurevel, by the aid of a cordial I have administered to him, has in some measure recovered his strength, and has written the name of the man in the King of Navarre's chamber. This name was M. de Mouy."

"Mouy!" murmured the queen, "I thought it was he. But this old man—eh, *cospetto!*—this old man is—" Catherine remained with her eyes fixed and her mouth open. Then, leaning toward the ear of the captain of the guards, who was by her side, "Look, M. de Nancey," she said; "look, but without seeming to do so. See Seigneur Lasco, the man who is speaking at this moment. Behind him do you see an old man with a white beard and dressed in black velvet?"

"Yes, Madame," replied the captain.

"Good; do not lose sight of him."

"He to whom the King of Navarre made a sign?"

"Yes; station yourself at the door with ten men, and when he comes out, invite him, in the king's name, to dinner. If he accept, conduct him to a chamber, and keep him prisoner; if he resist, seize him, dead or alive. Go! go!"

Fortunately, Henri, but little interested in Marguerite's address, had his eyes fixed on Catherine, and had not lost a single expression of her face. On seeing her look so steadily and so implacably at Mouy, he became uneasy; on seeing her give an order to the captain of the guards, he understood the whole matter.

It was at this moment that he made the sign which Nancey had observed, and which meant, "Save yourself; you are discovered!" Mouy comprehended the meaning of that gesture, which continued so fittingly the portion of Marguerite's discourse which had been addressed to him. He did not wait for the sign to be repeated; he mingled with the crowd and disappeared. But Henri was not quite reassured until Nancey returned, and he saw by Catherine's face that the officer had been unsuccessful.

The audience was finished. The king rose with difficulty, saluted the ambassadors, and retired, leaning on Ambroise Paré, who had been with him since his accident. Catherine, pale with rage, and Henri, silent with grief, followed him. As to the Due d'Alençon, he had been completely effaced during the ceremony; and Charles's eyes, which had been fixed on D'Anjou, had not once been turned toward him.

The new King of Poland felt himself lost. Carried off by those barbarians, far from his mother, he was like Antæus, that son of the Earth, who lost his strength when lifted in the arms of Hercules. Once beyond the frontier, he regarded himself as forever shut out from the throne of France. Instead of following the king, he retired to his mother's apartments. He found her not less gloomy and preoccupied than he was himself; for she was thinking of that fine head and mocking face which had been continually in her sight during the ceremony—of that Béarnais for whom Destiny seemed to make room by sweeping away before him kings, royal assassins, enemies, and obstacles.

On seeing her much-loved son, pale under his crown, crushed under his royal mantle, silently joining in supplication his beautiful hands which he had inherited from her, Catherine rose and went to him.

"Oh, Mother!" cried the king, "I am condemned to die in exile."

"My son," returned Catherine, "have you so soon forgotten René's prediction? Tranquillize yourself; you will not be there long."

"Mother, I entreat you," said the Duc d'Anjou, "on the least probability of the crown of France being vacant, inform me."

"My son," replied the queen, "until the day we both of us await, a horse shall be always saddled in my stable, and a courier ever in my antechamber ready to set out for Poland."

CHAPTER 13

Orestes and Pylades

Henri d'Anjou having departed, peace and happiness seemed to have returned to the Louvre. Charles, laying aside his melancholy, recovered his vigorous health, either hunting each day with Henri, or if prevented from following that sport, passing the time in discussing subjects relating to it and scolding his brother-in-law for the indifference he betrayed for hawking, declaring that he would be the most accomplished prince of his time, if he did but understand the management of falcons, gerfalcons, hawks, and tiercelets, as well as he did that of badgers and hounds. Catherine had returned to all the duties of a good mother. Kind and gentle toward Charles and D'Alençon, affectionate to Henri and Marguerite, gracious to Madame de Nevers and Madame de Sauve, she even carried her amiability so far as to visit Maurevel twice during the time he lay ill at his residence, situated in the Rue de la Cerisaie—on the pretext that he had been wounded while fulfilling her orders. Marguerite followed up her love affairs *à l'Espagnole.* Every evening she stood at her open window, and both by writing and gestures kept up a continual correspondence with La Mole; while in each of his letters the impatient young man reminded his lovely mistress of her promise to see him in the Rue Cloche Percée, in recompense for his exile.

There was but one lonely and discontented person in the Louvre, now become so calm and tranquil. That person was our friend Comte Annibal de Coconnas.

It was certainly something to know that La Mole still lived; it was much to continue to be favored by Madame de Nevers, the gayest and most fanciful of women. But all the happiness of the intimacy granted by the beautiful duchess, all the peace of mind which he gained from Marguerite in regard to the fortunes of their friend, were to the Piedmontese not equal to an hour with La Mole at La Hurière's inn before a pot of sweet wine, or indeed to one of those adventurous excursions through the regions of the city where an honest gentleman may easily get holes in his skin, in his purse, or in his coat.

Madame de Nevers—it must be confessed to the shame of humanity—endured impatiently this rivalry of La Mole. It was not that she disliked the Provençal. Quite the contrary. Led by that irresistible instinct which urges every woman to play the coquette with another woman's lover, especially when that woman is her friend, she had not spared La Mole the flashes of her emerald eyes, and Coconnas had sometimes envied the free hand-shakings and tokens of tenderness bestowed on his friend in those periods of caprice when the star of the Piedmontese seemed to pale in the sky of his beautiful mistress. But Coconnas, who would have cut the throats of fifteen persons for a single wink of the eye at his lady, was so little jealous of La Mole that often after these inconsistencies of the duchess he had whispered to him certain offers which had made the Provençal blush.

It resulted from this state of things that Henriette—whom the absence of La Mole deprived of all the advantages the society of Coconnas afforded her; that is to say, his inexhaustible gaiety and his endless entertaining caprices—came one day to beg of Marguerite to restore to her that necessary third party, in whose absence the mind and heart of Coconnas were gradually wasting away.

Marguerite, always compassionate, and besides urged by the prayers of La Mole and the desires of her own heart, made an appointment with Henriette for a meeting on the next day in the house with two doors, where they might thoroughly consider these matters without interruption.

Coconnas received with a very ill grace Henriette's summons to be in the Rue Tizon at half-past nine. Nevertheless, he went to the appointed place, where he found Henriette already arrived, and not a little offended at being there first.

"Fie, Monsieur!" cried she, as he entered, "what bad manners to make, I will not say a princess, but a woman wait in this way!"

"Wait?" replied Coconnas. "I like that! I'll wager you what you like that we are before our time."

"I was, yes."

"Bah! and so am I. I'll bet it isn't later than ten o'clock."

"Very well! my note said half-past nine."

"And therefore I left the Louvre at nine—for I am in the service of the Duc d'Alençon, I would say in passing, which will oblige me to leave you in an hour."

"And that pleases you?"

"Upon my soul, no! But M. d'Alençon is a surly and whimsical master; and if there is to be a scolding I would rather it would come from pretty lips like yours than from a crooked mouth like his."

"Come, now," said the duchess, "that is a little better. You say, then, that you left the Louvre at nine o'clock?"

"Oh, certainly, yes—intending to come straight here; but at the corner of the Rue de Grenelle I saw a man who looked like La Mole."

"Good! still La Mole."

"Always, with or without permission."

"Rude!"

"Ah!" said Coconnas, "we are beginning our compliments again."

"No; but finish your story."

"I am not anxious to tell it; but you asked me why I was late."

"Certainly; is it for me to arrive first?"

"Eh! You have no one to search for."

"You are assuming, my dear. But continue. At the corner of the Rue de Grenelle you saw a man who resembled La Mole. But what is that on your doublet—blood?"

"Good! that was a man who splashed me as he fell."

"You have been fighting?"

"I should say so."

"For your La Mole?"

"For whom would you have me fight—for a woman?"

"Thank you."

"I followed, then, that man who had the impudence to borrow the manner of my friend; I overtook him in the Rue Coquilière. I went in front of him and examined him closely by the light from a shop window. It was not he."

"Good! that was well done."

"Yes, but it was unlucky for him. 'Monsieur,' I said to him, 'you are a fool to allow yourself to bear a distant resemblance to my friend La Mole, who is an accomplished cavalier, while it is easy to see, on a near view, that you are only a vagabond.' Upon that he drew his sword, and I drew mine. At the third pass—see his bad manners!—he splashed me as he fell."

"And did you not afford him any help?"

"I was about to do so when a man passed on horseback. Ah, then, Duchess, I was sure it was La Mole. Unfortunately, the horse was going at a gallop. I ran after the horse; and the crowd which had gathered to see me fight ran after me. Now, as I might have been taken for a thief, followed as I was by that mob howling at my heels, I was obliged to turn and put them to flight; and so I lost a little time. Meanwhile the horseman had disappeared. I resumed the pursuit. I inquired, I demanded, giving the color of the horse; but *baste!* useless,—no one had noticed him. And so, tired out, I came here."

"Tired out!" said the duchess; "that was very kind in you."

"Listen, dear friend," said Coconnas turning carelessly in his armchair; "you are still about to persecute me with reference to La Mole. Well, you are wrong; for in short, friendship, you see (I wish I had his wit or his learning, that poor friend's; I should find some comparison which would make you feel my thought)—friendship, you see, is a star; while love—love—well, I have found the comparison—love is only a candle. You will tell me that there are many kinds—"

"Of loves?"

"No, of candles; and that among those different kinds some are preferable to others—the rose candle, for example. Agreed as to the rose—it is the best; but rose though it be, the candle is consumed, while the star shines forever. To that you will reply that when the candle is consumed one can light another."

"M. de Coconnas, you are a fool."

"La!"

"M. de Coconnas, you are impertinent."

"La! la!"

"M. de Coconnas, you are a knave."

"Madame, I warn you that you will make me regret La Mole three times as much."

"You no longer love me."

"On the contrary, Duchess, I idolize you; but you do not understand the thing. I can love you, cherish you, idolize you, and yet employ my spare time in eulogizing my friend!"

"You call the moments passed with me spare time!"

"I can't help it; that poor La Mole is forever in my thoughts!"

"And you prefer him to me! it is insulting. Come, Annibal, I detest you. Deal candidly with me; tell me that you prefer him to me. Annibal, I warn you that if you dare to prefer anything in the world to me—"

"Henriette, most lovely duchess! let me advise you, for the sake of your own tranquillity, not to ask unwise questions. I love you more than all other women, but I love La Mole more than all other men."

"Well answered!" said a strange voice, suddenly; and a large damask curtain being raised discovered a panel which, sliding back into the wall, and forming a mode of communication between the two apartments, revealed La Mole framed in that opening, like one of Titian's splendid paintings set in a gilded frame.

"La Mole!" exclaimed Coconnas, without noticing Marguerite, or taking time to thank her for the surprise she had arranged for him—"La Mole! my dear, dear friend!"

So saying, he threw himself into his friend's arms, knocking over the table that stood in his way, as well as the armchair on which he had been sitting.

La Mole returned his greetings with effusion; but in the midst of it all he turned to the Duchesse de Nevers and said, "You must pardon me, Madame, if the mention of my name has been allowed to disturb your happiness; certainly," continued he, regarding Marguerite with ineffable tenderness, "it has not been my fault that I have not sooner returned."

"You see, Henriette," said Marguerite, taking up the conversation, "I have kept my word; here he is!"

"Is it then only to the prayers of Madame the Duchess that I owe this happiness?" asked La Mole.

"To her prayers alone," replied Marguerite; then facing him, she added, "La Mole, I give you leave not to believe a word I say."

Meanwhile, Coconnas, after having embraced his friend and walked round and round him a dozen times, after even holding a light to his face, the better to gaze on his beloved features, suddenly turned toward Henriette and kneeling down, kissed the hem of her robe.

"Well, well!" said the Duchesse de Nevers, "I like that! you find me endurable at last?"

"*Mordi!*" replied Coconnas, "you are, as you always are to me, adorable. Only, I can now tell you so with a lighter heart; and I wish I had here a score of Poles, Sarmatians, and other barbarous hyperboreans, to make them confess that you are queen of the beautiful."

"Gently, gently, Coconnas," interposed La Mole, "and Madame Marguerite, then?"

"Oh! I take nothing back," answered Coconnas, with that half-comic air peculiarly his own; "Madame Henriette is queen of the beautiful, and Madame Marguerite is the beautiful among queens."

"Come, then, my beautiful queen!" said Madame de Nevers, perceiving that Coconnas had neither eyes nor ears for anyone but La Mole, "let us leave these tender friends to have an hour's chat together. M. de Coconnas will perhaps be a little more rational after that."

Marguerite whispered a few words to La Mole, who, whatever might have been his desire to see his friend once more, would have been quite content had the tenderness of Coconnas been less exacting. Coconnas meantime was trying, by force of protestations, to elicit a pleasant smile and a friendly word from the lips of Henriette—an effort easily successful.

Then the two women went into the adjoining chamber, where supper was awaiting them, and the two young men were left alone.

The first questions asked by Coconnas related to that fatal evening in which La Mole had been so near to losing his life. As La Mole proceeded in his narration, the Piedmontese shook with emotion. "And why," he asked, "instead of running away as you did, and causing me so much anxiety, did you not seek refuge with our master the duke, who would have received and protected you?"

"Our master!" said La Mole, in a low voice, "the Duc d'Alençon?"

"Yes, according to what he has told me, it is to him that you owe your life."

"I owe my life to the King of Navarre," replied La Mole.

"Oh, oh!" said Coconnas; "are you sure of it?"

"It is beyond a doubt."

"Oh, the good, the excellent king! but what part did the Duc d'Alençon play in the affair?"

"He held the cord with which I was to be strangled."

"*Mordi!* La Mole!" exclaimed Coconnas, springing up with violent energy; "are you sure of that? What! a pale-faced sickly looking prince, a currish mongrel, dare to strangle my friend!—*mordi!* by tomorrow he shall hear my opinion on the subject."

"Are you mad?"

"It is true, he might begin again—But what matter? the affair must not be passed over in this way."

"Come, come, Coconnas, calm yourself, and try not to forget that it is half-past eleven o'clock, and that you are in waiting tonight at the Louvre."

"What care I for that? Good! he may wait long ere he has my attendance. What, do you suppose I will ever again serve a man who has held a cord to murder my friend? You are jesting! No, no, the hand of Providence has reunited us, and from you I go no more. If you stay here I remain also."

"For the love of Heaven, Coconnas, mind what you are about; you are not drunk!"

"Luckily, for if I were I should set the Louvre on fire."

"Come, Annibal," replied La Mole, "be reasonable. Return yonder. The service is a sacred matter."

"Will you return with me?"

"Impossible."

"Are they still thinking of killing you?"

"I don't think so; I am of too little importance for them to have a settled plan against me. They undertook to kill me in a moment of caprice—that is all; the princes were on a lark that night."

"What do you propose to do, then?"

"I? nothing. I will stroll about; I will take a walk."

"Well, I will take a walk, like you; I will stroll with you—it is a charming occupation. Then, if they attack us, there will be two of us, and we will give them work to do. Ah, let him come on, your insect of a duke! I will pin him to the wall, like a butterfly!"

"But ask him for leave of absence, then."

"Yes, final."

"In that case, notify him that you leave him."

"Nothing more fitting. I consent to that. I will write to him."

"It is very improper, Coconnas, to write to him—a prince of the blood!"

"Yes, of the blood! of the blood of my friend. Take care!" cried Coconnas, rolling his eyes tragically—"take care that I don't make short work of matters of etiquette!"

"In fact," said La Mole to himself, "in a few days he will have no need of the prince nor of anyone; for if he is willing to go with us we will take him away."

Coconnas took the pen without further opposition from his friend, and hastily composed the following bit of eloquence:

MY LORD—There can be no doubt but that your Highness, versed in the writings of antiquity, is acquainted with the touching story of Orestes and Pylades, two heroes celebrated alike for their misfortunes and their friendship. My friend La Mole is not less unfortunate than was Orestes, and I am not less devoted than was Pylades. Affairs of the utmost importance to him demand my aid at this particular moment; it is therefore impossible for me to leave him. So that with the permission of your Highness, I will take a furlough, resolved as I am to follow the fortune of my friend whithersoever it may lead me. This will show your Highness how great is the force which tears me from your Highness's service, by reason of which I do not despair of obtaining forgiveness, and venture to continue to call myself, Monseigneur,

Your royal Highness's
most humble and most obedient

Annibal, Comte de Coconnas,
Inseparable friend of M. de la Mole.

This masterpiece being finished, Coconnas read it in a loud voice to La Mole, who shrugged his shoulders.

"Well, what do you think of it?" inquired Coconnas, who had not seen the movement, or feigned not to have seen it.

"Why, I say that M. d'Alençon will laugh at us."

"At us?"

"Conjointly."

"That is better, it seems to me, than to strangle us separately."

"Bah!" said La Mole, laughing; "perhaps the one will not prevent the other."

"Well, so much the worse! Come what will, I shall send the letter tomorrow morning. Where shall we go to find a bed on leaving here?"

"To Maître la Hurière's. You remember—that little chamber where you tried to murder me before we were Orestes and Pylades."

"Well, I will get our host to take my letter to the Louvre."

At this moment the panel was slid back.

"Well," inquired both princesses in the same breath; "and where are Orestes and Pylades?"

"*Mordi,* Madame!" replied Coconnas, "Pylades and Orestes are dying of hunger and of love."

It was, in fact, Maître la Hurière, who, at nine o'clock the following morning, carried to the Louvre the respectful missive of Comte Annibal de Coconnas.

CHAPTER 14

Orthon

Henri de Navarre, after the refusal of the Duc d'Alençon, which left everything undecided and in peril, even his very existence, had become, if possible, more intimate with the prince than he had been before; from which circumstance Catherine concluded that not only did the two princes understand each other, but also that they were engaged in some conspiracy.

She questioned Marguerite on the subject, but Marguerite was worthy of her mother; and so skillfully did the Queen of Navarre parry her mother's inquiries that, having answered to all, she left her more uncertain than before.

The Florentine had thus no guide but the spirit of intrigue she had brought with her from Tuscany; and the first conclusion she came to was that as the hated Béarnais derived the principal part of his strength from his alliance with the Duc d'Alençon, it would be expedient to separate them as speedily as possible.

From the instant in which she formed this resolution, Catherine continued to beset her son with the patience and skill of a fisherman who, having dropped his leads at some distance from the fish, gradually draws them together until his prey is surrounded on all sides.

Duc François was conscious of the increased affection shown him by his mother, whose advances he received with every manifestation of pleasure. As for Henri, he affected to know nothing of what was going on, but he kept a more watchful eye on his ally than he had hitherto done. Everybody seemed to await some event.

Now, while all were in that attitude of expectation, on a morning when the sun had risen with more than wonted splendor, and the rich balmy air was filled with the odor of a thousand flowers, a pale and sickly looking man came forth from a small house situated behind the Arsenal, and feebly dragged his way, supporting himself by a staff, toward the Rue de Petit Musc.

Having reached the Porte St. Antoine, he diverged from the boulevard and entered the Archery Garden, the man who kept the gate receiving him with every demonstration of respect.

No one was in the garden, which, as its name indicates, belonged to an association of archers. But had there been spectators present, the pale stranger would have well merited their commiseration and sympathy; for his long mustache and his military step, weakened by sickness and suffering, sufficiently indicated that he was some officer recently wounded, seeking to regain his strength by gentle exercise in the sunlight. Yet, strange to say, when the cloak with which (spite of the increasing warmth) the apparently harmless visitant was clad flew open, it displayed a pair of long pistols hanging to the silver clasps of his belt, which also sustained a dagger and a sword of colossal size, the latter of which hung heavily at his side, and with its ponderous sheath clattered against his shrunken and trembling legs. Besides all this, and for further increase of precautions, the lounger, solitary as he was, at every step cast a searching glance around, questioning every path, every bush, every ditch. Thus advancing into the garden, the man selected for a resting place a small covered arbor looking on the boulevards, from which it was separated only by a thick hedge and a small ditch, which formed a double barrier. Extending his weary limbs on a turfy bank within reach of a table, he beckoned the porter—who, in addition to the duties of concierge, exercised also the vocation of a vintner—and saying a few words, was quickly supplied with what appeared to be a species of cordial.

The invalid had been about ten minutes in his shady retreat, slowly discussing the draught brought to him by the concierge, when suddenly his countenance, notwithstanding its interesting pallor, assumed a fearful expression. He had just noticed the approach of a cavalier who, turning quickly around the corner of a street, advanced, wrapped in a large cloak, and stopped just before his eyes. Scarcely had the pale stranger in the arbor (who was no other than Maurevel) a little recovered from the agitation occasioned by the unexpected presence of the cavalier, when he observed that the latter was joined by a second person, dressed in the garb of a page.

Concealed beneath his leafy bower, Maurevel could see everything and hear everything without difficulty. And when the reader learns that the cavalier was Mouy, and that the young man was Orthon, he can judge whether Maurevel found employment for his eyes and ears.

Both looked carefully around them, while Maurevel held his breath lest a sound should escape him.

"You may speak now in safety, Monsieur," said the younger and more confident of the two; "we are quite secure here; none can either see or hear us."

" 'Tis well!" answered Mouy. "Now attend! you are to go to Madame de Sauve's, and should she be at home give this into her own hands; but if she be not in her apartments then place the letter where the king is accustomed to deposit his—behind the mirror. Wait at the Louvre; and if any reply is sent bring it, you know where. Should you not be charged with an answer, then meet me tonight, with a petronel, at the spot I pointed out to you, and which I have just left."

"Enough!" said Orthon; "I understand."

"I must now leave you," continued Mouy; "I have much to do during the day. It will be useless for you to go to the Louvre till he is there; and I have every reason to believe he will be engaged all day studying hawking. Go, and fear not to show yourself at the Louvre; you can say that being now quite recovered, you come to thank Madame de Sauve for the kind care she took of you during your illness."

Maurevel with fixed gaze, continued to listen till the perspiration gathered in large drops on his forehead. His first impulse had been to detach one of the pistols from his belt and take deadly aim at Mouy, but at that instant the sudden opening of the latter's cloak displayed a cuirass, firm and solid. Probably the ball would flatten on the cuirass, or would strike some part of the body where the wound might not be mortal. Then, he reflected, Mouy, vigorous and well armed, would have the advantage of him, wounded as he was; and with a sigh he drew back the pistol already pointed at the Huguenot. "How unfortunate," he murmured, "that I cannot stretch him dead on the spot, without any other witness than that young varlet, who would have served as a capital mark for my second pistol!"

Then, on the other hand, it occurred to him that the note sent by the page to Madame de Sauve might be better worth taking than even the life of the Huguenot chief.

"Well," said he, "be it so, then; you escape me this morning, but tomorrow I will settle all scores with you, if I pursue you to that hell from which you have sprung to ruin me, unless I first destroy you!"

At this instant, Mouy, folding his cloak around him, and concealing his features in its large folds, departed in the direction of the Temple, while Orthon took the road that conducted to the banks of the river.

Then Maurevel, rising with more vigor and agility than he had dared to hope for, regained the Rue de la Cerisaie, caused a horse to be saddled, and, weak as he was, and at the risk of again opening his newly closed wounds, he set off at full gallop toward the Rue St. Antoine, reached the quays, and darted into the Louvre.

Five minutes after he had passed the wicket, Catherine was in full possession of all that had occurred, and Maurevel had received the thousand golden crowns promised him for the arrest of the King of Navarre.

"Yes, yes!" exclaimed Catherine, exultingly, "either I am much deceived, or Mouy will turn out the black spot discovered by René in the horoscope of this cursed Béarnais."

A quarter of an hour after Maurevel, Orthon reached the Louvre, and having fearlessly shown himself as directed by Mouy, proceeded unmolested to the apartments of Madame de Sauve. There he found only Dariole, who informed him that her lady was occupied, by the queen's orders, in transcribing letters for her Majesty, who had summoned her for that purpose within the last five minutes.

"It does not signify," replied Orthon; "I can wait." Then, profiting by the freedom he had always been permitted to enjoy, he went into the adjoining chamber, which was the sleeping room of the baroness, and after assuring himself that he was unobserved, carefully deposited the note behind the looking glass. Just as he was withdrawing his hand from the mirror, Catherine entered the room. Orthon changed color, for he fancied that the quick, searching glance of the queen-mother was first directed to the glass.

"What are you doing here, my little fellow?" asked Catherine. "Seeking for Madame de Sauve, I suppose?"

"Yes, indeed, your Majesty; it is a long time since I saw her, and if I delay returning her my thanks, I fear she will think me ungrateful."

"You love Madame de Sauve, then, very much, do you not?"

"Oh, that I do, with all my heart! I can never forget the kindness Madame de Sauve condescended to bestow on a humble servitor like myself."

"And upon what occasion was it that she showed you all this care and attention?" inquired Catherine, feigning to be ignorant of what had befallen the youth.

"When I was wounded, Madame."

"Ah, poor child!" said Catherine, pityingly, "you have been wounded?"

"Yes, Madame."

"And when was that?"

"The night that they tried to arrest the King of Navarre. I was so terrified at the sight of the soldiers that I called out for help; one of them gave me a blow on the head, and I fell senseless to the ground."

"Poor child! and you are now quite recovered?"

"Oh, quite, Madame!"

"And that being the case," continued Catherine, "I suppose you are trying to get back into the service of the King of Navarre?"

"No, indeed, Madame; when the King of Navarre learned that I had presumed to resist your Majesty's orders, he dismissed me in heavy displeasure."

"Really!" said Catherine, with a tone expressive of the deepest interest. "Well, I will take the arrangement of that affair into my own hands; but if you are looking for Madame de Sauve, you will do so in vain. She is at this moment busily occupied in my apartments." Then, thinking that Orthon might not have had time to place his note behind the glass previous to her entrance, she returned to the adjoining chamber, in order to afford the requisite opportunity for his so doing.

But just as Orthon, uneasy at the unexpected arrival of the queen-mother, was asking himself whether the circumstance did not in some way forebode evil to his master, he heard three gentle taps against the ceiling—the very signal he was in the habit of using to warn his master of the approach of danger during his visits to Madame de Sauve. He started at the sound; a sudden light seemed to break in upon his mind, and he appropriated the warning to himself—danger was near, doubtless; and hastily springing toward the mirror, he withdrew the paper he had previously placed there.

Through a rent in the tapestried hangings, Catherine watched every movement of the youth; she saw him dart forward to the mirror, but whether to take away or to conceal the coveted paper, she could not detect. Returning to the apartment, with a smiling countenance she said, "What! here still, my little man? What are you waiting for, then? Did I not promise to take charge of your future prospects? Do you doubt my word?"

"God forbid, Madame!" replied Orthon; then, kneeling before the queen, he kissed the hem of her robe, and hastily quitted the room. As he went out he observed the captain of the guards waiting the orders of Catherine in the antechamber. This was far from calming his apprehensions; on the contrary, it increased the vague terror under which he already labored.

As soon as the folds of the massy curtain which hung before the door had closed on the form of Orthon, Catherine darted to the mirror; but vainly did she thrust her eager hand behind it. She found no letter, and yet she was sure that she had seen the youth approach the mirror—it was, then, to recover, and not to deposit the missive. Fatality gave an equal force to her adversaries. A child became a man the moment he contended against her. She shook the mirror, examined, sounded. Nothing there! "Oh, the poor wretch!" she cried. "I wished him no harm, but in withdrawing that note he hastens to his doom. Ho, there, M. de Nancey!"

The vibrating voice of the queen crossed the salon and penetrated even to the anteroom, where M. de Nancey awaited her orders. At the sound of his name thus pronounced, the captain of the guards lost not an instant in obeying the summons. "What is your Majesty's pleasure?" said he, on entering.

"Did you but now observe a youth—nay, a mere child—go hence?"

"I did, Madame."

"Call him back."

"By what name shall I address him?"

"By that of Orthon. Should he refuse to return, bring him back by force; but do not alarm him if he comes unresistingly. I must speak with him directly."

The captain of the guards darted out. Orthon had scarcely got halfway downstairs; for he was descending slowly in the hope of meeting on the stairs or seeing in some corridor the King of Navarre or Madame de Sauve. He heard himself called, and a cold shudder seized him, for he guessed who had sent for him. His first impulse was to fly, but with an accuracy of judgment above his years, he quickly perceived that flight would be certain ruin. He therefore stopped and inquired. "Who calls me?"

"I do—M. de Nancey," replied the captain of the guards, hurriedly descending the stairs.

"But I am in a very great hurry," replied Orthon.

"By order of her Majesty the queen-mother."

The terrified boy wiped the perspiration from his brow, and turned back, the captain following. As he entered the room where the queen-mother waited he trembled, and a deathly paleness came over him. The poor boy was as yet too young to exercise a more practiced control over himself. "Madame," he said, "you have done me the honor to recall me. How can I be of service to your Majesty?"

"I have recalled you, child," answered Catherine, with a bright and encouraging smile, "because your countenance pleases me; and having promised to interest myself in your welfare, I wish to do so at once. They accuse us of being forgetful. It is not our heart which is forgetful, but our mind, crowded by events. Now I have remembered that kings hold in their hands the fortune of men, and so I sent for you. Come, my child, follow me."

M. de Nancey, who took this scene seriously, regarded the tender manner of Catherine with great astonishment.

"Can you ride, little one?" asked Catherine.

"Yes, Madame."

"Then come into my cabinet, and I will give you a message to carry to St. Germain."

"I am at your Majesty's commands."

"Order a horse to be prepared, M. de Nancey."

The captain of the guards disappeared.

"Now then, boy!" said Catherine, leading the way and signing for Orthon to follow her.

The queen-mother descended a flight of stairs, then entered the corridor in which were situated the apartments of the Duc d'Alençon and the king, reached the winding staircase, again descended a flight of stairs, and opening a door leading to a circular gallery, of which none but the king and herself possessed the key, made Orthon pass through before her, then, entering after him, closed the door. This gallery formed a sort of rampart round a portion of the apartments occupied by the king and queen-mother, and resembled the corridor of the Castle of St. Angelo at Rome, or that of the Pitti Palace at Florence, designed to serve as a place of refuge in case of danger.

The door secured, Catherine and her companion found themselves enclosed in a dark corridor. They advanced a few steps, the queen leading the way and the page following, when suddenly Catherine turned round; and Orthon perceived on her countenance the same gloomy expression it had worn ten minutes previously. Her eyes, round, like those of the cat or panther, seemed to dart forth sparks of fire.

"Stop!" cried she.

Orthon felt a cold shiver pervade his frame; the damp, chill air of that unfrequented spot seemed to cling around him like an icy mantle; the floor seemed like the cover of a tomb; Catherine's look was pointed, so to speak, and penetrated the young man's breast. He recoiled and leaned all trembling against the wall.

"Where is the letter you were desired to give to the King of Navarre?"

"The letter?" stammered Orthon.

"Ay, the letter, which, in the event of not finding the king, you were instructed to place behind the mirror."

"Indeed, Madame," said Orthon, "I know not to what your Majesty alludes."

"The letter given you by M. de Mouy, about an hour since, behind the Archery Garden."

"Your Majesty is wholly mistaken or misinformed," answered Orthon; "I have no letter."

"You lie!" said Catherine. "Give me that letter, and I will fulfill the promise I have made you."

"What letter, Madame?"

"I will make you rich."

"I have no letter, Madame."

Catherine began to lose all patience. She ground her teeth with rage; then, suddenly checking herself, and assuming a bland smile, she said, "Give it to me, and you shall have a thousand crowns of gold."

"I have no letter, Madame."

"Two thousand crowns."

"Impossible. Since I have no letter, I cannot give you one."

"Ten thousand crowns, Orthon!"

Orthon, who perceived the rising anger of the queen, decided that the only chance remaining of preserving his master's secret was to swallow the disputed billet. With this design, he attempted to take it from his pocket; Catherine divined his intention and stopped him.

"There, there, my child!" said she, laughing, "that will do. Your fidelity, it seems, is above all temptation. Well, when royalty would secure to itself a faithful follower, it is necessary to try the devotedness of the heart it would attach. I now know what opinion to form of your zeal and faithfulness. Take this purse, in earnest of my future bounty, and carry the note to your master, with an intimation that after today I take you into my service. You may now depart; you can let yourself out by the door by which we entered; it opens from within."

So saying, Catherine placed a heavily filled purse in the hands of the astonished youth, walked on a few steps, and placed her hand against the wall.

But the young man stood hesitating. He could not believe that the danger which he had felt so near was withdrawn from him.

"Come, don't tremble so," said Catherine. "Haven't I said that you are free to go, and that if you are willing to return, your fortune is made?"

"Thanks, gracious madame!" murmured Orthon. "Then you pardon me?"

"I do more; I reward you as a faithful bearer of billets-doux—a pleasing messenger of love! Only you forget that your master is waiting for you."

"True!" said the youth, springing toward the door.

But scarcely had he advanced three steps when the floor gave way beneath his feet. He stumbled, extended his hands with a fearful cry, and disappeared in one of those horrible oubliettes of the Louvre of which Catherine had just touched the spring.

"Now, then," murmured Catherine, "thanks to this fool's obstinacy, I shall have to descend two hundred steps!"

The Florentine then returned to her apartments, whence she took a dark lantern, then returning to the gallery, closed the spring and opened the door of a spiral staircase, which seemed as though contrived to penetrate into the very bowels of the earth. Proceeding along the windings of this descent, she reached a second door, which, revolving on its hinges, admitted to the depths of the oubliette, where—crushed, bleeding, and mutilated by a fall of more than one hundred feet—lay the still palpitating form of poor Orthon; while on the other side of the wall forming the barrier of this dreadful spot the waters of the Seine were heard to ripple by, brought by a subterranean excavation to the foot of the staircase.

Having reached the damp and unwholesome abyss, which during her reign had witnessed numerous scenes like this, Catherine proceeded to search the corpse, eagerly seized the letter, ascertained by the lantern that it was the one she sought, thcn pushing the mangled body from her with her foot, she pressed a spring, the bottom of the oubliette sank down, and the corpse, sliding down by its own weight, disappeared toward the river.

Closing the door after her, she reascended, and returning to her cabinet, read the paper poor Orthon had so valiantly defended. It was conceived in these words:

This evening at ten o'clock, Rue de l'Arbre Sec, Hôtel de la Belle Etoile. Should you come, no reply is needed; if otherwise, say "No" to the bearer.

MOUY DE SAINT-PHALE.

As Catherine read these words, a smile of triumph curled her lip. She thought only of the victory she had gained, completely forgetting at what cost it had been won. And after all, what was Orthon? A faithful, devoted follower; a youth, a handsome and noble-minded youth—nothing more; of no weight in the balance in which the destinies of empires are suspended.

Having read the note, Catherine immediately returned to the apartments of Madame de Sauve, and placed it behind the mirror. As she returned, she found the captain of the guards in the corridor.

"Madame," said M. de Nancey, "according to your Majesty's orders, the horse is ready."

"My dear baron," said Catherine, "the horse is useless; I have talked with the boy and find that he is not sufficiently intelligent to be entrusted with the message I designed to send by him. I have therefore made him a little present, and dismissed him by the small side-wicket."

"But," persisted M. de Nancey, "that commission?"

"That commission?" Catherine repeated.

"Yes, the errand to St. Germain. Does your Majesty wish that I go myself, or shall I send one of my men?"

"No," said Catherine; "both you and your men, M. de Nancey, will have other work this evening." And Catherine returned to her apartments well assured that in the course of that evening she would hold in her hands the fate of that accursed King of Navarre.

The Hostelry of the Belle Etoile

Two hours after the event we have described, Madame de Sauve, having completed her attendance on the queen, entered her apartments. Henri followed her; and Dariole having informed him that Orthon had been there, he went to the glass and took the letter.

There was no address upon the letter.

"Henri is certain to go," Catherine had reflected; "for even did he not wish it, he cannot find the bearer to tell him so."

Catherine was right; Henri inquired after Orthon. Dariole told him that he had gone out with the queen-mother; but Henri felt no uneasiness, as he knew Orthon was incapable of betraying him. He dined as usual at the king's table, who rallied him upon the mistakes he had made that morning in hawking. Henri excused himself, alleging that he dwelt on the mountains, and not in the plains; but he promised Charles to study the noble art. Catherine was in an excellent humor; and when she rose from table, requested Marguerite to pass the evening with her.

At eight o'clock Henri took two of his gentlemen, went out by the Porte St. Honoré, entered again by the Tour de Bois, crossed the Seine at the ferry of the Nesle, went up the Rue St. Jacques, and there dismissed his companions, as if he were going to an amorous rendezvous. At the corner of the Rue des Mathurins he found a man on horseback, wrapped in a large cloak; he approached him.

"Mantes!" said the man.

"Pau!" replied the king.

The horseman immediately dismounted. Henri wrapped himself in the man's splashed mantle, sprang on his horse, rode down the Rue de la Harpe, crossed the Pont St. Michel, passed the Rue Barthélemy, crossed the river again on the Pont aux Meuniers, descended the quays, reached the Rue de l'Arbre Sec, and knocked at Maître la Hurière's.

La Mole was in a little chamber, writing a long love letter—to whom may be easily imagined. Coconnas was in the kitchen, watching half a dozen partridges roasting, and disputing with La Hurière as to whether they were done or not. At this moment Henri knocked. Grégoire went to take his horse, and the traveler entered, stamping on the floor as if to warm his feet.

"Eh!" said La Mole, continuing to write; "La Hurière, here is a gentleman who wants you."

La Hurière advanced, looked at Henri from head to foot; and as his large cloak did not inspire him with very great veneration, "Who are you?" he asked.

"Eh, *sang Dieu!*" returned Henri, pointing to La Mole. "I am, as the gentleman told you, a Gascon gentleman come to Paris to appear at court."

"What do you want?"

"A room and supper."

"Hum!" said La Hurière, "have you a lackey?"

It was, as we know, his usual question.

"No," Henri replied, "but I count on having one when I have made my fortune."

"I do not let a room to anyone unless he has a lackey."

"Even if I offer you a rose noble for the supper, and your own price for the room?"

"Oh, oh! you are very generous, my gentleman," said La Hurière, looking at Henri with suspicion.

"No; but expecting to sup here, I invited a friend of mine to meet me. Have you any good wine of Artois?"

"Henri de Navarre drinks no better."

"Ah, good! Here is my friend."

As he spoke, the door opened, and a gentleman somewhat older than the first, and having a long rapier at his side, entered.

"Ah, ah!" said he, "you are exact, my young friend. It is something for a man who has traveled two hundred leagues to be so punctual."

"Is this your friend?" asked La Hurière.

"Yes," replied the first, shaking hands with the young man with the rapier.

"Maître," said La Mole to La Hurière, "free us from these Huguenot fellows; Coconnas and I cannot converse together while they are there."

"Carry the supper into No. 2, on the third floor," said La Hurière. "Upstairs, gentlemen."

The two travelers followed Grégoire, who lit the way.

La Mole followed them with his eyes until they had disappeared; then turning, he saw Coconnas at the kitchen door. Two wide-open, staring eyes and a gaping mouth gave to his face a remarkable expression of astonishment. La Mole approached him.

"Mordi!" said Coconnas, "did you see?"

"What?"

"Those two gentlemen."

"Well?"

"I would swear that they are Henri de Navarre and the man in the red mantle."

"Swear if you wish, but not so loud."

"You also recognized them?"

"Certainly."

"What are they doing here?"

"Some love affair."

"You think so?"

"I am sure of it."

"I'll bet they are engaged in some conspiracy."

"Ah! you are foolish."

"But I tell you—"

"And I tell you that if they conspire, it is their own affair."

"Ah! that is true. At any rate," said Coconnas, "I am no longer in the services of M. d'Alençon; let them do as they please."

Meantime Henri and Mouy were installed in their chamber.

"Well, Sire," said Mouy, "have you seen Orthon?"

"No; but I found the note which he placed behind the mirror. I suppose he was frightened; the queen came in while he was there, and he went away without waiting for me. I had some fear about him, for Dariole told me the queen had a long conversation with him."

"Oh, there is no danger; he is very quick-witted. I will venture to say the queen did not learn much from him."

"Have you seen him yourself?"

"No, but he will come at midnight to attend me, armed with a good petronel; and he can tell us what took place as we walk along."

"And the man who was at the corner of the Rue Mathurins?"

"What man?"

"The man whose horse and cloak I have; are you sure of him."

"He is one of our most devoted associates; besides, he doesn't know that the affair is with your Majesty."

"We can discuss our business, then, in all security?"

"Without any doubt. Besides, La Mole is on guard."

"Good!"

"Well, Sire, what says M. d'Alençon?"

"He will not go; he says so distinctly. The departure of D'Anjou and the king's illness have changed all his plans."

"So it is he who made our plan miscarry?"

"Yes."

"He betrays us, then?"

"Not yet; but he is ready to do so on the first opportunity."

"Coward! traitor! Why did he not answer my letters?"

"In order to have proofs against you, and that you should have none against him. Meantime all is lost, is it not, Mouy?"

"On the contrary, all is won. You know all the party, except Condé's faction, were for you, and only used D'Alençon as a safe-guard. Well, since the day of the ceremony I have arranged everything. I shall have fifteen hundred horse ready in a week; they will be posted on the road to Pau; they will surely suffice?"

Henri smiled and laid his hand on his friend's shoulder. "Mouy," said he, "you, and you alone, know that the King of Navarre is not such a coward as men think."

"I know it, Sire; and I trust ere long all France will know it too. When do you hunt again?"

"In a week or ten days."

"Well, everything seems quiet now. The Duc d'Anjou has gone—we have no more occasion to think of him. The king gets better every day; the persecution against us has almost ceased. Play the amiable with the queen-mother and M. d'Alençon; tell the duke you cannot go without him, and try to make him believe you, which will be more difficult."

"Oh, he shall believe me!"

"Has he such confidence in you?"

"Not in me, but in the queen."

"And is the queen true to us?"

"I have ample proof of it; besides, she is ambitious."

"Well, three days before you hunt, tell me where it will be—at Bondy, at St. Germain, or at Rambouillet. Add that you are ready, and when you see La Mole spur on, follow him; once out of the forest, they must have fleet steeds to overtake us."

"Agreed."

"Have you money, Sire?"

Henri made the grimace he made all his life at that question. "Not much," said he; "but I believe Margot has."

"Well, whether it be yours or hers, bring all you can with you."

"And you—what do you propose to do meanwhile?"

"Since I have been pretty busy with the affairs of your Majesty, as you see, will your Majesty permit me to engage a little in my own affairs?"

"Certainly, Mouy; but what are your affairs?"

"Listen, Sire; Orthon tells me that yesterday he met near the Arsenal that brigand of a Maurevel, who, thanks to René's care, has recovered, and who warms himself in the sun, like the serpent that he is."

"Ah, I understand."

"You will be king someday, and will avenge yourself as a king; I am a soldier, and avenge myself as one. When all our little affairs are arranged, which will be in five or six days, I will walk round the Arsenal myself, and after giving him two or three rapier-thrusts, I shall leave Paris with a lighter heart."

"Do as you will. By the way, you are pleased with La Mole, are you not?"

"Ah! a charming fellow, who is devoted to you, body and soul, Sire, and on whom you can rely, as upon myself—brave—"

"And especially discreet. He must go with us to Navarre, Mouy, and once there we will see what we can do for him."

As Henri pronounced these words, the door flew open, and La Mole rushed in, pale and agitated.

"Quick! quick!" cried he, "the house is surrounded."

"Surrounded!" said Henri, rising, "by whom?"

"By the king's guards."

"Oh," said Mouy, drawing two pistols from his belt, "battle, then!"

"Pistols! and battle!—what can you do against fifty men?" said La Mole.

"He is right," said the king, "and if there were any means of retreat—"

"I know one," said La Mole, "if your Majesty will follow me."

"And Mouy—"

"Can follow us; but you must be quick."

Steps were heard on the stairs.

"It is too late," said Henri.

"If anyone could occupy them five minutes," said La Mole, "I could save the king."

"I will occupy them," said Mouy. "Go, Sire, go."

"But what will you do?"

"Oh, do not fear for me, Sire; only go!"

And Mouy rapidly concealed the king's plate, goblet, and napkin, so that it might seem he had supped alone.

"Come, Sire; come!" cried La Mole.

"Mouy! my brave Mouy," said Henri, offering his hand to the young man.

Mouy seized his hand, kissed it, pushed the door to, the instant they were outside, and bolted it.

"Yes, yes, I understand," said Henri; "he will allow himself to be taken while we escape. But who the devil can have betrayed us?"

"Quick! quick, Sire!" said La Mole, "they are on the stairs!"

At this moment the torches were visible on the stairs, and the rattling of arms was heard. La Mole guided the king in the darkness, and conducting him two stories higher, opened a door, which he shut and bolted, and opening the window, "Does your Majesty fear an excursion on the roofs?" said he.

"I, a chamois-hunter!"

"Well, then, follow me, and I will guide you."

And getting out of the window, La Mole clambered along the ridge, then passed along a gully formed by two roofs, at the end of which was the open window of a garret.

"Here we are, in port," said La Mole.

"So much the better," returned Henri, wiping the perspiration from his brow.

"Now, then," continued La Mole, "this garret communicates with a staircase, and the staircase with the street. I traveled the road on a more terrible night than this."

"Go on; go on!"

La Mole sprang into the open window, opened the door, found himself at the head of a winding staircase, and placing the cord that served as a baluster in Henri's hand, "Come, Sire," said he.

Henri had stopped before a window opposite the Belle Etoile; the stairs were crowded with soldiers, some with swords in their hands, others with torches. Suddenly the king saw a group descend the stairs, with Mouy in the midst; he had surrendered his sword, and descended quietly.

"Brave Mouy!" said the king.

"Faith, Sire, he seems very composed, and see, he even laughs! He must be meditating some good turn, for you know he laughs rarely."

"And the young man who was with you?"

"M. de Coconnas?" asked La Mole.

"Yes, M. de Coconnas. What has become of him?"

"Oh, Sire, have no uneasiness about him. On seeing the soldiers, he said to me, 'Do we risk anything?' 'Our heads,' I answered. 'And you will escape?' 'I hope so!' 'Well, then, so will I,' he answered; and I can assure you, Sire, that he will escape. When anyone takes Coconnas it will be because it is convenient to him to be taken."

"All is well, then," replied Henri. "Let us try to regain the Louvre."

"Nothing easier; wrap yourself in your mantle, for the street is full of people, and we shall pass for spectators."

They gained the Rue d'Averon, but in passing by the Rue des Pouliés, they saw Mouy and his escort cross the Place St. Germain l'Auxerrois.

"Ah!" said Henri, "they are taking him to the Louvre. The devil! the wicket will be closed; they will take the name of everyone who enters, and I shall be suspected of having been with him."

"Well, Sire," replied La Mole, "enter the Louvre in some other way."

"How the devil would you have me enter?"

"Hasn't your Majesty the Queen of Navarre's window?"

"Ventre-saint-gris! M. de la Mole, you are right, and I didn't think of it! But how shall I attract her attention?"

"Oh," said La Mole, bowing with an air of respectful gratitude, "your Majesty throws stones so well!"

M. de Mouy de Saint-Phale

This time Catherine had taken her precautions so well that she believed herself sure of her object.

Consequently about ten o'clock she had sent away Marguerite, quite convinced that the Queen of Navarre was ignorant of the plot against her husband, and went to the king and begged him to delay his retirement for the night. Puzzled by the air of triumph which in spite of her habitual dissimulation appeared on his mother's countenance, Charles questioned Catherine, who only said—

"I can make but one reply to your Majesty, and that is, you will this evening be delivered from two of your bitterest enemies."

Charles lowered his eyebrows, like a man who says to himself, "This is well; we shall see"; and whistling to his tall greyhound, who came to him, dragging his belly along the ground like a serpent, and placed his fine and intelligent head on his master's knee, he waited. After a few minutes, which Catherine passed with her eyes fixed and ears attentive, there was suddenly heard the noise of a pistol-shot in the courtyard of the Louvre.

"What noise is that?" inquired Charles, with a frown, while the hound rose up and pricked his ears.

"Nothing," Catherine replied, "it was only a signal."

"And what is the meaning of that signal?"

"It means that from this moment, Sire, your only, your real enemy is unable any longer to injure you."

"Have they been killing a man?" inquired Charles, looking at his mother with that eye of command which signified that assassination and mercy are two prerogatives pertaining to royal power.

"No, Sire, they have only arrested two."

"Oh," murmured Charles, "always hidden plots and plans in which the king has no part! *Mort diable!* Mother, I am an oldish boy, big enough to take care of myself, and want neither leading-strings nor swaddling-clothes. Go into Poland with your son Henri if you desire to reign; but here you are wrong, I tell you, to play the game you do."

"My son," replied Catherine, "this is the last time I meddle with your affairs; but this is an enterprise begun long ago, in which you have always said I was wrong, while I have labored to prove that I was right."

At this moment M. de Nancey begged an audience of the king, and there was a noise of footsteps in the vestibule, and the butts of muskets clattered on the floor.

"Let M. de Nancey enter," said the king, hastily.

M. de Nancey entered, saluted the king, and then, turning to the queen-mother, said, "Madame, your orders are executed; he is taken."

"What do you mean by *he?*" cried Catherine, much troubled; "have you only arrested one?"

"He was alone, Madame."

"Did he defend himself?"

"No, he was supping quietly in a room, and gave up his sword the moment it was demanded."

"Who is he?" asked the king.

"You will see," said Catherine. "Bring in the prisoner, M. de Nancey."

Mouy was introduced.

"Mouy!" exclaimed the king; "what is the matter now?"

"If, Sire," said Mouy, with perfect composure, "your Majesty would allow me that liberty, I would ask the same question."

"Instead of asking this question of the king," said Catherine, "have the kindness, M. de Mouy, to tell my son who was the man who was in the chamber of the King of Navarre on a certain night, and who on that night resisted the king's orders, like a rebel as he is, killed two of the guards, and wounded M. Maurevel."

"Yes," said Charles, frowning; "do you know the name of that man, M. de Mouy?"

"I do, Sire; does your Majesty desire to know it?"

"Yes, it would give me pleasure, I confess."

"Well, Sire, he is called Mouy de Saint-Phale."

"It was you, then?"

"It was, Sire."

Catherine, astonished at this audacity, recoiled before the young man.

"And how," inquired Charles IX, "dared you resist the orders of the king?"

"In the first place, Sire, I was ignorant that there was an order of your Majesty; then I saw only one thing, or rather but one man, M. Maurevel—the assassin of my father, the assailant of the admiral. I remembered that it was a year and a half since, in the very chamber in which we now are, on the evening of the twenty-fourth of August, your Majesty had promised me to do us justice on this murderer; and as since that time very grave events had occurred, I thought that perchance the king had been, in spite of himself, turned away from his desires. Seeing Maurevel within my reach, I believed Heaven had sent him there. Your Majesty knows the rest; I struck him down as a murderer, and fired at his men as robbers."

Charles made no reply; his friendship for Henri had for some time led him to look at things otherwise than he had been accustomed to, and sometimes even with terror. The queen-mother, in reference to the Saint Bartholomew, had set down in her memory observations which had fallen from her son, very much resembling remorse.

"But," observed the queen-mother, "what were you doing at that hour in the King of Navarre's apartments?"

"Oh," said Mouy, "it is a long story to tell, but if his Majesty has the patience to listen—"

"Yes," replied Charles, "I should wish to hear it."

"I will obey, Sire," said Mouy, bowing.

Catherine sat down, fixing an uneasy look on the young chief.

"We will listen," said Charles. "Here, Actælon!"

The dog resumed the place he had occupied before the prisoner had come in.

"Sire," said Mouy, "I came to his Majesty the King of Navarre as the deputy of our brethren, your faithful subjects of the Reformed religion—"

Catherine made a sign to Charles IX.

"Be quiet, Madame," he said; "I do not lose a word. Go on, M. de Mouy; go on."

"To inform the King of Navarre," continued Mouy, "that his abjuration had lost for him the confidence of the Huguenot party; but that nevertheless in remembrance of his father, Antoine de

Bourbon, and especially out of regard for the memory of his mother, the courageous Jeanne d'Albret, whose name is dear among us, the chiefs of the Reformed religion thought it a mark of deference due to him to beg him to relinquish his claims to the crown of Navarre."

"What said he?" asked Catherine, unable, in spite of her self-control, to receive this unexpected blow without wincing a little.

"Ah, ah!" said Charles, "but this crown of Navarre, which without my permission is made thus to jump from head to head, seems to belong a little to me."

"The Huguenots, Sire, recognize better than anyone the principle of suzerainty which your Majesty has just stated, and therefore hope to induce your Majesty to place the crown on some head which is dear to you."

"I!" said Charles; "on a head which is dear to me? *Mort diable!* of what head, then, do you speak, Monsieur? I do not understand you."

"Of the head of the Duc d'Alençon."

Catherine became as pale as death, and her eyes glared fiercely on Mouy.

"And did my brother d'Alençon know this?"

"Yes, Sire."

"And accepted the crown?"

"Subject to your Majesty's consent, to which he referred us."

"Ah, ah!" said Charles, "it is, indeed, a crown which would suit our brother D'Alençon wonderfully well! And that I should never have thought of it! Thanks, Mouy; thanks! when you have such ideas you will always be welcome at the palace."

"Sire, you would long since have been informed of all this, but for the unfortunate affair of the Louvre, which made me fear that I had fallen into disgrace with your Majesty."

"Yes; but," asked Catherine, "what said the King of Navarre to this proposal?"

"The king, Madame, yielded to the desire of his brethren, and his renunciation was ready."

"In this case," cried Catherine, "you must have that renunciation."

"I have, Madame," said Mouy; "and by chance I have it about me, signed by him, and dated."

"Of a date anterior to the affair in the Louvre?" inquired Catherine.

"Yes, of the previous evening, I think."

And Mouy drew from his pocket a renunciation in favor of the Duc d'Alençon, written and signed in Henri's hand, and bearing the date assigned to it.

"Faith! yes," said Charles, "and all is in due form."

"And what did Henri demand in return for this renunciation?"

"Nothing, Madame; the friendship of King Charles, he declared to us, would amply repay him for the loss of a crown."

Catherine bit her lips in anger and wrung her beautiful hands.

"This is all as complete as possible, Mouy," added the king.

"Then," asked the queen-mother, "if all was settled between you and the King of Navarre, for what purpose did you seek an interview with him this evening?"

"I, Madame! with the King of Navarre?" said Mouy. "He who arrested me will bear testimony that I was alone. Will your Majesty call him?"

"M. de Nancey," said the king; and the captain of the guards entered.

"M. de Nancey," said Catherine, quickly, "was M. de Mouy quite alone at the hostelry of the Belle Etoile?"

"In the chamber, yes, Madame; in the hostelry, no."

"Ah!" said Catherine, "who was his companion?"

"I know not if he were the companion of M. de Mouy, Madame; but I know he escaped by a back door after having prostrated two of my guards."

"And you recognized this gentleman, no doubt."

"I did not, but the guards did."

"And who was he?" inquired Charles IX.

"M. le Comte Annibal de Coconnas."

"Annibal de Coconnas!" repeated the king, gloomy and reflective. "He who made so terrible a slaughter of the Huguenots during the Saint Bartholomew?"

"M. de Coconnas, gentleman of the Duc d'Alençon," replied Nancey.

"Good! good!" said Charles. "You may withdraw, M. de Nancey; and another time, remember one thing."

"What is that, Sire?"

"That you are in my service, and will take orders from no one but me."

M. de Nancey retired backwards, bowing respectfully. Mouy smiled ironically at Catherine. There was a brief silence. The queen pulled the tassels of her *cordelière;* Charles caressed his dog.

"But what was your intention, Monsieur?" continued Charles. "Were you acting violently?"

"Against whom, Sire?"

"Why, against Henri or François or myself."

"Sire, we had the renunciation of your brother-in-law, the consent of your brother, and, as I had the honor to tell you, we were on the point of soliciting your Majesty's authority, when there happened this unfortunate affair of M. Maurevel's."

"Well, Mother, I see nothing wrong in all this. You were perfectly right, M. de Mouy, in asking for a king. Yes, Navarre may be, and ought to be, a separate kingdom. Moreover, this kingdom seems made expressly to endow my brother D'Alençon, who has always had so great a desire for a crown that when we wear our own he cannot withdraw his gaze from it. The only thing which opposed this coronation was Henriot's rights; but since Henriot voluntarily abdicates—"

"Voluntarily, Sire."

"It appears to be the will of God! M. de Mouy, you are free to return to your brethren, whom I have chastised—somewhat rudely, perchance, but that is between God and myself; and tell them that since they desire to have my brother, the Duc d'Alençon, for King of Navarre, the King of France accedes to their desires. From this moment Navarre is a kingdom, and its sovereign's name is François. I ask but a week for my brother to be ready to leave Paris with the éclat and pomp which appertain to a king. Go, M. de Mouy, go. M. de Nancey, allow M. de Mouy to retire. He is free."

"Sire," said Mouy, advancing a step, "will your Majesty allow me—"

"Yes," replied Charles. And he extended his hand to the young Huguenot. Mouy went on one knee, and kissed the king's hand.

"By the way," said Charles, as Mouy was about to rise, "have you not demanded from me justice on that ruffian Maurevel?"

"I have, Sire."

"I know not where he is, that I might render it to you, for he is in hiding; but if you meet him, take justice into your own hands. I authorize you to do so, and with all my heart."

"Oh, Sire!" exclaimed Mouy, "this is all I could desire. I know not where he is; but your Majesty may rest assured that I shall find him."

Mouy respectfully saluted the king and Catherine, and then retired uninterrupted. He made all haste to the hostelry of the Belle Etoile, where he found his horse; and three hours after he left Paris, the young man breathed in safety behind the walls of Mantes.

Catherine, bursting with rage, regained her apartments, whence she passed into those of Marguerite. There she found Henri in his dressing gown, as if just going to bed.

"Satan!" she muttered, "aid a poor queen, for whom God will do nothing more!"

CHAPTER 17

Two Heads for One Crown

"Request M. d'Alençon to come to me," said Charles, as his mother left him.

M. de Nancey hastened to M. d'Alençon's apartments, and delivered the king's message. The duke started when he heard it. He always trembled in Charles's presence, and the more so when he had reason to be afraid. Still, he went to his brother with all speed.

Charles was standing up, and whistling a hunting air. On entering, the Duc d'Alençon caught from the glassy eye of Charles one of those looks full of hatred which he so well understood.

"Your Majesty has asked for me," he said. "I am here, Sire. What is your Majesty's desire?"

"I desire to tell you, Brother, that in order to recompense you for the great friendship you bear me, I have resolved to do for you today the thing you most desire in all the world."

"For me?"

"Yes, for you. Ask yourself what that thing is of which you most frequently dream, without daring to ask for, and that thing I will give you."

"Sire," said François, "I swear to you that there is nothing I more desire than the continuance of the king's good health."

"Then you will be deeply gratified to know, D'Alençon, that the indisposition I experienced at the time when the Poles arrived has quite passed by. I have escaped, thanks to Henriot, a furious wild boar, who would have ripped me up, and I am so well as not to envy the healthiest man in my dominions; so that without being an unkind brother, you may wish for something else besides the continuation of my health, which is excellent."

"I desire nothing else, Sire."

"Oh! come now, François," continued Charles, impatiently; "you desire the crown of Navarre, and have had an understanding to that effect with Henriot and Mouy—with the first, that he would abdicate, and with the second, that he would secure it for you. Well, Henriot has renounced, Mouy has mentioned your wishes to me, and the crown to which you aspire—"

"Well?" said D'Alençon, in a trembling voice.

"Well, *mort diable!* it is yours."

D'Alençon turned ghastly pale, and then his face was suffused. The favor which the king granted him threw him at this moment into utter despair.

"But, Sire," he replied, palpitating with emotion, and in vain trying to recover his self-possession, "I have never desired, and certainly never sought for such a thing."

"That is possible," said the king, "for you are very discreet, Brother; but it has been desired and sought for you."

"Sire, I swear to you that I never—"

"Do not swear."

"But, Sire, do you then exile me?"

"Do you call that an exile, François? *Peste!* you are hard to please. What better thing could you hope for?"

D'Alençon bit his lips in despair.

"Faith!" continued Charles, affecting good nature, "I did not think you were so popular, François, and particularly with the Huguenots. Why, they really petition for you; and what better could I desire than a person devoted to me, a brother whom I love, and who is incapable of betraying me, at the head of a party who for thirty years has been in arms against us. This must calm everything as if by enchantment, to say nothing of the fact that we shall be all kings in the family. There will only be poor Henriot who will remain my friend, and nothing more. But he is not ambitious, and this title, which no one else covets, he will take."

"Oh, Sire, you mistake; I covet that title—a title to which no one has such right as I have. Henri is your brother only by marriage; I am your brother by blood and in heart, and I entreat you, Sire, keep me near you."

"No, no, François," replied Charles, "that would be unfortunate for you."

"How, Sire?"

"For a thousand reasons."

"But, Sire, have you a more faithful companion than I am? From my childhood I have never left your Majesty."

"I know it well, I know it well; and sometimes I have wished you farther off."

"What means your Majesty?"

"Oh, nothing, nothing! I know; I know. Ah, what glorious hunting you will have there, François; how I shall envy you! Do you know they chase the bear in the mountains there, as we do the boar here? You'll send us magnificent skins. You know they hunt there with the poniard, wait for the animal, excite and irritate him; he goes toward the hunter, and four paces off he rises on his hind-legs. Then they plunge the steel into his heart, as Henri did to the wild boar at our last hunt. You know it is dangerous work; but you are brave, François, and the danger would be real pleasure to you."

"Ah! your Majesty increases my trouble, for I shall no more hunt with you."

"*Corbœuf!* so much the better," said the king; "it does not suit either of us to hunt together—"

"What means your Majesty?"

"To hunt with me causes you such pleasure, and creates in you so much emotion that you, who are skill personified—you, who with any arquebus can bring down a magpie at a hundred paces—with a weapon of which you are such a perfect master failed at twenty paces to hit a wild boar, and broke the leg of my best horse! *Mort diable!* François, that makes one reflect, you must know!"

"Oh, Sire, think of my emotion," said D'Alençon, livid with agitation.

"Yes," replied Charles; "I guess what the emotion might be; and so I say, François, it is best for us to hunt at a distance from each other for fear of such emotions. You might, you know, in another emotion, kill the horseman instead of the horse, the king instead of the animal! When Montgomery killed our father, Henri II, by acci-dent—emotion, perhaps—the blow placed our brother François II on the throne, and sent our father Henri to St. Denys; a little in this way can do so much."

The duke felt the perspiration pour down his brow at this unexpected attack. The king had surmised all, and veiling his anger under a jesting tone, was perhaps more terrible than if he had poured out, hot from his lips, the hatred that consumed his heart; his revenge was proportioned to his rancor. In proportion as the one was sharpened, the other increased; and for the first time, D'Alençon felt remorse, or rather regret, for having meditated a crime that had not succeeded. He had sustained the struggle as long as he could; but at this last blow he bowed his head.

Charles fixed on him his vulture gaze, and watched closely every feeling that displayed itself in the young duke's countenance, as if he perused an open book. "Brother," said he, "we have declared our resolution; that resolution is immutable. You will go."

D'Alençon started; but Charles did not appear to observe it, and continued, "I wish that Navarre should be proud of having at its head a brother of the King of France. Gold, power, honor—you will have all that belongs to your birth, as your brother Henri had; and, like him," he added with a smile, "you will bless me from a distance. But no matter! blessings know no distance!"

"Sire—"

"Accept, or rather resign yourself. Once a king, we shall find for you a wife worthy of a son of France, who may—who knows?— bring you another throne."

"But," observed the Duc d'Alençon, "your Majesty forgets your good friend Henri."

"Henri!—why, I told you he does not desire the throne of Navarre; he has abandoned it. Henri is a jovial fellow, and not a pale-face, like you; he likes to amuse himself and laugh at his ease, and not weary himself, as we are compelled to do who wear crowns upon our heads."

"Your Majesty then desires me to occupy myself—"

"By no means. Do not in any way disturb yourself; I will arrange everything myself. Say not a word to anyone, and I will take upon myself to give publicity to everything. Go, François."

There was nothing to reply. The duke bowed and left the apartment, with rage devouring his heart. He was eager to find Henri, and talk with him of all that had taken place; but he could find only Catherine, for Henri avoided, while his mother sought him. The duke, seeing Catherine, endeavored to swallow his griefs and tried to smile. "Well, Madame," he said, "do you know the great news?"

"I know that there is an idea of making a king of you, Monsieur."

"It is a great kindness on the part of my brother, Madame; and I am inclined to think that a portion of my gratitude is due to you, although I confess that at bottom it gives me pain thus to despoil the King of Navarre."

"You are very fond of Henriot, my son, it appears."

"Why, yes, for some time we have been closely allied."

"Do you suppose that he loves you as much as you love him?"

"I hope so, Madame."

"Such a friendship is edifying, do you know?—especially among princes. Friendships of the court are not generally very solid, my dear François."

"Mother, consider that we are not only friends, we are almost brothers."

Catherine smiled in a peculiar manner. "Are there brothers, then, among kings?" she asked.

"Oh, we were neither of us kings when our alliance began. We had no prospect of being kings; that is what brought us together."

"Yes; but things are changed now. Who can say that you will not both be kings?"

Catherine saw, by the start and sudden color of the duke, that the shaft had hit the mark.

"He? Henriot king? and of what kingdom?"

"The most glorious in Christendom, my son."

"Ah!" said D'Alençon, growing very pale, "what do you mean?"

"What a good mother should say to a son; what you have thought of more than once, François."

"I?" said the duke, "I have thought of nothing, Madame, I swear to you!"

"I believe you; for your friend, your brother Henri, as you call him, is, under his apparent frankness, a very clever and wily person, who keeps his secrets better than you do yours, François. For instance, did he ever tell you that Mouy was his man of business?" And Catherine looked at François as though she would read his very heart.

François had but one virtue, or rather but one vice—dissimulation; he bore his mother's gaze unshrinkingly.

"Mouy!" said he, with surprise, and as if he uttered the name for the first time.

"Yes, the Huguenot, M. de Mouy de Saint-Phale—he who nearly killed Maurevel, and who is intriguing and raising an army to support your brother Henri against your family."

Catherine, unaware that François knew as much on this matter as herself, rose at these words, and would have gone out majestically, but François detained her.

"Mother," he said, "another word, if you please. How can Henri, with his feeble resources, carry on any war serious enough to disquiet my family?"

"Child," said the queen, smiling, "he is supported by more than thirty thousand men, who, the day he says the word, will appear as suddenly as if they sprang forth from the ground; and these thirty thousand men are Huguenots, remember—in other words, the bravest soldiers in the world. And then, he has a protector whom you have not been able, or have not chosen to conciliate."

"Who is that?"

"He has the king—the king, who loves him, pushes him on; the king, who, from jealousy against your brother of Poland, and from spite against you, seeks a successor outside of his family."

"The king? Do you think so?"

"Do you not see how he takes to Henriot, his dear Henriot?"

"Yes, Madame; yes."

"And how he is repaid in return? for this very Henriot, forgetting how his brother-in-law would have shot him on Saint Bartholomew's day, grovels to the very earth like a dog, and licks the hand which has beaten him."

"Yes," said François, "Henri is very humble with my brother Charles; and as the king is always rallying him as to his ignorance of hawking, he has begun to study it. It was only yesterday he asked me if I had not some books on that sport."

"Well," said Catherine, whose eyes glittered as if a sudden project had occurred to her—"well, and what reply did you make him?"

"That I would look in my library."

"Good! good!" answered Catherine; "he must have that book."

"But I have looked for it and cannot find it."

"I will find it; I will find it! and you will give it to him as coming from you."

"And what will that lead to?"

"Have you confidence in me, D'Alençon?"

"Yes, Mother."

"Will you obey me blindly in regard to Henri, whom you do not love, though you say you do?" D'Alençon smiled. "And whom I hate," continued Catherine.

"Yes, I will obey."

"Well, then, day after tomorrow come here for the book; I will give it to you, and you shall carry it to Henri, and—"

"And—"

"Leave the rest to Providence, or chance."

François bowed in acquiescence and left his mother's chamber.

Meanwhile, Marguerite received through La Mole a letter from Mouy addressed to the King of Navarre. As in politics the two illustrious allies had no secrets, she opened the missive and read it, and then, going quickly and silently along the secret passage, went in the King of Navarre's antechamber, no longer guarded since Orthon's disappearance.

That disappearance, of which we have not spoken since the moment when the reader saw it take place in a manner so tragical for poor Orthon, had greatly disturbed Henri. He had spoken about it to Madame de Sauve and to his wife; but neither of them knew more about it than he did. Only, Madame de Sauve had given him some information which made it clear to his mind that the poor boy had fallen a victim to some machination of the queen-mother, and that his narrow escape from arrest at the same time with Mouy was due to the same machination.

Any other than Henri would have kept silence; but Henri calculated cleverly, and saw that his silence would betray him. And thus he sought and inquired for Orthon everywhere, even in the presence of the king and the queen-mother, and of everyone, down to the sentinel at the wicket of the Louvre; but every inquiry was in vain. Henri appeared so affected by that loss, and so attached to the poor absent servitor that he declared that he would not have another in his place until entirely satisfied that he would not return.

The antechamber was therefore unoccupied. Henri turned round as the queen entered. "You, Madame?" he cried.

"Yes," replied Marguerite; "read quickly!" and she handed the open letter to him. It contained these lines:

SIRE—The moment has arrived for putting our plan of flight into execution.

Day after tomorrow there will be hawking on the banks of the Seine, from St. Germain to Maisons, all along the forest.

Go to this meeting, although it is only a hawking party. Put a good coat of mail under your doublet, your best sword by your side, and ride the fleetest horse in your stable.

About noon, when the sport is at its height, and the king is galloping after his falcon, get away alone, if you come alone; with the queen, if her Majesty will follow you.

Fifty of our party will be concealed in the Pavilion of François I, of which we have the key; no one will know that they are there, for they will come at night, and the shutters will be closed.

You will go by the Allée des Violettes, at the end of which I shall be on the watch; at the right of this road will be M. M. de la Mole and de Coconnas, with two horses, intended to replace yours if they should be fatigued.

Adieu, Sire! be ready, as we shall be.

"Now then, Sire," said Marguerite, "be a hero; it is not difficult. You have but to follow the route indicated, and create for me a glorious throne," said the daughter of Henri II.

An imperceptible smile rose to the thin lips of the Béarnais, as he kissed Marguerite's hand, and went out to explore the passage, humming the refrain of an old song:

> *"Cil qui mieux battit la muraille*
> *N'entra point dedans le chasteau."*

The precaution was good, for as he opened his bedchamber door the Duc d'Alençon opened that of his antechamber. Henri motioned to Marguerite with his hand, and then said aloud, "Ah, is it you, Brother? Welcome!"

The queen understood her husband's meaning, and went quickly into a dressing-closet, before the door of which hung a thick tapestry. D'Alençon entered with a timorous step, and looking around him, "Are we alone, Brother?" he asked in an undertone.

"Quite. But what ails you?—you seem upset."

"We are discovered, Henri!"

"How discovered?"

"Mouy has been arrested!"

"I know it."

"Well, Mouy has told the king all!"

"All what?"

"He said I was ambitious for the throne of Navarre, and was conspiring to obtain it."

"The dunderhead!" said Henri. "So that you are compromised, my dear brother! How is it, then, that you are not under arrest?"

"I cannot tell; the king jested with me, and offered me the throne of Navarre, hoping, doubtless, to draw from me a confession, but I said nothing."

"And you did well, *ventre-saint-gris!*" said the Béarnais. "Stand firm, for our lives depend on that."

"Yes," said François, "our position is difficult, and that is why I came to ask your advice, my brother. Ought I to flee or remain?"

"You have seen the king, and he has spoken to you?"

"Yes."

"Well, you must have ascertained his thoughts; act from your own inspiration."

"I would rather remain," said François.

Master of himself as he was, yet Henri allowed a movement of joy to escape him, and François observed it.

"Remain, then," said Henri.

"And you?"

"Why, if you remain, I have no motive for going; if you went I should follow you only out of devotion—that I might not part from a brother I love."

"So, then," said D'Alençon, "there is an end of all our plans, and you give way to the first evil fortune."

"I?" said Henri, "I do not call it evil fortune to remain here; thanks to my contented disposition, I am happy everywhere."

"Well, then," observed D'Alençon, "there's no more to be said; only, if you change your mind, let me know."

"*Corbleu!* I shall be sure to do that," replied Henri. "Have we not agreed to have no secrets from each other?"

D'Alençon said no more, and withdrew full of thought, for he believed he had seen the tapestry move at a certain moment; and indeed, scarcely was D'Alençon gone when Marguerite reappeared.

"What do you think of this visit?" inquired Henri.

"That there is something new and important; what it is, I will learn."

"In the meanwhile?"

"In the meanwhile, fail not to come to my apartments tomorrow evening."

"I will not fail, be assured, Madame," was the reply of Henri, kissing his wife's hand very gallantly.

With the same precaution she had used in coming, Marguerite returned to her own apartments.

CHAPTER 18

The Book of Venery

Thirty-six hours had elapsed since the events we have related. The Louvre clock had just struck four when D'Alençon, who, with all the rest of the court, had risen early, to prepare for the hunt, entered his mother's apartments. The queen was not in her chamber, but she had left orders that if her son came he was to wait. At the end of a few minutes she came out of a cabinet where she carried on her chemical studies, and into which no one ever entered. As she opened the door, a strong odor of some acrid perfume pervaded the room, and looking through the door of the cabinet, the duke perceived a thick white vapor, like that of some aromatic substance, floating in the air. He could not restrain a look of inquiry.

"Yes," said Catherine, "I burned some old parchments, and their smell was so offensive that I cast some juniper into the brazier." D'Alençon bowed. "Well," continued the queen, concealing beneath the sleeves of her *robe de chambre* her hand stained with large reddish spots, "anything new since yesterday?"

"Nothing."

"Have you seen Henri?"

"Yes."

"Will he go?"

"He refuses positively."

"The knave!"

"What do you say, Madame?"

"I say that he will go."

"You think so?"

"I am sure of it."

"Then he escapes us?"

"Yes," said Catherine.

"And you let him depart?"

"I not only suffer him, but, I tell you, it is necessary that he should leave the court."

"I do not understand you."

"Listen: a skillful physician, the same who gave me the book of venery you are about to present to the King of Navarre, has told me that he is on the point of being attacked with consumption—an incurable disease. Now, you will understand that if he be doomed to die of so cruel a disease, it is better that he should die away from us than under our eyes, at the court."

"Indeed, that would be too painful for us."

"Especially for Charles; whereas, if he die after having disobeyed him, he will look upon his death as a punishment from heaven."

"You are right, Mother," said François, with admiration; "it is better he should depart. But are you sure he will go?"

"All his measures are taken. The place of rendezvous is in the forest of St. Germain; fifty Huguenots are to escort him to Fontainebleau, where five hundred others await him."

"And does Margot accompany him?" asked D'Alençon.

"Yes; but upon Henri's death she will return to court, a widow and free."

"Are you sure that Henri will die?"

"The physician who gave me this book assured me of it."

"And where is this book?"

Catherine entered her cabinet, and returned instantly with the book in her hand.

"Here it is," said she.

D'Alençon looked at it, not without a certain feeling of terror.

"What is this book?" asked he, shuddering.

"I have already told you. It is a treatise on the art of rearing and training falcons, goshawks, and gerfalcons, written by a very learned man—Seigneur Castruccio Castracani, duke of Lucca."

"What am I to do with it?"

"Give it to your good friend Henriot, who, you told me, asked you for this book, or one like it, in order to study the science of hawking. As he is going to hawk this morning with the king, he will not fail to read some pages of it, so as to show the king that he is following his advice and taking lessons. The main thing is to give it to him personally."

"Oh, I dare not!" said D'Alençon, shuddering.

"Why not?" replied the queen; "it is a book like any other, except that it has lain by so long that the leaves stick together. Do not attempt to read it, for it can only be read by wetting the finger, and turning over each leaf, which occasions a great loss of time."

"So that it will be read only by a man who is anxious to learn?"

"Exactly so, my son; you understand?"

"Oh," said D'Alençon, "I hear Henri in the court. Give it to me, and I will avail myself of his absence to place it in his room; on his return he will find it there."

"I should much prefer that you gave it to him personally, François; it is more certain."

"I have already told you I dare not."

"Go, then; but at least place it where it can be easily seen."

"I will place it where he must see it. Will it be better to open it?"

"Yes, open it."

"Give it to me, then."

D'Alençon took with a trembling hand the book which Catherine held out to him with a hand that did not tremble.

"Take it," said she. "There is no danger, since I can handle it; besides, you have your gloves on."

D'Alençon wrapped the book in his mantle, as if still afraid.

"Make haste," continued the queen; "Henri may enter at any moment."

"You are right, Madame, I will go." And the duke left the apartment, trembling with emotion.

We have often introduced our readers into the apartments of the King of Navarre, and have made them witnesses of events that took place there—joyous or terrible accordingly as the protecting angel of the future King of France smiled or threatened. But those walls, stained with blood by murder, sprinkled with wine by revelry, scented with perfumes by love, had perhaps never seen a face so pale as the Duc d'Alençon's when he entered the apartments, the book in his hand.

On the wall hung Henri's sword; some links of mail were scattered on the floor; a well-filled purse and a poniard lay on the table; and the light ashes in the grate showed D'Alençon that Henri had put on a shirt of mail, collected what money he could, and burned all papers that might compromise him.

"My mother was right," thought D'Alençon. "He would betray me."

Doubtless this conviction gave him strength; for after having looked into all the corners and lifted the tapestry, after assuring himself that no one was thinking of what he might be doing, he took the book from under his cloak, placed it on the table, and then, with his gloved hand, and with a hesitation that betrayed his fears, he opened the book at an engraving. The instant he had done so he drew off his glove and cast it into the fire; the leather crackled, burned, and was soon reduced to a black and curled remnant. He waited until he had seen it consumed, and then hastily returned to his own apartments. As he entered he heard steps on the winding stair; and not doubting but that it was Henri, he quickly closed his door. Then he looked out of his window into the court below. Henri was not in that portion of the court visible from the window, and this strengthened François's belief that it was he whom he had just heard.

The duke sat down, took up a book, and tried to read. It was a History of France, from Pharamond to Henri II. But the duke could not fix his attention on it; the fever of expectation burned his veins; the throbbing of his temples sounded through all his brain. As one sees in a dream or in a magnetic trance, it seemed to him that he could see through the walls. His eyes appeared to plunge into the chamber of Henri, spite of the obstacles that separated it from him. In order to drive away the terrible object before his mind's eye, the duke vainly looked at his arms, his ornaments, his books; every detail of the engraving that he had seen but for a moment was before him still. It was a gentleman on horseback, recalling his falcon, in a flat landscape; then it was not only the book he saw, but the King of Navarre reading it, and wetting his thumb in order to turn over the pages. At this sight, fictitious and imaginary as it was, D'Alençon staggered against a table and covered his eyes with his hands, as if to hide the horrible vision.

Suddenly D'Alençon saw Henri in the court. He stopped a few moments to speak to the men who were loading two mules, ostensibly with his provisions for the chase, but really with the money and other things he wished to take with him; then, having given his orders, he advanced toward the door.

D'Alençon stood motionless; it was not Henri, then, he had heard mount the stairs. All those agonies, then, that he had suffered in the last quarter of an hour were groundless. What he had thought finished, or nearly so, was only about to begin. He opened his door and listened; this time there was no mistake—it was Henri. D'Alençon recognized his step, even to the peculiar jingle of his spurs. Henri's door opened, and then closed.

"Good!" said D'Alençon. "He has passed through the antechamber; he has entered his bedchamber; he has looked to see if his sword, his purse, and his poniard are there; then he has seen the book open on the table. 'What is this book?' he asks himself. 'Where has it come from? Who has brought it?' Then, seeing the engraving, he tries to read it and turns over the leaves." A cold sweat moistened the duke's brow. "Will he call for help?" said he. "Is the poison sudden? No; for my mother said he would die slowly of consumption."

Ten minutes passed by in these horrible reflections. D'Alençon could support it no longer; he rose, and passed through his chamber, which was already filled with gentlemen. "Good day, gentlemen," said he, "I am going to the king." And to distract his attention, to prepare an alibi, perhaps, D'Alençon descended to his brother's apartments. Why, he knew not. What had he to say? Nothing! It was not Charles he sought; it was Henri from whom he fled.

François crossed successively the salon and the sleeping room, without meeting anyone; he then thought Charles might be in his armory, and he opened the door.

Charles was seated at a table in an armchair of carved oak; his back was turned to the door by which François had entered. The duke approached silently. Charles was reading.

"Pardieu!" cried the king, "what an admirable book! I did not think there was such a work in France."

D'Alençon listened.

"Devil take the leaves!" said Charles, as, wetting his thumb, he turned them. "It seems as if the leaves had been stuck together purposely, to conceal the marvels they contain."

D'Alençon bounded forward. The book Charles was reading

was the same that D'Alençon had taken into Henri's room. A cry burst from his lips.

"Ah, it is you, D'Alençon!" said the king; "you are just in time to see the most admirable work on venery in the world."

D'Alençon's first idea was to snatch the book from his brother, but an infernal thought nailed him to his place. A frightful smile passed over his white lips; he put his hand before his eyes as if dazzled. Then, gradually recovering himself, but without moving a step backward or forward, "Sire," he asked, "how did this book come into your possession?"

"Oh, I went into Henriot's room to see if he was ready, and found this treasure, which I brought down with me to read at my ease."

And the king again moistened his finger, and again turned over the page.

"Sire," faltered D'Alençon, whose hair stood on end—"Sire, I have come to tell you—"

"Let me finish this chapter, François, and then tell me what you please. I have read, or rather devoured, fifty pages."

"My brother has tasted the poison five-and-twenty times," thought D'Alençon; "he is a dead man!"

François wiped the cold dew from his brow with a trembling hand, and waited in silence, as the king bade him, until he had finished the chapter.

CHAPTER 19

The Hawking Party

Charles read on; he seemed, indeed, to devour the pages. And each leaf, as we have said, whether because the book had been long exposed to dampness or for some other reason, adhered to the leaf next following.

D'Alençon gazed wildly on this terrible spectacle, of which he alone foresaw the consequence.

"Oh," murmured he, "what will happen now? Shall I go into exile and seek a visionary throne, while Henri, on the first intelligence of Charles's illness, will return to some fortress near Paris, whence he may come hither in an hour or two? so that before D'Anjou even hears of Charles's death the dynasty already will have been changed."

Instantly his plan with regard to Henri altered. It was Charles who had read the poisoned book; Henri must stay. He was less to be dreaded in the Bastille, or a prisoner at Vincennes, than as King of Navarre at the head of thirty thousand men.

The duke waited until Charles finished his chapter, and then, "Brother," said he, "I waited because you ordered me; but I have something of the greatest importance to say to you."

"Ah, the devil take you!" returned Charles, whose pale cheeks were becoming purple, either because he had read with too much fervor, or the poison was beginning to operate, "if you come and worry me, I'll get rid of you, as I have of the King of Poland."

"It is not on that subject I would speak to you. Your Majesty has touched me in my most sensitive point—that of my love for you as a brother, and my devotion as your subject; and I come to prove to you that I am no traitor."

434

"Well, well," said Charles, crossing his legs and throwing himself back on his chair; "some fresh report, some new nightmare?"

"No, Sire; a certainty—a plot, which only my ridiculous delicacy of sentiment has prevented my revealing to you."

"A plot! let us hear the plot."

"Sire," said François, "while your Majesty hawks in the plain of Vesinet, the King of Navarre will fly into the forest of St. Germain, where a troop of his friends await him, and will escape with them."

"I expected this!" cried Charles; "a fresh calumny against my poor Henriot! When will you leave him alone?"

"Your Majesty need not wait long to know whether what I say be true or false."

"Why not?"

"Because this evening he will be gone."

Charles rose. "Listen," said he; "I will once more seem to believe you; but mind, it is for the last time! Without there! summon the King of Navarre!"

A soldier was about to obey, when François stopped him. "That is a bad way to learn the truth," said he. "Henri will deny it, will give a signal, all his accomplices will conceal themselves, and my mother and myself will be accused of calumny."

Charles opened the window, for the blood was rushing into his head. Then, turning to D'Alençon, "What would you do, then?" asked he.

"Sire," said D'Alençon, "I would surround the wood with three detachments of light-horse, who, at a certain hour—at eleven o'clock, for example—should beat the forest, and drive everyone in it back upon the Pavilion of François I, which I would, as if casually, have appointed as the place for dinner. Then, when I saw Henri withdraw, I would follow him to the rendezvous, and capture him and his accomplices."

"A good idea enough!" returned Charles. "Call the captain of my guards."

D'Alençon drew from his doublet a silver whistle fastened to a chain of gold, and whistled. Nancey appeared. Charles gave him some orders in an undertone. Meanwhile Actæon, the greyhound, had dragged a book off the table and begun to tear it. Charles turned round and swore a terrible oath. The book was the precious treatise on venery, of which there existed but three copies in the world.

The chastisement was proportionate to the offense. Charles seized a whip and lashed the dog soundly; Actæon yelled and disappeared under a table covered with a large green cloth. The king picked up the book, and saw with joy that but one leaf was wanting, and that leaf not a page of text, but an engraving. He carefully placed it on a shelf beyond the reach of Actæon—D'Alençon looking on with anxiety; now that it had fulfilled its fearful task, he would have been glad to see it out of Charles's hands.

Six o'clock struck, and the king descended. He first closed the door of the armory, locked it, and put the key in his pocket, D'Alençon earnestly watching each movement; on his way downstairs he stopped, and passed his hand to his brow. "I do not know what is the matter with me," he said, "but I feel very weak."

D'Alençon's legs trembled not less than those of the king. "Perhaps," he faltered, "there is a thunderstorm in the air."

"A thunderstorm in January! you are mad," said Charles. "No, no; I feel a dizziness, my skin is dry. I am overfatigued, that's all." Then in an undertone he added, "They will kill me with their quarrels and their plots."

The fresh air, the cries of the huntsmen, and the noise of the horses and hounds, produced their ordinary effect upon the king; he breathed freely, and felt exhilarated. His first care was to look for Henri and Marguerite, who seemed, excellent spouses, as if they could not leave each other. On perceiving Charles, Henri spurred his horse, and in three bounds was beside him.

"Ah, ah, Henriot!" said Charles, "you are mounted as if you were going to hunt the stag, and yet you know we are only going to hawk." Then without awaiting a reply, "Forward, gentlemen!" cried he, frowning, and with a voice almost threatening; "we must be at the meet by nine."

Catherine was watching at a window, and only her pale face could be seen; her figure was concealed by the curtain.

At Charles's order, the whole cortège passed through the gate of the Louvre, and along the road to St. Germain, amid the acclamations of the people, who saluted their young king as he rode by on his horse whiter than snow.

"What did he say to you?" asked Marguerite of Henri.

"He felicitated me on the stoutness of my horse."

"Is that all?"

"Yes."

"He knows something, then."

"I fear so."

"Let us be cautious."

Henri's face was lighted up in reply with one of his cordial smiles, which meant for Marguerite, especially, "Be easy, my dear."

As for Catherine, when she had seen them all depart, she let fall the curtain. "This time," she murmured, "I think I have him." Then, to satisfy herself, after having waited for a few minutes she entered the King of Navarre's apartments, using her passkey. But she searched in vain for the book.

"D'Alençon has already taken it away," she said; "that is prudent." And she descended, convinced that this time her project had succeeded.

The king arrived at St. Germain. The sun, hitherto hidden by a cloud, lighted up the splendid cortège. Then, as if it had awaited this moment, a heron rose from the reeds with a mournful cry.

"Haw! haw!" cried Charles, unhooding his falcon.

The falcon, dazzled for a moment by the light, described a circle, then, suddenly perceiving the heron, dashed after it. However, the heron, which had risen a hundred yards before the beaters, had profited by the time occupied in unhooding the falcon to gain a considerable distance; he was therefore at least at a height of five hundred feet, and was still mounting rapidly.

"Haw! haw! Bec-de-Fer!" cried Charles, encouraging his falcon; "show us now your noble blood! haw! haw!"

As if he had understood that encouragement, the noble bird mounted like an arrow after the heron, which had now well-nigh disappeared.

"Ah, coward!" said Charles, putting his horse to its speed, and throwing back his head, so as not to lose sight of the chase; "courage, Bec-de-Fer!"

The contest was most curious. The falcon was rapidly nearing the heron; the only question was which in that first attack should be uppermost. Fear had better wings than courage. The falcon passed underneath; and the heron, profiting by his advantage, dealt him a blow with his long beak. The falcon staggered and seemed as if about to retreat, but soon recovering himself, went after the heron. The latter, pursuing his advantage, had changed the direction of his flight and sought the forest, endeavoring to escape by distance rather than by height; but the falcon followed him so closely that the heron was obliged again to mount, and in a few seconds the two birds were scarcely distinguishable.

"Bravo, Bec-de-Fer!" cried Charles, "see, he is uppermost!"

"Faith!" said Henri, "I confess I do not see the one or the other."

"Nor I," said Marguerite.

"If you can't see them, you may hear them—at least the heron," replied Charles. "Hark! he asks quarter." As he spoke, two or three plaintive cries were heard. "Look, look!" he cried, "and you will see them descend quicker than they went up."

As the king spoke, the two birds reappeared; the falcon was uppermost.

"Bec-de-Fer has him!" shouted Charles.

The heron, outflown by the falcon, no longer sought to defend himself; he descended rapidly, struck continually by the falcon. Suddenly he folded his wings and dropped like a stone; but his adversary did the same. And when the fugitive resumed his flight, he received a stroke that stunned him; he fell to the earth, and the falcon, uttering a note of victory, alighted near him.

"To the falcon! to the falcon!" cried Charles, galloping toward the place. But suddenly he stopped, and uttering a cry, let fall his bridle, and pressed his hand to his stomach. All the courtiers hastened up.

"It is nothing," said he, with inflamed features and haggard eyes. "But I felt as if a hot iron was passing through me just now; but it is nothing." And he galloped on.

D'Alençon turned pale.

"What is the matter now?" inquired Henri of Marguerite.

"I know not," replied she; "but did you see Charles? He was purple!"

"He is not so generally," said Henri.

They reached the place where the two birds were; the falcon was already eating the heron's brains. Charles sprang off his horse; but on alighting he was forced to seize the saddle to prevent himself from falling. The earth turned under him; he felt a strong inclination to sleep.

"My brother!" cried Marguerite, "what is the matter?"

"I feel," said Charles, "what Portia must have felt when she swallowed her burning coals. It seems as if my breath was aflame."

Meantime the falcon was reclaimed, and all the suite gathered round Charles.

"What is all this?" cried he. "Body of Christ! it is nothing, or at most only the sun that affects me. Unhood all the falcons! there go a whole flight of herons!"

Five or six falcons were instantly unhooded, while all the chase galloped along the bank of the river.

"Well, Madame, what say you?" asked Henri.

"That the moment is favorable, and that if the king does not look back, we may easily gain the forest."

Henri called the attendant who had the fallen heron in charge, and while the court swept on, remained behind, as if to examine the bird. At this moment, and as if to aid his plans, a pheasant rose. Henri slipped the jesses of his falcon; he had now the pretext of a chase on his own account to assist him.

CHAPTER 20

The Pavilion of François I

At the right of the Allée des Violettes is a long clearing, so far that it cannot be discovered from the high road, but yet the high road can be seen from the clearing.

In the middle of this clearing two men were lying on the grass, having a traveling-cloak spread beneath them, and at the side of each a long sword, and a musketoon (then called a petronel) with the muzzle turned from them. One of them was leaning on his knee and one hand, listening like a hare or a deer.

"It appears to me," said he, "that the hunt drew very close upon us just now. I heard the cries of the hunters as they cheered on the falcon."

"And now," said the other, who appeared to await events with much more philosophy than his comrade—"now I hear them no longer; they must be a long way off. I have already remarked that this is a bad place for observation. It is true one is not seen here, but neither can one see."

"What the devil would you have, my dear Annibal? We must wait quietly; the place hides us and our mules and horses very well; Mouy has selected a good spot, one which has all the concealments and privacy indispensable to a conspirator."

"Ah, good!" said the other gentleman; "that's the word, is it? Well, I expected it. So, then, we are conspiring?"

"We are not conspiring; we are serving the king and queen."

"Who are conspiring; and that, so far as we are concerned, comes to the same thing."

"Coconnas," replied La Mole, "I have already told you that I do not force you in the least degree to join me in this adventure, which a private sentiment unshared by you—and which you cannot share—urges me to undertake."

"Eh! *mordi!* who, then, says that you are forcing me? In the first place, I don't know a man who could force Coconnas into doing what he didn't wish to do; but do you suppose that I will let you go without following you, especially when I see you going to the devil?"

"Annibal! Annibal!" said La Mole, "I think I see down there her white horse. Oh! it is strange how the mere thought of her coming makes my heart beat!"

"Very odd!" said Coconnas, yawning; "my heart doesn't beat at all."

"It was not she," said La Mole. "What has happened, then? It was appointed for noon, I think."

"It has happened that it is not noon," said Coconnas, "that is all; and it appears that we have time for a nap." And so saying, Coconnas stretched himself on his mantle like a man who is about to add practice to precept; but as his ear touched the ground, he raised his finger and motioned La Mole to be silent.

Then a distant sound was heard, which at first was scarcely perceptible, and to unpracticed ears would have seemed to be only the wind, but to the cavaliers it was the distant galloping of horses.

La Mole sprang to his feet in a moment.

"Here they are!" said he. "Up!"

Coconnas rose more quietly; and then a regular, measured noise struck the ears of the two friends. The neighing of a horse made the horses they had ten paces distant prick up their ears; and in the road there passed like a white shadow a woman, who, turning toward them, made a particular signal and disappeared.

"The queen!" they exclaimed, both at once.

"What can this mean?" said Coconnas.

"And she did so with her arm," said La Mole, "which means, 'Immediately.' "

"She did so," said Coconnas, "which means, 'Depart.' "

"The signal means, 'Wait for me.' "

"It means, 'Away at once!' "

"Well," said La Mole, "let each act on his own conviction. Do you go; I will remain."

Coconnas shrugged his shoulders and lay down on the grass. At the same moment, in the opposite direction to that which the queen had followed, but in the same road, there passed at great speed a troop of horsemen whom the two friends recognized as Protestants. They disappeared rapidly.

"*Peste!* the thing becomes serious," said Coconnas, rising. "Let us go to the Pavilion of François I."

"No," replied La Mole; "by no means. If we are discovered, the attention of the king will be especially directed toward the pavilion, as that is the general rendezvous."

"Well, this time perhaps you are right," grumbled Coconnas.

Hardly had these words been uttered when a horseman passed like a flash of lightning amid the trees, and leaping over ditches, bushes, briars, and all obstacles, reached the young men. He had a pistol in each hand, and guided his horse in his furious career with his knees only.

"M. de Mouy!" exclaimed Coconnas, uneasy, and now more on the alert than La Mole; "M. de Mouy flying! Is it a retreat, then?"

"Quick! quick!" cried the Huguenot; "away with you! All is lost! I have come round to tell you so. To horse and away!"

"And the queen?" cried La Mole.

But the voice of the young man was lost in space; Mouy was already too far away to hear him.

Coconnas had soon made up his mind. While La Mole remained motionless, following Mouy with his eyes as he disappeared among the branches, he hastened to the horses, and leaping on his own, threw the bridle of the other to La Mole, and prepared to dash off. "Come, come!" he exclaimed, "let us be off, as Mouy advises, and Mouy is a sensible man. Away, away, La Mole!"

"One moment," said La Mole; "we came here for something."

"Unless it is to get hanged," replied Coconnas, "I would advise you to lose no more time. When M. de Mouy de Saint-Phale flies, all the world may fly."

"M. de Mouy de Saint-Phale," said La Mole, "is not charged to carry off the Queen Marguerite! M. de Mouy de Saint-Phale does not love the Queen Marguerite."

"*Mordi!* and he is quite right too, if that love were to lead him into such follies as I see you are meditating. May five hundred thousand devils of hell take the love which is likely to cost the lives of two brave gentlemen! '*Corne de bœuf!*' as King Charles says, we are conspiring, my dear fellow; and when men conspire, they should make off at the right time. Mount, mount, La Mole!"

"Escape, my dear fellow; I do not hinder you—I even urge you. Your life is more valuable than mine; defend, then, your life."

"It were better to say, 'Coconnas, let us be hanged together,' and not, 'Coconnas, escape alone.'"

"Bah! my friend," replied La Mole, "the cord is made for vagabonds, and not for gentlemen like us."

"I begin to think," said Coconnas, with a sigh, "that the precaution I have taken is not bad."

"What is that?"

"To make a friend of the executioner."

"You are gloomy, Coconnas."

"But, in short, what are we to do?" said the latter, impatiently.

"We are going to find the queen."

"Where is she?"

"I don't know. We are to find the king."

"Where is he?"

"I don't know; but we shall find him, and shall do—we two—what fifty men have not been able, or have not dared to do."

"You appeal to my vanity, Hyacinthe; it is a bad sign."

"Well, well, let us, then, to horse and away!"

"That's right."

La Mole turned round to lay his hand on the pommel of his saddle; but at the moment when he put his foot in the stirrup, a voice of command was heard, saying, "Halt there! surrender!"

At the same moment the figure of a man was seen behind an oak, then another, then thirty; they were the light dragoons dismounted, who were making their way quietly, and searching the forest.

"What did I tell you?" muttered Coconnas.

A muffled groan was La Mole's reply.

The light dragoons were within thirty paces of the two friends.

"Well, gentlemen," said the Piedmontese, "what is your pleasure?"

The lieutenant ordered his men to take aim at the two friends.

Coconnas continued in a low tone. "Mount, La Mole! there is time enough. Jump into your saddle as I have seen you do it a hundred times, and let us be off." Then, turning to the light dragoons, "Eh! what the devil, gentlemen, don't fire; you might kill friends." Then to La Mole, "Through the trees! their aim must be bad. They will fire, and miss us."

"Impossible," said La Mole. "We cannot take with us

Marguerite's horse and the two mules. That horse and those mules would compromise her, while by my answers I will remove all suspicion. Go, my friend, go!"

"Gentlemen," said Coconnas, drawing his sword and raising it in the air, "we surrender."

The soldiers raised their muskets.

"But why are we summoned to surrender?"

"That you must ask of the King of Navarre."

"What crime have we committed?"

"M. d'Alençon will inform you."

Coconnas and La Mole looked at each other. The name of their enemy mentioned at such a moment was not reassuring. Yet neither of them made any resistance. Coconnas was desired to alight from his horse, a movement which he executed without a word; then they were both placed in the center of the light dragoons, and took the route to the Pavilion of François I.

"You wished to see the Pavilion of François," said Coconnas to La Mole, when they saw through the trees the walls of a pretty Gothic building; "well, it seems that you are likely to see it."

La Mole made no reply, but only extended his hand to Coconnas. By the side of this beautiful pavilion, built in the time of Louis XII, and which was called after François because he always made it a *rendezvous de chasse,* was a hut built for the huntsmen and prickers, and which was now nearly concealed by the muskets, halberds, and swords in front of it. The prisoners were conducted to this hut.

We will now throw a little light on the gloomy position of the two friends, by stating what had occurred. The Protestant gentlemen had assembled, as was agreed, in the Pavilion of François I, of which we know Mouy had the key. Masters of the forest, as they believed, they had placed sentinels here and there, whom the light dragoons, having exchanged their white scarfs for red ones (a precaution due to the ingenious zeal of M. de Nancey), had laid hands upon without striking a blow.

The light dragoons continued their quest, keeping a good watch over the pavilion; but Mouy, who, as we have seen, was awaiting the king at the end of the Allée des Violette, had seen these red scarfs stealing along, and instantly suspected them. He hastily concealed himself, and remarked the vast circle they made in order to beat the forest and hem in the place of rendezvous. At the same moment, at the bottom of the principal alley, he had seen the white aigrettes and bright arquebuses of the king's bodyguard, and then the king himself, while in the opposite direction he observed the King of Navarre. Then he had made a sign of a cross with his hat, which was the signal agreed upon to indicate that all was lost. At this signal the King of Navarre turned back, and rapidly disappeared. Then Mouy, digging the two large rowels of his spurs into the sides of his horse, fled like the wind, and as he fled, gave those words of advice to La Mole and Coconnas which we have mentioned.

Now, the king, having noticed the departure of Henri and Marguerite, had come up, escorted by D'Alençon, expecting to see them both come from the hut, where he had desired all to be shut up who were found, not only in the pavilion, but in the forest.

D'Alençon, full of confidence, galloped close by the king, whose severe pain increased his ill-humor. Twice or thrice he had nearly fainted, and once had vomited blood. "Quick, quick!" he said, when he arrived. "Make haste; I want to return to the Louvre. Draw these heretics out of their lair. This is Saint Blaise's day, and he was cousin to Saint Bartholomew."

At these words of the king, all the pikes and arquebuses were in motion, and they compelled the Huguenots arrested in the forest or the pavilion to come out of the hut one after the other. But the King of Navarre, Marguerite, and Mouy were not among them.

"Well," said the king, "where is Henri? Where is Margot? You promised them to me, D'Alençon, and, *corbœuf!* I must have them found."

"We have not seen the King and Queen of Navarre, Sire," said M. de Nancey.

"But here they come," observed Madame de Nevers.

And at the same moment, at the farther extremity of a path which led down to the river appeared Henri and Marguerite, both as calm as if nothing had happened—both with their falcons on their wrists, and lovingly side by side on their horses, as they galloped along, while their steeds, like themselves, seemed to be caressing each other.

It was then that D'Alençon, furious, commanded the forest to be searched, and that La Mole and Coconnas were discovered. They had reached the circle which the guards closed in; only, as they were not sovereigns, they could not assume so cool an appearance as Henri and Marguerite. La Mole was too pale, and Coconnas was too red.

CHAPTER 21

The Examinations

The spectacle which presented itself to the friends, as they entered, was one of those that are never forgotten, though seen but once and for an instant. As we have already said, Charles had anxiously observed each prisoner as, one by one, they left the hut, expecting, with an intensity of interest equal to that of D'Alençon, to see the King of Navarre come forth. Their expectation was disappointed. But that was not enough; they must know what had become of him.

When, therefore, Henri and Marguerite were seen approaching from the end of a path, a mortal paleness seized D'Alençon, while the breast of Charles seemed to expand; for instinctively he wished that all that his brother had constrained him to do might fall back on D'Alençon himself.

"He will escape again!" murmured François, turning pale.

But at this moment the king was seized with such excruciating pains, such spasmodic agony throughout his frame that pressing a hand on each side, he shrieked aloud like a delirious man.

Henri hastened toward him; but by the time he had crossed the space that separated them, the paroxysm had passed away.

"Whence come you, Monsieur?" inquired the king, with a sternness of manner that frightened Marguerite.

"Why, from the chase, my brother," she replied.

"The chase was on the riverbank, and not in the forest."

"Sire," said Henri, "my falcon suddenly struck down a pheasant, at the very time when we had stopped to see the heron."

"And where is the pheasant?"

"Here it is, Sire; a fine bird, is it not?" And Henri, with his most innocent manner, presented to Charles his bird with the plumage of purple, red, and gold.

4 4 7

"Ah, ah!" exclaimed Charles; "but why did you not rejoin me when you had secured the pheasant?"

"Because the bird had directed his flight toward the park, Sire; so that when we returned to the river's side, we saw you more than a mile off, proceeding toward the forest. So we galloped after you, for since we belonged to your Majesty's hunting party, we didn't like to lose it."

"And were all these gentlemen invited also?" inquired Charles.

"What gentlemen?" inquired Henri, casting a look of inquiry around him.

"Eh, *pardieu!*" exclaimed Charles; "why, your Huguenot friends. They certainly have not been invited by me."

"No, Sire," answered Henri, "but perhaps they come at the bidding of M. d'Alençon."

"Mine?" said the Duc d'Alençon.

"Why, yes, Brother," returned Henri; "did you not announce yourself yesterday as King of Navarre? Well, the Huguenots who have sought you for their king have come to thank you for accepting the crown, and the king for giving it. Is it not so, gentlemen?"

"Yes, yes!" shouted a number of voices. "Long live the Duc d'Alençon! long live King Charles!"

"I am not King of the Huguenots!" said François, white with rage; and looking stealthily at Charles, he added, "And trust I never shall be!"

"No matter," interposed Charles; "you know, Henri, that I look upon this as very strange."

"Sire," cried the King of Navarre, firmly, "it looks—God forgive me!—as if I were undergoing an examination!"

"And if it were so, how would you answer?"

"That I am a king like yourself," replied Henri, proudly, "for it is not the crown, but birth, that confers royalty; and that I will answer to my brother and to my friend, but never to my judge."

"I only wish," muttered Charles, "that for once in my life I could hit upon what it was right to do."

"M. de Mouy is doubtless among those persons secured," cried the Duc d'Alençon. "Let him be brought before your Majesty; we shall then know all we require."

"Is M. de Mouy among the prisoners?" inquired the king.

Henri felt a momentary uneasiness, and exchanged glances with Marguerite; but it was of short duration.

No voice answered to the inquiry after Mouy.

"He is not among the parties arrested," said M. de Nancey; "some of my men fancy they saw him, but no one is certain on the subject."

An oath escaped from the lips of D'Alençon.

"Ha!" cried Marguerite, pointing to La Mole and Coconnas, who had heard all that had passed, and on whose wit and intelligence she felt she might reckon; "here, Sire, are two gentlemen in the service of M. d'Alençon. Question them; they will reply."

The duke felt the blow.

"I had them arrested purposely, to be enabled to prove that they neither of them belonged to me," answered the duke.

The king contemplated the two friends, and started at seeing La Mole again.

"Oh! oh! still that Provençal," said he.

Coconnas gracefully saluted.

"What were you doing when you were arrested?" asked Charles.

"Sire, we were planning deeds of love and war."

"What, with horses ready saddled, armed to the teeth, and every preparation made for flight?"

"Not so, Sire," replied Coconnas; "your Majesty is misinformed. We were lying beneath a sheltering beech, *sub tegmine fagi,* and might easily have ridden away had we entertained the slightest suspicion that we had been so unfortunate as to offend your Majesty. Now, gentlemen," continued he, turning toward the light-horsemen, "say candidly and fairly, on your honor as soldiers, could we or could we not have escaped, had such been our desire?"

"The fact is," answered the lieutenant, "that neither of these cavaliers made the slightest attempt at flight."

"Because their horses were too far off," said the Duc d'Alençon.

"Your pardon, Monseigneur," responded Coconnas, "but mine was under me, and my friend, Comte Lerac de la Mole, held his by the bridle."

"Is this true, gentlemen?" asked the king.

"It is true, Sire," replied the lieutenant; "upon seeing us approach, M. de Coconnas even got off his horse."

Coconnas looked at the king with a grim smile that seemed to say, "There, you see!"

"But what did all those led horses, those mules laden with cases and packages, signify, then?" asked François.

"How can we tell you?" replied Coconnas; "we are neither grooms nor squires. Ask these questions of the varlet who had charge of them."

"He is not to be found!" exclaimed the duke, furious.

"Most likely he was frightened and ran away," retorted Coconnas; "one cannot expect a clown to have the self-possession of a gentleman."

"Still the same system," said D'Alençon, grinding his teeth. "Fortunately, Sire, I told you beforehand that neither of these persons had been in my service for some days past."

"Is it possible," cried Coconnas, "that I have the misfortune no longer to form part of your Highness's retinue?"

"*Morbleu!* Monsieur, you know that better than anyone, since you yourself gave in your dismissal in a letter so impertinent that I have thought it proper to preserve it, and happily have it about me."

"Oh!" said Coconnas, "I hoped that your Highness had forgiven me for writing that letter under an impulse of vexation. I had just learned that your Highness had endeavored to strangle my friend La Mole in one of the corridors of the Louvre."

"What is that he says?" interrupted the king.

"At first I thought your Highness was alone in the affair; but afterwards I learned that three other persons—"

"Silence!" exclaimed Charles, "we have heard enough." Then, turning to the King of Navarre, he said, "Henri, your word not to escape?"

"I give it to your Majesty."

"Return to Paris with M. de Nancey, and remain in your chamber under arrest. As for you, Messieurs," continued he, speaking to the two friends, "give up your swords."

La Mole looked at Marguerite, who smiled; the young man immediately delivered his sword to the nearest officer, Coconnas following his friend's example.

"Has M. de Mouy been found?" inquired the king.

"No, Sire," answered M. de Nancey; "either he was not in the forest, or he has escaped."

"So much the worse," rejoined Charles; "but let us return to Paris. I am cold, and my head seems dizzy."

" 'Tis anger that excites you, Sire," observed François.

"It may be; but my eyes seem troubled. Where are the prisoners? I cannot distinguish anything. Is it so soon dark? Oh, mercy! help! help! I die! I die!"

So saying, the unfortunate king let go the reins of his horse, and fell backwards, wildly stretching forth his hands; while his terrified courtiers, alarmed at this sudden seizure, supported him.

Standing apart from the clustering nobles, François wiped the cold drops from his brow; for he alone of all the company knew the cause of Charles's violent attack. On the other side, the King of Navarre, already under the guard of M. de Nancey, looked on with increasing astonishment. "Eh! eh!" he murmured with that wonderful intuition which sometimes made him a man inspired, so to speak, "am I to find myself fortunate in being arrested in my flight?" He looked at Margot, whose eyes, dilated by surprise, wandered from him to the king, and from the king to him.

This time the king became insensible. A litter was brought, and he being extended on it was covered with a cloak taken from the shoulders of one of his attendants. The melancholy procession then proceeded toward Paris in a very different frame of mind from that in which it had departed thence in the morning. Then, a merry, jocund party had set forth, consisting of conspirators whose hearts beat high with hope, and a joyous monarch, promising himself many such days of princely enjoyment; their return displayed a dying king surrounded by rebel prisoners.

Marguerite, who throughout all this had not for an instant lost her self-possession, gave her husband a look of intelligence, then, passing so close to La Mole that he was enabled to catch the two brief words she uttered, she said, *"Mé déidé"* ("Fear nothing").

"What did she say?" asked Coconnas.

"She told me to fear nothing."

"So much the worse," murmured the Piedmontese; "so much the worse. It means that we are in a bad predicament. Every time when that word has been addressed to me encouragingly, I have received at the same moment a bullet somewhere, a sword thrust in my body, or a pot of flowers on my head. 'Fear nothing,' whether spoken in Hebrew, Greek, Latin, or French, I always understand to mean, 'Look out, down there!' "

"Now, gentlemen," exclaimed the captain of light-horse, "we are ready to start."

"Would it be a liberty," inquired Coconnas, "to ask where we are going?"

"I believe to Vincennes," replied the lieutenant.

"I would rather be going anywhere else," answered Coconnas; "but people are sometimes obliged to do things against their will."

The king recovered his senses during the journey, and even a portion of his strength. He declared himself equal to remounting his horse, but that was not permitted.

"Let Maître Ambroise Paré be immediately summoned," said Charles, as he reached the Louvre. Then, descending from his litter, he walked slowly toward his apartments, leaning on the arm of Tavannes, and strictly forbidding anyone to follow him.

All had observed his extreme gravity of look and manner. During the journey homewards he had appeared lost in reflection, not addressing a word to those around him. Still it was evident that the recently discovered conspiracy was not the subject of his thoughts, but that he was solely occupied with his own illness—a malady so strange, so sudden and severe, the symptoms of which reminded the spectators of those observed in the last sickness of François II.

Arrived in his chamber, Charles seated himself on a species of lounge, and supported his head on the cushions; then reflecting that there might be some little delay before the arrival of Maître Ambroise Paré, he determined to utilize his time while waiting. He clapped his hands; a guard appeared.

"Let the King of Navarre be informed that I desire to speak with him," said Charles.

The man bowed and departed.

The king was visited by a repetition of the distressing sufferings he had previously undergone. His head fell back; his ideas were crowded and confused till he could not separate one from the other; a sort of blood-colored vapor seemed to float before his eyes; his mouth was parched, and he had already, without quenching his thirst, emptied a carafe of water. During the almost lethargic state into which he had sunk, a sudden noise was heard of approaching footsteps; the door rolled back on its hinges, and Henri entered. M. de Nancey was following him, but remained in the antechamber. The King of Navarre waited until the door was closed behind him, and then went forward. "You sent for me, Sire," said he. "I am here."

The sound of the well-known voice effectively roused Charles, who, raising his languid head mechanically, held out his hand to Henri.

"Sire," observed Henri, whose hands remained at his sides, "your Majesty forgets that I am no longer your brother, but your prisoner."

"True, true," answered Charles, "and I thank you for having reminded me of it; but was there not also some promise on your part to answer me frankly when we should be alone?"

"I am ready to keep that promise. Question me, Sire."

The king poured some water into the palm of his hand and applied it to his temples. "First, then," said he, "tell me truly, Henri, how much of the charge brought against you by the Duc d'Alençon is true?"

"Half of it only. It was M. d'Alençon who was to have fled, and I who was to have accompanied him."

"And why should you have done so, Henri? Are you dissatisfied with my conduct toward you?"

"Far from it, Sire. Your Majesty is all goodness; and that God who reads the hearts of men sees in mine the deep affection I bear to my brother and my king."

"Yet," said Charles, "it seems to me not natural to fly from those we love, and who love us."

"So," said Henri, "I was not flying from those who love me, but from those who hate me. Am I permitted to speak openly?"

"Speak, Monsieur."

"Those here who hate me, Sire, are M. d'Alençon and the queen-mother."

"As for M. d'Alençon, I will not say you are wrong; but the queen-mother loads you with attentions."

"And it is precisely for that reason that I mistrust her; and a very good thing it is I was on my guard."

"Against the queen-mother?"

"Ay, the queen-mother, or those who are about her. You know that the misfortune of kings, Sire, is not always in being served too inefficiently; it sometimes consists in being served with too much zeal."

"Explain yourself. You have engaged yourself to tell me everything."

"Your Majesty wishes me to do so?"

"Continue."

"Your Majesty loves me, you have said?"

"That is to say, I did love you before your treason, Henriot."

"Let us suppose that you love me still, Sire."

"Very well."

"If you love me you will wish me to live, will you not?"

"I should have been in despair had misfortune overtaken you."

"Well, Sire, on two occasions your Majesty has barely escaped falling into despair."

"How is that?"

"Yes, for twice Providence alone saved my life. It is true that on the second occasion Providence assumed the features of your Majesty."

"And in what form did Providence appear on the first occasion?"

"In that of a man who would be astonished at finding himself identified with Providence—that of René. Yes; you, Sire, saved me from death by steel—"

Charles frowned, for he remembered the night when he had taken Henriot to the Rue des Barres. "And René?" he said.

"René saved me from death by poison."

"You are lucky, Henriot," said the king, attempting a smile, which sudden pain changed to a nervous contraction; "it is not his business."

"Two miracles, then, have saved me, Sire—a miracle of repentance on the part of the Florentine, a miracle of goodness on your part. Well, I confess to your Majesty my fear that Heaven may grow weary of working miracles, and I have wished to flee in obedience to the maxim, 'Help yourself, and Heaven will help you.' "

"Why have you not told me this before, Henri?"

"Had I said these words to you yesterday, I should have been an informer."

"And in saying them today?"

"Today it is another matter; I am accused, and I defend myself."

"Are you sure about that first attempt, Henriot?"

"As sure as of the second."

"And they really tried to poison you?"

"They attempted it."

"With what?"

"With an opiate."

"And how can one poison with an opiate?"

"Well, Sire, ask René. They can poison even with gloves."

Charles bent his brows; but by degrees the frown disappeared. "Yes, yes," he said, as if talking to himself, "it is the nature of created beings to flee from death; why, then, should not intelligence do what is done by instinct?"

"Well, Sire," said Henri, "have I been frank enough for you, and are you satisfied that I have told you all?"

"Yes, Henriot, yes; and you are a brave fellow. And you think, then, that your enemies have not given up, and that new attempts will be made against you?"

"Sire, every evening I am surprised to find myself still alive."

"It is because they know that I love you, Henriot, that they wish to kill you; but make yourself quite easy. They shall be punished for their evil intentions; meanwhile, you are free."

"Free to leave Paris?" asked Henri.

"No, no! you are well aware I cannot possibly do without you. Thousand names of a devil! I must have someone who loves me."

"Then if your Majesty prefers keeping me with you, at least grant me one favor."

"What is that?"

"Not to entertain me as a friend, but to detain me as a prisoner."

"A prisoner?"

"Eh! yes. Does not your Majesty see that it is your friendship that ruins me?"

"And you would prefer my hatred?"

"An apparent hatred, Sire. That hatred will save me. Let them see me in disgrace, and they will not care so much to see me dead."

"Henriot," said Charles, "I don't know what you wish—I

don't know what purpose you have in view; but if your wishes are not fulfilled, if you fail in accomplishing your purpose, I shall be much surprised."

"I may, then, rely on the severity of the king?"

"Yes."

"Then I shall be less uneasy. But what are your Majesty's orders?"

"Return to your apartments, Henriot. As for me, I am suffering. I will see my dogs, and go to bed."

"Sire," said Henri, "your Majesty should summon a physician. Your illness is perhaps more serious than you think."

"I have sent for Maître Ambroise Paré."

"Then I shall retire more satisfied."

"Upon my soul," said the king, "I verily believe that of all my family you are the only person who really loves me!"

"Is such your opinion, Sire?"

"Yes, upon my word."

"Very well. Give me in charge to M. de Nancey as a man to whom your anger allows only a month to live; it is a way to provide for my loving you a long time."

"M. de Nancey!" cried Charles.

The captain of the guards entered.

"M. de Nancey," said Charles, "I here commit to your keeping the most guilty man in my kingdom; you will answer for him with your life."

The officer bowed low; and with an air of consternation Henri followed him from the apartment.

CHAPTER 22

Actæon

Charles was alone, and much astonished not to have seen either of his faithful attendants—his nurse Madelon and his greyhound Actæon.

"Nurse has gone to sing her psalms with some Huguenot of her acquaintance," he said to himself; "and Actælon is still angry with me for the blow I gave him with my whip this morning."

Charles then took a wax candle and went into the nurse's apartment. She was not there, and he passed on into his armory; but as he went forward, a violent illness, such as he had already experienced, suddenly seized him. He suffered as if his entrails were perforated with a hot iron; an unquenchable thirst consumed him, and seeing a cup of milk on the table, he swallowed it at a draught. He then felt somewhat easier, and entered the armory. To his great astonishment, Actælon did not come to meet him. Had he been shut up? In that case he would have known that his master had returned from hunting, and would have howled to rejoin him.

Charles called, whistled; the animal did not appear. He advanced four paces, and as the light of the wax candle threw its beams to a corner of the cabinet, he saw a large mass extended on the floor. "Holloa, Actælon, holloa!" said he, whistling again.

The dog did not move. Charles hastened forward and touched him; the poor brute was stiff and cold. From his throat, contracted by pain, several drops of bile had fallen, mingled with a foamy and bloody slaver. The dog had found in the cabinet an old cap of his master's, and had died with his head resting on something that represented a friend.

At this spectacle, which made him forget his own sufferings, and restored to him all his energy, rage boiled in Charles's veins. He would have cried out, but encompassed in their greatness as they

457

are, kings are not free to yield to that first impulse in passion or in danger. He reflected that there might be some treason here, and was silent.

Charles knelt before his dog, and examined the dead carcass with an experienced eye. The eye was glassy, the tongue red, and covered with pustules; it was a strange disease, and made Charles shudder. He put on his gloves, opened the livid lips of the dog to examine the teeth, and remarked in the interstices some white-looking fragments clinging about the points of his sharp teeth. He took these fragments out, and at once saw that they were paper; near where the paper was, the inflammation was more violent, the gums were more swollen, and the skin appeared as if eaten by vitriol.

Charles looked around him attentively. On the carpet were lying several pieces of paper similar to that which he had already found in the dog's throat; one of the bits, larger than the others, presented the marks of an engraving on wood. Charles's hair stood erect on his head; he recognized a fragment of the engraving which represented a gentleman hawking, and it was that which Actælon had torn out of his book of venery.

"Ah," said he, turning pale, "the book was poisoned!" Then, suddenly calling up his recollections, "Thousand devils! I touched every page with my finger; and at every page I raised my finger to my lips to moisten it. These faintings—these pains—these vomitings! I am a dead man!" He remained for an instant motionless under the weight of this frightful idea; then, raising himself with a hoarse groan, he went hastily toward the door. "Let someone go instantly and with all dispatch," he cried, "to Maître René, and bring him here in ten minutes. Let one of you mount a horse and lead another one, that you may return the sooner. If Maître Ambroise Paré arrives, desire him to wait."

A guard started off on the run to obey the king's commands.

"Ah," muttered Charles, "if I put everybody to the torture, I will learn who gave this book to Henriot!" and with the perspiration on his brow, his hands clenched, his breast heaving, Charles remained with his eyes fixed on the body of his dead dog. Ten minutes afterwards, the Florentine rapped timidly and with some uneasiness at the king's door. There are certain consciences to which the sky is never clear.

"Enter!" said Charles.

The perfumer appeared. Charles went toward him with an imperious air and compressed lip.

"Your Majesty desired to see me," said René, trembling.

"You are a skillful chemist, are you not?"

"Sire—"

"And know all that the most skillful doctors know!"

"Your Majesty is pleased to flatter me."

"No, my mother tells me so; and, besides, I have confidence in you, and would rather consult you than anyone else. Look!" he continued, pointing to the carcass of the dead dog; "I beg you to look at that animal's mouth, and tell me of what death he has died."

While René, with a wax candle in his hand, was stooping down to the ground, as much to hide his emotion as to obey the king, Charles, standing up, with his eyes fixed on him, awaited with a feverish expectation easily to be imagined, the reply which would be his sentence of death or his assurance of safety.

René drew a kind of scalpel from his pocket, opened it, and with the point detached from the dog's mouth the morsels of paper adhering to the gums, looking long and attentively at the bile and blood exuding from the sore spots.

"Sire," he said in a tremulous voice, "here are very sad symptoms."

Charles felt an icy shudder run through his veins, and to his very heart. "Yes," he exclaimed; "the dog has been poisoned, has he not?"

"I fear so, Sire."

"And with what sort of poison?"

"I think a mineral poison."

"Can you ascertain to a certainty whether or not he has been poisoned?"

"Yes, on opening and examining the stomach."

"Open it, then; I wish the matter to be settled beyond doubt."

"I must call someone to assist me."

"I will assist you," said Charles. "If he has been poisoned, what symptoms shall we find?"

"Red blotches and herborizations in the stomach."

"Come, then, to work!"

René, with one stroke of the scalpel, opened the hound's body, while Charles, with one knee on the ground, held the light with a clenched and convulsive hand.

"See, Sire," said René; "see, here are evident traces. Here are the red blotches I mentioned; and these veins, turgid with blood, resembling the roots of certain plants, are what I meant by herborizations. I find here every symptom I anticipated."

"So the dog was poisoned?"

"Unquestionably, Sire."

"With mineral poison?"

"According to every appearance."

"And what would be a man's symptoms who by accident had swallowed such poison?"

"Great pains in the head, a feeling of burning in the stomach, as if he had swallowed hot coals, pains in the bowels, and vomiting."

"Would he be thirsty?" asked Charles.

"Parchingly thirsty."

" 'Tis so, then; 'tis so, then," muttered the king.

"Sire, I search in vain for the object of all these inquiries."

"Why search for it? You have no need to know. Only answer my questions."

"Let your Majesty question me."

"What is the antidote to administer to a man who had swallowed the same substance as my dog?"

René reflected an instant. "There are many mineral poisons," he replied; "and I should like to know precisely to what poison the inquiry relates. Has your Majesty any idea of the mode in which the poison was conveyed to the dog?"

"Yes," said Charles; "he has eaten the leaf of a book."

"The leaf of a book?"

"Yes."

"And has your Majesty that book?"

"Here it is," was Charles's answer, taking the hunting book from the shelf where he had placed it, and handing it to René. René gave a start of surprise, which did not escape the king's notice.

"He has eaten a leaf of this book?" stammered René.

"Yes, this one"; and Charles pointed out the torn leaf.

"Allow me to tear out another, Sire."

"Do so."

René tore out a leaf and held it to the wax candle. When it was lighted a strong smell of garlic diffused itself through the apartment. "He has been poisoned with a preparation of arsenic," he said.

"You are sure?"

"As if I had prepared it myself."

"And the antidote?"

René shook his head.

"What!" said Charles, in a hoarse voice, "do you know no remedy?"

"The best and most efficacious is white of eggs beaten in milk; but—"

"But what?"

"It must be instantly administered; if not—"

"If not—"

"It is a terrible poison, Sire," replied René.

"Yet it does not kill at once?" said Charles.

"No, but it kills surely—no matter how long the person is in dying, though sometimes that may be reduced to a calculation."

Charles leaned on the marble table. "Now," said he, touching René on the shoulder, "you know this book."

"I, Sire?" replied René, turning pale.

"Yes, you; for you betrayed yourself when you saw it."

"Sire, I swear to you—"

"Listen to me, René, and listen attentively. You poisoned the Queen of Navarre with gloves; you poisoned the Prince de Porcian with the smoke of a lamp; you tried to poison M. de Condé with a scented apple. René, I will have your flesh torn off your bones, shred by shred, with red-hot pincers, if you do not tell me to whom this book belongs."

The Florentine saw that he must not trifle with Charles's anger, and resolved to reply with audacity. "And if I tell the truth, Sire, who will guarantee me from not being more cruelly tortured than if I hold my tongue?"

"I will."

"Will you give me your royal word?"

"On my honor as a gentleman, your life shall be spared," said the king.

"Then this book belongs to me."

"To you?" replied Charles, starting, and gazing on him with bewildered eye.

"Yes, to me."

"And how did it leave your hands?"

"Her Majesty the queen-mother took it from my house."

"The queen-mother?" exclaimed Charles.

"Yes."

"And with what intention?"

"With the intention, as I believe, of having it sent to the King of Navarre, who had asked the Duc d'Alençon for a book of this description, that he might study hawking."

"Ah!" said Charles, "and is that it? I understand it all. This book, indeed, was in Henriot's chamber. There is a destiny, and I submit to it."

At this moment Charles was seized with a dry and violent cough, followed by another attack of pain in the stomach; he uttered two or three stifled groans, and fell back in his chair.

"What ails you, Sire?" asked René, alarmed.

"Nothing," said Charles, "except great thirst. Give me something to drink."

René poured out a glass of water, and presented it to Charles, who swallowed it at a draught. "Now," said he, taking a pen, and dropping it into the ink, "write in this book."

"What shall I write?"

"What I dictate: 'This book on hawking was given by me to the queen-mother, Catherine de Médicis. RENE.' "

The Florentine wrote and signed as he was commanded.

"You promised my life should be saved," said René.

"And on my part, I will keep my word."

"But," said René, "as to the queen-mother?"

"Oh," replied Charles, "that I have nothing to do with. If you are attacked, defend yourself."

"Sire, may I quit France when I find my life menaced?"

"I will reply to that in two weeks."

"But in the meantime——"

Charles bent his brows, and placed his finger on his livid lips.

"Rely on me, Sire," said René, who, too happy to escape so well, bowed, and left the room.

On René's departure the nurse appeared at her chamber door. "What is the matter, my Charlot?" she inquired.

"Nurse, I have been walking in the dew, and it has made me ill."

"You look very pale, Charlot."

"And feel very weak. Give me your arm, Nurse, as far as the bed"; and leaning on her, Charles went to his chamber.

"Now," said Charles, "I will put myself to bed without assistance."

"And if Maître Ambroise Paré comes?"

"You must tell him I am better and do not want him."

"But meanwhile what will you take?"

"Oh, a very simple medicine—whites of eggs beaten in milk. By the way, Nurse, poor Actælon is dead; tomorrow morning have him buried in a corner of the garden of the Louvre. He was one of my best friends, and I will raise a tomb over him—if I have time."

CHAPTER 23

Vincennes

According to the order given by Charles IX, Henri was the same evening conducted to Vincennes, that famous castle of which only a fragment now remains, but a fragment colossal enough to give an idea of its past grandeur.

At the postern of the prison they stopped. M. de Nancey alighted from his horse, opened the gate closed with a padlock, and respectfully invited the king to follow him. Henri obeyed without a word of reply. Every abode seemed to him safer than the Louvre, and ten doors closing on him were ten doors between him and Catherine de Médicis.

The royal prisoner crossed the drawbridge between two soldiers, passed the three doors at the ground floor and the three doors at the foot of the staircase, and then, still preceded by M. de Nancey, went up one flight of stairs. Arrived there, the captain of the guards, seeing that Henri was about to ascend still higher, said to him, "Monseigneur, halt!"

"Ah, ah!" said Henri, pausing; "it seems they will honor me with a place on the first floor."

"Sire," said M. de Nancey, "you will be treated as a crowned king."

"The devil!" said Henri to himself; "two or three stories higher would have been no humiliation to me. I shall be too comfortable here. They will surely suspect something."

"Is your Majesty willing to follow me?" said M. de Nancey.

"Ventre-saint-gris!" said the King of Navarre, "Monsieur, here there is no question of what I wish or do not wish; the question is, what does my brother Charles order? Does he order me to follow you?"

"Yes, Sire."

"In that case I follow you, Monsieur."

They entered a sort of corridor, at the extremity of which was a very large and gloomy chamber; Henri looked round him with considerable disquietude. "Where are we?" he inquired.

"In the chamber of torture, Monseigneur."

"Ah, ah!" replied the king; and he looked around with more interest.

There was a little of everything in this chamber—pitchers and trestles for the torture by water; wedges and mallets for the torture of the boot; moreover, there were stone benches for the unhappy wretches who awaited the torture, nearly all round the chamber; and above these seats, below them and on a level with them, were iron rings mortised into the walls.

"Ah, ah!" said Henri; "shall we soon reach my apartment?"

"Yes, Monseigneur; and here it is," said a figure in the dark, who approached and became distinguishable.

Henri thought he recognized the voice, and advancing, said, "Ah, is it you, Beaulieu? And what the devil are you doing here?"

"Sire, I have just been appointed governor of the fortress of Vincennes."

"Well, my dear friend, your début does you honor; a king for a prisoner is no bad beginning."

"Pardon me, Sire, but before I received you I had already received two gentlemen."

"Who may they be? Ah, your pardon! Perhaps I commit an indiscretion?"

"Monseigneur, I have not been bound to secrecy. They are M. de la Mole and M. de Coconnas."

"Ah, it is true; I saw them arrested, those poor gentlemen. And how do they sustain their great misfortune?"

"Very differently, Sire; the one is gay, the other sad—one sings, the other groans."

"And which of them groans?"

"M. de la Mole, Sire."

"Faith!" said Henri. "I understand better him who groans than him who sings. After what I have seen of it the prison doesn't seem to me very gay. And in what story are they lodged?"

"High up; on the fourth floor."

Henri sighed. It was there he wished to be.

"Now, then, M. de Beaulieu," said Henri, "have the kindness to show me my chamber. I am desirous of reaching it, as I am very much fatigued with my day's toil."

"Here, Monseigneur," said Beaulieu, showing Henri an open door.

"Number two!" said Henri, "and why not number one?"

"Because it is reserved, Monseigneur."

"Ah, ah! It appears, then, that you expect a prisoner of higher rank than mine."

"I have not said, Monseigneur, that it is a prisoner."

"And who is it, then?"

"I beg, Monseigneur, that you will not insist; for I shall be compelled to fail, by keeping silence, in the obedience which I owe you."

"Ah, that is another thing," said Henri, and he became even more pensive. He wondered who was to occupy number 1.

The governor, with a thousand apologies, installed Henri in his apartment, made many excuses for his deficiencies, and placing two soldiers at the door, retired.

"Now," said the governor, addressing the turnkey, "let us visit the others."

The turnkey preceded him, and traversing the hall of inquisition, they again passed through the corridor, and reached the staircase. M. de Beaulieu followed his guide up three pairs of stairs. On reaching the fourth story the turnkey opened successively three doors, each ornamented with two locks and three enormous bolts. He had scarcely touched the third door when they heard a joyous voice which exclaimed, "Eh, *mordi!* open, if it be only to give us a little air! Your stove is so warm that it stifles me here." And Coconnas, whom the reader has recognized by his favorite oath, made a bound to the door.

"One moment, my gentleman," said the turnkey; "I have not come to let you out, but to come in to you with the governor."

"Monsieur the Governor does me great honor," replied Coconnas, "and is most welcome."

M. de Beaulieu then entered, and extinguished Coconnas's cordial smile by one of those icy politenesses which belong to governors of fortresses, jailers, and executioners.

"Have you any money, Monsieur?" he inquired of his prisoner.

"I!" replied Coconnas. "Not a crown."

"Jewels?"

"I have a ring."

"Allow me to search you."

"Mordi!" cried Coconnas, reddening with anger.

"We must suffer everything for the service of the king!"

"Humph!" replied the Piedmontese, "they who rob on the Pont Neuf are, then, like you, in the service of the king. *Mordi!* I have been unjust, Monsieur; for until now I had taken them for thieves."

"Monsieur, good day!" said Beaulieu. "Jailer, lock the door!"

The governor went away, taking with him the ring—a beautiful emerald which Madame de Nevers had given to Coconnas to remind him of the color of her eyes. "Now for the other," he said, as he went out.

They crossed an empty apartment, and the game of three doors, six locks, and nine bolts was played all over again. The last door being opened, a sigh was the first sound that saluted the visitors. The chamber was even more gloomy than the one which M. de Beaulieu had just left. La Mole was seated in a corner, his head resting on his hand, and in spite of the visit and the visitors, was as motionless as if he did not observe them.

"Good evening, M. de la Mole," said Beaulieu.

The young man raised his head slowly.

"Good evening, Monsieur," he replied.

"Monsieur," continued Beaulieu, "I have come to search you."

"It is useless," replied La Mole; "I will give you all I have."

"What have you?"

"About three hundred crowns, these jewels, these rings." La Mole turned out his pockets, stripped his fingers, and took the clasp out of his hat.

"Have you nothing more?"

"Not that I know of."

"And that silk cord round your neck, what may that be?" asked the governor.

"Monsieur, it is not a jewel; it is a relic."

"You must give it to me."

"What! You require—"

"I am commanded to leave you only your garments, and a relic is not a garment."

La Mole made a movement of anger, which, in contrast with the melancholy and dignified manner which distinguished him, was especially impressive to those men accustomed to boisterous emotions. But he recovered himself almost immediately. "Very well, Monsieur," he said, "you shall see the thing you have demanded"; then turning away, as if to approach the light, he unfastened the pretended relic, which was in fact a medallion containing a portrait. The latter he took out of its case, pressed it to his lips, and having kissed it many times, pretended to drop it accidentally, and placing the heel of his boot upon it, crushed it to atoms.

"Monsieur!" said the governor, and he stooped to see if he could save from the ruin the unknown object which La Mole sought to keep from him; but the portrait was literally in powder.

"The king wished to have that trinket," said La Mole, "but he had no right to the portrait which it contained. Here, then, is the medallion; take it."

"Monsieur," said Beaulieu, "I shall complain to the king." And without taking leave of his prisoner in a single word, he withdrew, so angry that he left the turnkey to fasten the doors. The jailer took a few steps as if to go out, and observing that M. de Beaulieu had already descended several stairs, he said, turning to La Mole, "Faith, Monsieur, it was very well you gave me the hundred crowns at once, for which I am to give you leave to see and talk with your companion; for if you had not, the governor would have taken them with the other three hundred, and my conscience would then not have allowed me to do anything for you. But I have been paid in advance, and have promised you shall see your comrade, and an honest man always keeps his word. Only if you can avoid it, for your own sake as well as mine, do not talk politics."

La Mole came forth from his apartment, and found himself face-to-face with Coconnas who was walking up and down the flags of the intermediate chamber. The two friends threw themselves into each other's arms. The jailer pretended to wipe the corner of his eye, and then withdrew, to see that the prisoners were not surprised by anyone—or rather, to see that he himself was not surprised.

"Ah, here you are!" said Coconnas. "Has that brute of a governor visited you?"

"Yes, and you too, I presume?"

"And taken everything from you?"

"And from you too, eh?"

"Oh, I had not much—only a ring Henriette gave me."

"And money?"

"I had given all I possessed to that brave jailer to induce him to procure us this interview."

"Ah!" said La Mole, "it seems that he receives with both hands."

"You have also paid him?"

"I have paid him a hundred crowns."

"Better for us that our jailer should be a mercenary wretch."

"Certainly, we can make him do as we please, for money; and that, I trust, will not be lacking."

"Have you any idea what has happened?"

"Perfectly; we have been betrayed."

"By that scoundrelly Duc d'Alençon. I should have been right to twist his neck, you see."

"And do you think our position is serious?"

"I am afraid so."

"Then we may have to anticipate—the torture?"

"I will not hide from you that I have already thought so."

"And what shall you do in that case?"

"And you?"

"I shall be silent," replied La Mole, with a fevered blush, "if I can."

"And I," said Coconnas, "will tell them a few things."

"What things?" asked La Mole, eagerly.

"Oh, be easy; things that will prevent M. d'Alençon from sleeping quietly for some time."

La Mole was about to reply, when the jailer, who no doubt heard some noise, came suddenly into the chamber, and pushing each into his respective dungeon, locked them in again.

CHAPTER 24

The Figure of Wax

For a week Charles was confined to his bed by a slow fever, interrupted by fits like epilepsy. During these attacks his cries were terrible; then, when they were over, he sank back exhausted into the arms of his nurse. Henri was shut up in his chamber at the prison, and at his own request to Charles, no one was allowed to see him, not even Marguerite. It was, in the view of all, a complete disgrace. Catherine and D'Alençon breathed more freely, thinking him lost, and Henri ate and drank more at his ease, hoping he was forgotten. At court no one suspected the real cause of the king's illness. Maître Ambroise Paré and Mazille, his colleague, believed it to be inflammation of the coats of the stomach, and had prescribed a regimen which aided the operation of the drink prescribed by René, and which Charles received thrice a day from the hands of his nurse; it was the only nourishment he took.

La Mole and Coconnas were at Vincennes in close confinement. Marguerite and Madame de Nevers had made several attempts to see them or to send them a letter, but in vain.

One morning Charles felt rather better, and ordered that the court should be admitted. The doors were accordingly opened; and it was easy to see by his pale cheeks and the feverish glare of his eyes what great ravages disease had made on the young king. The royal chamber was soon filled with courtiers, curious and interested.

Catherine, D'Alençon, and Marguerite were informed that the king gave audience. They entered nearly at the same time—Catherine calm, D'Alençon smiling, Marguerite dejected. Catherine sat down by the side of the bed without remarking the look Charles gave her; D'Alençon stood at the foot; Marguerite leaned against a table. On seeing her brother thus worn by illness, she could not repress a sigh and a tear.

Charles, whom nothing escaped, saw the tear and heard the sigh, and made a motion of his head to Marguerite, unseen by all but her. This sign, slight as it was, gave courage to the poor queen, to whom Henri had not had time or perhaps had not chosen to say anything. She feared for her husband; she trembled for her lover. For herself she had no fear; she knew La Mole too well not to feel that she might fully rely upon him.

"Well, my dear son," said Catherine, "how are you now?"

"Better, Madame, better."

"And what say the physicians?"

"Oh, my physicians, they are very clever fellows," cried Charles, bursting into a discordant laugh; "I have great amusement in listening to their discussions about my malady."

"What my brother wants," observed François, "is to take the fresh air. The chase, which he is so fond of, would do him good."

"And yet," replied Charles, with a singular smile, "the last did me a great deal of harm."

Then, with an inclination of his head, he signified to the courtiers that the audience was at an end. D'Alençon bowed and withdrew. Marguerite seized Charles's wasted hand and kissed it tenderly, then left the apartment.

"Dear Margot!" murmured Charles.

Catherine remained; and Charles, seeing her alone with him, recoiled as if from a serpent. He knew to whom and to what his death was attributable. "Why do you stay, Madame?" asked he, with a shudder.

"I wish to speak to you of important matters, my son," returned Catherine.

"Speak, Madame," said Charles.

"Sire, you said just now that your doctors are very skillful."

"I say so still."

"But what have they done since you have been ill?"

"Nothing, that is true; but if you could have heard what they have said! In fact, Madame, one might wish to be ill only to have the opportunity of hearing so learned dissertations."

"Well, I suspect that clever as they are, they know nothing at all about your disorder."

"Really, Madame?"

"And that they treat the symptoms, instead of treating the cause."

"On my soul," replied Charles, astonished, "I think you are right!"

"Well, my son," continued Catherine, "as it is essential for my happiness and for the welfare of the kingdom that you should be cured as speedily as possible, I have assembled all the men skilled, not only in curing the diseases of the body, but those of the mind."

"What was the result?"

"That which I expected; I have the remedy that will cure not only your body, but your mind."

Charles trembled; he thought that his mother intended to give him a fresh poison, finding the first too slow in operation.

"Where is this remedy?" asked he.

"In the disease itself."

"Where is that situated?"

"Listen, my son," said the queen. "Did you never hear of secret enemies, who from a distance assassinate their victim?"

"By steel, or by poison?" demanded Charles, without for an instant losing sight of his mother's impassive face.

"No, by other means, sure but terrible."

"Explain yourself."

"My son," asked the Florentine, "do you believe in magic?"

"Fully," returned Charles, repressing a smile of incredulity.

"Well, then," continued Catherine, "from magic proceed all your sufferings. An enemy, who dared not attack you openly, has done so in secret; a terrible conspiracy, the more terrible that it was without accomplices, has been directed against your Majesty."

"Oh, no!" said Charles, shocked by that depth of cunning.

"Examine well, my son; recall certain projects of escape which might have assured the safety of your murderer."

"Murderer!" cried Charles; "murderer, do you say? Has any one, then, tried to kill me?"

"Yes, my son. You doubt it perhaps, but I have gained certain knowledge of it."

"I never doubt what you tell me," replied the king, sarcastically. "I am curious to know how they have sought to kill me."

"By magic."

"Explain yourself, Madame."

"If the conspirator I mean, and whom your Majesty suspects already in your mind—after having arranged his batteries, sure of success—had managed to slip away, perhaps no one ever would have known the cause of your Majesty's sufferings. But, happily, Sire, your brother watched over you."

"What brother?"

"D'Alençon."

"Ah, true!" said Charles, with a bitter laugh; "I forgot I had a brother. Well, continue, Madame."

"He very fortunately discovered the clue to the conspirator."

"Ah! I suppose you mean the King of Navarre, Mother?" replied Charles, wishing to see how far her dissimulation would go.

Catherine hypocritically cast down her eyes.

"I have had him arrested and sent to Vincennes for his escapade," continued the king. "Is he more culpable than I suspected, then?"

"Do you feel the fever that consumes you?" asked Catherine.

"Yes, to be sure," replied Charles, his brow darkening.

"Do you feel the fire that burns your stomach?"

"Ay, Madame," said Charles, with increasing gloom.

"Do you feel the shooting pains in your head?"

"Yes, yes, Madame. Oh, I feel all that! How well you describe my illness!"

"Well, look here." And she drew from under her mantle a little figure. The figure was of yellow wax, about ten inches high, clothed in a robe covered with golden stars, also of wax, and over this a royal mantle of the same material.

"What is this statue?" asked Charles.

"See what it has on the head," said Catherine.

"A crown," replied Charles.

"And in the heart—"

"A needle."

"Well, do you recognize yourself?"

"Myself!"

"Yes, yourself, in your royal robes, with the crown on your head."

"And who made this figure," asked the king, weary of the miserable farce—"the King of Navarre, of course?"

"No, Sire."

"No? then I do not understand you."

"I say no," replied Catherine, "because you perhaps ask the

question literally; had you put it in a different manner, I should have answered yes."

Charles made no answer. He tried to read the thoughts of that dark soul which ever closed itself before him at the moment he thought he was about to read.

"Sire," she continued, "this statue was found by the *procureur-général,* Laguesle, in the apartment of the man who led a horse for the King of Navarre on the day of the hawking party."

"M. de la Mole?"

"Himself. Now look at the needle in the heart, and the name written on the label attached to it."

"I see an *M,*" returned Charles.

"That means *'Mort'* [Death]; it is the magic formula."

"So, then, the person who seeks to kill me is M. de la Mole?" said Charles.

"Yes, he is the poniard; but behind the poniard is the hand that directs it."

"This, then, is the cause of my illness? The day the charm is destroyed my illness will cease? But what is to be done about it? for you know that, unlike you, I know nothing of charms and spells."

"The death of the conspirator destroys the charm. Its power ceases with his life."

"Really!" said Charles, with an air of astonishment.

"Did you not know that?"

"I am no sorcerer."

"But now you are convinced, are you not, of the cause of your illness?"

"Completely."

"You do not say so out of complaisance?"

"Oh, no! from the bottom of my heart."

"Heaven be praised!" said Catherine, as if she believed in God.

"Yes, Heaven be praised!" repeated Charles, ironically. "I know now the cause of my illness, and whom to punish."

"And we will punish——"

"M. de la Mole; you say he is the guilty party?"

"I say he is the instrument."

"Well, we will begin with him; and if he has an accomplice, he will confess."

"If he does not," muttered Catherine, "I have infallible means of making him. You will then, Sire, permit the process to begin?"

"I desire it, Madame, and the sooner the better."

Catherine pressed her son's hand, without understanding its nervous trembling as he pressed her own, and left the apartment without hearing his sardonic laugh, or the terrible imprecation which followed that laugh. The king asked himself whether it was prudent to allow that woman her freedom, since in a few hours she could do evil beyond remedy. At this moment he heard a rustling noise, and turning round, saw Marguerite lifting the tapestry of the door opening into the nurse's apartments.

"Oh, Sire, Sire!" cried Marguerite, "you know what she says is false."

"She? Who?" said Charles.

"Oh, Charles! it is terrible to accuse one's mother. I suspected that she was staying only to persecute them; but upon my life, upon your own, upon both our souls, I tell you that she lies!"

"Persecute them! whom does she persecute?"

Both of them instinctively spoke in a low tone; it would seem that they were afraid to hear each other.

"Henri, in the first place, your Henriot, who loves you, and is devoted to you."

"You think so, Margot?"

"I am sure of it."

"Well, and so am I."

"Why, then, did you arrest him, and send him to Vincennes?"

"Because he himself requested it."

"He requested it, Sire!"

"Oh, he has singular ideas—perhaps he is wrong, perhaps he is right; but he thought he should be more safe in disgrace than in favor, away from me than near me, at Vincennes than in the Louvre."

"Ah! I understand. He is safe, then?"

"As safe as a man can be for whose life Beaulieu answers with his own."

"Oh, thanks! but—"

"But what?"

"There is another person in whose welfare I am interested."

"Who is this person?"

"Sire, spare me; I scarce dare name him to my brother, much less to my king."

"M. de la Mole, is it not?"

"Alas, Sire, you wished once before to kill him; and he escaped only by a miracle."

"He had committed but one crime then, now he has committed two."

"Ah! he is not guilty of the second."

"But did you not hear what our good mother said, poor Margot?"

"I have already told you that what she said is false."

"Perhaps you do not know that a figure of wax has been seized at La Mole's?"

"Yes, my brother, I know it."

"That this figure is pierced to the heart by a needle, and that the needle carries a small banner inscribed with an *M?*"

"I know that also."

"That this figure has a royal robe on its shoulders, and a royal crown on its head?"

"I know all that."

"Well, then, what have you to say?"

"I have to say that this small image, which bears a royal robe on its shoulders, and a royal crown on its head, is the representation of a woman and not of a man."

"Bah!" said Charles; "and that needle piercing the heart?"

"It was a charm to win that woman's love, and not a spell to doom a man to death."

"But that letter *M?*"

"It does not mean *'Mort,'* as the queen-mother says."

"What, then, does it mean?" asked Charles.

"It means—it means the name of the woman loved by M. de la Mole."

"And that woman's name is—"

"MARGUERITE!" cried the queen, falling on her knees at Charles's bedside, and bathing his hand with tears.

"Silence, Margot!" said Charles, "you may in your turn be overheard."

"Oh, no matter!" cried the queen. "If all the world were present to hear me, I would declare it infamous to abuse the love of a gentleman by staining his reputation with a charge of murder."

"Margot, what if I should tell you that I know as well as you do who is guilty and who is not?"

"My brother!"

"What if I should tell you that La Mole is innocent?"

"You know it?"

"What if I should tell you that I know the real culprit?"

"The real culprit!" cried Marguerite. "A crime has been committed, then?"

"Yes; intentionally or unintentionally, a crime has been committed."

"Upon you?"

"Upon me."

"Impossible!"

"Impossible? Look at me, Margot."

Marguerite obeyed, and shuddered as she saw him so pale.

"Margot, I have not three months to live!"

"You, my brother, my Charles?"

"Margot, I am poisoned!"

Marguerite screamed.

"Silence!" said Charles; "it must be thought that I die by magic."

"You know who is guilty."

"Yes."

"You have said that it was not La Mole?"

"No, it is not he."

"And certainly it cannot be Henri—Great God! can it be—"

"Who?"

"My brother—D'Alençon?" murmured Marguerite.

"Perhaps."

"Or," Marguerite whispered, as if alarmed at what she was going to say, "our mother?"

Charles remained silent. Marguerite, however, read the answer in his eye, and sank into a chair.

"My God!" murmured she. "It is impossible!"

"Impossible?" said Charles, with a forced laugh. "It is a pity René is not here; he could tell you my story."

"René?"

"Yes; he would tell you, for example, that a woman to whom he dared refuse nothing, came to him to ask for a book on hunting from his library; that a subtle poison has been poured upon every page of that book; that the poison, destined for someone, I know not for whom, fell—by caprice of chance, or by chastisement of Heaven—into other hands than those for which it was intended. But since René is not here, if you wish to see the book, it is there in my cabinet; and you will see, in the handwriting of the Florentine, that that book, which still contains in its leaves the death of twenty persons, was given by him to his compatriot."

"Silence, Charles; in your turn, silence!" said Marguerite.

"You now see clearly that it must be believed that I have died by magic."

"But it is monstrous!" exclaimed Marguerite. "Pardon! pardon! You know he is innocent!"

"Yes, I know it; but the world must believe him guilty. Permit, then, the death of your lover; it is a small price to pay to save the honor of the house of France. I myself die that the secret may be preserved."

Marguerite saw that her only hope lay in her own resources, and withdrew, weeping.

Meantime Catherine had lost not an instant, but had written to Laguesle the following historical letter, which we give word for word, and which throws considerable light on this bloody drama:

MONSIEUR LE PROCUREUR—I have this evening been informed for certain that La Mole has committed sacrilege; many evil books and papers have been found in his apartments in Paris. See, therefore, the chief president, and inform him as soon as possible of the whole affair—of the waxen figure meant for the king, and which they have pierced to the heart.

CATHERINE.

CHAPTER 25

The Invisible Bucklers

The day after that on which Catherine had written this letter, the governor entered Coconnas's cell with an imposing cortège of two halberdiers and four black-gowned men. Coconnas was invited to descend into the room where Laguesle and two judges waited to interrogate him according to Catherine's instructions.

During the week he had passed in prison Coconnas had reflected deeply; besides that, he and La Mole, seeing each other daily, had agreed on the conduct they were to pursue, which was to persist in an absolute denial; and they were persuaded that with a little address the affair would take a more favorable turn. The charges could not weigh more heavily against them than against the others. Henri and Marguerite had made no attempt at flight; and he and La Mole could not be compromised in an affair the principals in which were at liberty (Coconnas was ignorant that Henri was in the same prison with themselves). Furthermore, the complaisance of his jailer apprised him that over his head there was extended a protection, which he called "invisible bucklers."

Up to this time the interrogations had been confined to the designs of the King of Navarre, his projects of flight, and the part the two friends had borne in these projects. Coconnas had constantly replied in a way more than vague, and much more than adroit; he was ready still to reply in a similar manner, and had prepared beforehand all his little repartees, when he suddenly found that the subject of interrogation was changed. The questions were now directed to several visits made to René, and one or more waxen figures made at La Mole's instigation. Prepared as he was, Coconnas believed that the accusation had lost much of its intensity, since it was no longer in reference to having betrayed a king, but to having made a figure of a queen, and this queen not more than from eight to ten inches high at most. He therefore replied with much vivacity that neither he nor his friend had played with a doll for many years; and he saw with much satisfaction that his replies more than once made the judges smile. His interrogatory concluded, he went up to his chamber singing so merrily that La Mole, for whom he made all this noise, drew from it the brightest auguries.

La Mole was brought down from his tower, as Coconnas had been, and saw with equal astonishment the new turn which the investigation took. He was questioned as to his visits to René. He replied that he had only once visited the Florentine. Then they asked him if he had not ordered a waxen figure. He replied that René had showed him such a figure ready-made. Then he was asked if this figure did not represent a man. He replied that it represented a woman. Then they inquired if the purpose of the charm was not to cause the death of this man. He replied that the purpose of the charm was to cause himself to be beloved by the woman.

These questions, put in a hundred different ways, were always replied to by La Mole in the same manner. The judges looked at one another with a kind of indecision, not knowing very well what to say or do, when a note brought to the *procureur-général* resolved the difficulty. It was in these words:

"If the accused denies, put him to the torture.—C."

The *procureur* put the note in his pocket, smiled at La Mole, and politely dismissed him. La Mole returned to his dungeon almost as assured, if not as joyous, as Coconnas. "I think all will now go well," he said.

An hour afterwards he heard footsteps, and saw a note which was slipped under his door, without seeing the hand that moved it. He took it up with a trembling hand, and almost died with joy as he recognized the writing.

"Courage!" said the billet. "I am watching over you."

"Ah! if she is watching," cried La Mole, kissing the note which a hand so dear had touched—"if she is watching, I am saved!"

In order that the reader may understand La Mole's confidence in that note, and the trust reposed by him and by Coconnas in what the Piedmontese called their "invisible bucklers," we must conduct him to that small house and to that chamber where so many scenes of intoxicating enjoyment, so many perfumes hardly evaporated, so many sweet remembrances now changed to griefs, weighed upon the heart of a woman lying back on a divan covered with velvet cushions.

"To be a queen—powerful, young, rich, beautiful—and suffer what I suffer!" she exclaimed; "oh, it is impossible!"

Then in her agitation, she rose, paced up and down, suddenly paused, pressed her burning forehead against an ice-cold marble slab, rose, pale, her face covered with tears, wrung her hands in agony, and fell back, fainting, into the nearest chair.

Suddenly the tapestry which separated the apartment in the Rue Cloche Percée from the apartment in the Rue Tizon was lifted up, and the Duchesse de Nevers appeared.

"Ah!" exclaimed Marguerite, "is it you? With what impatience I have awaited you. Well, what news?"

"Bad news—bad news, my dear friend! Catherine herself is hurrying on the trial, and is at this moment at Vincennes."

"And René?"

"Is arrested."

"And our prisoners?"

"The jailer informs me that they see each other daily. The day before yesterday they were searched; and La Mole broke your miniature to atoms rather than let them have it."

"Dear La Mole!"

"Annibal laughed in the teeth of the inquisitors."

"Worthy Annibal! And what happened then?"

"They were this morning interrogated as to the flight of the king, his projects of rebellion in Navarre; and they have told nothing."

"Oh, I knew they would keep silence; but silence will kill them just as much as if they spoke."

"Yes, but we must save them."

"You have thought over our plan, then?"

"I have occupied myself with it since yesterday."

"Well?"

"I have come to terms with Beaulieu. Ah, my dear queen, what a hard and greedy man! It will cost a man's life and three hundred thousand crowns."

"Only the life of a man and three hundred thousand crowns? Why, it is nothing!"

"Nothing! three hundred thousand crowns! Why, all your jewels and all mine will not be enough."

"Oh, that's nothing! The King of Navarre will pay something, the Duc d'Alençon pay something, my brother Charles must pay something, or if not—"

"Oh, you reason like a fool. I have them—the three hundred thousand crowns."

"You?"

"Yes, I."

"And how have you procured them?"

"Ah, that's telling!"

"Is it a secret?"

"For all the world except you."

"Oh, *mon Dieu!*" said Marguerite, smiling through her tears, "have you stolen them?"

"You shall judge."

"Well?"

"You remember that horrible Nantouillet?"

"The rich fellow, the usurer?"

"If you call him so."

"Well?"

"Well, one day seeing a certain woman pass, of blond complexion, green eyes, her hair dressed with three rubies, one on her brow, and the two others on her temples—a *coiffure* very becoming to her—that rich fellow, that usurer, not knowing that she was a duchess, called out, 'For three kisses I will replace those three rubies with three diamonds worth one hundred thousand crowns each.' "

"Well, Henriette?"

"Well, my dear, the diamonds are sold and delivered."

"Oh, Henriette, Henriette!" murmured Marguerite.

"Hold!" cried the duchess, with an accent of shamelessness at once naïve and sublime, revealing both the woman and the age, "hold! I love Annibal!"

"It is true," said Marguerite, smiling and blushing at the same time, "you love him much; you even love him too much"; and nevertheless she pressed her hand.

"Now then," continued Henriette, "thanks to our three diamonds, the three hundred thousand crowns and the man are ready."

"The man! what man?"

"The man who must be killed, to be sure. Have you already forgotten that there is a man to be killed?"

"And you have found the man you need?"

"Precisely so."

"At the same price?" asked Marguerite, with a smile.

"At that price I could have found a thousand," replied Henriette; "no, no, for five hundred crowns."

"You have found a man who is willing to be killed for five hundred crowns?"

"Certainly; one must live somehow."

"My dear friend, I no longer understand you. Come, speak plainly; riddles take too much time in our present situation."

"Well, listen. The jailer who has La Mole and Coconnas in keeping is an old soldier, who knows what a wound amounts to. He would willingly help in saving our friends, but doesn't want to lose his place. A poniard-blow skillfully placed will do the business. We shall give him a reward, the State an indemnity. In that way the worthy fellow will receive with both hands; he will renew the fable of the pelican."

"But," said Marguerite, "a wound with a poniard—"

"Be easy; it is Annibal who will give it."

"True," said Marguerite, smiling; "he gave La Mole three wounds with sword and poniard, and La Mole is not dead. There is, then, room for hope."

"Wretch! you deserve that I should drop the whole affair."

"Oh, no, no; tell the rest, I beg of you. How are we to save them?"

"Well, this is the plot. The chapel is the only place in the fortress where women not being prisoners are admitted. We shall hide behind the altar; under the cloth will be laid two daggers. The door of the sacristy will be previously opened. Coconnas will strike the jailer, who will fall down as if dead; we shall then appear, and each cast a cloak over the shoulders of our friend. We shall then fly with them by the small door of the sacristy, and as we shall have the password, we shall get out without difficulty."

"And once out?"

"Two horses will be in waiting at the door; they will jump on them, leave France, and reach Lorraine, whence they will occasionally return incognito."

"Oh, you restore me to life!" said Marguerite. "So we shall save them?"

"I almost would warrant it."

"And soon?"

"In three or four days; Beaulieu is to let us know."

"But if you were recognized in the vicinity of Vincennes, all our plans might be marred."

"How could anyone recognize me? I go as a nun, with a large hood over my face; so that no one sees even the end of my nose."

"We cannot take too many precautions."

"I know that well enough, *'mordi!'* as poor Annibal would say."

"Have you any news of the King of Navarre?"

"Yes, he was never happier, it appears. He laughs, sings, and eats, drinks, and sleeps well; all he asks is to be well guarded."

"He is right. And my mother?"

"I have told you that she pushes on the trial as fast as possible."

"Yes, but does she suspect anything in regard to us?"

"How do you think she could suspect anything? All who are in the secret are interested to keep it. Ah! I have learned that she notified the judges of Paris to hold themselves in readiness."

"Let us act quickly, Marguerite. If our poor captives should change their prison all must be begun again."

"Be easy; I am as eager as you are to see them at liberty."

"Oh, yes, I know it; and thanks, thanks a hundred times for what you have done!"

"Adieu, Marguerite! I am going to take the field again."

"Are you sure of Beaulieu?"

"I think so."

"Of the jailer?"

"He has promised."

"Of the horses?"

"They will be the best in the Duc de Nevers's stables."

"Henriette, I adore you!" And Marguerite threw her arms around her friend's neck; after which the two women separated, promising to see each other again next day and every day, at the same place and hour. These were the two charming and devoted creatures whom Coconnas, with so much reason, called the "invisible bucklers."

"Well, my brave friend," said Coconnas to La Mole, when they met after the examination in which for the first time the wax figure had been introduced, "everything seems going on as favorably as we could wish, and we shall ere long be at liberty."

"No doubt," answered La Mole; "and then the complaisance with which our jailers treat us abundantly proves that our noble friends are at work for us."

"To be sure they are," rejoined Coconnas; "and how could a queen or a princess better employ her riches than in procuring our freedom? Now let us go over our lesson a little. We are to be conducted to the chapel, where we shall be left in charge of our turnkey; we each find a dagger in the place indicated. I make a hole in the body of our guide——"

"Oh, not in the body!—you would rob him of his five hundred crowns; in the arm."

"Ah, yes, in the arm! That would ruin him, poor man! it would be clear enough that he was in collusion with us. No, no—in the right side, slipping skillfully along the ribs; it is a veritable wound, and harmless."

"Well, so much for that; then——"

"Then we barricade the door of the chapel by piling up the benches against it, while our two princesses emerge from their hiding places behind the altar, and Henriette opens the small side door!"

"And then," said La Mole, with that quivering voice which sounds like music from the lips—"and then we gain the forest. A good kiss to each makes us joyous and strong. Do you see us, Annibal, leaning forward on our fast horses, and bearing light burdens of anxiety? Oh, what a pleasant thing is fear!—fear in the open air, when one has at his side a good sword unsheathed, when one cries, 'Hurrah!' to his horse driven by the spur, who at each cry bounds and flies!"

"Yes," said Coconnas; "but fear between four walls—what do you say to that, La Mole? I can speak of it, for I have experienced something like that. When Beaulieu put his sallow face into my chamber for the first time, in the shade behind him I saw the gleaming of partisans, and there was the sinister sound of steel striking against steel. I swear to you, I thought at once of the Duc d'Alençon, and expected to see his villainous face between the villainous heads of two halberdiers. I was mistaken, and that was my only consolation."

"So," said La Mole, who followed his own glowing thoughts instead of attending his friend in his excursions through the field of fancy—"so they have provided everything, even the place of our retreat. We are going to Lorraine, dear friend. In fact, I should have preferred Navarre; in Navarre I should be near her. But Navarre is too remote; Nancey is better. Besides, there we shall be only eighty leagues from Paris. Do you know, Annibal, in leaving here I bear with me one regret."

"Ah, faith! no, indeed! As for me, I confess that I leave all mine here."

"Well, it is that we are not able to take our worthy jailer with us, instead of—"

"But he wouldn't be willing," said Coconnas; "it would cost him too much. Think of it; five hundred crowns from us, a recompense from the Government, promotion perhaps. How happily that fellow will live when I shall have killed him! But what is the matter?"

"Nothing—an idea that occurred to me."

"Not a comical idea, apparently, for you have turned frightfully pale."

"I was wondering why we are taken to the chapel."

"Why," said Coconnas, "to receive the sacraments; and in good time, it seems to me."

"But," answered La Mole, "they take to the chapel only those who are condemned to death or to torture."

"Truly," replied Coconnas, becoming pale in his turn, "this

deserves our attention; let us speak to the worthy fellow I am to carve my name upon with my dagger. Here, I say, turnkey!"

"Did you call?" said the man, who had been keeping watch at the top of the stairs.

"Come here."

"Here I am."

"It is settled that we are to make our escape from the chapel, is it not?"

"Hush!" said the turnkey, looking round him with terror.

"Don't be frightened—no one can hear you; speak out."

"Yes, Monsieur, from the chapel."

"They will take us to the chapel, then?"

"Certainly, it is the custom."

"It is the custom?"

"Yes; after a condemnation to death, it is the custom to allow the condemned to spend the night in the chapel."

Coconnas and La Mole exchanged looks of surprise and alarm.

"You think, then, that we shall be condemned to death?"

"Why, you think so yourselves, don't you—else why take the trouble to make arrangements for your flight?"

"There is reason in what he says," said Coconnas.

"We are playing a critical game, it seems," replied La Mole.

"And do I risk nothing?" said the jailer. "Suppose, in the excitement of the moment, Monsieur were to wound me in the wrong place."

"*Mordi!*" exclaimed Coconnas, "I only wish we could change places, and I had nothing more to fear than you have."

"Condemned to death!" said La Mole; "but that is impossible!"

"Impossible!" said the jailer, naïvely; "and why?"

"Hush!" said Coconnas; "I believe the door is opening down there."

"Oh, pray, pray, gentlemen, get into your cells! make haste!"

"And when will our trial take place?"

"Tomorrow at latest; but don't be uneasy—the friends who are interested for you shall be duly informed."

"Then let us bid adieu to each other, and to these walls."

The friends exchanged an affectionate embrace, and each retired to his place of confinement—La Mole sighing, Coconnas humming an air. Nothing unusual occurred until seven o'clock in the evening. Night descended, dark and rainy, on the donjon of Vincennes—just such weather as would have favored an escape. Coconnas's supper was brought, and eaten with his ordinary appetite; and he had well-nigh composed himself to sleep, while listening to the loud murmurs of the wind and the splashing rain as it drove heavily against the walls, when he was roused by a sound of persons passing to and fro from the chamber of La Mole.

In vain did Coconnas strain his listening powers; he could distinguish nothing. The time passed on; no one came near him. "Strange," murmured he, "that La Mole should receive so many visits, while I seem quite forgotten! perhaps La Mole felt himself suddenly taken ill, and called out for assistance. What can it mean?"

Three hours slowly passed away, and Coconnas, notwithstanding all his anxieties, was beginning again to sleep, when a turning of the lock startled him.

"Oh, oh!" he said, "it is already time for us to set out, and they are coming, no doubt, to conduct us to the chapel without any previous condemnation. *Mordi!* the night is most favorable—dark as a pit; I only hope the horses they give us will be able to find their way." He was about to ask some jocular question of the turnkey, who had by that time entered, when he saw the man put his finger to his lips, and roll his eyes in a significant manner.

Coconnas then perceived a dim outline of persons following the jailer, and quickly distinguished two figures wearing helmets, on which the smoking candle cast a yellow light. "Oh!" said he, in a low tone, "what is the meaning of all this? Where are we going, then?"

The jailer replied only with a sigh, which resembled a groan.

"Follow the halberdiers, Monsieur," said a voice, which at once made Coconnas aware that the soldiers were accompanied by an officer of some kind.

"And where is M. de la Mole?" inquired the Piedmontese. "What has become of him?"

"Follow the halberdiers!" repeated the same voice that had previously spoken.

There was nothing for him but to obey; without another word, therefore, Coconnas began to descend the spiral staircase. At the first floor the guards stopped; the door was opened, and a number of persons arrayed as judges and seated in judicial order presented themselves, while in the background Coconnas discerned the dim outline of a man with naked arms and a look that made a cold dew start to his forehead.

Still, concealing his alarm, he entered the chamber with an easy air, his head thrown a little on one side, and his hand on his hip, after the most approved manner of court gallants. As Coconnas advanced, he perceived La Mole sitting on a bench near the judges and officials. The guards led Coconnas to the front of the tribunal; arrived there, he stopped, turned round, and smilingly nodded to La Mole, then remained in a waiting attitude.

"What is your name?" inquired the president.

"Marc-Annibal de Coconnas," replied the Piedmontese, with gentlemanly grace, "Comte de Montpantier, Chenaux, and other places; but our titles are known, I presume."

"Where were you born?"

"At St. Colomban, near Suza."

"How old are you?"

"Twenty-seven years, three months."

"Good!" answered the president.

"He seems to be pleased with my account of myself," murmured Coconnas.

"Now, then," continued the president, "what was your motive in leaving the service of the Duc d'Alençon?"

"To rejoin my friend, M. de la Mole, who, when I left M. d'Alençon, had also left him some days previously."

"And what were you doing when arrested, the day of the chase?"

"Why, hunting, of course!" replied Coconnas.

"The king was also present at that chase, and there he was first attacked with the malady from which he now suffers."

"I know nothing about that; I was not near the king myself, and I did not even know he had been taken ill."

The judges looked at one another with an air of incredulity.

"Oh! you were ignorant of his Majesty's illness, were you?"

"Yes, completely so, and I regret to hear of it; for though the King of France is not my king, I have a great deal of sympathy for him."

"Really?"

"On my honor. I don't say as much for his brother, the Duc d'Alençon, for there, I must confess—"

"We have nothing to do with the Duc d'Alençon, Monsieur; our business relates to his Majesty—"

"Whose very humble servant I have already told you I am."

"Then, being his servant, as you say, be pleased to tell us what you know relative to a certain wax figure."

"Oh! what, we are going over that story again, are we?"

"If you have no objection."

"Pardieu! on the contrary, I prefer it; go on."

"How came this statue to be found in M. de la Mole's possession?"

"M. de la Mole's! No, no, you mean in René's possession."

"Then you acknowledge the existence of such an image?"

"I don't know whether it exists or not; I could tell you better if I saw it."

"Here it is. Is it the one you have previously seen?"

"It is."

"Write down," said the judge, "that the accused recognizes the statue as the one he has heretofore seen in the possession of M. de la Mole."

"No, no, no!" interposed Coconnas, "do not let us mistake one another; write that I say it is the same figure I saw at René's."

"Well, be it so—at René's; and on what day?"

"The only day La Mole and myself ever were at René's."

"You admit, then, having been there with M. de la Mole?"

"Why, I never denied it, did I?"

"Write down that the accused admits having gone to René's to work certain conjurations—"

"Holloa, ho! gently, gently, Monsieur President! Moderate your enthusiasm, I beg; I have not said one word of all that."

"You deny having gone to René's house to work conjurations?"

"I do; the conjuration that took place was by chance, and wholly unpremeditated."

"But still it took place?"

"Certainly; I cannot deny that something resembling the working of a charm did occur."

"Write down that the accused admits having gone to René's for the sake of obtaining a charm against the king's life."

"What! against the king's life!" exclaimed Coconnas. "It is an infamous lie; no such charm was ever made or sought for."

"There, gentlemen!" said La Mole, "you hear!"

"Silence!" vociferated the president; then, turning toward the clerk he said, "Against the king's life. Have you written it?"

"No, no!" cried Coconnas; "I said no such thing, and then the figure is not that of a man, but of a woman."

"What did I tell you, gentlemen?" inquired La Mole.

"M. de la Mole," said the president, "reply when you are questioned, but do not interrupt the interrogation of others."

"You say that the figure is that of a woman?" resumed the judge.

"Certainly I say it."

"Why, then, does it wear a royal crown and mantle?"

"*Pardieu!* for a very simple reason—because the figure was meant for—"

Here La Mole rose, and placed a finger on his lips.

"True!" said Coconnas; "I was beginning to relate matters with which these gentlemen have nothing at all to do."

"You persist, then, in your assertion that this waxen image was intended to represent a woman?"

"Yes, certainly, I persist."

"And you refuse to say who the woman was?"

"A woman in my own country," said La Mole, "whom I loved, and by whom I was desirous of being loved."

"You are not the person interrogated, M. de la Mole," exclaimed the president; "either be silent, or I shall be obliged to have you gagged."

"Gag!" said Coconnas. "What are you saying there, Monsieur in the black robe? You will gag my friend!—a gentleman! Come, now!"

"Bring in René!" said the *procureur-général*.

"Yes, yes, by all means, bring René," said Coconnas, "bring him in; we shall soon see who is right—you three, or we two."

René entered, pale, shrunken, and so altered that the two young men could scarcely recognize him. The wretched old man appeared more conscience-stricken and bowed down by the weight of the crime he was about to commit than by those he had already perpetrated.

"Maître René!" said the judge, "do you know the two accused persons here present?"

"I do," answered René, in a voice which betrayed his emotion.

"As having seen them where?"

"In various places, but more especially at my own house."

"How frequently at your house?"

"Only once."

As René proceeded, the countenance of Coconnas grew brighter; La Mole, on the other hand, as though warned by some presentiment of evil, looked graver than before.

"And on what occasion did they pay you a visit?"

René seemed to hesitate a moment, then said, "To order me to make a small waxen figure."

"Maître René," interrupted Coconnas, "permit me to tell you that you are making a little mistake."

"Silence, I command!" cried the president; then, turning toward René, he said, "And pray was this figure to represent a man or a woman?"

"A man," answered René.

Coconnas sprang up as though he had received an electric shock. "A man!" he said.

"A man," responded René, but in so feeble a voice that the president could scarcely hear him.

"And why was this statue clad in a royal mantle, with a crown on its head?"

"Because," replied René, "it represented a king."

"Infamous liar!" cried Coconnas, infuriated.

"Hold your peace, Coconnas!" interposed La Mole. "Let the man talk; everyone has a right to destroy his soul."

"But not the bodies of others!"

"And what is the signification of the needle found sticking in the heart of the image, with a small banner bearing the letter *M* at the end?"

"The needle is emblematical of the sword or dagger, and the letter *M* stands for *Mort*."

Coconnas sprang forward as though to strangle René, but was held back by the guards.

"That will do!" said the officer; "the tribunal is in possession of all it desires to know. Let the prisoners be reconducted to the waiting room."

"But," exclaimed Coconnas, "it is quite impossible to hear one's self accused of such crimes without protesting against them."

"Protest, Monsieur; no one hinders you. Guards, take the prisoners."

The officials seized upon La Mole and Coconnas, and led them away, each by a separate door. The *procureur-général* then signed to the man with bare arms, whom Coconnas had observed on entering, and said, "Do not go away, my good fellow, there will be work for you before the night is over."

"Which shall I begin with?" said the man, respectfully raising his cap.

"With that one!" answered the president, pointing to La Mole, whom they could still perceive, like a shadow between his two guards; then, approaching René, who stood in trembling expectation of being ordered back to his place of confinement in the Châtelet, "You have spoken well, my friend," he said to him; "be under no alarm. Both the king and the queen shall be made acquainted that it is to you they are indebted for coming at the real truth of this affair."

But this promise, instead of restoring René to strength, seemed to terrify him; and he replied only by a groan.

CHAPTER 27

The Torture of the Boot

It was only when he had been conducted to his new cell, and the door was closed upon him, that Coconnas, left to himself, and no longer sustained by his contention with the judges and his wrath against René, fell into a train of sad reflections. "It seems to me," he said, "that the affair is taking a bad turn, and that it is time to go for a little while to the chapel. I distrust condemnations to death; for unquestionably they are condemning us to death at this moment. I distrust especially condemnations to death pronounced secretly in a fortified castle before faces as ugly as are all those that surround me. They seriously intend to cut off our heads—hum! hum! I return to what I said; it is time to go to the chapel."

These words, uttered in a low tone, were followed by silence; and that silence was broken by a dull, stifled, wailing cry which was not like that of a human being. It seemed to pierce the thick wall and to vibrate on the iron bars.

Coconnas shuddered with terror, although he was so brave that his courage was nearly allied to that of wild beasts. He stood motionless, doubting whether what he had heard was not the wind, when he heard it again; and this time he was convinced not only that the voice was human, but that it was the voice of La Mole. At this voice, the Piedmontese forgot he was himself a prisoner confined by two doors, three gates, and a wall twelve feet thick; he rushed forward crying, "They are murdering someone here!"

But he encountered the wall so violently that the shock threw him back on a stone bench.

"Oh, they have killed him!" he repeated; "it is abominable! and to be without arms!"

He reached out his hands on every side. "Ah, that iron ring!" he said; "I will pull it from the wall, and then woe to him who

494

comes near me!" He rose, seized the iron ring, and with his first effort shook it so violently that it was evident that by two such efforts
he would secure it. But suddenly the door opened, and the light of
two torches invaded his cell.

The same voice that before had been so disagreeable to him
said, "Come, Monsieur, the court awaits you."

"Good!" said Coconnas; "to hear my sentence, I suppose."

"Yes, Monsieur."

"I breathe again; go on, Monsieur." And he followed the officer, who went in front, his black wand in his hand.

Spite of his expressed satisfaction, Coconnas glanced anxiously
on either side. "Oh," murmured he, "I do not see my worthy jailer;
I wish he were here."

On entering the chamber, Coconnas perceived the *procureur-
général,* who had conducted the prosecution with most palpable ani-
mosity, for Catherine had charged him to carry on the affair
earnestly. A curtain was drawn back and exposed the recesses of this
chamber; so terrible were these recesses, thus lighted up, that
Coconnas felt his knees tremble, and he exclaimed, "Oh, *mon
Dieu!*"

The sight before him was indeed alarming. The portion of the
apartment which had been concealed during the examination by a
curtain, now raised, seemed like the vestibule of hell. "Oh!" said
Coconnas, "the chamber of torture is prepared, and only awaits the
victim. What does this mean?"

"Kneel down, Marc-Annibal de Coconnas," said a voice;
"kneel down, and hear your sentence."

Against a summons of that kind the whole person of Coconnas
instinctively rebelled. But before he had time to collect his thoughts,
two strong hands laid hold of him, and forced him to his knees.

The voice continued: "Sentence of the court sitting at
Vincennes on Marc-Annibal de Coconnas, accused and convicted of
the crime of high treason; of an attempt to poison; of sacrilege and
magic against the person of the king; of a conspiracy against the
State; and of having driven a prince of the blood into rebellion by
his pernicious counsels."

At each of these charges Coconnas shook his head.

The judge continued: "In consequence of which, the aforesaid
Marc-Annibal de Coconnas will be taken from prison to the Place

St.-Jean-en-Grève, to be there decapitated; his property will be confiscated, his woods cut down, his château destroyed, and a post planted, with a copper-plate bearing an inscription recording his crime and punishment."

"As for my head," said Coconnas, "that I know is in jeopardy; but as for my woods and châteaux, I do not fear for them in the least, and I defy all your hatchets and pickaxes to harm them."

"Silence!" said the judge, and he continued: "And, moreover, the aforesaid Coconnas—"

"What!" interrupted Coconnas, "will they do anything more after cutting my head off? Oh, that seems to me rather severe!"

"No, Monsieur," replied the judge, *"before."*

He continued: "And the aforesaid Coconnas will undergo, before the execution of this sentence, the extraordinary torture, consisting of ten wedges—"

Coconnas started, and looked with flashing eyes at the judge. "For what?" cried he, finding only those simple words to express the flood of thoughts that rose upon his mind.

The torture was, in reality, ruin to Coconnas's hopes. He would not be taken to the chapel until after the torture, and the torture often occasioned death. It was especially likely to be fatal where the sufferer was brave and firm; for to him it would seem cowardly to yield a confession, and so long as he did not confess the torture would be not only continued, but increased.

The judge made no reply, but continued: "In order to compel him to name his accomplices and to confess his plots and machinations in detail."

"Mordi!" cried Coconnas, "this is infamous! this is cowardice!"

The judge, accustomed to the indignant protestations of the victims, made a sign. Coconnas, seized by the legs and arms, was overpowered and bound to the rack before he could even see who were the authors of this violence.

"Wretches!" shouted Coconnas, shaking, in a paroxysm of fury, the rack and the trestles in such a manner that his tormentors recoiled in alarm. "Scoundrels! torture me, shatter me, tear me in pieces—you will learn nothing, I swear to you! Ah! you think that with bits of wood and with bits of iron you will compel a gentleman of my name to speak. Come on, I defy you!"

"Clerk, prepare to write," said the judge.

"Yes, prepare to write," cried Coconnas; "and if you write all I tell you, you scoundrel, you will have something to do!"

"Will you confess?" asked the judge.

"No, not one word; go to the devil!"

"You may change your mind, Monsieur, during the preparations. Come, Maître, fit the boot to Monsieur."

At these words, a man holding a cord in his hand advanced toward him. It was Maître Caboche. A painful astonishment appeared on Coconnas's face; but instead of crying out, he remained motionless and silent, unable to withdraw his eyes from that forgotten friend who reappeared at such a moment. Caboche, without moving a muscle of his face, or appearing to recognize Coconnas, placed two planks between his legs, then two more outside, and bound them together with a cord. This formed what was called the "boot." In the "ordinary" torture, six wedges were used, which crushed the flesh; in the "extraordinary" torture ten were employed, which not only crushed the flesh, but broke the bones also.

Maître Caboche introduced the wedge between the planks, and then, with his mallet in his hand, looked at the judge.

"Will you confess?" asked the latter.

"Never!" returned Coconnas, although he felt a cold damp all over his brow.

"Proceed," said the judge.

Caboche raised his heavy mallet, and struck a tremendous blow on the wedge. Coconnas did not utter the slightest sound at this first wedge, which usually extorted a groan from the most resolute. On the contrary, his countenance expressed the greatest wonder, and he gazed in astonishment at Caboche, who, his arm raised, stood ready to repeat the blow.

"What was your intention in concealing yourself in the forest?" demanded the judge.

"To enjoy the fresh air."

"Proceed," said the judge.

Caboche struck again. Coconnas did not stir, but kept his eyes fixed on the executioner with the same expression of surprise. The judge frowned.

"He is indeed determined!" muttered he. "Has the wedge entered, Maître?"

Caboche stopped as if to examine it, and whispered to

Coconnas, "Cry out! cry out!" Then rising, "Up to the head, Monsieur," said he to the judge.

"Second wedge!" said the judge, quietly.

The words of Caboche explained all to Coconnas; the worthy executioner was rendering him the greatest service in his power. He was sparing him not only pain, but moreover the shame of a confession, by driving, in place of oak wedges, wedges of leather, with the top only of wood; he thus left him all his strength to mount the scaffold manfully.

"Oh, excellent Caboche!" muttered Coconnas, "fear nothing; I will cry out loud enough."

Caboche had introduced a second wedge, larger than the first, and at a sign from the judge struck as if he were going to demolish the donjon of Vincennes at a blow.

"Ah! ah! *hou! hou!*" roared Coconnas, with a great variety of intonations, "take care! you are breaking my bones!"

"Ah," said the judge, smiling, "the second seems to take effect."

Coconnas panted like the bellows of a forge.

"What were you doing in the forest?" repeated the judge.

"Eh, *mordi!* I have already told you. I was simply enjoying the fresh air."

"Proceed."

"Confess," whispered Caboche.

"What?"

"Anything; only confess."

And he dealt another blow on the wedge.

"Oh, oh!" cried Coconnas. "What do you wish to know, Monsieur? By whose order I was in the forest?"

"Yes."

"By the order of M. d'Alençon."

"Write that," said the judge.

"If I laid a snare for the King of Navarre," continued Coconnas, "I only obeyed my master's orders."

The clerk applied himself to writing down the confession.

"Ah, you denounced me, tallow-face!" thought Coconnas; "I will be even with you." And he related the visit of François to the King of Navarre, the interviews between Mouy and D'Alençon, and the history of the red mantle. He gave precise, terrible, incontestable evidence against D'Alençon making it seem all the while as though his statements were extorted from him only by the intensity of his sufferings—he grimaced, roared, and complained so naturally and in so many different tones; and the judge at last became terrified himself at having to record details so compromising to a prince of the blood.

"Ah," said Caboche, "here is a gentleman to whom it isn't necessary to speak more than once; and he gives the clerk enough to do. What, then, would he have said if the wedges had been of wood?"

The last wedge of the extraordinary was omitted; but without that nine had been used on Coconnas, which would have been sufficient to reduce his legs to a jelly. The judge withdrew, according so much advantage to Coconnas by reason of his confession, and left him alone with Caboche.

"Well," said the latter, "how do you find yourself, Monsieur?"

"Ah, excellent Caboche, I shall never forget what you have done for me!"

"You are right; for if they knew what I have done for you, I should soon take your place, and they would not amuse me with leathern wedges."

"But how came you to think?"

"I will tell you," said Caboche, twisting, for the sake of appearances, bandages of bloody linen about Coconnas's legs. "I knew you were arrested, that Queen Catherine wished to kill you; I guessed you would be put to the torture, and I took my measures accordingly."

"At the risk of what might happen to yourself?"

"Monsieur," replied Caboche, "you are the only gentleman who has ever given me his hand, and, executioner as I am, I have a heart; you shall see how I will perform my office tomorrow."

"Tomorrow?"

"Certainly, tomorrow."

"What office?"

Caboche stared. "You ask what office? Have you, then, forgotten the sentence?"

"Ah, true, I had forgotten all about that."

He had not forgotten it; but he was thinking of the chapel, the knife concealed beneath the napkin, of Henriette and the queen, of the door of the sacristy, the two horses that awaited them; of liberty, of the fresh air, of happiness and security beyond the bounds of France.

"Now," said Caboche, "I must get you from the rack to the litter. Do not forget that both your legs are broken, and that the least movement pains you."

"Ah! oh!" cried Coconnas, as the two assistants advanced.

"Take courage," said Caboche; "if you cry so now what will you do presently?"

"Maître Caboche," replied Coconnas, "I pray you lift me yourself, as I do not wish your two estimable acolytes to touch me."

"Place the litter near the rack," said Caboche.

The two assistants obeyed. Caboche then raised Coconnas in his arms as if he had been an infant, and placed him on the litter; but notwithstanding all his care, Coconnas uttered ferocious cries.

The jailer then appeared with a lantern. "To the chapel," said he.

The bearers and Coconnas started, after Coconnas had again given his hand to Caboche. The former grasp had been too useful to him for him to find any difficulty in repeating it.

CHAPTER 28

The Chapel

The mournful cortège crossed in silence the two drawbridges of the fortress and the courtyard which leads to the chapel, through the windows of which a pale light colored the white faces of the apostles in red robes.

Coconnas eagerly breathed the night air, although it was heavy with rain. He looked at the darkness, and rejoiced to see that everything conspired to favor the flight of himself and his companion. It required all his resolution, prudence, and self-control to restrain him from leaping off his litter when on entering the chapel he saw in the choir, and at three paces from the altar, a mass of something wrapped in a large white mantle. It was La Mole.

"Since we are once more reunited," said Coconnas, in a voice of affected languor, "carry me to my friend."

The porters, having no orders to the contrary, readily obeyed that request.

La Mole was gloomy and pale; his head reclined against the marble wall, and his black hair, bathed with profuse perspiration, which gave to his countenance the paleness of ivory, seemed to have stood up on his head and stiffened so.

On a sign from the turnkey, the two valets went to seek the priest whom Coconnas had asked for. This was the signal agreed upon.

Coconnas followed them with anxious eyes; but his was not the only ardent look fixed on them. Scarcely had they disappeared when two women rushed from behind the altar, and hastened rapidly toward the choir.

Marguerite hurried toward La Mole and seized him in her arms. La Mole uttered a terrible cry—a cry like those which Coconnas had heard in his cell.

"My God! what is the matter, then, La Mole?" said Marguerite, recoiling in terror.

La Mole uttered a deep groan, and put his hand to his eyes as if to avoid seeing Marguerite. Marguerite was even more alarmed by that silence and that gesture than by his cry of pain. "Oh!" she cried, "what is the matter, then? You are covered with blood!"

Coconnas, who had also rushed toward the altar, taken up the dagger, and had his arm round Henriette's waist, turned suddenly.

"Get up!" said Marguerite; "get up, I entreat you! You see the moment has arrived."

A smile, awful in its sadness, passed over La Mole's pale lips, which seemed as though they would never smile again.

"Beloved queen!" said the young man, "you have calculated without Catherine, and consequently without a crime. I have been put to the torture; my bones are broken, all my body is one wound, and the effort I make at this moment to press my lips upon your forehead causes me agony worse than death." And as he spoke, with great exertion, and ghastly pale, La Mole pressed his lips on the queen's brow.

"Torture!" cried Coconnas; "and so did I undergo it. But did not the executioner do for you what he did for me?" And Coconnas told all.

"Ah!" replied La Mole, "that is easily explained. You gave him your hand on the day of our visit; I forgot that all men were brothers, and was disdainful. God punishes me for my pride. God be praised!"

La Mole clasped his hands. Coconnas and the two ladies exchanged a look of indescribable horror.

"Come, come," said the jailer, who had been to the door to listen, and had returned; "come along! Do not lose any time, my dear M. de Coconnas. Give me my blow with the dagger, and manage it like a worthy, kind gentleman, for they will soon be here."

Marguerite was kneeling beside La Mole, like one of the reclining figures on a tomb, made after the likeness of that which the tomb encloses.

"Come, my dear friend," said Coconnas; "courage! I am strong, and will carry you. I can place you on your horse, or hold you on my own, if you cannot keep yourself erect in the saddle.

Come, let us go! let us go! You understand what the good fellow says: our lives are at stake."

La Mole made a superhuman, a sublime effort. "True," he said, "your life is at stake"; and he tried to rise. Annibal placed his arms under him and raised him up. La Mole during this time uttered only a low moaning; but at the moment when Coconnas left to go to the turnkey, and the sufferer was supported only by the arms of two women, his legs bent under him, and in spite of all the efforts of the weeping Marguerite, he fell like an inert mass, and the piercing shriek he could no longer repress made the chapel echo through all its gloomy vaults.

"You see," said La Mole, in an agony of distress; "you see, my queen; so leave me—leave me with one last adieu. I have not told anything, Marguerite; your secret is hidden in my love, and will die with me. Adieu, my queen, adieu!"

Marguerite, almost lifeless herself, threw her arms round that beautiful head, and imprinted on his brow a kiss that was almost holy.

"You, Annibal," said La Mole—"you who have been spared these agonies, who are young and may escape, fly, fly, my friend, and give me the consolation of knowing that you are in safety!"

"The hour is passing," exclaimed the jailer. "Come, gentlemen, make haste!"

Henriette endeavored to lead Annibal gently away; while Marguerite was on her knees before La Mole, her hair disheveled, and eyes overflowing with tears.

"Fly, Annibal!" repeated La Mole; "fly, and do not afford our enemies the joyful spectacle of the death of two innocent men."

Coconnas quietly disengaged himself from Henriette, who was urging him toward the door, and with a gesture so solemn as to be majestic, said, "Madame, first give the five hundred crowns we have promised to this man."

"Here they are," said Henriette.

Then turning toward La Mole and shaking his head sorrowfully, he said, "As for you, La Mole, you have done me an injury in thinking for one moment that I would leave you. Have I not sworn to live and die with you? But you are so great a sufferer, poor friend, that I forgive you." And he seated himself with a resolute air near his friend, toward whom he leaned his head, and whose forehead he touched with his lips. Then he drew gently to him, with the tenderness of a mother toward her child, the head of his friend, which glided from the wall, and rested on his breast.

Marguerite was gloomy; she had picked up the poniard which Coconnas had let fall.

"Oh, my queen!" cried La Mole, extending his hands as he comprehended her purpose, "do not forget that I die in order to destroy the slightest suspicion of our love."

"What, then, can I do for you," exclaimed Marguerite, in despair, "if I must not die with you?"

"You can do that," replied La Mole, "which will make death pleasant to me, so that it will approach me almost with a smiling face."

Marguerite clasped her hands, and looked inquiringly at him.

"Do you remember the evening, Marguerite, when in exchange for the life I offered you then, and today lay down for you, you made me a sacred promise?"

Marguerite started.

"Ah, you do remember!" said La Mole, "for you shudder."

"Yes, yes, I remember," said Marguerite; "and on my soul, Hyacinthe, I will keep that promise." She extended her hand toward the altar, as if a second time to call on God to witness her oath.

La Mole's face lighted up as if the vaulted roof of the chapel had opened and a celestial light had descended upon him.

"They are coming!" exclaimed the jailer.

Marguerite uttered a cry, and hastened toward La Mole, but for fear of increasing his agony, she paused trembling before him.

Henriette pressed her lips on Coconnas's brow, and said to him, "I understand you, my Annibal, and I am proud of you. I know the heroism that makes you die, and I love you for that heroism. Before God, I will always love you more than anything living! and what Marguerite has sworn to do for La Mole, although I know not what it is, I will also do for you." And she held out her hand to Marguerite.

"It is good in you to say that; thank you," replied Coconnas.

"Before you leave me, my queen," said La Mole, "one last favor; give me some souvenir, that I may kiss it as I mount the scaffold."

"Ah, yes!" cried Marguerite, "here, take this!" And she untied from her neck a small reliquary of gold, fastened to a chain of the same metal. "Here," she said, "is a holy relic which I have worn from my childhood. My mother put it round my neck when I was very little, and while she still loved me. It was given by our uncle, Pope Clement, and has never left me. Take it!"

La Mole took it, kissing it eagerly.

"They are opening the door," said the jailer. "Fly, ladies, fly!"

The two women hastened behind the altar, and disappeared. At the same moment the priest entered.

CHAPTER 29

The Place St.-Jean-en-Grève

It was seven o'clock in the morning; and the crowd was waiting, dense and riotous, in the squares, the streets, and upon the quays.

At six o'clock in the morning a tumbril—the same in which the two friends after their duel had been conveyed half dead to the Louvre—had set forth from Vincennes and slowly followed the Rue St. Antoine. On its route, the spectators, so huddled together that they crushed one another, seemed like statues, with their eyes fixed and their mouths open in wonderment. There was this day a heart-rending spectacle offered by the queen-mother to all the people of Paris.

In the tumbril we have mentioned as making its slow way from Vincennes were lying on some straw two young men, bareheaded and entirely clothed in black, leaning against each other. Coconnas supported on his knees La Mole, whose head appeared above the crossbars of the tumbril, and whose eyes looked vaguely around him.

The crowd, eager to see even to the bottom of the vehicle, pressed, drove, heaved, lifted itself upon stones, clung to angles of the walls, and appeared satisfied when it contrived to gain a look at the two bodies which were going from suffering to destruction.

It had been reported that La Mole would die without having confessed one of the charges imputed to him; while on the contrary, Coconnas, it was asserted, could not endure the torture, and had disclosed everything. So there were cries on all sides: "Look at the red one! It is he who confessed! It is he who owned everything! He is the coward who caused the death of the other, who is a brave fellow, and would not confess anything!"

The two young men heard all this—the one the praises, and the other the insults, which accompanied their funereal journey; and while La Mole pressed the hands of his friend, a sublime expression of disdain overspread the features of the Piedmontese, who from the foul tumbril gazed on the stupid mob as if he were looking down from a triumphal car. Misfortune had done its heavenly work—had ennobled the countenance of Coconnas, as death was about to render divine his soul.

"Are we nearly there?" asked La Mole; "for I can endure this no longer, my friend, and I feel as if I should faint."

"Rouse thee, rouse thee, La Mole! We are passing by the Rue Tizon and the Rue Cloche Percée. Look, look!"

"Oh, raise me, raise me, that I may once again behold that blessed house!"

Coconnas touched the executioner on the shoulder, as he sat on the tumbril and drove the horse. "Maître," he said, "do us the kindness to pause a moment in front of the Rue Tizon."

Caboche bowed his head in token of assent, and stopped. La Mole raised himself with a great effort, aided by Coconnas, and gazed with tearful eyes at the small house, now closed and silent as the tomb. A groan burst from his overcharged breast, and he said in a low voice, "Adieu, adieu, youth, love, life!" And his head fell on his breast.

"Courage!" said Coconnas; "we may perchance find all this above!"

"Do you think so?" murmured La Mole.

"I think so because the priest told me so, and more especially because I hope so. But do not faint, my friend, or these wretches will laugh at us."

Caboche heard these last words, and whipping his horse with one hand, he extended the other—unseen by anyone—to Coconnas. It contained a small sponge saturated with a stimulant so powerful that after having smelt it and having it rubbed over his brow, La Mole felt himself revived and reanimated. "Ah!" he said, "I am born again." And he kissed the reliquary suspended from his neck.

When they reached the quay they saw the scaffold, which was elevated considerably above the ground.

"My friend," said La Mole, "I wish to die first."

Coconnas again touched the headsman's shoulder. "Maître," said he, "my friend has suffered more than I have, and therefore has less strength than I. He says it would pain him too much to see me die first; and besides, if I were to die before him he would have no one to support him on the scaffold."

"Good, good!" said Caboche, wiping away a tear with the back of his hand; "be easy, it shall be as you desire."

"And with one blow, eh?" said the Piedmontese, in a low tone.

"Yes, with one blow."

" 'Tis well; if you have to repeat, repeat upon me."

The tumbril stopped. They had arrived. Coconnas put on his hat. A murmur like that of the waves of the sea reached the ears of La Mole. He tried to rise, but his strength failed him; and Caboche and Coconnas were compelled to support him under his arms.

The place was paved with heads, and the steps of the Hôtel de Ville seemed an amphitheater peopled with spectators; each window was filled with animated countenances. When they saw the handsome young man who could no longer support himself on his legs, bruised and broken, make a supreme effort to go unassisted to the scaffold, a vast sound was heard, like a cry of universal desolation; the men groaned, and the women uttered plaintive sighs.

"He was one of the grandest dons at the court," said one.

"How handsome he is! How pale he looks!" said the women. "He is the one who would not confess!"

"My friend," said La Mole, "I cannot support myself. Carry me!"

"Stay a moment," replied Coconnas.

He made a sign to the executioner, who moved aside; then, stooping, he lifted La Mole in his arms as if he had been an infant, and went up the steps to the scaffold with unfaltering foot, bore his burden firmly onto the platform, and put him down amid the frenzied shoutings and applause of the multitude. Coconnas returned the greeting by raising his hat from his head, and then threw it down on the scaffold beside him.

"Look round," said La Mole. "Do you see them anywhere?"

Coconnas glanced deliberately all around him, and when his eyes reached a certain spot, paused. Then, without turning his eyes, he touched his friend on the shoulder, saying, "Look, look, at the window of that little tower!" With his other hand he pointed out to La Mole the small building which still exists at the corner of the Rue de la Vannerie and the Rue Mouton—a remnant of past ages. Two women, clothed in black, were leaning on each other, somewhat retired from the window.

"Ah!" said La Mole, "I had but one fear, and that was to die without again seeing her. I have seen her again, and now I can die." And with his eyes steadfastly fixed on the small window, he lifted the reliquary to his lips, and covered it with kisses.

Coconnas saluted the two women with as much grace as if he were in a drawing room, and they replied to the two devoted men by shaking their handkerchiefs bathed in tears.

Caboche then touched Coconnas on his shoulder, and looked at him significantly. The Piedmontese replied, "Yes, yes." Then, turning to La Mole, he said to him, "One last embrace, dear friend, and die like a man! That will not be difficult for you, who are so brave."

"Ah," replied La Mole, "there will be no merit in me to die well, suffering the torments I do."

The priest approached and extended the crucifix to La Mole, who smiled and pointed to the reliquary he held in his hand.

"No matter," replied the priest, "still pray for strength from Him who suffered what you are about to suffer."

La Mole kissed the feet of the crucifix. "I am ready," said he.

"Can you hold your head upright?" asked Caboche, coming with his drawn sword behind La Mole, who was now on his knees.

"I hope so," was the reply.

"Then all will go well."

"But you," said La Mole, "will not forget what I requested of you; this reliquary will open the doors for you."

"Make yourself quite easy; and now try and hold your head up."

La Mole held his neck erect, and looking toward the little tower, said, "Adieu, Marguerite! bless—"

He did not finish; with one stroke of his keen and flashing sword Caboche severed from the body the head of La Mole, which rolled to Coconnas's feet. The body fell gently back, as if going to rest.

One cry arose from the lips of a thousand human beings; and among them Coconnas fancied he heard a shriek more piercing than all the rest.

"Thanks, good friend, thanks!" said Coconnas, extending his hand for the third time to the executioner.

"My son," said the priest to Coconnas, "have you nothing you would confess to God?"

"Faith! no, Father," replied the Piedmontese, "all I had to say I said to you yesterday." Then, turning to Caboche, he said, "Now then, headsman, my last friend, one more service!"

Before he knelt he turned on the multitude a look so calm, so full of resignation that a murmur of admiration came to soothe his ear and flatter his pride. Then, taking in his hands the head of his dear friend, and impressing a kiss on the purple lips, he gave one more look toward the little tower, and kneeling down, still holding the beloved head in his hands, he cried, "Now!"

He had scarcely uttered the word when Caboche with a sweep of his arm had cut his head from his body.

"It is time it was all over," said the worthy creature, trembling all over, "poor, poor fellow!"

He took with some difficulty from the clenched fingers of La Mole the reliquary of gold, and threw his cloak over the sad remains, which the tumbril had yet to convey to his abode.

The spectacle was over; the crowd dispersed.

CHAPTER 30

The Headsman's Tower

Night spread her mantle over the city, still shuddering under the recollection of this spectacle, the details of which passed from mouth to mouth, to sadden in every home the happy hour of the family supper.

In contrast to the city, which was silent and mournful, the Louvre was joyous, noisy, and illuminated. There was a grand fête at the palace—a fête commanded by Charles IX; a fête which he had ordered for that evening at the same time he had ordered the execution for the morning.

The Queen of Navarre had received on the previous evening the king's orders to be present; and in the hope that La Mole and Coconnas would escape in the night, in the conviction that all measures had been well taken for their safety, she had promised her brother to comply with his desire. But when she had lost all hope after the terrible scene in the chapel; after she had, from a last impulse of that deep love which was the most decided and enduring of her life, been present at the execution—she had firmly resolved that neither prayers nor threats should compel her to go to a boisterous festival at the Louvre the same day on which she had witnessed so terrible a scene at the Grève.

The king had on this day exhibited another proof of that power of will which no one perhaps ever displayed more energetically than Charles IX. In bed for a fortnight, weak as a dying man, ghastly as a corpse, he yet arose at five o'clock, and was attired in his gayest habiliments. It is true that during his toilet he had fainted three times. About eight o'clock he inquired after his sister, if any one had seen her or knew where she was. No one could answer satisfactorily, for the queen had gone to her apartments about eleven o'clock, and refused admittance to everybody.

But there was no refusal for Charles. Leaning on the arm of M.

de Nancey, he proceeded to the Queen of Navarre's apartments and entered suddenly by the secret door. Although he expected a melancholy sight, and had prepared himself for it, that which he beheld was even more distressing than he had anticipated.

Marguerite, half dead, was lying on the sofa, her head buried in the cushions. She neither wept nor prayed; ever since her return she had been groaning in bitter anguish. At the other corner of the chamber, Henriette de Nevers, that daring woman, lay stretched on the carpet, without consciousness. On returning from the Grève, her strength had failed, as had Marguerite's; and poor Gillonne went from one to the other without daring to speak a word of consolation.

Charles desired Nancey to await him in the corridor, and entered, pale and trembling. Neither of the women saw him. Gillone alone, who was at the moment endeavoring to revive Henriette, rose on her knee and looked at the king in terror. He made a sign with his hand, whereupon she rose, made an obeisance, and retired.

Charles now approached Marguerite, looked at her for a moment in silence, and then in a tone of which his harsh voice might have been thought incapable, said, "Margot, my sister!"

The queen started and turned round. "Your Majesty!" she said.

"Come, Sister, courage!"

Marguerite raised her eyes to heaven.

"Yes," said Charles; "I know all; but listen to me."

The queen made a sign that she listened.

"You promised me to come to the ball," said Charles.

"I?" exclaimed Marguerite.

"Yes; and after your promise, you are expected, and therefore if you do not come, everybody will be surprised at not seeing you."

"Excuse me, Brother," replied Marguerite; "you see how much I suffer."

"Exert yourself."

Marguerite endeavored for a moment to summon courage, and then suddenly giving way again, fell back upon the cushions. "No, no, I cannot go!" she said.

Charles took her hand, seated himself beside her on the sofa, and said, "You have just lost a dear friend, Margot, I know full well. But look at me, have not I lost all my friends, and, moreover, my mother? You have time to bewail as you now do; but I, in the midst of my severest griefs, am always forced to smile. You suffer, but look at me! I am dying. Well, then, Margot, come, courage! I demand it of you, my sister, in the name of our glory! Let us bear like a cross of suffering the fame of our house; let us bear it as the Lord bore His cross to the Mount of Calvary. And if on the way we falter like him, let us like him become again courageous and resigned."

"Oh, *mon Dieu! mon Dieu!*" exclaimed Marguerite.

"Yes," said Charles, answering her thought, "yes, the sacrifice is severe, my sister; but everyone has his trials—some of their honor, others of their life. Do you suppose that I, with my twenty-five years, and the most splendid throne in the world, do not regret dying? Well, then, look at me! My eyes, my complexion, my lips are those of a dying man; yet my smile—would not my smile make all the world believe that I still hope? But in a week, a month at most, you will weep for me, my sister, as you do for him who died to-day."

"My brother!" cried Marguerite, throwing her arms round Charles's neck.

"Come, dress yourself, dear Marguerite," said the king; "hide your paleness, and appear at the ball. I have desired that they should bring you some new jewels and ornaments worthy of your beauty."

"Oh, what are jewels and ornaments to me now?" exclaimed Marguerite.

"Life is long, Marguerite!" said Charles, with a smile, "at least, for you."

"No! no!"

"Sister, recollect one thing: it is sometimes by stifling, or rather dissimulating, our suffering that we show most honor to the dead."

"Well, Sire," said Marguerite, shuddering, "I will attend the ball."

A tear, rapidly dried upon his parched eyelid, moistened Charles's eye for a moment. He kissed his sister's brow, paused a moment before Henriette, who had not seen or heard him, and then retired, saying as he did so, "Poor girl!"

After the king's departure several pages entered, bearing boxes and caskets. Marguerite made a sign with her hand that they should be placed on the floor. The pages went out, and Gillonne alone remained.

"Get everything ready to dress me, Gillonne," said Marguerite.

The young girl looked at her mistress in astonishment.

"Yes," said Marguerite, in a tone of indescribable bitterness—"yes, I shall dress. I am going to the ball; they expect me. Make haste, then; the day will so be complete—the fête at the Grève in the morning, the fête at the Louvre in the evening."

"And the duchess?" asked Gillonne.

"Ah, she—she is quite happy; she can remain here; she can weep; she can suffer at her ease. She is not a king's daughter, a king's wife, a king's sister; she is not a queen. Help me to dress, Gillonne."

The young girl obeyed. The new ornaments sent by the king were splendid, and the dresses gorgeous. Marguerite had never been so beautiful. She looked at herself in a glass, and said, "My brother is right—a human being is a miserable creature."

Gillonne entered at this moment. "Madame," she said, "here is a man asking for you."

"Who is he?"

"I do not know, but he is very horrid-looking; his very appearance made me tremble."

"Go and ask his name," said Marguerite, turning pale.

Gillonne went out, and returning after a few minutes, said, "He would not tell his name, Madame, but begged me to give you this." And Gillonne handed to Marguerite the reliquary which she had given to La Mole the night before.

"Oh, bring him hither! bring him hither!" said the queen, eagerly; and she became even paler and colder than she had been before.

A heavy step was heard upon the floor, and then a man appeared on the threshold.

"You are—" said the queen.

"He whom you saw one day near Montfaucon, Madame, and who conveyed in his tumbril two wounded gentlemen to the Louvre."

"Yes, yes, I recognize you; you are Maître Caboche."

"Executioner of the provostry of Paris, Madame."

These were the only words which Henriette had heard of all those that had been spoken around her for the last hour. She then raised her pale face from her two hands, and looked at the headsman with her emerald eyes, which seemed to dart flames.

"And you come—" said Marguerite, tremulously.

"To remind you of the promise made to the younger of the two gentlemen—to him who charged me to return this reliquary to you. Do you recollect, Madame?"

"Yes, yes!" cried the queen, "and never shall more noble shade have nobler satisfaction. But where is it?"

"It is at my abode, with the body."

"Why did you not bring it?"

"I might have been stopped at the wicket of the Louvre, and compelled to open my cloak. What would have been said if a head had been discovered underneath it?"

"True, true; keep it at your house, and I will come for it tomorrow."

"Tomorrow, Madame; tomorrow!" said Maître Caboche. "It may be too late!"

"And why so?"

"Because the queen-mother desired me to keep for her experiments in magic the heads of the first two criminals I should execute."

"Oh, profanation! the heads of our beloved! Henriette," exclaimed Marguerite, running toward her friend, whom she found standing up as if a spring had placed her on her feet—"Henriette, my angel, do you hear what this man says?"

"Yes; and what are we to do?"

"We must accompany him"; and Marguerite threw a velvet cloak over her shoulders. "Come, come," she said; "we shall see them once more."

Marguerite ordered all the doors to be closed, and a litter to be brought to the private door; then she took Henriette by the arm, and going down the secret staircase, made a sign to Caboche to follow. At the door was her litter, and at the wicket they found Caboche's servant with a lantern.

Marguerite's bearers were trustworthy men, deaf and dumb, and surer than beasts of burden.

The litter went forward about ten minutes, preceded by Maître Caboche and his servant carrying the lantern; then it stopped. The executioner opened the door, while the servant went on. Marguerite alighted, and aided the Duchesse de Nevers. In their great grief, which thus tried them both, it was the nervous temperament that was the stronger.

"You may enter, ladies," said Caboche; "everybody is asleep in the tower."

In compliance with this invitation from the headsman, the two ladies, clinging to each other, passed through the entrance, and went along in darkness over a rugged and slippery pavement.

Caboche, with a torch in his hand, led them into a chamber, low, and blackened with smoke. In a conspicuous place was nailed to the wall a parchment sealed with the king's seal; it was the headsman's brevet. In a corner was a large sword with a long handle; it was the flaming sword of justice. Here and there were seen several large images, representing saints under different kinds of martyrdom.

Having arrived here, Caboche made a low bow. "Your Majesty will pardon me," he said, "if I have dared to penetrate to the Louvre and conduct you hither; but it was the last and earnest wish of the gentleman. So—"

"You have done well, Maître," said Marguerite; "and here is a recompense for your zealous service."

Caboche eyed sorrowfully the purse well filled with gold, which Marguerite placed on the table. "Gold! gold! always gold!" he muttered. "Alas, Madame, would that I could redeem at the price of gold the blood I have been compelled to shed today!"

"Maître," replied Marguerite, with painful hesitation, "I do not see—"

"No, Madame, no; they are not here. But it is a sad spectacle, which I might have spared you by carrying, concealed in a cloak, what you have come to seek."

"No," said Marguerite, who had read in the eyes of her friend the same resolution which she had formed—"no; show us the way; we will follow."

Caboche took the torch and opened an oak door, which, opening upon the staircase, led by a few steps into a cellar. At the same moment a current of air passed, which made sparks fly from the torch, and brought up with it the nauseous smell of damp and blood.

Henriette, white as a marble statue, leaned on the arm of her friend, who moved with a more assured step; but at the first stair she staggered. "I shall never be able," she exclaimed.

"When we really love, Henriette," replied the queen, "we love even beyond death itself."

It was a sight at the same time distressing and pathetic, to see those two women resplendent in youth, beauty, and attire, bending under this sordid and chalky vault, the weaker leaning on the stronger, and the stronger clinging to the headsman's arm.

They reached the lowest step. On the floor of this cellar lay two human forms covered with a large cloth of black serge. Caboche raised a corner of the cloth, and lowering his torch, said, "Look, your Majesty!"

In their black attire, the two young men lay side by side in the fearful symmetry of death. Their heads, placed close on their bodies, seemed to be divided from them only by a red circle round the neck. Death had not separated their hands, for either by accident, or by the pious care of the headsman, the right hand of La Mole rested in the left hand of Coconnas. There was a look of love beneath the eyelids of La Mole; there was a smile of disdain under those of Coconnas.

Marguerite knelt down beside her lover, and with her hands glittering with jewels gently raised the head of him she had loved so well.

The Duchesse de Nevers, leaning against the wall, could not take her eyes off that pale face she had so often gazed upon with joy and love.

"La Mole! dear La Mole!" murmured Marguerite.

"Annibal! Annibal!" cried the duchess, "so handsome, so proud, so brave, you will speak to me no more!" and a torrent of tears gushed from her eyes.

That woman, so disdainful, so bold, so insolent in happiness, who pushed skepticism to the extreme of doubt, and passion even to cruelty—that woman had never thought of death.

Marguerite then put into a bag embroidered with pearls and perfumed with the finest essences the head of La Mole, which looked still more striking when in contact with the velvet and gold, and whose beauty a peculiar preparation, used at the period in royal embalmings, could not fail to preserve. Henriette folded the head of Coconnas in the skirt of her mantle. And both, bending beneath their poignant sorrow, ascended the stairs, after one last lingering look at the loved remains which they were leaving to the mercy of an executioner, in this gloomy den of common criminals.

"Fear nothing, Madame," said Caboche, who comprehended

the look. "The gentlemen shall be buried in holy ground; this I swear to you."

"And you will have masses said for their souls, which this will pay for," said Henriette, taking from her neck a magnificent necklace of rubies, which she gave to the headsman.

They returned to the Louvre, and the queen, going to her own apartments, deposited the melancholy relic in the cabinet of her bedchamber, destined from that moment to be an oratory. Then, leaving Henriette in her room, the queen, paler and lovelier than ever, about ten o'clock entered the splendid ballroom—the same in which we saw the first chapter of our history open, some two years previously.

All eyes were turned toward her, and she supported the universal gaze with a proud and almost joyous look, for she had religiously accomplished the dying wish of her friend.

Charles, when he saw her, passed through the gilded throng, and said aloud, "Thanks, my dear sister!" and then, in a lower tone, "Mind! you have a spot of blood upon your arm."

"Of what consequence is that, Sire, if I have a smile upon my lips?"

CHAPTER 31

The Sweat of Blood

Some days after the terrible scene we have related—that is, on the 30th of May 1574—the court was at Vincennes, when suddenly a great noise was heard in the chamber of the king, who had been attacked with an increase of his disorder in the midst of the grand ball he had given the very day of the young men's execution, and by advice of his physicians had come to Vincennes for change of air.

It was eight o'clock in the morning; a small group of courtiers was assembled in the antechamber, when all at once a cry was heard, the nurse appeared at the door of the royal apartment, her eyes bathed in tears, and called out, "Help! help for the king!"

"The king is worse, then?" said Nancey, whom, as we have seen, Charles had released from the service of Catherine, and had attached to his own person.

"Oh, summon the doctors! summon the doctors!" cried the nurse.

Mazille and Ambroise Paré attended the king by turns, and Paré, having seen Charles fall asleep, had profited by the opportunity to retire for a few moments. Meantime Charles had broken into a profuse perspiration, and as he suffered from a relaxation of the capillary vessels, which occasions hemorrhage of the skin, this bloody sweat had alarmed the nurse, who, being a Protestant, declared it was a judgment for the blood shed in the massacre of Saint Bartholomew. Everyone hastened in search of the doctor, in order to display his zeal and activity.

A door suddenly opened, and Catherine appeared; she crossed the antechamber and entered the king's apartment. Charles was lying back upon the bed, his eyes closed, and his chest heaving; his body was covered with a reddish perspiration, and from the end of each finger hung a drop of blood.

At the sound of steps Charles looked up and beheld his mother. "Excuse me, Madame," said he, "I would die in peace."

"Die, my son," said Catherine, "in a passing attack of this wretched malady? Do you wish, then, to drive us to despair?"

"I tell you, Madame, that I perceive my soul going out of me. I tell you, Madame—death of all the devils!—that it is Death who approaches me. I feel what I feel, and I know what I tell you."

"Sire," said the queen, "your mind is diseased. Since the death of those two assassins, La Mole and Coconnas, your bodily sufferings ought to have abated; and as for your mental anguish, if I had ten minutes' conversation with you, I could prove—"

"Nurse," interrupted Charles, "let no one enter; the Queen Catherine de Médicis wishes to speak with her beloved son, Charles IX."

The nurse obeyed.

"This interview must have taken place," continued he, "sooner or later, and perhaps tomorrow it may be too late; but a third person must be present."

"Why?"

"Because, I repeat," said Charles, with a terrible solemnity, "death is at the door of this chamber, and may enter at any moment; and it is time, since last night I arranged my personal affairs, to put in order this morning the affairs of the kingdom."

"And who is this third person?"

"My brother, Madame; have him summoned."

"Sire," said the queen, "I see with pleasure that those denunciations, dictated by hate rather than wrested from suffering, have not left any prejudice on your mind. Nurse! Nurse!"

The nurse appeared.

"Nurse," said Catherine, "when M. de Nancey comes, order him in the king's name to summon M. d'Alençon."

Charles made a sign to the nurse to stay.

"I said my brother," he exclaimed.

Catherine's eyes glistened with rage, but an imperious gesture of Charles stopped her.

"I wish to speak with my brother Henri," continued he; "Henri alone is my brother—not the one who is king yonder, but the one who is a prisoner here. Henri shall know my last wishes."

"And do you think," cried the queen, daring (so great was her hate to Henri) to brave Charles's anger—"do you think that if you are really, as you say, dying, I will yield to anyone, to a stranger, my right as a queen and as a mother to be present at your last moments?"

"Madame," said Charles, "I am yet king; I yet command. I have told you that I wish to speak to my brother Henri; and will you not summon my captain of the guards? Thousand devils! I warn you that I am yet strong enough to go for him myself." And Charles half rose from the bed.

"Sire," cried Catherine, detaining him, "think what you do; as for me, the laws of nature and of etiquette alike bid me stay."

"By what title do you stay?"

"By that of your mother."

"You are no more my mother than D'Alençon is my brother."

"You rave, Monsieur," said Catherine. "Since when is she who gives life no longer the mother of him who has received it?"

"From the moment, Madame, when that unnatural mother takes what she gives," said Charles, trying to wipe from his lips a bloody foam.

"What mean you, Charles? I do not understand you," murmured Catherine, her eyes dilated with astonishment.

"You will understand me, Madame."

Charles felt under his pillow, and drew forth a small silver key. "Take this key; open my traveling-casket there, and you will find papers that will speak for me." He pointed to a casket of carved oak, fastened with a silver lock, that stood in the center of the apartment.

Catherine, controlled in spite of herself by Charles's superior attitude toward her, opened the casket; but no sooner had she done so than she recoiled as if she had seen a serpent inside it.

"What do you see that alarms you, Madame?" asked Charles.

"Nothing," said Catherine.

"Then put your hand in, and give me a book; for there is one there, is there not?"

"Yes," faltered Catherine.

"A book of venery?"

"Yes."

"Bring it to me."

Catherine, trembling in every limb, did as he bade her. "Fatality!" she murmured.

"Listen," continued Charles. "This book—I was foolish—I loved the chase above everything—I read this book too much. Do you understand, Madame?"

Catherine uttered a suppressed groan.

"It was a folly!" said Charles. "Burn it, Madame; the world must not know the weaknesses of kings."

Catherine advanced to the fire, cast the fatal book in, and stood, motionless and haggard, watching the blue flames that devoured the poisoned leaves of the volume. As it burned, a strong odor, like garlic, pervaded the apartment. The book was soon entirely consumed.

"And now, Madame," said the king, with irresistible majesty, "summon my brother."

Catherine, overwhelmed, crushed beneath a complicated emotion she could not analyze, left the room. "Curse him!" cried she, as she passed the threshold. "He triumphs! he reaches the goal! Curse him! curse him!"

"Henri! my brother Henri!" cried Charles, following his mother with his voice; "I wish to see him instantly, to speak about the regency."

At this moment Ambroise Paré entered by the opposite door. "Who has been burning arsenic here?" said he.

"I have," replied Charles.

CHAPTER 32

The Platform of the Donjon
at Vincennes

Henri de Navarre was walking alone on the terrace of the donjon. He knew the court was at the château, and it seemed to him that he could see through the walls Charles on his deathbed. It was a summer's eve. A broad ray of light bathed the distant plains, and gilded the stems of the old oaks in the forest.

But it was not on these objects that Henri fixed his attention; he was gazing, in thought, on the capital of France.

"Paris!" murmured he; "Paris! where the Louvre is—the Louvre, where the throne is! and here do these ramparts shut me out from thee, to confine me with my mortal enemy!"

As his thoughts wandered from Paris back to Vincennes, he saw on the left in a valley a man whose cuirass sparkled in the sunbeams. This man was on a splendid charger, and led another.

The king fixed his eyes upon this cavalier, and saw him draw his sword, place his handkerchief on it, and wave it in the air. Instantly the signal was repeated from the next hill, and continued until the king saw it extend all round the château. It was Mouy and his Huguenots, who, knowing the king was dying, and fearing lest Henri's life should be in danger, had come together in readiness to defend or to attack.

Henri shaded his eyes with his hand, and recognizing the cavalier, "Mouy!" he cried, as though his friend could hear him. And in his joy at finding himself thus surrounded by friends, he raised his hat and waved his scarf. All the handkerchiefs were again waved. "Ah, they wait for me!" said he. "I cannot join them. Why did I not do so when it was in my power?" And he made a despairing gesture, that Mouy returned by another, which meant, "I will wait."

At this moment Henri heard steps on the stairs. He suddenly

withdrew. The Huguenots understood the cause of that retreat. Swords were resheathed, and the handkerchiefs disappeared.

Henri saw, and not without a secret dread, his mortal foe, Catherine de Médicis, appear on the terrace. Behind her were two guards, who stopped at the head of the staircase.

"Oh," thought he, "it must be something important, indeed, that makes her come and seek me on the platform of the donjon of Vincennes."

Catherine sat down on a stone bench to recover her breath. Henri approached her. "Are you seeking me, Madame?" he asked.

"Yes," replied Catherine; "I wished to give you a proof of my attachment. The king is dying and wishes to see you."

"Me?" said Henri, starting with joy.

"Yes. He thinks that not content with desiring the throne of Navarre, you covet that of France also."

"Oh, Madame!"

"I know it is not true, but he believes it, and lays a snare for you."

"What will he, then, offer me?"

"How do I know?—impossibilities, perhaps."

"But you have no idea?"

"No; but I imagine, for instance—"

"What?"

"I imagine that believing you to entertain those ambitious views that have been reported to him, he wishes to gain from your own lips the proof of that ambition. Suppose that he should tempt you, as other men have been tempted, to secure a confession without recourse to torture; suppose," Catherine continued, looking fixedly at Henri, "that he should propose to you a share in the government—a regency, even."

Henri felt a thrill of joy pervade him, but he saw the snare and avoided it.

"Oh," said he, "the trick would be too palpable; offer me the regency, when there is yourself, when there is D'Alençon!"

"You will refuse it, then?" replied Catherine.

"The king is dead," thought Henri; "she has laid a trap for me.—I must hear what the king says, Madame, for you know all this is but supposition."

"Doubtless; but you can tell me your intentions."

"*Mon Dieu!*" said Henri, "I have no pretensions, and so can have no intentions."

"That is no answer," replied Catherine; "but to be short with you—for there is no time to lose—if you accept the regency you are a dead man."

"The king lives," thought Henri—"Madame," said he, firmly, "God will inspire me, for the hearts of kings are in his hands. I am ready to see his Majesty."

"Reflect, Monsieur!"

"During two years that I have been persecuted, and a month that I have been a prisoner," said Henri, gravely, "I have had time for reflection; and I have reflected, Madame. Favor me, therefore, by informing the king of my coming. These two guards would prevent my escape, even did I contemplate flight, which I do not."

Catherine saw she could do nothing more, and hastily descended.

No sooner had she disappeared than Henri made a sign to Mouy, that meant, "Draw nearer and be ready for any event." Mouy, who had dismounted, sprang into the saddle and advanced to within a musket-shot of the château. Henri thanked him by a gesture, and hastened after the queen. On the first landing he found the two sentinels awaiting him. A double troop of Swiss and light-horse guarded the court, and to enter or leave the château it was necessary to pass between two rows of halberds. Catherine was waiting there for him.

"Look!" said she, laying her hand on his arm; "this court has two gates. At this, behind the king's apartments, if you refuse the regency, a good horse and freedom await you; if you follow the dictates of ambition, you must come by this. What say you?"

"I say that if the king makes me regent, I, and not you, shall command these soldiers."

"Madman!" murmured Catherine; "be warned, and do not play at life and death with me!"

"Why not," said Henri, "since up to this time I have been the gainer?"

"Go to the king's apartments, Monsieur, since you will not listen to me," said Catherine, pointing to the stairs with one hand, while the other sought the handle of one of the poisoned daggers she wore at her girdle in the shagreen case which has become historical.

"Pass before me, Madame," said Henri; "until I am regent, you have the precedence."

Catherine, foiled at every point, made no resistance, but ascended the stairs before Henri.

CHAPTER 33

The Regency

The king had become impatient, and was on the point of sending Nancey in search of Henri, when the latter appeared. On seeing him, Charles uttered a cry of joy. Henri stood appalled as if in the presence of a corpse. The two doctors and the priest, who were with the king, instantly rose and left the chamber.

Charles was not greatly beloved, and yet all the courtiers in the antechamber were weeping. At the death of every king, good or bad, there are some persons who fear they shall lose by it.

Charles smiled mournfully. "Come here, Henriot," said he, holding out his hand to him; "come here. I was unhappy at not seeing you, for, believe me, I have often reproached myself with having tormented you; but a king cannot control events, and besides, my mother and D'Anjou and D'Alençon, and something else, which now that I am dying does not influence me, influenced me then—State policy."

"Sire," replied Henri, "I recollect only the love I have always borne you as my brother, and my respect for you as my king."

"Ah, you are right, and I am grateful to you for speaking so, Henriot; for in fact you have suffered much under my reign, without remembering that during its continuance your poor mother has died. But you have been able to see how I am pressed. Sometimes I resist; but sometimes also I yield through weariness. But, as you have said, let us speak no more of the past; it is the present which presses me now, and the future frightens me." And in saying these words the poor king hid his white face behind his fleshless hands. After a moment's silence he continued, "We must save the State; we must not let it fall into the hands of fanatics or women."

Charles spoke these words in a low tone, and yet Henri fancied he heard behind the curtain a suppressed exclamation of rage. Perhaps an opening in the wall, made at the instance of Charles himself, enabled Catherine to overhear the last conversation.

"Of women?" said Henri, anxious to provoke an explanation.

"Yes, for my mother would like to be regent until D'Anjou's return; but I tell you that he will not return."

"How, not return?" cried Henri, his heart beating joyfully.

"No, his subjects will not let him."

"But do you not think the queen-mother has already written to him?"

"Yes; but Nancey stopped the courier at Château-Thierry, and brought me the letter, in which she said I was dying. I wrote to Warsaw myself, and D'Anjou will be carefully watched, so that in all probability the throne will become vacant."

Another angry sound was heard behind the tapestry.

"She is there," thought Henri, "and is listening."

Charles heard nothing. "I die without male heirs," he continued. Then, stopping suddenly, he looked at the King of Navarre. "Do you recollect, Henriot," said he, "the little boy I showed you one night, sleeping peacefully in his cradle, and watched over by an angel? Alas, they will kill him also!"

"Oh, no, no!" cried Henri, with tears in his eyes; "I swear to you that I will watch over and protect him with my life."

"Thanks, Henriot, thanks!" said the king, gratefully; "I accept your promise. Do not make him a king—fortunately, he is not born to a throne—but make him happy. I leave him an ample fortune; as to rank, may he have his mother's nobility, that of the heart! Perhaps it would be better that he should be educated for the Church; he would inspire less apprehension. Oh! it seems to me I could die, if not happy, at least tranquil, could I have, to console me here, the child's caresses and the sweet face of the mother."

"Sire, could they not come?"

"Eh! they would never go out from here. Such is the lot of kings, Henriot. They can neither live nor die as they would. But since your promise I am more resigned."

Henri reflected. "I have promised," said he; "but can I fulfill my word?"

"What do you mean?"

"Shall I not be persecuted, and in more danger than he is, since I am a man, and he but an infant?"

"You are mistaken," said Charles. "After my death you will be great and powerful; and here is what will give you power."

At these words he drew a parchment from under his pillow. "Here!" said he.

Henri hastily glanced over the document adorned with the royal seal.

"The regency for me, Sire?" said he, turning pale with joy.

"Yes, until D'Anjou's return; and as he will not return, in all probability it is the throne I give you."

"The throne to me!" murmured Henri.

"You alone are worthy of it; you alone capable of governing. D'Alençon is a traitor; leave him in the prison to which I have consigned him. My mother will seek to kill you; banish her. D'Anjou, in three months, in four months, in a year perhaps, will leave Poland and come to contest your power; reply to him by a papal bull. I have already arranged that matter, through my ambassador, the Duc de Nevers, and you will receive the document shortly."

"Oh, my king!"

"You have but one thing to fear—civil war; but by remaining converted, you will avoid that. The Protestants can do nothing unless you are at their head, and Condé is not strong enough to contend against you. The King of France should be King of the Catholics, and not King of the Huguenots; for the King of France should be king of the majority. They say I feel remorse for the Bartholomew. Doubts, yes! remorse, no! They say I bleed at every pore the blood then shed; what flows from me is arsenic, and not blood."

"Oh, what do you mean, Sire?"

"Nothing; God will, if he think fit, avenge my death. I leave you a faithful parliament and a trusty army. They will protect you against your only enemies—my mother and D'Alençon."

At this moment the sound of arms and of military orders was heard in the vestibule.

"I am lost," murmured Henri.

"You fear; you hesitate," said Charles, with anxiety.

"I, Sire?" Henri replied. "No, I do not fear; no, I do not hesitate. I accept."

Charles pressed his hand; and as at that moment his nurse drew near with a potion which she had just prepared in a neighboring chamber, without being aware that within a few feet of where she was, the destiny of France was at stake, "Nurse," he said, "summon my mother and M. d'Alençon."

The King Is Dead!
God Save the King!

Catherine and D'Alençon, pale with fear and trembling with rage, entered a few minutes later. As Henri had conjectured, the queen had overheard all, and had in a few words acquainted D'Alençon with what had occurred. Henri stood by the head of the king's bed.

The king announced to them his will. "Madame," said he to his mother, "if I had a son he would be king, and you would be regent; in your stead, did you decline, the King of Poland; in his stead, did he decline, D'Alençon. But I have no son, and the throne belongs to D'Anjou, who is absent. Since he will sometime return to reclaim that throne, I do not wish him to find in his place a man who, with claims almost equal to his own, might dispute his rights, and so expose the kingdom to the danger of civil war. I do not make you regent because it would be painful for you to choose between your two sons. I do not make D'Alençon regent because he might say to D'Anjou, 'You had a throne; why have you abandoned it?' No; I have chosen a regent who can take the crown as a trust, and will keep it under his hand, and not on his head. Salute him, Madame; salute him, D'Alençon. It is the King of Navarre!" And with a gesture of supreme authority he himself saluted Henri. Catherine and D'Alençon made a motion between a shudder and a salute.

"Here, my Lord Regent," said Charles, "is the parchment that until the return of D'Anjou gives you command of the armies, the keys of the treasury, royal right and power."

Catherine devoured Henri with her eyes; D'Alençon trembled so that he could hardly stand. But that feebleness of the one and firmness of the other, instead of reassuring Henri, showed him that danger was at hand. Making a violent effort, he took the warrant from Charles, and drawing himself up to his full height, fixed his eyes on the queen as if to say, "Beware, I am your master!"

Catherine understood that look. "No, never!" said she; "never shall my race yield to a foreign one! Never shall a Bourbon reign while a Valois remains!"

"Mother!" cried Charles, sitting up, "take care! I am yet king—for only a short time, I am aware; but not much time is needed to give an order. It does not require much time to punish murderers and poisoners."

"Very well, give the order if you dare; I am going now to give mine. Come, François, come." And she left the room, followed by D'Alençon.

"Nancey!" cried Charles; "Nancey, arrest my mother; arrest my brother; arrest—" A stream of blood choked his utterance.

Nancey entered; he had heard only his name. The orders which followed, uttered in a voice less distinct, had been lost in space.

"Guard the door," said Henri, "and let no one enter!"

Nancey bowed, and left the apartment. Henri looked at the dying king. "The fatal moment has come," said he. "Shall I reign? Shall I live?"

"Live, Sire!" said a voice.

The tapestry of the alcove was lifted, and René's pale face appeared.

"René?" cried Henri.

"Yes, Sire."

"Your prediction was false, then; I shall not be king?"

"You shall be; but the time has not yet come."

"How do you know? Speak!"

"Listen!"

"I listen."

"Stoop!"

Henri leaned over the bed, and René did the same; between them lay the motionless body of the dying king.

"Listen!" said René. "Placed here by the queen-mother to undo you, I prefer to serve you, for I have faith in your horoscope; and I find it to be for the interest both of my body and of my soul to serve you."

"Is it the queen-mother who bade you tell me that?" said Henri, full of doubt and anxiety.

"No," said René; "but listen to a secret, which I alone know, and which I will disclose to you if you will swear upon this dying king to forgive me the death of your mother."

"I have already promised you once," said Henri, his face darkening.

"Promised, but not sworn," said René, making a movement to withdraw.

"I swear it," said Henri, extending his hand over the head of the king.

"Well, Sire," said the Florentine, hastily, "the King of Poland will soon be here!"

"No, for the king stopped the courier at Château-Thierry."

"The queen had sent three, by different routes."

"Oh, I am lost!" said Henri.

"A messenger arrived this morning from Warsaw. No one knows of Charles's illness there, and D'Anjou left that city without opposition. The courier preceded him only by a few hours."

"Oh, had I but eight days!" muttered Henri.

"You have not eight hours! did you not hear the noise of the arms in the vestibule? The soldiers will come even here to kill you."

"The king is not dead yet."

"No," said René, "but he will be in ten minutes; you have, then, ten minutes to live, perhaps less."

"What shall I do, then?"

"Fly instantly."

"How? If I cross the vestibule, they will kill me there."

"Listen! I risk everything for you; do not forget it."

"Be assured."

"Follow me through this passage; I will conduct you to the postern. Then, to give you time I will go and tell the queen that you are coming; they will think afterwards that you have discovered the secret door and escaped."

Henri stopped and kissed Charles's forehead.

"Adieu, my brother!" said he; "I will not forget your last wish was to see me king. Die in peace! In the name of my brethren I forgive you their blood you have spilled."

"Quick! quick!" said René; "he is coming to himself! Fly, before he opens his eyes; fly!"

"Nurse!" murmured Charles in a low tone, "Nurse!"

Henri seized Charles's sword, thenceforth useless to the dying king, placed in his breast the parchment that made him regent, pressed his lips again to Charles's forehead, and disappeared by the secret passage.

"Nurse!" cried the king, in louder tones, "Nurse!"

The good woman hastened to him. "What do you want, Charlot?" cried she.

"Nurse," said the king, his eyelids open and his eyes dilated in the terrible fixedness of death, "something has happened while I slept. I see a great light; I see God, our Master; I see the Lord Jesus; I see the blessed Virgin Mary. They pray for me; they intercede for me. The Lord all-powerful pardons me; he calls me. My God, my God, receive me into thy pity! My God, forget that I have been a king, for I come to thee without a scepter and without a crown! My God, forget the crimes of the king, in remembering the sufferings of the man! My God, I come!"

Charles, as he proceeded in the utterance of these words, raised himself more and more, as if to go forward in response to the voice which called him. After these last words, he breathed a sigh and fell back motionless and cold into his nurse's arms.

Meantime, Henri, guided by René, traversed the passage, passed through the postern, and springing on his horse, galloped toward the place where he knew he should find Mouy.

The sentinels, hearing the horse, moved forward and cried, "He flies; he flies!"

"Who flies?" said the queen, going to a window.

"The King of Navarre!"

"Fire on him! fire!" said the queen.

The sentinels leveled their pieces; but the king was out of reach.

"He flies!" said Catherine; "he is vanquished, then!"

"He flies!" muttered D'Alençon; "I am king, then!"

But at the same moment, and while François and his mother were at the window, the drawbridge creaked under the feet of horses; and preceded by a clash of arms and by a great noise, a young man, riding at a gallop, his hat in his hand, entered the court, crying,

"France!" followed by four gentlemen, covered, like himself, with sweat, dust, and foam.

"My son!" cried Catherine joyfully.

"My mother!" replied the young man, springing to the ground.

"D'Anjou!" exclaimed François, thunderstruck.

"Am I too late?" said Henri d'Anjou.

"No, you are just in time; and had God led you by the hand, your arrival could not have been more seasonable. Look; listen!"

At this moment Nancey appeared at the balcony of the king's apartments; all eyes were fixed on him. He broke a wand in two pieces and extended his arms, holding a fragment in either hand. "King Charles IX is dead! King Charles IX is dead! King Charles IX is dead!" cried he, three times. And he let fall the fragments of the wand.

"Long live King Henri III!" said Catherine, crossing herself— "long live King Henri III!"

All repeated the cry, with the exception of D'Alençon. "Ah! she has betrayed me," said he, tearing his breast with his fingernails.

"I have conquered," cried Catherine; "and the odious Béarnais will not reign!"

A year had elapsed since the death of Charles IX and the accession of his successor. King Henri III, happily reigning by the grace of God and of his mother Catherine, had gone in a fine procession in honor of Nôtre Dame de Clery. He had gone on foot with the queen, his wife, and all the court.

King Henri III was able to afford himself this little pastime, for no serious business occupied him at the moment. The King of Navarre was in Navarre, where he had so long desired to be, and they said was very much taken up with a beautiful girl of the blood of the Montmorencies, whom he called La Fosseuse (dimple-cheek). Marguerite was with him, sad and gloomy, and finding only in her beautiful mountains, not an amusement, but a soother of the two great griefs of human life—absence and death.

Paris was very quiet; and the queen-mother, really regent since her dear son Henri had become king, resided sometimes at the Louvre, sometimes at the Hôtel de Soissons.

One evening when she was deeply occupied in studying the stars with René, whose little treason she had never detected, and who had been reinstated in her favor after the false testimony he had so opportunely borne against La Mole and Coconnas, she was informed that a man desired to see her who said that he had a matter of the utmost importance to communicate. She went hastily to her oratory, and found M. Maurevel.

"He is here!" exclaimed the ancient captain of the petardeers, not giving Catherine time to address him, according to royal etiquette.

" 'He'? Who?" she asked.

"Who can it be, Madame, but the King of Navarre?"

"Here?" cried Catherine. "Here? He? Henri? And what is the madman doing here?"

"If appearances may be trusted, he has come to see Madame de Sauve; if probabilities are considered, he comes to conspire against the king."

"How do you know he is here?"

"Because I saw him enter a house yesterday, and, very soon afterwards Madame de Sauve joined him there."

"Are you sure it was he?"

"I waited until he came out; that is to say, a part of the night. At three o'clock the two lovers appeared. The king conducted Madame de Sauve to the wicket of the Louvre. There the porter, who is no doubt in her interest, admitted her; she entered without interruption, and the king returned, humming a tune, and with a step as free and unconcerned as if he were among his mountains in Béarn."

"And whither did he betake himself?"

"Rue de l'Arbre Sec, to the Hôtel de la Belle Etoile, the same inn where the two sorcerers lodged whom your Majesty executed last year."

"Why did you not come and inform me the moment you first saw him?"

"Because I was not quite sure of my man."

"While now—"

"Now I am."

"You saw him, then?"

"Plainly. I concealed myself at the wine shop in front of the house, and saw him enter the same place as on the previous night. Then, as Madame de Sauve was late, he imprudently put his face against the window on the first floor, and then I had no further doubt. Besides, a few moments afterwards Madame de Sauve came and rejoined him."

"And do you think they will remain, as they did last night, until three o'clock in the morning?"

"It is probable."

"Where is the house you mention?"

"Near the Croix des Petits Champs, close by St. Honoré."

"Very good!" replied Catherine. "Does M. de Sauve know your handwriting?"

"No," said Maurevel.

"Sit down there and write."

Maurevel obeyed.

"I am ready, Madame," said he.

Catherine dictated:

"While the Baron de Sauve is on service at the Louvre, his wife is with her lover in a house near the Croix des Petits Champs, Rue St. Honoré. The baron will recognize the house by a red cross on the wall."

"Well?" asked Maurevel.

"Now make a copy of this letter."

Maurevel did so.

"Now," continued the queen, "let this note be given by a skillful messenger to the baron, and let that messenger drop the other in the corridor of the Louvre."

"I do not understand."

Catherine shrugged her shoulders.

"You do not see that a husband who receives such a letter must be angry."

"In the King of Navarre's time he was not offended."

"Do you not know there is a great difference between a king and a plain lover? Besides, if he is not offended, you will be offended for him."

"I?"

"Yes; take four or six men, masked. You burst open the door; you surprise the lovers; you strike in the baron's name. And the next day, the letter found in the Louvre proves that it is the husband who revenged himself—only it happened that the lover was the King of Navarre; but who could think he was there, when everyone believed he was at Pau?"

Maurevel looked at Catherine with admiration, bowed, and withdrew.

Just as he left the Hôtel de Soissons, Madame de Sauve entered the house of the Croix des Petits Champs. Henri was waiting for her.

"Have you been followed?" said he.

"No," said Charlotte, "not that I am aware of."

"I think I have; not only tonight, but last evening also."

"Oh, Sire, you terrify me. I should be inconsolable if anything were to happen to you."

"Fear nothing, love," said the Béarnais, "three faithful followers watch over me."

"Only three? that is small protection, Sire."

"Three are sufficient when they are called Mouy, Saucourt, and Barthélemy."

"Mouy is then at Paris? Has he, like you, some poor woman madly in love with him?"

"No, but a mortal enemy, whose death he has sworn to compass. Nothing else but hate, my dear, makes men commit such follies as they commit in love."

"Thank you, Sire!"

"Oh, I do not speak of our present follies, but those past and to come. But let us leave off this conversation, for my time is short."

"You leave Paris, then?"

"Tonight."

"Your affairs in Paris are finished?"

"My only business was to see you."

"Gascon!"

"My love, it is true; but we have a few more hours to pass together and then we separate forever."

"Oh, Henri," said Charlotte, "nothing but my love lasts forever."

Meantime, as the King of Navarre had said, Mouy and his two companions were concealed in the neighborhood of the house. It was arranged that Henri should leave the house at twelve o'clock, that he and his companions should escort Madame de Sauve to the Louvre, and should go from thence to the Rue de Cerisaie, where Maurevel dwelt.

The three Huguenots had been on guard about an hour when they saw a man, followed at some distance by five others, approach the door of the house, and apply successively several keys to the lock.

At this sight, Mouy sprang from his concealment, and catching the man by the arm, "Stay!" said he, "you do not enter there!"

The man started, and his hat fell off. "M. de Mouy de Saint-Phale!" cried he.

"Maurevel!" thundered the Huguenot, brandishing his sword; "I sought you, and you come to find me!" But he did not forget Henri, and turning to the window, he whistled like the Béarnese shepherds. "That is sufficient," said he to Saucourt. "Now, then, murderer!" and he sprang toward Maurevel.

Maurevel had had time to draw a pistol from his belt, and leveling it at the young man, "This time," said the King's Killer, "you are dead."

But Mouy sprang on one side, and the ball passed by him. "It is my turn now!" cried he; and he dealt Maurevel so terrible a thrust with his rapier that although it hit his leather belt, the sharp point went through that obstacle and penetrated the flesh.

Maurevel uttered so piercing a cry that his followers thought he was killed, and ran away down the Rue St. Honoré.

Maurevel, seeing himself abandoned, took to flight, crying, "Help! help!" Mouy, Saucourt, and Barthélemy pursued him hotly.

As they entered the Rue de Grenelle, a man sprang out of a window on the first floor. It was Henri. Warned by Mouy's signal, and by the report of the pistol, that something had occurred, he hastened to the assistance of his friends. Active and vigorous, he dashed after them, sword in hand.

A cry guided him. It came from the Barrier des Sergens; it was Maurevel, who, hard pressed by Mouy, called again for help. He was forced to turn or else be run through the back. He turned, therefore, and thrust fiercely at Mouy and pierced his scarf; Mouy thrust in his turn, and a second time wounded him.

"He has it!" cried Henri, who had come up. "At him! at him, Mouy!"

Mouy needed no exhortation: he charged Maurevel again, who, pressing his hand over his wound, took to flight once more.

"Kill him quickly!" cried the king. "Here are his soldiers!"

Maurevel, breathless and exhausted, could go no farther; he fell on one knee, and presented his sword-point to Mouy.

"They are only two!" cried he. "Fire! fire!"

Saucourt and Barthélemy had been carried away in pursuit of the other soldiers, so that Mouy and the king found themselves opposed to four men.

"Fire!" cried Maurevel, while one of the soldiers prepared his arquebus.

"Yes; but first," said Mouy, "die! assassin, murderer, traitor, die!"

So saying, Mouy seized Maurevel's sword with one hand, and plunged his own so violently into his breast that he pinned him to the earth.

"Take care! take care!" cried Henri.

Mouy sprang back, leaving his sword in the body of Maurevel, for a soldier was in the act of firing at him. Henri instantly passed his sword through the soldier's body, who fell, uttering a cry. The two others betook themselves to flight.

"Come, Mouy, come!" said Henri. "We have not a moment to lose; if we are recognized, we are lost!"

"One moment, Sire, while I recover my sword. You do not suppose I would leave it sticking in the body of that scoundrel!"

He went toward Maurevel, who lay, to all appearance, deprived of the power of motion; but the moment that Mouy laid his hand on the hilt of the sword which had remained in his body, he raised himself, with the petronel in his hand, which the soldier had dropped as he fell, and placing the muzzle full against Mouy's breast, pulled the trigger. Mouy fell without a cry; he was killed outright.

Henri rushed toward Maurevel; but he had fallen again, and the king's sword pierced only a dead carcass.

It was necessary for him to flee; the noise had attracted a great number of persons, and the guard might arrive. Henri then looked among the spectators drawn together by the noise, to see if anyone was there whom he knew, and gave a cry of joy as he recognized Maître la Hurière.

"My dear La Hurière, look after Mouy, I pray you, although I have great fear that he is past hope. Have him taken to your house, and if he still lives, spare no expense; here is my purse. As to the other, leave the scoundrel to rot in the gutter like a dog!"

"But yourself?" said La Hurière.

"I have a farewell to make. I will hasten, and be back with you in ten minutes. Have my horses ready."

Henri then hastened away in the direction of the little house in the Croix des Petits Champs; but as he turned the corner, he stopped in great alarm.

There was a great crowd before the door.

"What has happened in this house?" inquired Henri.

"Oh," replied a bystander, "a terrible affair, Monsieur! A beautiful woman has been stabbed by her husband, to whom someone had sent a note, informing him that she was there with her lover."

"And the husband?" cried Henri.

"Has gone."

"The wife?"

"Is there still."

"Dead?"

"Not yet; but there is no hope."

"Oh," exclaimed Henri, "I am then accursed!" and he rushed into the house.

The room was filled with people, all surrounding the bed on which lay poor Charlotte, stabbed with two blows of a poniard. Her husband, who had for two years concealed his jealousy of Henri, had seized this opportunity of avenging himself.

"Charlotte, Charlotte!" cried Henri, falling on his knees at the bedside.

Charlotte opened her beautiful eyes, already veiled by death, and gave a cry which made the blood flow from her two wounds; and making an effort to rise, she said, "Oh, I was sure I could not die without seeing him once more!"

And as if she had awaited the moment of Henri's coming to die, she pressed her lips on the King of Navarre's forehead, and murmuring for the last time, "I love thee!" fell back and expired.

Henri could not remain a moment longer without his life being in jeopardy. He drew his dagger, cut off one of those long and fair tresses he had so often admired and pressed to his lips, and sobbing bitterly, amid the sobs of the lookers-on, who had no idea that their sympathies were excited for persons of such high estate, left the room.

"Friend, mistress," cried Henri, in despair, "all forsake me, all leave me, all fail me at once."

"Yes, Sire," said a man who had quitted the group before the house, and followed Henri; "but the throne is still left to you."

"René!" cried Henri.

"Yes, Sire, René, who still watches over you. The wretch Maurevel named you as he died. They know you are in Paris; the archers are seeking you. Fly!"

"And yet you say, René, that I, a fugitive, shall be king?"

"Look, Sire," said the Florentine, pointing out to the king a star which appeared alone, brilliant among the folds of a golden cloud; "it is not I who say so, but that!"

Henri sighed and disappeared in the darkness.

ABOUT THE AUTHOR

Alexandre Dumas was born July 24, 1802, at Villers-Cotterets, France, the son of Napoleon's famous mulatto general, Dumas. Alexandre Dumas began writing at an early age and found his first success in a play he wrote entitled *Henri III et sa cour* (1829). A prolific author, Dumas was also an adventurer and took part in the Revolution of 1830. Dumas is most famous for his brilliant historical novels, which were serialized in the popular press of the day. *Queen Margot* first appeared in the newspaper *La Presse* during the years 1843–1845, under the name *Marguerite de Valois* (it is also known as *La Reine Margot*) while *The Three Musketeers* and *The Count of Monte Cristo* were being published simultaneously in other dailies. Dumas made and lost several fortunes and died penniless on December 5, 1870.